Charles Gibbon

The Casquet of Literature

Vol. V

Charles Gibbon

The Casquet of Literature
Vol. V

ISBN/EAN: 9783337077693

Printed in Europe, USA, Canada, Australia, Japan

Cover: Foto ©Andreas Hilbeck / pixelio.de

More available books at **www.hansebooks.com**

THE CASQUET

OF

LITERATURE:

BEING

A SELECTION IN POETRY AND PROSE

FROM THE WORKS OF THE MOST ADMIRED AUTHORS.

EDITED,

WITH BIOGRAPHICAL AND LITERARY NOTES,

By CHARLES GIBBON,

AUTHOR OF "ROBIN GRAY," "FOR LACK OF GOLD," ETC

IN SIX VOLUMES.

VOL. V.

LONDON:

BLACKIE & SON, OLD BAILEY, E.C.:

GLASGOW AND EDINBURGH

1880.

GLASGOW:
W. G. BLACKIE AND CO., PRINTERS,
VILLAFIELD

CONTENTS OF VOL. V.

vi CONTENTS.

CONTENTS.   vii

LIST OF PLATES IN VOL. V.

THE CASQUET.

MOTHER RIGBY'S PIPE.

[Nathaniel Hawthorne, born in Salem, Massachusetts, 4th July, 1804; died in Plymouth, New Hampshire, 19th May, 1864. Novelist. He held various appointments under the American government, the most important of which was that of consul at Liverpool. His works are: *Twice-told Tales; Mosses from an Old Manse; The Scarlet Letter; The House of the Seven Gables; The Blithedale Romance* (in this novel he embodies his experience of the Brook Farm Community, of which he was a member for about a year); *The Marble Faun; The Snow Image*, and other Twice-told Tales; *Grandfather's Chair; The Wonder Book* for girls and boys; *Tanglewood Tales; Life of Franklin Pierce*, President of the United States; *Septimius*, a novel which, unhappily, he did not live to complete; *English and American Note Books*. The following story is one of seven, which in 1873 were published (King & Co.) for the first time in England by Mr. H. A. Page, accompanied by a singularly powerful biographical and critical study of the author. "The characteristics of Hawthorne which first arrest the attention," says Mr. R. W. Griswold, an American critic, "are imagination and reflection; and these are exhibited in remarkable power and activity in tales and essays, of which the style is distinguished for great simplicity, purity, and tranquillity." Of "Mother Rigby's Pipe," Mr. Page says: "Here we have an illustration of his (Hawthorne's) unique power of concentrating himself upon one point, and throwing down on it from all sides the most capricious lights of fancy; while yet never ceasing to moralize through a delicate medium of allegory. The meanings are profound enough, but the humour is of the finest, and relieves their presence; gently lighting up the whole now and then, suddenly as a smile will unexpectedly pass over a pensive countenance. It required no little skill so to use witchcraft as to gently satirize by means of it the artificialities and follies of the present."]

I.

"DICKON," cried Mother Rigby, "a coal for my pipe!"

The pipe was in the old dame's mouth when she said these words. She had thrust it there after filling it with tobacco, but without stooping to light it at the hearth, where indeed there was no appearance of a fire having been

kindled that morning. Forthwith, however, as soon as the order was given, there was an intense red glow out of the bowl of the pipe, and a whiff of smoke from Mother Rigby's lips. Whence the coal came, and how brought thither by an invisible hand, I have never been able to discover.

"Good!" quoth Mother Rigby, with a nod of her head, "thank ye, Dickon! And now for making this scarecrow. Be within call, Dickon, in case I need you again."

The good woman had risen thus early (for as yet it was scarcely sunrise), in order to set about making a scarecrow, which she intended to put in the middle of her corn-patch. It was now the latter week of May, and the crows and blackbirds had already discovered the little, green, rolled-up leaf of the Indian corn just peeping out of the soil. She was determined, therefore, to contrive as lifelike a scarecrow as ever was seen, and finish it immediately, from top to toe, so that it should begin its sentinel's duty that very morning. Now Mother Rigby (as everybody must have heard) was one of the most cunning and potent witches in New England, and might, with very little trouble, have made a scarecrow ugly enough to frighten the minister himself. But on this occasion, as she had awakened in an uncommonly pleasant humour, and was further dulcified by her pipe of tobacco, she resolved to produce something fine, beautiful, and splendid, rather than hideous and horrible.

"I don't want to set up a hobgoblin in my own corn-patch, and almost at my own doorstep," said Mother Rigby to herself, puffing out a whiff of smoke: "I could do it if I pleased, but I'm tired of doing marvellous things, and so I'll keep within the bounds of everyday business, just for variety's sake. Besides, there is no use in scaring the little children for a mile roundabout, though 'tis true I'm a witch."

It was settled, therefore, in her own mind, that the scarecrow should represent a fine gentleman of the period, so far as the materials at hand would allow. Perhaps it may be as well to enumerate the chief of the articles that went to the composition of this figure.

The most important item of all, probably, although it made so little show, was a certain broomstick, on which Mother Rigby had taken many an airy gallop at midnight, and which now served the scarecrow by way of a spinal column, or, as the unlearned phrase it, a backbone. One of its arms was a disabled flail which used to be wielded by Goodman Rigby, before his spouse worried him out of this troublesome world; the other, if I mistake not, was composed of the pudding stick and a broken rung of a chair, tied loosely together at the elbow. As for its legs, the right was a hoe handle, and the left an undistinguished and miscellaneous stick from the woodpile. Its lungs, stomach, and other affairs of that kind were nothing better than a meal bag stuffed with straw. Thus we have made out the skeleton and entire corporeity of the scarecrow, with the exception of his head; and this was admirably supplied by a somewhat withered and shrivelled pumpkin, in which Mother Rigby cut two holes for the eyes, and a slit for the mouth, leaving a bluish-coloured knob in the middle to pass for a nose. It was really quite a respectable face.

"I've seen worse ones on human shoulders, at any rate," said Mother Rigby. "And many a fine gentleman has a pumpkin head, as well as my scarecrow."

But the clothes, in this case, were to be the making of the man. So the good old woman took down from a peg an ancient plum-coloured coat of London make, and with relics of embroidery on its seams, cuffs, pocket-flaps, and button-holes, but lamentably worn and faded, patched at the elbows, tattered at the skirts, and threadbare all over. On the left breast was a round hole, whence either a star of nobility had been rent away, or else the hot heart of some former wearer had scorched it through and through. The neighbours said that this rich garment belonged to the Black Man's wardrobe, and that he kept it at Mother Rigby's cottage for the convenience of slipping it on whenever he wished to make a grand appearance at the governor's table. To match the coat there was a velvet waistcoat of very ample size, and formerly embroidered with foliage that had been as brightly golden as the maple leaves in October, but which had

now quite vanished out of the substance of the velvet. Next came a pair of scarlet breeches, once worn by the French governor of Louisbourg, and the knees of which had touched the lower step of the throne of Louis le Grand. The Frenchman had given these smallclothes to an Indian powwow, who parted with them to the old witch for a gill of strong waters, at one of their dances in the forest. Furthermore, Mother Rigby produced a pair of silk stockings and put them on the figure's legs, where they showed as unsubstantial as a dream, with the wooden reality of the sticks making itself miserably apparent through the holes. Lastly, she put her dead husband's wig on the bare scalp of the pumpkin, and surmounted the whole with a dusty three-cornered hat, in which was stuck the longest tail feather of a rooster.

Then the old dame stood the figure up in a corner of her cottage, and chuckled to behold its yellow semblance of a visage, with its nobby little nose thrust into the air. It had a strangely self-satisfied aspect, and seemed to say, "Come, look at me!"

"And you are well worth looking at, that's a fact!" quoth Mother Rigby, in admiration of her own handiwork! "I've made many a puppet since I've been a witch; but methinks this is the finest of them all. 'Tis almost too good for a scarecrow. And, by the by, I'll just fill a fresh pipe of tobacco, and then take him out to the corn-patch."

While filling her pipe, the old woman continued to gaze with almost motherly affection at the figure in the corner. To say the truth, whether it were chance, or skill, or downright witchcraft, there was something wonderfully human in this ridiculous shape, bedizened with its tattered finery; and as for the countenance, it appeared to shrivel its yellow surface into a grin—a funny kind of expression betwixt scorn and merriment, as if it understood itself to be a jest at mankind. The more Mother Rigby looked, the better she was pleased.

"Dickon," cried she sharply, "another coal for my pipe!"

Hardly had she spoken, when, just as before, there was a red-glowing coal on the top of the tobacco. She drew in a long whiff and puffed it forth again into the bar of morning sunshine which struggled through the one dusty pane of her cottage window. Mother Rigby always liked to flavour her pipe with a coal of fire from the particular chimney corner whence this had been brought. But where that chimney corner might be, or who brought the coal from it—further than that the invisible messenger seemed to respond to the name of Dickon—I cannot tell.

"That puppet yonder," thought Mother Rigby, still with her eyes fixed on the scarecrow, "is too good a piece of work to stand all summer in a corn-patch, frightening away the crows and blackbirds. He's capable of better things. Why, I've danced with a worse one, when partners happened to be scarce, at our witch meetings in the forest! What if I should let him take his chance among other men of straw and empty fellows who go bustling about the world?"

The old witch took three or four more whiffs of her pipe and smiled.

"He'll meet plenty of his brethren at every street-corner!" continued she. "Well; I didn't mean to dabble in witchcraft to-day, further than the lighting of my pipe; but a witch I am, and a witch I'm likely to be, and there's no use trying to shirk it. I'll make a man of my scarecrow, were it only for the joke's sake!"

While muttering these words, Mother Rigby took the pipe from her own mouth and thrust it into the crevice which represented the same feature in the pumpkin visage of the scarecrow.

"Puff, darling, puff!" said she. "Puff away, my fine fellow! your life depends upon it!"

This was a strange exhortation, undoubtedly, to be addressed to a mere thing of sticks, straw, and old clothes, with nothing better than a shrivelled pumpkin for a head; as we know to have been the scarecrow's case. Nevertheless, as we must carefully hold in remembrance, Mother Rigby was a witch of singular power and dexterity; and, keeping this fact duly before our minds, we shall see nothing beyond credibility in the remarkable incidents of our story. Indeed, the great difficulty will be at once got over, if we can only bring ourselves to believe that, as soon as the old dame bade him puff, there came a whiff of smoke from the scarecrow's mouth. It was the very feeblest of whiffs, to be sure; but it was followed by another and another, each more decided than the preceding one.

"Puff away, my pet! puff away, my pretty one!" Mother Rigby kept repeating, with her pleasantest smile. "It is the breath of life to ye; and that you may take my word for."

Beyond all question the pipe was bewitched. There must have been a spell either in the tobacco, or in the fiercely-glowing coal that so mysteriously burned on the top of it, or in the pungently aromatic smoke which exhaled from the kindled weed. The figure, after a few doubtful attempts, at length blew forth a volley of smoke extending all the way from the obscure corner into the bar of sunshine. There it eddied and melted away among the motes of dust. It seemed a convulsive effort; for the two or three next whiffs were fainter, although the coal still glowed and threw a gleam over the scarecrow's visage. The old witch clapped her skinny hands together, and smiled encouragingly upon her handiwork. She saw that the charm worked well. The shrivelled, yellow face, which heretofore had been no face at all, had already a thin, fantastic haze, as it were, of human likeness, shifting to and fro across it; sometimes vanishing entirely, but growing more perceptible than ever with the next whiff from the pipe. The whole figure, in like manner, assumed a show of life, such as we impart to ill-defined shapes among the clouds, and half deceive ourselves with the pastime of our own fancy.

If we must needs pry closely into the matter, it may be doubted whether there was any real change, after all, in the sordid, worn-out, worthless, and ill-jointed substance of the scarecrow; but merely a spectral illusion, and a cunning effect of light and shade so coloured and contrived as to delude the eyes of most men. The miracles of witchcraft seem always to have had a very shallow subtlety; and, at least, if the above explanation do not hit the truth of the process, I can suggest no better.

"Well puffed, my pretty lad!" still cried old Mother Rigby. "Come, another good stout whiff, and let it be with might and main. Puff for thy life, I tell thee! Puff out of the very bottom of thy heart; if any heart thou hast, or any bottom to it! Well done, again! Thou did'st suck in that mouthful as if for the pure love of it."

And then the witch beckoned to the scarecrow, throwing so much magnetic potency into her gesture that it seemed as if it must inevitably be obeyed, like the mystic call of the loadstone when it summons the iron.

"Why lurkest thou in the corner, lazy one?" said she. "Step forth! Thou hast the world before thee!"

Upon my word, if the legend were not one which I heard on my grandmother's knee, and which had established its place among things credible before my childish judgment could analyze its probability, I question whether I should have the face to tell it now.

In obedience to Mother Rigby's word, and extending its arm as if to reach her outstretched hand, the figure made a step forward —a kind of hitch and jerk, however, rather than a step—then tottered and almost lost its balance. What could the witch expect? It was nothing, after all, but a scarecrow stuck upon two sticks. But the strong-willed old beldam scowled, and beckoned, and flung the energy of her purpose so forcibly at this poor combination of rotten wood, and musty straw, and ragged garments, that it was compelled to show itself a man, in spite of the reality of things. So it stepped into the bar of sunshine. There it stood—poor devil of a contrivance that it was!—with only the thinnest vesture of human similitude about it, through which was evident the stiff, ricketty, incongruous, faded, tattered, good-for-nothing patchwork of its substance, ready to sink in a heap upon the floor, as conscious of its own unworthiness to be erect. Shall I confess the truth? At its present point of vivification, the scarecrow reminds me of some of the lukewarm and abortive characters, composed of heterogeneous materials, used for the thousandth time, and never worth using, with which romance writers (and myself, no doubt, among the rest) have so over-peopled the world of fiction.

But the fierce old hag began to get angry and show a glimpse of her diabolic nature (like a snake's head, peeping with a hiss out of her bosom), at this pusillanimous behaviour of the thing which she had taken the trouble to put together.

"Puff away, wretch!" cried she wrathfully. "Puff, puff, puff, thou thing of straw and emptiness! thou rag or two! thou meal bag! thou pumpkin head! thou nothing! Where shall I find a name vile enough to call thee by? Puff, I say, and suck in thy fantastic life along with the smoke; else I snatch the pipe from thy mouth and hurl thee where that red coal came from."

Thus threatened, the unhappy scarecrow had nothing for it but to puff away for dear life. As need was, therefore, it applied itself lustily to the pipe, and sent forth such abundant volleys of tobacco smoke that the small cottage became all vaporous. The one sunbeam struggled mistily through, and could but imperfectly define the image of the cracked and dusty window pane on the opposite wall. Mother Rigby, meanwhile, with one brown arm akimbo and the other stretched towards the figure, loomed grimly amid the obscurity with such port and expression as when she was wont to heave a ponderous nightmare on her victims, and stand at the bedside to enjoy

their agony. In fear and trembling did this poor scarecrow puff. But its efforts, it must be acknowledged, served an excellent purpose; for, with each successive whiff, the figure lost more and more of its dizzy and perplexing tenuity and seemed to take denser substance. Its very garments, moreover, partook of the magical change, and shone with the gloss of novelty and glistened with the skilfully embroidered gold that had long been rent away. And, half-revealed among the smoke, a yellow visage bent its lustreless eyes on Mother Rigby.

At last the old witch clinched her fist and shook it at the figure. Not that she was positively angry, but merely acting on the principle—perhaps untrue, or not the only truth, though as high a one as Mother Rigby could be expected to attain—that feeble and torpid natures, being incapable of better inspiration, must be stirred up by fear. But here was the crisis. Should she fail in what she now sought to effect, it was her ruthless purpose to scatter the miserable simulacre into its original elements.

"Thou hast a man's aspect," said she, sternly. "Have also the echo and mockery of a voice! I bid thee speak!"

The scarecrow gasped, struggled, and at length emitted a murmur, which was so incorporated with its smoky breath that you could scarcely tell whether it were indeed a voice or only a whiff of tobacco. Some narrators of this legend hold the opinion that Mother Rigby's conjurations and the fierceness of her will had compelled a familiar spirit into the figure, and that the voice was his.

"Mother," mumbled the poor stifled voice, "be not so awful with me! I would fain speak; but being without wits, what can I say?"

"Thou canst speak, darling, canst thou?" cried Mother Rigby, relaxing her grim countenance into a smile. "And what shalt thou say, quotha! Say, indeed! Art thou of the brotherhood of the empty skull, and demandest of me what thou shalt say? Thou shalt say a thousand things, and saying them a thousand times over, thou shalt still have said nothing! Be not afraid, I tell thee! When thou comest into the world (whither I purpose sending thee forthwith), thou shalt not lack the wherewithal to talk. Talk! Why thou shalt babble like a mill-stream, if thou wilt. Thou hast brains enough for that, I trow!"

"At your service, mother," responded the figure.

"And that was well said, my pretty one,"

answered Mother Rigby. "Then thou spakest like thyself, and meant nothing. Thou shalt have a hundred such set phrases, and five hundred to the boot of them. And now, darling, I have taken so much pains with thee, and thou art so beautiful, that, by my troth, I love thee better than any witch's puppet in the world; and I've made them of all sorts—clay, wax, straw, sticks, night-fog, morning-mist, sea-foam, and chimney-smoke. But thou art the very best. So give heed to what I say."

"Yes, kind mother," said the figure, "with all my heart!"

"With all thy heart!" cried the old witch, setting her hands to her sides and laughing loudly. "Thou hast such a pretty way of speaking. With all thy heart! And thou didst put thy hand to the left side of thy waistcoat as if thou really hadst one!"

So now, in high good humour with this fantastic contrivance of hers, Mother Rigby told the scarecrow that it must go and play its part in the great world, where not one man in a hundred, she affirmed, was gifted with more real substance than itself. And, that he might hold up his head with the best of them, she endowed him, on the spot, with an unreckonable amount of wealth. It consisted partly of a gold mine in Eldorado, and of ten thousand shares in a broken bubble, and of half a million of acres of vineyard at the North Pole, and of a castle in the air, and a château in Spain, together with all the rents and income therefrom accruing. She further made over to him the cargo of a certain ship, laden with salt from Cadiz, which she herself, by her necromantic arts, had caused to founder, ten years before, in the deepest part of mid-ocean. If the salt were not dissolved, and could be brought to market, it would fetch a pretty penny among the fishermen. That he might not lack ready money, she gave him a copper farthing of Birmingham manufacture, being all the coin she had about her, and likewise a great deal of brass, which she applied to his forehead, thus making it yellower than ever.

"With that brass alone," quoth Mother Rigby, "thou canst pay thy way over all the earth. Kiss me, pretty darling! I have done my best for thee."

Furthermore, that the adventurer might lack no possible advantage towards a fair start in life, this excellent old dame gave him a token by which he was to introduce himself to a certain magistrate, member of the council, merchant, and elder of the Church (the four capacities constituting but one man), who

stood at the head of society in the neighbouring metropolis. The token was neither more nor less than a single word, which Mother Rigby whispered to the scarecrow, and which the scarecrow was to whisper to the merchant.

"Gouty as the old fellow is, he'll run thy errands for thee, when once thou hast given him that word in his ear," said the old witch. "Mother Rigby knows the worshipful Justice Gookin, and the worshipful Justice knows Mother Rigby!"

Here the witch thrust her wrinkled face close to the puppet's, chuckling irrepressibly, and fidgetting all through her system with delight at the idea which she meant to communicate.

"The worshipful Master Gookin," whispered she, "hath a comely maiden to his daughter. And hark ye, my pet! Thou hast a fair outside, and a pretty wit enough of thine own. Yea, a pretty wit enough! Thou wilt think better of it when thou hast seen more of other people's wits. Now, with thy outside and thy inside, thou art the very man to win a young girl's heart. Never doubt it! I tell thee it shall be so. Put but a bold face on the matter; sigh, smile, flourish thy hat, thrust forth thy leg like a dancing master, put thy right hand to the left side of thy waistcoat, and pretty Polly Gookin is thine own!"

All this while the new creature had been sucking in and exhaling the vapoury fragrance of his pipe, and seemed now to continue this occupation as much for the enjoyment it afforded as because it was an essential condition of his existence. It was wonderful to see how exceedingly like a human being it behaved. Its eyes (for it appeared to possess a pair) were bent on Mother Rigby, and at suitable junctures it nodded or shook its head. Neither did it lack words suitable for the occasion: "Really! Indeed! Pray tell me! Is it possible! Upon my word! By no means! O! Ah! Hem!" and other such weighty utterances as imply attention, inquiry, acquiescence, or dissent on the part of the auditor. Even had you stood by and seen the scarecrow made, you could scarcely have resisted the conviction that it perfectly understood the cunning counsels which the old witch poured into its counterfeit of an ear. The more earnestly it applied its lips to the pipe the more distinctly was its human likeness stamped among visible realities, the more sagacious grew its expression, the more lifelike its gestures and movements, and the more intelligibly audible its voice. Its garments, too, glistened so much the brighter with an illusory magnificence. The very pipe, in which burned the spell of all this wonder-work, ceased to appear as a smoke-blackened earthen-stump, and became a meer-schaum, with painted bowl and amber mouth-piece.

It might be apprehended, however, that as the life of the illusion seemed identical with the vapour of the pipe, it would terminate simultaneously with the reduction of the tobacco to ashes. But the beldam foresaw the difficulty.

"Hold thou the pipe, my precious one," said she, "while I fill it for thee again."

It was sorrowful to behold how the fine gentleman began to fade back into a scarecrow while Mother Rigby shook the ashes out of the pipe and proceeded to replenish it from her tobacco-box.

"Dickon," cried she, in her high, sharp tone, "another coal for this pipe!"

No sooner said than the intensely red speck of fire was glowing within the pipe-bowl; and the scarecrow, without waiting for the witch's bidding, applied the tube to his lips and drew in a few short, convulsive whiffs, which soon, however, became regular and equable.

"Now, mine own heart's darling," quoth Mother Rigby, "whatever may happen to thee, thou must stick to thy pipe. Thy life is in it; and that, at least, thou knowest well, if thou knowest nought besides. Stick to thy pipe, I say! Smoke, puff, blow thy cloud; and tell the people, if any question be made, that it is for thy health, and that so the physician orders thee to do. And, sweet one, when thou shalt find thy pipe getting low, go apart into some corner, and (first filling thy-self with smoke) cry sharply, 'Dickon, a fresh pipe of tobacco!' and, Dickon, another coal for my pipe!' and have it into thy pretty mouth as speedily as may be. Else, instead of a gallant gentleman in a gold laced coat, thou wilt be but a jumble of sticks and tattered clothes, and a bag of straw, and a withered pumpkin! Now depart, my treasure, and good luck go with thee!"

"Never fear, mother!" said the figure, in a stout voice, and sending forth a courageous whiff of smoke, "I will thrive, if an honest man and a gentleman may!"

"O thou wilt be the death of me!" cried the old witch, convulsed with laughter. "That was well said. If an honest man and a gentleman may! Thou playest thy part to perfection. Get along with thee for a smart fellow; and I will wager on thy head, as a man of pith and substance, with a brain, and what they call a heart, and all else that a man

should have, against any other thing on two legs. I hold myself a better witch than yesterday, for thy sake. Did not I make thee? And I defy any witch in New England to make such another! Here; take thy staff along with thee!"

The staff, though it was but a plain oaken stick, immediately took the aspect of a gold-headed cane.

"That gold head has as much sense in it as thine own,".said Mother Rigby, "and it will guide thee straight to worshipful Master Gookin's door. Get thee gone, my pretty pet, my darling, my precious one, my treasure; and if anyone ask thy name, it is Feathertop. For thou hast a feather in thy hat, and I have thrust a handful of feathers into the hollow of thy head, and thy wig, too, is of the fashion they call Feathertop,—so be Feathertop thy name!"

And, issuing from the cottage, Feathertop strode manfully towards town. Mother Rigby stood at the threshold, well pleased to see how the sunbeams glistened on him, as if all his magnificence were real, and how diligently and lovingly he smoked his pipe, and how hand-somely he walked, in spite of a little stiffness of his legs. She watched him until out of sight, and threw a witch benediction after her darling, when a turn of the road snatched him from her view.

II.

Betimes in the forenoon, when the principal street of the neighbouring town was just at its acme of life and bustle, a stranger of very dis-tinguished figure was seen on the side-walk. His port as well as his garments betokened nothing short of nobility. He wore a richly-embroidered plum-coloured coat, a waistcoat of costly velvet, magnificently adorned with golden foliage, a pair of splendid scarlet breeches, and the finest and glossiest of white silk stockings. His head was covered with a peruke, so daintily powdered and adjusted that it would have been sacrilege to disorder it with a hat; which, therefore, (and it was a gold-laced hat, set off with a snowy feather), he carried beneath his arm. On the breast of his coat glistened a star. He managed his gold-headed cane with an airy grace peculiar to the fine gentleman of the period; and, to give the highest possible finish to his equip-ment, he had lace ruffles at his wrist, of a most ethereal delicacy, sufficiently avouching how idle and aristocratic must be the hands which they half concealed.

It was a remarkable point in the accoutrement of this brilliant personage, that he held in his left had a fantastic kind of a pipe, with an exquisitely painted bowl and an amber mouthpiece. This he applied to his lips as often as every five or six paces, and inhaled a deep whiff of smoke, which, after being retained a moment in his lungs, might be seen to eddy gracefully from his mouth and nostrils.

As may well be supposed, the street was all astir to find out the stranger's name.

"It is some great nobleman, beyond question," said one of the townspeople. "Do you see the star at his breast?"

"Nay; it is too bright to be seen," said another. "Yes; he must needs be a nobleman as you say. But by what conveyance, think you, can his lordship have voyaged or travelled hither? There has been no vessel from the old country for a month past; and if he have arrived overland from the southward, pray where are his attendants and equipage?"

"He needs no equipage to set off his rank," remarked a third. "If he came among us in rags, nobility would shine through a hole in his elbow. I never saw such dignity of aspect. He has the old Norman blood in his veins, I warrant him."

"I rather take him to be a Dutchman, or one of your high Germans," said another citizen. "The men of those countries have always the pipe at their mouths."

"And so has a Turk," answered his companion. "But, in my judgment, this stranger hath been bred at the French court, and hath there learned politeness and grace of manner, which none understand so well as the nobility of France. What gait, now! A vulgar spectator might deem it stiff—he might call it a hitch and a jerk—but, to my eye, it hath an unspeakable majesty, and must have been acquired by constant observation of the deportment of the Grand Monarque. The stranger's character and office are evident enough. He is a French ambassador, come to treat with our rulers about the cession of Canada."

"More probably a Spaniard," said another, "and hence his yellow complexion; or, most likely, he is from the Havanas, or from some port on the Spanish main, and comes to make investigation about the piracies which our governor is thought to connive at. Those settlers in Peru and Mexico have skins as yellow as the gold which they dig out of their mines."

"Yellow or not," cried a lady, "he is a beautiful man!—so tall, so slender! such a fine, noble face, with so well-shaped a nose, and all that delicacy of expression about the mouth. And, bless me, how bright his star is! It positively shoots out flames!"

"So do your eyes, fair lady," said the stranger, with a bow and a flourish of his pipe; for he was just passing at the instant. "Upon my honour, they have quite dazzled me."

"Was ever so original and exquisite a compliment?" murmured the lady, in an ecstacy of delight.

Amid the general admiration excited by the stranger's appearance, there were only two dissentient voices. One was that of an impertinent cur, which, after snuffing at the heels of the glistening figure, put its tail between its legs and skulked into its master's backyard, vociferating an execrable howl. The other dissentient was a young child, who squalled at the fullest stretch of his lungs, and babbled some unintelligible nonsense about a pumpkin.

Feathertop meanwhile pursued his way along the street. Except for the few complimentary words to the lady, and now and then a slight inclination of the head in requital of the profound reverences of the bystanders, he seemed wholly absorbed in his pipe. There needed no other proof of his rank and consequence than the perfect equanimity with which he comported himself, while the curiosity and admiration of the town swelled into a clamour around him. With a crowd gathering behind his footsteps, he finally reached the mansion-house of the worshipful Justice Gookin, entered the gate, ascended the steps of the front door, and knocked. In the interim, before his summons was answered, the stranger was observed to shake the ashes out of his pipe.

"What did he say in that sharp voice?" inquired one of the spectators.

"Nay, I know not," answered his friend. "But the sun dazzles my eyes strangely. How dim and faded his lordship looks all of a sudden! Bless my wits, what is the matter with me?"

"The wonder is," said the other, "that his pipe, which was out only an instant ago, should be all alight again, and with the reddest coal I ever saw. There is something mysterious about this stranger. What a whiff of smoke was that! Dim and faded did you call him? Why, as he turns about, the star on his breast is all ablaze."

"It is indeed," said his companion; "and it will go near to dazzle pretty Polly Gookin, whom I see peering at it out of the chamber window."

The door being now opened, Feathertop turned to the crowd, made a stately bend of his body like a great man acknowledging the reverence of the meaner sort, and vanished into the house. There was a mysterious kind of a smile, if it might not better be called a grin or grimace, upon his visage; but, of all the throng that beheld him, not an individual appears to have possessed insight enough to detect the illusive character of the stranger except a little child and a cur dog.

Our legend here loses somewhat of its continuity, and, passing over the preliminary explanation between Feathertop and the merchant, goes in quest of the pretty Polly Gookin. She was a damsel of a soft, round figure, with light hair and blue eyes, and a fair, rosy face, which seemed neither very shrewd nor very simple. This young lady had caught a glimpse of the glistening stranger while standing at the threshold, and had forthwith put on a laced cap, a string of beads, her finest kerchief, and her stiffest damask petticoat, in preparation for the interview. Hurrying from her chamber to the parlour, she had ever since been viewing herself in the large looking-glass and practising pretty airs—now a smile, now a ceremonious dignity of aspect, and now a softer smile than the former, kissing her hand likewise, tossing her head, and managing her fan; while within the mirror an unsubstantial little maid repeated every gesture, and did all the foolish things that Polly did, but without making her ashamed of them. In short, it was the fault of pretty Polly's ability rather than her will if she failed to be as complete an artifice as the illustrious Feathertop himself; and, when she thus tampered with her own simplicity, the witch's phantom might well hope to win her.

No sooner did Polly hear her father's gouty footsteps approaching the parlour door, accompanied with the stiff clatter of Feathertop's high-heeled shoes, than she seated herself bolt upright and innocently began warbling a song.

"Polly! daughter Polly!" cried the old merchant. "Come hither, child."

Master Gookin's aspect, as he opened the door, was doubtful and troubled.

"This gentleman," continued he, presenting the stranger, "is the Chevalier Feathertop,—nay, I beg his pardon, my Lord Feathertop,—who hath brought me a token of remembrance from an ancient friend of mine. Pay your duty to his lordship, child, and honour him as his quality deserves."

After those few words of introduction, the worshipful magistrate immediately quitted the room. But, even in that brief moment, had the fair Polly glanced aside at her father instead of devoting herself wholly to the brilliant guest, she might have taken warning of some mischief nigh at hand. The old man was nervous, fidgety, and very pale. Purposing a smile of courtesy, he had deformed his face with a sort of galvanic grin, which, when Feathertop's back was turned, he exchanged for a scowl, at the same time shaking his fist and stamping his gouty foot—an incivility which brought its retribution along with it. The truth appears to have been, that Mother Rigby's word of introduction, whatever it might be, had operated far more on the rich merchant's fears than on his goodwill. Moreover, being a man of wonderfully acute observation, he had noticed that the painted figures on the bowl of Feathertop's pipe were in motion. Looking more closely, he became convinced that these figures were a party of little demons, each duly provided with horns and a tail, and dancing hand in hand, with gestures of diabolical merriment, round the circumference of the pipe-bowl. As if to confirm his suspicions, while Master Gookin ushered his guest along a dusky passage from his private room to the parlour, the star on Feathertop's breast had scintillated actual flames, and threw a flickering gleam upon the wall, the ceiling, and the floor.

With such sinister prognostics manifesting themselves on all hands, it is not to be marvelled at that the merchant should have felt that he was committing his daughter to a very questionable acquaintance. He cursed, in his secret soul, the insinuating elegance of Feathertop's manners, as this brilliant personage bowed, smiled, put his hand on his heart, inhaled a long whiff from his pipe, and enriched the atmosphere with the smoky vapour of a fragrant and visible sigh. Gladly would poor Master Gookin have thrust his dangerous guest into the street; but there was a constraint and terror within him. This respectable old gentleman, we fear, at an earlier period of life, had given some pledge or other to the evil principle, and perhaps was now to redeem it by the sacrifice of his daughter.

It so happened that the parlour door was partly of glass, shaded by a silken curtain, the folds of which hung a little awry. So strong was the merchant's interest in witnessing what was to ensue between the fair Polly and the gallant Feathertop, that after quitting the room he could by no means refrain from peeping through the crevice of the curtain.

But there was nothing very miraculous to be seen; nothing—except the trifles previously noticed—to confirm the idea of a supernatural peril environing the pretty Polly. The stranger, it is true, was evidently a thorough and practised man of the world, systematic, and self-possessed, and therefore the sort of a person to whom a parent ought not to confide a simple young girl, without due watchfulness for the result. The worthy magistrate, who had been conversant with all degrees and qualities of mankind, could not but perceive every motion and gesture of the distinguished Feathertop come in its proper place; nothing had been left rude or native in him; a well-digested conventionalism had incorporated itself thoroughly with his substance and transformed him into a work of art. Perhaps it was this peculiarity that invested him with a species of ghastliness and awe. It is the effect of anything completely and consummately artificial, in human shape, that the person impresses us as an unreality, and as having hardly pith enough to cast a shadow upon the floor. As regarded Feathertop, all this resulted in a wild, extravagant, and fantastical impression, as if his life and being were akin to the smoke that curled upward from his pipe.

But pretty Polly Gookin felt not thus. The pair were now promenading the room; Feathertop with his dainty stride and no less dainty grimace; the girl with a native maidenly grace, just touched, not spoiled, by a slightly affected manner, which seemed caught from the perfect artifice of her companion. The longer the interview continued, the more charmed was pretty Polly, until, within the first quarter of an hour (as the old magistrate noted by his watch), she was evidently beginning to be in love. Nor need it have been witchcraft that subdued her in such a hurry; the poor child's heart, it may be, was so very fervent that it melted her with its own warmth as reflected from the hollow semblance of a lover. No matter what Feathertop said, his words found depth and reverberation in her ear; no matter what he did, his action was heroic to her eye. And by this time it is to be supposed there was a blush on Polly's cheek, a tender smile about her mouth, and a liquid softness in her glance; while the star kept coruscating on Feathertop's breast, and the little demons careered with more frantic merriment than ever about the circumference of his pipe-bowl. O, pretty Polly Gookin, why should these imps rejoice so madly that a silly

maiden's heart was about to be given to a shadow! Is it so unusual a misfortune, so rare a triumph?

By and by Feathertop paused, and, throwing himself into an imposing attitude, seemed to summon the fair girl to survey his figure and resist him longer if she could. His star, his embroidery, his buckles glowed at that instant with unutterable splendour; the picturesque hues of his attire took a richer depth of colouring; there was a gleam and polish over his whole presence betokening the perfect witchery of well-ordered manners. The maiden raised her eyes and suffered them to linger upon her companion with a bashful and admiring gaze. Then, as if desirous of judging what value her own simple comeliness might have side by side with so much brilliancy, she cast a glance towards the full length looking-glass in front of which they happened to be standing. It was one of the truest plates in the world, and incapable of flattery. No sooner did the images therein reflected meet Polly's eye than she shrieked, shrank from the stranger's side, gazed at him for a moment in the wildest dismay, and sank insensible upon the floor. Feathertop likewise had looked towards the mirror, and there beheld, not the glittering mockery of his outside show, but a picture of the sordid patchwork of his real composition, stripped of all witchcraft.

The wretched simulacrum! We almost pity him. He threw up his arms with an expression of despair that went further than any of his previous manifestations towards vindicating his claims to be reckoned human; for, perchance the only time since this so often empty and deceptive life of mortals began its course, an illusion had seen and fully recognized itself.

III.

Mother Rigby was seated by her kitchen hearth in the twilight of this eventful day, and had just shaken the ashes out of a new pipe, when she heard a hurried tramp along the road. Yet it did not seem so much the tramp of human footsteps as the clatter of sticks or the rattling of dry bones.

"Ha!" thought the old witch, "what step is that? Whose skeleton is out of its grave now, I wonder?"

A figure burst headlong into the cottage door. It was Feathertop! His pipe was still alight; the star still flamed upon his breast; the embroidery still glowed upon his garments; nor had he lost, in any degree or manner that could be estimated, the aspect that assimilated him with our mortal brotherhood. But yet, in some indescribable way (as is the case with all that has deluded us when once found out), the poor reality was felt beneath the cunning artifice. "What has gone wrong?" demanded the witch. "Did yonder sniffling hypocrite thrust my darling from his door? The villain! I'll set twenty fiends to torment him till he offer thee his daughter on his bended knees!"

"No, mother," said Feathertop despondingly; "it was not that."

"Did the girl scorn my precious one?" asked Mother Rigby, her fierce eyes glowing like two coals of Tophet. "I'll cover her face with pimples! Her nose shall be as red as the coal in my pipe! Her front teeth shall drop out! In a week hence she shall not be worth thy having!"

"Let her alone, mother," answered poor Feathertop; "the girl was half won; and me-thinks a kiss from her sweet lips might have made me altogether human. But," he added, after a brief pause, and then a howl of self-contempt, "I've seen myself, mother! I've seen myself for the wretched, ragged, empty thing I am! I'll exist no longer!"

Snatching the pipe from his mouth, he flung it with all his might against the chimney, and at the same instant sank upon the floor, a medley of straw and tattered garments, with some sticks protruding from the heap, and a shrivelled pumpkin in the midst. The eye-holes were now lustreless; but the rudely carved gap, that just before had been a mouth, still seemed to twist itself into a despairing grin, and was so far human.

"Poor fellow!" quoth Mother Rigby, with a rueful glance at the relics of her ill-fated contrivance. "My poor, dear, pretty Feathertop! There are thousands upon thousands of coxcombs and charlatans in the world, made up of just such a jumble of worn-out, for-gotten, and good-for-nothing trash as he was! Yet they live in fair repute, and never see themselves for what they are. And why should my poor puppet be the only one to know himself and perish for it?"

While thus muttering, the witch had filled a fresh pipe of tobacco, and held the stem between her fingers, as doubtful whether to thrust it into her own mouth or Feathertop's.

"Poor Feathertop!" she continued. "I could easily give him another chance and send him forth again to-morrow. But no; his feelings are too tender, his sensibilities too deep. He seems to have too much heart to bustle for his own advantage in such an empty and heartless world. Well! well! I'll

make a scarecrow of him after all. 'Tis an innocent and a useful vocation, and will suit my darling well; and if each of his human brethren had as fit a one, 'twould be better for mankind; and as for this pipe of tobacco, I need it more than he."

So saying, Mother Rigby put the stem between her lips. "Dickon!" cried she, in her high, sharp tone, "another coal for my pipe!"

THE LAST NIGHT AT HOME.

BY COVENTRY PATMORE.

O, Muse, who dost to me reveal
The mystery of the woman's life,
Relate how 'tis a maid might feel,
The night before she's crown'd a wife!
Lo, sleepless in her little bed,
She lies and counts the hours till noon.
Ere this, to-morrow, she'll be wed,
Ere this? Alas, how strangely soon!
A fearful blank of ignorance
Lies, manifest, across her way,
And shadows, cast from unknown chance,
Make sad and dim the coming day.
Her faithless dread she now discards,
And now remorseful memory flings
Its glory round the last regards
Of home and all accustom'd things.
Her father's voice, her mother's eyes
Accuse her treason; 'tis in vain
She thinks herself a wife, and tries
To comprehend the greater gain;
Her unknown fortune nothing cheers
Her loving heart's familiar loss,
And torrents of repentant tears
Their hot and smarting threshold cross.
When first within her bosom Love
Took birth, and beat his blissful wings,
It seem'd to lift her mind above
All care for other earthly things;
But, oh, too lightly did she vow
To leave for aye her happy nest;
And dreadful is the thought that now
Assaults her weak and shaken breast:
Ah, should her lover's love abate;
Ah, should she, miserable, lose
All dear regards of maiden state,
Dissolved by time and marriage dues!
And so her fears increase, till fear
O'erfilms her apprehensive eye
That she may swoon, with no one near,
And haply so, unmarried, die.
With instinct of her ignorance,
(The virgin's strength and veiled guide,)
She prays, and casts the reins of chance
To Love, nor recks what shall betide.

The Angel in the House.

THE GRANDMOTHER.

[Alfred Tennyson, D.C.L., F.R.S., born at Somerby, Lincolnshire, 1809; poet laureate. He was educated by his father, the late Rev. G. C. Tennyson, and at Trinity College, Cambridge, where in 1829 he gained the Chancellor's medal for his English poem entitled *Timbuctoo*. Two years before that event, he had published, in conjunction with his brother Charles, a small volume under the title of *Poems by Two Brothers*.[1] In 1830 he issued *Poems, chiefly Lyrical;* another volume, partly reprints, two years later, and a third in 1842. These were followed by *The Princess*, 1847; *In Memoriam*, 1850; *Ode on the Death of the Duke of Wellington*, 1852; *Maud, and other Poems*, 1855; *The Idylls of the King*, 1859; *Enoch Arden*, 1864; *The Holy Grail*, 1869; *The Window, or the Songs of the Wrens*, 1870, &c. Mr. Tennyson has added repeatedly to the *Idylls of the King* and the work was not completed until the publication of *Gareth* and *Lynette* in 1873. On the death of Wordsworth, he was appointed poet laureate.[2] *The Edinburgh Review* says: "The particular power by which Mr. Tennyson surpasses all recent English poets is precisely that of sustained perfection of style." He has obtained general recognition as the first of modern English poets. His complete works are published by Henry S. King & Co.

And Willy, my eldest-born, is gone, you say, little Anne?
Ruddy and white, and strong on his legs, he looks like a man.
And Willy's wife has written: she never was over-wise,
Never the wife for Willy: he wouldn't take my advice.

For, Annie, you see, her father was not the man to save,
Hadn't a head to manage, and drank himself into his grave.
Pretty enough, very pretty! but I was against it for one.
Eh!—but he wouldn't hear me—and Willy, you say, is gone.

Willy, my beauty, my eldest-born, the flower of the flock;
Never a man could fling him: for Willy stood like a rock.
"Here's a leg for a babe of a week!" says doctor; and he would be bound,
There was not his like that year in twenty parishes round.

Strong of his hands, and strong on his legs, but still of his tongue!
I ought to have gone before him: I wonder he went so young.
I cannot cry for him, Annie: I have not long to stay;
Perhaps I shall see him the sooner, for he lived far away.

Why do you look at me, Annie? you think I am hard and cold;
But all my children have gone before me, I am so old:
I cannot weep for Willy, nor can I weep for the rest;
Only at your age, Annie, I could have wept with the best.

[1] Wordsworth upon reading this volume at first thought Charles the better poet of the two; but afterwards altered his opinion.

[2] The duties and origin of this office are somewhat obscure. The poet laureate was to furnish the state with a measure of praise and verse twice a year. The Delphic laurel consecrated to Apollo in the mythology of the Greeks, or the garland of oak-leaves given to victors in the Roman Capitoline games, probably first suggested the literary distinction of poet laureate, which, with some variations of ceremonies, was maintained until the reign of Theodocius, who abolished it as a remnant of pagan superstition. The title was not used again until it was conferred upon Petrarch, who revived the spirit and studies of the age of Augustus. After Petrarch the title was bestowed on Philelphus, a satirical poet of the fifteenth century; then on Tasso; then on Quezno, the buffoon of Leo X.! and next upon Æneas Sylvius Piccolomini. The following anecdote is not without meaning: A poor poet, hoping for some reward, presented a panegyric to Pope Pius III., who sent him an epigram to this effect:—

"The poet in his own work aye finds his greatest need."

The poet retorted:—

"If thou wert so rewarded, thou wouldst be poor indeed!"

The following is a list of English poets laureate, but the appointment of the first two named is considered doubtful by some authorities: John Skelton, who died 1529; Edmund Spenser, died 1598-9; Samuel Daniel, who was appointed to the laureateship in the year of Spenser's death; Ben Jonson, appointed 1619; Sir William Davenant, 1637; John Dryden, 1668; dismissed the same year on account of being a Papist; Thomas Shadwell, 1688; Nahum Tate, 1692; Nicholas Rowe, 1715; Lawrence Eusden, 1718; Colley Cibber, 1730; W. Whitehead, 1757; Thomas Warton, 1785; Henry James Pye, 1790; Robert Southey, 1813 (the laurel was offered to Scott in this year and he declined it.; William Wordsworth, 1843; Alfred Tennyson, 1850. The dates given are those of the appointment, which was generally made immediately after the death of the preceding laureate

For I remember a quarrel I had with your father, my dear,
All for a slanderous story, that cost me many a tear.
I mean your grandfather, Annie: it cost me a world of woe,
Seventy years ago, my darling, seventy years ago.

For Jenny, my cousin, had come to the place, and I knew right well
Then Jenny had tript in her time: I knew, but I would not tell.
And she to be coming and slandering me, the base little liar!
But the tongue is a fire as you know, my dear, the tongue is a fire.

And the parson made it his text that week, and he said likewise,
That a lie which is half a truth is ever the blackest of lies,
That a lie which is all a lie may be met and fought with outright,
But a lie which is part a truth is a harder matter to fight.

And Willy had not been down to the farm for a week and a day;
And all things look'd half-dead, tho' it was the middle of May.
Jenny, to slander me, who knew what Jenny had been!
But soiling another, Annie, will never make oneself clean.

And I cried myself well-nigh blind, and all of an evening late
I climb'd to the top of the garth, and stood by the road at the gate.
The moon like a rick on fire was rising over the dale,
And whit, whit, whit, in the bush beside me chirrupt the nightingale.

All of a sudden he stopt: there past by the gate of the farm,
Willy,—he didn't see me,—and Jenny hung on his arm.
Out into the road I started, and spoke I scarce knew how;
Ah, there's no fool like the old one—it makes me angry now.

Willy stood up like a man, and look'd the thing that he meant;
Jenny, the viper, made me a mocking courtsey and went.
And I said, "Let us part: in a hundred years it'll all be the same,
You cannot love me at all, if you love not my good name."

And he turn'd, and I saw his eyes all wet, in the sweet moonshine:
"Sweetheart, I love you so well that your good name is mine.
And what do I care for Jane, let her speak of you well or ill;
But marry me out of hand: we two shall be happy still:"

"Marry you, Willy!" said I, "but I needs must speak my mind,
And I fear you'll listen to tales, be jealous and hard and unkind."
But he turn'd and claspt me in his arms, and answer'd, "No, love, no;"
Seventy years ago, my darling, seventy years ago.

So Willy and I were wedded: I wore a lilac gown;
And the ringers rang with a will, and he gave the ringers a crown.
But the first that ever I bare was dead before he was born,
Shadow and shine is life, little Annie, flower and thorn

That was the first time, too, that ever I thought of death.
There lay the sweet little body that never had drawn a breath.
I had not wept, little Anne, not since I had been a wife;
But I wept like a child that day, for the babe had fought for his life.

His dear little face was troubled, as if with anger or pain:
I look'd at the still little body—his trouble had all been in vain.
For Willy I cannot weep, I shall see him another morn:
But I wept like a child for the child that was dead before he was born.

But he cheer'd me, my good man, for he seldom said me nay:
Kind, like a man, was he; like a man, too, would have his way:
Never jealous—not he: we had many a happy year;
And he died, and I could not weep—my own time seem'd so near.

But I wish'd it had been God's will that I, too, then could have died:
I began to be tired a little, and fain had slept at his side.
And that was ten years back, or more, if I don't forget:
But as to the children, Annie, they're all about me yet.

Pattering over the boards, my Annie who left me at two,
Patter she goes, my own little Annie, an Annie like you:
Pattering over the boards, she comes and goes at her will,
While Harry is in the five-acre and Charlie ploughing the hill.

And Harry and Charlie, I hear them too—they sing to their team:
Often they come to the door in a pleasant kind of a dream.
They come and sit by my chair, they hover about my bed—
I am not always certain if they be alive or dead.

And yet I know for a truth, there's none of them left alive;
For Harry went at sixty, your father at sixty-five:
And Willy, my eldest born, at nigh threescore and ten;
I knew them all as babies, and now they're elderly men.

For mine is a time of peace, it is not often I grieve;
I am oftener sitting at home in my father's farm at eve:
And the neighbours come and laugh and gossip, and so do I;
I find myself often laughing at things that have long gone by.

To be sure the preacher says, our sins should make us sad:
But mine is a time of peace, and there is Grace to be had;
And God, not man, is the Judge of us all when life shall cease;
And in this Book, little Annie, the message is one of Peace.

And age is a time of peace, so it be free from pain,
And happy has been my life; but I would not live it again.
I seem to be tired a little, that's all, and long for rest;
Only at your age, Annie, I could have wept with the best.

So Willy has gone, my beauty, my eldest-born, my flower;
But how can I weep for Willy, he has but gone for an hour,—
Gone for a minute, my son, from this room into the next;
I, too, shall go in a minute.   What time have I to be vext?

And Willy's wife has written, she never was overwise.
Get me my glasses, Annie: thank God that I keep my eyes.
There is but a trifle left you, when I shall have passed away.
But stay with the old woman now: you cannot have long to stay.

A FAMILY IN LOVE.

[Mrs. Dinah Maria Mulock Craik, born at Stoke-upon-Trent, Staffordshire, 1826. She is distinguished as a writer of the best class of novels, but she is also the author of many tender, truthful, and inspiring poems. Her first novel, *The Ogilvies*, appeared in 1849, and was followed by *Olive; The Head of the Family; Alice Learmont*, a fairy tale ; *Agatha's Husband; John Halifax, Gentleman* (this is the most popular of all her works); *Nothing New*—a collection of eight tales, from which we take the following; *A Woman's Thoughts about Women; Studies from Life; A Life for a Life; Mistress and Maid*, &c. She has also written many books for children. Her chief works are published by Hurst and Blackett, her poems by Sampson Low, Marston, & Co. "We are always glad to welcome Miss Mulock. She writes from her own convictions, and she has the power not only to conceive clearly what it is that she wishes to say, but to express it in language effective and vigorous."—*Athenæum*.]

This is the age of complainings. Nobody suffers in silence; nobody breaks his or her heart in secrecy and solitude: they all take "the public" into their confidence—the convenient public, which, like murder,

> Hath no tongue, but speaks
> With most miraculous organ.

Of course it is neither the confider's fault nor yet the confidant's, if the winds sometimes whisper that king Midas has asses' ears.

Mine is no such confession. I have no gossip to retail of my neighbours: I am a very quiet gentleman, who prefer confining my interests and observations to my own household, my own immediate family. Ay, there lies my inevitable grief, there lurks my secret wrong; I am the unhappy elder brother of a family in love.

The fact dimly dawned upon me, widening by degrees, ever since I came home from India last year, and took upon myself the charge of my five sisters, aged from about—— But Martha might object to my particularizing. Good little Patty! what a merry creature she was when she went nutting and fishing with me. And what ugly caps she has taken to wearing, poor dear! And why can't she speak as gently when scolding the servants as I remember our sweet-voiced pretty mother used always to do? And why, in spite of their mutual position, will she persist in calling Mr. Green with a kind of frigid solemnity, " Mr. Green?" But he does not seem to mind it: probably he never was called anything else. He is a very worthy person, nevertheless, and I have a great respect for him. When my sister Martha—Miss Heathcote, as she

has been called from her cradle—by letter announced to me at Madras that she intended to relinquish that title for the far less euphonious one of Mrs. Green, I was, to say the least of it, surprised. I had thought, for various reasons (of no moment now), that my eldest sister was not likely to marry—I rather hoped she would not. We might have been so comfortable, poor Patty and I. However, I had no business to interfere with either her happiness or her destiny; so when, the first Sunday after my arrival at home, a cozy carriage drove up the avenue, and a bald, rather stout little man got out, to be solemnly introduced to me as " Mr. Green," I submitted to the force of circumstances, and to the duties of a brother-in-law.

He has dined with us every Sunday since. He and I are capital friends; regularly, when the ladies retire, he informs me what the Funds have been at, day by day during the past week, and which is the safest railway to buy shares in for the week following. A most worthy person, I repeat, will make a kind husband, and I suppose Martha likes him; but ——. However, poor girl, she is old enough to judge for herself, and it is no business of mine. Some time, before long, I shall give her away at the old parish church—quietly, without any show; I shall see her walk down the church-aisle with old Mr. Green—he in his best white waistcoat, and she in her sober gray poplin, which she insists on being married in—not the clear soft muslin and long lace veil I quite well remember seeing Patty working at and blushing over, we won't say how many years ago. Well, women are better married, they say; but I think I would rather have had Martha an old maid.

My second sister, Angeline, was fifteen when I left England; and the very loveliest creature I ever beheld. Everybody knew it, everybody acknowledged it. She could not walk down the street without people turning to look after her; she could not enter a room without creating a general whisper: " Who is she?"—The same thing continued as she grew up to womanhood. All the world was at her feet; every one said she would make a splendid marriage—become a countess at least; and I do believe Angeline herself had the fullest confidence in that probability. She refused lovers by the dozen: every letter I got told me of some new slaughter of Miss Angeline's. I would have pitied the poor fellows, only she was such a dazzling beauty, and no man falls out of love so safely as a man who falls in love with a beauty. I never heard that anybody died either by consumption, cord, or pistol, through the cruelty of my sister Angeline.

But, like most cruel damsels, she paid the penalty of her hard-heartedness; when I came home I found Angeline Heathcote Angeline Heathcote still. Beautiful yet, beautiful exceedingly; a walking picture, a visible poem: it was a real pleasure to me to have such a handsome creature about the house. Though people did say with a mysterious shake of the head, that handsome as she was, if I had only seen my sister two or three years ago! And Angeline herself became tenacious on the subject of new gowns, and did not like it to be generally known whether she or Charlotte was the elder. Good, plain, merry Charlotte, who never thought about either her looks or her age.

Yet Charlotte was the first that brought me into trouble—that trouble which I am now called upon to bemoan. I had not been at home three months, when there came a young gentleman—a very lively and pleasant young gentleman too—who sang duets with the younger girls, and made himself quite at home in my family circle. I myself did not much meddle with him, thought him a good-natured lad, and no more—until one fine morning he astonished me by requesting five minutes' conversation with me in my study. (Alas! such misfortunes come not singly—my study has never been safe from similar applications and conversations since.)

I was very kind to the young man; when he blushed I looked another way; when he trembled, I invited him to take a chair. I listened to his stammering explanations with the utmost patience and sympathy; I even tried to help him out with them—till he came to the last clause.

Now, I do say that a man who asks you for your purse, your horse, your friendship, after only four weeks' acquaintance, has considerable courage; but a man who, after that brief period since his introduction, comes and asks you for your *sister*—why, one's first impulse is to kick him down stairs.

Happily, I controlled myself. I called to mind that Mr. Cuthbert was a very honest young fellow, and that if he did choose to risk his whole future upon the result of a month's laughing, and singing, and dancing at balls—certainly it was his affair, not mine. My business solely related to Charlotte. I was just despatching it in the quickest and friendliest manner, by advising the young fellow to go back to college and not make a fool of himself in vain, when he informed me that my

consent only was required, since he and Charlotte had been a plighted couple for the space of three whole days!

I have always held certain crotchets on the paramount rights of lovers, and the wrong of interfering with any apparently sincere vows; so I sent for Lotty—talked with her; found she was just as foolish as he. That because he was the best waltzer, the sweetest tenor singer, and had the handsomest moustache she knew—our lively Charlotte was quite contented to dance through life with Mr. Cuthbert, and decidedly proud of having his diamond ring on her third finger, and being considered "engaged"—as indeed they were likely to remain, if their minds changed not, for the next ten years.

So, what could I do?—Nothing but deal with the young simpletons—if such they were—according to their folly. If true, their love would have time to prove itself such; if false, they would best find out that fact by its not being thwarted. I kissed away Lotty's tears, silly child! and next Sunday I had the honour of carving for brother-in-law elect No. 2.

It never rains but it pours. Whether Angeline was roused at once to indignation and condescension by Charlotte's engagement—which she was the loudest in inveighing against—or whether, as was afterwards reported to me, she was influenced by a certain statistical newspaper paragraph, maliciously read aloud by Mr. Cuthbert for general edification, that women's chances of matrimony were proved by the late census to diminish greatly between the ages of thirty and thirty-five; but most assuredly Angeline's demeanour changed. She stooped to be agreeable as well as beautiful. To more than one suitor whom she had of old swept haughtily by, did she now graciously incline; and the result was—partly owing to the gaieties of this autumn's election—that Miss Angeline Heathcote, the beauty of the country, held a general election on her own private account.

Alas for me! in one week I had no less than four hopeful candidates requesting "the honour of an interview" in my study.

Angeline's decision was rather dilatory—they were all such excellent matches; and, poor girl—with her beauty for her chief gift and with all the tinsel adoration it brought her, she had never been used to think of marriage as anything more than a mere worldly arrangement. She was ready to choose a husband as she would a wedding-gown—dispassionately, carefully, as the best out of a large selection of articles, each rich and good in its way, and warranted to wear. She had plenty of common sense, and an acute judgment; as for her heart——

"You see, Nigel," she said to me, when weighing the respective claims and merits of Mr. Archer and Sir Roland Griffith Jones—"you see, I never was sentimentally inclined. I want to be married. I think I should be better married than single. Of course, my husband must be a good man; also, he should be a wealthy man; because—well!—because I rather like show and splendour: they suit me."

And she glanced into the mirror at something which, certainly, if any woman has any excuse for the vanities of life, might have pleaded Angeline's.

"But," I argued—half sorrowfully, as when you see an ignorant child throwing gold away, and choosing sham jewels for their pitiful glistering, "you surely would think it necessary to love your husband?"

"Oh yes; and I like Sir Roland extremely—perhaps even better than Mr. Archer—though he has been fond of me so long, poor fellow! but he will get over it—all men do."

So, though the balance hung for a whole week doubtful, Heaven forgive the girl! but true love was not in her nature, and how can people see further than their lights go?—I was soon pretty certain that fate would decide the marriage question in favour of the baronet. As Lotty said, Angeline would look magnificent in the family diamonds as Lady Griffith Jones.

The Welsh cause triumphed; Mr. Archer quitted the field. He had been an old acquaintance; but—what was that to Sir Roland and £10,000 a year?

After Angeline's affair was settled, there came a lull in the family epidemic—possibly because the head of the family grew savage as a bear, and for a full month his spirit hugged itself into fierce misanthropy, or rather misogyny, contemning the whole female sex, especially such as contemplated, or were contemplated in, the unholy estate of matrimony. No wonder! I could not find peace in my own house; I had not my own sisters' society; not a single family fireside evening could I get from week's end to week's end; not a room could I enter without breaking in on some tête-a-tête; not a corner could I creep into without stumbling upon a pair of lovers. For a little while these fond couples kept on their good behaviour towards me—preserved a degree of reserve towards each other out of respect to the head of the house, the elder brother; but gra-

dually it deteriorated—ceased. Nay, I, who belong to the old generation—which was foolish enough to deem caresses hallowed things, that the mere pressure of a beloved woman's hand, not to speak of her sacred mouth, was a thing not to be made a public show of—never to be thought of without a tender reverence, a delicious fear—I, Nigel Heathcote, have actually seen two young men, strangers a little year ago, kiss my two sisters openly before their whole family—before their brother's very face.

My situation became intolerable. I fled the fireside; I took refuge in my study. Woe betide the next lover who should assail me there!

Surely that fatality would not again arrive for some time. When the elder ones were once married and away, surely I, and Constantia, and little Lizzie might live a few years in fraternal peace, unmolested by the haunting shadow of impending matrimony.

It occurred to me that in the interval of the weddings I would send for an old friend, a bachelor like myself—an honest manly fellow, who worked hard from circuit to circuit, and got barely one brief a year. Yes, Will Launceston would keep me company; and we would spend our days in the woods, and our evenings in my study, safe out of the way of lovers, weddings, and womankind.

I had just written to him, when my sister Martha came in with a very serious face, and told me "she wished for a little conversation with me."

Ominous beginning! But she was not a young man, and could not well attack me concerning any more of my sisters. At least so I congratulated myself—alas, too soon!

My sister settled herself by the fire with a serious countenance.

"My dear Nigel."

"My dear Martha."

"I wish to consult you on a matter which has recently come to my knowledge, and has given me much pain, and some anxiety."

"Indeed!" and I am afraid my tone was less sympathising than eager, since from her troubled nervous manner, I thought—I hoped, the matter in question indicated the secession of Mr. Green. "Go on. Is it about"—I stopped and corrected myself hypocritically—"about the girls?"

She assented.

"Whew!"—a disappointed whistle, faint and low. "Still go on. I'll listen to anything except another proposal."

Martha shook her head. "Alas, I fear it will never come to that! Brother, have you noticed?—but men never do—still, I myself have observed a great change in Constantia lately."

Now Constantia always was different from the other girls—liked solitude and books, talked little, and had a trick of reverie. In short, was what young people call "interesting," and old people "romantic"—the sort of creature who, did she grow up a remarkable woman, would have her youthful peculiarities carefully and respectfully noted, with "I always said there was a great deal in that girl;" but who, did she turn out nothing particular, would be laughed at, and probably would laugh at herself, for having been "very sentimental when she was young." Nevertheless, having at one time of my life shared that imputation, I was tender over the little follies of Constantia.

"I think the girl reads too much, and sits with her eyes too wide open, Martha;—is rather unsocial, likewise. She wanted to get out of the way of the weddings, and positively refused to be Angeline's bridemaid."

"Ah!" sighed Martha, "that's it. Poor foolish child, to think of falling in love——"

I almost jumped off my chair. "I'll not hear a word of it—I declare I will not! I'll keep the young fellow off my premises with man-traps and spring-guns. I'll go back to India if you tell me of another 'engagement.'"

"No chance of that;" and Martha shook her head more drearily than ever. "Poor child, I fear it is an unfortunate attachment!"

I brightened up—so much so that my sister looked, nay, gently hinted, her conviction that I was a "brute." She expected I would have been as sorry as she was!

"No, Martha; I am rather glad. Glad, after my experience of these 'fortunate' love-affairs, to find that one of my sisters has the womanly courage, unselfishness, and simplicity to conceive an 'unfortunate' attachment."

Perhaps this speech hurt Martha, and yet it need not. She and I both knew and respected one another's youth; and if we differed in opinion concerning our middle age, why—I was as likely to be wrong as she.

She did not at first reply; and then, without comment, she explained to me her uneasiness about Constantia. The girl had long played confidante to Mr. Archer in the matter of Angeline, and, as often happens, the confidante had unwittingly taken too great interest in one of her principles, until she found herself envying the lot of the other. When Mr.

Archer's dismissal finally broke off all his intercourse with our family, there was one of my sisters who missed him wearily, cruelly; and that was—not Angeline.

I was touched. Now, no doubt Constantia had been very foolish; no doubt she had nourished and encouraged this fancy, as romantic girls do, in moonlight walks and solitary dreams; hugging her pain, and deluding herself that it was bliss. Little doubt, likewise, that the feeling would wear itself out, or fade slowly away in life's stern truths; but at present it was a most sincere passion, sad and sore. Foolish and romantic as it might be, in itself and in its girlish demonstrations, I could not smile at it. It was a real thing, and as such to be respected.

Martha and I held counsel together, and acted on the result. We took Constantia under our special charge; we gave her books to read, visits to pay, work to do; keeping her as much as possible with one or other of us, and out of the way of the childish flirtation of Cuthbert and Charlotte, or the formal philandering of Sir Roland and the future Lady Griffith Jones. And if sometimes, as Lizzie told me—my little Lizzie, who laughed at love and lovers with the lightness of sixteen—Constantia grew impatient with Lotty's careless trifling, and curled her lip scornfully when Angeline paraded the splendours of her *trousseau*, we tried to lead the girl's mind out of herself, and out of dreamland altogether, as much as possible.

"But suppose," Lizzie sagely argued—"suppose, when Angeline is married, Mr. Archer should come back? He always liked Constantia extremely. She understood him far better than Angeline. Who knows but——"

I shook my head, and desired the little castle builder to hold her tongue.

She was our sole sharer of the secret; and I must say, though she laughed at her now and then, Lizzie was extremely loving and patient with Constantia. After a time, we left the two girls wholly to one another, more especially as my time was now taken up with my friend Launceston.

O the comfort, the relief, of the society of a man!—a real honest man—who had some sterling aim and object in life—some steady work to do—some earnest interest in the advance of the world, the duties and pursuits of his brother men: who was neither handsome, witty, nor accomplished; who rarely shone in ladies' society; in fact, rather eschewed it than otherwise. For, he said, nature had unfitted him to act the part of a mere admirer, and

18 A FAMILY IN LOVE.

adverse fortune forbade him to appear in the character of a lover; so he held aloof, keeping his own company and that of one or two old friends like myself.

I was fond of Launceston; I wished my family to like him too; but they were all too busy about their own affairs. Evening after evening I could not get any of my sisters to make tea for us, or give us a little music afterwards, except the pale, dull-looking Constantia, or my bonny rose of June, little Lizzie. At last we four settled into a small daily company, and went out together, read together, talked together continually. I kept these two younger ones as much as possible in our unromantic practical society, that not only my mind, but Launceston's, in its thorough cheerfulness and healthiness of tone, might unconsciously have a good influence upon Constantia.

The girl's spirit slowly began to heal. She set aside her dreaming, and took with all the energy of her nature to active work—women's work—charity school-teaching, village-visiting, and the like. She put a little too much "romance" into all she did still; but there was life in it, truth, sincerity.

"Miss Constantia will make an admirable lady-of-all-work," said Launceston in his quaint way, watching her with his kindly and observant eyes. "The world wants such. She will find enough to do."

And so she did: enough to steal her too from my side, almost as much as the three fiancées. The circle in my study dwindled gradually down to Lizzie, Launceston, and me.

We were excellent company still, we three. I had rarely had so much of my pet sister's society: I had never found it so pleasant. True, she was shyer than usual, probably from being with us two, older and wiser people—men likewise; but she listened to our wisdom so sweetly—she bore with our dry, long-worded learning so patiently—that my study never seemed itself unless I had the little girl seated at my feet, or sewing quietly in the window-corner. And then she was completely a "little girl;" had no forward ways—no love notions, or, ten times worse, marriage notions, crossing her innocent brain. I felt sure I could take her into my closest heart, form her mind and principles at my will, and one day make a noble woman of her, after the pattern of —— But I never mention that sacred name.

I loved Lizzie—loved her to the core of my heart. Sometimes with fatherly more than even brotherly pride, I used to talk to Launceston of the child's sweetness, but he always gave me short answers. It was his way. His

laconism in most things was really astonishing for a man under thirty.

One day, when Angeline's grand wedding was safely over, and the house had sunk into a pathetic quietness that reminded one of the evening after a funeral—at least so I thought—Launceston and I fell into a discussion, which stirred him into more demonstrativeness than usual. The subject was men, women, and marriages.

"I am convinced," he said, "that I shall never marry."

It was not my first hearing of this laudable determination; so I let it pass, merely asking his reasons.

"Because my conscience, principles, and feelings go totally against the system of matrimony, as practised in the world, especially the world of womankind—all the courting and proposing, the presents and the love-letters, the dinners to relatives and congratulations of friends, the marriage guests and marriage settlements, the white lace, white satin, and white favours, carriage, postilions, and all. Heigh-ho, Heathcote, what fools men are!"

I was just about to suggest the possibility of naming one, say two, wise individuals among our sex, when in stole a white fairy—my pretty Lizzie, in her bridemaid's dress. Her presence changed the current of conversation, until from some remark she made about a message Angeline had left us to the proper way of inserting her marriage in the Times newspaper to-morrow, our talk imperceptibly fell back into the old channel.

"I, like you, Launceston, hate the whole system of love and marrying. It is one great sham. Beginning when miss at school learns that it is the apex of feminine honour to be a bride—the lowest deep of feminine humiliation to die an old maid. Continuing when she, a young lady at home, counts her numerous 'offers;' taking pride in what ought to be to her a source either of regret or humiliation. Ending when, time slipping by, she drops into the usual belief that nobody ever marries her first love; so takes the best match she can find, and makes marriage, which is merely the visible crown and completion of love, the pitiful dishonoured substitute for it. I declare solemnly, I have seen many a wife whom I held to be scarcely better than—no wife at all."

I had forgotten my little sister's presence; but she did not seem to hear me—nor Launceston either, for that matter. His earnestness had softened down; he sat, very thoughtful, over against the window where Lizzie had taken her sewing. — What a pretty picture she made!

"Come here, my little girl," I said: "I should not like thee to go the way of the world; and yet I should be satisfied to give thee away some day, quietly, in a white muslin gown and a straw bonnet, to some honest man who loved thee,—and was loved so well, that Lizzie would never dream of marrying any other, but would have been quite content, if need be, to live an old maid for his sake to the end of her days. That's what I call love—eh, my girl?"

Lizzie drooped her head, blushing deeply. Of course; girls always do.

Launceston said, in a tone so low that I quite started, "Then you do believe in true love, after all?"

"It would be ill for me, or for any human being, if I did not. And I believe in it the more earnestly because of its numberless counterfeits. Nay"—and now when, after this gay marriage-morning, the evening was sinking gray and dull, my mind inclined pensively, even tenderly, to the sister who had gone, the other two sisters who were shortly going away from my hearth for ever—"nay, as since in the falsest creeds there lurks, I hope, a modicum of absolute truth, I would fain trust that in the poorest travesty or masquerade of love, one might find a fragment of the sterling commodity. Still, my Lizzie, dear, when all our brides are gone, let us congratulate ourselves that for a long time we shall have no more engagements."

"You object to engagements?" said Lizzie, speaking timidly and downfaced—as I rather like to see a young girl speak on this subject.

"Why, how should you like it yourself, my little maid? To be loved, wooed, and wedded in public, for the benefit of an amused circle of friends, neighbours, and connections. To have one's actions noticed, one's affairs canvassed, one's feelings weighed and measured; to be congratulated, condoled, and jested with—horrible! literally horrible. My wonder is that any true lovers can ever stand it."

"Perhaps you are right," said Launceston, vehemently. "No man ought to place the girl he loves in such a position. Whatever it costs him, he ought to leave her free—altogether free—and offer her nothing until he can offer her his hand, at once, and with no delay."

"Bless my soul, Launceston, what are you in such excitement about? Has anybody been offering himself to *your* sister? Because—you mistook me. Ask her, or Lizzie, or any good woman, if they would feel flattered by a gen-

tleman's acting in the way you suggest? As if his hand—with the ring in it—were everything to them, and himself and his true love nothing at all!"

Launceston laughed uneasily. "Well, but what did you mean? A—a friend of mine would like to know your opinion on this matter."

"My opinion is simply—an opinion. Every man is the best judge of his own affairs, especially love-affairs. As the Eastern proverb says, 'Let not the lions decide for the tigers.' But I think, did *I* love a woman"—(and it pleased me to know I was but speaking out *her* mind who years ago lived and died, in her fond simplicity wiser than any of these)— "did I love a woman, I would like to tell her so—just to herself, no more. And I would tell her so at once—whether I were poor or rich, prosperous or hopeless; whether we could be married next month, next year, or not for the next twenty years. If she loved me as I her, it would be no matter—we could wait. And meantime, I would like to give her my love to rest on—to receive the help and consolation of hers. I would like her to feel that through all chances and changes she and I were one; one neither for foolish child's-play nor headlong passion, but for mutual strength and support, holding ourselves responsible both to Heaven and each other for our life and our love. One, indissolubly, whether we were ever married or not; one in this world, and—we pray—one in the world everlasting."

Was I dreaming? Did I actually see my friend Launceston take, unforbidden, my youngest sister's hand, and hold it—firmly, tenderly, fast? Did I hear, with my own natural ears, Lizzie's soft little sob, not of grief certainly, as she slipped out of the room, as swift and silent as a moonbeam?

Eh! what? Good heavens! Was there ever any creature so blind as a middle-aged elder brother!

Well, as I told Launceston, it was half my own fault; and I must bear it stoically. Perhaps, on the whole, things might have been worse, for he is a noble fellow, and no wonder the child loves him. They cannot be married just yet—meanwhile, Lizzie and I keep the matter between ourselves. They are very happy —God bless them! and so am I.

. . . .

P.S.—Mr. Archer reappeared yesterday— looking quite well and comfortable! I see clearly that, one day not distant, I shall be left lamenting—the solitary residuum of a Family in Love.

ODE TO EVENING.

[William Collins, born at Chichester, 25th December, 1720; died 1756. After taking his bachelor's degree at Oxford he proceeded to London about 1744, where he found a friend in Dr. Johnson, who was himself, at the time, struggling to win a place in literature. Collins published his *Oriental Eclogues* whilst at college, and his *Odes* in 1746. It is said that the slowness of the sale of the *Odes* so irritated him that he burned the remaining copies of the edition. He became embarrassed and despondent, and although a legacy of £2000 relieved him from immediate necessities, he sunk into a sort of intellectual languour from which he sought relief in intoxication. He was for a time confined in a lunatic asylum, and afterwards retired to Chichester, where his sister attended him till his death. Campbell says that his "works will abide comparison with whatever Milton wrote under the age of thirty."]

If aught of oaten stop, or pastoral song,
May hope, O pensive Eve, to soothe thine ear
　　Like thy own modest springs,
　　Thy springs, and dying gales;

O nymph reserved, while now the bright-haired
　　　sun
Sits in yon western tent, whose cloudy skirts,
　　With brede ethereal wove,
　　O'erhang his wavy bed.

Now air is hush'd, save where the weak-eyed bat.
With short shrill shriek flits by on leathern wing,
　　Or where the beetle winds
　　His small but sullen horn.

As oft he rises, 'midst the twilight path,
Against the pilgrim borne in heedless hum:
　　Now teach me, maid composed,
　　To breath some softened strain,

Whose numbers stealing through thy darkening
　　　vale,
May not unseemly with its stillness suit,
　　As musing slow I hail
　　Thy genial loved return!

For when thy folding star arising shows
His paly circlet, at his warning lamp
　　The fragrant hours and elves
　　Who slept in buds the day,

And many a nymph who wreathes her brows with
　　　sedge,
And sheds the freshening dew, and lovelier still
　　The pensive pleasures sweet
　　Prepare thy shadowy car.

Then let me rove some wild and heathy scene,
Or find some ruin 'midst its dreary dells,
　　Whose walls more awful nod
　　By thy religious gleams.

Or if chill blustering winds, or driving rain
Prevent my willing feet, be mine the hut,
　　That from the mountain's side
　　Views wilds and swelling floods,

And hamlets brown, and dim discovered spires,
And hears their simple bell, and marks o'er all
　　Thy dewy fingers draw
　　The gradual dusky veil.

While Spring shall pour his showers, as oft he
　　　wont,
And bathe thy breathing tresses, meekest Eve!
　　While summer loves to sport
　　Beneath thy lingering light;

While sallow Autumn fills thy lap with leaves,
Or Winter, yelling through the troublous air,
　　Affrights thy shrinking train,
　　And rudely rends thy robes;

So long, regardful of thy quiet rule,
Shall Fancy, Friendship, Science, smiling Peace,
　　Thy gentlest influence own,
　　And love thy favourite name.

———

EUREKA.

BY DR. J. G. HOLLAND.

Whom I crown with love is royal;
　　Matters not her blood or birth;
She is queen, and I am loyal
　　To the noblest of the earth.

Neither place, nor wealth, nor title
　　Lacks the man my friendship owns;
His distinction, true and vital,
　　Shines supreme o'er crowns and thrones.

Where true love bestows its sweetness,
　　Where true friendship lays its hand,
Dwells all greatness, all completeness,
　　All the wealth of every land.

Man is greater than condition,
　　And where man himself bestows,
He begets and gives position
　　To the gentlest that he knows.

Neither miracle nor fable
　　Is the water changed to wine;
Lords and ladies at my table
　　Prove Love's simplest fare divine.

And if these accept my duty,
　　If the loved my homage own,
I have won all worth and beauty;
　　I have found the magic stone.

THE GARDENER OF THE MANOR.

[Hans Christian Andersen, born at Odense, 2d April, 1805; died at Rolighed, Copenhagen, 4th August, 1875. The Danish novelist. His father was a shoemaker, and too poor to give his son any education, save that afforded by the charity school; but after various struggles, Andersen was admitted to one of the government schools through the influence of Counsellor Collin, who was the first to suspect the genius of the youth. He tried the stage, wrote plays and failed; but he gradually earned reputation by his poems, and by his romances. Thanks to a government pension, he was enabled to travel in Europe and America. His principal works are: *The Improvisatore; O. T.; Only a Fiddler; The Sandhills of Jutland; Tales for Children; The Wild Swans*, a fairy tale; *The Tee Maiden; The Story of My Life*, &c. His tales for children have become popular in all languages; and the Leipsic editions of his works number thirty-five volumes.]

About one Danish mile from the capital stood an old manor-house, with thick walls, towers, and pointed gable-ends. Here lived, but only in the summer season, a rich and courtly family. This manor-house was the best and the most beautiful of all the houses they owned. It looked outside as if it had just been cast in a foundry, and within it was comfort itself. The family arms were carved in stone over the door; beautiful roses twined about the arms and the balcony; a grass-plot extended before the house with red-thorn and white-thorn, and many rare flowers grew even outside the conservatory. The manor kept also a very skilful gardener. It was a real pleasure to see the flower-garden, the orchard, and the kitchen-garden. There was still to be seen a portion of the manor's original garden, a few box-tree hedges cut in shape of crowns and pyramids, and behind these two mighty old trees almost always without leaves. One might always think that a storm or waterspout had scattered great lumps of manure on their branches, but each lump was a bird's-nest. A swarm of rooks and crows from time immemorial had built their nests here. It was a townful of birds, and the birds were the manorial lords here. They did not care for the proprietors, the manor's oldest family branch, nor for the present owner of the manor—these were nothing to them; but they bore with the wandering creatures below them, notwithstanding that once in a while they shot with guns in a way that made the birds' back-bones shiver, and made every bird fly up, crying, "Rak, Rak!"

The gardener very often explained to the master the necessity of felling the old trees, as they did not look well, and by taking them away they would probably also get rid of the screaming birds, which would seek another place. But he never could be induced either to give up the trees or the swarm of birds: the manor could not spare them, as they were relics of the good old times, that ought always to be kept in remembrance.

"The trees are the birds' heritage by this time!" said the master. "So let them keep them, my good Larsen." Larsen was the gardener's name, but that is of very little consequence in this story. "Haven't you room enough to work in, little Larsen? Have you not the flower-garden, the green-houses, the orchard, and the kitchen-garden?" He cared for them, he kept them in order and cultivated them with zeal and ability, and the family knew it; but they did not conceal from him that they often tasted fruits and saw flowers in other houses that surpassed what he had in his garden, and that was a sore trial to the gardener, who always wished to do the best, and really did the best he could. He was good-hearted, and a faithful servant.

The owner sent one day for him, and told him kindly that the day before, at a party given by some friends of rank, they had eaten apples and pears which were so juicy and well-flavoured, that all the guests had loudly expressed their admiration. To be sure, they were not native fruits, but they ought by all means to be introduced here, and to be acclimatized if possible. They learned that the fruit was bought of one of the first fruit-dealers in the city, and the gardener was to ride to town, and find out about where they came from, and then order some slips for grafting. The gardener was very well acquainted with the dealer, because he was the very person to whom he sold the fruit that grew in the manor-garden, beyond what was needed by the family. So the gardener went to town and asked the fruit-dealer where he had found those apples and pears that were praised so highly.

"They are from your own garden," said the fruit-dealer, and he showed him both the apples and the pears, which he recognized. Now, how happy the gardener felt! He hastened back to his master, and told him that the apples and pears were all from his own garden. But he would not believe it.

"It cannot be possible, Larsen. Can you get a written certificate of that from the fruit-dealer?" And that he could; and brought him a written certificate.

"This is certainly wonderful!" said the family.

And now every day were set on the table great dishes filled with beautiful apples and pears from their own garden; bushels and barrels of these fruits were sent to friends in the city and country—nay, were even sent abroad. It was exceedingly pleasant; but when they talked with the gardener, they said that the last two seasons had been remarkably favourable for fruits, and that fruits had done well all over the country.

Some time passed. The family were at dinner at court. The next day the gardener was sent for. They had eaten melons at the royal table which they found very juicy and well-flavoured; they came from his majesty's greenhouse. "You must go and see the court-gardener, and let him give you some seeds of those melons."

"But the gardener at the court got his melon-seeds from us," said the gardener, highly delighted.

"But then that man understands how to bring the fruit to a higher perfection," was the answer. "Each particular melon was delicious."

"Well, then, I really may feel proud," said the gardener. "I must tell your lordship that the gardener at the court did not succeed very well with his melons this year, and so, seeing how beautiful ours looked, he tasted them, and ordered from me three of them for the castle."

"Larsen, do not pretend to say that those were melons from our garden."

"Really, I dare say as much," said the gardener, who went to the court-gardener and got from him a written certificate to the effect that the melons on the royal table were from the manor. That was certainly a great surprise to the family, and they did not keep the story to themselves. Melon seeds were sent far and wide, in the same way as had been done with the slips, which they were now hearing had begun to take, and to bear fruit of an excellent kind. The fruit was named after the manor, and the name was written in English, German, and French.

This was something they never had dreamed of.

"We are afraid that the gardener will come to think too much of himself," said they; but he looked on it in another way: what he wished was to get the reputation of being one of the best gardeners in the country, and to produce every year something exquisite out of all sorts of garden stuff, and that he did. But he often had to hear that the fruits which he first brought, the apples and pears, were after all

the best. All other kinds of fruit were inferior to these. The melons, too, were very good, but they belonged to quite another species. His strawberries were very excellent, but by no means better than many others; and when it happened one year that his radishes did not succeed, they only spoke of them, and not of other good things he had made succeed.

It really seemed as if the family felt some relief in saying, "It won't turn out well this year, little Larsen!" They seemed quite glad when they could say, "It won't turn out well!"

The gardener used always twice a week to bring them fresh flowers, tastefully arranged, and the colours by his arrangements were brought out in stronger light.

"You have good taste, Larsen," said the owner, "but that is a gift from our Lord, not from yourself."

One day the gardener brought a great crystal vase with a floating leaf of a white water-lily, upon which was laid, with its long thick stalk descending into the water, a sparkling blue flower, as large as a sunflower.

"The sacred lotos of Hindostan!" exclaimed the family. They had never seen such a flower; it was placed every day in the sunshine, and in the evening under artificial light. Every one who saw it found it wonderfully beautiful and rare; and that said the most noble young lady in the country, the wise and kind-hearted princess. The lord of the manor deemed it an honour to present her with the flower, and the princess took it with her to the castle. Now the master of the house went down to the garden to pluck another flower of the same sort, but he could not find any. So he sent for the gardener, and asked him where he kept the blue lotos. "I have been looking for it in vain," said he. "I went into the conservatory, and round about the flower-garden."

"No, it is not there," said the gardener. "It is nothing else than a common flower from the kitchen-garden, but do you not find it beautiful? It looks as if it was the blue cactus, and yet it is only a kitchen-herb. It is the flower of the artichoke."

"You should have told us that at the time," said the master. "We supposed, of course, that it was a strange and rare flower. You have made us ridiculous in the eyes of the young princess! She saw the flower in our house and thought it beautiful. She did not know the flower, and she is versed in botany, too, but then that has nothing to do with kitchen-herbs. How could you take it into your head, my good

Larsen, to put such a flower up in our drawing-room? It makes us ridiculous."

And the magnificent blue flower from the kitchen-garden was turned out of the drawing-room, which was not at all the place for it. The master made his apology to the princess, telling her that it was only a kitchen-herb which the gardener had taken into his head to exhibit, but that he had been well reprimanded for it.

"That was a pity," said the princess, "for he has really opened our eyes to see the beauty of a flower in a place where we should not have thought of looking for it. Our gardener shall every day, as long as the artichoke is in bloom, bring one of them up into the drawing-room."

Then the master told his gardener that he might again bring them a fresh artichoke-flower. "It is, after all, a very nice flower," said he, "and a truly remarkable one." And so the gardener was praised again. "Larsen likes that," said the master; "he is a spoiled child."

In the autumn there came up a great gale, which increased so violently in the night that several large trees in the outskirts of the wood were torn up by the roots; and to the great grief of the household, but to the gardener's delight, the two big trees blew down, with all their birds'-nests on them. In the manor-house they heard during the storm the scream-ing of rooks and crows, beating their wings against the windows.

"Now I suppose you are happy, Larsen," said the master: "the storm has felled the trees, and the birds have gone off to the woods; there is nothing left from the good old days; it is all gone, and we are very sorry for it."

The gardener said nothing, but he thought of what he long had turned over in his mind, how he could make that pretty sunny spot very useful, so that it could become an ornament to the garden and a pride to the family. The great trees which had been blown down had shattered the venerable hedge of box, that was cut into fanciful shapes.

Here he set out a multitude of plants that were not to be seen in other gardens. He made an earthen wall, on which he planted all sorts of native flowers from the fields and woods. What no other gardener had ever thought of planting in the manor-garden he planted, giving each its appropriate soil, and the plants were in sunlight or shadow, ac-cording as each species required. He cared tenderly for them, and they grew up finely.

The juniper-tree from the heaths of Jutland rose in shape and colour like the Italian cypress; the shining, thorny Christ-thorn, as green in the winter's cold as in the summer's sun, was splendid to see. In the foreground grew ferns of various species; some of them looked as if they were children of the palm-tree; others, as if they were parents of the pretty plants called "Venus's golden locks" or "Maiden-hair." Here stood the despised burdock, which is so beautiful in its freshness that it looks well even in a bouquet. The burdock stood in a dry place, but below, in the moist soil, grew the colt's-foot, also a despised plant, but yet most picturesque, with its tall stem and large leaf. Like a candelabrum with a multitude of branches six feet high, and with flower over against flower, rose the mullein, a mere field plant. Here stood the woodroof and the lily of the valley, the wild calla and the fine three-leaved wood-sorrel. It was a wonder to see all this beauty.

In the front grew in rows very small pear-trees from French soil, trained on wires. By plenty of sun and good care they soon bore as juicy fruits as in their own country. Instead of the two old leafless trees was placed a tall flag-staff, where the flag of Dannebrog was displayed; and near by stood another pole, where the hop-tendril in summer or harvest-time wound its fragrant flowers; but in winter time, after ancient custom, oat-sheaves were fastened to it, that the birds of the air might find here a good meal in the happy Christmas-time.

"Our good Larsen is growing sentimental as he grows old," said the family; "but he is faithful, and quite attached to us."

In one of the illustrated papers there was a picture at New Years of the old manor, with the flag-staff and the oat-sheaves for the birds of the air, and the paper said that the old manor had preserved that beautiful old custom, and deserved great credit for it.

"They beat the drum for all Larsen's doings," said the family. "He is a lucky fellow, and we may almost be proud of having such a man in our service."

But they were not a bit proud of it. They were very well aware that they were the lords of the manor; they could give Larsen warning, in fact, but they did not. They were good people, and fortunate it is for every Mr. Larsen that there are so many good people like them.

Yes, that is the story of the Gardener of the Manor. Now you may think a little about it.

24

FABLES.

[Johann Gotthold Ephraim Lessing, born at Karmentz, Upper Lusatia, 1729; died, 1781. Critic, philosopher, and miscellaneous writer. *Laocoon, or the Limits of Painting and Poetry*, is regarded as a masterpiece of German criticism; and *Emilia Galotti* takes a prominent place in German tragedy. It was said of Lessing that "His style is the style of Roman architecture—the greatest solidity with the greatest simplicity."]

ZEUS AND THE SHEEP.

The sheep was doomed to suffer much from all the animals. She came to Zeus and prayed him to lighten her misery. Zeus appeared willing, and said to the sheep: I see indeed, my good creature, I have made thee too defenceless. Now choose in what way I may best remedy this defect. Shall I furnish thy mouth with terrible teeth and thy feet with claws.

Ah! no, said the sheep, I do not wish to have anything in common with the beasts of prey.

Or, continued Zeus, shall I infuse poison into thy spittle.

Alas! replied the sheep; the poisonous serpents are so hated.

What then shall I do? I will plant horns in thy forehead, and give strength to thy neck.

Not so, kind Father! I might be disposed to butt like the he-goat.

And yet, said Zeus, thou must thyself be able to injure others, if others are to beware of injuring thee.

Must I? sighed the sheep. O! then, kind Father, let me be as I am. For the ability to injure will excite, I fear, the desire. And it is better to suffer wrong than to do wrong.

Zeus blessed the good sheep, and from that time forth she forgot to complain.

THE BLIND HEN.

A hen which had become blind continued to scratch for food as she had been used. What availed it the industrious fool? Another hen, that could see, but wished to spare her tender feet, never forsook the side of the former, and without scratching enjoyed the fruit of scratching. For as often as the blind hen turned up a corn, the seeing one devoured it.

The laborious German compiles the *collectanea* which the witty Frenchman uses.

THE WOLF ON HIS DEATH-BED.

A wolf lay at the last gasp, and was reviewing his past life. It is true, said he, I am a

sinner, but yet, I hope, not one of the greatest. I have done evil, but I have also done much good. Once, I remember, a bleating lamb that had strayed from the flock came so near to me that I might easily have throttled it, but I did it no harm. At the same time I listened with the most astonishing indifference to the gibes and scoffs of a sheep, although I had nothing to fear from protecting dogs.

I can testify to all that, said his friend the fox, who was helping him prepare for death. I remember perfectly all the circumstances. It was just at the time when you were so dreadfully choked with that bone, which the good-natured crane afterwards drew out of your throat.

ÆSOP AND THE ASS.

Said the ass to Æsop: The next time you tell a story about me, let me say something that is right rational and ingenious.

You something ingenious! said Æsop; what propriety would there be in that? Would not the people say you were the moralist and I the ass?

HERCULES.

When Hercules was received into heaven he paid his respects to Juno before all the other divinities. The whole heaven and Juno were astonished. Dost thou show such preference to thine enemy? Yes, replied Hercules, even to her. It was her persecution alone that furnished the occasion of those exploits with which I have earned heaven.

Olympus approved the answer of the new god, and Juno was reconciled.

THE BOY AND THE SERPENT.

A boy played with a tame serpent. My dear little animal, said the boy, I would not be so familiar with thee had not thy poison been taken from thee. You serpents are the most malicious and ungrateful of all animals. I have read how it fared with a poor countryman who, in his compassion, took up a serpent—perhaps it was one of thy ancestors—which he found half-frozen under a hedge, and put it into his bosom to warm it. Scarcely had the wicked creature begun to revive, when it bit its benefactor; and the poor, kind countryman was doomed to die.

I am amazed, said the serpent. How partial your historians must be! Ours relate the affair very differently. Thy kind man thought the serpent was actually frozen, and, because it was one of the variegated sort, he put it into his bosom, in order, when he reached home, to strip off its beautiful skin. Was that right?

Ah! be still! replied the boy. When was there ever an ingrate who did not know how to justify himself?

True, my son, said his father, who had listened to the conversation. Nevertheless, when you hear of an extraordinary instance of ingratitude, be sure to examine carefully all the circumstances before you brand a human being with so detestable a fault. Real benefactors have seldom had ungrateful debtors;—no! I will hope, for the honour of humanity—never. But benefactors with petty, interested motives—they, my son, deserve to reap ingratitude instead of acknowledgments.

THE FAERIE QUEENE.

[Edmund Spenser, born in London, 1552; died in Westminster, 16th January, 1599. Educated at Cambridge; proceeded to Dublin in 1580 as private secretary to Arthur Lord Grey of Wilton; in the year following, he was appointed Clerk of Degrees and Recognizances in the Irish Court of Chancery, and also received a grant of land in Enniscorthy. In 1588 he became clerk to the council of Munster; resided some years at Kilcolman, in Cork, a ruined castle of the Earls of Desmond, whence he had to flee with his family during the insurrection of 1598. He made his way to London, and there died in straitened circumstances. The first part of the *Fairy Queen* was published in 1590, and the second in 1595. Hallam says: "Spenser is still the third name in the poetical literature of our country, and he has not been surpassed, except by Dante, in any other." Scott says: "Spenser I could have read forever. Too young to trouble myself about the allegory, I considered all the knights and ladies, and dragons and giants in their outward and exoteric sense; and God only knows how delighted I was to find myself in such society." Keble calls him "pre-eminently the sacred poet of his country."[1]]

UNA AND THE LION

Nought is there under heav'ns wide hollownesse,
That moves more deare compassion of mind,
Then beautie brought t'unworthie wretchednesse
Through envies snares, or fortunes freakes unkind.
I, whether lately through her brightnes blynd,
Or through alleageauce, and fast fealty,
Which I do owe unto all womankynd,
Feele my hart perst with so great agony,
When such I see, that all for pitty I could dy.

And now it is empassioned so deepe,
For fairest Unaes sake, of whom I sing,
That my frayle eies these lines with teares do steepe,
To thinke how she through guyleful handeling,
Though true as touch, though daughter of a king,
Though faire as ever living wight was fayre,
Though nor in word nor deede ill meriting,
Is from her knight divorced in despayre,
And her dew loves deryv'd to that vile witches shayre.

Yet she, most faithfull Ladie, all this while
Forsaken, wofull, solitarie mayd,
Far from all peoples preace, as in exile,
In wildernesse and wastfull deserts strayd,
To seeke her knight; who, subtily betrayd
Through that late vision which th'Enchaunter wrought,
Had her abandond. She, of nought affrayd,
Through woods and wastnes wide him daily sought;
Yet wished tydinges none of him unto her brought.

One day, nigh wearie of the yrkesome way,
From her unhastie beast she did alight;
And on the grasse her dainty limbs did lay
In secrete shadow, far from all mens sight:
From her fayre head her fillet she undight,
And layd her stole aside. Her angels face,
As the great eye of heaven, shyned bright,
And made a sunshine in the shady place;
Did never mortall eye behold such heavenly grace.

It fortuned, out of the thickest wood
A ramping Lyon rushed suddeinly,
Hunting full greedy after salvage blood;
Soone as the royall virgin he did spy,
With gaping mouth at her ran greedily,
To have attonce devourd her tender corse:
But to the pray when as he drew more ny,
His bloody rage aswaged with remorse,
And, with the sight amazd, forgat his furious forse.

In stead thereof he kist her wearie feet,
And lickt her lilly hands with fawning tong,
As he her wronged innocence did weet.
O, how can beautie maister the most strong,
And simple truth subdue avenging wrong!
Whose yielded pryde and proud submission,
Still dreading death, when she had marked long,
Her hart gan melt in great compassion;
And drizling teares did shed for pure affection

"The Lyon, Lord of everie beast in field,"
Quoth she, "his princely puissance doth abate,
And mightie proud to humble weake does yield,

---

[1] In a letter to Sir Walter Raleigh, Spenser explained the purpose of his poem:

"In that Faery Queene I meane glory in my generall intention, but in my particular I conceive the most excellent and glorious person of our soveraine the Queene (Elizabeth), and her kingdome in Faery land. And yet, in some places els, I doo otherwise shadow her. For considering she beareth two persons, the one of a most royall Queene or Empresse, the other of a most vertuous and beautifull Lady, this latter part in some places I doe expresse in Belphœbe, fashioning her name according to your owne excellent conceipt of Cynthia, (Phœbe and Cynthia being both names of Diana.) So in the person of Prince Arthure I sette

Forgetfull of the hungry rage, which late
Him prickt, in pittie of my sad estate:
But he, my Lyon, and my noble Lord,
How does he find in cruell hart to hate
Her, that him lov'd, and ever most adord
As the God of my life? why hath he me abhord?"

Redounding teares did choke th' end of her plaint,
Which softly eechoed from the neighbour wood;
And, sad to see her sorrowfull constraint,
The kingly beast upon her gazing stood:
With pittie calmd downe fell his angry mood.
At last, in close hart shutting up her payne,
Arose the virgin, borne of heavenly brood,
And to her snowy Palfrey got agayne,
To seeke her strayed Champion if she might attayne.

The Lyon would not leave her desolate,
But with her went along, as a strong gard
Of her chast person, and a faythfull mate
Of her sad troubles and misfortunes hard:
Still, when she slept, he kept both watch and ward;
And, when she wakt, he wayted diligent,
With humble service to her will prepard:
From her fayre eyes he tooke commandement,
And ever by her lookes conceived her intent.

After various adventures Una finds the Red-
cross knight, and proceeds with him to the
rescue of her parents:

THE KNIGHT AND THE DRAGON.

The knight with that old Dragon fights
Two days incessantly:
The third him overthrowes, and gayns
Most glorious victory.

High time now gan it wex for Una fayre
To thinke of those her captive Parents deare,
And their forwasted kingdom to repayre:
Whereto whenas they now approched neare,
With hartie wordes her knight she gan to cheare,
And in her modest manner thus bespake:
"Deare knight, as deare as ever knight was deare,
That all these sorrowes suffer for my sake,
High heven behold the tedious toyle ye for me take!

"Now are we come unto my native soyle,
And to the place where all our perilles dwell;
Here hauntes that feend, and does his dayly spoyle;
Therefore, henceforth, bee at your keeping well,
And ever ready for your foeman fell:
The sparke of noble corage now awake,
And strive your excellent selfe to excell:
That shall ye evermore renowmed make
Above all knights on earth, that batteill undertake."

And pointing forth, "Lo! yonder is," (said she)
"The brasen towre, in which my parents deare
For dread of that huge feend emprisond be;
Whom I from far see on the walles appeare,

forth magnificence in particular, which vertue, for
that (according to Aristotle and the rest) it is the perfection of all the rest, and conteineth in it them all,
therefore in the whole course I mention the deedes of
Arthure applyable to that vertue, which I write of in
that booke. But of the xii. other vertues, I make xii.
other knights the patrones, for the more variety of
the history: Of which these three bookes contayn
three.
"The first of the knight of the Redcrosse, in whome
I expresse Holynes: The seconde of Sir Guyon, in
whome I sette forth Temperaunce: The third of Brito-
martis, a Lady Knight, in whome I picture Chastity.
But because the beginning of the whole worke seemeth
abrupte and as depending upon other antecedents, it
needs that ye know the occasion of these three knights
severall adventures. For the methode of a Poet historical is not such as of an Historiographer. For an
Historiographer discourseth of affayres orderly as they
were donne accounting as well the times as the actions;
but a Poet thrusteth into the middest, even where it
most concerneth him, and there recoursing to the
thinges fore; aste, and divining of thinges to come,
maketh a pleasing Analysis of all.
"The beginning therefore of my history, if it were to
be told by an Historiographer should be the twelfth
booke, which is the last; where I devise that the Faery
Queene kept her Annuall feaste xii. dayes; uppon
which xii. severall dayes, the occasions of the xii. severall adventures hapned, which being undertaken by xii.
severall knights, are in these xii. bookes severally handled
and discoursed. The first was this. In the beginning of the feast, there presented him selfe a tall

clownishe younge man, who falling before the Queene
of Faries desired a boone (as the manner then was)
which during that feast she might not refuse; which
was that hee might have the atchievement of any
adventure, which during that feaste should happen:
that being graunted, he rested him on the floore, unfitte
through his rusticity for a better place. Soone after
entred a faire Ladye in mourning weedes, riding on a
white Asse, with a dwarfe behind her leading a warlike
steed, that bore the Armes of a knight, and his speare
in the dwarfes hand. Shee, falling before the Queene
of Faeries, complayned that her father and mother, an
ancient King and Queene, had bene by an huge dragon
many years shut up in a brasen Castle, who thence
suffred them not to yssew; and therefore besonght the
Faery Queene to assygne her some one of her knights
to take on him that exployt. Presently that clownish
person, upstarting, desired that adventure: whereat
the Queene much wondering, and the Lady much
gainesaying, yet he earnestly importuned his desire.
In the end the Lady told him, that unlesse that armour
which she brought, would serve him (that is, the
armour of a Christian man specified by Saint Paul, vi.
Ephes.) he could not succeed in that enterprise;
which being forthwith put upon him, with dewe furni-
tures thereunto, he seemed the goodliest man in al
that company, and was well liked of the Lady. And
eftesoones taking on him knighthood, and mounting
on that straunge Courser, he went forth with her on
that adventure."
This legend is the subject of one of the latest written
of Tennyson's *Idylls of the King*—namely, *Gareth and
Lynette.*

Whose sight my feeble soule doth greatly cheare:
And on the top of all I do espye
The watchman wayting tydings glad to heare;
That, (O my Parents!) might I happily
Unto you bring, to ease you of your misery!"

With that they heard a roaring hideous sownd,
That all the ayre with terror filled wyde,
And seemd uneath to shake the stedfast ground.
Eftsoones that dreadful Dragon they espyde,
Where stretcht he lay upon the sunny side
Of a great hill, himselfe like a great hill:
But, all so soone as he from far descryde
Those glistring armes that heven with light did fill,
He rousd himselfe full blyth, and hastned them untill.

Then badd the knight his Lady yede aloof,
And to an hill herselfe withdraw asyde;
From whence she might behold that battailles proof,
And eke be safe from daunger far descryde.
She him obayd, and turnd a little wyde.—
Now, O thou sacred Muse! most learned Dame,
Fayre ympe of Phœbus and his aged bryde,
The Nourse of time and everlasting fame,
That warlike handes ennoblest with immortall name;

O! gently come into my feeble brest;
Come gently, but not with that mightie rage,
Wherewith the martiall troupes thou doest infest,
And hartes of great Heroes doest enrage,
That nought their kindled corage may aswage:
Soone as thy dreadfull trompe begins to sownd,
The God of warre with his fiers equipage
Thou doest awake, sleepe never he so sownd;
And scared nations doest with horror sterne astownd.

Fayre Goddesse, lay that furious fitt asyde,
Till I of warres and bloody Mars doe sing,
And Bryton fieldes with Sarazin blood bedyde,
Twixt that great faery Queene and Paynim king,
That with their horror heven and earth did ring;
A worke of labour long, and endlesse prayse:
But now a while lett downe that haughtie string,
And to my tunes thy second tenor rayse,
That I this man of God his godly armes may blaze.

By this, the dreadful Beast drew nigh to hand,
Halfe flying and halfe footing in his haste,
That with his largenesse measured much land,
And made wide shadow under his huge waste,
As mountaine doth the valley overcaste.
Approching nigh, he reared high afore
His body monstrous, horrible, and vaste;
Which, to increase his wondrous greatnes more,
Was swoln with wrath and poyson, and with bloody
gore;

And over all with brasen scales was armd,
Like plated cote of steele, so couched neare
That nought mote perce; ne might his corse bee harmd
With dint of swerd, nor push of pointed speare:
Which as an Eagle, seeing pray appeare,
His aery plumes doth rouze, full rudely dight;
So shaked he, that horror was to heare:

For as the clashing of an Armor bright,
Such noyse h.s rouzed scales did send unto the knight.

His flaggy winges, when forth he did display,
Were like two sayles, in which the hollow wynd
Is gathered full, and worketh speedy way:
And eke the pennes, that did his pineons bynd,
Were like mayne yardes with flying canvas lynd;
With which whenas him list the ayre to beat,
And there by force unwonted passage fynd,
The cloudes before him fledd for terror great,
And all the hevens stood still amazed with his threat.

His huge long tayle, wownd up in hundred foldes,
Does overspred his long bras-scaly back,
Whose wreathed boughtes when ever he unfoldes,
And thick entangled knots adown does slack,
Bespotted as with shieldes of red and blacke,
It sweepeth all the land behind him farre,
And of three furlongs does but litle lacke;
And at the point two stinges in fixed arre,
Both deadly sharp, that sharpest steele exceeden farre.

But stinges and sharpest steele did far exceed
The sharpnesse of his cruel rending clawes:
Dead was it sure, as sure as death in deed,
What ever thing does touch his ravenous pawes,
Or what within his reach he ever drawes.
But his most hideous head my tongue to tell
Does tremble; for his deepe devouring jawes
Wyde gaped, like the griesly mouth of hell,
Through which into his darke abysse all ravin fell.

And, that more wondrous was, in either jaw
Three rankes of yron teeth enraunged were,
In which yett trickling blood, and gobbets raw,
Of late devoured bodies did appeare,
That sight thereof bredd cold congealed feare;
Which to increase, and all atonce to kill,
A cloud of smoothering smoke, and sulphure seare,
Out of his stinking gorge forth steemed still,
That all the ayre about with smoke and stench did fill.

His blazing eyes, like two bright shining shieldes,
Did burne with wrath, and sparkled living fyre:
As two broad Beacons, sett in open fieldes,
Send forth their flames far off to every shyre,
And warning give that enimies conspyre
With fire and sword the region to invade:
So flam'd his eyne with rage and rancorous yre:
But far within, as in a hollow glade,
Those glaring lampes were sett that made a dreadfull
shade.

So dreadfully he towardes him did pas,
Forelifting up a-loft his speckled brest,
And often bounding on the brused gras,
As for great joyance of his newcome guest.
Eftsoones he gan advance his haughty crest,
As chauffed Bore his bristles doth upreare:
And shoke his scales to battaile ready drest,
That made the Redcrosse knight nigh quake for feare,
As bidding bold defyaunce to his foeman neare.

The knight gan fayrely couch his steady speare,
And fiersely ran at him with rigorous might:
The pointed steele, arriving rudely theare,
His harder hyde would nether perce nor bight,
But, glauncing by, foorth passed forward right.
Yet sore amoved with so puissaunt push,
The wrathfull beast about him turned light,
And him so rudely, passing by, did brush
With his long tayle, that horse and man to ground did
          rush.

Both horse and man up lightly rose againe,
And fresh encounter towardes him addrest;
But th' ydle stroke yet backe recoyld in vaine,
And found no place his deadly point to rest.
Exceeding rage enflam'd the furious Beast,
To be avenged of so great despight;
For never felt his imperceable brest
So wondrous force from hand of living wight;
Yet had he prov'd the powre of many a puissant knight.

Then, with his waving wings displayed wyde,
Himselfe up high he lifted from the ground,
And with strong flight did forcibly divyde
The yielding ayre, which night too feeble found
Her flitting parts, and element unsound,
To beare so great a weight: he, cutting way
With his broad sayles, about him soared round:
At last, low stouping with unweldy sway,
Snatcht up both horse and man, to beare them quite
away.

Long he them bore above the subject plaine,
So far as Ewghen bow a shaft may send,
Till struggling strong did him at last constraine
To let them downe before his flightes end:
As hagard hauke, presuming to contend
With hardy fowle above his hable might,
His wearie pounces all in vaine doth spend
To trusse the pray too heavy for his flight;
Which, comming down to ground, does free it selfe by
fight.

He so disseized of his gryping grosse,
The knight his thrillant speare againe assayd
In his bras-plated body to embosse,
And three mens strength unto the stroake he layd;
Wherewith the stiffe beame quaked as affrayd,
And glauncing from his scaly necke did glyde
Close under his left wing, then broad displayd:
The percing steele there wrought a wound full wyde,
That with the uncouth smart the Monster lowdly
cryde.

He cryde, as raging seas are wont to rore
When wintry storme his wrathful wreck does threat;
The rolling billowes beate the ragged shore,
As they the earth would shoulder from her seat;
And greedy gulfe does gape, as he would eat
His neighbour element in his revenge:
Then gin the blustring brethren boldly threat
To move the world from off his stedfast henge,
And boystrous battaile make, each other to avenge.

The steely head stuck fast still in his flesh,
Till with his cruell clawes he snatcht the wood,
And quite a sunder broke.   Forth flowed fresh
A gushing river of blacke gory blood,
That drowned all the land whereon he stood;
The streame thereof would drive a water-mill:
Trebly augmented was his furious mood
With bitter sence of his deepe rooted ill,
That flames of fire he threw forth from his large nose-
thril.

His hideous tayle then hurled he about,
And therewith all enwrapt the nimble thyes
Of his froth-fomy steed, whose courage stout
Striving to loose the knott that fast him tyes,
Himselfe in streighter bandes too rash implyes.
That to the ground he is perforce constraynd
To throw his ryder; who can quickly ryse
From off the earth, with durty blood distaynd,
For that reprochfull fall right fowly he disdaynd;

And fiercely tooke his trenchand blade in hand,
With which he stroke so furious and so fell,
That nothing seemd the puissaunce could withstand:
Upon his crest the hardned yron fell,
But his more hardned crest was armd so well,
That deeper dint therein it would not make;
Yet so extremely did the buffe him quell,
That from thenceforth he shund the like to take,
But when he saw them come he did them still forsake.

The knight was wroth to see his stroke beguyld.
And smot againe with more outrageous might;
But backe againe the sparcling steele recoyld,
And left not any marke where it did light,
As if in Adamant rocke it had beene pight.
The beast, impatient of his smarting wound
And of so fierce and forcible despight,
Thought with his winges to stye above the ground:
But his late wounded wing unserviceable found

Then full of griefe and anguish vehement,
He lowdly brayd, that like was never heard:
And from his wide devouring oven sent
A flake of fire, that flashing in his beard
Him all amazd, and almost made afeard:
The scorching flame sore swinged all his face,
And through his armour all his body seard,
That he could not endure so cruell cace,
But thought his armes to leave, and helmet to unlace.

Not that great Champion of the antique world,
Whom famous Poetes verse so much doth vaunt,
And hath for twelve huge labours high extold,
So many furies and sharpe fits did haunt,
When him the poysoned garment did enchaunt,
When Centaures blood and bloudy verses charmd,
As did this knight twelve thousand dolours daunt,
Whom fyrie steele now burnt, that erst him armd;
That erst him goodly armd, now most of all him
harmd.

Faynt, wearie, sore, emboyled, grieved, brent,
With heat, toyle, wounds, armes, smart, and inward
 fire,
That never man such mischiefes did torment:
Death better were; death did he oft desire,
But death will never come when needes require.
Whom so dismayd when that his foe beheld,
He cast to suffer him no more respire,
But gan his sturdy sterne about to weld,
And him so strongly stroke, that to the ground him
 feld.

It fortuned, (as fayre it then befell)
Behynd his backe, unweeting, where he stood,
Of auncient time there was a springing well,
From which fast trickled forth a silver flood,
Full of great vertues, and for med'cine good:
Whylome, before that cursed Dragon got
That happy land, and all with innocent blood
Defyld those sacred waves, it rightly hot
The well of life, ne yet his vertues had forgot:

For unto life the dead it could restore,
And guilt of sinfull crimes cleane wash away;
Those that with sicknesse were infected sore
It could recure; and aged long decay
Renew, as one were borne that very day.
Both Silo this, and Jordan, did excell,
And th' English Bath, and eke the German Spau;
Ne can Cephise, nor Hebrus, match this well:
Into the same the knight back overthrowen fell.

Now gan the golden Phœbus for to steepe
His fierie face in billowes of the west,
And his faint steedes watred in Ocean deepe,
Whiles from their journall labours they did rest;
When that infernall Monster, having kest
His wearie foe into that living well,
Gan high advaunce his broad discoloured brest
Above his wonted pitch, with countenance fell,
And clapt his yron wings as victor he did dwell.

Which when his pensive Lady saw from farre,
Great woe and sorrow did her soule assay,
As weening that the sad end of the warre;
And gan to highest God entirely pray
That feared chaunce from her to turne away:
With folded hands, and knees full lowly bent,
All night shee watcht, ne once adowne would lay
Her dainty limbs in her sad dreriment,
But praying still did wake, and waking did lament.

The morrow next gan earely to appeare,
That Titan rose to runne his daily race;
But earely, ere the morrow next gan reare
Out of the sea faire Titans deawy face,
Up rose the gentle virgin from her place,
And looked all about, if she might spy
Her loved knight to move his manly pace:
For she had great doubt of his safety,
Since late she saw him fall before his enimy.

At last she saw where he upstarted brave
Out of the well, wherein he drenched lay:
As Eagle, fresh out of the ocean wave,
Where he hath lefte his plumes all hory gray,
And deckt himselfe with fethers youthly gay,
Like Eyas hauke up mounts unto the skies,
His newly-budded pineons to assay,
And marveiles at himselfe still as he flies:
So new this new-borne knight to battell new did rise.

Whom when the damned feend so fresh did spy,
No wonder if he wondred at the sight,
And doubted whether his late enimy
It were, or other new supplied knight.
He now, to prove his late-renewed might,
High brandishing his bright deaw-burning blade,
Upon his crested scalp so sore did smite,
That to the scull a yawning wound it made:
The deadly dint his dulled sences all dismaid.

I wote not whether the revenging steele
Were hardned with that holy water dew
Wherein he fell, or sharper edge did feele,
Or his baptized hands now greater grew.
Or other secret vertue did ensew;
Els never could the force of fleshly arme,
Ne molten mettall, in his blood embrew;
For till that stownd could never wight him harme
By subtilty, nor slight, nor might, nor mighty charme.

The cruell wound enraged him so sore,
That loud he yelled for exceeding paine;
As hundred ramping Lions seemd to rore,
Whom ravenous hunger did thereto constraine;
Then gan he tosse aloft his stretched traine,
And therewith scourge the buxome aire so sore,
That to his force to yielden it was faine;
Ne ought his sturdy strokes might stand afore,
That high trees overthrew, and rocks in peeces tore.

The same advauncing high above his head,
With sharpe intended sting so rude him smott,
That to the earth him drove, as stricken dead,
Ne living wight would have him life behott:
The mortall sting his angry needle shott
Quite through his shield, and in his shoulder seasd,
Where fast it stucke, ne would thereout be gott:
The griefe thereof him wondrous sore diseasd,
Ne might his rancling paine with patience be appeasd.

But yet, more mindfull of his honour deare
Then of the grievous smart which him did wring,
From loathed soile he can him lightly reare,
And strove to loose the far infixed sting:
Which when in vaine he tryde with struggeling,
Inflam'd with wrath, his raging blade he hefte,
And strooke so strongly, that the knotty string
Of his huge taile he quite a sonder clefte;
Five joints thereof he hewd, and but the stump him
 lefte.

Hart cannot thinke what outrage aud what cries,
With fowle enfouldred smoake and flashing fire,
The hell-bred beast threw forth unto the skies,
That all was covered with darknesse dire:
Then, fraught with rancour and engorged yro,
He cast at once him to avenge for all;
And, gathering up himselfe out of the mire
With his uneven wings, did fiercely fall
Upon his sunne-bright shield, and grypt it fast withall.

Much was the man encombred with his hold,
In feares to lose his weapon in his paw,
Ne wist yett how his talaunts to unfold;
Nor harder was from Cerberus greedy jaw
To plucke a bone, then from his cruell claw
To reave hy strength the gripped gage away:
Thrise he assayd it from his foote to draw,
And thrise in vaine to draw it did assay;
It booted nought to thinke to robbe him of his pray.

Tho, when he saw no power might prevaile,
His trusty sword he cald to his last aid,
Wherewith he fiersly did his foe assaile,
And double blowes about him stoutly laid,
That glauncing fire out of the yron plaid,
As sparkles from the Andvile use to fly,
When heavy hammers on the wedge are swaid:
Therewith at last he furst him to unty
One of his grasping feete, him to defend thereby.

The other foote, fast fixed on his shield,
Whenas no strength nor stroke mote him constraine
To loose, ne yet the warlike pledge to yield,
He smott thereat with all his might and maine,
That nought so wondrous puissaunce might sustaine:
Upon the joint the lucky steele did light, .
And made such way that hewd it quite in twaine;
The paw yett missed not his minisht might,
But hong still on the shield, as it at first was pight.

For griefe thereof and divelish despight,
From his infernall fournace forth he threw
Huge flames that dimmed all the hevens light,
Enrold in duskish smoke and brimstone blew:
As burning Aetna from his boyling stew
Doth belch out flames, and rockes in peeces broke,
And ragged ribs of mountaines molten new,
Enwrapt in coleblacke clowds and filthy smoke,
That al the land with stench and heven with horror
    choke.

The heate whereof, and harmefull pestilence,
So sore him noyd, that forst him to retire
A little backeward for his best defence,
To save his body from the scorching fire,
Which he from hellish entralles did expire.
It chaunst, (eternall God that chaunce did guide)
As he recoiled backeward, in the mire
His nigh forewearied feeble feet did slide,
And downe he fell, with dread of shame sore terrifide.

There grew a goodly tree him faire beside,
Loaden with fruit and apples rosy redd,
As they in pure vermilion had been dide,
Whereof great vertues over-all were redd :
For happy life to all which thereon fedd,
And life eke everlasting did befall :
Great God it planted in that blessed stedd
With his Almighty hand, and did it call
The tree of life, the crime of our first fathers fall.

In all the world like was not to be fownd,
Save in that soile, where all good things did grow
And fteely sprong out of the fruitfull grownd,
As incorrupted Nature did them sow,
Till that dredd Dragon all did overthrow.
Another like faire tree eke grew thereby,
Whereof whoso did eat, eftsoones did know
Both good and ill. O mournfull memory !
That tree through one mans fault hath doen us all to
    dy.

From that first tree forth flowd, as from a well
A trickling streame of Balme, most soveraine
And dainty deare, which on the ground still fell,
And overflowed all the fertile plaine,
As it had deawed bene with timely raine:
Life and long health that gracious ointment gave,
And deadly wounds could heale, and reare againe
The senselesse corse appointed for the grave:
Into that same he fell, which did from death him save.

For nigh thereto the ever damned Beast
Durst not approch, for he was deadly made,
And al that life preserved did detest;
Yet he it oft adventur'd to invade.
By this the drouping day-light gan to fade,
And yield his rowme to sad succeeding night,
Who with her sable mantle gan to shade
The face of earth and wayes of living wight,
And high her burning torch set up in heaven bright.

When gentle Una saw the second fall
Of her deare knight, who, weary of long fight
And faint through losse of blood, moov'd not at all,
But lay, as in a dreame of deepe delight,
Besmeard with pretious Balme, whose vertuous might
Did heale his woundes, and scorching heat a'lay;
Againe she stricken was with sore affright,
And for his safetie gan devoutly pray,
And watch the noyous night, and wait for joyous day.

The joyous day gan early to appeare;
And fayre Aurora from the deawy bed
Of aged Tithone gan herselfe to reare
With rosy cheekes. for shame as blushing red :
Her go'den locks for hast were loosely shed
About her eares, when Una her did marke
Clymbe to her charet, all with flowers spred,
From heven high to chace the chearelesse darke;
With mery note her lowd salutes the mounting larke.

Then freshly up arose the doughty knight,
All healed of his hurts and woundes wide,
And did himselfe to battaile ready dight;
Whose early foe awaiting him beside
To have devourd, so soone as day he spyde,
When now he saw himselfe so freshly reare,
As if late fight had nought him damnifyde,'
He woxe dismaid, and gan his fate to feare:
Nathlesse with wonted rage he him advaunced neare.

And in his first encounter, gaping wyde,
He thought attonce him to have swallowd quight,
And rusht upon him with outragious pryde;
Who him rencountring fierce, as hauke in flight,
Perforce rebutted backe. The weapon bright,
Taking advantage of his open jaw,
Ran through his mouth with so importune might,
That deepe emperst his darksom hollow maw,
And, back retyrd, his life blood forth with all did
draw.

So downe he fell, and forth his life did breath,
That vanisht into smoke and cloudes swift;
So downe he fell, that th' earth him underneath
Did grone, as feeble so great lond to lift;
So downe he fell, as an huge rocky clift,
Whose false foundacion waves have washt away,
With dreadfull poyse is from the mayneland rift,
And rolling downe great Neptune doth dismay:
So downe he fell, and like an heaped mountaine lay.

The knight him selfe even trembled at his fall,
So huge and horrible a masse it seemd;
And his deare Lady, that beheld it all,
Durst not approch for dread which she misdoemd;
But yet at last, whenas the direfull feend
She saw not stirre, off-shaking vaine affright
She nigher drew, and saw that joyous end:
Then God she prayd, and thankt her faithfull knight,
That had atchievde so great a conquest by his might.

FLOWERS.

Where are now the dreaming flowers,
Which of old were wont to lie,
Looking upwards at the Hours,
In the pale blue sky?

Where's the once red regal rose?
And the lily love-enchanted?
And the pensee, which arose
Like a thought earth-planted?

Some are wither'd—some are dead,
Others now have no perfume;
This doth hang its sullen head,
That hath lost its bloom.

Passions, such as nourish strife
In our blood, and quick decay,
Hang upon the flower's life,
Till it fades away.

THAT GENTLEMAN.

[Eliza Leslie, born in Philadelphia, 15th November, 1787; died in Gloucester, New Jersey. 2d January, 1858. Descended from a Scotch family. She was sister of the painter Charles Robert Leslie, R.A. She wrote and edited numerous works which obtained popularity; amongst them several cookery books. *The Young American; Atlantic Tales; Amelia, or a Young Lady's Vicissitudes; Althea Vernon; Henrietta Robinson;* and three series of *Pencil Sketches*—from which we quote—are her chief works. Professor Hart said: " Her writings are distinguished for vivacity and ease of expression, strong common sense, and right principle."]

On the third day, we were enabled to lay our course with a fair wind and a clear sky: the coast of Cornwall looking like a succession of low white clouds ranged along the edge of the northern horizon. Towards evening we passed the Lizard, to see land no more till we should descry it on the other side of the Atlantic. As Mr. Fenton and myself leaned over the taffrail, and saw the last point of England fade dimly from our view, we thought with regret of the shore we were leaving behind us, and of much that we had seen, and known, and enjoyed in that country of which all that remained to our lingering gaze was a dark spot so distant and so small as to be scarcely perceptible. Soon we could discern it no longer: and nothing of Europe was now left to us but the indelible recollections that it has impressed upon our minds. We turned towards the region of the descending sun—

"To where his setting splendours burn
Upon the western sea-maid's urn,"

and we vainly endeavoured to direct all our thoughts and feelings towards our home beyond the ocean—our beloved American home.

Our passengers were not too numerous. The lesser cabin was appropriated to three other ladies and myself. It formed our drawing-room; the gentlemen being admitted only as visitors. One of the ladies was Mrs. Calcott, an amiable and intelligent woman, who was returning with her husband from a long residence in England. Another was Miss Harriet Audley, a very pretty and very lively young lady from Virginia, who had been visiting a married sister in London, and was now on her way home under the care of the captain, expecting to meet her father in New York. We were much amused during the voyage with the coquetry of our fair Virginian as she aimed her arrows at nearly all the single gentlemen in turn, and with her frankness in openly talking of her designs and animadverting on their good or ill success. The gentlemen, with the usual vanity of their sex, always believed Miss Audley's attacks on their hearts to be made in earnest, and that she was deeply smitten with each of them in succession; notwithstanding that the smile in her eye was far more frequent than the blush on her cheek; and notwithstanding that rumour had asserted the existence of a certain cavalier in the neighbourhood of Richmond, whose constancy it was supposed she would eventually reward with her hand, as he might be considered, in every sense of the term, an excellent match.

Our fourth female passenger was Mrs. Cummings, a plump, rosy-faced old lady of remarkably limited ideas, who had literally passed her whole life in the city of London. Having been recently left a widow, she had broken up housekeeping, and was now on her way to join a son established in New York, who had very kindly sent for her to come over and live with him. The rest of the world was almost a sealed book to her, but she talked a great deal of the Minories, the Poultry, the Old Jewry, Cheapside, Long Acre, Bishopsgate Within and Bishopsgate Without, and other streets and places with appellations equally expressive.

The majority of the male passengers were pleasant and companionable—and we thought we had seen them all in the course of the first three days—but on the fourth, we heard the captain say to one of the waiters, " Juba, ask that gentleman if I shall have the pleasure of taking wine with him." My eyes now involuntarily followed the direction of Juba's movements, feeling some curiosity to know who " that gentleman " was, as I now recollected having frequently heard the epithet within the last few days. For instance, when almost every one was confined by sea-sickness to their state-rooms, I had seen the captain despatch a servant to inquire of that gentleman if he would have anything sent to him from the table. Also, I had heard Hamilton, the steward, call out—" There, boys, don't you hear that gentleman ring his bell—why don't you run spontaneously—jump, one of you, to number eleventeen." I was puzzled for a moment to divine which state-room bore the designation of eleventeen, but concluded it to be one of the many unmeaning terms that characterize the phraseology of our coloured people. Once or twice I wondered who that gentleman could be, but something else happened immediately to divert my attention.

Now when I heard Captain Santlow propose taking wine with him, I concluded that, of course, that gentleman must be visible in pro-

pria persona, and casting my eyes towards the lower end of the table, I perceived a genteel-looking man whom I had not seen before. He was apparently of no particular age, and there was nothing in his face that could lead any one to guess at his country. He might have been English, Scotch, Irish, or American; but he had none of the characteristic marks of either nation. He filled his glass, and bowing his head to Captain Santlow, who congratulated him on his recovery, he swallowed his wine in silence. There was an animated conversation going on near the head of the table, between Miss Audley and two of her beaux, and we thought no more of him.

At the close of the dessert, we happened to know that he had quitted the table and gone on deck, by one of the waiters coming down, and requesting Mr. Overslaugh (who was sitting atilt, while discussing his walnuts, with his chair balanced on one leg, and his head leaning against the wainscot) to let him pass for a moment, while he went into No. eleventeen for that gentleman's overcoat. I now found that the servants had converted No. 13 into eleventeen. By-the-bye, that gentleman had a state-room all to himself, sometimes occupying the upper and sometimes the under berth.

"Captain Santlow," said Mr. Fenton, "allow me to ask you the name of that gentleman."

"Oh! I don't know," replied the captain, trying to suppress a smile, "at least I have forgotten it—some English name ; for he is an Englishman—he came on board at Plymouth, and his indisposition commenced immediately. Mrs. Cummings, shall I have the pleasure of peeling an orange for you?"

I now recollected a little incident which had set me laughing soon after we left Plymouth, and when we were beating down the coast of Devonshire. I had been trying to write at the table in the ladies' cabin, but it was one of those days when

"Our paper, pen and ink, and we
Roll up and down our ships at sea."

And all I could do was to take refuge in my berth, and endeavour to read, leaving the door open for light and air. My attention, however, was continually withdrawn from my book by the sound of something that was dislodged from its place, sliding or falling, and frequently suffering destruction; though sometimes miraculously escaping unhurt.

While I was watching the progress of two pitchers that had been tossed out of the washing-stand, and after deluging the floor with water, had met in the ladies' cabin, and were rolling amicably side by side, without happening to break each other, I saw a barrel of flour start from the steward's pantry, and running across the dining-room, stop at a gentleman that lay extended in a lower berth with his room-door open, and pour out its contents upon him, completely enveloping him in a fog of meal. I heard the steward, who was busily engaged in mopping up the water that had flowed from the pitchers, call out, "Run, boys, run, that gentleman's smothering up in flour —go take the barrel off him—jump, I tell you."

How that gentleman acted while hidden in the cloud of flour, I could not perceive, and immediately the closing of the folding doors shut out the scene.

For a few days after he appeared among us, there was some speculation with regard to this nameless stranger, whose taciturnity seemed his chief characteristic. One morning while we were looking at the gambols of a shoal of porpoises that were tumbling through the waves and sometimes leaping out of them, my husband made some remark on the clumsy antics of this unsightly fish, addressing himself, for the first time, to the unknown Englishman, who happened to be standing near him. That gentleman smiled affably, but made no reply. Mr. Fenton pursued the subject—and that gentleman smiled still more affably, and walked away.

Nevertheless, he was neither deaf nor dumb, nor melancholy, but had only "a great talent for silence," and as is usually the case with persons whose genius lies that way, he was soon left entirely to himself, no one thinking it worth while to take the trouble of extracting words from him. In truth, he was so impracticable, and at the same time so evidently insignificant, and so totally uninteresting, that his fellow-passengers tacitly conveyed him to Coventry; and in Coventry he seemed perfectly satisfied to dwell. Once or twice Captain Santlow was asked again if he recollected the name of that gentleman; but he always replied with a sort of smile, "I cannot say I do—not exactly, at least—but I'll look at my manifest and see"—and he never failed to turn the conversation to something else.

The only person that persisted in occasionally talking to that gentleman, was old Mrs. Cummings; and she confided to him her perpetual alarms at "the perils of the sea," considering him a good hearer, as he never made any reply, and was always disengaged, and sitting and standing about, apparently at leisure, while the other gentlemen were oc-

cupied in reading, writing, playing chess, walking the deck, &c.

Whenever the ship was struck by a heavy sea, and after quivering with the shock, remained motionless for a moment before she recovered herself and rolled the other way, poor Mrs. Cummings supposed that we had run against a rock, and could not be convinced that rocks were not dispersed everywhere about the open ocean. And as that gentleman never attempted to undeceive her on this or any other subject, but merely listened with a placid smile, she believed that he always thought precisely as she did. She not unfrequently discussed to him, in an under tone, the obstinacy and incivility of the captain, who, she averred, with truth, had never in any one instance had the politeness to stop the ship, often as she had requested, nay, implored him to do so, even when she was suffering with sea-sickness, and actually tossed out of her berth by the violence of the storm, though she was holding on with both hands. . . .

In less than a fortnight after we left the English Channel we were off the banks of Newfoundland ; and, as is frequently the case in their vicinity, we met with cold foggy weather. It cleared a little about seven in the morning, and we then discovered no less than three icebergs to leeward. One of them, whose distance from us was perhaps a mile, appeared higher than the main-mast head, and as the top shot up into a tall column, it looked like a vast rock with a lighthouse on its pinnacle. As the cold and watery sunbeams gleamed fitfully upon it, it exhibited in some places the rainbow tints of a prism—other parts were of a dazzling white, while its sharp angular projections seemed like masses of diamonds glittering upon snow.

The fog soon became so dense that in looking over the side of the ship we could not discern the sea. Fortunately, it was so calm that we scarcely moved, or the danger of driving on the icebergs would have been terrific. We had now no other means of ascertaining our distance from them, but by trying the temperature of the water with a thermometer.

In the afternoon the fog gathered still more thickly round us, and dripped from the rigging, so that the sailors were continually swabbing the deck. I had gone with Mr. Fenton to the round-house, and looked a while from its windows on the comfortless scene without. The only persons then on the main-deck were the captain and the first mate. They were wrapped in their watch-coats, their hair and whiskers dripping with the fog dew. Most of the passengers went to bed at an early hour, and soon all was awfully still; Mrs. Cummings being really too much frightened to talk, only that she sometimes wished herself in Shoreditch, and sometimes in Houndsditch. It was a night of real danger. The captain remained on deck till morning, and several of the gentlemen bore him company, being too anxious to stay below. About day-break, a heavy shower of rain dispersed the fog—"the conscious vessel waked as from a trance"—a breeze sprung up that carried us out of danger from the icebergs, which were soon diminished to three specks on the horizon, and the sun rose bright and cheerfully.

Towards noon, the ladies recollected that none of them had seen that gentleman during the last twenty-four hours, and some apprehension was expressed lest he should have walked overboard in the fog. No one could give any account of him, or remember his last appearance; and Miss Audley professed much regret that now in all probability we should never be able to ascertain his name, as, most likely, he had "died and made no sign." To our shames be it spoken, not one of us could cry a tear at his possible fate. The captain had turned into his berth, and was reposing himself after the fatigue of last night; so we could make no inquiry of him on the subject of our missing fellow-passenger.

Mrs. Cummings called the steward, and asked him how long it was since he had seen anything of that gentleman. "I really can't tell, madam," replied Hamilton; "I can't pretend to charge my memory with such things. But I conclude he must have been seen yesterday—at least I rather expect he was."

The waiter Juba was now appealed to. "I believe, madam," said Juba—"I remember something of handing that gentleman the bread-basket yesterday at dinner—but I would not be qualified as to whether the thing took place or not, my mind being a good deal engaged at the time."

Solomon, the third waiter, disclaimed all positive knowledge of this or any other fact, but sagely remarked, "that it was very likely that gentleman had been about all yesterday as usual; yet still it was just as likely he might not; and there was only one thing certain, which was, that if he was not nowhere, he must, of course, be somewhere."

"I have a misgiving," said Mrs. Cummings, "that he will never be found again."

"I'll tell you what I can do, madam," exclaimed the steward, looking as if suddenly struck with a bright thought—"I can examine into No. eleventeen, and see if I can perceive him there." And softly opening the door of the state-room in question, he stepped back and said with a triumphant flourish of his hand —"There he is, ladies, there he is, in the upper berth, fast asleep in his double cashmere dressing-gown. I opinionate that he was one of the gentlemen that stayed on deck all night, because they were afraid to go to sleep on account of the icebergs—of course nobody noticed him — but there he is now, safe enough."

Instantly we proceeded *en masse* towards No. eleventeen, to convince ourselves: and there indeed we saw that gentleman lying asleep in his double cashmere dressing-gown. He opened his eyes, and seemed surprised, as well he might, at seeing all the ladies and all the servants ranged before the door of his room, and gazing in at him: and then we all stole off, looking foolish enough.

"Well," said Mrs. Cummings, "he is not dead, however,—so we have yet a chance of knowing his name from himself, if we choose to ask him. But I'm determined I'll make the captain tell it me, as soon as he gets up. It's all nonsense, this making a secret of a man's name." . . . .

After crossing the Banks we seemed to feel ourselves on American ground, or rather on American sea. As our interest increased on approaching the land of our destination, that gentleman was proportionally overlooked and forgotten. He "kept the even tenor of his way," and we had become scarcely conscious that he was still among us: till one day when there was rather a hard gale, and the waves were running high, we were startled, as we surrounded the luncheon table, by a tremendous noise on the cabin staircase, and the sudden bursting open of the door at its foot. We all looked up, and saw that gentleman falling down-stairs, with both arms extended, as he held in one hand a tall cane-stool, and in the other the captain's barometer, which had hung just within the upper door; he having involuntarily caught hold of both these articles, with a view of saving himself. "While his head, as he tumbled, went nicketty nock," his countenance, for once, assumed a new expression, and the change from its usual unvarying sameness was so striking, that, combined with his ludicrous attitude, it set us all to laughing. The waiters ran forward and assisted him to rise; and it was then found that the stool and the barometer had been the greatest sufferers; one having lost a leg, and the other being so shattered that the stair-carpet was covered with globules of quicksilver. However, he retired to his state-room, and whether or not he was seen again before next morning, I cannot positively undertake to say.

Next day we continued to proceed rapidly, with a fair wind, which we knew would soon bring us to the end of our voyage. The ladies' cabin was now littered with trunks and boxes, brought from the baggage room that we might select from them such articles as we thought we should require when we went on shore.

Near one o'clock I heard a voice announcing the light on the island of Neversink, and in a short time all the gentlemen were on deck. At daybreak Mr. Fenton came to ask me if I would rise and see the morning dawn upon our own country. We had taken a pilot on board at two o'clock, had a fine fair breeze to carry us into the Bay of New York, and there was every probability of our being on shore in a few hours.

Soon after sunrise we were visited by a news-boat, when there was an exchange of papers, and much to inquire and much to tell. We were going rapidly through the Narrows, when the bell rung for breakfast, which Captain Santlow had ordered at an early hour, as we had all been up before daylight. Chancing to look towards his accustomed seat, I missed that gentleman, and inquired after him of the captain. "Oh!" he replied, "that gentleman went on shore in the news-boat; did you not see him depart? He bowed all round before he went down the side."

"No," was the general reply, "we did not see him go." In truth we had all been too much interested in hearing, reading, and talking of the news brought by the boat.

"Then he is gone for ever," exclaimed Mrs. Cummings, "and we shall never know his name."

"Come, Captain Santlow," said Mr. Fenton, "try to recollect it. 'Let it not,' as Grumio says, 'die in oblivion, while we return to our graves inexperienced in it.'"

Captain Santlow smiled, and remained silent.

"Now, captain," said Miss Audley, "I will not quit the ship till you tell me that gentleman's name.—I cannot hold out a greater threat to you, as I know you have had a weary time of it since I have been under your charge. Come, I set not my foot on shore till I know the name of that gentleman, and also why you cannot refrain from smiling whenever you are asked about it."

"Well, then," replied Captain Santlow, "though his name is a very pretty one when you get it said, there is a little awkwardness in speaking it. So I thought I would save myself and my passengers the trouble. And partly for that reason, and partly to tease you all, I have withheld it from your knowledge during the voyage. But I can assure you he is a baronet."

"A baronet!" cried Miss Audley—"I wish I had known that before, I should certainly have made a dead set at him. A baronet would have been far better worth the trouble of a flirtation than you Mr. Williams, or you Mr. Sutton, or you Mr. Belfield, or any of the other gentlemen that I have been amusing myself with during the voyage."

"A baronet!" exclaimed Mrs. Cummings, "well, really—and have I been four weeks in the same ship with a baronet—and sitting at the same table with him,—and often talking to him face to face.—I wonder what Mrs. Thimbleby of Threadneedle Street would say if she knew that I am now acquainted with a baronet?"

"But what is his name, captain?" said Mr. Fenton; "still you do not tell us.'"

"His name," answered the captain, "is Sir St. John St. Ledger."

"Sir St. John St. Ledger!" was repeated by each of the company.

"Yes," resumed Captain Santlow—"and you see how difficult it is to say it smoothly. There is more sibilation in it than in any name I know.—Was I not right in keeping it from you till the voyage was over, and thus sparing you the trouble of articulating it, and myself the annoyance of hearing it? See, here it is in writing."

The captain then took his manifest out of his pocket-book, and showed us the words, "Sir St. John St. Ledger, of Sevenoaks, Kent."

"Pho!" said Mrs. Cummings, "where's the trouble in speaking that name, if you only knew the right way—I have heard it a hundred times—and even seen it in the newspapers. This must be the very gentleman that my cousin George's wife is always talking about. She has a brother that lives near his estate, a topping apothecary. Why, 'tis easy enough to say his name, if you say it as we do in England."

"And how is that?" asked the captain; "what can you make of Sir St. John St. Ledger?"

"Why, Sir Singeon Sillinger, to be sure;" replied Mrs. Cummings—"I am confident he would have answered to that name. Sir Singeon Sillinger of Sunnock—cousin George's wife's brother lives close by Sunnock in a yellow house with a red door."

"And have I," said the captain laughing, "so carefully kept his name to myself, during the whole passage, for fear we should have had to call him Sir St. John St. Ledger, when all the while we might have said Sir Singeon Sillinger!"

"To be sure you might," replied Mrs. Cummings, looking proud of the opportunity of displaying her superior knowledge of something. "With all your striving after sense you Americans are very ignorant people, particularly of the right way of speaking English. Since I have been on board, I have heard you all say the oddest things—though I thought there would be no use in trying to set you right. The other day there was Mr. Williams talking of the church of St. Mary le bon—instead of saying Marrow bone. Then Mr. Belfield says, Lord Cholmondeley, instead of Lord Chumley, and Col. Sinclair instead of Col. Sinkler; and Mr. Sutton says Lady Beauchamp, instead of Lady Beachum; and you all say Birmingham instead of Brummagem. The truth is, you know nothing about English names. Now that name, Trollope, that you all sneer at so much, and think so very low, why Trollope is quite genteel in England, and so is Hussey. The Trollopes and Husseys belong to great families. But I have no doubt of finding many things that are very elegant in England counted quite vulgar in America, owing to the ignorance of your people. For my part, I was particularly brought up to despise all manner of ignorance."

In a short time a steamboat came alongside, into which we removed ourselves, accompanied by the captain and the letter-bags; and we proceeded up to the city, where Mr. Fenton and myself were met on the wharf, I need not tell how, and by whom.

THE FOREIGN LAND.

A woman is a foreign land,
  Of which, though there he settle young,
A man will ne'er quite understand
  The customs, politics, and tongue.
The foolish hie them post-haste through,
  See fashions odd, and prospects fair,
Learn of the language, "How d'ye do,"
  And go and brag that they've been there.
The most for leave to trade apply,
  For once, at Empire's seat, her heart,
Then get what knowledge ear and eye
  Glean chancewise in the life-long mart.
And certain others, few and fit,
  Attach them to the Court, and see
The Country's best, its accent hit,
  And partly sound its polity.

COVENTRY PATMORE.

THE BLESSING.

[Rev. Thomas Brydson, was sometime minister of Levern Church, Renfrewshire, and wrote numerous minor poems.]

Dark is the sky with thunder-clouds,
  While breathes that aged one
His fervent gratitude to Heaven,
  Amid the mountains lone,
For the mercy of the present hour,
  And for the mercies shown
To him and his continually,
  In the seasons that are gone.

His little grandson calmly views
  The tempest gathering round;
For though the words cannot be heard,
  Yet, in their whisper'd sound,
The boy a heart-felt safety finds,
  And it seems holy ground
To his young eye, where they two sit
  On the gray rocky mound.

Not oft in crowded scenes of life,
  When the richest feasts are spread,
Does such accepted prayer arise
  As o'er the peasant's bread,
Who, at the close of every day,
  Rests a toil-wearied head,
Soothed by the hope that heaven remains
  When mortal life is fled.

A WARNING TO YOUTH OF BOTH SEXES.

BY THEODORE HOOK.[1]

My readers may know that to all the editions of Entick's *Dictionary*, commonly used in schools, there is prefixed "a table of words that are alike, or nearly alike, in sound, but different in spelling and signification." It must be evident that this table is neither more nor less than an early provocation to punning; the whole mystery of which vain art consists in the use of words, the sound and sense of which are at variance. In order, if possible, to check any disposition to punning in youth, which may be fostered by this manual, I have thrown together the following adaptation of Entick's hints to young beginners, hoping thereby to afford a warning, and exhibit a deformity to

[1] From *The Christmas Box*, edited by T. Crofton Croker, 1828.

be avoided, rather than an example to be followed; and at the same time showing the caution children should observe in using words which have more than one meaning.

PUNNING.

"My little dears, who learn to read, pray early learn to shun
That very silly thing indeed which people call a pun:
Read Entick's rules, and 'twill be found how simple an offence
It is, to make the self-same sound afford a double sense.

"For instance, *ale* may make you *ail*, your *aunt* an *ant* may kill,
You in a *vale* may buy a *veil*, and *Bill* may pay the *bill*.
Or if to France your *bark* you steer, at Dover, it may be,
A *peer appears* upon the *pier*, who, blind, still goes to *sea*.

"Thus one might say, when to a treat good friends accept our greeting,
'Tis *meet* that men who *meet* to eat should eat their *meat* when meeting.
Brawn on the board's no *bore* indeed, although from *boar* prepared;
Nor can the *fowl*, on which we feed, *foul* feeding be declared.

"Thus *one* ripe fruit may be a *pear*, and yet be *pared* again,
And still be *one*, which seemeth rare until we do explain.
It therefore should be all your aim to speak with ample care:
For who, however fond of game, would choose to swallow *hair!*

"A fat man's *gait* may make us smile, who has no *gate* to close:
The farmer sitting on his *style* no *stylish* person knows:
Perfumers men of *scents* must be; some *Scilly* men are bright;
A *brown* man oft deep *read* we see, a *black* a wicked *wight*.

"Most wealthy men good *manors* have, however vulgar they;
And actors still the harder slave, the oftener they *play:*
So poets can't the *baize* obtain, unless their tailors choose;
While grooms and coachmen, not in vain, each evening seek the *Mews.*

"The *dyer* who by *dying* lives, a *dire* life maintains;
The glazier, it is known, receives—his profits from his *panes:*
By gardeners *thyme* is *tied*, 'tis true, when spring is in its prime;
But *time* or *tide* won't wait for you, if you are *tied* for *time.*

"Then now you see, my little dears, the way to make a pun;
A trick which you, through coming years, should sedulously shun.
The fault admits of no defence; for wheresoe'er 'tis found,
You sacrifice the *sound* for *sense:* the sense is never *sound.*

"So let your words and actions too, one single meaning prove,
And, just in all you say or do, you'll gain esteem and love:
In mirth and play no harm you'll know, when duty's task is done;
But parents ne'er should let ye go un*pun*ish'd for a *pun!*"

THE MOUNTAIN OF MISERIES.

[Joseph Addison, born at Milston, near Amesbury, Wiltshire, 1st May, 1672; died at Holland House, Kensington, 17th June, 1719. He was the eldest son of Lancelot Addison, D.D., Dean of Lichfield. He was educated at the Charter House, where Richard Steele was his fellow-pupil, and afterwards at Oxford. His works are: *Remarks on Several Parts of Italy*, in 1701–3; *The Campaign*, a poem; *The Five Whig Examiners*, 1712; *Cato*, a tragedy, 1713; *Poems; The Drummer, or the Haunted House; Dissertations on the most Celebrated Roman Poets; Notes upon the Twelve Books of Paradise Lost*—collected from the *Spectator; On the Evidences of the Christian Religion*, &c. Macaulay said: "Addison is entitled to be considered not only as the greatest of the English essayists, but as the forerunner of the great English novelists. His best essays approach near to absolute perfection; nor is their excellence more wonderful than their variety." Thackeray said: "If Swift's life was the most wretched, I think Addison's was one of the most prosperous and beautiful—a life prosperous and beautiful—a calm death—an immense fame, and affection afterwards for his happy and spotless name." 1]

It is a celebrated thought of Socrates, that if all the misfortunes of mankind were cast into a public stock, in order to be equally distributed among the whole species, those who now think themselves the most unhappy would prefer the share they are already possessed of, before that which would fall to them by such a division. Horace has carried this thought a great deal further, and implies that the hardships or misfortunes we lie under are more easy to us than those of any other person would be, in case we could change conditions with him. As I was ruminating on these two remarks, and seated in my elbow-chair, I insensibly fell asleep; when, on a sudden, methought there was a proclamation made by Jupiter, that every mortal should bring in his griefs and calamities, and throw them together in a heap. There was a large plain appointed for this purpose. I took my stand in the centre of it, and saw with a great deal of pleasure the whole human species marching one after another and throwing down their several loads, which immediately grew up into a prodigious mountain that seemed to rise above the clouds.

There was a certain lady of a thin airy shape, who was very active in this solemnity. She carried a magnifying glass in one of her hands, and was clothed in a loose flowing robe, embroidered with several figures of fiends and spectres, that discovered themselves in a thousand chimerical shapes, as her garment hovered

in the wind. There was something wild and distracted in her look. Her name was *Fancy*. She led up every mortal to the appointed place, after having very officiously assisted him in making up his pack, and laying it upon his shoulders. My heart melted within me to see my fellow-creatures groaning under their respective burdens, and to consider that prodigious bulk of human calamities which lay before me. There were however several persons who gave me great diversion upon this occasion. I observed one bringing in a fardel very carefully concealed under an old embroidered cloak, which, upon his throwing it into the heap, I discovered to be poverty. Another, after a great deal of puffing, threw down his luggage, which, upon examining, I found to be his wife. There were multitudes of lovers saddled with very whimsical burdens composed of darts and flames; but, what was very odd, though they sighed as if their hearts would break under these bundles of calamities, they could not persuade themselves to cast them into the heap when they came up to it; but after a few faint efforts, shook their heads and marched away as heavy laden as they came. I saw multitudes of old women throw down their wrinkles, and several young ones who stripped themselves of a tawny skin. There were very great heaps of red noses, large lips, and rusty teeth. The truth of it is, I was surprised to see the greatest part of the mountain made up of bodily deformities. Observing one advancing towards the heap with a larger cargo than ordinary upon his back, I found upon his near approach that it was only a natural hump, which he disposed of with great joy of heart among this collection of human miseries. There were likewise distempers of all sorts, though I could not but observe that there were many more imaginary than real. One little packet I could not but take notice of, which was a complication of all the diseases incident to human nature, and was in the hand of a great many fine people: this was called the spleen. But what most of all surprised me was a remark I made, that there was not a single vice or folly thrown into the whole heap: at which I was very much astonished, having concluded within myself that every one would take this opportunity of getting rid of his passions, prejudices, and frailties. I took notice in particular of a very profligate fellow, who I did not question came laden with his crimes, but upon searching into his bundle I found that, instead of throwing his guilt from him, he had only laid down his memory. He was followed by another worthless rogue who flung away his modesty instead of his ignorance.

---

1 Addison contributed altogether 309 papers to the *Tatler, Spectator*, and *Guardian;* Steele contributed £10.

When the whole race of mankind had thus cast their burdens, the phantom which had been so busy on this occasion, seeing me an idle spectator of what passed, approached towards me. I grew uneasy at her presence, when of a sudden she held her magnifying glass full before my eyes. I no sooner saw my face in it, but was startled at the shortness of it, which now appeared to me in its utmost aggra' vation. The immoderate breadth of the features made me very much out of humour with my own countenance, upon which I threw it from me like a mask. It happened very luckily, that one who stood by me had just before thrown down his visage, which, it seems, was too long for him. It was indeed extended to a most shameful length; I believe the very chin was, modestly speaking, as long as my whole face. We had both of us an opportunity of mending ourselves, and all the contributions being now brought in, every man was at liberty to exchange his misfortune for those of another person.

I saw, with unspeakable pleasure, the whole species thus delivered from its sorrows: though at the same time, as we stood round the heap, and surveyed the several materials of which it was composed, there was scarce a mortal in this vast multitude who did not discover what he thought pleasures and blessings of life; and wondered how the owners of them ever came to look upon them as burdens and grievances.

As we were regarding very attentively this confusion of miseries, this chaos of calamity, Jupiter issued out a second proclamation, that every one was now at liberty to exchange his affliction, and to return to his habitation with any such other bundle as should be delivered to him.

Upon this, Fancy began again to bestir herself, and parcelling out the whole heap with incredible activity, recommended to every one his particular packet. The hurry and confusion at this time was not to be expressed. Some observations, which I made upon the occasion, I shall communicate to the public. A venerable gray-headed man, who had laid down the colic, and who I found wanted an heir to his estate, snatched up an undutiful son that had been thrown into the heap by his angry father. The graceless youth, in less than a quarter of an hour, pulled the old gentleman by the beard, and had like to have knocked his brains out; so that meeting the true father, who came towards him in a fit of the gripes, he begged him to take his son again, and give him back his colic; but they were incapable either of them to recede from the choice they had made.

A poor galley-slave, who had thrown down his chains, took up the gout in their stead, but made such wry faces, that one might easily perceive he was no great gainer by the bargain. It was pleasant enough to see the several exchanges that were made, for sickness against poverty, hunger against want of appetite, and care against pain.

The female world were very busy among themselves in bartering for features; one was trucking a lock of gray hairs for a carbuncle, another was making over a short waist for a pair of round shoulders, and a third cheapening a bad face for a lost reputation: but on all these occasions, there was not one of them who did not think the new blemish, as soon as she had got it into her possession, much more disagreeable than the old one. I made the same observation on every other misfortune or calamity, which every one in the assembly brought upon himself, in lieu of what he had parted with; whether it be that all the evils which befall us are in some measure suited and proportioned to our strength, or that every evil becomes more supportable by our being accustomed to it, I shall not determine.

I must not omit my own particular adventure. My friend with the long visage, had no sooner taken upon him my short face, but he made such a grotesque figure in it, that as I looked upon him I could not forbear laughing at myself, insomuch that I put my own face out of countenance. The poor gentleman was so sensible of the ridicule, that I found he was ashamed of what he had done: on the other side I found that I myself had no great reason to triumph, for as I went to touch my forehead I missed the place, and clapped my finger upon my upper lip. Besides, as my nose was exceeding prominent, I gave it two or three unlucky knocks as I was playing my hand about my face, and aiming at some other part of it. I saw two other gentlemen by me who were in the same ridiculous circumstances. These had made a foolish swop between a couple of thick bandy legs, and two long trapsticks that had no calves to them. One of these looked like a man walking upon stilts, and was so lifted up into the air above his ordinary height, that his head turned round with it, while the other made such awkward circles, as he attempted to walk, that he scarce knew how to move forward upon his new supporters. Observing him to be a pleasant kind of fellow, I stuck my cane in the ground, and told him I would lay him a bottle of wine that he did not march up to it on a line, that I drew for him, in a quarter of an hour.

The heap was at last distributed among the two sexes, who made a most piteous sight, as they wandered up and down under the pressure of their several burdens. The whole plain was filled with murmurs and complaints, groans and lamentations. Jupiter at length, taking compassion on the poor mortals, ordered them a second time to lay down their loads, with a design to give every one his own again. They discharged themselves with a great deal of pleasure, after which the phantom, who had led them into such gross delusions, was commanded to disappear. There was sent in her stead a goddess of a quite different figure; her motions were steady and composed, and her aspect serious but cheerful. She every now and then cast her eyes towards heaven, and fixed them upon Jupiter: her name was Patience. She had no sooner placed herself by the Mount of Sorrows, but, what I thought very remarkable, the whole heap sunk to such a degree, that it did not appear a third part so big as it was before. She afterwards returned every man his own proper calamity, and teaching him how to bear it in the most commodious manner, he marched off with it contentedly, being very well pleased that he had not been left to his own choice as to the kind of evils which fell to his lot.

Besides the several pieces of morality to be drawn out of this vision, I learned from it, never to repine at my own misfortunes, or to envy the happiness of another, since it is impossible for any man to form a right judgment of his neighbour's sufferings; for which reason also I have determined never to think too lightly of another's complaints, but to regard the sorrows of my fellow-creatures with sentiments of humanity and compassion.

HELEN'S TOMB.

At morn a dew-bathed rose I past,
  All lovely on its native stalk,
Unmindful of the noon-day blast,
  That strew'd it on my evening's walk.

So, when the morn of life awoke,
  My hopes sat bright on fancy's bloom,
Forgetful of the death-aimed stroke,
  That laid them in my Helen's tomb.

Watch there, my hopes! watch Helen sleep,
  Nor more with sweet-lipped Fancy rave,
But with the long grass sigh, and weep
  At dewy eve by Helen's grave.

ROBERT POLLOK.

THE FISHER-MAID.

BY THE AUTHOR OF "JOHN HALIFAX,
                 GENTLEMAN."

"If I were a noble lady,
    And he a peasant born,
With nothing but his good right hand
    'Twixt him and the world's scorn—
Oh, I would speak so humble,
    And I would smile so meek,
And cool with tears this fierce hot flush
    He left upon my cheek.
Sing heigh, sing ho, my bonnie, bonnie boat,
    Let's watch the anchor weighed:
For he is a great sea-captain,
    And I a fisher-maid.

"If I were a royal princess,
    And he a captive poor,
I would cast down these steadfast eyes,
    Unbar this bolted door,
And walking brave in all men's sight,
    Low at his feet would fall:
Sceptre and crown and womanhood,
    My love should take them all!
Sing heigh, sing ho, my bonnie, bonnie boat,
    Alone with sea and sky,
For he is a bold sea-captain,
    A fisher-maiden I.

"If I were a saint in heaven,
    And he a sinner pale,
Whom good men passed with face avert,
    And left him to his bale,
Mine eyes they should weep rivers,
    My voice reach that great Throne,
Beseeching—'Oh, be merciful!
    Make Thou mine own, Thine own!'
Sing heigh, sing ho, my bonnie, bonnie boat,
    Love only cannot fade:
Though he is a bold sea-captain,
    And I a fisher-maid."

Close stood the young sea-captain,
    His tears fell fast as rain,
"If I have sinned, I'll sin no more—
    God judge between us twain!"
The gold ring flashed in sunshine,
    The small waves laughing curled—
"Our ship rocks at the harbour bar,
    Away to the under world."—
"Farewell, farewell, my bonnie, bonnie boat!
    Now Heaven us bless and aid,
For my lord is a great sea-captain,
    And I was a fisher-maid."

Poems, 1872.

ELLEN.

BY MARY RUSSELL MITFORD.

Charlotte and Ellen Page were the twin daughters of the rector of N., a small town in Dorsetshire. They were his only children, having lost their mother shortly after their birth; and as their father was highly connected, and still more highly accomplished, and possessed good church-preferment with a considerable private fortune, they were reared and educated in the most liberal and expensive style. Whilst mere infants, they had been uncommonly beautiful, and as remarkably alike, as occasionally happens with twin sisters, distinguished only by some ornament of dress. Their very nurse, as she used to boast, could hardly tell her pretty "couplets" apart, so exactly alike were the soft blue eyes, the rosy cheeks, the cherry lips, and the curly light hair. Change the turquoise necklace for the coral, and nurse herself would not know Charlotte from Ellen. This pretty puzzle, this inconvenience, of which mammas and aunts and grandmammas love to complain, did not last long. Either from a concealed fall, or from original delicacy of habit, the little Ellen faded and drooped almost into deformity. There was no visible defect in her shape, except a slight and almost imperceptible lameness when in quick motion; but there was the marked and peculiar look in the features, the languor and debility, and above all, the distressing consciousness attendant upon imperfect formation; and, at the age of twenty years, the contrast between the sisters was even more striking than the likeness had been at two.

Charlotte was a fine, robust, noble-looking girl, rather above the middle height; her eyes and complexion sparkled and glowed with life and health, her rosy lips seemed to be made for smiles, and her glossy brown hair played in natural ringlets round her dimpled face. Her manner was a happy mixture of the playful and the gentle; frank, innocent, and fearless, she relied with a sweet confidence on everybody's kindness, was ready to be pleased, and secure of pleasing. Her artlessness and *naïveté* had great success in society, especially as they were united with the most perfect good breeding, and considerable quickness and talent. Her musical powers were of the most delightful kind; she sang exquisitely, joining to great taste and science a life, and freedom, and buoyancy quite unusual in that artificial personage, a young lady. Her clear and ringing notes had the effect of a milk-maid's song, as if a

mere ebullition of animal spirits; there was no resisting the contagion of Charlotte's glee. She was a general favourite, and above all, a favourite at home,—the apple of her father's eye, the pride and ornament of his house, and the delight and comfort of his life. The two children had been so much alike, and born so nearly together, that the precedence in age had never been definitely settled; but that point seemed very early to decide itself. Unintentionally, as it were, Charlotte took the lead, gave invitations, received visitors, sat at the head of the table, became in fact and in name Miss Page, while her sister continued Miss Ellen.

Poor Ellen! she was short and thin, and sickly, and pale, with no personal charm but the tender expression of her blue eyes and the timid sweetness of her countenance. The resemblance to her sister had vanished altogether, except when, very rarely, some strong emotion of pleasure, a word of praise, or a look of kindness from her father, would bring a smile and a blush at once into her face, and lighten it up like a sunbeam. Then, for a passing moment, she was like Charlotte, and even prettier,—there was so much of mind, of soul, in the transitory beauty. In manner she was unchangeably gentle and distressingly shy, shy even to awkwardness. Shame and fear clung to her like her shadow. In company she could neither sing nor play nor speak without trembling, especially when her father was present. Her awe of him was inexpressible. Mr. Page was a man of considerable talent and acquirement, of polished and elegant manners, and great conversational power—quick, ready, and sarcastic. He never condescended to scold; but there was something very formidable in the keen glance and the cutting jest, to which poor Ellen's want of presence of mind frequently exposed her—something from which she shrank into the very earth. He was a good man, too, and a kind father—at least he meant to be so—attentive to her health and comfort, strictly impartial in favours and presents, in pocket-money and amusements, making no difference between the twins, except that which he could not help, the difference in his love. But to an apprehensive temper and an affectionate heart, that was everything; and whilst Charlotte flourished and blossomed like a rose in the sunshine, Ellen sickened and withered like the same plant in the shade.

Mr. Page lost much enjoyment by this unfortunate partiality: for he had taste enough to have particularly valued the high endowments which formed the delight of the few friends to whom his daughter was intimately known. To them not only her varied and accurate acquirements, but her singular richness of mind, her grace and propriety of expression, and fertility of idea, joined to the most perfect ignorance of her own superiority, rendered her an object of as much admiration as interest. In poetry especially, her justness of taste and quickness of feeling were almost unrivalled. She was no poetess herself, never, I believe, even ventured to compose a sonnet; and her enjoyment of high literature was certainly the keener for that wise abstinence from a vain competition. Her admiration was really worth having. The tears would come into her eyes, the book would fall from her hand, and she would sit lost in ecstasy over some noble passage, till praise, worthy of the theme, would burst in unconscious eloquence from her lips.

But the real charm of Ellen Page lay in the softness of her heart and the generosity of her character: no human being was ever so free from selfishness, in all its varied and clinging forms. She literally forgot herself in her pure and ardent sympathy with all whom she loved, or all to whom she could be useful. There were no limits to her indulgence, no bounds to her candour. Shy and timid as she was, she forgot her fears to plead for the innocent, or the penitent, or even the guilty. She was the excuser-general of the neighbourhood, turned every speech and action the sunny side without, and often in her good-natured acuteness hit on the real principle of action, when the cunning, and the worldly-wise, and the cynical, and such as look only for bad motives, had failed. She had, too, that rare quality, a genuine sympathy not only with the sorrowful (there is a pride in that feeling, a superiority —we have all plenty of that), but with the happy. She could smile with those who smiled, as well as weep with those who wept, and rejoice in a success to which she had not contributed, protected from every touch of envy no less by her noble spirit than by her pure humility; she never thought of herself. So constituted, it may be imagined that she was, to all who really knew her, an object of intense admiration and love. Servants, children, poor people, all adored Miss Ellen. She had other friends in her own rank of life who had found her out—many; but her chief friend, her principal admirer, she who loved her with the most entire affection, and looked up to her with the most devoted respect, was her sister. Never was the strong and lovely tie of twin sisterhood more closely knit than in these two

charming young women. Ellen looked on her favoured sister with a pure and unjealous delight that made its own happiness, a spirit of candour and of justice that never permitted her to cast a shade of blame on the sweet object of her father's partiality: she never indeed blamed him, it seemed to her so natural that every one should prefer her sister. Charlotte, on the other hand, used all her influence for Ellen, protected and defended her, and was half tempted to murmur at an affection which she would have valued more, if shared equally with that dear friend. Thus they lived in peace and harmony, Charlotte's bolder temper and higher spirits leading and guiding in all common points, whilst on the more important, she implicitly yielded to Ellen's judgment. But when they had reached their twenty-first year a great evil threatened one of the sisters, arising (strange to say) from the other's happiness. Charlotte, the reigning *belle* of an extensive and affluent neighbourhood, had had almost as many suitors as Penelope; but, light-hearted, happy at home, constantly busy and gay, she had taken no thought of love, and always struck me as a very likely subject for an old maid; yet her time came at last. A young man, the very reverse of herself, pale, thoughtful, and gentlemanlike, and melancholy, wooed and won our fair Euphrosyne. He was the second son of a noble house, and bred to the church; and it was agreed between the fathers that as soon as he should be ordained (for he still wanted some months of the necessary age), and settled in a family-living held for him by a friend, the young couple should be married.

In the meanwhile Mr. Page, who had recently succeeded to some property in Ireland, found it necessary to go thither for a short time, and unwilling to take his daughters with him, as his estate lay in the disturbed districts, he indulged us with their company during his absence. They came to us in the bursting spring-time, on the very same day with the nightingale; the country was new to them, and they were delighted with the scenery and with our cottage life. We, on our part, were enchanted with our young guests. Charlotte was certainly the most amiable of enamoured damsels, for love with her was but a more sparkling and smiling form of happiness; all that there was of care and fear in this attachment fell to Ellen's lot; but even she, though sighing at the thought of parting, could not be very miserable whilst her sister was so happy.

A few days after their arrival we happened

to dine with our accomplished neighbours, Colonel Falkner and his sister. Our young friends of course accompanied us; and a similarity of age, of liveliness, and of musical talent speedily recommended Charlotte and Miss Falkner to each other. They became immediately intimate, and were soon almost inseparable. Ellen at first hung back. "The house was too gay, too full of shifting company, of titles, and of strange faces. Miss Falkner was very kind; but she took too much notice of her, introduced her to lords and ladies, talked of her drawings, and pressed her to sing; she would rather, if I pleased, stay with me, and walk in the coppice, or sit in the arbour, and one might read Spenser whilst the other worked—that would be best of all. Might she stay?"

"O, surely! but Colonel Falkner, Ellen, I thought you would have liked him?"

"Yes!——"

"That *yes* sounds exceedingly like *no.*"

"Why, is he not almost too clever, too elegant, too grand a man? Too mannered, as it were? Too much like what one fancies of a prince—of George IV. for instance—too high and too condescending? These are strange faults," continued she laughing; "and it is a curious injustice that I should dislike a man merely because he is so graceful that he makes me feel doubly awkward—so tall, that I am in his presence a conscious dwarf—so alive and eloquent in conversation that I feel more than ever puzzled and unready. But so it is. To say the truth, I am more afraid of him than of any human being in the world, except one. I may stay with you—may I not? and read of Una and of Britomart—that prettiest scene where her old nurse soothes her to sleep? I may stay?"

And for two or three mornings she did stay with me; but Charlotte's influence and Miss Falkner's kindness speedily drew her to Hollygrove, at first shyly and reluctantly, yet soon with an evident though quiet enjoyment; and we, sure that our young visitors could gain nothing but good in such society, were pleased that they should so vary the humble home-scene.

Colonel Falkner was a man in the very prime of life, of that happy age which unites the grace and spirit of youth with the firmness and vigour of manhood. The heir of a large fortune, he had served in the Peninsular War, fought in Spain and France, and at Waterloo, and, quitting the army at the peace, had loitered about Germany and Italy and Greece, and only returned on the death of his father, two or three years back, to reside on the family estate, where he had won "golden opinions from all

sorts of people." He was, as Ellen truly described him, tall and graceful, and well-bred almost to a fault; reminding her of that *beau ideal* of courtly elegance, George IV., and me, (pray reader, do not tell!) me, a little, a very little, the least in the world, of Sir Charles Grandison. He certainly did excel rather too much in the mere forms of politeness, in cloakings and bowings, and handings down stairs; but then he was, like both his prototypes, thoroughly imbued with its finer essence—considerate, attentive, kind, in the most comprehensive sense of that comprehensive word. I have certainly known men of deeper learning and more original genius, but never any one whose powers were better adapted to conversation, who could blend more happily the most varied and extensive knowledge with the most playful wit and the most interesting and amiable character. *Fascinating* was the word that seemed made for him. His conversation was entirely free from trickery and display—the charm was (or seemed to be) perfectly natural; he was an excellent listener; and when he was speaking to any eminent person—orator, artist, or poet—I have sometimes seen a slight hesitation, a momentary diffidence, as attractive as it was unexpected. It was this astonishing evidence of fellow-feeling, joined to the gentleness of his tone, the sweetness of his smile, and his studied avoidance of all particular notice or attention, that first reconciled Ellen to Colonel Falkner. His sister, too, a charming young woman, as like him as Viola to Sebastian, began to understand the sensitive properties of this shrinking and delicate flower, which, left to itself, repaid their kind neglect by unfolding in a manner that surprised and delighted us all. Before the spring had glided into summer, Ellen was as much at home at Holly-grove as with us; talked and laughed and played and sang as freely as Charlotte. She would indeed break off, if visibly listened to, either when speaking or singing; but still the ice was broken; that rich, low, mellow voice, unrivalled in pathos and sweetness, might be heard every evening, even by the colonel, with little more precaution, not to disturb her by praise or notice, than would be used with her fellow-warbler the nightingale.

She was happy at Holly-grove, and we were delighted; but so shifting and various are human feelings and wishes, that as the summer wore on, before the hay-making was over in its beautiful park, whilst the bees were still in its lime-trees, and the golden beetle lurked in its white rose, I began to lament that she had ever seen Holly-grove or known its master. It was clear to me, that, unintentionally on his part, unwittingly on hers, her heart was gone, and considering the merit of the unconscious possessor, probably gone for ever. She had all the pretty marks of love at that happy moment when the name and nature of the passion are alike unsuspected by the victim. To her there was but one object in the whole world, and that one was Colonel Falkner: she lived only in his presence; hung on his words; was restless, she knew not why, in his absence; adopted his tastes and opinions, which differed from hers as those of clever men so frequently do from those of clever women; read the books he praised, and praised them too, deserting our old idols, Spenser and Fletcher, for his favourites, Dryden and Pope; sang the songs he loved as she walked about the house; drew his features instead of Milton's, in a portrait which she was copying for me of our great poet—and finally wrote his name on the margin. She moved as in a dream—a dream as innocent as it was delicious!—but oh, the sad, sad waking! It made my heart ache to think of the misery to which that fine and sensitive mind seemed to be reserved. Ellen was formed for constancy and suffering—it was her first love, and it would be her last. I had no hope that her affection was returned. Young men, talk as they may of mental attractions, are commonly the slaves of personal charms. Colonel Falkner, especially, was a professed admirer of beauty. I had even sometimes fancied that he was caught by Charlotte's, and had therefore taken an opportunity to communicate her engagement to his sister. Certainly he paid our fair and blooming guest extraordinary attention; anything of gallantry or compliment was always addressed to her, and so for the most part was his gay and captivating conversation; whilst his manner to Ellen, though exquisitely soft and kind, seemed rather that of an affectionate brother. I had no hopes.

Affairs were in this posture when I was at once grieved and relieved by the unexpected recall of our young visitors. Their father had completed his business in Ireland, and was eager to return to his dear home, and his dear children; Charlotte's lover, too, was ordained, and was impatient to possess his promised treasure. The intended bridegroom was to arrive the same evening to escort the fair sisters, and the journey was to take place the next day. Imagine the revulsion of feeling produced by a short note, a bit of folded paper—the natural and redoubled ecstasy of Charlotte, the mingled emotions of Ellen. She wept bitterly; at first

she called it joy—joy that she should again see her dear father; then it was grief to lose her Charlotte; grief to part from me; but, when she threw herself in a farewell embrace on the neck of Miss Falkner, whose brother happened to be absent for a few days on business, the truth appeared to burst upon her at once in a gush of agony that seemed likely to break her heart. Miss Falkner was deeply affected: begged her to write to her often, very often; loaded her with the gifts of little price, the valueless tokens which affection holds so dear, and stole one of her fair ringlets in return.

"This is the curl which William used to admire," said she; "have you no message for poor William?"

Poor Ellen! her blushes spoke, and the tears which dropped from her downcast eyes; but she had no utterance. Charlotte, however, came to her relief with a profusion of thanks and compliments; and Ellen, weeping with a violence that would not be controlled, at last left Holly-grove.

The next day we, too, lost our dear young friends. Oh, what a sad day it was! how much we missed Charlotte's bright smile, and Ellen's sweet complacency! We walked about desolate and forlorn, with the painful sense of want and insufficiency, and of that vacancy in our home, and at our board, which the departure of a cherished guest is sure to occasion. To lament the absence of Charlotte, the dear Charlotte, the happiest of the happy, was pure selfishness; but of the aching heart of Ellen, my dearer Ellen, I could not bear to think—and yet I could think of nothing else, could call up no other image than her pale and trembling form, weeping and sobbing as I had seen her at Holly-grove; she haunted even my dreams.

Early the ensuing morning I was called down to the colonel, and found him in the garden. He apologized for his unseasonable intrusion; talked of the weather, then of the loss which our society had sustained; blushed and hesitated; had again recourse to the weather; and at last by a mighty effort, after two or three sentences began and unfinished, contrived, with an embarrassment more graceful and becoming than all his polished readiness, to ask me to furnish him with a letter to Mr. Page.

"You must have seen," said he, colouring and smiling, "that I was captivated by your beautiful friend; and I hope—I could have wished to have spoken first to herself, to have made an interest—but still if her affections are disengaged—tell me, you who must know, you who are always my friend, have I any chance? Is she disengaged?"

"Alas! I have sometimes feared this; but I thought you had heard—your sister at least was aware."

"Of what? It was but this very morning—aware of what?"

"Of Charlotte's engagement."

"Charlotte!—it is of Ellen, not her sister, that I speak and think! Of Ellen, the pure, the delicate, the divine! That whitest and sweetest of flowers, the jassmine, the myrtle, the tuberose among women," continued he, elucidating his similes by gathering a sprig of each plant, as he paced quickly up and down the garden walk—"Ellen, the fairest and the best; your darling and mine! Will you give me a letter to her father? And will you wish me success?"

"Will I! O how sincerely! My dear colonel, I beg a thousand pardons for undervaluing your taste—for suspecting you of preferring a damask rose to a blossomed myrtle; I should have known you better." And then we talked of Ellen, dear Ellen, talked and praised till even the lover's heart was satisfied. I am convinced that he went away that morning, persuaded that I was one of the cleverest women, and the best judges of character that ever lived.

And now my story is over. What need to say that the letter was written with the warmest zeal, and received with the most cordial graciousness—or that Ellen, though shedding sweet tears, bore the shock of joy better than the shock of grief—or that the twin sisters were married on the same day, at the same altar, each to the man of her heart, and each with every prospect of more than common felicity.

MY LADY'S PRAISE.

I would from truth my lady's praise supply,
Resembling her to lily and to rose;
Brighter than morning's lucid star she shows,
And fair as that which fairest is on high.
To the blue wave, I liken her, and sky,
All colour that with pink and crimson glows,
Gold, silver and rich stones: nay lovelier grows
E'en love himself, when she is standing by.
She passeth on so gracious and so mild,
One's pride is quench'd, and one of sick is well :
And they believe, who from the faith did err ;
And none may near her come by harm defiled.
A mightier virtue have I yet to tell;
No man may think of evil, seeing her.

GUIDO GUINICELLI (died 1276).

WOMAN'S LOVE.

[Lady Caroline Lamb, born 1785; died 1828. She was a daughter of the Earl of Besborough, and the wife of William Lamb, Lord Melbourne. She wrote a number of verses and three novels: *Glenarvon* (the hero of this novel was supposed to represent Lord Byron), *Graham Hamilton*, and *Ada Reis*. A romantic passion for Lord Byron embittered her latter years.]

Did ever man a woman love
And listen to her flattery,
Who did not soon his folly prove,
And mourning rue her treachery?

For were she fair as orient beams,
That gild the cloudless summer skies,
Or innocent as virgin's dreams,
Or melting as true lovers' eyes,

Or were she pure as falling dews,
That deck the blossoms of the spring,
Still, man, thy love she would misuse,
And from thy breast contentment wring.

Then trust her not though fair and young,
Man has so many true hearts grieved,
That woman thinks she does no wrong,
When she is false and he is deceived.

OF THE TRUTH OF PHYSIOGNOMY.

[Johann Caspar Lavater, born at Zurich, 14th November, 1741; died there, 2d February, 1801. Theologian and poet, but most widely known by his works on physiognomy.]

All countenances, all forms, all created beings, are not only different from each other in their classes, races, and kinds, but are also individually distinct.

Each being differs from every other being of its species. However generally known, it is a truth the most important to our purpose, and necessary to repeat, that, "There is no rose perfectly similar to another rose, no egg to an egg, no eel to an eel, no lion to a lion, no eagle to an eagle, no man to a man."

Confining this proposition to man only, it is the first, the most profound, most secure, and unshaken foundation-stone of physiognomy that, however intimate the analogy and similarity of the innumerable forms of men, no two men can be found who, brought together, and accurately compared, will not appear to be very remarkably different.

Nor is it less incontrovertible that it is equally impossible to find two minds, as two countenances, which perfectly resemble each other.

This consideration alone will be sufficient to make it received as a truth, not requiring farther demonstration, that there must be a certain native analogy between the external varieties of the countenance and form, and the internal varieties of the mind. Shall it be denied that this acknowledged internal variety among all men is the cause of the external variety of their forms and countenances? Shall it be affirmed that the mind does not influence the body, or that the body does not influence the mind?

Anger renders the muscles protuberant; and shall not therefore an angry mind and protuberant muscles be considered as cause and effect?

After repeated observation that an active and vivid eye and an active and acute wit are frequently found in the same person, shall it be supposed that there is no relation between the active eye and the active mind? Is this the effect of accident? Of accident! Ought it not rather to be considered as sympathy, an interchangeable and instantaneous effect, when we perceive that, at the very moment the understanding is most acute and penetrating and the wit the most lively, the motion and fire of the eye undergo, at that moment, the most visible change?

Shall the open, friendly, and unsuspecting eye and the open, friendly, and unsuspecting heart be united in a thousand instances, and shall we say the one is not the cause, the other the effect?

Shall nature discover wisdom and order in all things; shall corresponding causes and effects be everywhere united; shall this be the most clear, the most indubitable of truths; and in the first, the most noble of the works of nature, shall she act arbitrarily, without design, without law? The human countenance, that mirror of the Divinity, that noblest of the works of the Creator,—shall not motive and action, shall not the correspondence between the interior and the exterior, the visible and the invisible, the cause and the effect, be there apparent?

Yet this is all denied by those who oppose the truth of the science of physiognomy.

Truth, according to them, is ever at variance with itself. Eternal order is degraded to a juggler, whose purpose it is to deceive.

Calm reason revolts at the supposition that Newton or Leibnitz ever could have the coun-

tenance and appearance of an idiot, incapable of a firm step, a meditating eye; of comprehending the least difficult of abstract propositions, or of expressing himself so as to be understood; that one of these in the brain of a Laplander conceived his Theodica; and that the other in the head of an Esquimaux, who wants the power to number farther than six, and affirms all beyond to be innumerable, had dissected the rays of light, and weighed worlds.

Calm reason revolts when it is asserted that the strong man may appear perfectly like the weak, the man in full health like another in the last stage of a consumption, or that the rash and irascible may resemble the cold and phlegmatic. It revolts to hear it affirmed that joy and grief, pleasure and pain, love and hatred, all exhibit themselves under the same traits; that is to say, under no traits whatever, on the exterior of man. Yet such are the assertions of those who maintain physiognomy to be a chimerical science. They overturn all that order and combination by which eternal wisdom so highly astonishes and delights the understanding. It cannot be too emphatically repeated, that blind chance and arbitrary disorder constitute the philosophy of fools; and that they are the bane of natural knowledge, philosophy, and religion. Entirely to banish such a system is the duty of the true inquirer, the sage, and the divine.

All men (this is indisputable), absolutely all men, estimate all things whatever by their physiognomy, their exterior, temporary superficies. By viewing these on every occasion, they draw their conclusions concerning their internal properties.

What merchant, if he be unacquainted with the person of whom he purchases, does not estimate his wares by the physiognomy or appearance of those wares? If he purchase of a distant correspondent, what other means does he use in judging whether they are or are not equal to his expectation? Is not his judgment determined by the colour, the fineness, the superficies, the exterior, the physiognomy! Does he not judge money by its physiognomy! Why does he take one guinea and reject another? Why weigh a third in his hand? Does he not determine according to its colour, or impression; its outside, its physiognomy? If a stranger enter his shop, as a buyer or seller, will he not observe him? Will he not draw conclusions from his countenance? Will he not, almost before he is out of hearing, pronounce some opinion upon him, and say: "This man has an honest look," "That man has a pleasing, or forbidding, countenance?" What is it to the purpose whether his judgment be right or wrong? He judges. Though not wholly, he depends in part upon the exterior form, and thence draws inferences concerning the mind.

How does the farmer, walking through his grounds, regulate his future expectations by the colour, the size, the growth, the exterior; that is to say, by the physiognomy of the bloom, the stalk, or the ear of his corn; the stem, and shoots of his vine-tree? "This ear of corn is blighted," "That wood is full of sap; this will grow, that not," affirms he, at the first or second glance. "Though these vine-shoots look well, they will bear but few grapes." And wherefore? He remarks, in their appearance, as the physiognomist in the countenances of shallow men, the want of native energy. Does not he judge by the exterior?

Does not the physician pay more attention to the physiognomy of the sick than to all the accounts that are brought him concerning his patient? Zimmermann, among the living, may be brought as a proof of the great perfection at which this kind of judgment has arrived; and among the dead, Kempf, whose son has written a treatise on Temperament.

The painter —— Yet of him I will say nothing; his art too evidently reproves the childish and arrogant prejudices of those who pretend to disbelieve physiognomy.

The traveller, the philanthropist, the misanthrope, the lover, (and who not?) all act according to their feelings and decisions, true or false, confused or clear, concerning physiognomy. These feelings, these decisions, excite compassion, disgust, joy, love, hatred, suspicion, confidence, reserve, or benevolence.

Do we not daily judge of the sky by its physiognomy? No food, not a glass of wine or beer, not a cup of coffee or tea comes to table which is not judged by its physiognomy, its exterior, and of which we do not thence deduce some conclusion respecting its interior, good or bad properties.

Is not all nature physiognomy, superficies and contents; body, and spirit; exterior effect and internal power; invisible beginning and visible ending?

What knowledge is there, of which man is capable, that is not founded on the exterior; the relation that exists between visible and invisible, the perceptible and the imperceptible?

Physiognomy, whether understood in its most extensive or confined signification, is the origin of all human decisions, efforts, actions, expectations, fears, and hopes: of all pleasing and unpleasing sensations, which are occasioned by external objects.

From the cradle to the grave, in all conditions and ages, throughout all nations, from Adam to the last existing man, from the worm we tread on to the most sublime of philosophers, (and why not to the angel, why not to the Mediator Christ?) physiognomy is the origin of all we do and suffer.

Each insect is acquainted with its friend and its foe; each child loves and fears, although it knows not why. Physiognomy is the cause; nor is there a man to be found on earth who is not daily influenced by physiognomy; not a man who cannot figure to himself a countenance which shall to him appear exceedingly lovely, or exceedingly hateful; not a man who does not more or less, the first time he is in company with a stranger, observe, estimate, compare, and judge him, according to appearances, although he might never have heard of the word or thing called physiognomy; not a man who does not judge of all things that pass through his hands, by their physiognomy; that is, of their internal worth by their external appearance.

The art of dissimulation itself, which is adduced as so insuperable an objection to the truth of physiognomy, is founded on physiognomy. Why does the hypocrite assume the appearance of an honest man, but because that he is convinced, though not perhaps from any systematic reflection, that all eyes are acquainted with the characteristic marks of honesty.

What judge, wise or unwise, whether he confess or deny the fact, does not sometimes in this sense decide from appearances? Who can, is, or ought to be, absolutely indifferent to the exterior of persons brought before him to be judged?[1] What king would choose a minister without examining his exterior, secretly at least, and to a certain extent? An officer will not enlist a soldier without thus examining his appearance, his height out of the question. What master or mistress of a family will choose a servant without considering the exterior, no matter whether their judgment be or be not just, or whether it be exercised unconsciously?

I am wearied of citing instances so numerous, and so continually before our eyes, to prove that men, tacitly and unanimously, confess the influence which physiognomy has over their sensations and actions. I feel disgust at being obliged to write thus, in order to convince the learned of truths with which every child is or may be acquainted.

[1] Franciscus Valesius says—Sed legibus etiam civilibus, in quibus iniquum sit censere esse aliquid futile aut varium, cautum est; ut si duo homines inciderent in criminis suspicionem, is primum torqueatur qui sit aspectu deformior.

He that hath eyes to see, let him see; but should the light, by being brought too close to his eyes, produce frenzy, he may burn himself by endeavouring to extinguish the torch of truth. I use such expressions unwillingly, but I dare do my duty, and my duty is boldly to declare that I believe myself certain of what I now and hereafter shall affirm; and that I think myself capable of convincing all real lovers of truth, by principles which are in themselves incontrovertible. It is also necessary to confute the pretensions of certain literary despots, and to compel them to be more cautious in their decisions. It is therefore proved, not because I say it, but because it is an eternal and manifest truth, and would have been equally truth, had it never been said, that, whether they are or are not sensible of it, all men are daily influenced by physiognomy; that, as Sultzer has affirmed, every man, consciously or unconsciously, understands something of physiognomy; nay, that there is not a living being that does not, at least after its manner, draw some inferences from the external to the internal; that does not judge concerning that which is not, by that which is apparent to the senses. This universal, though tacit confession, that the exterior, the visible, the superficies of objects, indicates their nature, their properties, and that every outward sign is the symbol of some inherent quality, I hold to be equally certain and important to the science of physiognomy.

LOVE CEREMONIOUS.

Keep your undrest, familiar style
  For strangers, but respect your friend,
Her most, whose matrimonial smile
  Is and asks honour without end.
'Tis found, and needs it must so be,
  That life from love's allegiance flags,
When love forgets his majesty
  In sloth's unceremonious rags.
Let love make home a gracious Court;
  There let the world's rude, hasty ways
Be fashion'd to a loftier port,
  And learn to bow and stand at gaze;
And let the sweet respective sphere
  Of personal worship there obtain
Circumference for moving clear,
  None treading on another's train.
This makes that pleasures do not cloy,
  And dignifies our mortal strife
With calmness and considerate joy,
  Befitting our immortal life.

            COVENTRY PATMORE

THE BRIGAND'S WIFE.

The following incident was related by the wife of one of the notorious brothers Vardarelli:[1]—

" Yes, it is a sad life for us women; and yet

[1] "These three brothers were natives of the province of Abruzzo, but had of late years selected Apulia as the theatre best adapted to their system of depredation; its vast uninclosed plains, occasionally interspersed with patches of underwood, but in no part offering obstacles to the rapidity of their movements, the rare occurrence of large towns, the magnitude of the farms, or masserias, where they were sure to find provisions, forage, and booty united; all these circumstances combining with their local knowledge of the country, and the terror which they had impressed on its inhabitants, had rendered their power sufficiently formidable to resist, or at least elude, the means pursued by government for their destruction. Well armed and accoutred, and excellently mounted, their troop, in number exceeding forty, was also trained to the most rigid discipline; and Don Gaetano, the elder of the three brothers, as well as commander of the band, displayed an activity and skill worthy of a nobler profession. It should be observed that they seldom attacked travellers; and their outrages were generally unsullied by cruelty, except in some cases of revenge for breach of promise; but this false glare of generosity and forbearance, as well as the ample rewards which they bestowed on their spies and abettors, and the acts of charity by which they endeavoured to propitiate the feelings of the poorer class, rendered them only a more destructive scourge to the community at large. A person who had been a severe sufferer by their misdeeds, very justly observed to me, that it was very easy to give a hundred ducats to the poor out of a thousand stolen from the rich; and as their generosity could be estimated by this rule only, the motives of it may be duly appreciated. . . .
"Their marches, generally performed in the night-time, were so incredibly rapid, that the terror they inspired was equalled only by the astonishment created by operations apparently supernatural; and they have been known to have remained two or three days in one of these farms before the inmates of those adjoining have been aware of their proximity. During this time they usually feasted on whatever the premises afforded, always obliging their inhabitants to partake of whatever fare was prepared for them, through fear of poison. On one occasion of this nature, when the principal agents of the farm excused themselves from eating meat because it was a fast day, Don Gaetano approved their forbearance, which, he assured them, quite agreed with his practice in general; but alleged his mode of life and the uncertainty of his dinner-hour as an apology for the infraction of it. On removing from the scene of action, they always took with them what money could be collected, and as much grain as their horses could carry."—*A Tour through the Southern Provinces of the Kingdom of Naples*, by the Hon. Richard Keppel Craven. The Vardarelli band, after serving for a time under the government as a sort of mountain police, was ultimately destroyed by the soldiers, in consequence of some misunderstanding. A few escaped, and returned to their old ways.

we are gay enough at times, when our masters are in good humour, rejoicing over the success of some expedition. In youth we admire the strength of our lovers, and listen with delight to the stories of their exploits, of their triumphs over the soldiers. We never see them as criminals: to us they appear only as men oppressed by bad laws, and bravely asserting their independence at the hazard of their lives. They are heroes to us, not criminals. But by-and-by, as we grow older and have husbands, perhaps children, in the band, we learn what fear is. When we feel that we are hunted from pass to pass, sheltering in caves, or en-camping on the bare mountain—then we begin to understand that we belong to an outcast race, and we tremble at every halloo lest it prove the intimation of a surprise which may mean death to all. When we find wild revels followed by days of hunger; when we find our husbands so haunted by the dread of treachery that they suspect us and each other, then we know that there is no home, no rest anywhere for us, and we envy the happy lot of the wives of the poor shepherds.

"Our men have less time than us to think of these things, and so, no doubt, they are less sensible of the miserable condition in which we live. I am grateful to the holy mother that no children were given to me, and yet I love children: their happy ignorance of the crime and danger which surround us some-times helps me to forget them too. No, these tears are not for one lost, but for one saved; if regret makes my eyes dim, my heart is full of joy. The child whose memory I cherish was a stranger's; but he became very precious to me.

"The band had been absent two days; we women had been commanded to await them in one of our most secure hiding-places—a huge long cavern which had two outlets. The men returned laden with booty taken from the carriage of a rich nobleman. Gaetano came last.

"'A prize for you, wife!' he said, and flung a trembling child into my arms.

"'Mother!' sobbed the little one, and I shuddered, thinking that his one word told a cruel story. But it was not so bad as I feared. I looked at Gaetano, and he, understanding me, answered,

"'No, there has been no one much hurt; it was a nurse who was with him, and she has been sent back to Naples to demand ransom for the little signor. A pretty little fellow, is he not?—he quite takes to you—and worth a pretty sum.'

"I was relieved. The child clung to my neck as if he felt sure of protection from me. He had been much frightened and much fatigued by the journey to the cavern. A shout from the men, who were by this time busy feasting at the farther end of the cave, startled him, and he looked over my shoulder trembling. I kissed him and coaxed him to sit down on a box beside me, telling him that he would soon be with his mother again. His little head fell back on my knee, and he slept peace-fully.

"Gaetano threw down the papers he had been examining, and stretching himself upon a pile of wrappers, looked with smiling satisfaction at the child. He had demanded a high ransom, knowing that the mother would be ready to give anything for the recovery of her son, and he felt sure that all he had asked would be granted.

"Some days passed and little Elio was begin-ning to feel at ease in his strange home, although he could not be persuaded to leave my side. I loved the child; and that was why he so soon became contented in the cavern. The message from Naples was delivered to Gaetano, and I saw that he was angry and disappointed. The message told him that the boy Elio was not the son of the rich nobleman but of one of his servants, and that the amount required to ran-som him was too large.

"The band refused to believe this story, and declared that it was a trick to gain time in order to attack them. They were ready and resolved to take the usual horrible means of as-serting their power: the little one was doomed. I looked to Gaetano; but he could not help me; chief as he was he dare not break the law of the band. I turned to the men. I do not know what were my words, but I held up the poor child and implored them in the name of the dear Virgin to spare him; but they would not yield. Then I spoke wildly, and promised them a greater reward than that they had ex-pected if they would only be merciful and give me time to go myself to Naples. I suppose they pitied me, and perhaps—Heaven grant that it was so—they were moved by the sweet face of the child; at anyrate they agreed. Gaetano would have had me give up all thought of what seemed to be a useless journey; but he too consented at length when he saw how earnest was my determina-tion.

"I had no fears for myself; the only dread which haunted me was that any harm done to me would be the signal for the destruction of Elio. But Heaven was very kind. I was per-

mitted to see the nobleman and he listened to
me. He was pleased to say that he admired
me for what I had done; and that for my sake
he would do much to rescue Elio. He assured
me that the child, although a great pet of the
family, was the offspring of a faithful servant
now dead. But he agreed to pay half the ransom demanded, and to obtain for the Vardarelli band a free pardon on condition that they
should take service under the government.
Oh, how brave and light my heart was then.
My wild promise was fulfilled, and I brought
to the band a greater reward than they could
ever have expected; for by the tiny hands of
the child they had spared, they were themselves
saved."

PEACE.

BY PROFESSOR WILSON.

I could believe that sorrow ne'er sojourned
Within the circle of these sunny hills;
That this small lake, beneath the morning light,
Now lying so serenely beautiful,
Ne'er felt one passing storm, but on its breast
Retained for aye the silent imagery
Of those untroubled heavens.

How still yon isle,
Scarcely distinguished from its glimmering shadow
In the water pure as air! Yon little flock
How snow-white! lying on the pastoral mount,
Basking in the sunshine. That lone fisherman,
Who draws his net so slowly to the shore,
How calm an image of secluded life!
While the boat moving with its twinkling oars,
On its short voyage to yon verdant point,
Fringed with wild birch-wood, leaves a shining track
Connecting by a pure and silvery line
The quiet of both shores.

So deep the calm
I hear the solitary stock-dove's voice
Moaning across the lake, from the dark bosom
Of yon old pine grove. Hark, the village clock
Tolls soberly! And, 'mid the tufted elms,
Reveals the spire still pointing up to heaven.
I travel on unto the noisy city,
And on this sunny bank mine hour of rest
Stream-like has murmured by—yet shall the music
Oft rise again—the lake, hills, wood, and grove,
And that calm House of God. Sweet Vale, Farewell!

ITALIAN BANDITTI.

[Charlotte A. Waldie, born 1788; died 1859. Her
grandfather was a schoolfellow of Sir Walter Scott at
Kelso. Lockhart, in his Life of Scott, mentions the
work from which the following extract is made:—"I
remember the pleasure with which he [Sir Walter] read,
late in life, Rome in the Nineteenth Century, an ingenious
work produced by one of Mr. Waldie's grand-daughters,
and how comically he depicted the alarm with which
his ancient friend would have perused some of its
delineations of the high-places of Popery." Miss Waldie
also wrote, At Home and Abroad, Three Days in Belgium,
and other sketches of travel. In 1822 she married Mr.
Eaton, banker, Stamford. Her sister, Miss E. A.
Waldie (who became the wife of Admiral Watts), was
the authoress of several similar works, but she obtained
repute chiefly by her paintings in oil and water colours.]

Frascati, Nov. 11, 1818.

Consternation fills this little peaceful town.
Yesterday evening Lucien Buonaparte's villa
was entered by a gang of banditti;—but I
must tell you the story in order as it happened.
About four in the afternoon *Monsignore* (as
the old priest of the family is through courtesy
called) set out to take his accustomed walk;
and, unluckily for himself, directed his steps
up the hill to the ruins of ancient Tusculum;
when, suddenly from the bushes which shade
the cavity of the amphitheatre, two armed
robbers sprang out, dragged him among the
thickets, where four others were lying in am-
bush; and having stripped him of his watch,
money, and clothes, they tied his hands behind
his back, and gave him notice, that the first
moment he attempted to speak or make the
smallest noise would be the last of his life.
They kept him prisoner there till after sunset,
when they crept through the wood to the house,
and made a halt among the thick laurels and
shrubs close to it. In the meantime the dinner-
bell rang, the family sat down to table, but as
Monsignore was not to be found, a servant was
sent into the pleasure-ground in search of him,
who left the house door unfastened. The banditti softly made their approaches. Five of
them entered unseen and unheard, and the
sixth stayed to guard the door. Monsignore
seized this moment to betake himself to his
heels, and gained a remote outhouse, where he
buried himself overhead among straw, and was
found many hours after more dead than alive.
In the meantime the five robbers, with their
fire-arms presented, cautiously advanced into
the house; but they were soon descried by the
servants, whose shrieks they stilled in a moment by the menace of instant death if they
moved a step or uttered a sound. One maid-

servant, however, escaped, and gave the alarm to the party in the dining-room, who all fled in different directions to conceal themselves, excepting the unfortunate secretary, who had previously left the room to inquire into the cause of the tumult, and was seized on his way down stairs by the robbers, who mistook him for the prince; and, in spite of his protestations, was carried off, together with the head butler, and a poor *Facchino*,[1] whom they encountered on the grounds, to the mountain above Velletri, a distance of seven miles, without stopping.

This morning the captured *Facchino*, like another Regulus, has been sent as ambassador, or *charge d'affaires*, from the banditti to the prince, to propose terms which are, to deliver up their prisoners on the payment of a ransom of 4000 crowns; or, on the non-payment of it within four-and-twenty hours, to shoot them. Lucien Buonaparte sent back one half of their demand in money, and an order on his banker for the rest. The robbers sent back the order torn through the middle, with a further demand of 4000 crowns in hard money, besides the 2000 they had already received, under pain of the immediate death of their prisoners. The prince received this insolent mandate in his palace at Rome, where he took refuge this morning, and has been obliged to obey it.

I wonder the government do not feel ashamed that such outrages should be perpetrated within ten miles of Rome, and that they should be obliged to admit delegates from banditti into the very seat of government—the capital itself. A detachment of troops, and about two hundred armed peasants, levied by Lucien Buonaparte, are ready for the pursuit of the villains the moment their captives are released—but till then they dare not move; for the *eyrie* on which they have perched themselves commands a view of the whole country in every direction, and they have sworn to put the prisoners to death the moment they see the approach of an armed man. The Pope's soldiers, indeed, it would seem, are not much to be depended upon themselves, for it is not long since the guard from the Trinita de Monti, and the Porta del Popolo, at Rome, walked off one fine moonlight night, with their arms and accoutrements, to the hills, and joined a party of banditti.

It was the intention of the banditti who entered Lucien Buonaparte's villa to have seized both him and his daughter, who had been betrothed that very day to Prince Ercolani, a young Bolognese nobleman; and had they succeeded, their demands would have had no bounds.

[1] Porter or out-door labourer.

Frascati, Nov. 29.

After a captivity of two days and a half the prisoners returned, and the troops and armed peasantry instantly began the pursuit. The mountain on which they were stationed, it is said, was previously completely surrounded with guards, and every part of it has been searched, an immense reward has been offered for the apprehension even of one of them—but all in vain. No traces of them have been discovered; and Lucien Buonaparte, in addition to the ransom, has had to pay an immense sum to the peasantry he hired, without the satisfaction of bringing the offenders to justice.

The unfortunate secretary has been confined to bed ever since, partly from the effects of fright, fatigue, and cold, and partly from a wound he received in his forehead in the scuffle, when he was first taken prisoner. The captured butler and Facchino, whom I have seen, say that the robbers did not treat them ill, and gave them plenty of food; more, indeed, than they could eat; for, it may be supposed, that in such a situation their appetite could not be very keen. Neither could they enjoy much repose, surrounded with cocked carabines. The captain of those banditti, who was a remarkably little man, used to say to them, with great politeness, "We shall really be sorry to murder you, gentlemen; but if the prince does not send the money, we must do it—our *honour* is engaged."

They knew, indeed, too well, he would keep his word; for it is not long since a poor young woman was carried off between Velletri and Terracina, and the ransom they required not being paid, she was murdered, and her body left on the mountains.

Nor is this the only exploit of the sort in this neighbourhood. A few weeks ago, a Roman gentleman and his daughters were taking a walk after mass on a Sunday, close to the town of Palestrina, when a party of banditti rushed upon them and carried them off to the mountains. The poor old man, who was asthmatic, and unable to keep pace with the rapidity of the flight, was brutally murdered before the eyes of his unfortunate daughters, whose ransom enriched these monsters with the wealth of the man they had slain.

About two months ago, a bride, on the day of her nuptials, was carried off from a villa near Albano, while sitting at table surrounded by her husband and relations, and after passing a night on the mountain, she was liberated on the payment of a heavy ransom, without insult or injury.

RINGAN AND MAY.

BY JAMES HOGG.

I heard a laverock singing with glee,
And oh but the bird sang cheerilye;
Then I aakit at my true love Ringan,
If he kend what the bonnie bird was singing?
Now, my love Ringan is blithe and young,
But he has a fair and flattering tongue;
And oh, I'm fear'd I like ower weel
His tales of love, though kind and leal!
So I said to him, in scornful ways,
"You ken nae word that wee burd says!"
Then my love he turn'd about to me,
And there was a smile in his pawky ee;
And he says, "My May, my dawtied dow.
I ken that strain far better nor you;
For that little fairy that lilts so loud,
And hangs on the fringe of the sunny cloud,
Is telling the tale, in chants and chimes,
I have told to thee a thousand times.
I will let thee hear how our strains accord,
And the laverock's sweet sang, word for word:

INTERPRETATION OF THE LARK'S SONG.

"'Oh, my love is bonnie and mild to see,
As sweetly she sits on her dewy lea,
And turns up her cheek and clear gray eye,
To list what's saying within the sky!
For she thinks my morning hymn so sweet,
Wi' the streamers of heaven aneath my feet,
Where the proud goshawk could never won,
Between the gray cloud and the sun—
And she thinks her love a thing of the skies,
Sent down from the holy paradise,
To sing to the world, at morn and even,
The sweet love songs in the bowers of heaven.
"'Oh, my love is bonnie, and young, and chaste,
As sweetly she sits in her mossy nest!
And she deems the birds on bush and tree,
As nothing but dust and droul to me.
Though the robin warble his waesome churl,
And the merle gar all the greenwood dirl,
And the storm-cock touts on his towering pine,
She trows their songs a mock to mine;
The linty's cheip a ditty tame,
And the shilfa's everlasting rhame;
The plover's whew a solo drear,
And the whilly-whaup's ane shame to hear;
And, whenever a lover comes in view,
She cowers beneath her screen of dew.
"'Oh, my love is bonnie! her virgin breast
Is sweeter to me nor the dawning east;
And well do I like at the gloaming still,
To dreep from the lift or the lowering hill,
And press her neat as white as milk,
And her breast as soft as the downy silk.'"

Now when my love Ringan had warbled away
To this base part of the laverock's lay,
My heart was like to burst in twain,
And the tears flow'd from mine eyne like rain;
At length he said, with a sigh full lang,
"What ails my love at the laverock's sang?"
Says I, "He's ane base and wicked bird,
As ever rose from the dewy yird;
It's a shame to mount on his morning wing,
At the yetts of heaven sic sangs to sing;
And all to win with his amorous din,
A sweet little virgin bird to sin,
And wreck, with flattery and song combined,
His dear little maiden's peace of mind!
O, were I her, I would let him see
His songs should all be lost on me!"
Then my love took me in his arms,
And 'gan to laud my leifou charms;
But I would not so much as let him speak,
Nor stroke my chin, nor kiss my cheek:
For I fear'd my heart was going wrang,
It was so mov'd at the laverock's sang.
Yet still I lay with an upcast ee,
And still he was singing sae bonnilye,
That, though with my mind I had great strife,
I could not forbear it for my life,
But, as he hung on the heaven's brow,
I said, I ken not why, nor how,
"What's that little deevil saying now?"
Then my love Ringan, he was so glad,
He leugh till his folly pat me mad;
And he said, "My love, I will tell you true,
He seems to sing that strain to you;
For it says, 'I will range the yird and air
To feed my love with the finest fare;
And when she looks from her bed to me,
With the yearning love of a mother's ee,
O, then I will come, and draw her nearer,
And watch her closer, and love her dearer,
And we never shall part till our dying day,
But love and love on for ever and aye!'"
Then my heart it bled with a thrilling pleasure
When it learn'd the laverock's closing measure,
And it rose, and rose, and would not rest,
And would hardly bide within my breast.
Then up I rose, and away I sprung,
And said to my love with scornful tongue,
That it was ane big and burning shame;
That he and the lark were both to blame;
For there were some lays so soft and bland
That breast of maiden could not stand;
And if he lay in the wood his lane,
Quhill I came back to list the strain
Of an amorous bird among the broom,
Then he might lie quhill the day of doom!
But for all the sturt and strife I made,
For all I did, and all I said,
Alas! I fear it will be lang
Or I forget that wee burd's sang!
And langer still or I can flee
The lad that told that sang to me!

AMERICAN NOVELS.

BY T. S. PERRY.

We have often wondered that the people who raise the outcry for the "Great American Novel" did not see that, so far from being of any assistance to our fellow-countryman who is trying to win fame by writing fiction, they have rather stood in his way by setting up before him a false aim for his art, and by giving the critical reader a defective standard by which to judge his work. Whenever this so-longed-for novel does appear, we may be sure that our first impression will not be that it is American. It may be American, without a doubt, but it will not be ostentatiously so; that will not be its chief merit. If it is written in this country and about this country, there will be of course a flavour of the soil, which is to be desired, but the epicure does not want his coffee muddy. There is an American nature, but then there is human nature underlying it, and to that the novel must be true before anything else. That is what is of importance; it is that alone which makes the novel great, which causes it to be read in all times and in all countries. If the author so far forgets this, his first duty, as to imagine that the simple rehearsal of the barrenest external phenomena of life and nature in this country can be of any real interest to the reader, he makes as great a mistake as would an actor who should fancy that nothing more was needed for representing Hamlet than to dress in black, wear a light wig, and to powder his cheeks to look pale. It is the bane of realism, as of all *isms*, to forget that it represents only one important side of truth, and to content itself, as complacently as an advocate, with seeing its own rules obeyed, and, generally, with the narrowest construction of the law. By insisting above all things on the novel being American, we mistake the means for the end; we have a perfect right to demand accuracy in the writer,—in spite of Mrs. Spofford we cannot read about castles in New England,—but we should not regard it as anything but the merest machinery, the least part of a novel; it is a *sine qua non*, to be sure, but so in man is the spinal marrow; we think no more of a friend on account of his having a spinal marrow. So long as we over-estimate the value of his formal accuracy, it will be possible for any one to prove to his own satisfaction and to ours that such and such a novel is the best. "See here," he will say, "So-and-

so makes the Connecticut River two hundred and fifty miles long, while 'Civis Americanus' gives it its proper length; and then 'Geographicus' says on page 343, just before the Boston horse-car conductor declares his love to the Nova Scotia servant of the selectman, that Vermont has thirty-five inhabitants to the square mile; he was thinking of New Hampshire; he's no novelist." No one fancies a novel that can be proved to be better than another, like a manual of geometry. Nor do we care for one that loses its value at every census. It may be well that novels should be of temporary interest, but they should at least outlast the year's almanac.

It might not be amiss to pause for a moment to consider the origin of this expression, "The great American novel." Critics would differ about the great English novel or the great French novel; why should America have one? Nevertheless, novelists have striven for this prize, genial critics have imperilled their reputations by rashly awarding it to various writers, who have as rapidly faded into oblivion, and we are as far from unanimity about it as we ever were. We imagine that it is a term that has come down to us from the time, a generation or two ago, when, America having an army and navy, consideration in the eyes of Europe for its material strength and future importance, the absence of a fully developed literature was keenly felt. Literature, too, was considered a branch of manufactures, and not a thing of growth. We were to have an American Byron; possibly, with good Presidents and a proper tariff, an American Shakspeare; and then the public, detecting the great differences between the society of Europe and that of this country, cried aloud for the novel that should do for us what Fielding had already, and Thackeray has since, done for England. That this should be done is indeed desirable; but our hopes will be vain unless our writers, with keener vision than the public, see the uselessness of a mere outside resemblance to their models.

That a novel is not good by simply being un-American, one can see by recalling a by no means unreadable story—*Miss Van Kortland*—that appeared about four or five years ago. The effect of reading to excess the modern English novel was here clearly seen. There was the general air of English country life barely disguised by American names. Congress was made exactly like Parliament. It was an English bottom sailing under American colours. Of the elaborate Americanism of *Lady Judith* we need not speak. The reader could not help being reminded of the Yankees in *Punch's* caricatures, who would be arrested as suspicious characters in the backwoods of Maine, nor could their apt use of "old hoss" save them. Such hybrids we may trust will be soon forgotten; but in vastly the greater number of the American novels of the present day we find perhaps equally damaging faults, although of a different kind. Let us take, for example, Mr. De Forest's novels. In his writings we find a great deal that is American, but not so much that goes to the making of a really great novel. His stories have certain undeniable merits, and if the great American novel needed only to be American, he would easily bear off the palm. *Miss Ravenel's Conversion; Overland; Kate Beaumont,* are three novels that could have been written in no other country; but such geographical criticism wholly leaves their real value out of the question, as if Charles Reade were to be exalted for having written the "great Australian novel," *Never Too Late to Mend,* or De Foe for his "great Juan Fernandez novel." In the true novel the scene, the incidents, are subordinated to the sufferings, actions, and qualities of the characters. They are for the time living beings, and our greatest sympathy is necessarily given to those who deserve it from some internal reason, not from the number of miles they may have travelled, or the number of times they have been shot at in the dark. Such incidents lend an interest, it is true, but it is not of the highest kind. The geology, the botany, the ethnography, may be accurate to date, the reader may be in perpetual shivers from the urgency of the dangers that threaten every one in the novel, but the real story lies beneath the hats and bonnets of those concerned, not in the distant cataracts that wet them, nor the bullets that scar them. It would seem as if the author had contented himself too readily with but one side, and that not the most valuable, of the novelist's work. He should retain the skill that he now possesses and use it, not as a thing of lasting value in itself, but as aid to the representation of what is more genuine art. We should be sorry, however, if we did not do justice to the vividness with which he has drawn many of his side-characters, especially in his latest novels and in many of his less ambitious magazine sketches. As a simple narrator he is deserving of much praise; he can draw admirably the less important personages, so that one only notices more sharply his smaller degree of success when he undertakes to represent the more difficult character, a man under the influence of some all-controlling passion. What he can see he can write down for our reading, and that is certainly a rare gift, but his eye is stronger than his imagination. It is when he comes to this more delicate part of his work that the reader is disappointed, and all the more, as we have said, from his skill elsewhere.

Of the society novel this is the more common form. One takes the manly A and represents some possible complications of his "heart-agony," and that of the lovely C, from the persecution of flinty-hearted parents, loss of money, jealousy, &c. One would be averse to saying that his own country cannot supply as good material for such novels as any other. There are here pretty women and good men. In spite of our race for wealth, our early marriages, our bolting our meals and consequent dyspepsia, the devious course of what is strangely called the tender passion may still be observed by those who watch their kind. Lovers languish and rejoice, hearts threaten to break and then grow indifferent, as truly here as in any German village, where the full moon shines every night of the year. But can any one name a good American love-story? With the exception of *Esmond* it might be hard to find one in the language; but let us consider America alone. What are the American novels of society, in which we might suppose love-making would have full sway? Those of Mrs. Stowe suggest themselves at once. We cannot believe that her popularity is due entirely to her wonderful success with *Uncle Tom's Cabin.* To her youngest readers that book must be already a thing of the past; but we fancy that is because she has succeeded in catching certain traits of American life that she is so widely read. Besides, with all her faults, she is a humourist, and is often entertaining enough; but what could be more ignoble than her last two novels of society, *Pink and White Tyranny* and *My Wife and I.* It is profound criticism to call Thackeray a cynic; perhaps Mrs. Stowe is one in disguise, but no man would dare to show his head in a drawing-room after describing such a character as the heroine of the last of these novels. One would have to be disappointed in love a great many times before young ladies made upon him such an impression of furbelowed, curled, food-despising, thin-voiced flirts as one finds here. The men are the infant heroes of Mrs. Sherwood's tales grown up. As for the manners of these people, their giggling, their love-making, it is what one imagines to be the romance of a "calico and neck-tie ball." For example we find in chapter xxx. of *My Wife and I:*—

"'O you know'—this inextricable puzzle, —what does ail a certain person? Now he didn't come at all last night, and when I asked Jim Fellows where his friend was (one must pass the compliment of inquiring, you know), he said, "Henderson had grown dumpy lately," and he couldn't get him out anywhere.'

"'Well, Eva, I'm sure I can't throw any light on the subject. I know no more than you.'

"'Now, Ida, let me tell you, this afternoon when we stopped in the park, I went into that great rustic arbour on the top of the hill there, and just as we came in on one side, I saw him in all haste hurrying out on the other, as if he were afraid to meet me.'

"'How very odd!'

"'Odd! well, I should think it was; but what was worse, he went and stationed himself on a bench under a tree where he could hear and see us, and there my lord sat—perhaps he thought I didn't see him, but I did.'

"'Lillie and Belle Forester and Wat Jerrold were with me, and we were having such a laugh! I don't know when I have had such a frolic, and how silly it was of him to sit there glowering like an owl in an ivy-bush, when he might have come out and joined us, and had a good time! I'm quite out of patience with the creature, it's so vexatious to have him act so!'"

Further on we find:—

(*Enter* ALICE *with empressement.*)

"'Girls, what do you think? Wat Sydney come back and going to give a great croquet party out at Clairmont, and of course we are all invited with notes in the most resplendent style, with crest and coat of arms, and everything—perfectly "*mag.*" There's to be a steamboat, with a band of music, to take the guests up, and no end of splendid doings: *marquées* and tents and illuminations and fireworks, and to return by moonlight after all's over; isn't it lovely? I do think Wat Sydney's perfectly splendid, and it's all on your account, Eva, I know it is,'" &c. &c.

And so they artlessly prattle on. This is by no means an extract, which, taken away from its context, seems unduly ridiculous; far from it, it is a very good specimen of the whole tone of the book. Be these the manners of good society? Is there nothing nobler in life than a horse-car flirtation? Is it necessary

that society novels should be like fashion plates, with the same jaunty ease and simpering gentility that mark those illustrations of the happy life of the rich and great? If the people are tawdrily dressed, if their talk is empty enough to shame the silliest schoolgirl that ever chattered until she gasped for breath, if their manners are either rude or pompously haughty, how can one take a genuine interest in the story? Let their manners be as bad as possible, their clothes and grammar in tatters, provided they have one trait, one quality, be it one that makes or mars human beings, and then we can read the story. To be interested in characters in fiction, as with human beings in life, our sympathy must be aroused; for beings who simply giggle and pout, indifference is kindness.

Most American writers are afraid of their heroes and heroines. They give them homes by the side of imaginary rivers, in impossible cities. They are as shy of fairly introducing their characters as if we were all strangers at a watering-place hotel, and were very nervous about tainting our tender gentility. That this is the result of attempting to represent in this country, with its changing, uncertain classes, what in England is clear enough from its fixed social laws, is highly probable. But a novel to be good may well let good society alone. The best that Mrs. Stowe has done leaves the dancing master out entirely. For the English novel the task is greatly simplified by the fact that every man in that country is much more closely connected with the whole social system than is the case with us. In their novels we are introduced to distinct characters, say to a barrister, an officer, a young lord. Besides, whatever personal characteristics may belong to each of these persons, they all stand in a certain definite relation to society at large. Each carries a certain atmosphere with him. With us when we read about a lawyer in one of our stories, nothing more is told us than if we were informed that he always wore Roman scarfs, perhaps not so much. We have all sorts of lawyers; no one man is a representative of the class. Occasionally we find that a good word is given to an omniscient professor who sits by a lamp and dabbles in Sanskrit, botany, metaphysics, chemistry, anatomy, zoology, &c. &c. He generally wears a long beard, has acquired patience by his severe studies, and is especially remarkable for the unexpected way in which he makes an offer of marriage after nourishing an untold and unsuspected love for a long time, while he pretended to be looking out words in the dictionary. Occasionally, we say, this representative of the quiet ideal appears in fiction, but he is an uncertain and artificial creation. In spite of the young girl's rapture over hops at West Point, an officer is not always an entrancing lover in fiction. There is, possibly, a vague Bohemian glamour around the artist, but even that is by no means certain. Since in general this deficiency exists, the task of the writer is rendered more difficult. Our Democracy certainly equalizes us: it enlists us, as it were, into a vast army, but a peaceful, unheroic army; and to make any fictitious person interesting the author is put to the greater task of distinctly drawing his character as a man: he gets no aid from his surroundings. One would say that the natural tendency of the American novelist would be toward romance; that the very uniformity of our social life would offer nothing tempting to the writer, unless, indeed, to the satirist, who should turn to ridicule the shallowness, greedy pretence, and emptiness which he might see about him. In spite of the contumely that is thrown upon the frivolities of fashion in *Pink and White Tyranny* and in *My Wife and I*, it may be said that it is not given to every one to be a satirist. No satire is keener than that which tells the truth. One is only tender about his favourite vice. To call a selfish man a murderer, or a pirate, would be as idle as to write odes in praise of an honest clerk. And so in these stories Mrs. Stowe has overshot her mark by caricaturing what only needed to be shown in its real dulness to appear worthless. To her, and to many others, American society seems frivolous, but it is only exalted when a writer wastes his powder by attacking it as he would a dangerously false religion.

While the American writer finds these difficulties in the way of the "novel of society," it may be just that those tales should be considered that take up man from some other point of view than that which controls the respectable matron who is making out a list of invitations for her daughter's party. There are the dry-humoured Yankees, the Yankee-despising, self praising Westerners, and the lordly Southrons, who hate both. What has been done with such characters as these?

In hardly any book do we get more of the Yankee than in the novel *Margaret*, by Sylvester Judd. It is a story of life in New England nearly a hundred years ago, and although it stands in about the same relation to most novels that Burton's *Anatomy of Melancholy* does to ordinary manuals of

anatomy, it has a certain interest of its own. This is, to be sure, hardly great enough to beguile the reader to the reading of the book, which is written in defiance of every rule of literary composition; but yet, in spite of a crabbed style, as rough as a corduroy road, of tedious and impossible conversations, of great delays in the telling of the story, the reader can readily see a sincerity in the writer that is often much less evident in the works of much cleverer writers. As an example of its artistic crudeness we quote the following conversation:—

"Another day Mr. Evelyn came to the Pond. Margaret watched his approach with composure, and returned his greeting without confusion. 'You have been at the Head,' said she, 'and I must take you to other places to-day. First the Maples.'

"'This is a fine mineralogical region,' said he, as they entered the spot. 'I wish I had a hammer.'

"'I will get one,' said she. 'Let me go for it.'

"'You are not in health, you told me, and you do not look very strong. I must go by all means. I will be back in a trice. You will have quite as much walking as you can master before the day is through.'

"'I fear I shall be more tired wandering than in going.'

"'See this,' said he, exposing a hollow stone filled with rare crystals which he found and broke during her absence.

"'I thank you, I thank you,' she replied. 'The master has given me an inkling of geology, but I never imagined such beauty was hidden here.'

"'With definite forms and brilliant texture these gems vegetate in the centre of his rough rusty stone.'

"'Incomparable mystery! New anagogics! I begin to be in love with what I understand not.'

"'Humanity is like that.'

"'What is humanity?'

"'It is only another name for the world that you asked me about.'

"'I am perplexed by the duplicity of words. He is humane who helps the needy.'

"'That is one form of humanity. I use the term as expressing all men collectively viewed in their better light. Much depends upon this light phase, or aspect, what subjectively to us is by the Germans called standpoint. Indian's Head, in one position, resembles a human face; in another, quite as much a fish's tail. Man, like this stone, is geodic,—such stones, you know, are called geodes.'

"'Have you the skill to discover them?'

"'It is more difficult to break than to find them. Yet if I could crack any man as I do this stone, I should open to crystals.'

"'Any man?'

"'All men.'

"'Passing wonderful! I would run a thousand miles for the hammer! I have been straining after the stars, how much there is in the stones! Most divine earth, henceforth I will worship thee! Geodic Androids! What will the master say?'

"'I see traces of more gems in these large rocks. Let me rap here, and lo! a beryl; there is an agate, yonder is a growth of garnets.'

"'Let me cease to be astonished, and only learn to love.'

"'An important lesson, and one not too well-learned.'

"'Under this tree I will erect a temple to the god of rocks. Was there any such? Certes, I remember none.'

"'The god of rocks is God.'

"'You sport enigmas. Let us to Diana's Walk.'"

We will not follow them. Their talk flows on as easily and naturally as in the extract given above, closely resembling the conversations in the chapters in the phrase-book for advanced pupils. But with all these obvious faults, and an almost impossible plot, the writer shows a genuine love of nature, and an appreciation of character that is really poetical. It is a book that is good in spite of itself, but yet it is barely readable. Its merits are those that are hardly evident enough to tempt the ordinary reader, who, naturally enough, wishes the way made easy before him. He takes a novel as he takes a walk, for amusement; he does not care for ruggedness,—that wearies him, every day life gives him that,—any more than he does for an afternoon stroll through the thicket of the untrodden forest.

In Dr. Holmes' novels,—if we can call them novels,—in spite of his way of treating his characters like pathological or anatomical specimens, and in Mr. Henry Ward Beecher's *Norwood*, we find the humorous Yankee admirably given. But, while *Elsie Venner* is in its way a well constructed romance, and Hiram in *Norwood* is an amusingly and accurately drawn character, neither novel deserves the highest praise. They are both very clever attempts by men who are not novelists. Sam Lawson, in Mrs. Stowe's *Old Town Stories*, is an extremely amusing person. This lady has certainly, to a remarkable extent, the power of detecting the humorous side of what she sees, and of representing it. The Yankee in her writings is an admirable copy of an original that can be found in almost every New England village,—a man, namely, of greater or less worthlessness, but with a wisdom, or rather shrewdness, that makes him far superior to the ordinary people around him. It is part of the novelist's work to introduce just such characters. They are, so to speak, picturesque, and yet true to nature. Of the immense superiority of a story that contains one personage that is really a human being, it would be needless to speak. Most novels leave as shadowy an impression of the genuineness of their heroes and heroines upon the minds of their readers, as does the pictured Quaker of the advertisements of the soundness of his religious views. But the introduction of a character that is only of dramatic importance, that is to say, who is more truly drawn as a representative of a class than as a human being, does not of itself make a good novel. The reader is more easily satisfied with a superficial sketch in the former case than he would be in the latter. A man may be well drawn as a village loafer, he may give us the very impression that the genuine idler makes upon us, and to do this is no light task; it is one for which a writer deserves high praise, and this no one would deny to Mrs. Stowe. But there is beyond this a feeling in the reader's mind that he has a right to expect a solution of more difficult characters, a representation not only of one or two persons, but also of some probable and well-connected incidents. In the better sort of novels we get some human beings, but we also demand a story, a plot that shall be probable and interesting. One character, no matter if very life-like, in an awkwardly constructed story is as out of place as would be a poet on a desert island. But still it cannot be denied that it is the drawing of a character which is the most difficult part of the novelist's task, and if he succeeds he has thereby the surest hold upon his readers. If he fails in this, he fails indeed, for even the most imaginative are cold to the dangers that threaten even the most carefully dressed puppets. But a well-drawn character, one which we feel to be an accurate representation of what a human being might be, one who seems to us not merely what we fancy fellow-travellers, for instance, are, but who is a consistent creation, moved by passion, with feelings of his own, and his own special temptations, who may differ entirely from ourselves, but yet of the truth of whose delineation every one can instinctively be sure, is a rare person in fiction. ·For creating him there are no infallible rules, any more than there are for painting a good portrait in oils. It all depends upon the writer's brains. But if he is successful, if he creates a character with whom we can feel any sympathy, although the feeling may not be one of admiration, we are sure that the writer has done something of which he may well be proud.

The great novel is yet unwritten. · We hope that he who shall attempt to write it will see the simplicity, the singleness of the problem that lies before him. The surer he is of this, the better will be his work. The less conscious he is of trying to be American, the more truly will he succeed in being so. Self-consciousness does not make a strong character, and so it is with this quality of the novelist. Lay the scene on the limitless prairie or in limited Fifth Avenue, but let the story rise above its geographical boundaries; let the characters be treated as human beings, not simply as inhabitants of such or such a place, with nothing to distinguish them from the beasts that perish, except certain peculiarities of dress and language. They must dwell somewhere, but they must be something besides citizens. Fantastic creatures dwelling in pure ether are not what the reader demands, but beings true, not to fashion, but to those higher laws and passions that alone are real, that exist above all the petty, accidental caprice of time and place. The real novelist, he who is to write the "great American novel," must be a poet; he must look at life, not as the statistician, not as the census taker, nor yet as the newspaper reporter, but with an eye that sees, through temporary disguises, the animating principles, good or bad, that direct human existence; these he must set before us, to be sure, under probable conditions, but yet without mistaking the conditions for the principles. He must idealize. The idealizing novelist will be the real novelist. All truth does not lie in facts. —*North American Review.*

AUTHORITY.

Authority intoxicates,
And makes mere sots of magistrates;
The fumes of it invade the brain,
And make men giddy, proud, and vain:
By this the fool commands the wise,
The noble with the base complies,
The sot assumes the rule of wit,
And cowards make the brave submit.
         SAMUEL BUTLER.

LIFE'S PILGRIMAGE.

[Jorge Manrique, a Spanish poet of the 15th century, whose principal poems were written between 1450 and 1474. In the *Edinburgh Review* the late George Moir said that the following poem " is surpassed by nothing in the Spanish language, except the odes of Luis de Leon."]

O! let the soul its slumber break,
Arouse its senses and awake,
         To see how soon
Life with its glories glides away,
And the stern footstep of decay
         Comes stealing on.

How pleasure, like the passing wind,
Blows by, and leaves us nought behind
         But grief at last;
How still our present happiness
Seems, to the wayward fancy, less
         Than what is past.

And while we eye the rolling tide,
Down which our flying minutes glide
         Away so fast;
Let us the present hour employ,
And deem each future dream of joy
         Already past.

Let no vain hope deceive the mind—
No happier let us hope to find
         To-morrow than to-day.
Our golden dreams of yore were bright,
Like them the present shall delight,—
         Like them decay.

Our lives like hasting streams must be,
That into one engulfing sea
         Are doomed to fall:
The Sea of Death, whose waves roll on,
O'er king and kingdom, crown and throne,
         And swallow all.

Alike the river's lordly tide,
Alike the humble riv'lets glide
         To that sad wave;
Death levels poverty and pride,
And rich and poor sleep side by side
         Within the grave.

Our birth is but a starting place,
Life is the running of the race,
         And death the goal;
There all our steps at last are brought,
That path alone, of all unsought,
         Is found of all.

Say then, how poor and little worth
Are all those glittering toys of earth
         That lure us here;

Dreams of a sleep that death must break,
Alas! before it bids us wake
    Ye disappear.

Long ere the damps of death can blight,
The cheek's pure glow of red and white
    Hath passed away:
Youth smiled, and all was heav'nly fair,
Age came and laid his finger there,
    And where are they?

Where are the strength that mocked decay,
The step that rose so light and gay,
    The heart's blithe tone?—
The strength is gone, the step is slow,
And joy grows weariness and woe,
    When age comes on.
    Translated by George Moir.

THE FOUNTAIN OF BEAUTY.

[Mrs. Lydia Maria Child, born in Medford, Massachusetts, 11th February, 1802. One of the most earnest and successful advocates of the anti-slavery cause, and the author of numerous tales and sketches. Her chief works are: *Hobomok,* a tale of early times; *The Rebels; The Frugal Housewife; The History of Woman; Biographies of Good Wives; Philothea,* a novel; *Looking Towards Sunset;* and numerous works on the slave question.]

In ancient times two little princesses lived in Scotland, one of whom was extremely beautiful, the other dwarfish, dark-coloured, and deformed. One was named Rose, and the other Marion. The sisters did not live happily together. Marian hated Rose, because she was handsome, and everybody praised her. She scowled and her face absolutely grew black when anybody asked her how her pretty little sister Rose did; and once she was so wicked as to cut off all her glossy, golden hair, and throw it into the fire. Poor Rose cried bitterly about it, but she did not scold or strike her sister; for she was an amiable, gentle little being as ever lived. No wonder all the family and all the neighbourhood disliked Marion; and no wonder her face grew uglier and uglier every day. The Scots used to be a very superstitious people, and they believed the infant Rose had been blessed by the fairies, to whom she owed her extraordinary beauty and exceeding goodness.

Not far from the castle where the princesses resided was a deep grotto, said to lead to the Palace of Beauty, where the Queen of the Fairies held her court. Some said Rose had fallen asleep there one day when she had grown tired of chasing a butterfly, and that the Queen had dipped her in an immortal fountain, from which she had risen with the beauty of an angel.[1] Marion often asked questions about this story, but Rose always replied that she had been forbidden to speak of it. When she saw any uncommonly brilliant bird or butterfly, she would sometimes exclaim, "Oh how much that looks like fairyland!" But when asked what she knew about fairyland, she blushed and would not answer.

Marion thought a great deal about this. "Why cannot I go to the Palace of Beauty?" thought she; "and why may I not bathe in the Immortal Fountain!"

One summer's noon, when all was still save the faint twittering of the birds, and the lazy hum of the insects, Marion entered the deep grotto. She sat down on a bank of moss; the air around her was as fragrant as if it came from a bed of violets; and with a sound of far-off music dying on her ear, she fell into a gentle slumber. When she awoke it was evening; and she found herself in a small hall, where opal pillars supported a rainbow roof, the bright reflection of which rested on crystal walls, and a golden floor inlaid with pearls. All around between the opal pillars stood the tiniest vases of pure alabaster, in which grew a multitude of brilliant and fragrant flowers; some of them, twining around the pillars, were lost in the floating rainbow above. The whole of this scene of beauty was lighted up by millions of fire-flies, glittering about like wandering stars. While Marion was wondering at all this, a little figure of rare loveliness stood before her. Her robe was of green and gold; her flowing gossamer mantle was caught up on one shoulder with a pearl, and in her hair was a solitary star composed of five diamonds, each no bigger than a pin's point. And thus she sung:—

    "The Fairy Queen
    Hath rarely seen
    Creature of earthly mould,
    Within her door,
    On pearly floor,
    Inlaid with shining gold.
    Mortal, all thou see'st is fair,
    Quick thy purposes declare!

As she concluded, the song was taken up and thrice repeated by a multitude of soft voices in the distance. It seemed as if birds and insects joined the chorus—the clear voice of the thrush was distinctly heard; the cricket kept time with his tiny cymbal; and ever and anon,

---

[1] There was a superstition that whoever slept on fairy ground was carried away by the fairies.

between the pauses, the sound of a distant cascade was heard, whose waters fell in music.

All these delightful sounds died away, and the Queen of the Fairies stood patiently awaiting Marion's answer. Courtesying low, and with a trembling voice, the little maiden said, "Will it please your majesty to make me as handsome as my sister Rose?" The Queen smiled: "I will grant your request," she said, "if you will promise to fulfil all the conditions I impose. Marion eagerly promised that she would. "The Immortal Fountain," replied the Queen, "is on the top of a high, steep hill; at four different places fairies are stationed around it, who guard it with their wands; none can pass them except those who obey my orders. Go home now: for one week speak no ungentle word to your sister—at the end of that time come again to the grotto."

Marion went home light of heart. Rose was in the garden watering the flowers; and the first thing Marion observed was that her sister's sunny hair had suddenly grown as long and beautiful as it had ever been. The sight made her angry, and she was just about to snatch the water-pot from her hand with an angry expression; but she remembered the fairy, and passed into the castle in silence. The end of the week arrived, and Marion had faithfully kept her promise. Again she went to the grotto. The Queen was feasting when she entered the hall. The bees brought honey-comb and deposited it on the small rose-coloured shells which adorned the crystal table; gaudy butterflies floated about the head of the queen, and fanned her with their wings; the cucullo and the lantern-fly stood at her side to afford her light; a large diamond beetle formed her splendid footstool, and when she had supped, a dew-drop, on the petal of a violet, was brought for her royal fingers.

When Marion entered, the diamond sparkles on the wings of the fairies faded, as they always did in the presence of anything not perfectly good; and in a few moments all the Queen's attendants vanished away, singing as they went—

> " The Fairy Queen
> Hath rarely seen
> Creature of earthly mould,
> Within her door,
> On pearly floor,
> Inlaid with shining gold."

"Mortal! hast thou fulfilled thy promise?" asked the Queen. "I have," replied the maiden. "Then follow me." Marion did as she was directed, and away they went, over beds of violets and mignonette. The birds

warbled above their heads, butterflies cooled the air, and the gurgling of many fountains came with a refreshing sound. Presently they came to the hill on the top of which was the Immortal Fountain. Its foot was surrounded by a band of fairies clothed in green gossamer, with their ivory wands crossed to bar the ascent. The Queen waved her wand over them, and immediately they stretched their thin wings and flew away. The hill was steep; and far, far up they went, and the air became more and more fragrant, and more and more distinctly they heard the sound of the waters falling in music. At length they were stopped by a band of fairies clothed in blue, with their silver wands crossed. "Here," said the Queen, "our journey must end. You can go no farther until you shall have fulfilled the orders I shall give you. Go home now; for one month do by your sister in all respects as you would wish to have her do by you, were you Rose and she Marion." Marion promised, and departed. She found the task harder than the first had been. She could help speaking, but when Rose asked for any of her playthings she found it difficult to give them gently and affectionately, instead of pushing them along; when Rose talked to her she wanted to go away in silence; and when a pocket mirror was found in her sister's room, broken into a thousand pieces, she felt sorely tempted to conceal that she did the mischief. But she was so anxious to be made beautiful that she did as she would be done by.

All the household remarked how Marion had changed. "I love her dearly," said Rose, "she is good and amiable." "So do I," and "So do I," said a dozen voices. Marion blushed, and her eye sparkled with pleasure. "How pleasant it is to be loved," thought she.

At the end of the month she went to the grotto. The fairies in blue lowered their silver wands, and flew away. They travelled on: the path grew steeper and steeper, but the fragrance of the atmosphere was redoubled, and more distinctly came the sound of the waters falling in music. Their course was stayed by a troop of fairies in rainbow robes and silver wands tipped with gold. In face and form they were far more beautiful than anything Marion had yet seen. "Here we must pause," said the Queen; "this boundary you cannot yet pass." "Why not?" asked the impatient Marion. "Because those must be very pure who pass the rainbow fairies," replied the Queen. "Am I not very pure?" said Marion; "all the folks at the Castle tell me how good I have grown."

"Mortal eyes see only the outside," answered the Queen; "but those who pass the rainbow fairies must be pure in thought as well as in action. Return home—for three months never indulge an envious or wicked thought. You shall then have a sight of the Immortal Fountain." Marion was sad at heart; for she knew how many envious thoughts and wrong wishes she had suffered to gain power over her.

At the end of the three months she again visited the Palace of Beauty. The Queen did not smile when she saw her, but in silence led the way to the Immortal Fountain. The green fairies and the blue fairies flew away as they approached, but the rainbow fairies bowed low to the Queen, and kept their gold-tipped wands firmly crossed. Marion saw that the silver specks on their wings grew dim, and she burst into tears. "I knew," said the Queen, "that you could not pass this boundary. Envy has been in your heart, and you have not driven it away. Your sister has been ill, and in your heart you wished that she might die, or rise from the bed of sickness deprived of her beauty. But be not discouraged; you have been several years indulging wrong feelings, and you must not wonder that it takes many years to drive them away."

Marion was sad as she wended her way homeward. When Rose asked her what was the matter, she told her that she wanted to be very good, but she could not. "When I want to be good I read my Bible and pray," said Rose; "and I find God helps me to be good." Then Marion prayed that God would help her to be pure in thought; and when wicked feelings rose in her heart she read her Bible, and they went away.

When she again visited the Palace of Beauty the Queen smiled, and touched her playfully with her wand, then led the way to the Immortal Fountain. The silver specks on the wings of the rainbow fairies shone bright as she approached them, and they lowered their wands and sung as they flew away—

"Mortal, pass on,
Till the goal is won,—
For such I ween
Is the will of our Queen—
Pass on! Pass on!"

And now every footstep was on flowers that yielded beneath their feet, as if their pathway had been upon a cloud. The delicious fragrance could almost be felt, yet it did not oppress the senses with its heaviness; and loud, clear, and liquid came the sound of the waters as they fell in music. And now the cascade is

seen leaping and sparkling over crystal rocks; a rainbow arch rests above it, like a perpetual halo; the spray falls in pearls, and forms fantastic foliage about the margin of the fountain. It has touched the webs woven among the grass, and they have become pearl-embroidered cloaks for the Fairy Queen. Deep and silent, below the foam, is the Immortal Fountain! Its amber-coloured waves flow over a golden bed; and as the fairies bathe in it, the diamonds in their hair glance like sunbeams on the waters.

"Oh let me bathe in the fountain!" cried Marion, clasping her hands in delight. "Not yet," said the Queen. "Behold the purple fairies with golden wands that guard its brink!" Marion looked, and saw beings far lovelier than any her eye had ever rested on. "You cannot pass them yet," said the Queen. "Go home; for one year drive away all evil feelings, not for the sake of bathing in the fountain, but because goodness is lovely and desirable for its own sake. Purify the inward motive, and your work is done."

This was the hardest task of all. For she had been willing to be good, not because it was right to be good, but because she had wished to be beautiful. Three times she sought the grotto, and three times she left it in tears; for the golden specks grew dim at her approach, and the golden wands were still crossed, to shut her from the Immortal Fountain. The fourth time she prevailed. The purple fairies lowered their wands, singing—

"Thou hast scaled the mountain,
Go bathe in the fountain,
Rise fair to the sight
As an angel of light,—
Go bathe in the fountain!"

Marion was about to plunge in, but the Queen touched her, saying, "Look into the mirror of the waters. Art thou not already as beautiful as heart can wish?"

Marion looked at herself, and she saw that her eye sparkled with new lustre, that a bright colour shone through her cheeks, and dimples played sweetly about her mouth. "I have not touched the Immortal Fountain," said she, turning in surprise to the Queen. "True," replied the Queen; "but its waters have been within your soul. Know that a pure heart and clean conscience are the only Immortal Fountain of Beauty."

When Marion returned, Rose clasped her to her bosom, and kissed her fervently. "I know all," said she; "though I have not asked you a question. I have been in fairyland, disguised as a bird, and I have watched all your steps. When you first went to the grotto I begged the Queen to grant your wish."

Ever after that the sisters lived lovingly together. It was the remark of every one, "How handsome Marion has grown. The ugly scowl has departed from her face, and the light of her eye is so mild and pleasant, and her mouth looks so smiling and good-natured, that to my taste, I declare, she is as handsome as Rose."

THE LOVERS.

[Robert Pollok, A.M., born at Muirhouse, Eaglesham, Renfrewshire, 1799; died near Southampton, 15th September, 1827. Educated at the Glasgow University for the ministry; licensed to preach in 1827; but only appeared once in the pulpit. He died on his way to Italy in search of health. Besides his poem he wrote three tales of the Covenanters—*Helen of the Glen; The Persecuted Family;* and *Ralph Gemmell.* Professor Wilson said: "*The Course of Time* for so young a man was a vast achievement. . . . He had much to learn in composition, and, had he lived, would have looked almost with humiliation on much that is at present eulogized by his devoted admirers. But the soul of poetry is there." The poem was received with remarkable favour here and in America. The seventy-eighth thousand was published by Blackwood in 1868. The following is from the fifth book.]

It was an eve of Autumn's holiest mood;
The corn-fields, bathed in Cynthia's silver light,
Stood ready for the reaper's gathering hand,
And all the winds slept soundly. Nature seemed,
In silent contemplation, to adore
Its Maker. Now and then, the aged leaf
Fell from its fellows, rustling to the ground;
And, as it fell, bade man think on his end.
On vale and lake, on wood and mountain high,
With pensive wing outspread, sat heavenly Thought,
Conversing with itself. Vesper looked forth,
From out her western hermitage, and smiled;
And up the east, unclouded, rode the Moon,
With all her stars, gazing on earth intense,
As if she saw some wonder walking there.

Such was the night, so lovely, still, serene,
When, by a hermit thorn that on the hill
Had seen a hundred flowery ages pass,
A damsel kneeled to offer up her prayer,
Her prayer nightly offered, nightly heard.
This ancient thorn had been the meeting-place
Of love, before his country's voice had called
The ardent youth to fields of honour, far
Beyond the wave: and hither now repaired,
Nightly, the maid, by God's all-seeing eye
Seen only, while she sought this boon alone—
Her lover's safety and his quick return.
In holy humble attitude she kneeled,

And to her bosom, fair as moonbeam, pressed
One hand, the other lifted up to heaven.
Her eye, upturned, bright as the star of morn,
As violet meek, excessive ardour streamed,
Wafting away her earnest heart to God.
Her voice, scarce uttered, soft as Zephyr sighs
On morning lily's cheek, though soft and low,
Yet heard in heaven, heard at the mercy-seat.
A tear-drop wandered on her lovely face;
It was a tear of faith and holy fear,
Pure as the drops that hang at dawning-time
On yonder willows by the stream of life.
On her the Moon looked steadfastly; the Stars,
That circle nightly round the eternal Throne,
Glanced down, well-pleased; and Everlasting Love
Gave gracious audience to her prayer sincere.

O had her lover seen her thus alone,
Thus holy, wrestling thus, and all for him!
Nor did he not; for ofttimes Providence,
With unexpected joy the fervent prayer
Of faith surprised. Returned from long delay,
With glory crowned of righteous actions won,
The sacred thorn, to memory dear, first sought
The youth, and found it at the happy hour,
Just when the damsel kneeled herself to pray.
Wrapt in devotion, pleading with her God,
She saw him not, heard not his foot approach.
All holy images seemed too impure
To emblem her he saw. A seraph kneeled,
Beseeching for his ward, before the Throne,
Seemed fittest, pleased him best. Sweet was the thought!
But sweeter still, the kind remembrance came,
That she was flesh and blood, formed for himself,
The plighted partner of his future life.
And as they met, embraced, and sat, embowered
In woody chambers of the starry night,
Spirits of love about them ministered,
And God, approving, blest the holy joy!

A QUESTION OF GRAVITY.

BY W. M. PRAED.

The advancement of knowledge is the triumph of truth, and, as such, is the eventual interest of mankind; inasmuch as the extension of reason is by its very definition the necessary object of rational beings. Timid theologians have trembled on the confines of some topics which might lead to dangerous discovery; forgetful that religion and truth, if not identical, are at least inseparable. Some nice and sensitive chemists have forborne the search of the *ne plus ultra* in alchemy, dreading that as gold is the great fountain of wickedness on earth, the indefinite increase of that metal might be the unlimited multiplication of human evil: but forgetting that in all human affairs, from fluids up to theories, there is a specific gravity in all things which keeps constant the level of terrestrial operations, and prevents the restless brain of man from raising any edifice, in brick or discovery, high enough to be the ruin of his own species. To me, however, the one consideration, that the eternal search of knowledge and truth is the very object of our faculties, has been the main-spring of my life, and although my individual sufferings have been far from light, yet at their present distance the contemplation gives me pleasure, and I have the satisfaction to reflect that I am now in possession of an art which is continually employed, day and night, for the benefit of the present generation and of ages yet to come.

I was born in the Semlainogorod of Moscow; and for ten years applied intensely to chemistry. I confess the failure of many eminent predecessors prevented my attempting the philosopher's stone; my whole thoughts were engaged on the contemplation of gravity—on that mysterious invisible agent which pervaded the whole universe—which made my pen drop from my fingers—the planets move round the sun—and the very sun itself, with its planets, moons, and satellites, revolve for ever, with myriads of others, round the final centre of universal gravity—that mysterious spot, perhaps the residence of those particular emanations of Providence which regard created beings. At length I discovered the actual ingredients of this omnipresent agent. It is little more than a combination of carbon, oxygen, hydrogen, and azote; but the proportions of these constituent parts had long baffled me, and I still withhold them from my species for obvious reasons.

Knowledge is power,—and the next easy step from the discovery of the elements was the decomposition of gravity, and the neutralization of its parts in any substance at my pleasure. I was more like a lunatic than a rational chemist;—a burning furor drove me to an immediate essay of my art, and stripped me of the power and will to calculate on consequences. Imagine me in my laboratory. I constructed a gravitation-pump—applied it to my body—turned the awful engine, and stood in an instant the first of all created beings—devoid of weight! Up sprung my hair—my arms swung from my sides above the level of my shoulders, by the involuntary action of the muscles; which were no longer curbed by the re-action of their weight. I laughed like a fool or a fiend, closed my arms carefully to my side, compressed or concealed my bristling hair under my cap, and walked forth from my study to seek some re-

tired spot in the city where I might make instant experiment of a jump. With the greatest difficulty I preserved a decent gait; I walked with the uneasy unsteady motion of a man in water whose toes might barely reach the bottom: conscious as I was of my security, I felt every instant apprehensive of a fall. Nothing could have reconciled me to the disagreeable sensation I experienced, but the anticipation of vaulting unfettered into the air. I stood behind the cathedral of the Seven Towers; nobody was near—I looked hurriedly around, and made the spring! I rose with a slow, uniform motion,—but, gracious Heaven! imagine my horror and distress when I found that nothing but the mere resistance of the air opposed my progress; and when at last it stopped my flight, I found myself many hundred feet above the city—motionless, and destitute of every means of descent. I tore my hair, and cursed myself, for overlooking so obvious a result. My screams drew thousands to the singular sight. I stretched my arms towards the earth and implored assistance. Poor fool! I knew it was impracticable.

But conceive the astonishment of the people! I was too high to be personally known;—they called to me and I answered; but they were unable to catch the import, for sound, like myself, rises better than it falls. I heard myself called an angel, a ghost, a dragon, a unicorn, and a devil. I saw a procession of priests come under me to exorcise me; but had Satan himself been free of gravity, he had been as unable to descend at their bidding as myself. At length the fickle mob began to jeer me—the boys threw stones at me, and a clever marksman actually struck me on the side with a bullet; it was too high to penetrate—it merely gave me considerable pain, drove me a few feet higher, and sunk again to the ground. Alas! I thought, would that it had pierced me, for even the weight of that little ball would have dragged me back to earth. At length the shades of evening hid the city from my sight; the murmur of the crowd gradually died away, and there I still was, cold, terrified, and motionless—nearer to heaven than such a fool could merit to rise again. What was to be the end of this! I must starve and be stared at!

Imagine my joy when a breeze sprung up, and I felt myself floating in darkness over the town: but even now new horrors seized me;—I might be driven downwards into the Moskwa and drowned; I might be dashed against the cathedral and crushed. Just as I thought on this my head struck violently against the great bell of Boris Godunuff;—the blow and the deep intonation of the bell deprived me for some minutes of life and recollection. When I revived, I found I was lying gently pressed by the breeze against the balustrades: I pulled myself carefully along the church, pushed myself down the last column, and run as straight as my light substance would permit me to my house. With far greater joy than when I had been disrobed of it, I speedily applied a proper condensation of gravity to my body, fell on my knees to thank Heaven for my deliverance, and slunk into bed, thoroughly ashamed of my day's performance. The next day, to escape suspicion, I joined the re-assembled crowd, looking upward as serious as the rest, gazed about for yesterday's phenomenon, and I daresay was the only one who felt no disappointment in its disappearance.

Any one would imagine that, after this trial, I should have burned my pump and left gravity to its own operations. But no! I felt I was reserved for great things;—such a discovery was no every-day occurrence, and I would work up every energy of my soul rather than relinquish this most singular, though frightful, field of experiment.

I was too cautious to deprive myself again entirely of gravity. In fact, in my late experiment, as in others, when I talk of extracting my gravity *entirely*, I mean just enough to leave me of the same weight as the atmosphere. Had I been lighter than that, I should have risen involuntarily upward like an air-bubble in a bucket. Even as it was, I found myself inclined to rise and fall with every variation of the atmosphere, and I had serious thoughts of offering myself to the university as a barometer, that, by a moderate salary, I might pass the remainder of my days in tranquillity and honour. My object now was merely to render myself as light as occasion required: besides, I found that by continual contact with the earth and atmosphere I always imbibed gradually a certain portion of weight, though by extremely slow and imperceptible degrees; for the constituent parts of gravity which I have mentioned enter largely, as every chemist knows, into the composition of all earths and airs: thus, in my late essay, I should certainly have eventually descended to earth without the intervention of the breeze; indeed, I should probably have been starved first, though my body would have at last sunk down for the gratification of my friends.

Three furred coats and a pair of skates I gained by leaping at fairs in the Sloboda, and subsistence for three weeks by my inimitable performance on the tight-rope; but when at last

I stood barefoot on a single needle, and balanced myself head downwards on a bodkin, all Moscow rung with applause. But the great object of all my earthly hopes was to gain the affections of a young widow in the Kremlin, whose heart I hoped to move by the unrivalled effects of my despair. I jumped head-foremost from a chair on the hard floor; twice I sprung into a well, and once I actually threw myself from the highest spire in Moscow. I always lay senseless after my falls, screamed at my revival, and counterfeited severe contusions. But in vain! I found my person or pretensions disagreeable to her. The truth is, it did not escape the notice of the people that I was destitute of weight; and although I took care to show myself publicly with a proper gravity, even with an additional stone weight, strange stories and whispers went forth about me; and when my feats of agility, and frightful, though not fatal, falls were recollected, it became generally believed that I had either sold myself to the devil, or was myself that celebrated individual. I now began to prepare myself for immediate escape, in case I should be legally prosecuted. I had hitherto been unable, when suspended in the air, to lower myself at my pleasure; for I was unable to make my pump act upon itself, and therefore, when I endeavoured to take it with me, its own weight always prevented my making any considerable rise. I have since recollected, indeed, that had I made two pumps, and extracted the weight from one by means of the other, I might have carried the light one up with me, and filled myself by its means with gravity when I wished to descend. However, this plan, as I said, having escaped my reflection, I set painfully about devising some method of carrying about gravity with me in a neutralized state, and giving it operation and energy when it should suit my convenience. After long labour and expensive experiments, I hit upon the following simple method:—

You will readily imagine that this subtle fluid, call it gravitation, or weight, or attraction, or what you will, pervading as it does every body in nature, impalpable and invisible, would occupy an extremely small space when packed in its pure and unmixed state. I found, after decomposing it, that besides the gases I mentioned before, there always remained a slight residuum, incombustible and insoluble. This was evidently a pure element, which I have called by a termination common among chemists, "gravium." When I admitted to it the other gases, except the azote of the atmosphere, it assumed a creamy consistence, which might be called "essential oil of gravitation:" and finally, when it was placed in contact with the atmosphere, it imbibed azote rapidly, became immediately invisible, and formed pure weight. I procured a very small elastic Indian-rubber bottle, into which I infused as much oil of gravity as I could extract from myself, carefully closed it, and squeezed it flat; and I found that by placing over the orifice an extremely fine gauze and admitting the atmosphere through it (like the celebrated English Davy lamp), as the bottle opened by its own elasticity, the oil became weight; and when I squeezed it again the azote receded through the gauze and left the weightless oil. I was now in possession of the ultimatum of my inquiries, the means of jumping into the air without any weight, and the power of assuming it when I wished to descend. What I feared came to pass: I was indicted as a sorcerer and condemned to be hung; I concealed my bottle under my arm, ascended the scaffold, avowed my innocence, and was turned off. I counterfeited violent convulsions, but was careful to retain just weight enough to keep the rope tight. In the evening, when the populace had retired, I gently extricated my neck, walked home, and prepared to leave my country.

At Petersburg I heard that Captain Khark of Voronetz was about to sail to India to bombard a British fortress. I demanded an interview.

"Sir," said I, "I am an unhappy man, whose misfortunes have compelled him to renounce his country. I am in possession of an art by which I can give you accurate intelligence of everything going on in the fortress you are to attack; and I offer you my services, provided you will give me a passage and keep my secret."

I saw by his countenance he considered me an impostor.

"Sir," I said, "promise me secrecy, and you shall behold a specimen of my art."

He assented. I squeezed the little bottle under my arm, sprung upward, and played along the ceiling, to his great amaze. He was a man of honour, and kept his promise; and in six months we arrived off the coast of Coromandel. Here I made one of the greatest mistakes in my life. I had frequently practised my art during the first part of the voyage for the amusement of the sailors; and instead of carrying my gravity-bottle with me, I used to divest myself of just sufficient gravity to leap mast-high, and descend gently on the deck; and by habit I knew the exact quantity which

was requisite in northern climes. But when I had ascended to view the fortress near the equator, I found too late that I had extracted far too much, and for this reason:— If you hold an orange at its head and stalk by the forefinger and thumb, and spin it with velocity, you will see that small bodies would be thrown with rapidity from those parts which lie midway between the finger and thumb, while those that are nearer are far less affected by the rotatory motion. It was just so with me. I had been used to descend in the northern climates with a very slight weight; but I now found that in the equatorial regions I was thrown upward with considerable strength. A strong sea-breeze was blowing. I was borne rapidly away from the astonished crew, passed over the fortress, narrowly escaped being shot, and found myself passing in the noblest manner over the whole extent of India. Habit had entirely divested me of fear, and I experienced the most exquisite delight in viewing that fine country spread out like a map beneath me. I recognized the scenes of historical interest. There rolled the Hydaspes by the very spot where Porus met Alexander. There lay the track of Mahmoud the great Gaznevide. I left the beautiful Kashmir on the right. I passed over the head-quarters of Persia in her different ages, Herat, Ispahan, Kamadan. Then came Arbela on my right, where a nation, long cooped up in a country scarce larger than Candia, had overthrown the children of the great Cyrus, and crushed a dynasty whose sway reached uninterrupted for 2000 miles. I saw the tomb of Gordian on the extreme frontier of his empire—a noble spot for the head of a nation of warriors. I skimmed along the plain where Crassus and Galerius, at the interval of three hundred years, had learned on the same unhappy field that Rome could bleed. A strong puff from the Levant whirled me to the northward, and dropped me at length on a ridge of Mount Caucasus, fatigued and hungry. I assuaged my hunger with mountain mosses, and slept a few hours as well as the extreme cold would permit me. On waking, the hopelessness of my situation distressed me much. After passing over so many hot countries, where the exhalations from the earth had enabled my body to imbibe gravitation more rapidly than usual, I had gradually moved northward, where the centrifugal force of the earth had much decreased.

From these two causes, and in this wild country, without the means of chemically assisting myself, I now found my body too heavy to trust again to the winds—intrenched as I was between the Black Sea and the Caspian, but without weight to give firmness to my step; without the lightness of a fowl I had all its awkward weakness in water. The savage natives cast lots for me, and 1 became a slave. My strange lightness was a source of mirth to all, even to my fellow-servants; and I found, by experience, how little weight a man bears in society who has lost his gravity. When I attempted to dig, I rose without effect on my spade. Sometimes when I bore a load of wood on my shoulders it felt so top-heavy, that upon the slightest wind I was sure to tumble over— and then I was chastised: my mistress one day hoisted me three miles by a single kick on the breech. But however powerless against lateral pressure, it was observed with amaze how easily I raised the vast weights under which the most powerful men in the country sunk; for, in fact, my legs being formed to the usual capabilities of mankind, had now little or no weight of body to support; I was therefore enabled to carry ten or twelve stone in addition to a common burden. It was this strength that enabled me to throw several feet from the earth a native who had attacked me. He was stunned by the fall, but, on rising, with one blow he drove me a hundred yards before him. I took to my heels, determined, if possible, to escape this wretched life. The whole country was on foot to pursue me, for I had doubly deserved death; I had bruised a freeman, and was a fugitive slave. But notwithstanding the incredible agility of these people in their native crags, their exact knowledge of the clefts in the hills, the only passes between the eternal snows, and my own ignorance, I utterly baffled their pursuit by my want of weight, and the energy which despair supplied me. Sometimes when they pressed hardest on me I would leap up a perpendicular crag twenty feet high, or drop down a hundred. I bent my steps towards the Black Sea, determined, if I could reach the coast, to seek a passage to some port in Cathenoslaw, and retire where I might pass the remainder of my life under a feigned name, with at least the satisfaction of dying in the dominions of my legitimate sovereign, Alexander.

Exhausted and emaciated I arrived at a straggling village, the site of the ancient Pityus. This was the last boundary of the Roman power on the Euxine, and to this wretched place state exiles were frequently doomed. The name became proverbial; and, I understand, has been so far adopted by the English that the word " Pityus" is, to this day, most adapted to the lips of the banished. In a small vessel we

sailed for Azof; but when we came off the Straits of Caffa, where the waters of the Don are poured into the Euxine, a strong current drove us on a rock, and in a fresh gale the ship went speedily to pieces. I gave myself up for lost, and heard the crew, one after the other, gurgle in the waves and scream their last, while I lay struggling and buffeting for life. But after the first hurry for existence I found I had exhausted myself uselessly, for my specific gravity being so trifling I was enabled to lie on the surface of the billows without any exertion, and even to sit upon the wave as securely as a couch. I loosened my neckcloth, and spreading it wide with my hands and teeth, I trusted myself to the same winds that had so often pelted me at their mercy, and always spared me. In this way I traversed the Euxine. I fed on the scraps that floated on the surface—sometimes dead fish, and once or twice on some inquisitive stragglers whose curiosity brought them from the deep to contemplate the strange sail. Two days I floated in misery, and a sleepless night; by night I dared not close my eyes for fear of falling backward—and by day I frequently passed objects that filled me with despair — fragments of wrecks; and then I looked on my own sorry craft: once I struck my feet against a drowned sailor, and it put me in mind of myself. At last I landed safe on the beach between Odessa and Otchacow, traversed the Ukraine, and by selling the little curiosities I had picked up on my passage, I have purchased permission to reside for the rest of my days unknown and unseen in a large forest near Minsk. Here, within the gray crumbling walls of a castle that fell with the independence of this unhappy country, I await my end. I have left little to regret at my native Moscow; neither friends, nor reputation, nor lawful life; and I had failed in a love which was dearer to me than reputation—than life—than gravity itself. I have established an apparatus on improved principles to operate on gravity; and I am now employed, day and night, for the benefit, not more of the present generation than of all mankind that are to come. In fact, I am laboriously and unceasingly extracting the gravitation from the earth in order to bring it nearer the sun; and though by thus diminishing the earth's orbit, I fear I shall confuse the astronomical tables and calculations, I am confident I shall improve the temperature of the globe. How far I have succeeded may be guessed from the recent errors in the almanacs about the eclipses, and from the late mild winters.

THE SCHOOLMISTRESS.

[William Shenstone, born at the Leasowes, Hales
Owen, Shropshire, 1714; died there, 1763. His rural
tastes rendered the gardens of the Leasowes even more
famous than the proprietor's poetry. His poems chiefly
relate to ideal shepherds, and are marked by many
affectations; but *The Schoolmistress*, from which we
quote, will preserve his memory by its simple fidelity
to nature. Goldsmith said of it: "This poem is one of
those happinesses in which a poet excels himself, as
there is nothing in all Shenstone which anyway approaches it in merit."]

IN IMITATION OF SPENSER.

Ah me! full sorely is my heart forlorn,
To think how modest worth neglected lies,
While partial Fame doth with her blasts adorn
Such deeds alone as pride and pomp disguise,
Deeds of ill sort, and mischievous emprise :
Lend me thy clarion, goddess! let me try
To sound the praise of Merit ere it dies,
Such as I oft have chaunced to espy
Lost in the dreary shades of dull obscurity.

In ev'ry village mark'd with little spire,
Embow'red in trees, and hardly known to fame,
There dwells, in lowly shade and mean attire,
A matron old, whom we Schoolmistress name,
Who boasts unruly brats with birch to tame ;
They grieven sore, in piteous durance pent,
Aw'd by the pow'r of this relentless dame,
And oft-times, on vagaries idly bent,
For unkempt hair, or task unconn'd, are sorely shent.

And all in sight doth rise a birchen tree,
Which Learning near her little dome did stowe,
Whilom a twig of small regard to see,
Tho' now so wide its waving branches flow,
And work the simple vassals mickle woe ;
For not a wind might curl the leaves that blew,
But their limbs shuddered, and their pulse beat low,
And as they look'd they found their horror grew,
And shap'd it into rods, and tingled at the view.

Near to this dome is found a patch so green,
On which the tribe their gambols do display,
And at the door impris'ning board is seen,
Lest weakly wights of smaller size should stray,
Eager, perdie, to bask in sunny day !
The noises intermix'd which thence resound,
Do Learning's little tenements betray,
Where sits the dame, disguis'd in look profound,
And eyes her fairy throng, and turns her wheel around.

Her cap, far whiter than the driven snowe,
Emblem right meet of decency does yield ;
Her apron dy'd in grain, as blue, I trowe,
As is the harebell that adorns the field ;
And in her hand, for sceptre, she does wield

Tway birchen sprays, with anxious fear entwin'd,
With dark distrust, and sad repentance fill'd,
And stedfast hate, and sharp affliction join'd,
And fury uncontroll'd, and chastisement unkind.

A russet stole was o'er her shoulders thrown,
A russet kirtle fenc'd the nipping air ;
'Twas simple russet, but it was her own :
'Twas her own country bred the flock so fair ;
'Twas her own labour did the fleece prepare,
And, sooth to say, her pupils, rang'd around,
Thro' pious awe did term it passing rare,
For they in gaping wonderment abound,
And think no doubt, she been the greatest wight on
    ground.

Albeit no flatt'ry did corrupt her truth,
Ne pompous title did debauch her ear,
Goody, good woman, gossip, n'aunt, forsooth,
Or dame, the sole additions she did hear ;
Yet these she challeng'd, these she held right dear :
Ne would esteem him act as mought behove
Who should not honour'd eld with these revere ;
For never title yet so mean could prove,
But there was eke a mind which did that title love.

One ancient hen she took delight to feed,
The plodding pattern of the busy dame.
Which ever and anon, impell'd by need,
Into her school, begirt with chickens, came,
Such favour did her past deportment claim ;
And if neglect had lavish'd on the ground
Fragment of bread, she would collect the same :
For well she knew, and quaintly could expound,
What sin it were to waste the smallest crumb she found.

Herbs too she knew, and well of each could speak,
That in her garden sipp'd the silv'ry dew,
Where no vain flow'r disclos'd a gaudy streak,
But herbs for use, and physic, not a few,
Of gray renown, within those borders grew ;
The tufted basil, pun-provoking thyme,
Fresh baum, and marygold of cheerful hue,
The lowly gill, that never dares to climb,
And more I fain would sing, disdaining here to rhyme.

Yet euphrasy may not be left unsung,
That gives dim eyes to wander leagues around,
And pungent radish biting infant's tongue,
And plantain ribb'd, that heals the reaper's wound,
And marj'ram sweet, in shepherd's posie found,
And lavender, whose spikes of azure bloom
Shall be, erewhile, in arid bundles bound,
To lurk amidst the labours of her loom,
And crown her kerchiefs clean with mickle rare per-
    fume.

And here trim rosemarine, that whilom crown'd
The daintiest garden of the proudest peer,
Ere, driv'n from its envy'd site, it found
A sacred shelter for its branches here,
Where edg'd with gold its glitt'ring skirts appear.

f

O wassel days! O customs meet and well!
Ere this was banish'd from its lofty sphere;
Simplicity then sought this humble cell,
Nor ever would she more with thane and lordling dwell.

Here oft the dame, on Sabbath's decent eve,
Hymned such psalms as Sternhold forth did mete;
If winter 'twere, she to her hearth did cleave,
But in her garden found a summer-seat:
Sweet melody! to hear her then repeat
How Israel's sons, beneath a foreign king,
While taunting foemen did a song entreat,
All for the nonce untuning ev'ry string,
Uphung their useless lyres—small heart had they to
sing.

For she was just, and friend to virtuous lore,
And pass'd much time in truly virtuous deed;
And in those elphins' ears would oft deplore
The times when Truth by Popish rage did bleed,
And tortious death was true Devotion's meed;
And simple Faith in iron chains did mourn,
That nould on wooden image place her creed;
And lawny saints in smould'ring flames did burn:
Ah! dearest Lord! forfend thilk days should ere return.

In elbow-chair, like that of Scottish stem,
By the sharp tooth of cank'ring Eld defac'd,
In which, when he receives his diadem,
Our sov'reign prince and liefest liege is plac'd,
The matron sate, and some with rank she grac'd,
(The source of children's and of courtiers' pride!)
Redress'd affronts, for vile affronts there pass'd,
And warn'd them not the fretful to deride,
But love each other dear, whatever them betide.

Right well she knew each temper to descry,
To thwart the proud, and the submiss to raise,
Some with vile copper prize exalt on high,
And some entice with pittance small of praise,
And other some with baleful sprig she 'frays:
Ev'n absent, she the reins of pow'r doth hold,
While with quaint arts the giddy crowd she sways;
Forewarn'd, if little bird their pranks behold,
'Twill whisper in her ear, and all the scene unfold.

. . . .

Yet nurs'd with skill, what dazzling fruits appear!
Ev'n now sagacious foresight points to show
A little bench of heedless bishops here,
And there a chancellour in embryo,
Or bard sublime, if bard may e'er be so,
As Milton, Shakespeare, names that ne'er shall die!
Tho' now he crawl along the ground so low,
Nor weeting how the Muse should soar on high,
Wisheth, poor starv'ling elf! his paper kite may fly.

But now Dan Phœbus gains the middle sky,
And Liberty unbars her prison-door,
And like a rushing torrent out they fly,
And now the grassy cirque has cover'd o'er
With boist'rous revel rout and wild uproar;

A thousand ways in wanton rings they run,
Heav'n shield their short-liv'd pastimes, I implore!
For well may Freedom, erst so dearly won,
Appear to British elf more gladsome than the sun.

Enjoy, poor imps! enjoy your sportive trade,
And chase gay flies, and cull the fairest flow'rs,
For when my bones in grass-green sods are laid,
For never may ye taste more careless hours
In knightly castles or in ladies' bow'rs.
O vain to seek delight in earthly thing!
But most in courts, where proud Ambition tow'rs;
Deluded wight! who weens fair peace can spring
Beneath the pompous dome of kesar or of king.

AN ITALIAN LOVE-STORY.

BY SCIPIONE BARGAGLI.

Among other families, gentle ladies, that in times gone by are known to have ornamented our native city, one of the most noble, perhaps, was the Saracini; a house which still preserves unsullied its ancient worth and splendour. In the long list of names that constituted its different branches, we find mention of one Ippolito, the sole surviving heir of a distinguished cavalier. At the period we are about to refer to, he numbered no more than eighteen years, was extremely graceful and handsome in his person, of elevated mind and intellect, and much esteemed by his friends and fellow-citizens for the vivacity and courtesy of his manners. Now it fell out, as is most frequently the case with youths of a fine temperament, that he became deeply enamoured of one of the most beautiful and attractive girls in all the city, whose surpassing charms and accomplishments were celebrated wherever she had been seen. Her name was Gangenova, the youngest of three daughters left to the care of a widowed mother, the relict of Messer Reame Salimbeni, whose family ranked among the first in Sienna, for numerous services rendered to the republic in periods of the greatest peril, though now, along with its arms and palaces, become altogether extinct; nothing of its past grandeur remaining but the name. The delight of all her relations, as well as of the society in which she moved, it was no wonder then that the fair Gangenova should so far have enthralled the soul of young Ippolito, that, by frequent contemplation of her beauties and accomplishments, he resolved to run all hazards in order to win her love. Nor had he, in the few opportunities permitted him of conversing with her, any reason for despair, since he rightly interpreted the tones and looks with which she occasionally addressed him. But in consequence of the very strict superintendence of her mother, which was exercised with greater severity over Gangenova than over her elder sisters, the interviews of the lovers were very rare; a system of intolerance so little in accordance with the open and ardent character of Ippolito, that, despising the very particular forms and ceremonies which it exacted, he was apt to grow impatient for the enjoyment of a more unconstrained society with the object he adored. With this view he made known his wishes to the young lady's mother, leaving the terms of their future union, in the most liberal manner, wholly to her, and beseeching her only to grant him a little more of the society of her he loved. What was his surprise to receive a direct refusal, on the ground that it was the lady's duty, as a mother, to attend first to the disposal of her two elder sisters! an answer that threw the young lover into a paroxysm of mingled rage and despair.

The grief of Gangenova was little less than his own, and her affection, gathering strength by opposition, was indulged with double freedom upon receiving the sanction of such an offer. Aware at the same time that her lover's conduct, in attempting to obtain an interview, added only to the jealous caution of her mother, she was at a loss in what way to proceed, being so closely watched as scarcely to be allowed to breathe the air, much less to partake of the innocent sports and amusements to which young persons of her age are attached. It was impossible, however, to preserve so strict a watch as to deprive them of all kind of mutual intelligence; and Ippolito became acquainted with her unhappy situation. She even entreated of him, in pity to her, that he would discontinue his assiduous attentions, and either absent himself, or feign absence, during a short period, from the city, as she grew fearful of the extremities to which her friends in their anger might proceed. At the same time, she besought him to consider this as a proof of regard, not of coldness or indifference, as she would ever endeavour to show herself grateful, and worthy of the high opinion that he had so kindly and nobly avowed for her.

These tidings served at once to increase the passion that Ippolito already entertained, and the unhappiness he felt in being the unwilling cause of the least portion of suffering to her he loved, when he felt as if he could gladly have sacrificed his life to her happiness and repose. Still he exulted in the idea that she returned his affection, and he tried to flatter himself with the prospect of brighter days to come.

And in order to convince her of the purity and disinterestedness of his attachment, he resolved, however difficult the task, to obey her wishes, and to leave for a while his native place, giving out that he was gone upon a pilgrimage to the shrine of San Jacomo of Galicia. He was moreover desirous of thus proving the sincerity of the affection of her he loved, and of ascertaining whether her regard was likely to increase or diminish by distance; and with this view, having arranged his affairs, and bid adieu to all his friends, as if on the eve of a long voyage, he assumed his pilgrim's dress, and, to the surprise and grief of all his acquaintance, left the city. When the unhappy maiden heard of his departure, she shed many tears, regretting that she had ever proposed so harsh and trying an alternative, and upbraided herself as the sole cause of every sinister event that might chance to follow, never having imagined it possible that he would venture upon so painful and hazardous a journey. And in this she reasoned well, for when Ippolito had pursued his way until about sunset, he abandoned the great road, and, striking into one of the thickest woods near at hand, he there deposited his pilgrim's mantle, cowl, and staff; then retracing his steps in another dress, he entered, about the hour when the gates were closed, without observation, into Sienna. Proceeding direct to the abode of an old nurse, the only person whom he had admitted into his secret counsel, he there provided himself with everything requisite for his purpose.

Now near the church of San Lorenzo, was a little country seat, with a small orchard attached, belonging to Ippolito; both of which he had presented to his aged nurse, who, on her side, had always felt the same affection for him as for an only child. Next to this little tenement lay a spacious and beautiful garden, the property of the mother of the fair Gangenova, Ippolito's beloved mistress; and here with her daughters she was often accustomed to take the air, and enjoy the fragrance of the new-blown flowers. "Surely," thought the gentle and enamoured boy, "here at least we shall hardly be suspected; nobody will believe me bold enough to seek her under her mother's very wing; let us only find an opportunity of conversing with each other, and I cannot fail to discover some means of bringing our difficulties to a happy termination." And solely for this object did he keep himself concealed, like a bird that shuns the eye of day, within the bounds of his little cottage ground; never venturing forth except late in the evening, when, scaling a lofty wall, he descended into the garden of his beloved Gangenova, and approached close under her chamber windows. Up the side of these there chanced to flourish a lofty and lovely mulberry-tree, one of whose spacious branches overshadowed the apartment in which she lay, and where her mother kept her, as being the youngest of her charges, constant company by night. Under its shade, likewise, Ippolito was wont to take his evening station, eager to avail himself of any opportunity of beholding or discovering himself to the object of his attachment. In this way he was soon convinced that the sole chance he had of profiting by his situation was about the hour of sunrise, when he observed the fair girl appear on the balcony overlooking the garden, on which were placed a number of beautiful plants, interspersed with lilies and violets, from which she would cull some of the sweetest to deck her lovely breast and hair. There too he observed her amuse herself with a pretty linnet which had nested itself in the noble tree, and which, won by her sweet encouragement, would hop into the window and nestle in her bosom ; and it was then his delight to watch her thousand gentle looks and motions, and to imagine how delicious it would be to appropriate to himself the whole of those kisses and caresses. Often had he been on the point of accosting her, however great the risk, when her mother, her sisters, or some one in attendance, suddenly appearing, would dash all his hopes, and compel him to be doubly cautious, lest a discovery should be the cause of fresh restraints over his beloved. He next resolved to avail himself of the assistance of his kind old nurse, who, under a variety of pretences, obtained admission into the mother's house, of which she took advantage to gain the ear of the young lady, and inform her of all that her lover had done for her sake ; of his passionate attachment and devotion, so well worthy a return, and his extreme desire of beholding her once more. Finding her equally delighted and surprised with what she had already heard, the nurse ventured to reveal to Gangenova the place of her Ippolito's concealment; and the pleasure she experienced on finding that he was so near became almost too much for her to support. "Has he not, indeed, deserted me then? is he not really journeying far away, over seas, and in a foreign land, on my account? Oh, dear nurse, tell him that his image is engraven on my soul; that I am too blessed, too happy, and never more would give him reason to complain!" Upon hearing these words, the good old dame, thinking that she had happily succeeded in her mission, returned as fast as

she could, in order not to forget the least portion of the message, which she well knew would carry such joy to the soul of the young lover.

Ippolito preserved the utmost caution in his proceedings, and it was not long before fortune seemed to favour his wishes ; for keeping watch one evening very assiduously, he saw the arrival of a messenger, bearing tidings that the wife of one of the old lady's brothers was taken suddenly ill, and entreated to see the mother of Gangenova without a moment's delay. She was thus compelled to set out, and leave her precious charge, for one night at least, to her own discretion ; and Ippolito believed that he had at length an opportunity of convincing himself of the reality of his beloved girl's affection for him, by inducing her to embrace the long-wished occasion, and to secure their happiness by flying together, and uniting their fate in one. Fired with the hope, he hastened to his usual station, underneath the mulberry-tree that overspread her chamber windows; and in order better to attract her attention, he shook some of its boughs, imagining that her beloved bird, if nestling there, would fly to her, and by its little cries and flutterings, lead her to appear on the balcony. Not succeeding, however, in this, he hastily ascended the tree, when soon the affrighted bird, flying with timid cries into some neighbouring shrubs, uttered such loud and sorrowful tones as to startle the gentle girl out of her slumber, who fearing some sad accident had befallen it, hastily ran to the window. With a simple veil thrown over her neck and bosom, and her fine bright tresses carelessly yet gracefully arranged, she appeared in the eyes of her enchanted lover rather like a vision than a creature of mortal beauty, while a mingled look of anxiety and tenderness was impressed upon her countenance. Solicitous for the fate of her little companion, she cast her eyes eagerly on all sides, when, instead of her pretty linnet, the accents of Ippolito, eager to dissipate her alarm, met her ears. The next moment she beheld him nearly at her side, and he succeeded almost in reaching her chamber window, while he attempted to prevent her crying out by addressing her in the lowest and sweetest tone: "Fear not, my gentle Gangenova; it is your Ippolito who speaks ; fear not, either for yourself or your little favourite, for soon he will resume his blithesome notes, secure and happy as before. But mine, alas, how different a fate! though far more fond, a thousand times more passionately devoted to you, serving you so long and faithfully. Had you the heart then, my sweetest, to think I was now taking my woful pilgrimage far from thee, through remote and strange parts; perhaps gone upon my everlasting journey? Oh, no, no, I knew you had not, and I have been near you day and night, ever since the period when I left my friends to go upon my feigned pilgrimage. For, alas, when I cannot turn my thoughts from you for a moment, how could I wilfully bend my steps another way? how could I find a moment's repose till I had laid my wearied limbs and my burdened heart as near you as I could possibly venture, without quite breaking upon your hallowed rest? Hath not our poor nurse told you all I have done and suffered for your sake; my lonely days, and sorrowing, yet delicious nights, passed amidst the scenes you have loved, among the very trees, and fruits, and flowers where you have wandered? nay, in these lofty and verdant branches, that so richly and beauteously overshadow the sanctuary of my love? Often have I seen you, at the glimpse of dawn, gathering flowers, or caressing your bird; yet venturing not to intrude, afraid of calling down still further anger from your jealous guardians upon your innocent head. But my fond and unceasing vows have wearied Heaven at last: your mother is gone, and the hour arrived that is to repay us for a world of anxiety and dread; the fear of losing thee, and all that promised to make life sweet to me. Yet our time is precious, and I came to gather from thine own lips that thou dost indeed honour me with thy love; that thou wilt deign to receive my plighted vows and loyalty unto death. And this I would entreat in the name of all my anguish, all my fears for thee; by the horror of a rival's arms; and by thine own surpassing beauties, that amidst all our city's charms, have alone succeeded in rivetting my enchanted sight. Yet I know how all unworthy I am; how much better and longer thou deservest to be sought ere won. Still thou knowest my whole life and bearing, though thou canst not form an idea of the sighs and tears I have poured for thee. Pity me then; and with pity let love and reason, let all the heavenly gifts you possess, plead in my favour, and induce you to receive me as your favoured and honoured lord."

Here he ceased, waiting with eager and trembling looks for a reply: while the beautiful Gangenova, overpowered on her side by a thousand wild and sweet emotions, was almost unable to articulate a word. Having descended into the balcony, on her sudden alarm, to recover her favourite bird, she had attempted, on first hearing Ippolito's voice, to fly; yet

surprise and terror chained her to the spot; for, having read the fabled metamorphoses of plants into mortals, and human beings into plants, on hearing a voice from the mulberry-tree her blood began to run cold, and her attempt to call out died away ere it passed her lips. Yet there was something in the tone that convinced her she need not fear, and gradually recovering her confidence, her heart seemed actually to swim in a tide of rapture, before her noble lover had concluded his passionate appeal. "Dear Ippolito," she at length replied, "it grieves me that we are so situated that it would be dangerous to tell all I have thought and felt since last we met and parted, much less the delight I have at finding you safe and near me once more. But, alas! this is no place for you; speed away, I beseech you, and think me neither hasty nor unkind, as indeed, I esteem all your love and goodness to me as tenderly as I ought. But I fear for you, my kind Ippolito, and I entreat you to bid me one adieu, and let me see you safely depart." At this moment hearing a noise in the antechamber, and fearful lest her sisters should approach, Gangenova hastily drew back, while Ippolito, imagining that it proceeded from her room, and hearing a rustling noise continue for some time, was seized with sudden suspicions of some rival being harboured there, either by her sisters or the fair Gangenova herself. Maddened by this idea he no longer remained master of himself, and in his attempt to reach her window from the tree, so as to obtain a view of what was passing, such was the hurry of his spirits, that, missing his footing, he fell to the ground.

Startled at the terrific sound, the fair girl again rushed forward, bending as far as possible over the balcony, and calling on the name of Ippolito in a subdued and gentle tone: but no longer did the sound reach his enraptured ear, where he lay deprived of sense upon the cold earth. Suspense and terror seized upon the heart of the tender girl when she received no answer; love urged her to afford him her immediate assistance, while fear of discovery restrained her steps. Unable, however, longer to control her fears for his safety, she hastily descended into the garden by a back staircase rarely made use of, having remained from ancient times as a retreat in seasons of trouble, and having its outlet at the extreme part of the garden. And there, alas! she found him stretched under the mulberry-tree, lying cold and pallid, apparently deprived not only of sense but of life itself.

Almost as insensible as he, she threw herself

at his side. Upon recovering her consciousness, showers of tears expressed the intensity
of her sufferings; her cries would have moved
rocks and beasts of prey to pity, such were the
piteous tones in which these words were uttered:
"Sweet heavens, what dreadful thing hath
happened! What malignant star hath struck
with death one of the best and noblest hearts
that ever beat! O where is the soul that but
now shone in thy face? Wretch that I am,
shall I never behold it more! Art thou fled,
for ever fled, sweet guardian of my honour, my
love, and peace! But what will betide them
now, when every tongue will be busy with my
fame? Whither shall I turn for help, reduced
to such sad extremities as I now am?" And
while, abandoned to her woe, the hapless girl
thus poured her lamentations to the night, she
never ceased her endeavours to restore the object of them by every means in her power,
rubbing his heart and temples, joining his
hands and lips to her own, and trying to
breathe her soul into his. Finding that he
yet gave no signs of life, she sweetly folded
him in her arms, and bathed his inanimate
features with her tears. Ippolito's soul, just
on the point of taking wing, seemed to welcome
so much bliss; and suddenly recovering his
suspended powers, he heard the sweet words
she uttered, and found himself alive in her
arms. It was then he felt himself amply repaid for all the trials he had undergone; the
sweetness and ecstasy of the reward far surpassing all he had been able to conceive, in
breathing his vows thus closely into her ear.
The moment before she was about to transfix
her breast with her lover's sword in a paroxysm
of despair; the next she found herself pressed
to his breathing bosom, receiving, as it were,
the gift of two lives restored to her at once.
For some time they both remained doubtful
whether to believe that all was real, and gazed
upon each other as if in a dream, until the
fresh spirit of their joy being somewhat abated,
they sat down by each other, side by side,
with that serene and ineffable pleasure which
the imagined certainty of their bliss inspired.
But it was destined, alas, to be of short duration; a voice was heard calling upon the name
of Gangenova, gradually approaching nearer
and nearer, so that they were compelled to
part almost without bidding each other adieu.
The poor girl hastened trembling by the same
path that she had left the house: she fancied,
in the disorder of her spirits, that she suddenly
heard the terrific howlings of wild beasts, accompanied by the most dismal screams and
cries; and such was the impression they made

upon her imagination, just after having taken
leave of Ippolito, as to deprive her of the power
of motion. It was long before she recovered
even strength enough to regain her apartment,
and with panting breast and dishevelled hair,
she threw herself upon the couch, still unable
to banish the terrific ideas that haunted her
imagination.

In the meanwhile the sisters of Gangenova,
being likewise freed from the superintendence
of their mother, had been innocently enjoying
themselves in their chamber, frequently calling
the fair girl by her name to come and join in
their diversion. Paying little heed to their
silence, they continued for some time to amuse
themselves with their games, until one of them,
by way of adding a little novelty to the scene,
crept forward in the dark, intending to surprise
her in her own room. Still receiving no reply,
she ran for a light, and on returning found her
sister stretched upon the bed, resembling rather
a lifeless statue than a breathing human form.
Calling her second sister in great alarm, they
made eager inquiries into the cause of her agitation, feeling assured that something extraordinary must have happened. The poor girl
was equally unwilling and unable to reply, and
her sisters, in some anxiety, despatched a
messenger for their mother, who lost no time
in returning to resume her maternal charge.
With a little more authority, she insisted upon
knowing the cause of her alarm, and upbraided
her sisters severely for not keeping a more
vigilant watch. Gangenova declared herself
quite unable to account for the manner in
which she had been affected, and the others
professed equal ignorance as to the cause of her
indisposition. In this dilemma her mother
had recourse to the advice of the most expert
physicians the city had to boast, which brought
no alleviation however to her daughter's alarming symptoms; not one of them being able to
discover that her illness was owing to some
sudden surprise, while she, far more jealous of
her fair fame than of her life, concealed from
every one the real cause of her sufferings.
Growing rapidly worse, she became extremely
anxious to behold once more her beloved Ippolito; and recollecting the old nurse, she instantly sent for her, entreating that she would,
as soon as possible, acquaint him with her
situation, and find some means by which they
might at least meet to take an eternal farewell.

Upon receiving these sad tidings Ippolito
grew deadly pale and trembled, though at the
same moment he hastened to comply with her
wishes. He assumed the dress of a poor

traveller, with a false beard, so as to render it almost impossible to recognize him, and set out to beg alms at several houses adjacent to that of his beloved. As he approached the latter, the lady of the mansion herself made her appearance, half wild and distracted at the situation of her loveliest daughter. Informed of the occasion of her grief, the wily pilgrim, availing himself of the circumstance, bade her not despair, as the power of the Lord was infinite, and his goodness equal to his power. Moreover, with his aid, he had himself become skilled in all the virtues of almost all the plants under the sun, and had devoted his knowledge of herbs and juices to the relief of his unhappy fellow-creatures, besides possessing secrets adapted to every species of disease. The poor credulous old lady raised her hands to heaven in gratitude upon hearing such consolatory words, vowed that he had been peculiarly sent by Providence, and insisted that he should be instantly introduced to her unhappy girl.

The moment Ippolito beheld her he perceived that the tidings he had received were indeed too true. So much was he shocked, that he could with difficulty support his character; more particularly when he saw, from the brightening features of his beloved, that she instantly recognized him. Taking, then, the hand of the suffering girl within his own, as if to feel how fast her life-blood ebbed, he begged her attendants to stand apart, while he proceeded to try his secret prayers and charms in his own way. Ippolito was thus enabled to learn the real source of her illness from her own lips. Beholding him with a mixture of tenderness and pity, that added momentary lustre to her dying charms, she attempted, in those low soft tones he so much loved, to infuse balm into his wounded spirit. Painfully sensible of the extent of his loss, Ippolito from very grief was unable to utter a word, much less to ask the needful questions of his beloved. Wildly pressing his hand, she besought him never to forget the tender love he had borne her, and which she had seldom been happy enough to tell him how warmly and deeply she returned. "For joyful, oh, very joyful, my Ippolito," she continued, "would my departure have been to me before now, had not solicitude for your fate detained me. As it is, I die content, nay grateful, for two unexpected benefits: the one to have seen you thus, to hear you, and to feel your hand in mine; and the other, to know that I lived, and that I died, beloved by my most noble and faithful-hearted Ippolito!"

It was now that the latter attempted to console and encourage her, declaring it would be his only pride to fulfil her wishes in the minutest point; but here his voice failing him, through his fast-coming tears and sobs, he laid his aching head down by the side of his beloved's, and there remaining for a short time, as he breathed forth a soul-distracting adieu; he raised it again painfully, passed his hand over his eyes, and looking his last look, left the apartment. He then joined her weeping mother, and so far from holding out any hope, he said that pity for the sad and dying state in which he had found the poor patient had drawn scalding tears from his eyes. And he had not long been gone, before the gentle spirit of his love, as if unable to continue longer without him, prepared to take wing, and in a few hours actually fled, as if to prepare in some happier scene a mansion of rest for their divided loves. For the wretched Ippolito, though able to bear up long enough to behold the beloved one consigned to earth, had no sooner witnessed all the virtues and charms he had so fondly esteemed and loved for ever entombed in the vault of the Salimbeni, than just as the ceremony was about to close, he fell dead at the foot of her marble monument. So strange and sudden an event threw the surrounding company, by whom it was regarded as little less than a miracle, into the utmost surprise and confusion, all of them believing that Ippolito Saracini was then on his way to the shrine of San Giacomo of Galicia. His unhappy parents hearing of this his untimely end, hastened to join their tears with those of the mother of the beauteous Gangenova, by whose side the faithful Ippolito was laid.

CHANGE.

Youth's fairy-land recedes, and year by year
   Less brightly do sweet memories to the soul
Come o'er the widening interval so drear,
   Like gales o'er parched desert The control
Of after customs in life's pilgrimage
   Takes from us, with the relish, the regret
For what we deem'd we never should forget
To love :—Then strangely in extremest age
   The early past appears, and all between
Fades traceless from remembrance.—It is not
As some might deem, a mockery in our lot
   That thus we change, just e'er death close the scene.
Oh, no! 'tis foretaste of the coming heav'n,
Where more than youthful joy will unto man be giv'n

Thomas Brydson.

LAMENT FOR THE DECLINE OF CHIVALRY.

[Thomas Hood, born in London, 1798; died 3d May, 1845. Humourist and novelist. He began the business of life as clerk in a counting-house; then proceeded to learn the art of engraving under his uncle, Robert Sands; and finally he adopted the profession of letters. Frequent ill-health marred his prospects, although his works rapidly obtained the popularity which they still possess. A pension of £100 a year was offered to him by government when too late to be of service to him personally; but at his request it was continued to his wife. He was sometime editor of the *London Magazine*, the *New Monthly Magazine*, and for one year of the *Gem*, an annual in which first appeared *The Dream of Eugene Aram*. To *Punch*, amongst other valuable contributions, he gave *The Song of the Shirt*. His chief works are: *Odes and Addresses to Great People; Whims and Oddities; Hood's Own; Hood's Comic Miscellany; Up the Rhine; Tylney Hall*, a novel; *Our Family*, a novel, not completed, &c. "Hood's verse, whether serious or comic, was ever pregnant with materials for thought. Well may we say, in the words of Tennyson, 'Would he could have stayed with us!' for never could it be more truly recorded of any one that, 'he was a fellow of infinite jest, of most excellent fancy.'"—D. M. Moir.]

Well hast thou cried, departed Burke,
All chivalrous romantic work
　　Is ended now and past!—
That iron age—which some have thought
Of mettle rather overwrought—
　　Is now all over-cast!

Ay—where are those heroic knights
Of old—those armadillo wights
　　Who wore the plated vest,—
Great Charlemagne and all his peers
Are cold—enjoying with their spears
　　An everlasting rest!

The bold king Arthur sleepeth sound,
So sleep his knights who gave that Round
　　Old Table such eclat!
Oh, Time has pluck'd the plumy brow!
And none engage at Turneys now
　　But those that go to law!

Grim John o' Gaunt is quite gone by,
And Guy is nothing but a Guy,
　　Orlando lies forlorn!—
Bold Sidney, and his kidney—nay,
Those "early champions"—what are they
　　But "knights without a morn."

No Percy branch now perseveres
Like those of old in breaking spears—
　　The name is now a lie!—
Surgeons, alone, by any chance,
Are all that ever couch a lance
　　To couch a body's eye!

Alas for Lion-Hearted Dick!
That cut the Moslems to the quick,
　　His weapon lies in peace:
Oh, it would warm them in a trice,
If they could only have a spice
　　Of his old mace in Greece!

The famed Rinaldo lies a-cold,
And Tancred too, and Godfrey bold,
　　That scaled the holy wall!
No Saracen meets Paladin,
We hear of no great *Suladin*,
　　But only grow the small!

Our *Cressys* too have dwindled since
To penny things—at our Black Prince
　　Historic pens would scoff:
The only one we moderns had,
Was nothing but a Sandwich lad,
　　And measles took him off!

Where are those old and feudal clans,
Their pikes, and bills, and partizans;
　　Their hauberks—jerkins—buffs?
A battle was a battle then,
A breathing piece of work; but men
　　Fight now—with powder puffs!

The curtal-axe is out of date!
The good old cross-bow bends—to Fate,
　　'Tis gone—the archer's craft!
No tough arm bends the springing yew,
And jolly draymen ride, in lieu
　　Of death, upon the shaft!

The spear—the gallant tilter's pride,
The rusty spear, is laid aside,
　　Oh, spits now domineer!
The coat of mail is left alone,—
And where is all chain armour gone?
　　Go ask at Brighton Pier.

We fight in ropes, and not in lists,
Bestowing hand-cuffs with our fists,
　　A low and vulgar art!
No mounted man is overthrown!
A tilt! It is a thing unknown—
　　Except upon a cart!

Methinks I see the bounding barb,
Clad like his chief in steely garb,
　　For warding steel's appliance!
Methinks I hear the trumpet stir!
'Tis but the guard to Exeter,
　　That bugles the "Defiance."

In cavils when will cavaliers
Set ringing helmets by the ears,
　　And scatter plumes about?
Or blood - if they are in the vein?
That tap will never run again—
　　Alas, the *Casque* is out!

No iron crackling now is scored
By dint of battle-axe or sword,
To find a vital place—
Though certain doctors still pretend,
A while, before they kill a friend,
To labour through his case!

Farewell, then, ancient men of might!
Crusader, errant-squire, and knight!
Our coats and custom soften,—
To rise would only make you weep—
Sleep on, in rusty-iron sleep,
As in a safety-coffin!

ORATORY.

[Henry, Lord Brougham, born at Edinburgh, 19th September, 1778; died at Cannes, 7th May, 1868. He was one of the founders of the *Edinburgh Review* (1802); he distinguished himself at the bar—notably as the advocate of Queen Caroline; he won high repute in parliament; he became lord-chancellor in 1830; and he rendered important service to the cause of education by his share in the organization of mechanics' institutes, and in establishing the Society for the Diffusion of Useful Knowledge. He wrote upon almost every subject, and wrote well. His *Works, Critical, Historical, Philosophical, Scientific, and Rhetorical*, have been published in ten volumes; and his *Contributions to the Edinburgh Review* have been issued in three volumes by Griffin & Co. The following extract is from his review of the works of Demosthenes, of which the French critic M. Villemain declared him to be "the best of modern interpreters." Brougham also wrote a novel, *Arthur Lunel*, which was not published until five years after his death.[1]]

We must be permitted to dwell yet a little upon a topic, in itself truly inexhaustible—the prodigious merit of the immortal original (works of Demosthenes). And we pursue this course the rather in these times, when a corrupt or a careless eloquence so greatly abounds, that there are but few public speakers who give any attention to their art, excepting those who debase it by the ornaments of a most vicious taste. Not, indeed, that the two defects are often kept apart; for some men appear to bestow but little pains upon the preparation of the vilest composition that ever offended a classical ear, although it displays an endless variety of far-fetched thoughts, forced metaphors, unnatural expressions, and violent perversions of ordinary language;—in a word, it

[1] A feeble denial of the authorship was raised in some quarters; but there appears to be little doubt that Brougham wrote the novel, although he kept it in manuscript whilst he lived.

is worthless without the poor merit of being elaborate; and affords a new instance how wide a departure may be made from nature with very little care, and how apt easy writing is to prove hard reading.

Among the sources of this corruption may clearly be distinguished as the most fruitful, the habit of extempore speaking, acquired rapidly by persons who frequent popular assemblies, and, beginning at the wrong end, attempt to speak before they have studied the art of oratory, or even duly stored their minds with the treasures of thought and of language, which can only be drawn from assiduous intercourse with the ancient and modern classics. The truth is, that a certain proficiency in public speaking may be attained with nearly infallible certainty by any person who chooses to give himself the trouble of frequently trying it, and can harden himself against the pain of frequent failures. Complete self-possession and perfect fluency are thus acquired, almost mechanically, and with little or no reference to the talents of him who becomes possessed of them. If he is a man of no capacity, his speeches will of course be very bad; but though he be a man of genius, they will not be eloquent. A sensible remark or a fine image may frequently occur; but the loose and slovenly and poor diction, the want of art in combining and disposing his ideas, the inability to bring out many of his thoughts, and the utter incompetency to present any of them in the best and most efficient form, will deprive such a speaker of all claims to the character of an orator, and reduce him to the level of an ordinary talker. The same man, had he never spoken in public, would have possessed the same powers of convincing or expounding, provided he were only called upon to exert them in conversation with one or two persons. Perhaps the habit of speaking may have taught him something of arrangement, and a few of the simplest methods of producing an impression; but beyond these first steps he cannot possibly proceed by this empirical process: and his diction is sure to be much worse than if he had never made the attempt—clumsy, redundant, incorrect, unlimited in quantity, but of no value. Such a speaker is never in want of a word, and hardly ever has one that is worth having.

It is a very common error to call this natural eloquence: it is the reverse; it is neither natural nor eloquence. A person under the influence of strong passions or feelings, and pouring forth all that fills his mind, produces a powerful effect on his hearers, and frequently attains, without any art, the highest beauties of rhetoric.

The language of the passions flow easily: but it is concise and simple, and the opposite of that wordiness which we have been describing. The untaught speaker, who is also unpractised, and utters according to the dictates of his feelings, now and then succeeds perfectly; but, in those instances, he would not be the less successful for having studied the art; while that study would enable him to succeed equally in all that he delivers, and give him the same control over the feelings of others, whatever might be the state of his own. Herein, indeed, consists the value of the study; it enables a man to do at all times what nature only teaches upon rare occasions.

Now, we cannot imagine any better corrective to the faults of which we are complaining in the eloquence of modern times, than the habitual contemplation of those exquisite models which the ancients have left us; and especially the more chaste beauties of Greek composition. Its perfect success, both in moving the audience to whom it was addressed, and the readers in all ages who studied it, cannot be denied; its superiority to all that has ever been produced in other countries is confessed. There may be some use, therefore, in observing how certainly it was the result of intense labour—labour previously bestowed to acquire the power, and the utmost care used in almost every exercise of that power. Without somewhat both of this discipline and this sedulous attention, it would be as vain to think of emulating those divine originals, by dint of a habit of fluent speech attained through much careless practice, as to attempt painting like Raphael without having learned to draw, and by the help of some mechanical contrivance.

The extreme pains which the most illustrious of the Greeks bestowed upon their compositions, are evinced by all the accounts transmitted to us of the course of education deemed requisite to form an orator, and by the well-known anecdotes of the steps by which both Demosthenes, and, after his example, Cicero and some of his contemporaries, trained themselves to rhetorical habits. . . .

But let us come to Demosthenes himself. His extreme care in composing his orations is as well known as the sedulous discipline which he underwent to learn the art; and, notwithstanding the facility which he must have acquired, both by this preparation and by long and constant practice, he was averse, in an extraordinary degree, to extempore speaking. Plutarch relates this of him; and, notwithstanding the great excellence which is ascribed to his unpremeditated harangues in the same

passage, there may be some suspicion that his reluctance to "trust his success to fortune," affected his execution upon certain occasions—perhaps in the memorable debate with Philip, of which the orator's illustrious rival has left us so lively and so cutting a description. His anxiety in preparing may, however, be further estimated by the circumstance of his having left a collection of exordia, or introductions, almost resembling that "*volumen proœmiorum*," which we know Cicero to have kept ready by him, from the pleasant mistake that he committed in sending one to Atticus as the beginning of his treatise *De Gloriâ*, when he had before used it for the *Third Book of the Academic Questions*.[1] It may justly be conceived that Demosthenes was not likely to have a book of introductions, so unconnected with any particular subject as to be applicable to any speech. This rather befitted Sallust, or Cicero himself, than the close reasoning, business-like Athenian. Yet in whatever way we account for it, and though we suppose that most of the exordia in question were written in the prospect of making some particular speech, when time was wanting to compose the whole, the fact of fifty-six of these pieces remaining, only two or three of which exist in their connection with any of his known orations, seems to prove, incontestably, the laborious nature of the process by which he reached and kept his vast pre-eminence in eloquence. . . .

From the detailed examination into which we have entered of these repetitions, two conclusions may be drawn, both highly illustrative of the degree in which oratory among the Greeks was considered as an art demanding the utmost care, and calculated to exhibit the mere display of skill, as well as to attain more important objects. In the first place, we find that the greatest of all orators never regarded the composition of any sentence worthy of him to deliver, as a thing of easy execution. Practised, as he was, and able surely, if any man ever was, by his mastery over language, to pour out his ideas with facility, he elaborated every passage with almost equal care. Having the same ideas to express, he did not, like our easy and fluent moderns, clothe them in different language for the sake of variety; but reflecting that he had, upon the fullest deliberation, adopted one form of expression as the best, and because every other must needs be

---

[1] He tells him, as soon as he discovers the mistake, to cancel the exordium, and prefix another, which he sends, taken from the same collection.—*Ep. ad Att.* xvi. 6.

worse, he used it again without any change, unless further labour and more trials had enabled him in any particular to improve the workmanship. They who speak or write with little or no labour to themselves, and proportionably small satisfaction to others, would, in similar circumstances, find it far easier to compose anew, than to recollect or go back to what they had finished on a former occasion. Not so the mighty Athenian, whom we find never disdaining even to make use of half a sentence which he had once happily wrought, and treasured up as complete; nay, to draw part of a sentence from one quarter and part from another, applying them by some slight change to the new occasion, and perhaps adding some new member—thus presenting the whole, in its last form, made of portions fabricated at three different periods, several years asunder. Nothing can more strikingly demonstrate how difficult, in the eyes of the first of all orators and writers, that composition was, which so many speakers and authors, in all after ages, have thought the easiest part of their task.

But another inference may be drawn from the comparisons into which we have entered. If they prove the extreme pains taken by the orator, they illustrate as strikingly the delicate sense of rhetorical excellence in the Athenian audience; and seem even to show that they enjoyed a speech as modern assemblies do a theatrical exhibition, a fine drama or piece of music, which, far from losing by repetition, can only produce its full effect after a first, or even a second representation has made it thoroughly understood. It seems hardly possible, on any other supposition, to account for many of the repetitions in Demosthenes. A single sentence, or even a passage of some length, if it contained nothing very striking, might be given twice to a court or a popular assembly in modern times after no great interval of time; but who could now venture upon making a speech, about two-thirds of which had been spoken at different times, and nearly half of it upon one occasion the very year before? This would be impossible, how little soever there might be of bold figures, and other passages of striking effect. But we find Demosthenes repeating, almost word for word, some of his most striking passages—those which must have been universally known, and the recurrence of which might have been foreseen by the context. It seems to modern readers hardly possible to conceive that the functions of the critic thus performed by the Athenians should not have interfered with the capacity of actors or

judges, in which it was certainly the orator's business chiefly to address them; and that the warmth of feeling, arising from a sense of the reality of all they were hearing, should not sometimes have been cooled by the recollection of the very artificial display they were witnessing. Yet no fact in history is more unquestionable than the union of the two capacities in the Athenian audience—their exquisite discrimination and high relish of rhetorical beauties, with their susceptibility of the strongest emotions which the orator could desire to excite. The powers of the artist become, no doubt, all the more wonderful on this account; and no one can deny that he was an artist, and trusted as little to inspiration as Clairon and the other actors, of whose unconcern during the delivery of passages which were convulsing the audience so many striking anecdotes are preserved. In the whole range of criticism there is not, perhaps, a more sound remark than that of Quintilian, which has sometimes been deemed paradoxical, only because it is profound, in his celebrated comparison of the Greek and Roman masters—*Curæ plus in illo, in hoc naturæ.*

PROGRESS.

BY WILLIAM ALLINGHAM.

"Give back my youth!" the poets cry,
"Give back my youth!"—so say not I.
Youth play'd its part with us; if we
Are losers, should we gainers be
By recommencing, with the same
Conditions, all the finish'd game?
If we see better now, we are
Already winners just so far,—
And merely ask to keep our winning.
Wipe out loss, for a new beginning!
This may come, in Heaven's good way,
How, no mortal man shall say;
But not by fresh-recover'd taste
For sugar-plums, or valentines,
Or conjuring back the brightest day
Which gave its gift and therefore shines.
Win or lose, possess or miss,
There cannot be a weaker waste
Of memory's privilege than this—
To dwell among cast-off designs,
Stages, larvæ of yourself,
And leave the true thing on the shelf.
The Present-Future, wherewith blend
Hours that hasten to their end.

CLARISSA HARLOWE.

[Samuel Richardson, born in Derbyshire, 1689; died
in London, 4th July, 1761, and was buried in St. Bride's
Church. He was the son of a joiner; his father intended
him for the church, but finding the expense of education
was too great, bound him apprentice to a printer in
London. Having served his apprenticeship and worked
several years as a journeyman, he set up as a master
printer. His care and diligence earned success. He
obtained the printing of the journals of the House of
Commons; in 1754 he was chosen master of the Sta
tioners' Company; and in 1760 he purchased a moiety
of the patent of printer to the king, which added much
to his revenue. From his youth he had been an active
letter-writer, and his services in that capacity had been
frequently required by his friends of both sexes; in his
business he found it useful to be able to oblige the booksellers by writing for them prefaces and dedications.
He was asked by two publishers to write a book of
familiar letters "on the useful concerns in common
life." He gave them Pamela, which appeared in 1740
—the author being then fifty years of age. The work
was received with enthusiasm. Eight years afterwards
he issued Clarissa Harlowe, and five years later (1753)
the History of Sir Charles Grandison. "This last production," Scott says, "has neither the simplicity of the
two first volumes of Pamela, nor the deep and overwhelming interest of the inimitable Clarissa, and must,
considering it as a whole, be ranked considerably beneath both these works." "The publication of Clarissa
(eight volumes) raised the fame of the author to the
height. And high as his reputation stood in his own
country, it was even more exalted in those of France
and Germany." The work is still regarded as one of
the most important contributions to English fiction.]

[Clarissa was a young lady of high Christian
principle, beloved by everybody. Her grandfather had bequeathed to her his fortune; and
her avaricious brother and sister, fearing that
their uncles John and Anthony Harlowe might
also make her their heiress, were ready to find
any means of bringing her into disgrace. She
was commanded to marry a man she could not
like; she refused, and this was attributed to
her preference for an unprincipled fellow,
Lovelace. She had been induced to correspond
with the latter to prevent an encounter
between him and her brother. Lovelace persuaded her to grant him a private interview,
and he then succeeded in abducting her. He
conveyed her to a vicious house in London, and
there, after every other means had failed, she
was rendered insensible by means of drugs. On
recovering, she escaped from the place to the
house of an honest tradesman. On her way to
church she was discovered by some of Lovelace's
agents, who, thinking to oblige their master,
caused her to be arrested on pretence of debt;
but Lovelace obtained her release the moment
this new cruelty became known to him. She
returned to her lodgings to die. Her only sin

had been that of disobedience to her parents,
but they would not hear her prayers for pardon
and for a last blessing. Various circumstances
rendered it impossible for her chief friend and
correspondent, Miss Howe, to attend her, and
she was therefore obliged to depend upon
strangers. Whilst in the direst distress, her
exalted ideas of virtue compelled her to refuse
the hand of the man who had betrayed her,
although his family joined their prayers to his
that she would accept the only possible repara-
tion for the wrong which had been done her.
The writer of the following letters, Belford,
had been a companion of Lovelace, but, impressed by the noble character of Clarissa, he
had determined upon a new life. Colonel
Morden, her cousin, had returned to England
too late to save her.]

MR. BELFORD, TO ROBERT LOVELACE, ESQ.

FRIDAY NOON, July 21.

This morning I was admitted, as soon as I
sent up my name, into the presence of the
divine lady. Such I may call her; as what I
have to relate will fully prove.

She had had a tolerable night, and was much
better in spirits, though weak in person; and
visibly declining in looks.

Mrs. Lovick and Mrs. Smith [the landlady]
were with her; and accused her, in a gentle
manner, of having applied herself too assiduously to her pen for her strength, having
been up ever since five. She said she had
rested better than she had done for many
nights: she had found her spirits free, and
her mind tolerably easy: and having, as she
had reason to think, but a short time, and
much to do in it, she must be a good housewife
of her hours.

She had been writing, she said, a letter to
her sister, but had not pleased herself in it;
though she had made two or three essays: but
that the last must go.

By hints I had dropped from time to time, she
had reason, she said, to think that I knew
everything that concerned her and her family;
and if so, must be acquainted with the heavy
curse her father had laid upon her; which had
been dreadfully fulfilled in one part, as to her
prospects in this life, and that in a very short
time; which gave her great apprehensions of
the other part. She had been applying herself
to her sister, to obtain a revocation of it. "I
hope my father will revoke it," said she, "or
I shall be very miserable—Yet" (and she gasped
as she spoke, with apprehension)—"I am
ready to tremble at what the answer may be;
for my sister is hard-hearted."

I said something reflecting upon her friends; as to what they would deserve to be thought of, if the unmerited imprecation were not withdrawn—— Upon which she took me up, and talked in such a dutiful manner of her parents as must doubly condemn them (if they remain implacable) for their inhuman treatment of such a daughter.

She said, I must not blame her parents: it was her dear Miss Howe's fault to do so. But what an enormity was there in her crime, which could set the best of parents (they had been to her, till she disobliged them) in a bad light, for resenting the rashness of a child from whose education they had reason to expect better fruits! There were some hard circumstances in her case, it was true; but my friend could tell me, that no one person, throughout the whole fatal transaction, had acted out of character but herself. She submitted therefore to the penalty she had incurred. If they had any fault, it was only that they would not inform themselves of some circumstances which would alleviate a little her misdeed; and that supposing her a more guilty creature than she was, they punished her without a hearing.

Lord!—I was going to curse thee, Lovelace! How every instance of excellence, in this all-excelling creature, condemns thee;—thou wilt have reason to think thyself of all men the most accursed, if she die!

I then besought her, while she was capable of such glorious instances of generosity and forgiveness, to extend her goodness to a man whose heart bled in every vein of it for the injuries he had done her; and who would make it the study of his whole life to repair them.

The women would have withdrawn when the subject became so particular. But she would not permit them to go. She told me that if after this time I was for entering with so much earnestness into a subject so very disagreeable to her, my visits must not be repeated. Nor was there occasion, she said, for my friendly offices in your favour; since she had begun to write her whole mind upon that subject to Miss Howe, in answer to letters from her, in which Miss Howe urged the same arguments, in compliment to the wishes of your noble and worthy relations.

"Meantime, you may let him know," said she, "that I reject him with my whole heart:—yet, that, although I say this with such a determination as shall leave no room for doubt, I say it not, however, with passion. On the contrary, tell him that I am trying to bring my mind into such a frame as to be able to pity him [poor perjured wretch! what has he

not to answer for!]; and that I shall not think myself qualified for the state I am aspiring to, if, after a few struggles more, I cannot forgive him too: and I hope," clasping her hands together, uplifted as were her eyes, "my dear earthly father will set me the example my Heavenly one has already set us all; and, by forgiving his fallen daughter, teach her to forgive the man, who then, I hope, will not have destroyed my eternal prospects, as he has my temporal!"

Stop here, thou wretch!—But I need not bid thee!——For I can go no further.

You will imagine how affecting her noble speech and behaviour were to me at the time when the bare recollecting and transcribing them obliged me to drop my pen. The women had tears in their eyes. I was silent for a few moments. At last, "Matchless excellence! inimitable goodness!" I called her with a voice so accented, that I was half-ashamed of myself, as it was before the women. But who could stand such sublime generosity of soul in so young a creature, her loveliness giving grace to all she said? "Methinks," said I [and I really, in a manner involuntarily, bent my knee], "I have before me an angel indeed. I can hardly forbear prostration, and to beg your influence to draw me after you to the world you are aspiring to! Yet—but what shall I say?—only, dearest excellence, make me, in some small instances, serviceable to you, that I may (if I survive you) have the glory to think I was able to contribute to your satisfaction while among us."

Here I stopped. She was silent. I proceeded—"Have you no commission to employ me in; deserted as you are by all your friends; among strangers, though, I doubt not, worthy people? Cannot I be serviceable by message, by letter-writing, by attending personally, with either message or letter, your father, your uncles, your brother, your sister, Miss Howe, Lord M., or the ladies his sisters? Any office to be employed to serve you, absolutely independent of my friend's wishes, or of my own wishes to oblige him? Think, madam, if I cannot?"

"I thank you, sir, very heartily I thank you: but in nothing that I can at present think of, or at least resolve upon, can you do me service. I will see what return the letter I have written will bring me. Till then——"

"My life and my fortune," interrupted I, "are devoted to your service. Permit me to observe, that here you are, without one natural friend; and (so much do I know of your unhappy case) that you must be in a manner destitute of the means to *make* friends——."

She was going to interrupt me, with a prohibitory kind of earnestness in her manner.

"I beg leave to proceed, madam; I have cast about twenty ways how to mention this before, but never dared till now. Suffer me, now that I have broken the ice, to tender myself as your *banker* only. I know you will not be obliged: you *need* not. You have sufficient of your own, if it were in your hands; and from *that*, whether you live or die, will I consent to be reimbursed. I do assure you that the unhappy man shall never know either *my* offer or *your* acceptance—Only permit me this small——"

And down behind her chair I dropped a bank-note of £100 which I had brought with me, intending somehow or other to leave it behind me: nor shouldst thou ever have known it, had she favoured me with the acceptance of it; as I told her.

"You give me great pain, Mr. Belford," said she, "by these instances of your humanity. And yet, considering the company I have seen you in, I am not sorry to find you capable of such. Methinks I am glad, for the sake of human nature, that there could be but *one* such man in the world, as he, you, and I know. But as to your kind offer, whatever it be, if you take it not up, you will greatly disturb me. I have no need of your kindness. I have effects enough, which I never can want, to supply my present occasions: and, if needful, can have recourse to Miss Howe. I have promised that I would—so, pray, sir, urge not upon me this favour. Take it up yourself. If you mean me peace and ease of mind, urge not this favour." And she spoke with impatience.

"I beg, madam, but one word——"

"Not one, sir, till you have taken back what you have let fall. I doubt not either the *honour* or the *kindness* of your offer; but you must not say one word more on this subject. I cannot bear it."

She was stooping, but with pain. I therefore prevented her; and besought her to forgive me for a tender which, I saw, had been more discomposing to her than I had hoped (from the purity of my intentions) it would be. But I could not bear to think that such a mind as hers should be distressed: since the want of the conveniences she was used to abound in might affect and disturb her in the divine course she was in.

"You are very kind to me, sir," said she, "and very favourable in your opinion of me. But I hope that I cannot now be easily put out

of my present course. My declining health will more and more confirm me in it. Those who arrested and confined me, no doubt thought they had fallen upon the ready method to distress me so as to bring me into all their measures. But I presume to hope that I have a mind that cannot be debased, in *essential instances*, by *temporal calamities*: little do those poor wretches know of the force of innate principles" ("forgive my own *implied* vanity," was her word), "who imagine that a prison, or penury, can being a right-turned mind to be guilty of a wilful baseness, in order to avoid such *short-lived evils*."

She then turned from me towards the window, with a dignity suitable to her words; and such as showed her to be more of soul than of body, at that instant.

What magnanimity!—No wonder a virtue so solidly founded could baffle all thy arts:—and that it forced thee (in order to carry thy accursed point) to have recourse to those unnatural ones which robbed her of her charming senses.

The women were extremely affected, Mrs. Lovick especially; who said whisperingly to Mrs. Smith, "We have an angel, not a woman, with us, Mrs. Smith!"

I repeated my offers to write to any of her friends; and told her that, having taken the liberty to acquaint Dr. H. with the cruel displeasure of her relations, as what I presumed lay nearest her heart, he had proposed to write himself, to acquaint her friends how ill she was, if she would not take it amiss.

It was kind in the *doctor*, she said: but begged that no step of that sort might be taken without her knowledge or consent. She would wait to see what effects her letter to her sister would have. All she had to hope for was, that her father would revoke his malediction, previous to the last blessing she should then implore: for the rest, her friends would think she could not suffer too much; and she was content to suffer: for now, nothing could happen that could make her wish to live.

Mrs. Smith went down; and, soon returning, asked if the lady and I would not dine with her that day; for it was her wedding-day. She had engaged Mrs. Lovick, she said; and should have nobody else if we would do her that favour.

The charming creature sighed, and shook her head.—"*Wedding-day*," repeated she, 'I wish you, Mrs. Smith, many happy wedding-days!—But you will excuse *me*."

Mr. Smith came up with the same request. They both applied to me.

On condition the *lady* would, I should make no scruple; and would suspend an engagement: which I actually had.

She then desired they would all sit down. "You have several times, Mrs. Lovick and Mrs. Smith, hinted your wishes that I would give you some little history of myself: now, if you are at leisure, that this gentleman, who, I have reason to believe, knows it all, is present, and can tell you if I give it justly or not, I will oblige your curiosity."

They all eagerly, the man Smith too, sat down; and she began an account of herself, which I will endeavour to repeat as nearly in her own words as I possibly can: for I know you will think it of importance to be apprised of her manner of relating your barbarity to her, as well as what her sentiments are of it; and what room there is for the hopes your friends have in your favour for her.

"At first when I took these lodgings," said she, "I thought of staying but a short time in them; and so, Mrs. Smith, I told you: I therefore avoided giving any other account of myself than that I was a very unhappy young creature, seduced from good friends, and escaped from very vile wretches.

"This account I thought myself obliged to give, that you might the less wonder at seeing a young creature rushing through your shop into your back apartment, all trembling and out of breath; an ordinary garb over my own; craving lodging and protection; only giving my bare word, that you should be handsomely paid: all my effects contained in a pocket-handkerchief.

"My sudden absence for three days and nights together, when arrested, must still further surprise you: and although this gentleman, who, perhaps, knows more of the darker part of my story than I do myself, has informed you (as you, Mrs. Lovick, tell me) that I am only an *unhappy*, not a *guilty* creature; yet I think it incumbent upon me not to suffer honest minds to be in doubt about my character.

"You must know, then, that I have been in one instance (I had like to have said but in one instance; but that was a capital one) an undutiful child to the most indulgent of parents: for what some people call cruelty in them is owing but to the excess of their love, and to their disappointment, having had reason to expect better from me.

"I was visited (at first, with my friends' connivance) by a man of birth and fortune, but of worse principles, as it proved, than I believed any man could have. My brother, a very headstrong young man, was absent at that

time; and when he returned (from an old grudge, and knowing the gentleman, it is plain, better than I knew him) entirely disapproved of his visits: and, having a great sway in our family, brought other gentlemen to address me: and at last (several having been rejected) he introduced one extremely disagreeable: in every *indifferent* person's eyes disagreeable. I could not love him. They all joined to compel me to have him; a rencounter between the gentleman my friends were set against, and my brother, having confirmed them all his enemies.

"To be short; I was confined, and treated so very hardly that, in a rash fit, I appointed to go off with the man they hated. A wicked intention, you'll say! But I was greatly provoked; nevertheless I repented, and resolved not to go off with him: yet I did not mistrust his honour to me neither; nor his love; because nobody thought me unworthy of the latter, and my fortune was not to be despised. But foolishly (wickedly and contrivingly, as my friends still think, with a design, as they imagine, to abandon them) giving him a private meeting, I was tricked away: poorly enough tricked away, I must needs say; though others who had been first guilty of so rash a step as the meeting of him was, might have been so deceived and surprised as well as I.

"After remaining some time at a farmhouse in the country, and behaving so well to me all the time with honour, he brought me to handsome lodgings in town till still better provision could be made for me. But they proved to be (as he indeed knew and designed) at a vile, a very vile creature's; though it was long before I found her to be so, for I knew nothing of the town or its ways.

"There is no repeating what followed: such unprecedented vile arts!—For I gave him no opportunity to take me at any disreputable advantage."

And here (half covering her sweet face with her handkerchief put to her tearful eyes) she stopped.

Hastily, as if she would flee from the hateful remembrance, she resumed:—"I made escape afterwards from the abominable house in his absence, and came to yours: and this gentleman has almost prevailed on me to think that the ungrateful man did not connive at the vile arrest: which was made, no doubt, in order to get me once more to those wicked lodgings: for nothing do I owe them, except I were to pay them."—[She sighed, and again wiped her charming eyes—adding in a softer, lower voice] —"*for being ruined.*"

"Indeed, madam," said I, "guilty, abominably guilty, as he is in all the rest, he is innocent of this last wicked outrage."

"Well, and so I wish him to be.—That evil, heavy as it was, is one of the slightest evils I have suffered.—But hence you'll observe, Mrs. Lovick (for you seemed this morning curious to know if I were not a wife), that I *never was married*.—You, Mr. Belford, no doubt, knew before that I am no wife: and now I never will be one. Yet I bless God that I am not a guilty creature!

"As to my parentage, I am of no mean family; I have in my own right, by the intended favour of my grandfather, a fortune not contemptible: independent of my *father*, if I had pleased; but I never will please.

"My father is very rich. I went by another name when I came to you first: but that was to avoid being discovered to the perfidious man: who now engages, by this gentleman, not to molest me.

"'My real name you now know to be Harlowe: *Clarissa* Harlowe. I am not yet twenty years of age.

"I have an excellent mother, as well as father; a woman of family, and fine sense—worthy of a better child!—They both doated upon me.

"I have two good uncles: men of great fortunes; jealous of the honour of their family, which I have wounded.

"I was the joy of their hearts; and, with theirs and my father's, I had three houses to call my own; for they used to have me with them by turns, and almost kindly to quarrel for me: so that I was two months in the year with the one; two months with the other; six months at my father's; and two at the houses of others of my dear friends, who thought themselves happy in me· and whenever I was at any one's, I was crowded upon with letters by all the rest, who longed for my return to them.

"In short, I was beloved by everybody. The poor—I used to make glad *their* hearts: I never shut my hand to any distress, wherever I was—But now I am poor myself!

"So, Mrs. Smith—so, Mrs. Lovick—I am *not* married. It is but just to tell you so. And I am now, as I ought to be, in a state of humiliation and penitence for the rash step which has been followed by so much evil. God, I hope, will forgive me, as I am endeavouring to bring my mind to forgive all the world, even the man who has ungratefully, and by dreadful perjuries [Poor wretch! he thought all his wickedness to be *wit!*], reduced to this

a young creature who had *his* happiness in her *view*, and in her *wish*, even beyond this life; and who was believed to be of rank, and fortune, and expectations, considerable enough to make it the *interest* of any gentleman in England to be faithful to his vows to her. But I cannot expect that my parents will forgive me: my refuge must be death; the most painful kind of which I would suffer rather than be the wife of one who could act by me as the man has acted upon whose birth, education, and honour, I had so much reason to found better expectations.

"I see," continued she, "that I, who once was every one's delight, am now the cause of grief to every one—You, that are strangers to me, are moved for me!—'Tis kind!—But 'tis time to stop.—Your compassionate hearts, Mrs. Smith and Mrs. Lovick, are too much touched."—[For the women sobbed, and the man was also affected.]—"It is barbarous in me, with my woes, thus to sadden your wedding-day." Then turning to Mr. and Mrs. Smith—"May you see many happy ones, honest, good couple!—How agreeable is it to see you both join so kindly to celebrate it, after many years are gone over you!—I once—But no more!—All my prospects of felicity, as to this life, are at an end. My hopes, like opening buds or blossoms in an over-forward spring, have been nipped by a severe frost!—blighted by an eastern wind!—But I can but *once die*; and if life be spared me but till I am discharged from a heavy malediction, which my father in his wrath laid upon me, and which is fulfilled literally in every article relating to this world; that, and a last blessing, are all I have to wish for; and death will be welcomer to me than rest to the most wearied traveller that ever reached his journey's end."

And then she sunk her head against the back of her chair, and, hiding her face with her handkerchief, endeavoured to conceal her tears from us.

Not a soul of us could speak a word. Thy presence, perhaps, thou hardened wretch, might have made us ashamed of a weakness which perhaps thou wilt deride *me* in particular for, when thou readest this!

She retired to her chamber soon after, and was forced, it seems, to lie down. We all went down together: and, for an hour and half, dwelt upon her praises; Mrs. Smith and Mrs. Lovick repeatedly expressing their astonishment that there could be a man in the world capable of offending, much more of wilfully injuring, such a lady; and repeating, that they had an angel in their house. — I thought they had; and that as assuredly as there is a devil under the roof of good Lord M I hate thee heartily!—By my faith I do!—Every hour I hate thee more than the former!

J. BELFORD.

THURSDAY NIGHT.

I may as well try to write; since, were I to go to bed, I shall not sleep. I never had such a weight of grief upon my mind in my life, as upon the demise of this admirable woman, whose soul is now rejoicing in the regions of light. You may be glad to know the particulars of her happy exit. I will try to proceed; for all is hush and still; the family retired; but not one of them, and least of all her poor cousin, I daresay, to rest.

At four o'clock, as I mentioned in my last, I was sent for down; and as thou usedst to like my descriptions, I will give thee the woful scene that presented itself to me as I approached the bed.

The colonel was the first that took my attention, kneeling on the side of the bed, the lady's right hand in both his, which his face covered, bathing it with his tears; although she had been comforting him, as the woman since told me, in elevated strains, but broken accents.

On the other side of the bed sat the good widow, her face overwhelmed with tears, leaning her head against the bed's head in a most disconsolate manner; and turning her face to me as soon as she saw me, "O! Mr. Belford," cried she, with folded hands—"the dear lady—" A heavy sob permitted her not to say more.

Mrs. Smith, with clasped fingers and uplifted eyes, as if imploring help from the only Power which could give it, was kneeling down at the bed's feet, tears in large drops trickling down her cheeks.

Her nurse was kneeling between the widow and Mrs. Smith, her arms extended. In one hand she held an ineffectual cordial, which she had just been offering to her dying mistress; her face was swollen with weeping (though used to such scenes as this), and she turned her eyes towards me as if she called upon me by them to join in the helpless sorrow; a fresh stream bursting from them as I approached the bed.

The maid of the house, with her face upon her folded arms, as she stood leaning against the wainscot, more audibly expressed her grief than any of the others.

The lady had been silent a few minutes, and speechless, as they thought, moving her lips without uttering a word; one hand, as I said, in her cousin's. But when Mrs. Lovick on

my approach pronounced my name, "O! Mr. Belford," said she, with a faint inward voice, but very distinct nevertheless—"Now!—Now!" [in broken periods she spoke]—"I bless God for his mercies to his poor creature—will all soon be over—A few—a very few moments—will end this strife—And I shall be happy!

"Comfort here, sir,"—turning her head to the colonel—"Comfort my cousin—See! the blame—able kindness—He would not wish me to be happy—so soon!"

Here she stopped for two or three minutes, earnestly looking upon him: then resuming, "My dearest cousin," said she, "be comforted—what is dying but the common lot?—The mortal frame may seem to labour—but that is all!—It is not so hard to die as I believed it to be!—The preparation is the difficulty—I bless God I have had time for that—The rest is worse to beholders than to me!—I am all blessed hope—Hope itself." She looked what she said, a sweet smile beaming over her countenance.

After a short silence, "Once more, my dear cousin," said she, but still in broken accents, "commend me most dutifully to my father and mother."—There she stopped. And then proceeding—"To my sister—to my brother—to my uncles—And tell them I bless them with my parting breath—for all their goodness to me—Even for their displeasure, I bless them—Most happy has been to me my punishment here! Happy indeed!"

She was silent for a few moments, lifting up her eyes, and the hand her cousin held not between his. Then, "O death!" said she, "where is thy sting?" [The words I remember to have heard in the burial service read over my uncle and poor Belton.] And after a pause—"It is good for me that I was afflicted!" Words of Scripture, I suppose.

Then turning towards us, who were lost in speechless sorrow—"O dear, dear gentlemen," said she, "you know not what foretastes—what assurances—" And there she again stopped, and looked up, as if in a thankful rapture, sweetly smiling.

Then turning her head towards me—"Do you, sir, tell your friend that I forgive him! —And I pray to God to forgive him!"—Again pausing, and lifting up her eyes, as if praying that he would. "Let him know how happily I die:—and that such as my own, I wish to be his last hour."

She was again silent for a few moments: and then resuming—"My sight fails me!—Your voices only—" [for we both applauded her Christian, her divine frame, though in accents as broken as her own;] "and the voice of grief is alike in all.—Is not this Mr. Morden's hand?" pressing one of his with that he had just let go.—"Which is Mr. Belford's?" holding out the other. I gave her mine. "God Almighty bless you both," said she, and make you both in your last hour—for you *must* come to this—happy as I am!"

She paused again, her breath growing shorter; and, after a few minutes, "And now, my dearest cousin, give me your hand—Nearer—still nearer—" drawing it towards her; and she pressed it with her dying lips—"God protect you, dear, dear sir—And once more, receive my best and most grateful thanks—And tell my dear Miss Howe—and vouchsafe to see, and to tell my worthy Norton—She will be one day, I fear not, though now lowly in her fortunes, a saint in heaven—Tell them both that I remember them with thankful blessings in my last moments!—And pray God to give them happiness *here* for many, many years, for the sake of their friends and lovers; and an heavenly crown *hereafter;* and such assurances of it as I have, through the all-satisfying merits of my blessed Redeemer."

Her sweet voice and broken periods methinks still fill my ears, and never will be out of my memory.

After a short silence, in a more broken and faint accent—"And you, Mr. Belford," pressing my hand, "may God preserve you, and make you sensible of all your errors!—You see, in me, how all ends—May *you* be—" And down sunk her head upon her pillow, she fainting away, and drawing from us her hands.

We thought she was then gone; and each gave way to a violent burst of grief.

But soon showing signs of returning life, our attention was again engaged; and I besought her, when a little recovered, to complete in my favour her half-pronounced blessing. She waved her hand to us both, and bowed her head six several times, as we have since recollected, as if distinguishing every person present; not forgetting the nurse and the maid-servant; the latter having approached the bed, weeping, as if crowding in for the divine lady's last blessing; and she spoke faltering and inwardly—"Bless—bless—bless—you all—And—now—And now—" [holding up her almost lifeless hands for the last time] "Come—O come—Blessed Lord—JESUS!"

And with these words, the last but half pronounced, expired:—such a smile, such a charming serenity overspreading her sweet face at

the instant; as seemed to manifest her eternal happiness already begun.

O, Lovelace!—But I can write no more.

. . . .

I resume my pen to add a few lines.

While warm, though pulseless, we pressed each her hand with our lips; and then retired into the next room.

We looked at each other with intent to speak: but, as if one motion governed, as one cause affected both, we turned away silent.

The colonel sighed as if his heart would burst: at last, his face and hands uplifted, his back towards me, "Good Heaven!" said he to himself, "support me!—And is it thus, O flower of nature!"—Then pausing—"And must we no more—*Never more!*—My blessed, blessed cousin!" uttering some other words, which his sighs made inarticulate:—And then, as if recollecting himself—"Forgive me, sir!—Excuse me, Mr. Belford!" And, sliding by me, "Anon I hope to see you, sir."—And down stairs he went, and out of the house, leaving me a statue.

When I recovered I was ready to repine at what I *then* called an unequal dispensation; forgetting her happy preparation, and still happier departure; and that she had but drawn a common lot; triumphing in it, and leaving behind her every one less assured of happiness, though equally certain that the lot would one day be their own.

She departed exactly at forty minutes after six o'clock, as by her watch on the table.

And thus died Miss CLARISSA HARLOWE, in the blossom of her youth and beauty: and who, her tender years considered, has not left behind her her superior in extensive knowledge and watchful prudence; nor hardly her equal for unblemished virtue, exemplary piety, sweetness of manners, discreet generosity, and true Christian charity: and these all set off by the most graceful modesty and humility; yet on all proper occasions manifesting a noble presence of mind, and true magnanimity: so that she may be said to have been not only an ornament to her sex, but to human nature.

A better pen than mine may do her fuller justice. Thine, I mean, O Lovelace! For well dost thou know how much she excelled in the graces both of mind and person, natural and acquired, all that is woman. And thou also canst best account for the causes of her immature death, through those calamities which in so short a space of time, from the highest pitch of felicity (every one in a manner adoring her), brought her to an exit so happy for herself, but, that it was so *early*, so much to be deplored by all who had the honour of her acquaintance.

This task, then, I leave to thee: but now I can write no more, only that I am a sympathizer in every part of thy distress, except (and yet it is cruel to say it) in that which arises from thy guilt.

ONE O'CLOCK FRIDAY MORNING.

. . . .

TRANSLATION OF A LETTER FROM F. J. DE LA TOUR, TO JOHN BELFORD, ESQ., NEAR SOHO SQUARE, LONDON.

SIR, TRENT, DEC. 18, N.S.

I have melancholy news to inform you of, by order of the Chevalier Lovelace. He showed me his letter to you before he sealed it; signifying, that he was to meet the Chevalier Morden on the 15th. Wherefore, as the occasion of the meeting is so well known to you, I shall say nothing of it here.

I had taken care to have ready within a little distance a surgeon and his assistant, to whom, under an oath of secrecy, I had revealed the matter (though I did not own it to the two gentlemen); so that they were prepared with bandages, and all things proper. For well was I acquainted with the bravery and skill of my chevalier: and had heard the character of the other: and knew the animosity of both. A post chaise was ready, with each of their footmen, at a little distance.

The two chevaliers came exactly at their time: they were attended by Monsieur Margate (the colonel's gentleman) and myself. They had given orders over-night, and now repeated them in each other's presence, that we should observe a strict impartiality between them: and that if one fell, each of us should look upon himself, as to any needful help or retreat, as the servant of the survivor, and take his commands accordingly.

After a few compliments both the gentlemen, with the greatest presence of mind that ever I beheld in men, stripped to their shirts, and drew.

They parried with equal judgment several passes. My chevalier drew the first blood, making a desperate push, which, by a sudden turn of his antagonist, missed going clear through him, and wounded him on the fleshy part of the ribs of his right side; which part the sword tore out, being on the extremity of the body: but before my chevalier could recover himself, the colonel, in return, pushed him into the inside of the left arm, near the shoulder: and the sword (raking his breast as it passed) being followed by a great effusion of blood, the colonel said, "Sir, I believe you have enough."

My chevalier swore —— he was not hurt: 'twas a pin's point: and so made another pass at his antagonist; which he, with a surprising dexterity, received under his arm, and ran my dear chevalier into the body: who immediately fell, saying, "The luck is yours, sir—O my beloved Clarissa!—Now art thou—" Inwardly he spoke three or four words more. His sword dropped from his hand. Mr. Morden threw his down, and ran to him, saying in French—"Ah, Monsieur! you are a dead man!—Call to God for mercy!"

We gave the signal agreed upon to the footmen, and they to the surgeons, who instantly came up.

Colonel Morden, I found, was too well used to the bloody work; for he was as cool as if nothing extraordinary had happened, assisting the surgeons, though his own wound bled much. But my dear chevalier fainted away two or three times running, and vomited blood besides.

However, they stopped the bleeding for the present; and we helped him into the voiture: and then the colonel suffered his own wound to be dressed; and appeared concerned that my chevalier was between whiles (when he could speak and struggle) extremely outrageous.—Poor gentleman! he had made quite sure of victory!

The colonel, against the surgeon's advice, would mount on horseback to pass into the Venetian territories; and generously gave me a purse of gold to pay the surgeons; desiring me to make a present to the footman, and to accept of the remainder as a mark of his satisfaction in my conduct, and in my care and tenderness of my master.

The surgeons told him that my chevalier could not live over the day.

When the colonel took leave of him Mr. Lovelace said, "You have well revenged the dear creature."

"I have, sir," said Mr. Morden: "and perhaps shall be sorry that you called upon me to this work, while I was balancing whether to obey or disobey the dear angel."

"There is a fate in it!" replied my chevalier —"a cursed fate!—or this could not have been'—But be ye all witnesses, that I have provoked my destiny, and acknowledge that I fall by a man of honour."

"Sir," said the colonel, with the piety of a confessor (wringing Mr. Lovelace's hand), "snatch these few fleeting moments, and commend yourself to God."

And so he rode off.

The voiture proceeded slowly with my chevalier; yet the motion set both his wounds bleeding afresh; and it was with difficulty they again stopped the blood.

We brought him alive to the nearest cottage; and he gave orders to me to despatch to you the packet I herewith send sealed up; and bid me write to you the particulars of this most unhappy affair; and give you thanks in his name for all your favours and friendships to him.

Contrary to all expectation, he lived over the night: but *suffered much,* as well from his *impatience* and *disappointment,* as from his *wounds;* for he seemed *very unwilling to die.*

He was delirious, at times, in the two last hours; and then several times cried out, as if he had seen some frightful spectre, "Take her away! take her away!" but named nobody. And sometimes praised some lady (that Clarissa, I suppose, whom he had invoked when he received his death's wound), calling her, "Sweet excellence! Divine creature! Fair sufferer!"— and once he said, "Look down, blessed spirit, look down!"—and there stopped—his lips, however, moving.

At nine in the morning he was seized with convulsions, and fainted away; and it was a quarter of an hour before he came out of them.

His few last words I must not omit, as they show an ultimate composure which may administer some consolation to his honourable friends.

"*Blessed*—" said he, addressing himself no doubt to Heaven; for his dying eyes were lifted up—a strong convulsion prevented him for a few moments saying more—but recovering, he again with great fervour (lifting up his eyes, and his spread hands) pronounced the word "*blessed:*" then, in a seeming ejaculation, he spoke inwardly so as not to be understood: at last he distinctly pronounced these three words,

"LET THIS EXPIATE."

And then, his head sinking on his pillow, he expired, at about half an hour after ten.

He little thought, poor gentleman! his end so near: so had given no direction about his body. I have caused it to be embowelled, and deposited in a vault, till I have orders from England.

This is a favour that was procured with difficulty; and would have been refused had he not been an Englishman of rank, a nation with reason respected in every Austrian government—for he had refused ghostly attendance, and the sacraments in the Catholic way. May his soul be happy, I pray God!

F. J. DE LA TOUR.

THE PLEASURES OF IMAGINATION.

[Mark Akenside, M.D , born at Newcastle-on-Tyne, 9th November, 1721 ; died in London, 23d June, 1770. Educated in Edinburgh and at Leyden. Whilst still a youth he contributed to the *Gentleman's Magazine.* His principal poem, *The Pleasures of Imagination,* first appeared in 1744, and won for the author a distinguished position amongst the poets of the day. He wrote a number of odes and short pieces, the most notable of which are the lines *To Curio,* a satire; *To the Country Gentlemen of England; Hymn to the Naiads;* and *The Cuckoo.* The Rev. Alexander Dyce said of *The Pleasures of Imagination,* from which our extract is taken—" If some passages are not lighted up with poetic fire, they glow with rhetorical beauty; while ingenious illustration and brilliant imagery enliven and adorn the whole."[1]]

Oh! blest of Heaven, whom not the languid songs
Of Luxury, the Siren! not the bribes
Of sordid Wealth, nor all the gaudy spoils
Of pageant Honour can seduce to leave
Those ever-blooming sweets, which, from the store
Of Nature, fair Imagination culls,
To charm the enlivened soul! What tho' not all
Of mortal offspring can attain the heights
Of envied life ; though only few possess
Patrician treasures or imperial state;
Yet Nature's care, to all her children just,
With richer treasures and an ampler state,
Endows at large whatever happy man
Will deign to use them. His the city's pomp,
The rural honours his. Whate'er adorns
The princely dome, the column and the arch,
The breathing marbles and the sculptured gold,
Beyond the proud possessor's narrow claim,
His tuneful breast enjoys. For him, the Spring
Distils her dews, and from the silken gem
Its lucid leaves unfolds; for him, the hand
Of Autumn tinges every fertile branch
With blooming gold, and blushes like the morn.
Each passing hour sheds tribute from her wings;
And still new beauties meet his lonely walk,
And loves unfelt attract him. Not a breeze
Flies o'er the meadow, not a cloud imbibes
The setting sun's effulgence, not a strain
From all the tenants of the warbling shade
Ascends, but whence his bosom can partake
Fresh pleasure, unreproved. Nor thence partakes
Fresh pleasure only: for the attentive mind,
By this harmonious action on her powers,

1 In private life Akenside's manners were somewhat stiff: "when he walked in the streets he looked for all the world like one of his own alexandrines set upright," was a saying of the actor Henderson. He disliked reference to his parentage, because his father was a butcher. Smollett took the poet as his model for the pedantic doctor, whose dinner after the manner of the ancients is so humorously described in *Peregrine Pickle.* See *Casquet,* page 96, vol. iii.

Becomes herself harmonious: wont so long
In outward things to meditate the charm
Of sacred order, soon she seeks at home
To find a kindred order, to exert
Within herself this elegance of love,
This fair inspired delight: her tempered powers
Refine at length, and every passion wears
A chaster, milder, more attractive mein.
But if to ampler prospects—if to gaze
On Nature's form, where, negligent of all
Thess lesser graces, she assumes the port
Of that Eternal Majesty that weighed
The world's foundations—if to these the mind
Exalts her daring eye, then mightier far
Will be the change, and nobler. Would the forms
Of servile custom cramp her generous powers?
Would sordid policies, the barbarous growth
Of ignorance and rapine, bow her down
To tame pursuits, to indolence and fear?
Lo! she appeals to Nature, to the winds
And rolling waves, the sun's unwearied course,
The elements and seasons: all declare
For what the Eternal Maker has ordained
The powers of man: we feel within ourselves
His energy divine: he tells the heart,
He meant, he made us to behold and love
What he beholds and loves, the general orb
Of life and being; to be great like him,
Beneficent and active. Thus the men
Whom Nature's works can charm, with God himself
Hold converse; grow familiar, day by day,
With his conceptions, act upon his plan,
And form to his, the relish of their souls.

THE DARIEN SCHEME.

BY SIR WALTER SCOTT.

Human character, whether national or individual, presents often to our calm consideration the strangest inconsistencies; but there are few more striking than that which Scotchmen exhibit in their private conduct, contrasted with their views when united together for any general or national purpose. In his own personal affairs the Scotchman is remarked as cautious, frugal, and prudent in an extreme degree, not generally aiming at enjoyment or relaxation till he has realized the means of indulgence, and studiously avoiding those temptations of pleasure to which men of other countries most readily give way. But when a number of Scotchmen associate for any speculative project, it would seem that their natural caution becomes thawed and dissolved by the union of their joint hopes, and that their imaginations are heated and influenced by any splendid prospect held out to them. They appear, in particular, to lose the power of calculating and adapting their means to the end which they desire to accomplish, and are readily induced to aim at objects magnificent in themselves, but which they have not, unhappily, the wealth or strength necessary to attain. Thus the natives of Scotland are often found to attempt splendid designs, which, shipwrecked for want of the necessary expenditure, give foreigners occasion to smile at the great error, and equally great misfortune of the nation—I mean their pride and their poverty. There is no greater instance of this tendency to daring speculation, which rests at the bottom of the coldness and caution of the Scottish character, than the disastrous history of the Darien colony.

Paterson, a man of comprehensive views and great sagacity, was the parent and inventor of this memorable scheme. In youth he had been an adventurer in the West Indies, and it was said a *buccaneer*, that is, one of a species of adventurers nearly allied to pirates, who, consisting of different nations, and divided into various bands, made war on the Spanish commerce and settlements in the South seas, and among the West Indian islands. In this roving course of life Paterson had made himself intimately acquainted with the geography of South America, the produce of the country, the nature of its commerce, and the manner in which the Spaniards governed that extensive region.

On his return to Europe, however, the schemes which he had formed respecting the New World were laid aside for another project, fraught with the most mighty and important consequences. This was the plan of that great national establishment, the Bank of England, of which he had the honour to suggest the first idea. For a time he was admitted a director of that institution, but it befell Paterson as often happens to the first projectors of great schemes. Other persons, possessed of wealth and influence, interposed, and, taking advantage of the ideas of the obscure and unprotected stranger, made them their own by alterations and improvements more or less trivial, and finally elbowed the inventor out of all concern in the institution, the foundation of which he had laid.

Thus expelled from the Bank of England, Paterson turned his thoughts to the plan of settling a colony in America; a country so favoured in point of situation, that it seemed to him formed to be the site of the most flourishing commercial capital in the universe.

The two great continents of North and South America are joined together by an isthmus, or narrow tract of land, called Darien. This neck of land is not above a day's journey in breadth, and as it is washed by the Atlantic Ocean on the eastern side, and the Great Pacific Ocean on the west, the isthmus seemed designed by nature as a common centre for the commerce of the world. Paterson ascertained, or at least alleged that he had ascertained, that the isthmus had never been the property of Spain, but was still possessed by the original natives, a tribe of fierce and warlike Indians, who made war on the Spaniards. According to the law of nations, therefore, any state had a right of forming a settlement in Darien, providing the consent of the Indians was first obtained; nor could their doing so be justly made subject of challenge even by Spain, so extravagantly jealous of all interference with her South American provinces. This plan of a settlement, with so many advantages to recommend it, was proposed by Paterson to the merchants of Hamburgh, to the Dutch, and even to the Elector of Brandenburgh; but it was coldly received by all these states.

The scheme was at length offered to the merchants of London, the only traders probably in the world who had the means of realizing the splendid visions of Paterson. But when the projector was in London, endeavouring to solicit attention to his plan, he became intimate with the celebrated Fletcher of Salton. This gentleman, one of the most accomplished men and best patriots whom Scotland has produced in any age, had, nevertheless, some notions of her interests which were more fanciful than real, and, anxious to do his country service, did not sufficiently consider the adequacy of the means by which her welfare was to be obtained. He was dazzled by the vision of opulence and grandeur which Paterson unfolded, and thought of nothing less than securing, for the benefit of Scotland alone, a scheme which promised to the state which should adopt it the keys, as it were, of the New World. The projector was easily persuaded to give his own country the benefit of his scheme of colonization, and went to Scotland along with Fletcher. Here the plan found general acceptation, and particularly with the Scottish administration, who were greatly embarrassed at the time by the warm prosecution of the affair of Glencoe, and who easily persuaded King William that some freedom and facilities of trade granted to the Scotch would divert the public attention from the investigation of a matter not very creditable to his majesty's reputation any more than to their own. Stair, in particular, a party deeply interested, gave

the Darien scheme the full support of his eloquence and interest, in hope to regain a part of his lost popularity.

The Scottish ministers obtained permission, accordingly, to grant such privileges of trade to the Scotch as might not be prejudicial to that of England. In June, 1695, these influential persons obtained a statute from Parliament, and afterwards a charter from the crown, for creating a corporate body, or stock company, by name of the Company of Scotland trading to Africa and the Indies, with power to plant colonies and build forts in places not possessed by other European nations, the consent always of the inhabitants of the places where they settled being obtained.

The hopes entertained of the profits to arise from this speculation were in the last degree sanguine; not even the Solemn League and Covenant was signed with more eager enthusiasm. Almost every one who had or could command any sum of ready money, embarked it in the Indian and African Company; many subscribed their all; maidens threw in their portions, and widows whatever sums they could raise upon their dower, to be repaid an hundred fold by the golden shower which was to descend upon the subscribers. Some sold estates to vest the money in the Company's funds, and so eager was the spirit of speculation, that when eight hundred thousand pounds formed the whole circulating capital of Scotland, half of that sum was vested in the Darien stock.

But it was not the Scotch alone whose hopes were excited by the rich prospects held out to them. An offer being made by the managers of the Company to share the expected advantages of the scheme with English and foreign merchants, it was so eagerly grasped at, that three hundred thousand pounds of stock was subscribed for in London within nine days after opening the books. The merchants of Hamburgh and of Holland subscribed two hundred thousand pounds.

Such was the hopeful state of the new Company's affairs, when the English jealousy of trade interfered to crush an adventure which seemed so promising. The idea which then and long afterwards prevailed in England, was that all profit was lost to the British empire which did not arise out of commerce exclusively English. The increase of trade in Scotland or Ireland they considered not as an addition to the general prosperity of the united nations, but as a positive loss to England. The commerce of Ireland they had long laid under severe shackles, to secure their own predominance; but it was not so easy to deal with Scotland, who had not only a separate legislature, but acknowledged no subordination or fealty to England, being to all effects a foreign country, though governed by the same king.

This new species of rivalry on the part of an old enemy was both irritating and alarming. The English had hitherto thought of the Scotch as a poor and fierce nation, who, in spite of fewer numbers and far inferior resources, was always ready to engage in war with her powerful neighbour; and it was embarrassing and provoking to find the same nation display, in spite of its proverbial caution, a hardy and ambitious spirit of emulating them in the paths of commerce.

These narrow-minded, unjust, and ungenerous apprehensions prevailed so widely throughout the English nation, that both Houses of Parliament joined in an address to the king, stating that the advantages given to the newly-erected Scottish Indian and African Company, would insure that kingdom so great a superiority over the English East India Company, that a great part of the stock and shipping of England would be transported to the north, and Scotland would become a free port for all East Indian commodities, which they would be able to furnish at a much cheaper rate than the English. By this means, it was said, England would lose all the advantages of an exclusive trade in the eastern commodities, which had always been a great article in her foreign commerce, and sustain infinite detriment in the sale of her domestic manufactures. The king, in his gracious answer to this address, acknowledged the justice of its statements, though as void of just policy as of grounds in public law. It bore, that "the king had been ill served in Scotland, but hoped some remedies might still be found to prevent the evils apprehended." To show that his resentment was serious against his Scottish ministers, King William deprived Stair of his office as secretary of state. Thus a statesman, who had retained his place in spite of the bloody deed of Glencoe, was deprived of it for attempting to serve his country by extending her trade and national importance.

The English Parliament persisted in the attempt to find remedies for the evils which they were pleased to apprehend from the Darien scheme, by appointing a committee of inquiry, with directions to summon before them such persons as had, by subscribing to the Company, given encouragement to the progress of an undertaking so fraught, as they alleged, with danger to the trade of England. These persons being called before Parliament, and menaced with impeachment, were compelled to renounce their connection with the undertaking, which was thus deprived of the aid of English subscriptions, to the amount, as already mentioned, of three hundred thousand pounds. Nay, so eager did the English Parliament show themselves in this matter, that they even extended their menace of impeachment to some native-born Scotchmen, who had offended the House by subscribing their own money to a Company formed in their own country and according to their own laws.

That this mode of destroying the funds of the concern might be yet more effectual, the weight of the king's influence with foreign states was employed to diminish the credit of the undertaking, and to intercept the subscriptions which had been thence obtained. For this purpose the English envoy at Hamburgh was directed to transmit to the senate of that commercial city a remonstrance on the part of King William, accusing them of having encouraged the commissioners of the Darien Company; requesting them to desist from doing so; intimating that the plan, said to be fraught with many evils, had not the support of his majesty; and protesting that the refusal of the senate to withdraw their countenance from the scheme would threaten an interruption to the friendship which his majesty desired to cultivate with the good city of Hamburgh. The senate returned to this application a spirited answer:—"The city of Hamburgh," they said, "considered it as strange that the King of England should dictate to them, a free people, with whom they were to engage in commercial arrangements; and were yet more astonished to find themselves blamed for having entered into such engagements with a body of his own Scottish subjects, incorporated under a special act of Parliament." But as the menace of the envoy showed that the Darien Company must be thwarted in all its proceedings by the superior power of England, the prudent Hamburghers, ceasing to consider it as a hopeful speculation, finally withdrew their subscriptions. The Dutch, to whom William could more decidedly dictate, from his authority with the states of Holland as stadtholder, and who were jealous, besides, of the interference of the Scotch with their own East Indian trade, adopted a similar course without remonstrance: and thus the Company, deserted both by foreign and English associates, were crippled in their undertaking, and left to their own limited resources.

The managers of the scheme, supported by the general sense of the people of Scotland, made warm remonstrances to King William on the hostile interference of his Hamburgh envoy. In William's answer he was forced meanly to evade what he was resolved not to grant, and yet could not in equity refuse. "The king," it was promised, "would send instructions to his envoy not to make use of his majesty's name or authority for obstructing their engagements with the city of Hamburgh." The Hamburghers, on the other hand, declared themselves ready to make good their subscriptions if they had any assurance from the King of England that in so doing they would be safe from his threatened resentment. But in spite of repeated promises, the envoy received no power to make such declaration. Thus the Darien Company lost the advantage of support to the extent of two hundred thousand pounds subscribed in Hamburgh and Holland, and that by the personal and hostile interference of their own monarch, under whose charter they were embodied.

Scotland, left to her unassisted resources, would have acted with less spirit but more wisdom in renouncing her ambitious plan of colonization, sure as it now was to be thwarted by the hostile interference of her unfriendly neighbours. But those engaged in the scheme, comprising great part of the nation, could not be expected easily to renounce hopes which had been so highly excited, and enough remained of the proud and obstinate spirit with which their ancestors had maintained their independence to induce the Scotch, even when thrown back on their own limited means, to determine upon the establishment of their favourite settlement at Darien in spite of the desertion of their English and foreign subscribers, and in defiance of the invidious opposition of their powerful neighbours. They caught the spirit of their ancestors, who, after losing so many dreadful battles, were always found ready, with sword in hand, to dispute the next campaign.

The contributors were encouraged in this stubborn resolution by the flattering account which was given of the country to be colonized, in which every class of Scotchmen found something to foster their hopes and to captivate their imagination. The description given of Darien by Paterson was partly derived from his own knowledge, partly from the report of buccaneers and adventurers, and the whole was exaggerated by the eloquence of an able man pleading in behalf of a favourite project. The climate was represented as healthy and mild, the tropical heats being mitigated by the height of the country, and by the shade of extensive forests, which yet presented neither

thicket nor underwood, but would admit a horseman to gallop through them unimpeded. Those acquainted with trade were assured of the benefits of a safe and beautiful harbour, where the advantages of free commerce and universal toleration would attract traders from all the world, while the produce of China, Japan, the Spice Islands, and Eastern India, brought to the bay of Panama in the Pacific Ocean, might be transferred by a safe and easy route across the Isthmus to the new settlement, and exchanged for all the commodities of Europe. "Trade," said the commercial enthusiast, "will beget trade—money will beget money—the commercial world shall no longer want work for their hands, but will rather want hands for their work. This door of the seas, and key of the universe, will enable its possessors to become the legislators of both worlds and the arbitrators of commerce. The settlers at Darien will acquire a nobler empire than Alexander or Cæsar, without fatigue, expense, or danger, as well as without incurring the guilt and bloodshed of conquerors." To those more vulgar minds, who cannot separate the idea of wealth from the precious metals, the projector held out the prospect of golden mines. The hardy Highlanders, many of whom embarked in the undertaking, were to exchange their barren moors for extensive savannahs of the richest pasture, with some latent hopes of a creagh (or foray) upon Spaniards or Indians. The lowland laird was to barter his meagre heritage and oppressive feudal tenure for the free possession of unlimited tracts of ground, where the rich soil, three or four feet deep, would return the richest produce for the slightest cultivation. Allured by these hopes, many proprietors actually abandoned their inheritances, and many more sent their sons and near relations to realize their golden hopes, while the poor labourers, who desired no more than bread and freedom of conscience, shouldered their mattocks and followed their masters in the path of emigration.

Twelve hundred men, three hundred of whom were youths of the best Scottish families, embarked on board of five frigates, purchased at Hamburgh for the service of the expedition; for the king refused the Company even the trifling accommodation of a ship of war which lay idle at Burntisland. They reached their destination in safety, and disembarked at a place called Acta, where, by cutting through a peninsula, they obtained a safe and insulated situation for a town called New Edinburgh, and a fort named Saint Andrew. With the fond remembrance of their native land, the colony itself was called Caledonia. They were favourably received by the native princes, from whom they purchased the land they required. The harbour, which was excellent, was proclaimed a free port; and in the outset the happiest results were expected from the settlement.

The arrival of the colonists took place in winter, when the air was cool and temperate; but with the summer returned the heat, and with the heat came the diseases of a tropical climate. Those who had reported so favourably of the climate of Darien had probably been persons who had only visited the coast during the healthy season, or mariners who, being chiefly on ship-board, find many situations healthy which prove pestilential to Europeans residing on shore. The health of the settlers, accustomed to a cold and mountainous country, gave way fast under the constant exhalations of the sultry climate, and even a more pressing danger arose from the want of food. The provisions which the colonists had brought from Scotland were expended, and the country afforded them only such supplies as could be procured by the precarious success of fishing and the chase.

This must have been foreseen; but it was never doubted that ample supplies would be procured from the English provinces in North America, which afforded superabundance of provisions, and from the West India colonies, which always possessed superfluities. It was here that the enmity of the king and the English nation met the unfortunate settlers most unexpectedly and most severely. In North America, and in the West India Islands, the most savage pirates and buccaneers, men who might be termed enemies to the human race, and had done deeds which seemed to exclude them from intercourse with mankind, had nevertheless found repeated refuge — had refitted their squadrons, and, supplied with every means of keeping the sea, had set sail in a condition to commit new murders and piracies. But no such relief was extended to the Scotch colonists at Darien, though acting under a charter from their sovereign, and establishing a peaceful colony according to the law of nations, and for the universal benefit of mankind.

The governors of Jamaica, Barbadoes, and New York published proclamations, setting forth, that whereas it had been signified to them (the governors) by the English secretary of state that his majesty was unacquainted with the purpose and design of the Scotch settlers at Darien (which was a positive falsehood), and that it was contrary to the peace entered into with his majesty's allies (no European power having complained of it), and that the governors of the said colonies had been commanded not to afford them any assistance; therefore, they did strictly charge the colonists over whom they presided to hold no correspondence with the said Scots, and to give them no assistance of arms, ammunition, provisions, or any other necessary whatsoever, either by themselves or any others for them; as those transgressing the tenor of the proclamation would answer the breach of his majesty's commands at their highest peril.

These proclamations were strictly obeyed: and every species of relief, not only that which countrymen may claim of their fellow-subjects, and Christians of their fellow-Christians, but such as the vilest criminal has a right to demand, because still holding the same human shape with the community whose laws he has offended—the mere supply, namely, of sustenance, the meanest boon granted to the meanest beggar, was denied to the colonists of Darien.

Famine aided the diseases which swept them off in large numbers; and undoubtedly they who thus perished for want of the provisions for which they were willing to pay, were as much murdered by King William's government as if they had been shot in the snows of Glencoe. The various miseries of the colony became altogether intolerable, and after waiting for assistance eight months, by far the greater part of the adventurers having died, the miserable remainder abandoned the settlement.

Shortly after the departure of the first colony, another body of fifteen hundred men, who had been sent out from Scotland, arrived at Darien under the hope of finding their friends alive and the settlement prosperous. This reinforcement suffered by a bad passage, in which one of their ships was lost and several of their number died. They took possession of the deserted settlement with sad anticipations, and were not long in experiencing the same miseries which had destroyed and dispersed their predecessors. Two months after they were joined by Campbell of Finnab with a third body of three hundred men, chiefly from his own Highland estate, many of whom had served under him in Flanders, where he had acquired an honourable military reputation. It was time the colony should receive such support, for, in addition to their other difficulties, they were now threatened by the Spaniards.

Two years had elapsed since the colonization of Darien had become matter of public discussion, and notwithstanding their feverish jealousy of their South American settlements, the

Spaniards had not made any remonstrance against it. Nay, so close and intimate was the King of Spain's friendship with King William that it seems possible he might never have done so unless the colonists had been disowned by their sovereign as if they had been vaga-bonds and outlaws. But finding themselves so treated by their prince, the Spaniards felt themselves invited in a manner to attack them, and not only lodged a remonstrance against the settlement with the English cabinet, but seized one of the vessels wrecked on the coast, confiscated the ship, and made the crew pri-soners. The Darien Company sent an address to the king by the hands of Lord Basil Hamil-ton, remonstrating against this injury; but William, who studied every means to discoun-tenance the unfortunate scheme, refused, under the most frivolous pretexts, to receive the peti-tion. This became so obvious that the young nobleman determined that the address should be received in season or out of season, and tak-ing a public opportunity to approach the king as he was leaving the saloon of audience, he obtruded himself and the petition upon his notice, with more bluntness than ceremony. "That young man is too bold," said William; but, doing justice to Lord Basil's motive, he presently added, "if a man can be too bold in the cause of his country."

The fate of the colony now came to a crisis. The Spaniards had brought from the Pacific a force of sixteen hundred men, who were stationed at a place called Tubucantee, waiting the arrival of an armament of eleven ships with troops on board, destined to attack Fort Saint Andrew. Captain Campbell, who, by the unanimous con-sent of the settlers, was chosen to the supreme military command, marched against them with two hundred men, surprised and stormed their camp, and dispersed their army with consider-able slaughter. But in returning from this successful expedition he had the mortification to learn that the Spanish ships had arrived before the harbour, disembarked their troops, and invested the place. A desperate defence was maintained for six weeks, until loss of men, want of ammunition, and the approach of fa-mine, compelled the defenders to an honourable surrender. The survivors of this unhappy set-tlement were so few and so much exhausted, that they were unable to weigh the anchor of the vessel in which they were to leave the fatal shore, without assistance from the conquering Spaniards.

Thus ended the attempt of Darien, an enter-prise splendid in itself, but injudicious, because the beyond the force of the whole territory little

nation by which it was undertaken. Paterson survived the disaster, and even when all was over endeavoured to revive the scheme by allow-ing the English three-fourths in a new stock company. But national animosities were too high to suffer his proposal to be listened to. He died at an advanced age, poor and neglected.

The failure of this favourite project, deep sorrow for the numbers who had fallen, many of whom were men of birth and blood, the regret for pecuniary losses, which threatened national bankruptcy, and indignation at the manner in which their charter had been dis-regarded, all at once agitated from one end to the other a kingdom, which is to a proverb proud, poor, and warm in their domestic at-tachments. Nothing could be heard through-out Scotland but the language of grief and of resentment. Indemnification, redress, revenge, were demanded by every mouth, and each hand seemed ready to vouch for the justice of the claim. For many years no such universal feel-ing had occupied the Scottish nation. King William remained indifferent to all complaints of hardship and petitions of re-dress, unless when he showed himself irritated by the importunity of the supplicants, and hurt at being obliged to evade what it was im-possible for him, with the least semblance of justice, to refuse. The motives of a prince, naturally just and equitable, and who, him-self the president of a great trading nation, knew well the injustice which he was commit-ting, seem to have been, first, a reluctance to disoblige the King of Spain, but secondly, and in a much greater degree, what William might esteem the political necessity of sacrificing the interests of Scotland to that of her jealous neigh-bours. But what is unjust can never be in a true sense necessary, and the sacrifice of prin-ciple to circumstances will, in every sense, and in all cases, be found as unwise as it is unworthy.

Two or three Novels, two or three Toys;
Two or three Misses, two or three Boys;
Two or three Aldermen reading Gazettes,
Two or three Lovers arranged in sets;
Two or three Ladies throwing the dice,
And two or three 'Squires promoting the vice;
Two or three Aristocrats, silent and proud;
Two or three Democrats, silly and loud;
Two or three Parsons as black as a crow;
Two or three Soldiers, more smart than a beau;
Two or three Brokers, all fresh from 'Change Alley;
Two or three Clerks, with their Susan and Sally;
Two or three Beauties, full-dressed for the season;
And as many Old Women dressed quite out of reason.

THE LIFE BEYOND.

BY GERALD MASSEY.

Although its features fade in light of unimagined bliss,
We have shadowy revealings of the Better World in this.

A little glimpse, when Spring unveils her face and opes her eyes,
Of the Sleeping Beauty in the soul that wakes in Paradise.

A little drop of Heaven in each diamond of the shower,
A breath of the Eternal in the fragrance of each flower!

A little low vibration in the warble of Night's bird,
Of the praises and the music that shall be hereafter heard!

A little whisper in the leaves that clap their hands and try
To glad the heart of man, and lift to heaven his thankful eye!

A little semblance mirror'd in old Ocean's smile or frown
Of His vast glory who doth bow the heavens and come down!

A little symbol shining through the worlds that move at rest
On invisible foundations of the broad almighty breast!

A little hint that stirs and thrills the wings we fold within,
And tells of that full heaven *yonder* which must *here* begin!

A little springlet welling from the fountain-head above,
That takes its earthly way to find the ocean of all love!

A little silver shiver in the ripple of the river
Caught from the light that knows no night for ever and for ever!

A little hidden likeness, often faded and defiled,
Of the great, the good All-father, in His poorest human child!

Although the best be lost in light of unimagined bliss,
We have shadowy revealings of the Better World in this.

THE UNIVERSITY OF GOTTINGEN.

A STUDENT'S LAMENT.

BY THE RIGHT HON. GEORGE CANNING.

Whene'er with haggard eyes I view
 This dungeon that I'm rotting in,
I think of those companions true,
Who studied with me at the U-
 niversity of Gottingen.

There first for thee my passion grew,
 My sweet Matilda Pottingen!
She was the daughter of my Tutor, Law Professor at the U-
 niversity of Gottingen.

Sweet 'kerchief, checked with heavenly blue,
 Which once my love sat knotting in:
Alas! Matilda then was true—
At least I thought so, at the U-
 niversity of Gottingen.

Barbs! Barbs! alas, how swift ye flew,
 Her neat post-waggon trotting in:
Ye bore Matilda from my view—
Forlorn I languished at the U-
 niversity of Gottingen.

This faded form, this pallid hue,
 This blood my veins are clotting in—
My years are many—they were few,
When first I entered at the U-
 niversity of Gottingen.

Sun, moon, and thou, vain world, adieu!
 That kings and priests are plotting in,
Doomed here to starve on water gru-
el, never shall I see the U-
 niversity of Gottingen.

auld woman's very frail and very ill; I hae to
tak a' sort o' things oot to her the nicht frae
the doctor's, after selling the cow, and it's no
in the power o' things that her dochter, industrious as she is, should be able to get them for
her otherwise."

Thomas again turned aside, and drew his
sleeve across his eyes. Having inquired the
price sought for the cow, he handed the money
to the seller, and gave the animal in charge
to one of his herdsmen. He left the market
earlier than usual, and directed his servant
that the cow should be taken to Westruther.

It was drawing towards gloaming before
Thomas approached the habitation of the widow;
and, before he could summon courage to enter
it for the first time, he sauntered for several
minutes backward and forward on the moor,
by the side of the Blackadder, which there
silently wends its way as a dull and simple
burn through the moss. He felt all the awkwardness of an old man struggling beneath the
influence of a young feeling. He thought of
what he should say, how he should act, and
how he would be received. At length he had
composed a short introductory and explanatory
speech which pleased him. He thought it contained both feeling and delicacy (according to
his notions of the latter) in their proper proportions, and after repeating it three or four
times over by the side of the Blackadder, he
proceeded towards the cottage, still repeating
it to himself as he went. But, when he raised
his hand and knocked at the door, his heart
gave a similar knock upon his bosom, as though
it mimicked him; and every idea, every word
of the introductory speech, which he had studied
and repeated again and again, short though it
was, was knocked from his memory. The door
was opened by Margaret, who invited him to
enter. She was beautiful as when he first beheld her—he thought more beautiful—for she
now spoke to him. Her mother sat in an arm-
chair by the side of the peat fire, and was supported by pillows. He took off his bonnet,
and performed an awkward but his best salutation.

"I beg your pardon," said he hesitatingly,
"for the liberty I have taken in calling upon
you. But—I was to Kelso the day—and"——
He paused, and turned his bonnet once or twice
in his hands. "And," he resumed, "I observed, or rather I should say, I learned that
ye intended to sell your cow, but I also heard
that ye was very ill, and "——Here he made
another pause. "I say I heard that ye was
very ill, and I thocht it would be a hardship
for ye to part wi' crummie, and especially at

a time when ye are sure to stand maist in need
o' every help. So I bought the cow; but, as I
say, it would be a very great hardship for ye
to be without the milk, and what the cheese
may bring, at a time like this; and therefore
I hae ordered her to be brocht back to ye, and
ane o' my men will bring her hame presently.
Never consider the cow as mine, for a bachelor
farmer like me can better afford to want the
siller, than ye can to want yer cow; and I
micht hae spent it far mair foolishly, and wi'
less satisfaction. Indeed, if ye only but think
that good I've dune, I'm mair than paid."

"Maister Hardie," said the widow, "what
have I, a stranger widow woman, done to deserve this kindness at your hands? Or how is
it in the power o' words for me to thank ye?
He who provided for the widow and the fatherless will not permit you to go unrewarded,
though I cannot. O Margaret, hinny," added
she, "thank our benefactor as we ought to
thank him, for I cannot."

Fair Margaret's thanks were a flood of tears.
"Oh, dinna greet!" said Thomas; "I would
ten times ower rather no hae bocht the cow,
but hae lost the siller, than I would hae been
the cause o' a single tear rowin' doun yer bonnie
cheeks."

"O, sir," answered the widow, "but they
are tears o' gratitude that distress my bairn,
and nae tears are mair precious."

I might tell how Thomas sat down by the
peat-fire between the widow and her daughter,
and how he took the hand of the latter, and
entreated her to dry up her tears, saying that
his chief happiness would be to be thought
their friend, and to deserve their esteem. The
cow was brought back to the widow's, and
Thomas returned to Tollishill with his herdsman. But from that night he became almost
a daily visitor at the house of Mrs. Lylestone.
He provided whatever she required—all that
was ordered for her. He spoke not of love to
Margaret; but he wooed her through his kindness to her mother. It was perhaps the most
direct avenue to her affections. Yet it was not
because Thomas thought so that he pursued
this course, but because he wanted confidence
to make his appeal in a manner more formal
or direct.

The widow lingered many months; and all
that lay within the power of human means he
caused to be done for her, to restore her to
health and strength, or at least to smooth her
dying pillow. But the last was all that could
be done. Where death spreadeth the shadow
of his wing, there is no escape from sinking
beneath the baneful influence of its shade.

Mrs. Lylestone, finding that the hour of her departure drew near, took the hand of her benefactor, and when she had thanked him for all the kindness which he had shown towards her, she added —

"But, O sir, there is one thing that makes the hand of death heavy. When the sod is cauld upon my breast, who will look aft. r my puir orphan —my bonny faitherless and mo- therless Margaret? Where will she find a hame?"

"O mem," said Thomas, "if the like o' me durst say it, she needna hae far to gang to find a hame and a heart too. Would she only be mine, I would be her protector a' that I have should be hers."

A gleam of joy brightened in the eye of the dying widow.

"Margaret!" she exclaimed faintly; and Margaret laid her face upon the bed and wept. "O my bairn' my puir bairn!" continued her mother, "shall I see ye protected and pro- vided for before I am 'where the wicked cease from troubling, and the weary are at rest,' which canna be lang noo?"

Thomas groaned—tears glistened in his eyes—he held his breath in suspense. The moment of trial, of condemnation or acquittal, of happiness or misery, had arrived. With an eager impatience he waited to hear her answer. But Margaret's heart was prepared for his pro- posal. He had first touched it with gratitude —he had obtained her esteem; and where these sentiments prevail in the bosom of a woman whose affections have not been bestowed upon another, love is not far distant—if it be not between them, and a part of both.

"Did ever I disobey you, mother?" sobbed Margaret, raising her parent's hand to her lips.

"No, my bairn, no!" answered the widow. And raising herself in the bed, she took her daughter's hand and placed it in the hand of Thomas Hardie.

"Oh!" said he, "is this possible? Does my bonny Margaret really consent to make me the happiest man on earth? Shall I hae a gem at Tollishill that I wadna exchange for a mon- arch's diadem!"

It is sufficient to say that the young and lovely Margaret Lylestone became Mrs. Hardie of Tollishill; or, as she was generally called, "Midside Maggie." Her mother died within three months after their marriage, but died in peace, having, as she said, "seen her dear bairn blessed wi' a leal and a kind guidman, and ane that was weel to do."

For two years after their marriage, and not a happier couple than Thomas and Midside

Maggie was to be found on all the long Lam- mermoors, in the Merse, nor yet in the broad Lothians. They saw the broom and the heather bloom in their season, and they heard the mavis sing before their dwelling; yea, they beheld the snow falling on the mountains, and the drift sweeping down the glens; but while the former delighted, the latter harmed them not, and from all they drew mutual joy and happi- ness. Thomas said that "Maggie was a match- less wife;" and she that "he was a kind, kind husband."

But the third winter was one of terror among the hills. It was near the new year; the snow began to fall on a Saturday, and when the fol- lowing Friday came the storm had not ceased. It was accompanied by frost and a fierce wind, and the drift swept and whirled like awful pillars of alabaster down the hills, and along the glens—

"Sweeping the flocks and herds."

Fearful was the wrath of the tempest on the Lammermoors. Many farmers suffered se- verely, but none more severely than Thomas Hardie of Tollishill. Hundreds of his sheep had perished in a single night. He was brought from prosperity to the brink of adversity.

But another winter came round. It com- menced with a severity scarce inferior to that which had preceded it, and again scores of his sheep were buried in the snow. But February had not passed, and scarce had the sun entered what is represented as the astronomical sign of the *two fish* in the heavens, when the genial influence of spring fell with almost summer warmth upon the earth. During the night the dews came heavily on the ground, and the sun sucked it up in a vapour. But the herbage grew rapidly, and the flocks ate of it greedily, and licked the dew ere the sun rose to dry it up. It brought the murrain amongst them: they died by hundreds; and those that even fattened, but did not die, no man would pur- chase; or, if purchased, it was only upon the understanding that the money should be re- turned if the animals were found unsound. These misfortunes were too much for Thomas Hardie. Within two years he found himself a ruined man. But he grieved not for the loss of his flocks, nor yet for his own sake, but for that of his fair young wife, whom he loved as the apple of his eye. Many, when they heard of his misfortunes, said that they were sorry for bonny Midside Maggie.

But, worst of all, the rent-day of Thomas Hardie drew near; and for the first time since he had held a farm, he was unable to meet his landlord with his money in his hand. Margaret beheld the agony of his spirit, and she knew its cause. She put on her Sunday hood and kirtle; and professing to her husband that she wished to go to Lauder, she took her way to Thirlestane Castle, the residence of their proud landlord, before whom every tenant in arrear trembled. With a shaking hand she knocked at the hall door, and after much perseverance and entreaty, was admitted into the presence of the haughty earl. She curtsied low before him.

"Well, what want ye, my bonny lass?" said Lauderdale, eyeing her significantly.

"May it please yer lordship," replied Margaret, "I am the wife o' yer tenant, Thomas Hardie o' Tollishill; an' a guid tenant he has been to yer lordship for twenty years and mair, as yer lordship maun weel ken."

"He has been my tenant for more than twenty years, say ye?" interrupted Lauderdale; "and ye say ye are his wife: why, looking on thy bonny face, I should say that the heather hasna bloomed twenty times on the knowes o' Tollishill since thy mother bore thee. Yet ye say ye are his wife! Beshrew me, but Thomas Hardie is a man o' taste. Arena ye his daughter?"

"No, my lord; his first, his only, an' his lawfu' wife—an' I would only say, that to ye an' yer faither before ye, for mair than twenty years, he has paid his rent regularly an' faithfully; but the seasons hae visited us sairly, very sairly, for twa years successively, my lord, an' the drift has destroyed, an' the rot rooted oot oor flocks, sae that we are hardly able to haud up oor heads among oor neebors, and to meet yer lordship at yer rent-day is oot o' oor power; therefore hae I come to ye to implore ye, that we may hae time to gather oor feet, an' to gie yer lordship an' every man his due, when it is in oor power."

"Hear me, guidwife," rejoined the earl; "were I to listen to such stories as yours, I might have every farmer's wife on my estates coming whimpering and whinging, till I was left to shake a purse wi' naething in't, and allowing others the benefit o' my lands. But it is not every day that a face like yours comes in the shape o' sorrow before me; and for ae kiss o' your cherry mou' (and ye may take my compliments to your auld man for his taste) ye shall have a discharge for your half-year's rent, and see if that may set your husband on his feet again."

"Na, yer lordship, na!" replied Margaret: "it would ill become ony woman in my situation in life, an' especially a married ane, to be daffin with sic as yer lordship. I am the wife o' Thomas Hardie, wha is a guid guidman to me, an' I cam here this day to entreat ye to deal kindly wi' him in the day o' his misfortune."

"Troth," replied Lauderdale—who could feel the force of virtue in others, though he did not always practise it in his own person—"I hae heard o' the blossom o' Tollishill before, an' a bonny flower ye are to blossom in an auld man's bower; but I find ye modest as ye are bonny, an' upon one condition will I grant yer request. Ye hae tauld me o' yer hirsels being buried wi' the drift, an' that the snaw has covered the May primrose on Leader braes; now it is Martinmas, an' if in June ye bring me a snow-ball, not only shall ye be quit o' yer back rent, but ye shall sit free in Tollishill till Martinmas next. But see that in June ye bring me the snow-ball or the rent."

Margaret made her obeisance before the earl, and, thanking him, withdrew. But she feared the coming of June; for to raise the rent even then she well knew would be a thing impossible, and she thought also it would be equally so to preserve a snow-ball beneath the melting sun of June. Though young she had too much prudence and honesty to keep a secret from her husband; it was her maxim, and it was a good one, that "there ought to be no secrets between a man and his wife, which the one would conceal from the other." She therefore told him of her journey to Thirlestane, and of all that had passed between her and the earl. Thomas kissed her cheek, and called her his "bonny, artless Maggie;" but he had no more hope of seeing a snow-ball in June than she had, and he said, "the bargain was like the bargain o' a crafty Lauderdale."

Again the winter storms howled upon the Lammermoors, and the snow lay deep upon the hills. Thomas and his herdsmen were busied in exertions to preserve the remainder of his flocks; but one day, when the westling winds breathed with a thawing influence upon the snow-clad hills, Margaret went forth to where there was a small, deep, and shadowed ravine by the side of the Leader. In it the rivulet formed a pool, and seemed to sleep, and there the gray trout loved to lie at ease; for a high dark rock, over which the brushwood grew, overhung it, and the rays of the sun fell not upon it. In the rock, and near the side of the stream, was a deep cavity, and Margaret formed a snow-ball on the brae top, and she rolled it slowly down into the shadowed glen, till it attained the magnitude of an avalanche in miniature. She trode upon it, and pressed it firmly together, till it obtained almost the hardness and consistency of ice. She rolled it far into the cavity, and blocked up the mouth of the aperture, so that neither light nor air might penetrate the strange coffer in which she had deposited the equally strange rent of Tollishill. Verily, common as ice-houses are in our day, let not Midside Maggie be deprived of the merit of their invention.

I have said that it was her maxim to keep no secret from her husband; but, as it is said, there is no rule without an exception, even so it was in the case of Margaret, and there was one secret which she communicated not to Thomas, and that was—the secret of the hidden snow-ball.

But June came, and Thomas Hardie was a sorrowful man. He had in no measure overcome the calamities of former seasons, and he was still unprepared with his rent. Margaret shared not his sorrow, but strove to cheer him, and said—

"We shall hae a snawba' in June, though I climb to the top o' Cheviot for it."

"O my bonny lassie," replied he—and he could see the summit of Cheviot from his farm —"dinna deceive yersel' wi' what could only be words spoken in jest; but, at ony rate, I perceive there has been nae snaw on Cheviot for a month past."

Now, not a week had passed, but Margaret had visited the aperture in the ravine, where the snow-ball was concealed, not through idle curiosity to perceive whether it had melted away, but more effectually to stop up every crevice that might have been made in the materials with which she had blocked up the mouth of the cavity.

But the third day of the dreadful month had not passed, when a messenger arrived at Tollishill from Thirlestane with the abrupt mandate—"*June has come!*"

"And we shall be at Thirlestane the morn," answered Margaret.

"O my doo," said Thomas, "what nonsense are ye talking!—that isna like ye, Margaret; I'll be in Greenlaw Jail the morn; and oor bits o' things in the hoose, and oor flocks will be seized by the harpies o' the law; and the only thing that distresses me is, what is to come o' you, hinny."

"Dinna dree the death ye'll never dee," said Margaret affectionately; "we shall see, if we be spared, what the morn will bring."

"The fortitude o' yer mind, Margaret," said Thomas, taking her hand; and he intended to have said more, to have finished a sentence in

admiration of her worth, but his heart filled, and he was silent.

On the following morning Margaret said unto him—

"Now, Thomas, if ye are ready, we'll gang to Thirlestane. It is aye waur to expect or think o' an evil than to face it."

"Margaret, dear," said he, "I canna comprehend ye—wherefore should I thrust my head into the lion's den? It will soon enough seek me in my path."

Nevertheless she said unto him, "Come," and bade him be of good heart; and he rose and accompanied her. But she conducted him to the deep ravine, where the waters seem to sleep and no sunbeam ever falls; and, as she removed the earth and the stones, with which she had blocked up the mouth of the cavity in the rock, he stood wondering. She entered the aperture, and rolled forth the firm mass of snow, which was yet too large to be lifted by hands. When Thomas saw this he smiled, and wept at the same instant, and he pressed his wife's cheek to his bosom, and said—

"Great has been the care o' my poor Margaret; but it is o' no avail; for though ye hae proved mair than a match for the seasons, the proposal was but a jest o' Lauderdale."

"What is a man but his word?" replied Margaret; "and him a nobleman too."

"Nobility are but men," answered Thomas, "and seldom better men than ither folk. Believe me, if we were to gang afore him wi' a snawba' in oor hands, we should only get lauched at for oor pains."

"It was his ain agreement," added she; "and, at ony rate, we can be naething the waur for seeing if he will abide by it."

Breaking the snowy mass she rolled up a portion of it in a napkin, and they went towards Thirlestane together; though often did Thomas stop by the way, and say—

"Margaret, dear, I'm perfectly ashamed to gang upon this business; as sure as I am standing here, as I have tauld ye, we will only get oorselves lauched at."

"I would rather be lauched at," added she, "than despised for breaking my word; and if oor laird break his noo, wha wadna despise him?"

Harmonious as their wedded life had hitherto been, there was what might well nigh be called bickerings between them on the road; for Thomas felt or believed that she was leading him on a fool's errand. But they arrived at the castle of Thirlestane, and were ushered into the mansion of its proud lord.

"Ha!" said the earl as they entered, "bonny

landlord with his money in his hand. Margaret beheld the agony of his spirit, and she knew its cause. She put on her Sunday hood and kirtle; and professing to her husband that she wished to go to Lauder, she took her way to Thirlestane Castle, the residence of their proud landlord, before whom every tenant in arrear trembled. With a shaking hand she knocked at the hall door, and after much perseverance and entreaty, was admitted into the presence of the haughty earl. She curtsied low before him.

"Well, what want ye, my bonny lass?" said Lauderdale, eyeing her significantly.

"May it please yer lordship," replied Margaret, "I am the wife o' yer tenant, Thomas Hardie o' Tollishill; an' a guid tenant he has been to yer lordship for twenty years and mair, as yer lordship maun weel ken."

"He has been my tenant for more than twenty years, say ye?" interrupted Lauderdale; "and ye say ye are his wife: why, looking on thy bonny face, I should say that the heather hasna bloomed twenty times on the knowes o' Tollishill since thy mother bore thee. Yet ye say ye are his wife! Beshrew me, but Thomas Hardie is a man o' taste. Arena ye his daughter?"

"No, my lord; his first, his only, an' his lawfu' wife—an' I would only say, that to ye an' yer faither before ye, for mair than twenty years, he has paid his rent regularly an' faithfully; but the seasons hae visited us sairly, very sairly, for twa years successively, my lord, an' the drift has destroyed, an' the rot rooted oot oor flocks, sae that we are hardly able to haud up oor heads among oor neebors, and to meet yer lordship at yer rent-day is oot o' oor power; therefore hae I come to ye to implore ye, that we may hae time to gather oor feet, an' to gie yer lordship an' every man his due, when it is in oor power."

"Hear me, guidwife," rejoined the earl: "were I to listen to such stories as yours, I might have every farmer's wife on my estates coming whimpering and whinging, till I was left to shake a purse with naething in't, and allowing others the benefit o' my lands. But it is not every day that a face like yours comes in the shape o' sorrow before me; and for ae kiss o' your cherry mou' (and ye may take my compliments to your auld man for his taste) ye shall have a discharge for your half-year's rent, and see if that may set your husband on his feet again."

"Na, yer lordship, na!" replied Margaret: "it would ill become ony woman in my situation in life, an' especially a married ane, to be

daffin with sic as yer lordship. I am the wife o' Thomas Hardie, wha is a guid guidman to me, an' I cam here this day to entreat ye to deal kindly wi' him in the day o' his misfortune."

"Troth," replied Lauderdale—who could feel the force of virtue in others, though he did not always practise it in his own person—"I hae heard o' the blossom o' Tollishill before, an' a bonny flower ye are to blossom in an auld man's bower; but I find ye modest as ye are bonny, an' upon one condition will I grant yer request. Ye hae tauld me o' yer hirsels being buried wi' the drift, an' that the snaw has covered the May primrose on Leader braes; now it is Martinmas, an' if in June ye bring me a snow-ball, not only shall ye be quit o' yer back rent, but ye shall sit free in Tollishill till Martinmas next. But see that in June ye bring me the snow-ball or the rent."

Margaret made her obeisance before the earl, and, thanking him, withdrew. But she feared the coming of June; for to raise the rent even then she well knew would be a thing impossible, and she thought also it would be equally so to preserve a snow-ball beneath the melting sun of June. Though young she had too much prudence and honesty to keep a secret from her husband; it was her maxim, and it was a good one, that "there ought to be no secrets between a man and his wife, which the one would conceal from the other." She therefore told him of her journey to Thirlestane, and of all that had passed between her and the earl. Thomas kissed her cheek, and called her his "bonny, artless Maggie;" but he had no more hope of seeing a snow-ball in June than she had, and he said, "the bargain was like the bargain o' a crafty Lauderdale."

Again the winter storms howled upon the Lammermoors, and the snow lay deep upon the hills. Thomas and his herdsmen were busied in exertions to preserve the remainder of his flocks; but one day, when the westling winds breathed with a thawing influence upon the snow-clad hills, Margaret went forth to where there was a small, deep, and shadowed ravine by the side of the Leader. In it the rivulet formed a pool, and seemed to sleep, and there the gray trout loved to lie at ease; for a high dark rock, over which the brushwood grew, overhung it, and the rays of the sun fell not upon it. In the rock, and near the side of the stream, was a deep cavity, and Margaret formed a snow-ball on the brae top, and she rolled it slowly down into the shadowed glen, till it attained the magnitude of an avalanche in miniature. She trode upon it, and pressed it firmly together, till it obtained almost the hardness and consistency of ice. She rolled it far into the cavity, and blocked up the mouth of the aperture, so that neither light nor air might penetrate the strange coffer in which she had deposited the equally strange rent of Tollishill. Verily, common as ice-houses are in our day, let not Midside Maggie be deprived of the merit of their invention.

I have said that it was her maxim to keep no secret from her husband; but, as it is said, there is no rule without an exception, even so it was in the case of Margaret, and there was one secret which she communicated not to Thomas, and that was—the secret of the hidden snow-ball.

But June came, and Thomas Hardie was a sorrowful man. He had in no measure overcome the calamities of former seasons, and he was still unprepared with his rent. Margaret shared not his sorrow, but strove to cheer him, and said—

"We shall hae a snawba' in June, though I climb to the top o' Cheviot for it."

"O my bonny lassie," replied he—and he could see the summit of Cheviot from his farm—"dinna deceive yersel' wi' what could only be words spoken in jest; but, at ony rate, I perceive there has been nae snaw on Cheviot for a month past."

Now, not a week had passed, but Margaret had visited the aperture in the ravine, where the snow-ball was concealed, not through idle curiosity to perceive whether it had melted away, but more effectually to stop up every crevice that might have been made in the materials with which she had blocked up the mouth of the cavity.

But the third day of the dreadful month had not passed, when a messenger arrived at Tollishill from Thirlestane with the abrupt mandate—"*June has come!*"

"And we shall be at Thirlestane the morn," answered Margaret.

"O my doo," said Thomas, "what nonsense are ye talking!—that isna like ye, Margaret; I'll be in Greenlaw Jail the morn; and oor bits o' things in the hoose, and oor flocks will be seized by the harpies o' the law; and the only thing that distresses me is, what is to come o' you, hinny."

"Dinna dree the death ye'll never dee," said Margaret affectionately; "we shall see, if we be spared, what the morn will bring."

"The fortitude o' yer mind, Margaret," said Thomas, taking her hand; and he intended to have said more, to have finished a sentence in admiration of her worth, but his heart filled, and he was silent.

On the following morning Margaret said unto him—

"Now, Thomas, if ye are ready, we'll gang to Thirlestane. It is aye waur to expect or think o' an evil than to face it."

"Margaret, dear," said he, "I canna comprehend ye—wherefore should I thrust my head into the lion's den? It will soon enough seek me in my path."

Nevertheless she said unto him, "Come," and bade him be of good heart; and he rose and accompanied her. But she conducted him to the deep ravine, where the waters seem to sleep and no sunbeam ever falls; and, as she removed the earth and the stones, with which she had blocked up the mouth of the cavity in the rock, he stood wondering. She entered the aperture, and rolled forth the firm mass of snow, which was yet too large to be lifted by hands. When Thomas saw this he smiled, and wept at the same instant, and he pressed his wife's cheek to his bosom, and said—

"Great has been the care o' my poor Margaret; but it is o' no avail; for though ye hae proved mair than a match for the seasons, the proposal was but a jest o' Lauderdale."

"What is a man but his word?" replied Margaret; "and him a nobleman too."

"Nobility are but men," answered Thomas, "and seldom better men than ither folk. Believe me, if we were to gang afore him wi' a snawba' in oor hands, we should only get lauched at for oor pains."

"It was his ain agreement," added she; "and, at ony rate, we can be naething the waur for seeing if he will abide by it."

Breaking the snowy mass she rolled up a portion of it in a napkin, and they went towards Thirlestane together; though often did Thomas stop by the way, and say—

"Margaret, dear, I'm perfectly ashamed to gang upon this business; as sure as I am standing here, as I have tauld ye, we will only get oorselves lauched at."

"I would rather be lauched at," added she, "than despised for breaking my word; and if oor laird break his noo, wha wadna despise him?"

Harmonious as their wedded life had hitherto been, there was what might well nigh be called bickerings between them on the road; for Thomas felt or believed that she was leading him on a fool's errand. But they arrived at the castle of Thirlestane, and were ushered into the mansion of its proud lord.

"Ha!" said the carl as they entered, "bonny

Midside Maggie and her auld guidman! Well, what bring ye?—the rents o' Tollishill, or their equivalent?" Thomas looked at his young wife, for he saw nothing to give him hope on the countenance of Lauderdale, and he thought that he pronounced the word "*equivalent*" with a sneer.

"I bring ye snaw in June, my lord," replied Margaret, "agreeably to the terms o' yer bargain; and I'm sorry, for your sake and oors, that it hasna yet been in oor power to bring gowd instead o't."

Loud laughed the earl as Margaret unrolled the huge snowball before him; and Thomas thought unto himself, "I said how it would be." But Lauderdale, calling for his writing materials, sat down and wrote, and he placed in the hands of Thomas a discharge, not only for his back rent, but for all that should otherwise be due at the ensuing Martinmas.

Thomas Hardie bowed and bowed again before the earl, low and yet lower, awkwardly and still more awkwardly; and he endeavoured to thank him, but his tongue faltered in the performance of its office. He could have taken his hand in his and wrung it fervently, leaving his fingers to express what his tongue could not; but his laird was an earl, and there was a necessary distance to be observed between an earl and a Lammermoor farmer.

"Thank not me, goodman," said Lauderdale, "but thank the modesty and discretion o' yer winsome wife."

Margaret was silent; but gratitude for the kindness which the earl had shown unto her husband and herself took deep root in her heart. Gratitude, indeed, formed the predominating principle in her character, and fitted her even for acts of heroism.

The unexpected and unwonted generosity of the earl had enabled Thomas Hardie to overcome the losses with which the fury of the seasons had overwhelmed him, and he prospered beyond any farmer on the hills. But, while he prospered, the Earl of Lauderdale, in his turn, was overtaken by adversity. The stormy times of the civil wars raged, and it is well known with what devotedness Lauderdale followed the fortunes of the king. When the Commonwealth began he was made prisoner, conveyed to London, and confined in the Tower. There nine years of captivity crept slowly and gloomily over him; but they neither taught him mercy to others, nor to moderate his ambition, as was manifested when power and prosperity again cast their beams upon him. But he now lingered in the Tower, without prospect or hope of release, living upon the bare sustenance of a prisoner, while his tenants dwelt on his estates, and did as they pleased with his rents, as though they should not again behold the face of a landlord.

But Midside Maggie grieved for the fate of him whose generosity had brought prosperity, such as they had never known before, to herself and to her husband; and, in the fulness of her gratitude, she was ever planning schemes for his deliverance; and she urged upon her husband that it was their duty to attempt to deliver their benefactor from captivity, as he had delivered them from the iron grasp of ruin when misfortune lay heavily on them. Now, as duly as the rent-day came, from the Martinmas to which the snow-ball had been his discharge, Thomas Hardie faithfully and punctually locked away his rent to the last farthing, that he might deliver it into the hands of his laird, should he again be permitted to claim his own; but he saw not in what way they could attempt his deliverance, as his wife proposed.

"Thomas," said she, "there are ten lang years o' rent due, and we hae the siller locked away. It is o' nae use to us, for it isna oors; but it may be o' use to him. It would enable him to fare better in his prison, and maybe to put a handfu' o' gowd into the hands o' his keepers, and thereby to escape abroad, and it wad furnish him wi' the means o' living when he was abroad. Remember his kindness to us, and think that there is nae sin equal to the sin o' ingratitude."

"But," added Thomas, "in what way could we get the money to him? for, if we were to send it, it would never reach him, and, as a prisoner, he wouldna be allooed to receive it."

"Let us tak it to him oorsels, then," said Margaret.

"Tak it oorsels!" exclaimed Thomas in amazement, "a' the way to London! It is oot o' the question a'thegither, Margaret. We wad be robbed o' every plack before we got halfway; or if we were even there, hoo, in a' the world, do ye think we could get it to him, or that we would be allooed to see him?"

"Leave that to me," was her reply; "only say ye will gang, and a' that shall be accomplished. There is nae obstacle in the way but the want o' yer consent. But the debt, and the ingratitude o' it thegither, hang heavy upon my heart."

Thomas at length yielded to the importunities of his wife, and agreed that they should make a pilgrimage to London, to pay his rent to his captive laird; though how they were to carry the gold in safety through an unsettled country, a distance of more than three hundred miles, was a difficulty he could not overcome. But Margaret removed his fears; she desired him to count out the gold, and place it before her; and when he had done so, she went to the meal-tub and took out a quantity of pease and of barley meal mixed, sufficient to knead a goodly fadge or bannock; and when she had kneaded it, and rolled it out, she took the golden pieces and pressed them into the paste of the embryo bannock, and again she doubled it together, and again rolled it out, and kneaded into it the remainder of the gold. She then fashioned it into a thick bannock, and placing it on the hearth, covered it with the red ashes of the peats.

Thomas sat marvelling, as the formation of the singular purse proceeded, and when he beheld the operation completed, and the bannock placed upon the hearth to bake, he only exclaimed, "Weel, woman's ingenuity dings a'! I wadna hae thocht o' the like o' that, had I lived a thousand years! O Margaret, hinny, but ye are a strange ane."

"Hoots," replied she, "I'm sure ye micht easily hae imagined that it was the safest plan we could hae thocht upon to carry the siller in safety; for, I am sure, there isna a thief between the Tweed and Lon'on toun that would covet or carry awa a bear bannock."

"Troth, my doo, and I believe ye're richt," replied Thomas; "but wha could hae thocht o' sic an expedient? Sure there never was a bannock baked like the bannock o' Tollishill."

On the third day after this, an old man and a fair lad, before the sun had yet risen, were observed crossing the English Border. They alternately carried a wallet across their shoulders, which contained a few articles of apparel and a bannock. They were dressed as shepherds, and passengers turned and gazed on them as they passed along; for the beauty of the youth's countenance excited their admiration. Never had Lowland bonnet covered so fair a brow. The elder stranger was Thomas Hardie, and the youth none other than his Midside Maggie.

I will not follow them through the stages of their long and weary journey, nor dwell upon the perils and adventures they encountered by the way. But on the third week after they had left Tollishill, and when they were beyond the town called Stevenage, and almost within sight of the metropolis, they were met by an elderly military-looking man, who, struck with the lovely countenance of the seeming youth, their dress, and way-worn appearance, ac-

costed them, saying, "Good morrow, strangers; ye seem to have travelled far. Is this fair youth your son, old man?"

"He is a gay sib freend," answered Thomas.

"And whence come ye?" continued the stranger.

"Frae Leader Haughs, on the bonny Borders o' the north countrie," replied Margaret.

"And whence go ye?" resumed the other.

"First tell me wha ye may be that are sae inquisitive, interrupted Thomas, in a tone which betrayed something like impatience.

"Some call me George Monk," replied the stranger mildly, "others Honest George. I am a general in the Parliamentary army." Thomas reverentially raised his hand to his bonnet, and bowed his head.

"Then pardon me, sir," added Margaret, "and if ye indeed be the guid and gallant general, sma' offence will ye tak at onything that may be said amiss by a country laddie. We are tenants o' the Lord o' Lauderdale, whom ye now keep in captivity; and though we mayna think as he thinks, yet we never faund him but a guid landlord; and little guid, in my opinion, it can do ony body to keep him, as he has been noo for nine years, caged up like a bird. Therefore, though oor ain business that has brocht us up to London should fail, I winna regret the journey, since it has afforded me an opportunity o' seeing yer Excellency, and soliciting yer interest, which maun be poocrfu', in behalf o' oor laird, and that ye would release him frae his prison; and, if he michtna remain in this countrie, obtain permission for him to gang abroad."

"Ye plead fairly and honestly for yer laird, fair youth," returned the general; "yet, though he is no man to be trusted, I needs say he hath had his portion of captivity measured out abundantly; and, since ye have minded me of him, ere a week go round I will think of what may be done for Lauderdale." Other questions were asked and answered—some truly, and some evasively; and Thomas and Margaret, blessing Honest George in their hearts, went on their way rejoicing at having met him.

On arriving in London she laid aside the shepherd's garb in which she had journeyed, and resumed her wonted apparel. On the second day after their arrival she went out upon Tower Hill, dressed as a Scottish peasant girl, with a basket on her arm; and in the basket were a few ballads, and the bannock of Tollishill. She affected silliness, and, acting the part of a wandering minstrel, went singing her ballads towards the gate of the Tower. Thomas followed her at a distance. Her appearance interested the guard; and as she stood singing before the gate—"What want ye, pretty face?" inquired the officer of the guard. "Your alms, if you please," said she, smiling innocently, "and to sing a bonny Scotch sang to the Laird o' Lauderdale."

The officer and the sentinels laughed; and, after she had sung them another song or two, she was permitted to enter the gate, and a soldier pointed out to her the room in which Lauderdale was confined. On arriving before the grated windows of his prison she raised her eyes towards them, and began to sing "*Leader Haughs.*" The wild, sweet melody of his native land drew Lauderdale to the windows of his prison-house, and in the countenance of the minstrel he remembered the lovely features of Midside Maggie. He requested permission of the keeper that she should be admitted to his presence; and his request was complied with.

"Bless thee, sweet face!" said the earl, as she was admitted into his prison; "and you have not forgotten the snow-ball in June?" And he took her hand to raise it to his lips.

"Hooly, hooly, my guid lord," said she, withdrawing her hand; "my fingers were made for nae sic purpose—Thomas Hardie is here"—and she laid her hand upon her fair bosom; "though now standing without the yett o' the Tower." Lauderdale again wondered, and, with a look of mingled curiosity and confusion, inquired—"Wherefore do ye come; and why do ye seek me?" "I brocht ye a snawba' before," said she, "for yer rent—I bring ye a bannock noo." And she took the bannock from the basket, and placed it before him."

"Woman," added he, "are ye really as demented as I thocht ye but feigned to be, when ye sang before the window."

"The proof o' the bannock," replied Margaret, "will be in the breakin' o't."

"Then, goodwife, it will not be easily proved," said he—and he took the bannock, and, with some difficulty, broke it over his knee; but when he beheld the golden coins that were kneaded through it, for the first, perhaps the last and only time in his existence, the Earl of Lauderdale burst into tears, and exclaimed—"Well, every bannock has its maik, but the bannock o' Tollishill! Yet, kind as ye hae been, the gold is useless to ane that groans in hopeless captivity."

"Yours has been a long captivity," said Margaret; "but it is not hopeless; and if honest General Monk is to be trusted, from what he tauld me not three days by-gane, be-

fore a week gae roond ye will be at liberty to go abroad, and there the bannock o' Tollishill may be o' use."

The wonder of Lauderdale increased, and he replied—"Monk will keep his word; but what mean ye of him?"

And she related to him the interview they had had with the general by the way. Lauderdale took her hand, a ray of hope and joy spread over his face, and he added—"Never shall ye rue the bakin' o' the bannock, if auld times come back again."

Margaret left the Tower singing as she had entered it, and joined her husband, whom she found leaning over the railing around the moat, and anxiously waiting her return. They spent a few days more in London, to rest and to gaze upon its wonders, and again set out upon their journey to Tollishill. General Monk remembered his promise; within a week the Earl of Lauderdale was liberated, with permission to go abroad, and there, as Margaret had intimated, he found the bannock of Tollishill of service.

A few more years passed round, during which old Thomas Hardie still prospered; but during those years the Commonwealth came to an end, the king was recalled, and with him, as one of his chief favourites, returned the Earl of Lauderdale. And when he arrived in Scotland clothed with power, whatever else he forgot, he remembered the bannock of Tollishill. Arrayed in what might have passed as royal state, and attended by fifty of his followers, he rode to the dwelling of Thomas Hardie and Midside Maggie; and when they came forth to meet him he dismounted, and drew forth a costly silver girdle of strange workmanship, and fastened it round her jimp waist, saying—"Wear this, for now it is my turn to be grateful, and for your husband's life, and your life, and the life of the generation after ye" (for they had children), "ye shall sit rent free on the lands ye now farm. For, truly, every bannock had its maik, but the bannock o' Tollishill."

Thomas and Margaret felt their hearts too full to express their thanks; and ere they could speak, the earl, mounting his horse, rode towards Thirlestane; and his followers, waving their bonnets, shouted—"Long live Midside Maggie, queen of Tollishill."

Such is the story of "The Bannock o' Tollishill;" and it is only necessary to add, for the information of the curious, that I believe the silver girdle may be seen until this day, in the neighbourhood of Tollishill, and in the possession of a descendant of Midside Maggie, to whom it was given.

THE SHIPWRECK.

[William Falconer, born in Edinburgh, 11th February, 1732; lost at sea in the *Aurora* frigate, December, 1769. His father was a barber and wig maker in the Netherbow, and afterwards a grocer, but always unfortunate in business. When about fourteen the poet was sent to sea. In 1750 he was second mate on board the *Britannia*, which, on the passage from Alexandria to Venice, was shipwrecked on the coast of Greece. Only three of the crew survived, of whom Falconer was one; and it was this incident which inspired his poem. He served some time as midshipman in the Royal Navy, then was appointed purser, and was engaged in that capacity in the *Aurora* when it was lost on the passage to India. The *Shipwreck* first appeared in 1762. and was received with high favour by the public. The most important of his other poems are: *The Demagogue; A Poem, sacred to the Memory of H.R.H. Frederic Prince of Wales; Ode on the Duke of York's Second Departure from England as Rear-admiral; To Miranda; The Fond Lover;* and *The Description of a Ninety-gun Ship.* The Rev. John Mitford, in his life of Falconer prefixed to the Aldine edition of the *Shipwreck*, says of that poem: "It is a singularly elegant production of a person who had received no education beyond the mere elements of language, and who was subsequently occupied in the severe duties and business of a seafaring life —equally without learning or leisure. The poetical powers of Falconer, in whatever rank they may be placed, were the gift of nature." Falconer compiled a valuable Marine Dictionary (1769).[1]]

The moment fraught with fate approaches fast!
While thronging sailors climb each quivering mast;
The ship no longer now must stem the land,
And "Hard a starboard!" is the last command:
While every suppliant voice to Heaven applies,
The prow, swift wheeling, to the westward flies;
Twelve sailors, on the fore-mast who depend,
High on the platform of the top ascend:
Fatal retreat! for, while the plunging prow
Immerges headlong in the wave below,
Down prest by watery weight the bowsprit bends,
And from above the stern deep-crashing rends:
Beneath her bow the floating ruins lie;
The fore-mast totters, unsustained on high;
And now the ship, forelifted by the sea,
Hurls the tall fabric backward o'er her lee;
While, in the general wreck, the faithful stay
Drags the main top-mast by the cap away:
Flung from the mast, the seamen strive in vain,
Through hostile floods, their vessel to regain;
Weak hope, alas! they buffet long the wave,
And grasp at life though sinking in the grave;
Till all exhausted, and bereft of strength,

[1] It is said that Mr. Murray, founder of the famous publishing house, asked Falconer in 1768 to join him in the business. Mr. Murray wrote to him: "Many blockheads in the trade are making fortunes, and did we not succeed as well as they, I think it must be imputed only to ourselves." It is not known why Falconer declined this advantageous offer.

O'erpowered they yield to cruel fate at length;
The burying waters close around their head,
They sink! for ever numbered with the dead.
Those who remain the weather shrouds embrace,
Nor longer mourn their lost companions' case;
Transfixt with terror at the approaching doom,
Self-pity in their breasts alone has room:
Albert, and Rodmond, and Palemon, near
With young Arion, on the mast appear;
E'en they, amid the unspeakable distress,
In every look distracting thoughts confess,
In every vein the refluent blood congeals,
And every bosom mortal terror feels;
Begirt with all the horrors of the main
They viewed the adjacent shore, but viewed in vain:
Such torments, in the drear abodes of hell,
Where sad despair laments with rueful yell,
Such torments agonize the damned breast,
That sees remote the mansions of the blest.

It comes! the dire catastrophe draws near,
Lashed furious on by destiny severe:
The ship hangs hovering on the verge of death,
Hell yawns, rocks rise, and breakers roar beneath!
O yet confirm my heart, ye Powers above!
This last tremendous shock of fate to prove;
The tottering frame of reason yet sustain,
Nor let this total havoc whirl my brain;
Since I, all trembling in extreme distress,
Must still the horrible result express.

In vain, alas! the sacred shades of yore
Would arm the mind with philosophic lore;
In vain they'd teach us, at the latest breath
To smile serene amid the pangs of death:
Immortal Zeno's self would trembling see
Inexorable fate beneath the lee;
And Epictetus at the sight, in vain
Attempt his stoic firmness to retain:
Had Socrates, for godlike virtue famed,
And wisest of the sons of men proclaimed,
Spectator of such various horrors been,
E'en he had staggered at this dreadful scene.

In vain the cords and axes were prepared,
For every wave now smites the quivering yard;
High o'er the ship they throw a dreadful shade,
Then on her burst in terrible cascade;
Across the foundered deck o'erwhelming roar,
And foaming, swelling, bound upon the shore.
Swift up the mountain billow now she flies,
Her shattered top half-buried in the skies;
Borne o'er a latent reef the hull impends,
Then thundering on the marble crags descends:
Her ponderous bulk the dire concussion feels,
And o'er upheaving surges wounded reels—
Again she plunges! hark! a second shock
Bilges the splitting vessel on the rock—
Down on the vale of death, with dismal cries,
The fated victims shuddering cast their eyes
In wild despair; while yet another stroke
With strong convulsion rends the solid oak:
Ah Heaven!—behold her crashing ribs divide!
She looses, parts, and spreads in ruin o'er the tide.

Oh, were it mine with sacred Maro's art
To wake to sympathy the feeling heart,
Like him, the smooth and mournful verse to dress
In all the pomp of exquisite distress;
Then, too severely taught by cruel fate,
To share in all the perils I relate,
Then might I, with unrivalled strains, deplore
The impervious horrors of a leeward shore.
As o'er the surf the bending main-mast hung,
Still on the rigging thirty seamen clung:
Some on a broken crag were struggling cast,
And there by oozy tangles grappled fast;
Awhile they bore the o'erwhelming billows' rage,
Unequal combat with their fate to wage;
Till all benumbed, and feeble, they forego
Their slippery hold, and sink to shades below:
Some, from the main yard-arm impetuous thrown
On marble ridges, die without a groan:
Three with Palemon on their skill depend,
And from the wreck on oars and rafts descend;
Now on the mountain-wave on high they ride,
Then downward plunge beneath the involving tide;
Till one, who seems in agony to strive,
The whirling breakers heave on shore alive:
The rest a speedier end of anguish knew,
And prest the stony beach—a lifeless crew!
Next, O unhappy chief! the eternal doom
Of Heaven decreed thee to the briny tomb:
What scenes of misery torment thy view!
What painful struggles of thy dying crew!
Thy perished hopes all buried in the flood
O'erspread with corses, red with human blood!
So pierced with anguish hoary Priam gazed,
When Troy's imperial domes in ruin blazed;
While he, severest sorrow doomed to feel,
Expired beneath the victor's murdering steel—
Thus with his helpless partners to the last,
Sad refuge! Albert grasps the floating mast.
His soul could yet sustain this mortal blow,
But droops, alas! beneath superior woe;
For now strong nature's sympathetic chain
Tugs at his yearning heart with powerful strain:
His faithful wife, for ever doomed to mourn
For him, alas! who never shall return,
To black adversity's approach exposed,
With want, and hardships unforeseen, inclosed;
His lovely daughter, left without a friend
Her innocence to succour and defend,
By youth and indigence set forth a prey
To lawless guilt, that flatters to betray—
While these reflections rack his feeling mind,
Rodmond, who hung beside, his grasp resigned;
And, as the tumbling waters o'er him rolled,
His outstretched arms the master's legs enfold:
Sad Albert feels their dissolution near,
And strives in vain his fettered limbs to clear,
For death bids every clenching joint adhere:
All faint, to Heaven he throws his dying eyes,
And "Oh protect my wife and child!" he cries—
The gushing streams roll back the unfinished sound,
He gasps! and sinks amid the vast profound.

Five only left of all the shipwrecked throng
Yet ride the mast which shoreward drives along;
With these Arion still his hold secures
And all assaults of hostile waves endures:
O'er the dire prospect as for life he strives,
He looks if poor Palemon yet survives—
"Ah wherefore, trusting to unequal art,
Didst thou, incautious! from the wreck depart?
Alas! these rocks all human skill defy;
Who strikes them once, beyond relief must die:
And now sore wounded, thou perhaps art lost
On these, or in some oozy cavern lost:"
Thus thought Arion; anxious gazing round
In vain, his eyes no more Palemon found—
The demons of destruction hover nigh,
And thick their mortal shafts commissioned fly:
When now a breaking surge, with forceful sway,
Two, next Arion, furious tears away;
Hurled on the crags, behold they gasp, they bleed!
And groaning, cling upon the elusive weed:
Another billow bursts in boundless roar!
Arion sinks! and memory views no more.
Ha! total night and horror here preside,
My stunned ear tingles to the whizzing tide;
It is their funeral knell! and gliding near
Methinks the phantoms of the dead appear!

TALES OF THE ARABIANS.

[Jean Charles Leonard Simonde de Sismondi, born at Genoa, 9th May, 1773; died 25th June, 1842. Historian and miscellaneous writer. His chief works are: *Historical View of the Literature of the South of Europe* (from which we quote), translated by Thomas Roscoe; *History of the Crusades against the Albigenses in the 13th Century*; *History of the French*; *The Battles of Cressy and Poictiers*; *Religious Opinions during the 19th Century*; *Julie Sevère*, an historical novel, &c.]

IF the eastern nations possess not the epic or the drama, they have been the inventors of a style of poetry which is related to the epic, and which supplies amongst them the place of the drama. We owe to them those tales of which the conception is so brilliant, and the imagination so rich and varied; tales which have been the delight of our infancy, and which at a more advanced age we never read without feeling their enchantment anew. Every one is acquainted with the *Arabian Nights' Entertainments;* but, if we may believe the French translator, we do not possess the six-and-thirtieth part of the great Arabian collection. This prodigious collection is not confined merely to books, but forms the treasure of a numerous class of men and women, who, throughout the whole extent of the Mohammedan dominion, in Turkey, Persia, and even to the extremity of India, find a livelihood in reciting these tales to crowds who delight to forget, in the pleasing dreams of imagination, the melancholy feelings of the present moment. In the coffee-houses of the Levant one of these men will gather a silent crowd around him. Sometimes he will excite terror or pity, but he more frequently pictures to his audience those brilliant and fantastic visions which are the patrimony of eastern imaginations. He will even occasionally provoke laughter, and the severe brows of the fierce Mussulmans will only unbend upon an occasion like this. This is the only exhibition of the kind in all the Levant, where these recitations supply the place of our dramatic representations. The public squares abound with these story-tellers, who fill up the heavy hours of the seraglio. The physicians frequently recommend them to their patients, in order to soothe pain, to calm agitation, or to produce sleep after long watchfulness; and these story-tellers, accustomed to sickness, modulate their voices, soften their tones, and gently suspend them, as sleep steals over the sufferer.

The imagination of the Arabs, which shines in all its brilliancy in these tales, is easily distinguished from the imagination of the chivalric nations, though it is easy to perceive a certain resemblance between them. The supernatural world is the same in both, but the moral world is different.

The Arabian tales, like the romances of chivalry, convey us into the fairy-realms, but the human personages which they introduce are very dissimilar.

These tales had their birth, after the Arabians, yielding the empire of the sword to the Tartars, the Turks, and the Persians, had devoted themselves to commerce, literature, and the arts. We recognize in them the style of a mercantile people, as we do that of a warlike nation in the romances of chivalry. Riches and artificial luxuries dispute the palm with the splendid gifts of the fairies. The heroes unceasingly traverse distant realms, and the interests of merchandise excite their active curiosity, as much as the love of renown awakened the spirit of the ancient knights. Besides the female characters, we find in these tales only four distinct classes of persons—princes, merchants, monks or calenders, and slaves. Soldiers are scarcely ever introduced upon the stage. Valour and military achievements in these tales, as in the records of the East, inspire terror, and produce the most desolating effects, but excite no enthusiasm. There is, on this account, in the Arabian tales something less noble and heroic than we usually expect in compositions of this nature. But, on the other hand, we must consider that these story-tellers are our masters in the art of producing, sustaining, and unceasingly varying the interest of this kind of fiction; that they are the creators of that brilliant mythology of fairies and genii, which extends the bounds of the world, multiplies the riches and strength of human nature, and which, without striking us with terror, carries us into the realms of marvels and of prodigies. It is from them that we have derived that intoxication of love, that tenderness and delicacy of sentiment, and that reverential awe of women, by turns slaves and divinities, which have operated so powerfully on our chivalrous feelings. We trace their effects in all the literature of the south, which owes to this cause its mental character. Many of these tales had found their way into our poetical literature long before the translation of the *Arabian Nights*. Some of them are to be met with in our old Fabliaux, in Boccaccio, and in Ariosto; and these very tales which have charmed our infancy, passing from tongue to tongue, and from nation to nation, through channels frequently unknown, are now familiar to the memory, and form the delight of the imagination of half the inhabitants of the globe.

THE CHARM.

BY SEBASTIAN EVANS.[1]

When at Easter on thy lea
First thick-legged lamb thou see,—
If upon the greenwood side
Brock or crafty fox be spied,
    Goodman, turn thy money!

If the magpie, or the jay,
Or the lapwing cross thy way,
Or the raven from his oak
Ban thee hoarsely with his croak,
    Goodman, turn thy money!

If when at the hearth thou sit
Spark from out the fire should flit,—
If, when wintry tempest beat,
Candle wear a winding sheet,
    Goodman, turn thy money!

If the wizard's ring appear
Round the moon, or if thou see her
Full or new,—or, worse mishap,
New with old upon her lap,
    Goodman, turn thy money!

[1] *Brother Fabian's MS. and other Poems* (Macmillan & Co.)

If the salt thou chance to spill,
Token sure of coming ill,—
If thirteen sit down to sup,
And thou first have risen up,
  Goodman, turn thy money!

Goodman true, wouldst fend thyself
From witchcraft and midnight elf?
Wouldst thou dree no fairy harm?
Keep in mind my simple charm,
  Goodman, turn thy money!

Goodman, learn my charm and verse,
Learn to carry poke or purse!
And, that not in vain thou learn,
Somewhat keep therein to turn!—
  Goodman, turn thy money!
                    Quoth Fabian.

———

A POPULAR AUTHOR'S MISERIES.

"——I'll print it,
And shame the rogues."—POPE.

My friend Fosbrook,—Dick Fosbrook—for the abbreviation which his good-fellowship had won for him at Westminster and Cambridge did not desert him upon his entrance into the real man and woman world of society—was a very excellent personage. He was something more substantial than a mere "good fellow;" he was a well-informed, sensible man, with more originality of talent than a reserved disposition permitted to rise to the surface. His shyness at length took refuge behind a title-page; that which he found no courage to say, he resolved to write. "Some sin, his parents' or his own," indeed, had dipped him in ink very early in life; his infant elegy upon his mother's favourite tabby had been wept over by every maiden aunt of the house of Fosbrook: his translations had been applauded by Busby; his prize-poems had been printed at Cambridge; he had lodged in the same house with Lord Byron; his grandmother was a Hayley; his bankers, Rogers, Towgood, & Co. Such a concatenation of impulses was irresistible, and Dick Fosbrook became an author! One fatal and highly unpoetical stumble befell him upon the very brink of Helicon. He married!—neither a muse, nor a Madame Dacier; but a very pretty girl,—reasonably rich, and unreasonably silly;—a professional alliance, however, for she was the daughter of a master in Chancery, and was already at the bar.
The duties of his legal vocation did not at present interfere with his homage to the Nine;

or, as his wife persisted in calling them, the foolish virgins. He wrote, he published, and wrote and published again; and if "the learned world said nothing to his paradoxes," he was equally taciturn as to the amount of the printer's bill, which he annually pocketed with a genuine Christmas groan! He flattered himself he wrote for immortality; that post-obit bond, the dishonouring of which falls so lightly on our feelings!—and his wife and her relations, who regarded authorship as a lawless and cabalistic calling, inimical to the interests of church and state, and an increasing family, exulted in the premature deaths which unfailingly awaited his literary progeny. I dined with him once or twice at this period of his domestic felicity and public misfortunes, and I never beheld a happier or more contented man; he laughed at my bad jokes upon withered laurels, and Lethe, and the stream of Time; he told me that the indulgent public was a dunce, "sans ears, sans eyes, sans taste, sans everything;" while his wife, half aside, whispered to me that the ingratitude of this senseless dunce had nearly alienated his mind from his former unprofitable studies.
"Sur ces entrefaites," my own equally profitless pursuits led me to the Continent; and in the course of the three years I was vagabondizing through Italy, an incidental paragraph in Galignani's Journal bore honourable mention of "Mr. Fosbrook, the popular author!" "Poor Dick!" said I, involuntarily, "no relation of thine, I fear!"
Yet 'twas the same—the very Dick I knew! One of his least meritorious works had made what is called a hit; he was now the "darling of the Muses;" and what is better still, of the booksellers; one of the literary ephemera, basking in the transient sunshine of modern fame.
Soon afterwards I landed at Dover, and after the due proportion of wrangling at the custom-house, and grumbling at the divers instalments of tough beef-steaks and muddy wine, wherewith Messrs. Wright defy the patience of the returning exile, I arrived in town—heard the muffin-bell once more—that

———"Squilla di lontano
Che paja 'l giorno pianger che si muore!"

—and deposited myself and my yellow valet, Gioacchino, in an hotel in Brook Street. The next day I wandered to my old club, which was grown as fine and uncomfortable as "Ninette à la cour;" heard my contemporaries observe, as they glanced towards a mirror, that I was miserably altered; lost my way in a wilderness of new streets, and my footing in a plunge through the puddles of a macadamized square; and just as I was recovering my equilibrium of body, if not of temper, I perceived a lank, rueful visage, gazing sympathizingly upon my mischance. 'Twas a strangely familiar face—'twas Fosbrook's; not Dick's, but the "popular author's!"

His dolorous physiognomy expanded into smiles on this unexpected recognition. He took my arm, and my way onwards, and we turned literally and figuratively to the passages of our youth, till he almost became Dick again by the force of reminiscence. Nay! had it not been for the deferential salutation of two wise men, two very learned pundits, and the raised hats of a bustling Westminster-ward Member or two, whom we met scuffling down Regent Street, his popularity and his authorship would have been forgotten between us. "Dine with me to-morrow," said he at parting, "we shall be alone, and can gossip over our Trinity days."

"With all my heart," I answered. "At five—in Gower Street?"

"No, no! at seven, in Curzon Street;" but the words came not trippingly from his tongue.

The morrow came, and I was delighted to find that, among the various removes of the day, dear Old Bond Street had not changed its town residence, although "almost ashamed to know itself;" and as I re-paraded my daily walks and ancient neighbourhood, I was startled by the sight of poor Fosbrook's face frowning in all the panes of the print-shops. There, at least, he was no Dick of mine; for his worthy countenance was distorted into a most cynical sneer, and he looked as blue and yellow as an Edinburgh review. Rain came on, and I was driven to the cruel refuge of a morning-visit; when, having excused myself from an impromptu dinner invitation, through my "pre-engagement to my friend Mr. Fosbrook,"— "The popular author?"—I was amused to find that even to be his friend was a rising point in the thermometer of fashion; and my intervention was humbly prayed to render him my friend's friend too. Poor Fosbrook! I remember the time when I scarcely contrived to procure a third man to make up dummy whist with him; he was considered a chartered bore, by right divine, and according to the most approved authorities!

It was, however, with a feeling nearly amounting to respect for his new honours that I trod lightly upon the creaking step of my hackney-coach at the door of his new mansion, and was ushered by a sulky butler into a very literary-looking drawing-room. Over the marble sphinx-

ed chimney-piece hung a fine portrait of its master in oils, and by Lawrence! and over a buhl secretaire a spirited sketch by Hayter —being the original of the authorial print of the Bond Street windows. Poor Fosbrook! I remember the time when a paltry profile was the only copy of his countenance! Several proofs of splendid new engravings were "ordered to lie on the table," beside a few presentation copies of the latest works of the day. "Are they good for anything?' said I to Dick, who found me with a volume in my hands.

"I really cannot take upon me to say," he replied gravely, and with the air of a man who is afraid of committing himself. "One of the worst consequences of scribbling ourselves is, that we have no leisure to look over these light productions, which are sometimes far from unamusing?"

"We!"—thinks I to myself, editorial; while Richard (I will never Dick him any more) turned to the final page of the several works, and determined their length as the standard of their merits.

A very light production now entered the room—Mrs. Fosbrook; looking as dressy as the frontispiece of "La Belle Assemblée." But if her gown were couleur de rose, her brow was black as Erebus; the honours which had made him sad had made her cross. I did not care; I had never abbreviated her name; so as it was the May of a London summer, I turned for consolation towards a fire bright enough to roast St. Lawrence. This movement necessitated a glance towards the card-rack, and I observed that its prominent features were "At Homes" from L. House and D. House, and a "requests the honour" from the Dowager Lady C. "Ah! ah!" said I to myself, "your popular author is ever a diner out."

I trust my friend Fosbrook was an habitual one; or at least, that he did not affect to be "L'Amphitryon ou l'on dine." The solid joint and solid pudding of St. Pancras had been ill-exchanged, in his menu, for the unapproachable filets and fricandeaux of St. George's; and hot sauterne and iced Lafitte were abominable substitutes for the old Madeira and old port of old times. By the time the cloth and the lady were withdrawn I was as much out of humour as Mrs. Fosbrook with popular authorship. To judge by the lowering brow of my host, his feelings were turned to as doleful a key as my own. As we were tête-à-tête, I ventured an apostrophe to the memory of the Gower Street port; it was a fortunate digression: the butler was summoned; the cork squeaked beneath the screw, and Richard was himself again!

"You have an excellent house here, Fosbrook!"

"Why, yes;—the situation is good, and the distribution be' er; yet somehow or other, even in my perfection of a 'gentleman's room,' I always regret my Crusoe's cave in Gower Street. There I was never interrupted by importunate idlers; my books, ungilt and unprisoned behind the glittering wires of a library, came at my call; in short, I was able to read, and think, and write, as I liked."

"And as others liked," said I, courteously. "My return to England has discovered to me an old friend in the most popular author of the day."

Fosbrook literally shuddered at the word. "No more of that, an thou lovest me!" exclaimed he in a tone of acute sensibility. "Keep the name for the first dog you wish to see hanged."

"Pho! pho!" said I, "the mere cant of affected modesty! You have won your laurels bravely; do not wear them like a coward. They were long, it is true, in putting forth their verdant honours; but now it would seem as 'Birnam wood were come to Dunsinane.'"

Fosbrook shook his head despondingly; and his whole air was so completely that of Matthews' admirable hypochondriac, that, spite of myself, I burst into a hearty fit of laughter. By good luck it proved contagious, and having roared and shouted "à qui mieux mieux," a happy tone of confidence was immediately established between us.

"The fact is, my dear fellow," resumed Fosbrook, lowering his voice, "that I have led the life of a galley slave since I came to my title—."

"Title?"

"Of popular author! a title good for nothing but to expose one without redress to the insolence of every scribbler whose pen is the channel of his venom. No one presumes to insult a gentleman, or to tell a man that he is a fool; but a popular author is the property of the public—'its goods, its chattels, its ox, its ass, its everything!'—a culprit stuck up in the pillory of celebrity to be pelted by all the ragamuffins of the times."

"And yet I can remember your eyes being upturned towards the Temple of Fame, as a devotee gazes upon the sanctuary."

"Ay, ay; I looked at it through a telescope:

"'Tis distance lends enchantment to the view!'

and the farther the better! I had not then assumed the 'foolscap uniform turned up with ink;' I had not donned the livery of the booksellers to 'fetch and carry sing song up and

down.' I published, it is true—but what then? The sin lay dormant between you and me and the press! I lived secure from criticism—not a reptile of a magazine deigned to tickle me with its puny antennæ. My wife, however angry, borrowed no sarcasms from the leading reviews—'I found not Jeffrey's satire on her lips—I slept the next night well—was free—was happy.' On the strength of my uncut pages I passed for a literary man in my own select circle; my family took me for a genius, and my servants for a conjuror;—but now—my pages and myself are cut together."

"My dear Dick!" said I soothingly, for he had really talked himself into a fit of irritation, "remember how often and how philosophically you have declared yourself indifferent to the award of criticism."

"There you have me on the hip. My wife's family, and all the generation of bores at that, my former end of the town, are constantly reminding me that it is idle to value public opinion, since I have often proved to them that the world is an overgrown booby; to which I can only reply, like Benedict, that 'When I said I would die a bachelor, I did not think I should live to be married.' When I wrote the public down an ass, I little expected to become a popular author!"

"But after all," I observed, "these are mere trivial vexations compared with the glories of the daily incense burned upon your altars—of the solid gains achieved by your exertions."

"I will show some of the daily incense," said Fosbrook, opening his pocket-book; "unfortunately it is made to be read first and burned afterwards. It is a paragraph from a morning paper."

"Lege, Dick, lege."

"We copy the following interesting intelligence from the Newcastle Mercury:—'Mr. Fosbrook the popular author. We are happy to be the first to congratulate our townsmen upon the near and dear claim we can boast upon the parentage of this celebrated man. Richard Toppletoe, formerly a master tailor in North Lane, but at the period of his decease a much respected member of our corporation, proves to have been his maternal grandfather. Many still surviving among us retain a lively remembrance of the full-buckled flaxen wig and brocaded waistcoat of old Toppletoe; and there can be little doubt that from this eccentric knight of the shears Mr. Fosbrook derives much of his originality of mind, his baptismal name, and private fortune.'"

"Very provoking, certainly," said I, perceiving that some comment was unavoidable.

"Till I read that cursed paragraph," observed Fosbrook, "I had always believed and proclaimed myself to be of irreproachable descent, and the heir of an old Northumbrian family; had I never become a popular author I should have remained in ignorance that I had a Toppletoe for my mother! But listen to another of these precious bulletins of the state of my reputation.

"'Bow Street. Mr. Fosbrook.—Another instance of the irregularities of genius came this morning before the attention of the bench. The above popular author, returning from a deep carouse with some brother wits—some choice spirits, who appear to have been partial to proof spirits—chancing to unite the rampart valour of Othello with the disastrous plight of Cassio, fell into an outrageous affray with the guardians of the night—('Guardians! I wish they would make her a ward in Chancery!' ejaculated Dick)—and was at length victoriously lodged in the watchhouse. Our worthy chief magistrate considerately gave this delicate case a hearing in his private room; and after a few pertinent (qy. *im?*) observations to the delinquent upon the respect due to public decency, even from the *genus irritabile*, he fined him five shillings, and dismissed him with costs; judging, probably, that Mr. Fosbrook had already received poetical justice in the shape of two black eyes.'"

"Very provoking," said I again. "And did you pass the night in the watchhouse?"

"Not I. I appeared before Sir Richard as a witness in favour of an Irish applewoman whom I had caught the parish beadle in the act of maltreating, by virtue of some Street Bill. Unfortunately, I was recognized by some dirty reporter, who doubled his morning's pay by compounding this scurrilous attack."

"But of course you remonstrated with the editor?"

"I did; and my very forbearing letter produced a second paragraph, headed 'Mr. Fosbrook. We are authorized by this gentleman to state that he did not appear before Sir Richard Birnie with *two* black eyes.'"

"Well, well!" said I, "these idle slanders, if they filch from you your good name, do not steal the trash from your purse. Think of the solid profits, my dear Dick."

"I do, and with regret; for they are all gone. Every poor relation (Toppletoes in particular), and every literary acquaintance I had in the world, gave me the preference of their first application for a loan, on the second edition of my last work; nor does there exist a literary institution, or an establishment for the encouragement of the fine arts, for which my guineas have not been peremptorily claimed. Meanwhile, my law has long since left me in the lurch, and my father-in-law abhors me because I play shorts. He has persuaded my wife to send the boys to school lest I should undermine their morals, for the old gentleman holds that all modern authors are atheists."

"But what is become of your orthodox friend, the Dean of —— ?"

"We have not been on speaking terms these six months—he is persuaded he can detect my hand in the anatomization of his emancipation pamphlet in the new review."

"And Lorimer, our college chum?"

"Has basely deserted my cause; he goes about 'with his hand in his breeches' pocket, like a crocodile,' whispering that I have been puffed beyond my strength; that I have no stamina for the tug of war, and shall run away, *à la* Goderich, at the first shot. All my old friends affect to suppose that I have risen above them; and since I have been noticed by half a dozen rhyming lords, my wife's relations say I am grown fine, and have given over inviting me; while Sophia, as if in retribution, will never visit half a mile from Russell Square—the land of ancestors! She is gone there to-night."

"Mrs. Fosbrook gone out!" I exclaimed. "Then come with me to the opera; we shall be in time for Brocard."

"Willingly—I have a silver ticket."

We rose from table; the butler was hastily summoned, and entered with a huge and portentous packet in either hand. Dick broke the seal of the largest and read aloud—

"Albemarle Street.
"Dear Sir,—I beg to forward you the number of the —— Review, which appeared this day, and which contains some strictures on your new work. Permit me to say that I consider them highly illiberal, and that I have always thought the editor an envious little man.—I have the honour to be, &c. &c. &c."

"Don't read the article, my dear Dick. Pray don't. It will only make you bilious."

"I will not," he replied, resolutely tossing it aside. "Martin—call a coach."

"I beg your pardon, sir," replied the man, presenting the other pistol—packet I would say—"Mr. Colburn's printer has been waiting impatiently these two hours. He says it is the 24th of the month."

"The devil!" exclaimed the unhappy Fosbrook in dismay. "Well, my dear fellow, you must go and see Brocard without me; it is not the first time my patience has been 'put to the proof.'"

I left him alone with his glory; but sympathy forbade my attempting the opera. I went home to bed, where, thanks to Dick's deplorable destiny, or deplorable claret, I had an excruciating nightmare;—and the most appalling vision suggested by its influence was, that I had attained to the honours of a popular author!—*New Monthly Magazine.*

THE LOVER REFUSED.

[Sir Thomas Wyatt, born at Allington Castle, Kent, 1503; died at Sherborn, 11th October, 1542. He is called the elder to distinguish him from his son of the same name who was involved in the rebellion in the reign of Queen Mary. He was sometime a favourite of Henry VIII., but was imprisoned on account of his friendship for Anne Boleyn. "He is reported to have occasioned the Reformation by a joke, and to have planned the fall of Cardinal Wolsey by a seasonable story." His latter years were passed in rural enjoyments at Allington Castle.]

The answer that you made to me, my dear,
When I did sue for my poor heart's redress,
Hath so appall'd my countenance, and my cheer,
That in this case I am all comfortless,
Since I of blame no cause can well express.

I have no wrong where I can claim no right,
Nought ta'en me from where I have nothing had,
Yet of my woe I cannot so be quite,
Namely since that another may be glad
With that, that thus in sorrow makes me sad.

Yet none can claim (I say) by former grant
That knoweth not of any grant at all;
And by desert, I dare well make a vaunt
Of faithful will, there is nowhere that shall
Bear you more truth, more ready at your call.

Now good, then, call again that bitter word,
That touch'd your friend so near with plagues of pain,
And say, my dear, that it was said in bord.
Late or too soon, let it not rule the gain
Wherewith free will doth true desert retain.

CONTRARIETIES OF LOVE.

I find no peace, and all my war is done;
I fear and hope, I burn and freeze like ice;
I fly aloft, yet can I not arise,
And nought I have, and all the world I season,
That locks nor loseth, holdeth me in prison,
And holds me not, yet can I 'scape no wise,
Nor lets me live, nor die at my devise;
And yet of death it giveth me occasion.
Without eye I see, without tongue I plain,
I wish to parish, yet I ask for health;
I love another and I hate myself;
I feed me in sorrow, and laugh in all my pain.
Lo, thus displeaseth me, both death and life,
And my delight is causer of this strife.

SIR THOMAS WYATT.

A TALE OF THE OLD GORBALS.

[Alexander Whitelaw, born in Glasgow about 1796, died there in 1846. He was assistant to Dr. Robert Watt in the preparation of the *Bibliotheca Britannica*, and wrote a number of the lives in Chambers' *Biographical Dictionary of Eminent Scotsmen*. He edited the *Casquet of Literary Gems* and the *Republic of Letters*—two admirable works which suggested the present compilation; *The Book of Scottish Song*—the most complete collection of Scottish songs yet published; and *The Book of Scottish Ballads*, which included the collections of Scott, Motherwell, Jamieson, and Peter Buchan. He was the author of *St. Kentigern*, a tale of the city of St. Mungo, and of many minor poems and prose sketches. Good taste and a sincere devotion to literature are apparent in his work; and he was amongst the first to recognize and to proclaim the genius of Wordsworth.]

The old barony of Gorbals, which now forms an important suburb of Glasgow, was in former times celebrated for its manufactory of swords, harquebusses, and other implements of war. People who could not command the real Ferraras were accustomed to uphold the blades of the Gorbals, as being little inferior to them in temper and delicacy of edge; and its harquebusses or hand-guns were on all hands admitted to equal those of Ghent, Milan, or Paris. Dim shadows of this ancient renown may be traced down even to the present day. Families still exist who through a long line of ancestry have figured as gunsmiths, cutlers, or turners; and it is a remarkable fact, that till about the beginning of this century the only individuals in the west of Scotland who manufactured guns were to be found in this old barony.

During the wars between England and Scotland, few places were busier or merrier than the Gorbals, or *Gorbells* as it was then called—a name perhaps derived in some way from *corbells*, a term used in fortification and architecture. But at no time had it ever presented such an appearance of business and bustle as when the Regent Murray, in the year 1568, was lying at Glasgow with his forces, and news arrived of the escape of Queen Mary from Lochleven Castle. Night and day the smithy's furnace belched forth its sparkling smoke, and the cutler's wheel found no pause to its gyrations. The Laird of Elphinston was at that period Baron of the Gorbals, and formed one of the confederated lords who had compelled Mary to renounce her crown, and nominated Murray to the regency during the minority of her infant son. His castle or rather tower (which the modern Goths of the Gorbals first converted into a police office and afterwards abandoned and dismantled) was situated in the heart of the village; and as it had a chapel attached to it, and numerous buildings belonging to the ecclesiastics,[1] he was able to accommodate a large proportion of the regent's followers. It was here, on the 12th of May, 1568, that the regent's army rendezvoused, and from this place it issued to meet and give battle to the queen's forces, who were, with their unfortunate lady, on their way to Dumbarton Castle. The queen's road from Hamilton to that stronghold passed through the village of Langside, a place not two miles south from the Gorbals, and there Murray pitched his camp, with the resolution of disputing the passage. The result is well known. The queen's army was defeated, and she herself—obliged to flee—sought shelter and protection in England, where, to the everlasting infamy of her cousin Elizabeth, she only found a prison, an axe, and a block.

In Glasgow the sound of the cannon was distinctly heard, and from some of its elevations the movements even of the hostile armies were seen. Most of the people were of the reformed religion, and therefore in favour of the regent and his army; but still there were many hearts that sympathized with the cause of their young and beautiful queen, for, whatever wicked men may say, she had ever been gentle and generous to her people—no acts of oppression had stained her reign—and even in that which she held dearest—her religion—she had displayed more tolerance a thousand times than those who opposed her, and who boasted a purer faith. For two or three hours a dreadful anxiety prevailed as to the result of the contest, and rumours of every kind were afloat, till at first stragglers, and at length a portion of the regent's army, announced too truly that Mary Queen of Scotland was miserably defeated, and fleeing like a hunted deer before her savage subjects.

Though many wished such a result, there was little rejoicing over it; for however the queen's cause might be disliked while her fortunes were doubtful, now that she was driven to the wall and overtaken by calamity, old prejudices gave way to compassion, and all her grace and generosity—her youth, her beauty, and her accomplishments—her kind looks, words, and actions to high and low alike, even when insulted by rude and uncivil tongues, were remembered in her favour.

The women, especially, who are ever strong in gentle pity, and who judge of the right and wrong of a cause merely as it affects their own feelings, began to wail for their poor young queen, and some of them hesitated not to use the privilege of their tongues in attacking her triumphant enemies. As party after party of the regent's army returned to the Gorbals—some of them wiping their bloody swords on their horses' manes—they were saluted by such exclamations as these:

"Hech, sirs! hech, sirs! bonny wark ye've been at, nae doubt, and manly—chasing out o' the kingdom a poor bit lassie, that was just owre gude for ye—and a' to favour that bastard brither o' hers, wha might think shame to haud up his head in honest men's company, seeing the way he has used her! Gae wa', and sing psalms, ye ill-faured loons, now that your dirty day's darg's owre; for, after what ye have done, ye dinna deserve to look a bonny lassie in the face again!"

Besides a sympathy in the fate of the queen, there were other causes at work to check any strong exultation over the victory. Many of the victors themselves had friends and relations in the queen's army, and now that the fervour of the combat was over a very natural interest arose regarding them. In this situation was Baron Elphinston, whose young son, Master Patrick as he was called, had, in the teeth of his father's will, espoused the cause of Queen Mary. Master Patrick was a universal favourite throughout the barony, being handsome, generous, brave, and accessible; and deep was the interest which all felt as to his probable fate. Rumours were abroad that he had fallen in the field, and some even went so far as to affirm, that they had seen him lying desperately wounded; but no certain or satisfactory intelligence could be gained respecting him, and several days passed over in this tantalizing state.

It might be nearly a week after the battle, when the excitement it created had in some measure subsided, that a numerous and heterogeneous party were assembled in the large hall of Mrs. Ogilvie's hostelry, which was dignified by the sign of the Boar's Head, and which then formed the only house of public entertainment in the Gorbals.[2] Many of the wounded had been carried there; and upon the numerous benches which graced the hall might be seen some lying with bandaged heads, or

---

[1] This place is still distinguished by the name of the Chapel Close.

[2] The building of this ancient hostelry was taken down years ago, and a common place house erected in its stead. In the new building, there was a small tavern which retained the sign of the Boar's Head.

freshly amputated limbs, among whom stalked a chirurgeon, or physician, inquiring into their different cases. Others, apparently unhurt, were formed into clusters, and enjoying themselves over their "mugs of nappy ale," in discussing the signs of the times, and the accidents of the day. In one corner sat a core of cutlers, —fellows of infinite dexterity in giving an edge to a sword—who, after the great exertions which the battle called forth, thought themselves entitled to no measured relaxation. They were reckless dogs, all—caring little for any cause—and dividing their time between violent exertion at their grinding wheels, and violent drinking at the Boar's Head, the last being by far the heaviest work of the two. In spite of invalids, or any other consideration, one of them was singing, with clenched fists, shut teeth, and gleaming eye, the following ditty, which received no attention from any but his own company, who cheered him on by such exclamations as—"Well done, Ralph Munn! —Go on, my pretty fellow!"

Three things that do make a man lean—
Small beer, bread and cheese, and a bold quean,
            And sing Fal!
Three things that do make a man fat—
Roast beef, boiled beef, and the ale tap,
            And sing Fal!

(Burthen)— It's an auld sang, and a true sang,
            Neir let man trust woman too lang!
(Chorus)—Fal-lal-lillillilla, Fal-lal-lillillilla, &c. &c.[1]

It would be impossible to convey to the reader any conception of the maniacal fury with which the chorus of "Fal-lal-lillillilla" was received. The cutlers simultaneously rose, and, flinging up their arms to heaven, screamed it out in yells that drowned every other noise in the hostelry. But they were speedily checked by the remonstrances of the landlady. "For shame, sirs! yelling at sic a rate, and your poor young mistress lying in a sick bed!"

"What! is pretty Mistress Martha ailing?" said one of the cutlers; for Martha, the daughter of their mistress, who carried on the business on the death of their master, was a mighty favourite with the workmen.

"Ailing? She has not had a hale hour ever since the battle—and it sets ye ill to be sitting there routing, as if there were na a sair head or a sair heart in the town."

"Nay, landlady, we did not know anything was wrong—and here we shall drink a bumper to pretty Martha's health; and if any one says she is not the prettiest as well as best

---

[1] This was the favourite song of the Gorbals cutlers.

lady on both sides of the water, we shall hold his nose to the roughening stone."

"Well, that's spoken like civil gentlemen," said the landlady. "And now I will be able to let myself be heard. Dr. Macclutch!" she exclaimed, at the top of her voice. "Where's the doctor? Ay, doctor, there's an express here for you. You're to gang and wait on the baron without delay. Poor gentleman! I doubt he's takin' his son's death to heart."

The doctor—an officious, formal, good-natured man—was not a little gratified to find that he was in demand in such a high quarter, and particularly that the fact was made known to so many auditors. He buckled up a wound which he had been dressing, with little attention to the wry faces of his patient, and adjusting his cloak about him, proceeded with all decent dexterity to wait upon Baron Elphinston.

The baron ushered him into one of his private apartments. "My son, doctor," said the baron—"poor Patrick—has at length been found. Some of my own knaves, whose hearts he had gained, have, it seems, been keeping him in hiding ever since the battle, for he was sorely wounded, and he instructed them not to disclose his situation. But he was yesterday seized with a giddy fever in consequence of his wounds, and his attendants became so alarmed as at length to lay the truth before me. I have seen him, doctor; but he is insensible to everything. Now, I have sent for you that you may attend him; but chiefly, as a trustworthy man, that you may have him conveyed to some more fitting and salubrious place than the hovel which he now occupies. He cannot be brought here without discovery, filled as the place now is by so many of the queen's enemies; and if he were taken, not even my influence could protect him from fine or imprisonment, or perhaps from death. Upon your fidelity, as I said, I rely, as well as upon your skill in treating him according to his need."

"My lord," said the doctor, "nothing would more gratify me than to shelter and treat Master Patrick under my own poor roof. But since the combat at Langside my house has been frequently searched, in the hope of finding some of the queen's friends, who might be driven to seek my skill in chirurgery. I therefore could not insure him safety with me; but I bethink me of a worthy and charitable lady, who is furnished with all accommodations, and who would be proud to give him protection. May I mention the widow of good old Master Menzies, who made so much fame

and money by his skill in cutting not only weapons of war but chirurgical instruments?"

"An excellent worthy woman," said the baron, "and rich withal. She is, I believe, of better lineage than her husband was; yet she disdains not to continue his business, through his workmen, and to keep up his ancient credit as a grinder in iron. Hie thee, good doctor, and make arrangements with all speed, for I shall not be at ease till poor Patrick is removed to a comfortable and safe dwelling."

The doctor found the widow in all respects agreeable—nay, eager to receive Master Patrick under her roof, "not only," as she said, "because of the honour it conferred on her humble dwelling, but because of the affection which she, in common with everybody, bore him:"—and accordingly, under cloud of night, the young master was unconsciously conveyed to the richly-furnished and commodious mansion of Mrs. Menzies. The strictest secresy was enjoined and promised. "Indeed," said the old lady, "I cannot even acquaint my daughter Martha, for she, poor girl, is so unwell that she will not listen to anything. And it has occurred to me, doctor, as being in some degree fortunate, that your presence should be required here, for I wish to consult with you about my daughter's present unhappy state. She does not eat as much as would serve a sparrow, but lies tossing a-bed all day, fetching heavy sighs, and moaning in a most pitiful manner. I sent for Mrs. Ogilvie of the Boar's Head, who is skilled in all sorts of complaints, but Martha could not be prevailed on to take one single cup of her vegetable waters."

"I always supposed Mrs. Martha to be a sensible girl," said the doctor, "and now I know it. These vegetable waters, my good lady, are nothing but a devilish compound of syrup and poisonous roots, enough to sicken a dromedary, let alone a Christian. What, indeed, can Mrs. Ogilvie know of the noble arts of physic and chirurgery? Only let me see the young lady, and I will administer such medicaments as will, under Heaven's blessing, restore her to her wonted lustihood."

"If she would only take them," sighed the mother; "but alas! doctor, I fear me you would not commend her good sense, did you hear her foolish and inappropriate conversation, and see the manner in which she sometimes behaves. Indeed, I often think that the late unhappy battle has turned her head. She is ever inquiring about it, and takes no thought of household matters. Nay, she would be out one morning to search for the dead, as

she said, and she talked so wildly that I was obliged to make fast the door of her chamber. And when I have found her weeping, and asked her why she did so, she has answered, 'Is it not enough to make all people weep, to think of father fighting against son?'—and then she would say that all her tears could not wash out the dear blood that was shed at Langside."

"The case is not a little alarming," said the doctor, putting on one of his foreboding looks: "yet I would fain comfort myself with the hope that the poor young lady is not entirely crazed, and that proper treatment may yet bring her into her right judgment. Lead me to her incontinently, good Mrs. Menzies, for I doubt she is in a critical situation."

Martha was sitting by the bed-side, in a languishing and disconsolate posture, as her mother ushered in worthy Dr. Macclutch. She little expected the visit of a physician, and still less wished it; for her trouble was beyond the reach of doctors and drugs.

"Here, Martha, I have brought you our excellent friend Dr. Macclutch, to inquire into your state," said the mother.

"How is my fair young lady?" was the salutation of the good-natured leech.

"I am well—quite well—indeed, I am," said Martha, for the appearance of the doctor merely annoyed her.

"You look, it is true, in lusty health," was the answer, "and are in no measure emaciated: yet, my good young lady, these are but deceiving symptoms, and not at all to be trusted. Your worthy mother informs me that you are ailing: what is it you complain of?"

"I complain of nothing, doctor—of nothing," she added, weeping, "but a wretched world—a world full of strife and evil passions—where worth perishes, and hope is ever blasted—where might makes right, and love, and truth, and honour are trampled to the dust—where father fights against son, and the best blood of all the land is shed like water."

"True, lady, we must all lament the late unhappy struggle, by which I myself have been greatly embarrassed; but now that Mary, umquhile queen, has fled to England, we may look for peaceful and happy days."

"You may—I never can; for that which made life sweet to me, and the earth beautiful, is for ever lost, and no hope—no wish—remains to my poor fancy, except the grave."

The doctor now began to be assured that his patient's head was affected. "Suffer me, my dear young lady," he said, "to feel your pulse.

Ay, it is rather feverish, and we must phlebotomize. Where lies your chief ailment?" Martha almost instinctively pressed her hand on her heart, while the doctor, unseen by her, touched his forehead significantly with his finger. At this last sign the poor mother fell a crying. "O Martha, love! what makes you lose your senses, and speak in that way? will you break my heart altogether! And what makes that weary battle afflict you so? You have lost no friend, and had no hand in it. If you had been cut on the head, you might have had some cause for raving, as poor Master Patrick is doing"—

"Hush!" said the doctor, holding out his hand, and the old lady checked herself instantaneously. But a name had struck the ear of Martha, too deeply cherished to pass unnoticed. "Master Patrick!" she exclaimed, rising eagerly from her seat, "What said you of the young Master Elphinston?—Is he not lost—slain—dead? Or,—O merciful God!—does he yet live and breathe?"

"The young Master Patrick," stammered out the doctor, "is a gentleman of whom, my good young lady, it would be indecorous—I mean imprudent, to speak, seeing that his worthy father, the Baron"—

"He lives!" interrupted Martha. "Say that he lives, or my heart will burst!"

"That the young master lives," returned the doctor, "may be predicated or indeed affirmed, without breaking faith, or saying in what lady's house he lives, or what learned chirurgeon has been intrusted with his critical case."

"Enough—he lives," murmured Martha, sinking back into her chair, while her face, which before was highly flushed, became deadly pale. "But he is wounded," she added, recovering herself, after a pause—"dying, perhaps—I know it all—and under *your* care, doctor. I can see that—but in *what* lady's house? Is it indeed so? *Here? within these walls?* Do I guess aright, or is my head in truth deranged?"

"Who could have told you?" said the simple chirurgeon. "I am sure unless your mother has"—

"Nay, doctor," said the old lady, "blame me not, for unless it was yourself even now, I am sure—But, in truth, we have nothing to fear from Martha, and if it gives her comfort to know that young Master Patrick is under this roof, why should we withhold it?"

"Why, indeed, dearest mother?" said Martha, sinking into her arms, and giving vent to her feelings in a flood of tears. "Leave me,"

she added, "leave me for a little, until this foolish weakness is over. Master Patrick, you know, was an old friend—an acquaintance, whom we all thought lost, and blame me not if I should be moved to hear of his safety. Leave me for a little, that I may compose myself."

Scarcely had the mother and physician left the apartment—scarcely had the door closed upon them, ere Martha was on her knees, breathing a silent but heartfelt thanksgiving to Heaven, for restoring to this world of hope him upon whom all her happiness rested. She rose from her devotion with calm and elevated feelings, and proceeded to dress herself in simple attire. "I will attend him," she said to herself, "and administer to his wants; for what hand but mine should soothe his aching head?"

The young Master Elphinston had not had a conscious moment from the time he had been brought under the roof of Mrs. Menzies. The fever which had seized his brain was at its height, and he continued to rave as if he were still in the midst of the battle. But when Martha entered his apartment, and knelt by his bedside, he became suddenly silent, and gazed earnestly at her.

"Do you know *me*, Master Patrick?" she whispered tenderly, as she parted the raven locks that hung dishevelled over his burning brow.

"I know you," said the young man. "You are a vision from heaven of my own Martha, come to mock me when the battle's lost. But do not leave me, for even in dreams, and on the bloody field, would I see that sweet face!"

"O Patrick! this is no dream—no vision! You have been sorely wounded, and now lie in safety under my mother's roof."

"Ay, we fought it bravely—inch by inch. But where's the traitor brother? Has he escaped the sword? Down with the bastard—bastard in body and soul! And *she*—our queen! whither doth she flee? Are ye men, that ye would hunt the stricken deer? O, shame on your recreant souls! One bold struggle yet, my noble fellows, and the day is ours! Cowards! Do you shrink before these rebels? Follow me! The Queen—the Queen!" ■

"Alas! his mind still lingers in the giddy fight," said the mother. "Speak to him, Martha, of home."

But Martha could not speak; her heart was swelling, and she was obliged to bury her face in the clothes and sob aloud.

"Who weeps?" continued the young master. "Is it thee, Martha, my own love? You were ever tender-hearted, and well may weep to see the banner of our queen stricken in the dust. To horse! Did I not say I would save her? Ha, my father! why do you hold my arm? I dare not strike thee nor curse thee; but let me away! Would you have me play laggard in the fight, old man, and stain your family scutcheon? It must not be—let me off! Who is this that dares to hold me down! Knave! ruffian! who are you?"

"Your very good friend, Dr. Macclutch, Master Patrick," said the doctor, who was exerting himself strenuously to keep the young man in bed.

"Macclutch! Ha, ha, ha! That is good. How goes your market, doctor? Do you still poison as well as ever? Who is so fortunate as to be your grave-digger? What are your burial charges? Have you brought the coffin with you? Don't pinch it—who cares for fir—give the poor creature elbow-room; 'tis all he will ever require, since you have relieved him of his complaints. A fee? You will find it in his clenched fist. It won't open without the knife. Bravely done! What signify the fingers and thumbs of a dead man? But the teeth!—secure the teeth, doctor: they go for something, and, to speak truth, you have need of a few yourself. Hollo! Have you got a wife? Is she good at the needle, for she will be kept busy with shrouds."

"This, dear Master Patrick," said the doctor, somewhat mortified, "is good Mrs. Menzies, in whose house you are, and this is her daughter, Mrs. Martha."

"Martha!" echoed Patrick, sinking back in feebleness upon his couch, for his fits of raving were but of short duration; "Martha! I know it all. She is dead, for the doctor has been here, and I have seen her vision. Then, what have I to live for, since love and glory have departed from this earth. Come again, sweet vision! and hang over me in my dreams." And thus murmuring, he gradually fell into a slumber.

Two or three days passed over in this state, during which Martha was unwearied in her attendance at the sick bed of the young master. In the evenings the baron regularly visited his son, and spent several hours in his presence; for Patrick, although he had offended him by espousing the cause of Queen Mary, had all along been the favourite of his father. At length the danger of the fever was overcome by a vigorous constitution, and the young master became gradually conscious of his situation. It was to him a delightful feeling to find himself tended by the one whom he loved best, and though weak and emaciated, never had he experienced so much calm bliss as during the days of his convalescence.

"For such a nurse," he said, "it is worth being unwell. And O Martha! when I am fairly better, my first care will be to make you mine for ever. You fear my father; but he is too deeply interested in me to stand in the way of my happiness, and were it otherwise, he must now know your excellence, and be proud to call you his daughter."

It was after a week or two had elapsed, and Patrick was so far recovered as to be able to walk about, although he still confined himself to the house, that the Baron Elphinston requested a private interview with Dr. Macclutch.

"I have sent for you, good doctor," he said, "in order to express my satisfaction at the attention you have paid poor Patrick during his severe illness, and the fidelity with which you have otherwise conducted yourself. This is but a poor recompense for your services," he added, placing a purse in the doctor's hand. "Nay, put it up. It was not on that account alone that I sent for you. What I wished to consult you about was another matter. During the height of Patrick's fever he repeatedly made use of expressions by which I could discern that he was deeply attached to the daughter of Mrs. Menzies, and indeed he has himself this morning stated so to me, and implored my sanction to their union. At another time, and under other circumstances, I might have strongly objected to such a union; but Patrick's happiness, I see, so much depends on its accomplishment, that I cannot refuse his request, especially now that Heaven has so mercifully restored him to me. Besides, I have had occasion to admire the conduct of the young lady during his long illness, and if she may not be, in point of lineage, a proper match to the young Master of Elphinston, she is in every other respect all that I could wish. Even in lineage, she is not altogether deficient, for, as you may be aware, she is well connected by the female side, and—what perhaps you may think of more consequence, in these troublous times, to the younger son of a poor baron—she is possessed, I am given to understand, of a very handsome dowry."

"My lord," said the doctor, "it gives me great satisfaction to know that you are inclined to sanction the espousals of Master Patrick and Mrs. Martha; for a more worthy and deserving young lady is not to be found in the kingdom.

and as you well remark, she has a heavy tocher of her own—a pretty penny, believe me."

"Good Master John Knox," interrupted the baron, "has been exerting himself stoutly with the regent to procure pardons for many of the queen's friends. By his intercession the Hamiltons have been reprieved from the death of traitors, and to his kindness I owe a manumission which I received yesterday of Patrick's attainder, in consideration, as it stated, of his youth and of his father's services in the right cause. Partick is therefore now at liberty; and I have been thinking that, in the event of his marriage, he might take possession of the small estate of Polmadie, which his mother by will has left him. As to the young lady's mother, I have not yet consulted with her on the matter, but I doubt she will be very unwilling to part with her daughter, seeing that none other of the family remains."

"She will indeed be very lonely," said the doctor, "and of that I have been led to speak with her very frequently in private, when I observed the attachment of Master Patrick and Mrs. Martha."

"So—so," said the baron, smiling, "you have been already condoling with the widow on the subject, and you could not do less surely, doctor, than offer to cherish and comfort her in her apprehended loneliness, by taking her to wife."

"I will not deny, my lord, that some such understanding may exist between us," said the doctor, blushing as deeply as a bachelor of fifty could blush.

"Then all is well,—and we shall make two weddings of it at once, my old buck !" said the baron, poking the sides of the confused doctor with humorous glee.

The marriages, however, did not take place at the same time. The young master and the fair Martha were first espoused, and great was the rejoicing of the whole barony; for, in addition to the usual excitement of a marriage, the people were delighted at the restoration of their favourite, whom they had accounted lost, and at his union with one of their own native children. But great as was the rejoicing on this occasion, it did not equal the uproar which took place six weeks afterwards, when worthy Dr. Macclutch was united to widow Menzies. Every fire-arm was then in requisition to welcome the auspicious morn ; mummeries, in which the cutlers played a distinguished part, were enacted on the streets; and the walls of the Boar's Head shook with dancing and revelry for three successive nights.

WELL AND ILL WORKING.

[Nicholas Grimoald or Grimbold, died about 1563, the second English poet after Surrey who wrote in blank verse. He was the author of a Latin tragedy, *John the Baptist*, and of numerous translations from the Greek and Latin poets.]

In working well, if travail you sustain,
Into the winds shall lightly pass the pain,
But of the deed, the glory shall remain,
And cause your name with worthy wights to reign.
In working wrong, if pleasure you attain,
The pleasure soon shall fade, and void as vain :
But of the deed throughout the life the shame
Endures, defacing you with foul defame,
And still torments the mind both night and day,
No length of time the spot can wash away.
Flee then ill suading pleasure's baits untrue,
And noble virtue's fair renown pursue.

———

DEATH OF SOCRATES.

[Plato, an Athenian, born B.C. 429 ; died B.C. 347. He was a disciple of Socrates, and after an adventurous career, serving some time as a slave, he settled at Athens. The following is from an old translation of the *Phædo.*]

Having talked awhile, he arose, and went into an inner room to wash himself: and Crito following him, enjoined us to stay and expect his return. We therefore expected, discoursing among ourselves of the things that had been commemorated by him, and conferring our judgments concerning them. And we frequently spake of the calamity that seemed to impend on us by his death: concluding it would certainly come to pass, that, as sons deprived of their father, so should we disconsolately spend the remainder of our life. After he had been washed, and his children were brought to him (for he had two sons very young, and a third, almost a youth), and his wives also were come, he spake to them before Crito, and gave them his last commands: so he gave order to his wives and children to retire. Then he came back to us. By this time day had declined almost to the setting of the sun; for he had stayed long in the room where he washed himself. Which done, he returned, and sate to repose himself, not speaking much after that. Then came the Minister of the Eleven, the executioner; and addressing himself to him, "I do not believe, Socrates," said he, "that I shall reprehend that in you which I am wont to reprehend in others; that they are angry with me, and curse me, when by command of the magistrates (whom I am by my office obliged to obey) I come and give notice to them that they must now drink the poison; but I know you to be at all times, and chiefly at this, a man both generous and most mild and civil, and the best of all men that ever came into this place, so that I may be assured that you will not be displeased with me, but (you know the authors) with them rather. Now therefore (for you know what message I come to bring), farewell, and endeavour to suffer as patiently and calmly as you can what cannot be avoided:" then breaking forth into tears, he departed.

And Socrates converting his eyes upon him, "And farewell thou too," saith he: "we will perform all things." Then turning to us again, "How civil this man is," saith he; "all this time of my imprisonment he came to me willingly, and sometimes talked with me respectfully, and hath been the best of all that belong to the prison; and now how generously doth he weep for me! But, Crito, let us spare him, and let some other bring hither the deadly draught, if it be already bruised; if not, let him bruise it."

Then said Crito, "I think the sun shines upon the tops of the mountains, and is not yet quite gone down;[1] and I have seen some delay the drinking of the poison much longer: nay more, after notice had been given them that they ought to despatch, they have supped, and drank largely too, and talked a good while with their friends; be not then so hasty; you have yet time enough."

"Those men of whom you speak, Crito," saith he, "did well; for they thought they gained so much more of life; but I will not follow their example, for I conceive I shall gain nothing by deferring my draught till it be later in the night; unless it be to expose myself to be derided for being desirous, out of too great love of life, to prolong the short remainder of it. But well, get the poison prepared quickly, and do nothing else till that be despatched."

Crito hearing this, beckoned to a boy that was present; and the boy going forth, and employing himself a while in bruising the poison, returned with him who was to give it, and who brought it ready bruised in a cup: upon whom Socrates casting his eye, "Be it so, good man," said he: "tell me (for thou art well skilled in these matters), what is to be done?"

"Nothing," saith he, "but after you have drank, to walk, until a heaviness comes upon your legs and thighs, and then to sit: and this you shall do."

And with that he held forth the cup to Socrates, which he readily receiving, and being perfectly sedate, "O Echecrates," without trembling, without change either in the colour or in the air of his face, but with the same aspect, and countenance intent and stern (as was usual to him), looking upon the man: "what sayest thou," saith he, "may not a man offer some of this liquor in sacrifice?"

"We have bruised but so much, Socrates," saith he, "as we thought would be sufficient."

"I understand you," saith he: "but yet it is both lawful and our duty to pray to the gods, that our transmigration from hence to them may be happy and fortunate." Having spoke these words, and remained silent [for a minute or two], he easily and expeditely drank all that was in the cup. Then many of us endeavoured what we could to contain our tears, but when we beheld him drinking the poison, and immediately after, no man was able longer to refrain from weeping: and while I put force upon myself to suppress my tears, they flowed down my cheeks drop after drop. So, covering my face, I wept in secret: deploring not his, but my own hard fortune, in the loss of so great a friend and so near a kinsman. But Crito, no longer able to contend with his grief, and to forbid his tears, rose up before me. And Apollodorus first breaking forth into showers of tears, and then into cries, howlings, and lamentations, left no man from whom he extorted not tears in abundance; Socrates himself only excepted: who said,

"What do ye, my friends? truly I sent away the women for no other reason but lest they should in this kind offend. For I have heard, that we ought to die with good men's gratulation: but re-compose yourselves, and resume your courage and resolution." Hearing this, we blushed with shame, and suppressed our tears. But when he had walked awhile, and told us that his thighs were grown heavy and stupid; he lay down upon his back; for so he who had given him the poison had directed him to do. Who a little time after, returns, and feeling him, looked upon his legs and feet: then pinching his foot vehemently, he asked him if he felt it? and when he said no, he again pinched his legs; and turning to us, told us, that now Socrates was stiff with cold: and touching him, said he would die so soon as the poison came up to his heart; for the parts about his heart were already grown stiff.

---

[1] By the Athenian law no man was to be put to death until after sunset, lest the sun, for which they had a singular veneration, might be displeased at the sight.

Then Socrates, putting aside the garment wherewith he was covered; "We owe," saith he, "a cock to Æsculapius: but do ye pay him, and neglect not to do it." And these were his last words. "It shall be done," saith Crito: "but see if you have any other command for us." To whom he gave no answer: but soon after fainting, he moved himself often [as in suffering convulsions]. Then the servant uncovered him: and his eyes stood wide open; which Crito perceiving, he closed both his mouth and his eyes. This, Echecrates, was the end of our friend and familiar, a man, as we in truth affirm, of all whom we have by use and experience known, the wisest and most just.

____

WINTER.

[Thomas Sackville, born at Buckhurst, Withiam, Sussex, 1527; died at Whitehall, 19th April, 1608. Statesman and poet. He became the first Lord Buckhurst and Earl of Dorset, Lord High Treasurer, Chancellor of the University of Oxford, and author of the first genuine English tragedy—*Ferrex and Porrex*, afterwards called *Gorboduc*, and acted before Queen Elizabeth at Whitehall by students of the Inner Temple. As a poet he is best known as the originator of the *Mirror or Magistrates,*¹ in which all the illustrious but unfortunate characters of English history were to pass in review before the poet, who, conducted by Sorrow, descends like Dante into hell. For this work Sackville wrote the *Induction* and one legend, which is the life of Henry Stafford, Duke of Buckingham. The following stanzas are from the *Induction*]

The wrathful winter 'proaching on a pace,
With blust'ring blasts had all ybared the treen,
And old Saturnus with his frosty face
With chilling cold had pierc'd the tender green:
The mantels rent, wherein enwrapped been
The gladsome groves that now lay overthrown,
The tapets torn, and every bloom down blown.

The soil that erst so seemly was to seen
Was all despoiléd of her beauty's hue;
And sweet fresh flowers (wherewith the summer's queen
Had clad the earth) now Boreas blasts down blew,
And small fowls flocking, in their song did rue
The winter's wrath, wherewith each thing defaced
In woeful wise bewailed the summer past.

Hawthorn had lost his motley livery,
The naked twigs were shivering all for cold:
And dropping down the tears abundantly,
Each thing, methought, with weeping eye me told
The cruel season, bidding me withhold
Myself within, for I was gotten out
Into the fields whereas I walk'd about.

¹ This work supplied Shakspeare and other dramatists with many scenes and suggestions.

____

And sorrowing I to see the summer flowers,
The lively green, the lusty leas forlorn,
The sturdy trees so shattered with the showers,
The fields so fade that flourish'd so beforne;
It taught me well all earthly things be born
To die the death, for nought long time may last:
The summer's beauty yields to winter's blast.

____

LITTLE TOMMY TUCKER.

[Elizabeth Stuart Phelps, daughter of the late Mrs. E. S. Phelps, of Boston, who wrote numerous successful works for the young. Miss Phelps has written many short tales for the principal American magazines, and several novels. Her most popular works are: *The Gates Ajar; Hedged In;* and *Men, Women, and Ghosts,* from which we quote (London: Sampson Low, Marston & Co.)]

There were but three persons in the car; a merchant, deep in the income list of the *Traveller,* an old lady with two bandboxes, a man in the corner with his hat pulled over his eyes.

Tommy opened the door, peeped in, hesitated, looked into another car, came back, gave his little fiddle a shove on his shoulder, and walked in.

"Hi! Little Tommy Tucker
      Plays for his supper,"

shouted the young exquisite lounging on the platform in tan-coloured coat and lavender kid gloves.

"O Kids, you're there, are you? Well, I'd rather play for it than loaf for it, *I* had," said Tommy, stoutly.

The merchant shot a careless glance over the top of his paper at the sound of this *petit dialogue,* and the old lady smiled benignly; the man in the corner neither looked nor smiled.

Nobody would have thought, to look at that man in the corner, that he was at that very moment deserting a wife and five children. Yet that is precisely what he was doing. A villain? O no, that is not the word. A brute? Not by any means. A man, weak, unfortunate, discouraged, and selfish, as weak, unfortunate, and discouraged people are apt to be; that was the amount of it. His panoramas never paid him for the use of his halls. His travelling tin-type saloon had trundled him into a sheriff's hands. His petroleum speculations had crashed like a bubble. His black and gold sign, *F. Harmon, Photographer,* had swung now for nearly a year over the dentist's rooms, and he had had the patronage of precisely six old women and three babies. He had drifted to the theatre in the evenings, he did not care now to remember how many times—the fellows asked him, and it made him forget his troubles; the next morning his empty purse would gape at him, and Annie's mouth would quiver. A man must have his glass too, on Sundays, and—well, perhaps a little oftener. He had not always been fit to go to work after it; and Annie's mouth would quiver. It will be seen at once that it was exceedingly hard on a man that his wife's mouth should quiver. "Confound it! Why couldn't she scold or cry? These still women aggravated a fellow beyond reason."

Well, then the children had been sick; measles, whooping-cough, scarlatina, mumps, he was sure he did not know what not; every one of them from the baby up. There was medicine, and there were doctor's bills, and there was sitting up with them at night—their mother usually did that. Then she must needs pale down herself, like a poorly-finished photograph; all her colour and roundness and sparkle gone; and if ever a man liked to have a pretty wife about it was he. Moreover she had a cough, and her shoulders had grown round, stooping so much over the heavy baby, and her breath came short, and she had a way of being tired. Then she never stirred out of the house—he found out about that one day; she had no bonnet, and her shawl had been cut up into blankets for the crib. The children had stopped going to school. "They could not buy the new arithmetic," their mother said, half under her breath. Yesterday there was nothing for dinner but Johnny-cake, nor a large one at that. To-morrow the saloon rents were due. Annie talked about pawning one of the bureaus. Annie had had great purple rings under her eyes for six weeks.

He would not bear the purple rings and quivering mouth any longer. He hated the sight of her, for the sight stung him. He hated the corn-cake and the untaught children. He hated the whole dreary, dragging, needy home. The ruin of it dogged him like a ghost, and he should be the ruin of it as long as he stayed in it. Once fairly rid of him, his scolding and drinking, his wasting and failing, Annie would send the children to work, and find ways to live. She had energy and invention, a plenty of it in her young, fresh days, before he came across her life to drag her down. Perhaps he should make a golden fortune, and come back to her some summer day with a silk dress and servants, and make it all up; in theory this was about what he expected to do. But if his ill-luck

went westward with him, and the silk dress never turned up, why, she would forget him, and be better off, and that would be the end of it.

So here he was, ticketed and started, fairly bound for Colorado, sitting with his hat over his eyes, and thinking about it.

"Hm-m. Asleep," pronounced Tommy, with his keen glance into the corner. "Guess I'll wake him up."

He laid his cheek down on his little fiddle—you don't know how Tommy loved that little fiddle, and struck up a gay, rollicking tune—

"I care for nobody and nobody cares for me."

The man in the corner sat quite still. When it was over he shrugged his shoulders.

"When folks are asleep they don't hist their shoulders, not as a general thing," observed Tommy. "We'll try another."

Tommy tried another. Nobody knows what possessed the little fellow, the little fellow himself least of all; but he tried this:—

"We've lived and loved together,
Through many changing years."

It was a new tune, and he wanted practice, perhaps.

The train jarred and started slowly; the gloved exquisite, waiting hackmen, baggage-masters, coffee-counter, and station walls slid back; engine-house and prison towers, and labyrinths of tracks slipped by; lumber and shipping took their place, with clear spaces between, where sea and sky shone through. The speed of the train increased with a sickening sway; old wharves shot past, with the green water sucking at their piers; the city shifted by and out of sight.

"We've lived and loved together,"

played Tommy in a little plaintive wail,

"We've lived and loved"——

"Confound the boy!" Harmon pushed up his hat with a jerk, and looked out of the window. The night was coming on. A dull sunset lay low on the water, burning like a bale-fire through the snaky trail of smoke that went writhing past the car windows. Against lonely signal-houses and little deserted beaches the water was plashing drearily, and playing monotonous basses to Tommy's wail:—

"Through many changing years,
Many changing years."

It was a nuisance this music in the cars. Why didn't somebody stop it? What did the child mean by playing that? They had left the city far behind now. He wondered how far. He pushed up the window fiercely, venting the passion of the music on the first thing that came in his way, and thrust his head out to look back. Through the undulating smoke, out in the pale glimmer from the sky, he could see a low, red tongue of land, covered with the twinkle of lighted homes. Somewhere there, in among the quivering warmth, was one— What was that boy about now? Not "Home, sweet home?" But that was what Tommy was about.

They were lighting the lamps now in the car. Harmon looked at the conductor's face, as the sickly yellow flare struck on it, with a curious sensation. He wondered if he had a wife and five children; if he ever thought of running away from them; what he would think of a man who did; what most people would think; what she would think. She!—ah, she had it all to find out yet.

"There's no place like home,"

said Tommy's little fiddle,

"O, no place like home."

Now this fiddle of Tommy's may have had a crack or so in it, and I cannot assert that Tommy never struck a false note; but the man in the corner was not fastidious as a musical critic: the sickly light was flickering through the car, the quiver on the red flats was quite out of sight, the train was shrieking away into the west—the baleful, lonely west—which was dying fast now out there upon the sea, and it is a fact that his hat went slowly down over his face again, and that his face went slowly down upon his arm.

There, in the lighted home out upon the flats, that had drifted by for ever, she sat waiting now. It was about time for him to be in to supper; she was beginning to wonder a little where he was; she was keeping the coffee hot, and telling the children not to touch their father's pickles; she had set the table and drawn the chairs; his pipe lay filled for him upon the shelf over the stove. Her face in the light was worn and white—the dark rings very dark; she was trying to hush the boys, teasing for their supper; begging them to wait a few minutes, only a few minutes, he would surely be here then. She would put the baby down presently, and stand at the window with her hands—Annie's hands once were not so thin —raised to shut out the light—watching, watching.

The children would eat their supper; the table would stand untouched, with his chair in its place; still she would go to the window, and stand watching, watching. Oh, the long night that she must stand watching, and the days, and the years!

"Sweet, sweet home,"

played Tommy.

By and by there was no more of "Sweet Home."

"How about that cove with his head lopped down on his arms?" speculated Tommy, with a business-like air.

He had only stirred once, then put his face down again. But he was awake, awake in every nerve; and listening, to the very curve of his fingers. Tommy knew that; it being part of his trade to learn how to use his eyes.

The sweet, loyal passion of the music—it would take worse playing than Tommy's to drive the sweet, loyal passion out of Annie Laurie—grew above the din of the train!—

"'Twas there that Annie Laurie
Gave me her promise true."

She used to sing that, the man was thinking —this other Annie of his own. Why, she had been his own, and he had loved her once. How he had loved her! Yes, she used to sing that when he went to see her on Sunday nights, before they were married—in her pink, plump, pretty days. Annie used to be very pretty.

Gave me her promise true,"

hummed the little fiddle.

"That's a fact," said poor Annie's husband, jerking the words out under his hat, "and kept it too, she did."

Ah, how Annie had kept it! The whole dark picture of her married years—the days of work and pain, the nights of watching, the patient voice, the quivering mouth, the tact and the planning and the trust for to-morrow, the love that had borne all things, believed all things, hoped all things, uncomplaining—rose into outline to tell him how she had kept it.

"Her face it is the fairest
That e'er the sun shone on,"

suggested the little fiddle.

That it should be darkened for ever, the sweet face! and that he should do it—he, sitting here, with his ticket bought, bound for Colorado.

"And ne'er forget will I,"

murmured the little fiddle.

He would have knocked the man down who had told him twenty years ago that he ever should forget; that he should be here to-night, with his ticket bought, bound for Colorado.

But it was better for her to be free from him. He and his cursed ill-luck were a drag on her and the children, and would always be. What was that she had said once?

"Never mind, Jack, I can bear anything as long as I have you."

And here he was, with his ticket bought, bound for Colorado.

He wondered if it were ever too late in the day for a fellow to make a man of himself. He wondered—

"And she's a' the world to me,
And for bonnie Annie Laurie
I'd lay me down and dee,"

sang the little fiddle, triumphantly.

Harmon shook himself, and stood up. The train was slackening; the lights of a way-station bright ahead. It was about time for supper and his mother, so Tommy put down his fiddle and handed around his faded cap.

The merchant threw him a penny and returned to his tax-list. The old lady was fast asleep with her mouth open.

"Come here," growled Harmon, with his eyes very bright. Tommy shrank back, almost afraid of him.

"Come here," softening, "I won't hurt you. I tell you, boy, you don't know what you've done to-night."

"Done, sir?" Tommy couldn't help laughing, though there was a twinge of pain at his stout little heart, as he fingered the solitary penny in the faded cap. "Done? Well, I guess I've waked you up, sir, which was about what I meant to do."

"Yes, that is it," said Harmon, very distinctly, pushing up his hat, "you've waked me up. Here, hold your cap."

They had puffed into the station now and stopped. He emptied his purse into the little cap, shook it clean of paper and copper alike, was out of the car and off the train before Tommy could have said Jack Robinson.

"My eyes!" gasped Tommy, "that chap had a ticket for New York, sure! Methuselah! Look a here! One, two, three—must have been crazy; that's it, crazy."

"He'll never find out," muttered Harmon, turning away from the station lights, and striking back through the night for the red flats and home. "He'll never find out what he has done, nor, please God, shall she."

It was late when he came in sight of the house; it had been a long tramp across the tracks, and hard; he being stung by a bitter

wind from the east all the way, tired with the monotonous treading of the sleepers, and with crouching in perilous niches to let the trains go by.

She stood watching at the window, as he had known that she would stand, her hands raised to her face, her figure cut out against the warm light of the room.

He stood still a moment and looked at her, hidden in the shadow of the street, thinking his own thoughts. The publican, in the old story, hardly entered the beautiful temple with more humble step than he his home that night.

She sprang to meet him, pale with her watching and fear.

"Worried, Annie, were you? I haven't been drinking; don't be frightened—no, not the theatre either this time. Some business, dear; business that delayed me. I'm sorry you were worried, I am, Annie. I've had a long walk. It is pleasant here. I believe I'm tired, Annie."

He faltered, and turned away his face.

"Dear me," said Annie, "why, you poor fellow, you are all tired out. Sit right up here by the fire, and I will bring the coffee. I've tried so hard not to let it boil away, you don't know, Jack; and I was so afraid something had happened to you."

Her face, her voice, her touch, seemed more than he could bear for a minute, perhaps. He gulped down his coffee, choking.

"Annie, look here." He put down his cup, trying to smile and make a jest of the words. "Suppose a fellow had it in him to be a rascal, and nobody ever knew it, eh?"

"I should rather not know it, if I were his wife," said Annie, simply.

"But you couldn't care anything more for him, you know, Annie?"

"I don't know," said Annie, shaking her head with a little perplexed smile, "you would be just Jack, any how."

Jack coughed, took up his coffee-cup, set it down hard, strode once or twice across the room, kissed the baby in the crib, kissed his wife, and sat down again, winking at the fire.

"I wonder if He had anything to do with sending him," he said presently, under his breath.

"Sending whom?" asked puzzled Annie.

"Business, dear, just business. I was thinking of a boy who did a little job for me to-night, that's all."

And that is all that she knows to this day about the man sitting in the corner, with his hat over his eyes, bound for Colorado.

PEACE.

BY MRS. H. B. STOWE.

When winds are raging o'er the upper ocean,
And billows wild contend with angry roar,
'Tis said, far down beneath the wild commotion,
That peaceful *stillness* reigneth evermore.

Far, far beneath, the noise of tempest dieth,
And silver waves chime ever peacefully,
And no rude storm, how fierce soe'er he flieth,
Disturbs the Sabbath of that deeper sea.

So to the heart that knows thy love, O Purest,
There is a temple, sacred evermore,
And all the babble of life's angry voices
Die in hushed stillness at its peaceful door.

Far, far away, the roar of passion dieth,
And loving thoughts rise calm and peacefully,
And no rude storm, how fierce soe'er he flieth,
Disturbs the soul that dwells, O Lord, in thee.

O, rest of rests! O, peace serene, eternal!
Thou ever livest; and thou changest never,
And in the secret of thy presence dwelleth
Fulness of joy—for ever and for ever.

MARY HAMILTON.

[Robert Macnish, M.D., LL.D., born in Glasgow, 15th February, 1802; died there, January, 1837. He earned distinction as a writer of short tales in *Blackwood's Magazine*, under the pseudonym of "A Modern Pythagorean." His chief works are: *The Anatomy of Drunkenness; The Philosophy of Sleep; The Book of Aphorisms;* and the *Introduction to Phrenology.* His tales, with a biography by D. M. Moir, were published shortly after his death. One critic said of him: "There was always a spring of life about him, that vivified his pages and animated and delighted his readers."]

During the persecutions in Scotland, consequent upon the fruitless attempt to root out Presbyterianism and establish Episcopacy by force, there lived one Allan Hamilton, a farmer, at the foot of the Lowther mountains in Lanarkshire. His house was situated in a remote valley, which, though of small extent, was beautiful and romantic, being embosomed on all sides by hills covered to their summits with rich verdure. Around the house was a considerable piece of arable ground, and behind it a well-stocked orchard and garden. A few tall trees grew in front, waving their ample foliage over the roof, while at each side of the door was a little plot planted with honeysuckle, wall-flower, and various odoriferous shrubs.

The owner of this neat mansion was a fortunate man; for the world had hitherto gone well with him, and if he had lost his wife—an affliction which sixteen years had mellowed over—he was blessed with an affectionate and virtuous daughter. He had two male and as many female servants to assist him in his farming operations; and so well had his industry been rewarded, that he might be considered one of the most prosperous husbandmen in that part of the country.

Mary Hamilton, his only child, was, at the time we speak of, nineteen years of age. She was an extremely handsome girl, and, though living in so remote a quarter, the whole district of the Lowthers rang with the fame of her beauty. But this was the least of her qualifications; for her mind was even fairer than her person; and on her pure spirit the impress of virtue and affection was stamped in legible characters.

Allan, though a religious man, was not an enthusiast; and, from certain prudent considerations, had forborne to show any of that ardent zeal for the faith which distinguished many of his countrymen. He approved secretly in his heart of the measures adopted by the Covenanters, and inwardly prayed for their success; but these matters he kept to his own mind, reading his Bible with his daughter at home, and not exposing himself or her to the machinations of the persecuting party.

It was on an August evening, that he and his daughter were seated together in their little parlour. He had performed all his daily labours, and had permitted his servants to go to some rural meeting several miles off. Being thus left undisturbed, he enjoyed with her that quiet rest so grateful after a day spent in toil. The day had been remarkably beautiful; but towards nightfall the heavens were overcast with dark clouds, and the sun had that sultry glare which is so often the forerunner of a tempest. When this luminary disappeared beneath the mountains, he left a red and glowing twilight behind him; and over the firmament a tissue of crimson clouds was extended, mingled here and there with black vapours. The atmosphere was hot, sickening, and oppressive, and seemed to teem with some approaching convulsion.

"We shall have a storm to-night," Allan remarked to his daughter. "I wish that I had not let the servants out; they will be overtaken in it to a certainty as they cross the moors."

"There is no fear of them, father," replied Mary; "they know the road well; and at any rate the tempest will be over before they think of stirring from where they are."

Allan did not make any answer, but continued looking through the window opposite to which he was placed. He could see from it the mountain of Lowther, the highest in Lanarkshire: its huge shoulders and top were distinctly visible, standing forth in grand relief from the red clouds above and behind it. The last rays of the sun, bursting from the rim of the horizon, still lingered upon the hill, and, casting over its western side a broad and luminous glare, gave to it the appearance of a burnished pyramid towering from the earth. This gorgeous vision, however, did not continue long. In a few minutes the mountain lost its ruddy tint, and the sky around it became obscurer. Shortly afterwards a huge sable cloud was observed hovering over its summit. "Look, Mary," cried Allan to his daughter, "did you ever see anything grander than this? Look at yon black cloud that hangs over Lowther." Mary did so, and saw the same thing as was remarked by her father. The cloud came down slowly and majestically, enveloped the summit of the mountain, and descended for some way upon its sides. At last, when it had firmly settled, confirming, as it were, its dismal empire, a flash of fire was seen suddenly to issue from the midst of it. It revealed for an instant the summit of Lowther; then vanishing with meteor-like rapidity, left everything in the former state of gloom. Mary clung with alarm to her father.

"Hush, my dear," said Allan, pressing her closely to him, "and you will hear the thunder." He had scarcely pronounced the word when a clap was heard, so loud that the summit of the mountain appeared to be rent in twain. The terrific sound continued some time, for the neighbouring hills caught it up, and re-echoed it to each other, till it died away in the distance. A succession of flashes and peals from different quarters succeeded, and in a short time a deluge of rain poured down with the utmost violence.

The two inmates did not hear this noise without alarm. The rain beat loudly upon the windows, while, every now and then, fearful peals of thunder burst overhead. Without, no object was visible: darkness alone prevailed, varied at intervals with fierce glares of lightning. Thereafter gusts of wind began to sweep with tumult through the glen; and the stream which flowed past the house was evidently swollen, from the increased noise of its current rushing impetuously on.

The tempest continued to rage with unabated

violence, when a knock was heard at the door. Allan opened it, expecting to find his domestics; but to his astonishment and dismay he beheld the Rev. Thomas Hervey, one of the most famous preachers of the Covenant. He was a venerable old man, and seemed overcome with fatigue and want, for he was pale and drooping, while his thin garments were drenched with rain. Now, though Allan Hamilton would yield to no man in benevolence, he never, on any occasion, felt so disposed as at present to outrage his own feelings, and cast aside the godlike virtue of charity. Mr. Hervey, like many other good men, was proscribed by the ruling powers; and persecution then ran so high that to grant him a night's lodging amounted to a capital crime. Many persons had already been shot for affording this slight charity to the outlawed Covenanters: Allan himself had been an unwilling witness of this dreadful fact. It was not, therefore, with his usual alacrity that he welcomed in the wayworn stranger. On the contrary, he held the door half shut, and in a tone of embarrassment asked him what was wanted.

"I see, Mr. Hamilton," said the minister calmly, "that you do not wish I should cross your threshold. You ask me what I want. Is that Christian? What can anyone want in a night like this, but lodgment and protection? If you grant it to me, I shall pray for you and yours; if you refuse it, I can only shake the dust off my feet and depart, albeit it be to death."

"Mr. Hervey," said Allan, "you know your situation and you know mine. I would be loath to treat the meanest thing that breathes as I have now treated you; but you are an outlawed man, and a lodging for one night under my roof is as much as my life is worth. Was it not last month I saw one of my nearest neighbours cruelly slain for doing a less thing —even for giving a morsel of bread to one of your brethren? Mr. Hervey, I repeat it, and with sorrow, that you know my situation, and that for the sake of my poor daughter and myself I have no alternative."

"Yes, I know your situation," answered the preacher, drawing himself up indignantly. "You are one of those faint-hearted believers who, for the sake of ease and temporal gain, have deserted that glorious cause for which your fathers have struggled. You are one of those who can stand by coolly and see others fight the good fight—and when they have overcome you will doubtless enjoy the blessed fruits of their combating. You have held back in the time of need: you have abetted prelacy and persecution, in so far as you have not set your shoulder to the wheel of the Covenant. Now, when a humble forwarder of that holy cause craves from you an hour of shelter, you stand with your door well-nigh closed and refuse him admittance. I leave God to judge of your iniquity, and I quit your inhospitable and unchristian mansion."

He was moving off, when Mary Hamilton, who had listened with a beating heart to this colloquy, rushed forward and caught him by the arm. Her beautiful eyes were wet with tears, and she looked at her parent with an expression in which entreaty and upbraiding were mingled together.

"You will not turn out this poor old man, father? indeed you will not. You were only jesting. Come in, Mr. Hervey; my father did not mean what he said;"—and she led him in by the hand, pushing gently back Allan, who still stood by the door. "Now, Mr. Hervey, sit down there and dry yourself; and, father, shut the door."

"Thank you, my fair maiden," said the minister. "The Lord, for this good deed, will aid you in your distresses. You have shown that the old may be taught by the young; and I pray that this lesson of charity which you have given to your father, may not turn out to your scathe or his."

Allan said nothing: he felt that the part he had acted was hardly a generous one, although perhaps justified by the stern necessity of the times. His heart was naturally benevolent, and in the consciousness of self-reproach every dread of danger was obliterated.

The first attention of him and Mary was directed to their guest. His garments having been thoroughly dried, food was placed before him, of which he partook, after returning thanks to God in a lengthened grace, for so disposing towards him the hearts of his creatures. When he had finished the repast, he raised his face slightly towards heaven, closed his eyes, and clasping his hands together, fervently implored the blessings of providence on the father of that mansion and his child. When he had done this he took a small Bible from his pocket, and read some of the most affecting passages of the Old Testament, descanting upon them as he went along: how God fed Elijah in the wilderness; how he conducted the Israelites through their forty years of sojourn; how Daniel, by faith, remained unhurt in the lions' den; and how Shadrach, Meshach, and Abednego walked through the fiery furnace, and not even their garments were touched by the flames. Allan and Mary lis-

tened with the most intense interest to the old man, whose voice became stronger, whose form seemed to dilate, and whose eyes were lit up with a sort of prophetic rapture, as he threw his spirit into those mysteries of Holy Writ.

After having concluded this part of his devotions, and before retiring to rest, he proposed that evening prayer should be offered up. Each accordingly knelt down, and he commenced in a strain of ardent and impassioned language. He deplored the afflicted state of God's kirk; prayed that the hearts of those who still clung to it might be confirmed and made steadfast; that confidence might be given to the wavering; that those who from fear or worldly considerations had held off from the good cause, might be taught to see the error of their ways; and that all backsliders might be reclaimed, and become goodly members of the broken and distressed Covenant. "O Lord!" continued he, "thou who hast watched over us in all time—who from thy throne in the highest heaven hast vouchsafed to hearken to the prayers of thy servants, thou wilt not now abandon us in our need. We have worshipped thee from the depths of the valley, and the rocks and hills of the desert have heard our voices calling upon thy name. 'Where is your temple, ye outcast remnant?' cry the scorners. We answer, O Lord! that we have no temple but such as thou hast created; and yet from that tabernacle of the wilderness hast thou heard us, though storms walked around. We have trod the valley of the shadow of death, and yet thou hast been a light in our path; we have been chased like wild beasts through the land, yet thy spirit hath not deserted us; armed men have encompassed us on all sides, threatening to destroy, yet our hearts have not failed; neither have the prison nor the torture had power to make us abjure thy most holy laws."

During the whole of his supplication, which he poured forth with singular enthusiasm, the storm continued without, and distant peals of thunder were occasionally heard. This convulsion of elements did not, however, distract his thoughts; on the contrary, it rendered them more ardent; and in apostrophizing the tempest he frequently arose to a pitch of wild sublimity. Mary listened with deep awe. Her feelings, constitutionally warm and religious, were aroused, and she sobbed with emotion. Allan Hamilton, though not by nature a man of imagination, was also strongly affected; he breathed hard, and occasionally a half-suppressed groan came from his breast. He could not help feeling deep remorse for the lukewarmness he had shown to the great cause then at stake.

The night, though fearfully tempestuous, did not prevent slumber from falling on the eyes of all. Each slept soundly, and the old minister, perhaps, more so than any. Many months had elapsed since he had stretched himself on such a couch as that which Mary Hamilton had prepared for him; for he was a dweller in the desert, and had often lain upon the heath, with no other shelter than his plaid afforded. His slumbers, therefore, were delicious; but they were not long, for no sooner had the morning light begun to peep through the window of his chamber than he was up and at his devotions. Allan, though an early riser, was still in bed, and not a little astonished when he heard his door open and saw the old man walk softly up to his side.

"Hush! Allan Hamilton, do not awaken the dear maiden, your daughter, in the next room. I have come to thank you and bid you farewell. The morning sun is up, and I may not tarry longer here, consistent with my own safety or yours. There are spies through all the country, but peradventure I have escaped their observation. I am going a few miles off near the Clyde, to meet sundry of my flock who are to assemble there. May God bless you, and send better times to this afflicted land."

When Allan and his daughter sat down to their homely breakfast, the morning presented a pleasing contrast to the previous night. The sky was perfectly clear and serene. Every mountain sparkled, and the earth had a peculiar freshness diffused over its surface. The few clouds visible were at a great elevation, and were hurrying away, as if not to leave a stain on the transparent concave of heaven. There was little wind on the lower regions, scarcely sufficient to ruffle the surface of a slumbering lake. The dampness of the grass, the clay washed from the pebbles, and the rivulet swollen and turbid, were the only relics of the tempest. The weather continued beautifully serene, and when the sun was at his height, one of the finest days was presented that ever graced this most gorgeous month of the year.

It was about the middle of the day when Mary, who happened to look out, perceived six armed troopers approaching. They were on foot, their broadswords hanging at their sides, and carbines swung over their shoulders. In addition to this, each had a couple of pistols stuck in his belt. As soon as she saw them she ran in to her father with manifest looks of alarm, and informed him of their approach.

Allan could not help feeling uneasy at this intelligence; for the military were then universally dreaded, and whenever a number were seen together, it was almost always on some errand of destruction. He went to the door; but just as he reached it the soldiers were on the point of entering. The leader of the body he recognized to be the ferocious Captain Clobberton, who had rendered himself universally infamous by his cruelties; and who, it was reported, had in his career of persecution caused no less than seventeen persons to be put to death in cold blood, without even the formality of a trial. He was one of the chief favourites of Dalzell, who used to call him his "lamb." This man's aspect did not belie his heart, for it was fierce, lowering, and cruel. His companions, with a single exception, seemed well suited to their leader, and fit instruments to carry his bloody mandates into execution. Allan, when he confronted this worthy agent of tyranny, turned back, followed by him and his crew into the house.

"Shut the door, my dear chucks," cried Clobberton; "we must have some conversation with this godly man. So, Mr. Hamilton, you have taken up with that pious remnant: you have turned a psalm-singer, eh! Come, don't stare at me as if you saw an owl: answer my question—yes or no."

Allan looked at him with a steady eye. "Captain Clobberton, you have asked me no question. I shall not scruple to answer anything which may be justly demanded of me."

"Answer me, then, sir," continued the captain: "were you not present at the field-preaching near Lanark, when one of the king's soldiers was slain in attempting, with several others, to disperse it?"

"I was not," answered Allan; "I never in my life attended a field-preaching."

"Or a conventicle!"

"Nor a conventicle either."

"Do you mean to deny that you are one of that precious hypocritical set, who preach their absurd and treasonable jargon in defiance of the law? In a word, do you deny that you are one of the sworn members of the Covenant?"

"I do deny it, stoutly."

"Acknowledge it, and save your wretched life. Acknowledge it, or I will confront you with a proof which will perhaps astonish you, and cost you more than you are aware of."

"I will tell no untruth, even to save my life."

"Then on your own stupid head rest the consequences. Do you know one Hervey, a preacher?"

"I do," said Allan, firmly.

"Ha, here it comes! you have then spoken to that man, most godly Allan?"

"I have spoken to him."

"He has been in your house?"

"I do not mean to deny that he has."

"Has he not sung psalms in your house, and prayed in your house, and lodged in your house? Eh?—and was it not last night that these doings were going on?"

"I will gainsay nothing of what you have said."

"Then, Allan Hamilton," said the other, "I tell you plainly that you have harboured a traitor; and that unless you deliver him up, or tell where he may be found, I shall hold you guilty of treason, and punish you accordingly."

"The Lord's will be done!" answered Hamilton, with a deep sigh. "What I did was an act of common charity. The old man applied to me in his distress; and it would have been cruel to have closed my door against him. Wreak your will upon me as it pleases you. Where he has gone I know not ; and though I did know, I would hardly consider myself justified in telling you."

"Then we shall make short work with you !" rejoined Clobberton with an oath. "Ross, give him ten minutes to say his prayers, and then bind up his eyes. It is needless to palaver with him. We have other jobs of a like kind to manage to-day."

Here Mary, who stood in a corner listening with terrified heart, uttered a loud scream when she heard her father's doom pronounced. She rushed forth into the middle of the room, and fell upon her knees before Clobberton.

"O! Captain, do not slay my father ! Take *my* life. It was *my* fault alone that the old man was let into the house. My father refused to admit him. Take *my* life and save *his*. I shall be his murderess if he die—for I brought him into this trouble."

She continued some moments in this attitude, gazing up at him with looks of fear and entreaty, and clasping his knees. He had, however, been too long accustomed to scenes of this afflicting nature to be much moved ; and he extricated himself from the unhappy girl with brutal rudeness. She fell speechless at his feet.

"Confound the wench! was there ever seen the like of it! She takes me for one of your chicken-hearted milksops: out of the way with the ninny."

He was about to lay rough hands upon her, when a trooper stepping forward raised her gently up and placed her on a seat. This was

the only one of Clobberton's followers whose appearance was at all indicative of humanity. He was a handsome and strongly built young man of six feet. His countenance was well formed; but its expression was rather dissolute, and rendered stern, apparently by the prevalence of some fierce internal passion. The marks of a generous heart were, notwithstanding, imprinted upon its bold outlines; and whoever looked upon him could not help thinking that his natural disposition had been perverted by the wicked characters and scenes among which he was placed.

"Captain," said he, "I do not see the use of shooting this old fool. I begin to feel that we have had a surfeit of this work. Besides, if what the girl declares is correct, there is no great matter of treason in the case. At all events, I would vote to leave the business to the Justiciary."

"Graham," said Clobberton, eying him sternly, "give me none of your cursed whining palaver. What the —— is your liver made of? When there is anything in the way of justice to be done, you are as mealy and cream-faced as if you saw the devil. A fine fellow to wear the king's uniform! If you say another word," added he, with a frightful oath, "I'll have you reported to the general!"

"Captain," said Graham, stepping modestly but firmly forward, "you may speak of me as you please; you are my officer—(though neither you nor any man of the regiment need be told, that when my service was needed in real danger I was never behind); but I cannot stand by unmoved and see downright butchery. If you have anything to urge against this man, let him be brought to Edinburgh, and there tried by the commission, which will punish him severely enough, in all conscience, if he be really guilty. I have assisted in some of these murders; but my conscience tells me that I have done wrong: and, whatever the consequences be, I shall assist at them no more."

"Ay!" said Clobberton, "you are a pretty dainty fellow—fitter to strut about in regimentals before wenches than behave like a man; but, Mr. John Graham, let me tell you that your eloquence, instead of retarding, has hastened the fate of this rascally traitor. And, let me tell you farther, that on my arrival at head-quarters I shall have you arraigned for mutiny and disobedience of orders.—Ross, blindfold Hamilton and lead him out."

His command was instantly executed; while Mary, in a fit of distraction, flew up to her father, cast her arms round his neck, and kissed him with the most heart-rending affliction.

"My father, my father, I am your murderess! I will die with you! Ye cruel-hearted men, will none of you save him from this bloody death?"

"My dear Mary, may God protect you and send you a happier lot than mine," was all that the unhappy parent could articulate. He was then torn from her with violence, and hurried out to the green before the house. Mary, on this separation, fell into a short swoon; on awaking from which she found herself in the chamber with no one except Graham. His face was flushed with anger, and he walked impatiently up and down. By a sudden impulse she ran to the window, and the first sight which caught her eye was her father kneeling down, and opposite to him the four troopers, seemingly waiting for the signal of Clobberton, who looked intently at his watch. At this terrifying spectacle, and in an agony of desperation, she threw herself on her knees before the soldier.

"Young man—young man, save my father's life! O try, at least, to save him! I will love you, and work for you, and be your slave for ever! Blessings on your kind heart, you will do it—yes, you will do it!"

And she rose up and threw her arms round his neck, and kissed him on the cheek. A tear rolled from Graham's manly eye, and his soul was moved with compassion for the lovely being who clung to him and implored him so feelingly. He turned an instant to the window.

"Let me go, my dear—the accursed miscreant is putting up his watch and has told them to present; there is not a second to lose."

Without saying another word, he unslung his carbine, rushed to the open air—and shot Clobberton dead on the spot.

The troopers were confounded at this sudden action. They lowered the weapons which they had that instant raised to their shoulders, and stood for some time gazing confusedly at each other—then at Graham—then at the body of their captain. When they recovered their self-possession they raised up the latter to see if any spark of life remained. He was perfectly dead. The following colloquy then ensued between them.

Russell. "Whoy, I thinks as how he be dead."

Smith. "Dead! ay as dead as Julius Cæsar. I wonder what old Dalzell will say when he hears of his dear *lamb* being butchered thus."

Russell. "Now, domn it, Smith, don't speak ill of the coptain. He was a worthy man, that is to say, after his own fashion; and no one

ever sarved his country better in the way of ridding it of crop-eared preachers: he was worth a score of hangmen."

Ross. "Gentlemen, there is no occasion to stand jesting and talking nonsense. Here is as pretty a piece of murder as ever was committed; and it remains for us to decide what we will do, first with the traitor Hamilton, and secondly with the murderer Graham."

Graham. "Whatever you do with me, I hope you will not harm that poor man. Let him go, and thus do a charitable action for once in your lives."

Russell. "I always, do you zee, gentlemen, goes with the majority. Domn it, shoot or not is all one to Dick Russell. If you make up your minds to let him go scot free, whoy, I'se not oppose it."

Jones. "Well, well, let him go and sing psalms in his own canting fashion."

The fact is, these men were getting sick of shedding innocent blood, and although ready to spill more on being ordered, rather shunned it than otherwise—especially when their victims were unresisting.

"I see, comrades, you are agreed to let the old fool go unharmed," said Ross. Then walking up to Allan, who still knelt—his daughter, with her arms around him, awaiting in terrible suspense the result of their deliberation—"Get up," said he, "and bless your stars; but take care in future of your treasonable covenanting tricks under the cloak of charity. It is not every day you will get a young fellow to shoot your executioner and save your life. As for you, Graham," turning to his companion, "I hold you prisoner. You must accompany us to head-quarters, and there take your trial for this business. You have committed a black murder on the body of your officer; and if we failed to bring you up, old Dalzell would have us shot like so many picts the minute after."

Graham's carbine and pistols were immediately taken from him, and his hands tied behind his back by the remaining troopers.

"Farewell, young woman," said he to Mary, who looked at him with tears of gratitude: "farewell! I have saved your father's life and forfeited my own: don't forget Jack Graham."

The unfortunate girl was distracted at this heart-rending sight; and she rushed forward to entreat his guards to give him liberty. One of them presented his carbine at her.

"Off, mistress; blast my heart, if it were not for your pretty face I would send an ounce of cold lead through you. What, haven't we spared your father's life, and you would have us connive at the escape of a murderer, to the risk of our own necks!"

"Do not distress yourself about me, my sweet girl," cried Graham—"farewell, once more!"

And she turned back weeping, while the troopers held their way towards the western outlet of the valley.

Mary was too generous to be happy in the safety even of her father, when that was bought with the life of his brave deliverer. When Graham was taken away she felt a pang as if he had been led to execution. Instead, therefore, of indulging in selfish congratulation, her whole soul was taken up in the romantic and apparently hopeless scheme of extricating him from his danger. There was not a moment to lose; and she asked her father if he could think of any way in which a rescue might be attempted.

"Mary, my dear, I know of none," was his answer. "We live far from any house, and before assistance could be procured they would be miles beyond our reach."

"Yes, father, there is a chance," said she with impatience. "Gallop over to Allaster Wilson's on the other side of the hills. He is a strong and determined man, and, as well as some of his near neighbours, is accustomed to contest. You know he fought desperately at Drumclog; and though he blamed you for not joining the cause, he will not be loath to assist in this bitter extremity."

Allan at these words started up, as if awakened from a reverie. "That will do, my dear bairn. I never thought of it; but your understanding is quicker than mine. I shall get out the horse; follow me, on foot, as hard as you can."

This was the work of a minute. The horse was brought from the stable, and Allan lashed him to his full speed across the moor. Most fortunately he arrived at Allaster's house as the latter was on the point of leaving it. He carried a musket over his shoulder, and a huge claymore hung down from a belt girded around his loins.

"You have just come in time," said this stern son of the Covenant, after Allan had briefly related to him what had happened. "I am on my way to hear that precious saint, Mr. Hervey, hold forth. You see I am armed to defend myself against temporal foes, and so are many others of my friends and brethren in God, who will be present on that blessed occasion. Come away, Allan Hamilton: you are one of the timid and faint-hearted flock of Jacob, but we will aid you as you wish, and

peradventure save the young man who has done you such a good turn."

They went on swiftly to a retired spot at the distance of half a mile: it was a small glen nearly surrounded with rocks. There they beheld the Reverend Mr. Hervey standing upon a mound of earth, and preaching to a congregation, the greater part of the males of which were armed with muskets, swords, or pikes; they formed, as it were, the outworks of the assembly, the women, old men, and children being placed in the centre. These were a few of the devoted Christians who, from the rocks and caves of their native land, sent up their fearless voices to heaven—who, disowning the spiritual authority of a tyrannic government, thought it nowise unbecoming or treasonable to oppose the strong arm of lawless power with its own weapons; and who finally triumphed in the glorious contest—establishing that pure religion, for which posterity has proved, alas, too ungrateful! In the pressing urgency of the case Allaster did not scruple to go up to the minister in the midst of his discourse. Such interruptions, indeed, were common in these distracted times, when it was necessary to skulk from place to place, and perform divine worship as if it was an act of treason against the state. Mr. Hervey made known to his flock in a few words what had been communicated to him, taking care to applaud highly the scheme proposed by Wilson. There was no time to be lost, and, under the guidance of Allaster, the whole of the assemblage hurried into a gorge of the mountains through which the troopers must necessarily pass. As the route of the latter was circuitous, time was allowed to this sagacious leader to arrange his forces. This he did by placing all the armed men, about twenty-five in number, in two lines across the pass. Those who were not armed, together with the women and children, were sent to the rear. When, therefore, the soldiers came up, they found to their surprise a formidable body ready to dispute the passage.

"What means this interruption?" said Ross, who acted the part of spokesman to the rest. Whereupon Mr. Hervey advanced in front—"Release," said he, "that young man whom ye have in bonds."

"Release him!" replied Ross. "Would you have us release a murderer? Are you aware that he has shot his officer?".

"I am aware of it," Mr. Hervey answered, "And I blame him not for the deed. Stand forth, Allan Hamilton, and say if that is the soldier who saved your life—and you, Mary Hamilton, stand forth likewise."

Both, to the astonishment of the soldiers, came in front of the crowd. "That," said Allan, "is the man, and may God bless him for his humanity." "It is the same," cried his daughter; "I saw him with these eyes shoot the cruel Clobberton. On my knees I begged him to sue for mercy, and his kind heart had pity upon me, and saved my father."

"Soldiers," said Mr. Hervey, "I have nothing more to say to you. That young man has slain your captain, but he has done no murder. His deed was justifiable; yea, it was praiseworthy, in so far as it saved an upright man, and rid the earth of a cruel persecutor. Deliver him up and go away in peace, or peradventure ye may fare ill among these armed men who stand before you."

The troopers consulted together for a short time, till, seeing that resistance would be utter madness against such odds, they reluctantly let go their prisoner. The first person who came up to him was Mary Hamilton. She loosened the cords that tied him, and presented him with conscious pride to those of her own sex who were assembled round.

"Good bye, Graham!" cried Ross, with a sneer. "You have bit us once, but it will puzzle you to do so again. We shall soon *harry* you and your puritanical friends from your strongholds. An ell of strong hemp is in readiness for you at the Grassmarket of Edinburgh. Take my defiance for a knave, as you are?" added he, with an imprecation.

He had scarcely pronounced the last sentence when Graham unsheathed the weapon which hung at his side, sprang from the middle of the crowd, and stood before his defier.

"Ross, you have challenged me, and you shall abide it—draw!"

Here there was an instantaneous movement among the Covenanters, who rushed in between the two fierce soldiers, who stood with their naked weapons, their eyes glancing fire at each other. Mary Hamilton screamed aloud with terror, and cries of "Separate them!" were heard from all the women. Mr. Hervey came forward and entreated them to put up their swords, and he was seconded by most of the old men; but all entreaties were in vain. They stood fronting each other, and only waiting for free ground to commence their desperate game.

"Let me alone," said Graham furiously to some who were attempting to draw him back; "am I to be bearded to my teeth by that swaggering ruffian?"

"Come on, my sweet cock of the Covenant," cried Ross, with the most insulting derision, "you or any one of your canting crew—or a dozen of you, one after the other."

"Let Graham go," was heard from the deep stern voice of Allaster Wilson; "let him go, or I will meet that man with my own weapon. Mr. Hervey, your advice is dear to us all, and well do we know that the blood of God's creatures must not be shed in vain; but has not that man of blood openly defied us, and shall we hinder our champion from going forward to meet him? No, let them join in combat and try which is the better cause. If the challenger overcomes, we shall do him no harm, but let him depart in peace; if he be overcome, let him rue the consequences of his insolence."

This proposition, though violently opposed by the women and the aged part of the crowd, met the entire approbation of the young men. Each felt himself personally insulted, and allowed, for a time, the turbulent passions of his nature to get the better of every milder feeling. A space of ground was immediately cleared for the combat, the friends of Ross being allowed to arrange matters as they thought fit. They went about it with a coolness and precision which showed that to them this sort of pastime was nothing new. "All is right—fall on," was their cry, and in a moment the combatants met in the area. The three troopers looked on with characteristic *sang froid*, but it was otherwise with the rest of the by-standers, who gazed upon the scene with the most intense interest. Some of the females turned away their eyes from it, and among them Mary Hamilton, who almost sunk to the earth, and was with difficulty supported by her father.

The combat was desperate, for the men were of powerful strength, and of tried courage and skill in their weapons. The blows were parried for some time on both sides with consummate address, and neither could be said to have the advantage. At length, after contending fiercely, Ross exhibited signs of exhaustion—neither guarding himself, nor assaulting his opponent so vigorously as at first. Graham, on noticing this, redoubled his efforts. He acted now wholly on the offensive, sending blow upon blow with the rapidity of lightning. His last and most desperate stroke was made at the head of his enemy. The sword of the latter, which was held up in a masterly manner to receive it, was beat down by Graham's weapon, which descended forcibly upon his helmet. This blow proved decisive, and Ross fell senseless upon the ground. His conqueror immediately wrested the weapon from him, while a shout was set up by the crowd in token of victory. The troopers looked mortified at this result of the duel, which was by them evidently unexpected. Their first care was to raise up their fellow-comrade. On examination, no wound was perceived upon his head. His helmet had been penetrated by the sword, which however did not go farther. His own weapon had contributed to deaden the blow, by partially arresting that of Graham in its furious descent. It was this only which saved his life. In a few minutes he so far recovered as to get up and look around him. The first object which struck him was his opponent standing in the ring wiping his forehead.

"Well, Ross," said one of his companions, "I always took you to be the best swordsman in the regiment; but I think you have met your match."

"My match? confound me!" returned the vanquished man, "I thought I would have made minced meat of him. There, for three years have I had the character of being one of the best men in the army at my weapon, and here is all this good name taken out of me in a trice. Blast my eyes, how mortifying—and to loose my good sword too!"

"Here is your sword, Ross, and keep it," said Graham. "You have behaved like a brave man; and I honour such a fellow, whether he be my friend or foe. Only don't go on with your insolent bragging—that is all the advice I have to give you; nor call any man a knave till you have good proof that he is so."

"Well, well, Graham," answered the other, "I retract what I said ; I have a better opinion of you than I had ten minutes ago. Take care of old Dalzell—his *lambs* will be after you, and you had better keep out of the way. Take this advice in return for my weapon which you have given me back. It would, after all, be a pity to tuck up such a pretty fellow as you are; although I would care very little to see your long-faced acquaintances there dangling by the necks. Give us your hand for old fellowship, and shift your quarters as soon as you choose. Good bye." So saying, he and his three comrades departed.

After these doings, it was considered imprudent for the principal actors to remain longer in this quarter. Mr. Hervey retired about twenty miles to the northward, in company with Allan Hamilton and his daughter, and Allaster Wilson. Graham went by a circuitous route to Argyleshire, where he secreted himself so judiciously, that though the agents of government got information of his being in that county, they could never manage to lay hand upon him. These steps were prudent in all parties; for the very day after the rescue a strong body of dragoons was sent to the Lowthers to apprehend the above-named persons. They behaved with great cruelty, burning the cottages of numbers of the inhabitants, and destroying their cattle. They searched Allan Hamilton's house, took from it everything that could be easily carried away, and such of his cattle as were found on the premises. Among other things, they carried off the body of the sanguinary Clobberton, which they found in the spot where it had been left, and interred it in Lanark churchyard with military honours. None of the individuals, however, whom they sought for were found.

For a short time after this, the persecution raged with great violence in the south of Lanarkshire; but happier days were beginning to dawn; and the arrival of King William and dethronement of the bigoted James put an end to such scenes of cruelty. When these events occurred, the persecuted came forth from their hiding-places. Mr. Hervey, among others, returned to the Lowthers, and enjoyed many happy days in this seat of his ministry and trials. Allan and his daughter were among the first to make their appearance. Their house soon recovered its former comfort ; and in the course of time every worldly concern went well with them. Mary, however, for a month or more after their return, did not feel entirely satisfied. She was duller than was her wont; and neither she nor her father could give any explanation why it should be so. At this time a tall young man paid them a visit, and, strange to say, she became perfectly happy. This visitor was no other than the wild, fighting fellow Graham—now perfectly reformed from his former evil courses, by separation from his profligate companions, and by the better company and principles with which his late troubles had brought him acquainted.

A few words more will end our story. This bold trooper and the beautiful daughter of Allan Hamilton were seen five weeks thereafter going to church as man and wife. It was allowed that they were the handsomest couple ever seen in the Lowthers. Graham proved a kind husband ; and it is hardly necessary to state that Mary was a most affectionate and exemplary wife. Allan Hamilton attained a happy old age, and saw his grandchildren ripening into fair promise around him. His daughter, many years after his death, used to repeat to them the story of his danger and escape which we have here imperfectly related. The tale is not fictitious. It is handed down in tradition over the upper and middle wards of Lanarkshire, and with a consistency which leaves no doubt of its truth.

COUNT UGOLINO.

[Dante Alighieri, born at Florence, May, 1265; died at Ravenna, July or September, 1321. The author of the *Divina Commedia*, or *The Vision of Hell, Purgatory, and Paradise*. He also wrote the *Vita Nuova*, the *Convito*, or *The Banquet*, and other works; but it is by the *Vision* that his memory is perpetuated. The following is from Cary's translation.[1] Of the many English versions of this poem Longfellow's is the most recent. Count Ugolino, who relates his sufferings to the poet, was the chief of one of three parties who were competing for the sovereignty of Pisa. By treachery he became victor, only to be himself betrayed by the Archbishop Ruggieri, who reported to the people that their castles had been sold to the citizens of Florence and of Lucca. The count was seized, cast into prison with two of his sons and two grandsons, and they were all starved to death.[2]]

His jaws uplifting from their fell repast,
That sinner wiped them on the hairs o' the head,
Which he behind had mangled, then began:
"Thy will obeying, I call up afresh
Sorrow past cure; which, but to think of, wrings
My heart, or ere I tell on't. But if words
That I may utter shall prove seed, to bear
Fruit of eternal infamy to him,
The traitor whom I gnaw at, thou at once
Shalt see me speak and weep. Who thou mayest be
I know not, nor how here below art come:
But Florentine thou seemest of a truth,
When I do hear thee. Know, I was on earth
Count Ugolino, and the Archbishop he
Ruggieri. Why I neighbour him so close,
Now list. That through effect of his ill thoughts
In him my trust reposing, I was ta'en
And after murder'd, need is not I tell.
What therefore thou canst not have heard, that is,
How cruel was the murder, shalt thou hear,
And know if he have wrong'd me. A small grate
Within that mew, which for my sake the name
Of famine bears, where others yet must pine,
Already through its opening several moons
Had shown me, when I slept the evil sleep
That from the future tore the curtain off.
This one, methought, as master of the sport,
Rode forth to chase the gaunt wolf, and his whelps,
Unto the mountain which forbids the sight
Of Lucca to the Pisan. With lean brachs
Inquisitive and keen, before him ranged

[1] Rev. Henry Francis Cary, M.A., born at Birmingham, 1772; died in London, 14th August, 1844. Educated at Oxford; sometime vicar of Bromley Abbat's, Staffordshire; and afterwards assistant-librarian in the British Museum. In his latter years he enjoyed a pension of £200 a year from government. He won much reputation by his translations, and especially by his version of *The Divine Comedy*, which Southey said was "a translation of magnitude and difficulty, executed with perfect fidelity and admirable skill."

[2] This is the subject of one of Sir Joshua Reynold's most powerful paintings.

Lanfranchi with Sismondi and Gualandi.
After short course the father and the sons
Seem'd tired and lagging, and methought I saw
The sharp tusks gore their sides. When I awoke
Before the dawn, amid their sleep I heard
My sons (for they were with me) weep and ask
For bread. Right cruel art thou, if no pang
Thou feel at thinking what my heart foretold;
And if not now, why use thy tears to flow?
Now had they waken'd; and the hour drew near
When they were wont to bring us food; the mind
Of each misgave him through his dream, and I
Heard, at its outlet underneath lock'd up
The horrible tower: whence, uttering not a word,
I look'd upon the visage of my sons.
I wept not: so all stone I felt within.
They wept: and one, my little Anselm, cried,
'Thou lookest so! Father, what ails thee?' Yet
I shed no tear, nor answer'd all that day
Nor the next night, until another sun
Came out upon the world. When a faint beam
Had to our doleful prison made its way,
And in four countenances I descried
The image of my own, on either hand
Through agony I bit; and they, who thought
I did it through desire of feeding, rose
O' the sudden, and cried, 'Father, we should grieve
Far less, if thou wouldst eat of us: thou gavest
These weeds of miserable flesh we wear:
And do thou strip them off from us again.'
Then, not to make them sadder, I kept down
My spirit in stillness. That day and the next
We all were silent. Ah, obdurate earth!
Why open'dst not upon us? When we came
To the fourth day, then Gaddo at my feet
Outstretch'd did fling him, crying, 'Hast no help
For me, my father!' There he died; and e'en
Plainly as thou seest me, saw I the three
Fall one by one 'twixt the fifth day and sixth:
Whence I betook me, now grown blind, to grope
Over them all, and for three days aloud
Call'd on them who were dead. Then, fasting got
The mastery of grief." Thus having spoke,
Once more upon the wretched skull his teeth
He fastened like a mastiff's 'gainst the bone,
Firm and unyielding.
                    The Inferno—Canto xxxiii.

THE MIGRATIONS OF A SOLAN GOOSE.

BY MISS CORDET.

"Well, Bryce," said Mrs. Maxwell one day to her housekeeper, "what has the gamekeeper sent this week from Maxwell Hall?"

"Why, madam, there are three pair of partridges, a brace of grouse, a woodcock, three hares, a couple of pheasants, and a solan goose."

"A solan goose!" ejaculated the lady;

"what could induce him to think I would poison my house with a solan goose?"

"He knows it is a dish that my master is very fond of," replied Mrs. Bryce.

"It is more than your mistress is," retorted the lady; "let it be thrown out directly before Mr. Maxwell sees it."

The housekeeper retired, and Mrs. Maxwell resumed her cogitations, the subject of which was how to obtain an introduction to the French noblesse who had recently taken up their abode in Edinburgh.

"Gracious me!" said she, as she hastily rung the bell, "how could I be so stupid?—there is nothing in the world that old Lady Crosby is so fond of as a solan goose, and I understand she knows all the French people, and that they are constantly with her.—Bryce," she continued, as the housekeeper obeyed her summons, "is the goose a fine bird?"

"Very fine indeed, madam; the beak is broken, and one of the legs is a little ruffled, but I never saw a finer bird."

"Well, then, don't throw it away, as I mean to send it to my friend Lady Crosby, as soon as I have written a note."

Mrs. Bryce once more retreated, and Mrs. Maxwell, having selected a beautiful sheet of note-paper, quickly penned the following effusion:

"My dear Lady Crosby,—Permit me to request your acceptance of a solan goose, which has just been sent me from Maxwell Hall. Knowing your fondness for this bird, I am delighted at having it in my power to gratify you. I hope that you continue to enjoy good health. This is to be a very gay winter. By the bye, do you know any one who is acquainted with the French noblesse? I am dying to meet with them. Ever, my dear Lady Crosby, yours truly,   M. MAXWELL."

Lady Crosby being out when this billet reached her house, it was opened by one of her daughters.

"Bless me, Maria!" she exclaimed to her sister, "how fortunate it was that I opened this note; Mrs. Maxwell has sent mamma a solan goose!"

"Dreadful!" exclaimed Eliza; "I am sure if mamma hears of it she will have it roasted immediately, and Captain Jessamy, of the Lancers, is to call to-day, and you know a roasted solan goose is enough to contaminate a whole parish.—I shall certainly go distracted!"

"Don't discompose yourself," replied Maria; "I shall take good care to send it out of the house before mamma comes home; meanwhile,

I must write a civil answer to Mrs. Maxwell's note. I daresay she will not think of alluding to it; but if she should, mamma, luckily, is pretty deaf, and may never be a bit the wiser."

"I think," said Eliza, "we had better send the goose to the Napiers, as they were rather affronted at not being asked to our last musical party; I daresay they will make no use of it, but it looks attentive."

"An excellent thought," rejoined Maria. No sooner said than done; in five minutes the travelled bird had once more changed its quarters.

"A solan goose!" ejaculated Mrs. Napier, as her footman gave her the intelligence of Lady Crosby's present. "Pray, return my compliments to her ladyship, and I feel much obliged by her polite attention. Truly," continued she, when the domestic had retired to fulfil this mission, "if Lady Crosby thinks to stop our mouths with a solan goose, she will find herself very much mistaken. I suppose she means this as a peace-offering for not having asked us to her last party. I suppose she was afraid, Clara, my dear, you would cut out her clumsy daughters with Sir Charles."

"If I don't, it shall not be my fault," replied her amiable daughter. "I flirted with him in such famous style at the last concert, that I thought Eliza would have fainted on the spot. But what are you going to do with the odious bird?"

"Oh, I shall desire John to carry it to poor Mrs. Johnstone."

"I wonder, mamma, that you would take the trouble of sending all the way to the Canongate for any such purpose; what good can it do you to oblige people who are so wretchedly poor?"

"Why, my dear," replied the lady, "to tell you the truth, your father, in early life, received such valuable assistance from Mr. Johnstone, who was at that time a very rich man, as laid the foundation of his present fortune. Severe losses reduced Mr. Johnstone to poverty; he died, and your father has always been intending, at least promising to do something for the family, but has never found an opportunity. Last year, Mrs. Johnstone most unfortunately heard that he had it in his power to get a young man out to India, and she applied to Mr. Napier on behalf of her son, which, I must say, was a very ill-judged step, as showing that she thought he required to be reminded of his promises, which, to a man of any feeling, must always be a grating circumstance; but I have often observed, that poor people have very little delicacy in such points; however, as your papa fancies sometimes that these people have a sort of claim on him, I am sure he will be glad to pay them any attention that costs him nothing."

Behold, then, our hero exiled from the fashionable regions of the West, and laid on the broad of his back on a table, in a small but clean room, in a humble tenement in the Canongate, where three hungry children eyed with delight his fat legs, his swelling breast, and magnificent pinions.

"Oh, mamma, mamma," cried the children, skipping round the table, and clapping their hands, "what a beautiful goose! how nice it will be when it is roasted! You must have a great large slice, mamma, for you had very little dinner yesterday. Why have we never any nice dinners now, mamma?"

"Hush, little chatter-box," said her brother Henry, a fine stripling of sixteen, seeing tears gather in his mother's eyes.

"My dear boy," said Mrs. Johnstone, "it goes to my heart to think of depriving these poor children of their expected treat, but I think we ought to send this bird to our benefactress, Lady Bethune. But for her, what would have become of us? While the Napiers, who owe all they have to your worthy and unfortunate father, have given us nothing but empty promises, she has been a consoling and ministering angel, and I should wish to take this opportunity of showing my gratitude; trifling as the offering is, I am sure it will be received with kindness."

"I am sure of it," replied Henry; "and I will run and buy a few nuts and apples to console the little ones for losing their expected feast."

The children gazed with lengthened faces as the goose was carried from their sight, and conveyed by Henry to the house of Lady Bethune, who, appreciating the motives which had dictated the gift, received it with benevolent kindness.

"Tell your mother, my dear," said she to Henry, "that I feel most particularly obliged by her attention, and be sure to say that Sir James has hopes of procuring a situation for you; and if he succeeds, I will come over myself to tell her the good news."

Henry bounded away as gay as a lark, while Lady Bethune, after having given orders to her butler to send some bolls of potatoes, meal, and a side of fine mutton, to Mrs. Johnstone, next issued directions for the disposal of the present she had just received.

"La, madam!" exclaimed Mrs. Bryce, as she once more made her appearance before her mistress, "if here be not our identical solan goose come back to us, with Lady Bethune's compliments! I know him by his broken beak and ruffled leg; and as sure as eggs are eggs, that's my master's knock at the door!"

"Run, Bryce! fly!" cried Mrs. Maxwell in despair; "put it out of sight! give it to the house-dog!"

Away ran Mrs. Bryce with her prize to Towler; and he, not recollecting that he had any favour to obtain from any one, or that he had any dear friends to oblige, received the present very gratefully, and, as he lay in his kennel,

"Lazily mumbled the bones of the dead,"

thus ingloriously terminating the migrations of a solan goose.

THE KNIGHT'S TALE.

[Geoffrey Chaucer, born in London, 1328; died there 25th October, 1400. "The Father of English poetry" There are few authentic records of his life; but it seems to be generally accepted that he studied at Oxford and Cambridge; visited the Continent—as a soldier, according to some accounts—entered the Inner Temple to study law, and was "fined two shillings for beating a Franciscan friar in Fleet Street;" was a favourite of John of Gaunt, Duke of Lancaster, whose sister-in-law became his wife; and he received an annuity of twenty marks from Edward III. He was appointed comptroller of wool at the port of London, and was sent as an envoy to Genoa. At another time he was sent to France to treat of a marriage between Richard, Prince of Wales, and a daughter of the French king. In the early years of the reign of Richard II. he became involved in political disturbances, and fled to Holland. He returned to London soon after, and was committed to the Tower, but was released on disclosing the names of his associates in the late conspiracy. He subsequently became master of the works at Westminster, and soon after at Windsor. He was buried in Westminster Abbey, near the chapel of St. Bennet. His chief poems are: The Canterbury Tales; The Romaunt of the Rose, translated from the French; Troilus and Creseide; The Court of Love; The Complaint of Pitie; The Assembly of Foules; The House of Fame; The Legend of Good Women; The Flower and the Leaf; Chaucer's Dream, &c. Thomas Warton wrote: "His genius was universal, and adapted to themes of unbounded variety; and his merit was not less in painting familiar manners with humour and propriety, than in moving the passions, and representing the beautiful or grand objects of nature with grace and sublimity." In the following extracts, the orthography is, as far as possible, modernized.]

[Theseus, Duke of Athens, captured in war two cousins of Thebes, Palamon and Arcite, and condemned them to perpetual imprisonment. From the window of their cell the prisoners saw Emelie, sister of the queen, and

love of her filled their hearts. This caused
the first misunderstanding that had ever arisen
between these faithful friends. Arcite was
released from prison, but exiled from the realms
of Theseus.]

"O dear cousin Palamon, quod he,
Thine is the victory of this aventure;
Full blissfully in prison to enduro:
In prison? Nay certes, but in paradise.
Well hath fortune yturned thee the dice,
That hath the sight of her, and I the absence.
For possible is, since thou hast her presence,
And art a knight, a worthy and an able,
That by some chance, since fortune is changeable,
Thou mayest to thy desire sometime attain:
But I that am exiled, and barreyne
Of all grace, and in so great despair,
That there n' is water, earth, fire ne air,
Ne creature that of them maked is,
That may me help or comfort in this.
    Alas! why plainen men so in commune
Of purveance, of God, or of fortune,
That giveth them full oft in many a guise
Much better than they can themselves devise?
Some man desireth for to have richess,
That cause is of his murder or great sickness;
And some man would out of his prison fain,
That in his house is of his servants slain.
Infinite harms ben in this matere;
We wot never what thing we prayen here."

[Arcite at length returned in disguise to
Athens, and entered the Duke's household as a
servant, where he was privileged to see his lady
every day. He became a favourite and was pro-
moted, but not discovered. Palamon, meanwhile, escaped from prison, and, whilst hiding in
the woods, encountered his rival. They were to
engage in a duel, but were interrupted by
Theseus, who, upon learning the truth, appointed a tournament in which the knights
might decide their claims to the lady. The
day came: Arcite had placed himself under
the protection of Mars; Palamon had obtained
that of Venus. A hundred knights followed
each leader.]

Up goth the trumpets and the melodie;
And to the lists ride the companie
By ordinance, through the city large,
Hanging with cloth of gold and not with serge.
Full like a lord this noble Duke can ride,
And these two Thebans upon either side;
And after rode the queen and Emelie;
And after them of ladies another companie;
And after them of commons after their degree.
And thus they passeden through that city,
And to the lists comen they be-time:
It was not of the day yet fully prime,

When set was Theseus full rich and high,
Ipolita, the queen, and Emelie,
And other ladies in degrees about.
Unto the seats presseth all the rout,
And westward thorough the gates of Mart,
Arcite, and eke the hundred of his part,
With banners red, is enter'd right anon;
And in that same moment Palamon
Is, under Venus, eastward in the place,
With banner white and hardy cheer and face.
    In all the world to seeken up and down,
So even without variation,
There never were such companies twey;
For there was none so wise that coulde say
That any had of other advantage
Of worthiness, nor of estate, nor of visage,
So even were they chosen for to guess:
And in two ranges (ranks) fair they them 'dress.
When that their names read were every one,
That in their number guile were there none;
Then were the gates shut and cried was loud—
"Do now your devoir, young knightes proud."
    The heralds left their pricking up and down.
Now ringin trumpets loud and clarion.
There is no more to say, but east and west
In goeth the spears steadily in the rest;
There, see men who can joust and who can ride:
In goeth the sharp spur into the side:
There shiveren shaftes upon shieldes thick:
He feeleth through the hearte soon the prick:
Up springen speais twenty foot on hight;
Out gon the swordes as the silver bright:
The helms they to-hewen and to-shred;[1]
Out burst the blood with stern streames red;
With mighty maces the bones they to-breste;[2]
He through the thickest of the throng 'gan thrust:
There stumble steedes strong, and down can fall:
He rolleth under foot as doth a ball:
He presseth on his foe with a truncheon,
And he him hurtleth with his horse adown:
He through the body hurt is and sith then take
Maugre his head, and brought unto the stake,
As forword (agreement) was, right there he must
Another lad is on that other side;   [abide;
And sometime bids them, Theseus, to rest,
Them to refresh and drinken if them lest (list).
    Full oft a-day have these same Thebans two
Together met and wrought each other woe:
Unhorsed hath each other of them twey,
There was no tiger in the vale of Galgopley,
When that her whelp is stole when it is lite (little),
So cruel on the hunt as is Arcite,
For jealous heart, upon this Palamon:
Nor in Belmarie there n' is so fell lion
That hunted is, or for his hunger wud (mad),
Ne of his prey desireth so the blood,
As Palamon to slay his foe Arcite:
The jealous strokes on their helmets bite:
Out runneth blood on both their sides red.

---

[1] To hew and cut to pieces.   [2] Broke in pieces.

Sometime an end there is of every deed:
For ere the sun unto the reste went
The strong King Emetrius 'gan hent [1]
This Palamon as he fought with Arcite,
And made his sword deep in his flesh to bite;
And by the force of twenty is he take,
Unyielding, and is drawen to the stake:
And in the rescue of this Palamon
The strong King Ligurgius is borne adown:
And King Emetrius, for all his strength,
Is borne out of his saddle his sworde's length,
So hit him Palamon ere he were take:
But all for nought, he was brought to the stake.
His hardy heart might him holpen nought;
He must abiden when that he was caught
By force and eke by composition.
    Who sorroweth now, but woeful Palamon,
That must no more go again to fight?
And when that Theseus had seen that sight,
Unto the folk that foughten thus each one
He cried, "Ho!—no more, for it is done.
I will be true judge and not partie.
Arcite of Thebes shall have Emelie,
That by his fortune hath her fairly won."
    Anon there is a noise of people begun
For joy of this, so loud and high withal,
It seemed that the liftes (skies) would fall.
    What can now fair Venus do above?
What saith she now? what doth this queen of love
But weepeth so for wanting of her will,
Till that her teares in the liftes fill.
She said, "I am a-shamèd, doubtless."
    Saturnus said, "Daughter, hold thy peace:
Mars hath his will, his knight hath all his boon,
And by mine head, thou shalt be eased soon."
    The trump'ters with the loud minstrelsy,
The heralds that so loudly yell and cry,
Ben in their joy for weal of Dan[2] Arcite.
But hearkeneth me and stay the noise a lite,
What a miracle there befell anon.
    This fierce Arcite hath off his helm ydone,
And on his courser for to show his face
He pricketh end long in the large place,
Looking upward upon this Emelie,
And she again cast him a friendly eye,
(For women as to speaken in commune,
They follow all the favour of fortune)
And was all his in cheer as in heart.
    Out of the ground a fury infernal start —
From Pluto sent at the request of Saturne—
For which his horse for fear 'gan to turn,
And leapt aside and foundered as he leap;
And ere that Arcite may take any kepe (care)
He pitched him on the pomel (top) of his head,
That in the place he lay as he were dead.

[Arcite, dying, sent for Emelie and Palamon.]

"Alas the woe, alas the paines strong
That I for you have suffered and so long!
Alas the death, alas my Emelie!
Alas, departing of our companie!
Alas mine hearte's queen, alas my wife!
Mine hearte's lady, ender of my life!
What is this world, what asken men to have?
Now with his love, now in his cold grave
Alone withouten any companie.
Farewell my sweet, farewell mine Emelie!
And soft, take me in your armes twey,
For love of God, and hearkeneth what I say.
    "I have here with my cousin Palamon
Had strife and rancour many a day agone
For love of you, and eke for jelousie;
And Jupiter so wis my soule gie [3]
To speaken of a servant properly,
With all circumstances truely,
That is to say, truth, honour, and knighthede,
Wisdom, humbl'ess, estate and high kindrede.
Freedom, and all that 'longeth to that art,
So Jupiter have of my soule part,
As in this world right now we know I non'
So worthy to be loved as Palamon,
That serveth you, and will do all his life;
And if that ever ye shall be a wife,
Forget not Palamon, that gentle man."
    And with that word his speech to fail began. . . .
But on his lady yet cast he his eye;
His last word was, "Mercy, Emelie."

Infinite ben the sorrows and the tears
Of old folk and folk of tender years,
In all the town for death of this Theban—
For him there weepeth both child and man.

[Emelie, Palamon, and Theseus were the
chief mourners for the dead knight, and their
grief endured long. But—]

By processe and by length of certain years,
All stenten is the mourning and the tears.

[The Duke summoned Emelie and Palamon
to his presence, and spoke thus:—]

"The first Mover of the cause above
When he first made the fair chain of love,
Great was th' effect and high was his intent;
Well wist he why and what thereof he meant;
For which that fair chain of love he bond
The fire, the water, the air, and eke the lond,
In certain bonds that they may not flee:
That same Prince and Mover eke (quod he)
Hath 'stablisht in this wretched world adoun
Certain of days and duration
To all that are engendered in this place. . . .
    "Lo, the oak that hath so long a nourishing
From the time that it 'ginneth first to spring,

---

[1] Catch or attack; Emetrius being one of Arcite's
supporters.　　　　　　　　　[2] Lord.

[3] So direct me.

And hath so long a life, as we may see,
Yet at the last wasted is the tree.
Considereth eke how that the harde stone
Under our feet, on which we tread and go'n,
It wasteth as it lie'h by the way;
The broad river sometime waxeth dry;
The great towns see we wane and wend:
Then may we see that all thing hath an end.
  Of man and woman see we well also,
That wendeth in one of this termes two:
That is to say, in youth or else in age,
He must be dead, the king as shall a page;
Some in his bed, some in the deep sea,
Some in the large field as men may see:
There helpeth nought, all goeth thilke way:
Then may I say that all thing shall die.
What maketh this but Jupiter the king,
The which is prince and cause of all thing.
Converting all unto his proper will,
From which it is derived, sooth to tell?
And here against no creature alive,
Of no degree, availeth for to strive.
  Then is it wisdom, as it thinketh me,
To maken virtue of necessitie,
And take it well, that we may not eschew,
And namely that that to us all is due;
And whoso grudgeth ought he doeth follie.
And rebel is to him that all may gi'e.
And certainly a man hath most honour
To dien in his excellence and flower,
When he is siccar of his good name;
Then hath he done his friend, ne him, no shame;
And gladder ought his friend ben of his death
When with honour is yielded up his breath,
Than when his name appalled (made pale) is for age,
For all forgotten is his vassalage;
Then is it best as for a worthy fame,
To dien when a man is best of name.
The contrary of all this is wilfulness.
Why grudge·n we? Why have we heaviness,
That good Arcite, of chivalry the flower,
Departed is with worship and honour,
Out of this foule prison of this life?
Why grudgeth here his cousin and his wife
Of his welfare, that loven him so well?
Can he them thank? Nay, God wot, never a del,
That both his soul and eke himself offend,
And yet they may their lustres not amend.
  "What may I conclude of this long serie,
But after woe I rede us to be merry,
And thanken Jupiter of all his grace;
And ere that we departen from this place,
I rede that we make of sorrows two
One perfect joy lasting evermo:
And looking now where most sorrow is herein,
There will we first amenden and begin.
  "Sister (quod he) this is my full assent,
With all th' advice here of my parlement,
That gentle Palamon, your owen knight,
That serveth you with heart, and will, and might,
And ever hath done since first time you him knew,

That ye shall of your grace upon him rue,
And take him for your husband and for lord:
Lend me your hand, for this is our accord.
  "Let see now of your womanly pitee,
He is a kinge's brother's son, pardee;
And though he were a poor bachelere,
Since he hath served you so many a year,
And had for you so great adversity,
It must be considered, trusteth me,
For gentle mercy ought to pessen right."
  Then said he thus to Palamon, the knight:
"I trow there needeth little sermoning
To maken you assenten to this thing.
Come near, and take your lady by the hond."
  Betwixen them was maked anon the bond
That highte matrimony or marriage,
By all the council of the baronage.
And thus with bliss and eke with melody
Hath Palamon ywedded Emelie;
And God, that all this world hath wrought,
Send him his love that hath it dear ybought.
For now is Palamon in alle weal,
Living in bliss, in richess, and in heal';
And Emelie him loveth so tenderly,
And he her serveth so gentilly,
That never was there no word them between
Of jealousy, ne of none other tene (grief).
  Thus endeth Palamon and Emelie,
And God save all this fair companie.

FEATHERED LIFE IN AMERICA.

[John Burroughs, an American ornithologist, who, following in the footsteps of Wilson and Audubon, is helping to extend our knowledge of the characteristics of the winged tribes. The following is from an article in the New York Galaxy Magazine, August, 1869.]

Years ago, when quite a youth, I was rambling in the woods one Sunday with my brothers, gathering black-birch, wintergreens, &c., when, as we reclined upon the ground, gazing vaguely up into the trees, I caught sight of a bird that paused a moment on a branch above me, the like of which I had never before seen or heard of. It was probably the blue yellow-backed warbler, as I have since found this to be a common bird in those woods; but to my young fancy it seemed like some fairy bird, so curiously marked was it, and so new and unexpected. It seemed like an integral part of the green beech woods. I saw it a moment as the flickering leaves parted, noted the white spot in its wing, and it was gone. How the thought of it clung to me afterward! It was a revelation. It was the first intimation I had had that the woods we know so well held birds that we knew not at all. Were our eyes and ears so dull, then? There was the robin, the blue-jay, the blue-bird, the yellow-bird, the cherry-bird, the cat-bird, the chipping-bird, the woodpecker, the high-hole, an occasional red-bird, and a few others, in the woods or along their borders, but who ever dreamed that there were still others that not even the hunters saw, and whose names no one had ever heard?

When, one summer day later in life, I took my gun and went to the woods again in a different, though perhaps a less simple spirit, I found my youthful vision more than realized. There were indeed other birds, plenty of them, singing, nesting, breeding, among the familiar trees, which I had before passed by unheard and unseen.

It is a surprise that awaits every student of ornithology, and the thrill of delight that accompanies it, and the feeling of fresh, eager inquiry that follows, can hardly be awakened by any other pursuit. Take the first step in ornithology, procure one new specimen, and you are ticketed for the whole voyage. There is a fascination about it quite overpowering. It fits so well with other things—with fishing, hunting, farming, walking, camping-out—with all that takes one to the fields and woods. One may go a blackberrying and make some rare discovery; or, while driving his cow to pasture, hear a new song, or make a new observation. Secrets lurk on all sides. There is news in every bush. Expectation is ever on tip-toe. What no man ever saw before may the next moment be revealed to you. What a new interest the woods have! How you long to explore every nook and corner of them! You would even find consolation in being lost in them. You could then hear the night birds and the owls, and in your wanderings might stumble upon some unknown specimen.

In all excursions to the woods or to the shore, the student of ornithology has an advantage over his companions. He has one more resource, one more avenue of delight. He, indeed, kills two birds with one stone, and sometimes three. If others wander, he can never go out of his way. His game is everywhere. The cawing of a crow makes him feel at home, while a new note or a new song drowns all care. Audubon, on the desolate coast of Labrador, is happier than any king ever was; and on shipboard is nearly cured of his sea-sickness when a new gull appears in sight.

One must taste it to understand or appreciate its fascination. The looker-on sees nothing to inspire such enthusiasm. Only a little feathers

and a half-musical note or two; why all this ado? "Who would give a hundred and twenty dollars to know about the birds?" said an Eastern governor, half contemptuously, to Wilson, as the latter solicited a subscription to his great work. Sure enough. Bought knowledge is dear at any price. The most precious things have no commercial value. It is not, your excellency, mere technical knowledge of the birds that you are asked to purchase, but a new interest in the fields and woods, a new moral and intellectual tonic, a new key to the treasure-house of nature. Think of the many other things your excellency would get; the air, the sunshine, the sylvan fragrance and coolness, and the many respites from the knavery and turmoil of political life.

The ornithologists divide and subdivide the birds into a great many families, orders, genera, species, &c., which, at first sight, are apt to confuse and discourage the reader. But any unprofessional person can acquaint himself with most of our song birds by keeping in mind a few general divisions, and observing the characteristics of each. By far the greater number of our land birds are either Warblers, Vireos, Fly-catchers, Thrushes, or Finches.

The Warblers are, perhaps, the most puzzling. These are the true Sylvia, the real wood-birds. They are small, very active, but feeble songsters, and, to be seen, must be sought for. In passing through the woods, most persons have a vague consciousness of slight chirping, semi-musical sounds in the trees overhead. In most cases these sounds proceed from the Warblers. Throughout the Middle and Eastern States, half a dozen species or so may be found in almost every locality, as the red-start,[1] the Maryland yellow-throat, the yellow-warbler (not the common goldfinch, with black cap and black wings and tail), the hooded-warbler, the black and white creeping-warbler; or others, according to the locality and the character of the woods. In pine or hemlock woods, one species may predominate; in maple or oak woods, or in mountainous districts, another. The subdivision of ground warblers, the most common members of which are the Maryland yellow-throat, the Kentucky-warbler, and the mourning-ground warbler, are usually found

---

[1] I am aware that the red-start is generally classed among the Fly-catchers, but its song, its form, and its habits are in every respect those of a Warbler. Its main fly-catcher mark is its beak, but the *musica*, or proper it presents little or no resemblance to the general observer.

in low, wet, bushy or half-open woods, often on, and always near the ground.

Audubon figures and describes over forty different Warblers. More recent writers have divided and subdivided the group very much, giving new names to new classifications. But this part is of interest and value only to the professional ornithologist.

The finest songster among the Sylvia, according to my notions, is the black-throated greenback. Its song is sweet and clear, but brief.

The rarest of the species are Swainson's warbler, said to be disappearing; the cerulean-warbler, said to be abundant about Niagara; and the mourning-ground warbler, which I have found breeding about the headwaters of the Delaware in New York.

The Vireos, or Greenlets, are a sort of connecting-link between the Warblers and the true Fly-catchers, and partake of the characteristics of both.

The red-eyed vireo, whose sweet soliloquy is one of the most constant and cheerful sounds in our woods and groves, is, perhaps, the most noticeable and abundant species. The Vireos are a little larger than the Warblers, and are far less brilliant and variegated in colour.

There are four species found in most of our woods, viz. the red-eyed vireo, the white-eyed vireo, the warbling-vireo, and the solitary-vireo—the red-eyed and warbling being most abundant, and the white-eyed being the most lively and animated songster. I meet the latter bird only in the thick, bushy growths of low, swampy localities, where, eluding the observer, it pours forth its song with a sharpness and a rapidity of articulation that are truly astonishing. This strain is very marked, and, though inlaid with the notes of several other birds, is entirely unique. The iris of this bird is white, as that of the red-eyed is red, though in neither case can this mark be distinguished at more than two or three yards. In most cases, the iris of birds is a dark-hazel, which passes for black.

The basket-like nest, pendent to the low branches in the woods, which the falling leaves of autumn reveal to all passers, is, in most cases, the nest of the red-eyed, though the solitary constructs a similar tenement, but in much more remote and secluded localities.

The general colour of this group of birds is very light ash beneath, becoming darker above, with a tinge of green. The red-eyed has a crown of a bluish tinge.

Most birds exhibit great alarm and distress, usually with a strong dash of anger, when you

approach their nests; but the demeanour of the red-eyed on such an occasion is an exception to this rule. The parent birds move about softly amid the branches above, eyeing the intruder with a curious, innocent look, uttering now and then a subdued note or plaint, solicitous and watchful, but making no demonstration of anger or distress.

The birds, no more than the animals, like to be caught napping, but I remember, one autumn day of coming upon a red-eyed vireo that was clearly oblivious to all that was passing around it. It was a young bird, though full grown, and it was taking its *siesta* on a low branch in a remote heathery field. Its head was snugly stowed away under its wing, and it would have fallen an easy prey to the first hawk that came along. I approached noiselessly, and when within a few feet of it paused to note its breathings, so much more rapid and full than our own. A bird has greater lung capacity than any other living thing, hence more animal heat, and life at a higher pressure. When I reached out my hand and carefully closed it around the winged sleeper, its sudden terror and consternation almost paralyzed it. Then it struggled and cried piteously, and when released hastened and hid itself in some near bushes. I never expected to surprise it thus a second time.

The Fly-catchers are a larger group than the Vireos, with stronger-marked characteristics. They are not properly Songsters, but are classed by some writers as Screechers. Their pugnacious dispositions are well known, and they not only fight among themselves but are incessantly quarrelling with their neighbours. The king-bird, or tyrant fly-catcher, might serve as the type of the order.

The common pewee excites the most pleasant emotions, both on account of its plaintive note and its exquisite mossy nest.

The phœbe-bird is the pioneer of the Fly-catchers, and comes in April, sometimes in March. It comes familiarly about the house and out-buildings, and usually builds beneath hay-sheds or under bridges.

The Fly-catchers always take their insect prey on the wing, by a sudden darting or swooping movement; often a very audible snap of the beak may be heard.

These birds are the least elegant, both in form and colour, of any of our feathered neighbours. They have short legs, a short neck, large heads, and broad flat beaks, with bristles at the base. They often fly with a peculiar quivering movement of the wings, and when at rest oscillate their tails at short intervals.

There are found in the United States nineteen species. In the middle and eastern districts one may observe in summer, without any special search, about five of them, viz., the king-bird, the phœbe-bird, the wood-pewee, the great-crested fly-catcher (distinguished from all others by the bright ferruginous colour of its tail), and the small green-crested fly-catcher.

The Thrushes are the birds of real melody, and will afford one more delight perhaps than any other class. The robin is the most familiar example. Their manners, flight, and form are the same in each species. See the robin hop along upon the ground, strike an attitude, scratch for a worm, fix his eye upon something before him or upon the beholder, flip his wings suspiciously, fly straight to his perch, or sit at sundown on some high branch carolling his sweet and honest strain, and you have seen what is characteristic of all the Thrushes. Their carriage is pre-eminently marked by grace, and their songs by melody.

Beside the robin, which is in no sense a wood-bird, we have in New York the wood-thrush, the hermit-thrush, the veery or Wilson's thrush, the olive-backed thrush, and, transiently, one or two other species not so clearly defined.

The wood-thrush and the hermit stand at the head as songsters, no two persons, perhaps, agreeing as to which is the superior.

The cast of their songs is so much alike, that any but an experienced observer might easily confound the two. But hear them both at the same time and the difference is quite marked. The song of the hermit is on a higher key, and is more simple, and more wild and ethereal. His instrument is a silver horn, which he winds in the most solitary places. The song of the wood-thrush is more golden and leisurely. Its tone comes nearer to that of some rare stringed instrument.

One feels that perhaps the wood-thrush has more compass and power, if he would only let himself out. His tone is certainly richer; but, on the whole, I am inclined to think that he falls a little short of the pure, serene, hymn-like strain of the hermit.

Under the general head of Finches Audubon describes over sixty different birds, ranging from the sparrows to the grosbeaks, and including the buntings, the linnets, the snow-birds, the cross-bills, and the red-birds.

We have nearly or quite a dozen varieties of the sparrow in the Atlantic States, but perhaps no more than half that number would be discriminated by the unprofessional observer. The song-sparrow, which every child knows, comes first, at least his voice is first heard. And can there be anything more fresh and pleasing than this first simple strain heard from the garden fence, or a near hedge, on some bright, still March morning?

The field or vesper-sparrow, called also grass-finch, and bay-winged sparrow, a bird slightly larger than the song-sparrow, and of a lighter gray colour, is abundant in all our upland fields and pastures, and is a very sweet song-ster. It builds upon the ground, without the slightest cover or protection, and also roosts there. Walking through the fields at dusk I frequently start them up almost beneath my feet. When disturbed by day they fly with a quick, sharp movement, showing two white quills in the tail. The traveller along the country roads disturbs them earthing their wings in the soft dry earth, or sees them skulking and flitting along the fences in front of him. They run in the furrow in advance of the team, or perch upon the stones a few rods off. They sing much after sundown, hence the aptness of the name vesper-sparrow, which a recent writer, Wilson Flagg, has bestowed upon them.

In the meadows and low wet lands the savannah-sparrow is met with, and may be known by its fine, insect-like song. In the swamp, the swamp-sparrow.

The fox-sparrow, the largest and handsomest species of this family, comes to us in the fall, from the north, where it breeds. Likewise the tree or Canada-sparrow, and the white-crowned and white-throated sparrows.

The social-sparrow, alias "hair-bird," alias "red-headed chipping-bird," is the smallest of the sparrows, and, I believe, the only one that builds in trees.

A favourite sparrow of my own, but little noticed by bird writers, is the wood, or bush-sparrow, usually called spizella pusilla by the ornithologists. Its size and form are nearly that of the socialis, but in colour it is less distinctly marked, being of a duller reddish tinge. It prefers remote bushy fields, where its song is one of the sweetest to be heard. Its strain is sometimes very noticeable, especially early in spring. I have sat in the still leafless April woods when one of these birds would suddenly strike up, sending its voice through the woods like a clear soft whistle. On such an occasion, of course, its song is all the more noticeable and charming for being projected upon such a broad unoccupied page of silence. This song is like the words fe-o, fe-o, fe-o, few, few, few, fee, fee, fee, uttered at first high and leisurely, but running very rapidly toward the close, which is low and soft.

The Finches, as a class, all have short conical bills, with tails more or less forked. The purple-finch heads the list in varied musical ability.

Beside the groups of our more familiar birds which I have thus hastily outlined, there are numerous other groups, more limited in specimens, but comprising some of our best-known songsters. The Bobolink, for instance, has properly no congener. The famous Mockingbird of the Southern States belongs to a genus which has but two other representatives in the Atlantic States, viz. the Cat-bird and the long-tailed or ferruginous Thrush.

The Wrens are a large and interesting family, and as songsters are noted for vivacity and volubility. The more common species are the house-wren, the wood-wren, the marsh-wren, the great Carolina-wren, and the winter-wren, the latter perhaps deriving its name from the fact that it breeds in the north. It is an exquisite songster, and pours forth its notes so rapidly, and with such sylvan sweetness and cadence, that it seems to *go off* like a musical alarm.

Wilson called the Kinglets Wrens, but they have little to justify the name except their song, which is of the same continuous, gushing, lyrical character as that referred to above. Dr. Brewer was entranced with the song of one of these tiny minstrels in the woods of New Brunswick, and thought he had found the author of the strain in the blackpoll-warbler. He seems loath to believe that a bird so small as either of the kinglets could possess such vocal powers. It may indeed have been the winter-wren, but from my own observation I believe the golden-crowned kinglet quite capable of such a performance.

The Cuckoo, of which we have two species, the yellow-billed and black-billed, the latter abounding in New York, and the former further south, is an interesting bird, though no more a songster than a crow is. Its characteristic sound is a long loud call, which it repeats with a peculiar weird and monkish effect in the depths of the forest. It sometimes suggests the distant voice of a turkey. When near at hand it is like this, *k-k-k-kow, kow, kow-ow, kow-ow, kow-ow.* Like all natural sounds it has a charm of its own, and soon becomes associated in the mind with all that is delightful in summer days and woods. The European species is larger than ours, and differently marked; but its habits and call resemble those of our black-billed so closely that

Wordsworth's lines have the same beauty and accuracy in America that they have in England.

O blithe new-comer! I have heard,
I hear thee and rejoice;
O cuckoo! shall I call thee bird?
Or but a wandering voice?

While I am lying on the grass,
Thy loud note smites my ear!
From hill to hill it seems to pass,
At once far off and near!

Thrice welcome darling of the spring!
Even yet thou art to me
No bird, but an invisible thing—
A voice, a mystery.

More recent writers and explorers have added to Audubon's list over three hundred new species, the greater share of which belong to the northern and western parts of the continent. Audubon's observations were confined mainly to the Atlantic and Gulf States and the adjacent islands; hence the Western or Pacific birds were but little known to him, and are only briefly mentioned in his works.

As the paramount question in the life of a bird is the question of food, perhaps the most serious troubles our feathered neighbours encounter are early in the spring, after the supply of fat, with which nature stores every corner and by-place of the system, thereby anticipating the scarcity of food, has been exhausted; and the sudden and severe changes in the weather which occur at this season make unusual demands upon their vitality. No doubt many of the earlier birds die from starvation and exposure at this season. Among a troop of Canada-sparrows which I came upon one March day, all of them evidently much reduced, one was so feeble that I caught it in my hand.

During the present season a very severe cold spell, the first week in March, drove the blue-birds to seek shelter about the houses and out-buildings. As night approached, and the winds and the cold increased, they seemed filled with apprehension and alarm, and in the outskirts of the city came about the windows and doors, crept behind the blinds, clung to the gutters and beneath the cornice, flitted from porch to porch, and from house to house, seeking in vain for some safe retreat from the cold. The street pump, which had a small opening just over the handle, was an attraction which they could not resist. And yet they seemed aware of the insecurity of the position, for no sooner would they stow themselves away into the interior of the pump, to the number of six or eight, than they would come rushing out again, as if apprehensive of some approaching danger. Time after time the cavity was filled and re-filled, with blue and brown intermingled, and as often emptied. Presently they tarried longer than usual, when I made a sudden sally and captured three, that found a warmer and safer lodging for the night in the cellar.

In the fall birds and fowls of all kinds become very fat. The squirrels and mice lay by a supply of food in their dens and retreats; but the birds, to a considerable extent, especially our winter residents, carry an equivalent in their own systems, in the form of adipose tissue. I killed a red-shouldered hawk one December, and on removing the skin found the body completely encased in a coating of fat one-quarter of an inch in thickness. Not a particle of muscle was visible. This coating not only serves as a protection against the cold, but supplies the waste of the system when food is scarce, or fails altogether.

The crows at this season are in the same condition. It is estimated that a crow needs at least half a pound of meat per day, but it is evident that for weeks and months during the winter and spring they must subsist on a mere fraction of this amount. I have no doubt a crow or hawk, when in their fall condition, would live two weeks without a morsel of food passing their beaks; a domestic fowl will do as much. One January I unwittingly shut a hen under the floor of an out-building, where not a particle of food could be obtained, and where she was entirely unprotected from the severe cold. When the luckless Dominick was discovered, about eighteen days afterward, she was brisk and lively, but fearfully pinched up, and as light as a bunch of feathers. The slightest wind carried her before it. But by judicious feeding she was soon restored.

The circumstance of the blue-birds being emboldened by the cold, suggests the fact that the fear of man, which now seems like an instinct in the birds, is evidently an acquired trait, and foreign to them in a state of primitive nature. Every gunner has observed, to his chagrin, how wild the pigeons become after a few days of firing among them; and, to his delight, how easy it is to approach near his game in new or unfrequented woods. Professor Baird tells me that a correspondent of theirs visited a small island in the Pacific Ocean, situated about two hundred miles off Cape St. Lucas, to procure specimens. The island was but a few miles in extent, and had probably never been visited half a dozen times by human beings. The naturalist found the birds and water-fowls so tame that it was but a waste of ammunition to shoot them. Fixing a noose on the end of a long stick, he captured them by putting it over their necks and hauling them in to him. In some cases not even this contrivance was needed. A species of mocking-bird in particular, larger than ours, and a splendid songster, made itself so familiar as to be almost a nuisance, hopping on the table where the collector was writing, and scattering the pens and paper. Eighteen species were found, twelve of them peculiar to the island.

Thoreau relates that in the woods of Maine, the Canada jay will sometimes make its meal with the lumbermen, taking the food out of their hands.

Yet, notwithstanding the birds have come to look upon man as their natural enemy, there can be little doubt that civilization is on the whole favourable to their increase and perpetuity, especially to the smaller species. With man come flies and moths, and insects of all kinds in greater abundance; new plants and weeds are introduced, and, with the clearing up of the country, are sowed broadcast over the land.

The larks and snow-buntings that come to us from the north, subsist almost entirely upon the seeds of grasses and plants; and how many of our more common and abundant species are field birds, and entire strangers to deep forests?

In Europe some birds have become almost domesticated, like the house-sparrow, and in our own country the cliff-swallow seems to have entirely abandoned ledges and shelving rocks as a place to nest, for the eaves and projections of farms and other out-buildings.

The European house-sparrow, by the way, has been introduced with entire success in this country, and in New York and the adjacent cities is already quite numerous, and is rapidly increasing. Before I was aware of this fact I was much puzzled, a couple of years ago, by a bird I saw in the streets of Jersey City. I had occasion one June morning, at a very early hour, to walk from the depot out into the suburbs toward Bergen Hill, and all along the streets, picking up food about the feet of the horses, alighting on the curb-stones, and on the houses, quite unmindful of the passers-by, feeding their young with much chattering, and quarrelling with the martins, with loud squeaking, my attention was attracted by these strange birds, evidently sparrows. The figures of some of the rarer species of buntings, like henslows and the black-throated, kept recurring dimly to my mind, but only to make the puzzle more puzzling, as both these species are shy field birds. The matter remained a mystery till I heard of the introduction of this house-sparrow. These birds are said to be performing a rare service in the parks of New York, and for the fruit growers round about, by utterly exterminating the canker-worm, and other pests of this kind. I hear they have been introduced in the island of Cuba, with like beneficial results. An importer in Havana, indignant at the duties imposed upon his feathered freight, liberated the birds in the faces of the custom-house officials, when they showed themselves masters of the situation, and at once made themselves at home. Attempts to introduce the English skylark into this country have been less successful, owing largely to the extent to which the birds suffer on the passage over.

———

THE MANGO-TREE.

[The Rev. Charles Kingsley, born at Holne Vicarage, Devon, 12th June, 1819; died at the Parsonage, Eversley, 23d January, 1875. Educated at Cambridge, where, subsequently, he filled the chair of modern history for several years (1859–69). He was chaplain in ordinary to the Queen, and to the Prince of Wales and canon of Chester. In the church and in literature he worked with much industry; and his interest in the labouring classes found fervent expression in his books. He won high distinction as preacher, poet novelist, and miscellaneous writer. His chief works (published by Macmillan & Co) are: *The Saint's Tragedy, and other Poems; Alton Locke*, Tailor and Poet —a novel which obtained much favour, and helped to earn for the writer the name of the "Chartist parson;" *Yeast; Westward, Ho! Hypatia; Glaucus; Two Years Ago; The Water Babies; Hereward*, the Last of the English; *The Heroes: or Greek Fairy Tales; Miscellanies; At Last*, a Christmas in the West Indies, &c. &c. He also published several volumes of sermons.]

He wiled me through the furzy croft;
  He wiled me down the sandy lane.
He told his boy's love, soft and oft,
  Until I told him mine again.

We married, and we sailed the main;
  A soldier and a soldier's wife.
We marched through many a burning plain;
  We sighed for many a gallant life.

But his—God keep it safe from harm.
  He toiled, and dared, and earned command,
And those three stripes upon his arm
  Were more to me than gold or land.

Sure he would win some great renown:
  Our lives were strong, our hearts were high.
One night the fever struck him down.
  I sat, and stared, and saw him die.

I had his children—one, two, three.
  One week I had them, blithe and sound.
The next—beneath this mango-tree,
  By him in barrack burying-ground.

I sit beneath the mango-shade;
  I live my five years' life all o'er—
Round yonder stems his children played;
  He mounted guard at yonder door.

'Tis I, not they, am gone and dead.
  They live; they know; they feel; they see.
Their spirits light the golden shade
  Beneath the giant mango-tree.

All things, save I, are full of life:
  The minas, pluming velvet breasts;
The monkeys, in their foolish strife;
  The swooping hawks, the swinging nests.

The lizards basking on the soil,
  The butterflies who sun their wings;
The bees about their household toil,
  They live, they love, the blissful things.

Each tender purple mango shoot,
  That folds and droops so bashful down;
It lives, it sucks some hidden root;
  It rears at last a broad green crown.

It blossoms; and the children cry—
  "Watch when the mango-apples fall."
It lives; but rootless, fruitless, I—
  I breathe and dream;—and that is all.

Thus am I dead; yet cannot die:
  But still within my foolish brain
There hangs a pale blue evening sky;
  A furzy croft; a sandy lane.

———

MODERN GALLANTRY.

BY CHARLES LAMB.

In comparing modern with ancient manners, we are pleased to compliment ourselves upon the point of gallantry—a certain obsequiousness, or deferential respect, which we are supposed to pay to females as females.

I shall believe that this principle actuates our conduct when I can forget that in the nineteenth century of the era from which we date our civility, we are but just beginning to leave off the very frequent practice of whipping females in public, in common with the coarsest male offenders.

I shall believe it to be influential when I can shut my eyes to the fact that in England women are still occasionally—hanged.

I shall believe in it when actresses are no longer subject to be hissed off a stage by gentlemen.

I shall believe in it when Dorimant hands a fish-wife across the kennel; or assists the apple-woman to pick up her wandering fruit, which some unlucky dray has just dissipated.

I shall believe in it when the Dorimants in humbler life, who would be thought in their way notable adepts in this refinement, shall act upon it in places where they are not known, or think themselves not observed—when I shall see the traveller for some rich tradesman part with his admired box-coat, to spread it over the defenceless shoulders of the poor woman who is passing to her parish on the roof of the same stage-coach with him, drenched in the rain—when I shall no longer see a woman standing up in the pit of a London theatre, till she is sick and faint with the exertion, with men about her seated at their case, and jeering at her distress; till one that seems to have more manners or conscience than the rest significantly declares, "she should be welcome to his seat if she were a little younger and handsomer." Place this dapper warehouseman, or that rider, in a circle of their own female acquaintance, and you shall confess you have not seen a politer-bred man in Lothbury.

Lastly, I shall begin to believe that there is some such principle influencing our conduct, when more than one-half of the drudgery and coarse servitude of the world shall cease to be performed by women.

Until that day comes, I shall never believe this boasted point to be anything more than a conventional fiction; a pageant got up between the sexes, in a certain rank, and at a certain time of life, in which both find their account equally.

I shall be even disposed to rank it among the salutary fictions of life, when in polite circles I shall see the same attentions paid to age as to youth, to homely features as to handsome, to coarse complexions as to clear—to the woman as she is a woman, not as she is a beauty, a fortune, or a title.

I shall believe it to be something more than a name, when a well-dressed gentleman in a well-dressed company can advert to the topic of *female old age* without exciting, and intending to excite, a sneer;—when the phrases "antiquated virginity," and such a one has "overstood her market," pronounced in good company, shall raise immediate offence in man, or woman, that shall hear them spoken.

Joseph Paice, of Bread-street-hill, merchant, and one of the directors of the South Sea Company—the same to whom Edwards, the Shakspeare commentator, has addressed a fine sonnet—was the only pattern of consistent gallantry I have met with. He took me under his shelter at an early age, and bestowed some pains upon me. I owe to his precepts and example whatever there is of the man of business (and that is not much) in my composition. It was not his fault that I did not profit more. Though bred a Presbyterian, and brought up a merchant, he was the finest gentleman of his time. He had not *one* system of attention to females in the drawing-room, and *another* in the shop or at the stall. I do not mean that he made no distinction. But he never lost sight of sex, or overlooked it in the casualties of a disadvantageous situation. I have seen him stand bare-headed—smile if you please—to a poor servant-girl, while she has been inquiring of him the way to some street—in such a posture of unforced civility as neither to embarrass her in the acceptance nor himself in the offer of it. He was no dangler, in the common acceptation of the word, after women: but he reverenced and upheld, in every form in which it came before him, *womanhood*. I have seen him—nay, smile not—tenderly escorting a market-woman, whom he had encountered in a shower, exalting his umbrella over her poor basket of fruit, that it might receive no damage, with as much carefulness as if she had been a countess. To the reverend form of Female Eld he would yield the wall (though it were to an ancient beggar-woman) with more ceremony than we can afford to show our grandams. He was the Preux Chevalier of Age; the Sir Calidore, or Sir Tristan, to those who have no Calidores or Tristans to defend them. The roses, that had long faded thence, still bloomed for him in those withered and yellow cheeks.

He was never married, but in his youth he paid his addresses to the beautiful Susan Winstanley—old Winstanley's daughter of Clapton—who, dying in the early days of their courtship, confirmed in him the resolution of perpetual bachelorship. It was during their short courtship, he told me, that he had been one day treating his mistress with a profusion of civil speeches—the common gallantries—to which kind of thing she had hitherto manifested no repugnance—but in this instance with no effect. He could not obtain from her a decent acknowledgment in return. She rather seemed to resent his compliments. He could not set it down to caprice, for the lady had always shown herself above that littleness. When he ventured on the fol'owing day, finding her a little better humoured, to expostulate with her on her coldness of yesterday, she confessed with her usual frankness, that she had no sort of dislike to his attentions; that she could even endure some high-flown compliments; that a young woman placed in her situation had a right to expect all sort of civil things said to her; that she hoped she could digest a dose of adulation, short of insincerity, with as little injury to her humility as most young women: but that—a little before he had commenced his compliments—she had overheard him by accident, in rather rough language, rating a young woman who had not brought home his cravats quite to the appointed time, and she thought to herself, "As I am Miss Susan Winstanley, and a young lady—a reputed beauty, and known to be a fortune—I can have my choice of the finest speeches from the mouth of this very fine gentleman who is courting me; but if I had been poor Mary Such-a-one (*naming the milliner*), and had failed of bringing home the cravats to the appointed hour—though perhaps I had sat up half the night to forward them—what sort of compliments should I have received then?—And my woman's pride came to my assistance; and I thought, that if it were only to do *me* honour, a female like myself might have received handsomer usage: and I was determined not to accept any fine speeches, to the compromise of that sex, the belonging to which was, after all, my strongest claim and title to them."

I think the lady discovered both generosity and a just way of thinking in this rebuke which she gave her lover; and I have sometimes imagined that the uncommon strain of courtesy, which through life regulated the actions and behaviour of my friend towards all of womankind indiscriminately, owed its happy origin to this seasonable lesson from the lips of his lamented mistress.

I wish the whole female world would entertain the same notion of these things that Miss Winstanley showed. Then we should see something of the spirit of consistent gallantry; and no longer witness the anomaly of the same man—a pattern of true politeness to a wife—of cold contempt, or rudeness, to a sister—the idolater of his female mistress—the disparager and despiser of his no less female aunt, or unfortunate—still female—maiden cousin. Just so much respect as a woman derogates from her own sex, in whatever condition placed—her handmaid or dependant—she deserves to have diminished from herself on that score; and probably will feel the diminution, when youth, and beauty, and advantages not inseparable from sex, shall lose of their attraction. What a woman should de-

mand of a man in courtship, or after it, is first —respect for her as she is a woman;—and next to that—to be respected by him above all other women. But let her stand upon her female character as upon a foundation; and let the attentions incident to individual preference be so many pretty addjtaments and ornaments —as many, and as fanciful as you please—to that main structure. Let her first lesson be —with sweet Susan Winstanley—to *reverence her sex.*

WOMAN'S INCONSTANCY.

[Sir **Robert Aytoun**, born in Fifeshire, 1570; died in London, March, 1638. A courtier and poet, a friend of Ben Jonson, and acquainted with all the wits of his time. He served James I. and Charles I., and was knighted by the first-named monarch. He was an ancestor of W. Edmondstone Aytoun. Several of his poems are quoted in Watson's *Scottish Poems*, 1706–11, and in Ritson's *Caledonian Muse*.]

I lov'd thee once, I'll love no more,
    Thine be the grief, as is the blame;
Thou art not what thou wert before,
    What reason I should be the same?
He that can love unlov'd again
Hath better store of love than brain:
God send me love my debts to pay,
While unthrifts fool their love away.

Nothing could have my love o'erthrown,
    If thou hadst still continued mine:
Yea, if thou hadst remain'd thy own,
    I might perchance have yet been thine:
But thou thy freedom did recal,
That if thou might elsewhere enthral;
And then how could I but disdain
A captive's captive to remain?

When new desires had conquer'd thee,
    And chang'd the object of thy will,
It had been lethargy in me,
    Not constancy, to love thee still.
Yea, it had been a sin to go
And prostitute affection so;
Since we are taught our prayers to say
To such as must to others pray.

Yet do thou glory in thy choice,
    Thy choice of his good fortune boast;
I'll neither grieve nor yet rejoice
    To see him gain what I have lost.
The height of my disdain shall be
To laugh at him, to blush for thee,
To love thee still, but go no more
A-begging at a beggar's door.[1]

---

[1] Burns took from this poem the idea for his song "I do confess thou art sae fair."

CHURCH OF ST. LAWRENCE

ROTTERDAM.

BY ALEXANDER WHITELAW.

Rotterdam is the birth-place of Desiderius Erasmus, the reviver of learning, and within its magnificent cathedral sleep the patriotic De Wittses. These are the first thoughts which, to the man of letters, occur regarding Rotterdam, yet they are small matters in the eyes of its honest inhabitants, who value their town for its more substantial attractions—its comprehensive canals, its accommodating wharfs, its many-piled stores, and its heavy-sterned argosies. The merchant there is the honourable of the earth. This claim to distinction is not founded alone on his individual resources or aggrandizement: he has, in most cases, a long line of ancestry to boast of, being himself but the latest link of an unbroken family chain, which reaches back to the brightest ages of the Dutch republic. He is no upstart speculator—no builder of his own fortune. His father and his father's father held the same situation which he holds, and he only continues a business the foundations of which were laid ages before he was born. To this circumstance may be attributed much of that repose and placidity which characterize the Dutch merchant. He has not, as others have, his way to make in the world; his road is carved out for him, his path smoothed; and he is consequently free from that anxiety and bustle which mark his less favoured fellow-traders.

Of all the families of Rotterdam that of the Slows was one of the most ancient, and had from time immemorial possessed a reputable store and wharf near the cathedral of St. Lawrence.[1] Its latest descendant was Mynheer Van Double Slow, in whose person the name was like to become extinct. Mynheer had married, it is true, but the only result was a daughter, who could not be supposed to support either the name or the mercantile distinction of the family. This circumstance harassed Mynheer, so far as it was possible for a man of his enviable disposition to be harassed. He loved Agatha, but he lamented that he had no son to continue the honours of his line. In the absence of one, he took under his pro-

tection a young man distantly related to him, whom he instructed in all the mysteries of his merchandise. This young man was named Carl Van Speed, and was in every respect worthy of the patronage bestowed on him. As he lived under the same roof with his master, and sat at the same table, he had every opportunity of cultivating an intimacy with the daughter. The consequence was that they fell speedily in love with one another, which was the more remarkable, that nothing could be more natural or appropriate.

Whether the father wished or contemplated this result, no one could gather from his conversation, for more silent and unfathomable than Delphic oracle was Mynheer Van Double Slow. He was, indeed, the most philosophic of Dutch Pythagoreans. Not only was he never known to utter an unnecessary word, but he even refrained from articulating those which were necessary. An explanation from him was hopeless—the human pyramid! To speak, interfered with the business of his life, which was to smoke. Yet three smokes were all that he required in the day—one, when he rose till breakfast-time—another, from breakfast-time till dinner-time—and another, from dinner-time till he went to bed. In bed he was never known to use the meerschaum, except when he happened to be awake!

Agatha, his daughter, bore the same relation to her father that a rainbow does to a cloud. She owed her existence to him, yet was sprightly and beautiful as he was sombre and gross. No maiden of Rotterdam stepped so lightly—laughed so merrily—or held in her bosom so generous a spirit.

"My father loves you, Carl," she said one day to her lover, who was insisting on their speedy union; "I know it from the manner in which he puffs in your face; but it is almost hopeless to expect that he will ever exert himself so far as to approve of our marriage. I sometimes imagine he is on the eve of advising it, but his resolution dies away in the smoke of the pipe. Still, let us give him four weeks of trial longer, and if in that time he says nothing, why I suppose we may—just marry without him."

All the world of Rotterdam visit the tea-gardens once a week. Parties are there held of every description; for a Dutchman's home is sacred from friendly intrusions, and it is only in public where he displays his hospitality. Mynheer Van Double Slow was not-behind the world of Rotterdam. He had a favourite bower in the tea-gardens, where, with his daughter and her lover, he regularly spent his

---

[1] The church, which has been recently restored, is a brick structure of 1472 in the later Gothic style. The interior is of fine proportions, and contains numerous monuments of Dutch naval heroes. Its organ possesses three keyboards, 72 stops, and 4762 pipes, the largest of which is 32 feet long and 17 inches diameter.

Saturday afternoons. While he enjoyed himself with his schnaps and meerschaum, Carl played divinely on the fiddle, and Agatha danced like an angel. The old man generally indicated his satisfaction by a grunt or an extra prolific puff; but on the first week after the resolution of Agatha recorded above, he approached the subject on which the lovers' souls were bent.

"Carl, my prince," he said, "would you wish to mary?"

Carl's heart leaped to his mouth, as he bowed an acquiescent affirmative—but the oracle had spoken, and not another word issued from the lips of Mynheer Van Double Slow!

Next Saturday, Mynheer again enjoyed his meerschaum in his favourite bower—again Carl played divinely on the fiddle—and again Agatha danced like an angel. Again, also, was Mynheer moved to open his mouth.

"Agatha, my dove," he said, "would you?"

Agatha blushed and curtsied an affirmative —but the oracle had spoken, and not another word issued from the lips of Mynheer Van Double Slow!

Another Saturday came with its usual enjoyments, and again did Mynheer open his mouth.

"In that case," he said, laying down his pipe, "you had better"——

He took up his pipe again—lay back in his seat—and sacrificed the sentence in beatific puffs.

The fourth Saturday came. Carl played more divinely than ever on the fiddle, and Agatha danced with tenfold grace and vigour. Mynheer had at length reached his goal. He opened his mouth, and concluded his last week's sentence.

——"marry one another," he said.

"We are married already, father," said Agatha. "This morning we went to the church of St. Lawrence, and took our vows."

"That's good children," said Mynheer Van Double Slow, relapsing into his pipe, as of old.

Months have now passed. Mynheer Van Double Slow still spends his Saturday afternoons in the bower, and Carl Van Speed still plays divinely on the fiddle, but Agatha is scarcely so nimble in the dance. People shake their heads, and talk of the march of intellect, which only means that the SPEEDS are likely to supplant the SLOWS.

——

THE NIGHT BEFORE THE WEDDING; OR, TEN YEARS AFTER.

[Alexander Smith, born in Kilmarnock, 31st December, 1830; died at Wardie, Edinburgh, 5th January, 1867. He was the son of a pattern designer and was apprenticed to that business; but before he had attained his majority he had written the *Life Drama*, which secured for him immediate recognition as a poet of high promise, thanks to the enthusiasm of the Rev. George Gilfillan. He was then appointed secretary to the University of Edinburgh, which appointment afforded him a settled income and some leisure for composition. *City Poems* (from which we quote) and *Edwin of D irn* were his next important poetical works (Macmillan & Co.) His chief prose writings were: *Dreamthorpe; Alfred Haggart's Household;* and *A Summer 'in Skye.* "On the whole, then, we think Mr. Smith a true poet, and a poet of no common order."—*North British Review.*]

The country ways are full of mire,
The boughs toss in the fading light,
The winds blow out the sunset's fire,
And sudden droppeth down the night.
I sit in this familiar room,
Where mud-splashed hunting squires resort;
My sole companion in the gloom
This slowly dying pint of port.

'Mong all the joys my soul hath known,
'Mong errors over which it grieves,
I sit at this dark hour alone,
Like autumn 'mid his wither'd leaves.
This is a night of wild farewells
To all the past; the good, the fair;
To-morrow, and my wedding bells
Will make a music in the air.

Like a wet fisher tempest-tost,
Who sees throughout the weltering night
Afar on some low-lying coast
The streaming of a rainy light,
I saw this hour,—and now 'tis come;
The rooms are lit, the feast is set;
Within the twilight I am dumb,
My heart fill'd with a vague regret.

I cannot say, in Eastern style,
Where'er she treads the pansy blows;
Nor call her eyes twin-stars, her smile
A sunbeam, and her mouth a rose.
Nor can I, as your bridegrooms do,
Talk of my raptures. Oh, how sore
The fond romance of twenty-two
Is parodied ere thirty-four!

To-night I shake hands with the past,—
Familiar years, adieu, adieu!
An unknown door is open cast,
An empty future wide and new

Stands waiting. O ye naked rooms,
Void, desolate, without a charm,
Will Love's smile chase your lonely glooms,
And drape your walls, and make them warm.

The man who knew, while he was young,
Some soft and soul-subduing air,
Melts when again he hears it sung,
Although 'tis only half so fair.
So love I thee, and love is sweet
(My Florence, 'tis the cruel truth),
Because it can to age repeat
That long-lost passion of my youth.

Oh, often did my spirit melt,
Blurred letters, o'er your artless rhymes!
Fair tress, in which the sunshine dwelt,
I've kissed thee many a million times!
And now 'tis done.—My passionate tears,
Mad pleadings with an iron fate,
And all the sweetness of my years,
Are blacken'd ashes in the grate.

Then ring in the wind, my wedding chimes;
Smile, villagers, at every door;
Old churchyard, stuff'd with buried crimes,
Be clad in sunshine, o'er and o'er;
And youthful maidens, white and sweet,
Scatter your blossoms far and wide;
And with a bridal chorus greet
This happy bridegroom and his bride.

"This happy bridegroom!" there is sin
At bottom of my thankless mood:
What if desert alone could win
For me, life's chiefest grace and good?
Love gives itself; and if not given,
No genius, beauty, state, or wit,
No gold of earth, no gem of heaven,
Is rich enough to purchase it.

It may be, Florence, loving thee,
My heart will its old memories keep;
Like some worn sea-shell from the sea,
Fill'd with the music of the deep,
And you may watch, on nights of rain,
A shadow on my brow encroach;
Be startled by my sudden pain,
And tenderness of self-reproach.

It may be that your loving wiles
Will call a sigh from far-off years;
It may be that your happiest smiles
Will brim my eyes with hopeless tears;
It may be that my sleeping breath
Will shake, with painful visions wrung;
And, in the awful trance of death,
A stranger's name be on my tongue.

Ye phantoms, born of bitter blood,
Ye ghosts of passion, lean and worn,
Ye terrors of a lonely mood,
What do you here on a wedding-morn?
For, as the dawning sweet and fast
Through all the heaven spreads and flows,
Within life's discord rude and vast,
Love's subtle music grows and grows.

And lighten'd is the heavy curse,
And clearer is the weary road;
The very worm the sea-weeds nurse
Is cared for by the Eternal God.
My love, pale blossom of the snow,
Has pierced earth wet with wintry showers,—
O may it drink the sun, and blow,
And be follow'd by all the year of flowers!

Black Bayard from the stable bring;
The rain is o'er, the wind is down,
Round stirring farms the birds will sing,
The dawn stand in the sleeping town,
Within an hour. This is her gate,
Her sodden roses droop in night,
And—emblem of my happy fate—
In one dear window there is light.

The dawn is oozing pale and cold
Through the damp east for many a mile;
When half my tale of life is told
Grim-featured Time begins to smile.
Last star of night that lingerest yet
In that long rift of rainy gray,
Gather thy wasted splendours, set,
And die into my wedding-day.

THE DILEMMA.

BY H. G. BELL.

"By St. Agatha! I believe there is something in the shape of a tear in those dark eyes of mine, about which the women rave so unmercifully," said the young Fitzclarence, as, after an absence of two years, he came once more in sight of his native village of Malhamdale.

He stood upon the neighbouring heights, and watched the curling smoke coming up from the cottage chimneys in the clear blue sky of evening, and saw the last beams of the setting sun playing upon the western walls of his father's old baronial mansion, and, a little farther off, he could distinguish the trees and pleasure-grounds of Sir Meredith Appleby's less ancient seat. Then he thought of Julia Appleby, the baronet's only child, his youthful playmate, his first friend, and his first love; and as he thought of her, he sighed. I wonder why he sighed! When they parted two years before, sanctioned and encouraged by their respective parents (for there was nothing the old people wished more than a union between the families), they had sworn eternal fidelity, and plighted their hearts irrevocably to each other. Fitzclarence thought of all this, and again he sighed. Different people are differently affected by the same things. After so long an absence many a man would, in the exuberance of his feelings, have thrown himself down upon the first bed of wild flowers he came to, and spouted long speeches to himself out of all known plays. Our hero preferred indulging in the following little soliloquy:—

"My father will be amazingly glad to see me," said he to himself; "and so will my mother, and so will my old friend the antediluvian butler Morgan ap-Morgan, and so will the pointer Juno, and so will my pony Troilus;—a pretty figure, by-the-by, I should cut now upon Troilus, in this gay military garb of mine, with my sword rattling between his legs, and my white plumes streaming in the air like a rainbow over him! And Sir Meredith Appleby, too, with his great gouty leg, will hobble through the room in ecstacy as soon as I present myself before him;—and Julia—poor Julia, will blush, and smile, and come flying into my arms like a shuttle-cock. Heigho!—I am a very miserable young officer. The silly girl loves me; her imagination is all crammed with hearts and darts; she will bore me to death with her sighs, and her tender glances, and her allusions to time past, and her hopes of time to come, and all the artillery of a love-sick child's brain. What, in the name of the Pleiades, am I to do? I believe I had a sort of penchant for her once, when I was a mere boy in my nurse's leading-strings; I believe I did give her some slight hopes at one time or other; but now—O Rosalind! dear —delightful"——

Here his feelings overpowered him, and pulling a miniature from his bosom, he covered it with kisses. Sorry am I to be obliged to confess that it was not the miniature of Julia.

"But what is to be done?" he at length resumed. "The poor girl will go mad; she will hang herself in her garters; or drown herself, like Ophelia, in a brook under a willow. And I shall be her murderer! I, who have never yet knocked on the head a single man in the field of battle, will commence my warlike operations by breaking the heart of a woman. By St. Agatha! it must not be; I must be true to my engagement. Yes! though I become myself a martyr, I must obey the dictates of

honour. Forgive me, Rosalind, beautiful object of my adoration! Let not thy Fitzclarence"——

Here his voice became again inarticulate; and, as he winded down the hill, nothing was heard but the echoes of the multitudinous kisses he continued to lavish on the little brilliantly-set portrait he held in his hands.

Next morning Sir Meredith Appleby was just in the midst of a very sumptuous breakfast (for notwithstanding his gout, the baronet contrived to preserve his appetite), and the pretty Julia was presiding over the tea and coffee at the other end of the table, immediately opposite her papa, with the large long-eared spaniel sitting beside her, and ever and anon looking wistfully into her face, when a servant brought in, on a little silver tray, a letter for Sir Meredith. The old gentleman read it aloud; it was from the Elder Fitzclarence:

"My dear friend, Alfred arrived last night. He and I will dine with you to-day. Yours, Fitzclarence."

Julia's cheeks grew first as white as her brow, and then as red as her lips. As soon as breakfast was over, she retired to her own apartment, whither we must, for once, take the liberty of following her.

She sat herself down before her mirror, and deliberately took from her hair a very tasteful little knot of fictitious flowers, which she had fastened in it when she rose. One naturally expected that she was about to replace this ornament with something more splendid—a few jewels, perhaps; but she was not going to do any such thing. She rung the bell; her confidential attendant, Alice, answered the summons.

"La! ma'am," said she, "what is the matter? You look as ill as my aunt Bridget."

"You have heard me talk of Alfred Fitzclarence, Alice, have you not?" said the lady, languidly, and at the same time slightly blushing.

"O! yes, ma'am, I think I have. He was to be married to you before he went to the wars."

"He has returned, Alice, and he will break his heart if he finds I no longer love him. But he has been so long away; and Harry Dalton has been so constantly with me; and his tastes and mine are so congenial;—I'm sure you know, Alice, I am not fickle, but how could I avoid it? Harry Dalton is so handsome, and so amiable!"

"To be sure, ma'am, you had the best right to choose for yourself; and so Mr. Fitzclarence must just break his heart if he pleases, or else fight a desperate duel with Mr. Dalton, with his swords and guns."

"O! Alice, you frighten me to death. There shall be no duels fought for me. Though my bridal bed should be my grave, I shall be true to my word. The bare suspicion of my inconstancy would turn poor Alfred mad. I know how he dotes upon me. I must go to the altar, Alice, like a lamb to the slaughter. Were I to refuse him, you may depend upon it, he would put an end to his existence with five loaded pistols. Only think of that, Alice; what could I say for myself, were his remains found in his bed next morning?"

History does not report what Alice said her mistress might, under such circumstances, say for herself; but it is certain that they remained talking together till the third dinner-bell rang.

The Fitzclarences were both true to their engagements, but notwithstanding every exertion on the part of the two old gentlemen, they could not exactly bring about that "flow of soul" which they had hoped to see animating the young people. At length, after the cloth was removed, and a few bumpers of claret had warmed Sir Meredith's heart, he said boldly,

"Julia, my love, as Alfred does not seem to be much of a wine-bibber, suppose you show him the improvements in the gardens and hot-houses, whilst we sexagenarians remain where we are, to drink to the health of both, and talk over a few family matters."

Alfred, thus called upon, could not avoid rising from his seat, and offering Julia his arm. She took it with a blush, and they walked off together in silence.

"How devotedly he loves me!" thought Julia, with a sigh. "No, no, I cannot break his heart."

"Poor girl!" thought Alfred, bringing one of the curls of his whiskers more killingly over his cheek; "her affections are irrevocably fixed upon me; the slightest attention calls to her face all the roses of Sharon."

They proceeded down a long gravel walk, bordered on both sides with fragrant and flowery shrubs; but, except that the pebbles rubbed against each other as they passed over them, there was not a sound to be heard. Julia, however, was observed to hem twice, and we have been told that Fitzclarence coughed more than once. At length the lady stopped, and plucked a rose. Fitzclarence stopped also, and plucked a lily. Julia smiled; so did Alfred. Julia's smile was chased away by a sigh; Alfred

immediately sighed also. Checking himself, however, he saw the absolute necessity of commencing a conversation.

"Miss Appleby!" said he at last.

"Sir?"

"It is two years, I think, since we parted."

"Yes; two years on the fifteenth of this month."

Alfred was silent. "How she adores me!" thought he; "she can tell to a moment how long it is since we last met."—There was a pause.

"You have seen, no doubt, a great deal since you left Malhamdale?" said Julia.

"O! a very great deal," replied her lover. Miss Appleby hemmed once more, and then drew in a vast mouthful of courage.

"I understand the ladies of England and Ireland are much more attractive than those of Wales."

"Generally speaking, I believe they are."

"Sir!"

"That is—I mean, I beg your pardon—the truth is—I should have said—that—that—you have dropped your rose."

Fitzclarence stooped to pick it up; but in so doing, the little miniature which he wore round his neck escaped from under his waistcoat, and though he did not observe it, it was hanging conspicuous on his breast, like an order, when he presented the flower to Julia.

"Good heavens! Fitzclarence, that is my cousin Rosalind."

"Your cousin Rosalind! where? how?—the miniature! It is all over with me! The murder is out! Lord bless me! Julia, how pale you have grown; yet hear me! be comforted. I am a very wretch; but I shall be faithful; do not turn away, love; do not weep; Julia! Julia! what is the matter with you?—By Jove! she is in hysterics; she will go distracted! Julia! I will marry you, I swear to you by"——

"Do not swear by anything at all," cried Julia, unable any longer to conceal her rapture, "lest you be transported for perjury. You are my own—my very best Alfred!"

"Mad, quite mad," thought Alfred.

"I wear a miniature too," proceeded the lady: and she pulled from the loveliest bosom in the world the likeness, set in brilliants, of a youth provokingly handsome, but not Fitzclarence.

"Julia!"

"Alfred!"

"We have *both* been faithless!"

"And now we are both happy."

"By St. Agatha! I am sure of it. Only I

cannot help wondering at your taste, Julia;
that stripling has actually no whiskers!"
"Neither has my cousin Rosalind; yet you
found her resistless."
"Well, I believe you are right; and, besides,
de gustibus—I beg your pardon, I was going
to quote Latin."

THE ISLAND OF THE SCOTS.

[William Edmondstoune Aytoun, D.C.L., born in
Edinburgh, 21st June, 1813 ; died at Blackhills, Elgin,
4th August, 1865. He was a descendant of Sir Robert
Aytoun, a poet who lived in the reigns of James I. and
Charles I. He studied at the university of his native city,
and was called to the bar in 1840. He gave early indi-
cation of his taste for literature, and in 1832 issued a
small volume, entitled *Poland, Homer, and other Poems.*
He was appointed professor of belles-lettres and rhetoric in the Edinburgh University in 1845 ; and his
services to the Conservative party were recognized in
1852 by his appointment as sheriff of Orkney. As
joint author with Mr Theodore Martin of the *Bon
Gaultier Ballads,*[1] and by his *Lays of the Scottish Cavaliers,*
Professor Aytoun won for himself a distinguished place in
literature. He was for a number of years a regular
contributor to *Blackwood's Magazine;* and he produced
many translations, chiefly from the German poets
Uhland and Goethe. Of his other works the most
notable are: *Firmilian,* a spasmodic tragedy by T.
Percy Jones—a satire upon the spasmodic school of
poetry ; *Bothwell,* a poem ; *Norman Sinclair,* a novel ;
Life and Times of Richard I. (1840) ; and he edited a
collection of Scottish Ballads. Mr. T. Martin, who was
Aytoun's partner in many bright sketches, poems, and
translations, and who has written the biography of his
friend, says : "Fashions in poetry may alter, but so long
as the themes with which they deal have an interest
for his countrymen, his *Lays* will find, as they do now,
a wide circle of admirers. His powers as a humourist
were perhaps greater than as a poet. They have certainly been more widely appreciated. His immediate
contemporaries owe him much, for he has contributed
largely to that kindly mirth without which the strain
and struggle of modern life would be intolerable."[2]]

The Rhine is running deep and red,
    The island lies before—
"Now is there one of all the host
    Will dare to venture o'er?

For not alone the river's sweep
    Might make a brave man quail:
The foe are on the further side,
    Their shot comes fast as hail.
God help us, if the middle isle
    We may not hope to win!
Now is there any of the host
    Will dare to venture in?"

"The ford is deep, the banks are steep,
    The island-shore lies wide:
Nor man nor horse could stem its force,
    Or reach the further side.
See there! amidst the willow-boughs
    The serried bayonets gleam;
They've flung their bridge—they've won the
        isle;
    The foe have crossed the stream !
Their volley flashes sharp and strong—
    By all the saints! I trow
There never yet was soldier born
    Could force that passage now !"

So spoke the bold French Mareschal
    With him who led the van,
Whilst rough and red before their view
    The turbid river ran.
Nor bridge nor boat had they to cross
    The wild and swollen Rhine,
And thundering on the other bank
    Far stretched the German line.
Hard by there stood a swarthy man
    Was leaning on his sword,
And a saddened smile lit up his face
    As he heard the Captain's word.
"I've seen a wilder stream ere now
    Than that which rushes there;
I've stemmed a heavier torrent yet,
    And never thought to dare.
If German steel be sharp and keen,
    Is ours not strong and true?
There may be danger in the deed,
    But there is honour too."

The old lord in his saddle turned,
    And hastily he said—
"Hath bold Duguesclin's fiery heart
    Awakened from the dead?

---

[1] "Some of the best of these were exclusively Aytoun's,
such as "The Massacre of the M'Pherson," "The Rhyme
of Sir Lancelot Bogle," "The Broken Pitcher," "The
Red Friar and Little John," "The Lay of Mr. Colt,"
and that best of all imitations of the Scottish ballad,
"The Queen in France."—*Biography by T. Martin.*

[2] This poem is founded upon an exploit performed by
a company of Scottish gentlemen, who, having been
officers in the army of Dundee, escaped to France upon
the defeat of that general, and took service under the
standard of the French King. A work published in
London in 1714, entitled *An Account of Dundee's
Officers after they went to France,* by an Officer of the

Army, thus describes the adventure: "In December,
1697, General Stirk, who commanded for the Germans,
appeared with 16,000 men on the other side of the Rhine,
which obliged the Marquis de Sell to draw out all the
garrisons in Alsace, who made up about 4000 men ; and
he encamped on the other side of the Rhine, over against
General Stirk, to prevent his passing the Rhine and
carrying a bridge over into an island in the middle of
it, which the French foresaw would be of great prejudice
to them. For the enemy's guns, placed on that island,
would extremely gall their camp, which they could not
hinder for the deepness of the water, and their wanting
of boats—for which the Marquis quickly sent; but

Thou art the leader of the Scots—
Now well and sure I know,
That gentle blood in dangerous hour
Ne'er yet ran cold nor slow,
And I have seen thee in the fight
Do all that mortal may:
If honour is the boon ye seek,
It may be won this day—
The prize is in the middle isle,
There lies the adventurous way.
And armies twain are on the plain,
The daring deed to see—
Now ask thy gallant company
If they will follow thee!"

Right gladsome looked the Captain then,
And nothing did he say,
But he turned him to his little band—
Oh few, I ween, were they!
The relics of the bravest force
That ever fought in fray.
No one of all that company
But bore a gentle name,
Not one whose fathers had not stood
In Scotland's fields of fame.

All they had marched with great Dundee
To where he fought and fell,
And in the deadly battle strife
Had venged their leader well:
And they had bent the knee to earth
When every eye was dim,
As o'er their hero's buried corpse
They sang the funeral hymn;
And they had trod the Pass once more,
And stooped on either side
To pluck the heather from the spot
Where he had dropped and died;
And they had bound it next their hearts,
And ta'en a last farewell
Of Scottish earth and Scottish sky,
Where Scotland's glory fell.
Then went they forth to foreign lands
Like bent and broken men,
Who leave their dearest hope behind,
And may not turn again.

"The stream," he said, "is broad and deep,
And stubborn is the foe—
You island-strength is guarded well—
Say, brothers, will ye go?

---

arriving too late, the Germans had carried a bridge over into the island, where they had posted above 500 men, who, by order of their engineers, intrenched themselves; which the company of officers perceiving, who always grasped after honour, and scorned all thoughts of danger, resolved to wade the river, and attack the Germans in the island; and for that effect, desired Captain John Foster, who then commanded them, to beg of the Marquis that they might have liberty to attack the Germans in the island; who told Captain Foster, when the boats came up, they should be the first that attacked. Foster courteously thanked the Marquis, and told him they would wade into the island, who shrunk up his shoulders, prayed God to bless them, and desired them to do what they pleased." Whereupon the officers, with the other two Scottish companies, made themselves ready; and, having secured their arms round their necks, waded into the river hand-in-hand, "according to the Highland fashion," with the water as high as their breasts; and, having crossed the heavy stream, fell upon the Germans in their intrenchment. These were presently thrown into confusion, and retreated, breaking down their own bridges, whilst many of them were drowned. This movement, having been made in the dusk of the evening, partook of the character of a surprise; but it appears to me a very remarkable one, as having been effected under such circumstances, in the dead of winter, and in the face of an enemy who possessed the advantages both of position and of numerical superiority. The author of the narrative adds:—"When the Marquis de Sell heard the firing and understood that the Germans were beat out of the island, he made the sign of the cross on his face and breast, and declared publicly that it was the bravest action that ever he saw, and that his army had no honour by it. As soon as the boats came, the Marquis sent into the island to acquaint the officers

that he would send them both troops and provisions, who thanked his excellency, and desired he should be informed that they wanted no troops, and could not spare time to make use of provisions, and only desired spades, shovels, and pickaxes, wherewith they might intrench themselves—which were immediately sent to them. The next morning, the Marquis came into the island, and kindly embraced every officer, and thanked them for the good service they had done his master, assuring them he would write a true account of their honour and bravery to the court of France, which, at the reading his letters, immediately went to St. Germains, and thanked King James for the services his subjects had done on the Rhine."

The company kept possession of the island for nearly six weeks, notwithstanding repeated attempts on the part of the Germans to surprise and dislodge them; but all these having been defeated by the extreme watchfulness of the Scots, General Stirk at length drew off his army, and retreated. "In consequence of this action," says the chronicler, "that island is called at present Isle d'Ecosse, and will in likelihood bear that name until the general conflagration."

Two years afterwards, a treaty of peace was concluded; and this gallant company of soldiers, worthy of a better fate, was broken up and dispersed. At the time when the narrative, from which I have quoted so freely, was compiled, not more than sixteen of Dundee's veterans were alive. The author concludes thus:—"And thus was dissolved one of the best companies that ever marched under command! Gentlemen who, in the midst of all their pressures and obscurity, never forgot they were gentlemen; and whom the sweets of a brave, a just, and honourable conscience rendered perhaps more happy under those sufferings than the most prosperous and triumphant in iniquity, since our minds stamp our happiness."

From home and kin for many a year
   Our steps have wandered wide,
And never may our bones be laid
   Our fathers' graves beside.
No children have we to lament,
   No wives to wail our fall;
The traitor's and the spoiler's hand
   Have reft our hearths of all.
But we have hearts, and we have arms,
   As strong to will and dare
As when our ancient banners flew
   Within the northern air.
Come, brothers! let me name a spell
   Shall rouse your souls again,
And send the old blood bounding free
   Through pulse and heart and vein.
Call back the days of bygone years—
   Be young and strong once more;
Think yonder stream, so stark and red,
   Is one we've crossed before.
Rise, hill and glen! rise, crag and wood!
   Rise up on either hand—
Again upon the Garry's banks,
   On Scottish soil we stand!
Again I see the tartans wave,
   Again the trumpets ring;
Again I hear our leader's call—
   'Upon them for the King!'
Stayed we behind that glorious day
   For roaring flood or linn?
The soul of Græme is with us still—
   Now, brothers! will ye in?"

No stay—no pause   With one accord
   They grasped each other's hand,
Then plunged into the angry flood,
   That bold and dauntless band.
High flew the spray above their heads,
   Yet onward still they bore,
Midst cheer, and shout, and answering yell,
   And shot, and cannon-roar—
"Now, by the Holy Cross! I swear,
   Since earth and sea began,
Was never such a daring deed
   Essayed by mortal man!"

Thick blew the smoke across the stream,
   And faster flashed the flame:
The water plashed in hissing jets
   As ball and bullet came.
Yet onwards pushed the Cavaliers
   All stern and undismayed,
With thousand armed foes before,
   And none behind to aid.
Once, as they neared the middle stream,
   So strong the torrent swept,
That scarce that long and living wall
   Their dangerous footing kept.
Then rose a warning cry behind,
   A joyous shout before:

"The current's strong—the way is long—
   They'll never reach the shore!
See, see! they stagger in the midst,
   They waver in their line!
Fire on the madmen! break their ranks,
   And whelm them in the Rhine!"

Have you seen the tall trees swaying
   When the blast is sounding shrill,
And the whirlwind reels in fury
   Down the gorges of the hill?
How they toss their mighty branches,
   Struggling with the tempest's shock;
How they keep their place of vantage,
   Cleaving firmly to the rock?
Even so the Scottish warriors
   Held their own against the river;
Though the water flashed around them,
   Not an eye was seen to quiver;
Though the shot flew sharp and deadly,
   Not a man relaxed his hold:
For their hearts were big and thrilling
   With the mighty thoughts of old.
One word was spoke among them,
   And through the ranks it spread—
"Remember our dead Claverhouse!"
   Was all the Captain said.
Then, sternly bending forward,
   They wrestled on awhile,
Until they cleared the heavy stream,
   Then rushed towards the isle.

The German heart is stout and true,
   The German arm is strong;
The German foot goes seldom back
   Where armèd foemen throng.
But never had they faced in field
   So stern a charge before,
And never had they felt the sweep
   Of Scotland's broad claymore.
Not fiercer pours the avalanche
   Adown the steep incline,
That rises o'er the parent-springs
   Of rough and rapid Rhine—
Scarce swifter shoots the bolt from heaven
   Than came the Scottish band
Right up against the guarded trench,
   And o'er it sword in hand.
In vain their leaders forward press—
   They meet the deadly braud!

O lonely island of the Rhine—
   Where seed was never sown,
What harvest lay upon thy sands,
   By those strong reapers thrown?
What saw the winter-moon that night,
   As, struggling through the rain,
She poured a wan and fitful light
   On marsh, and stream, and plain?

A dreary spot with corpses strewn,
And bayonets glistening round;
A broken bridge, a stranded boat,
A bare and battered mound;
And one huge watchfire's kindled pile,
That sent its quivering glare
To tell the leaders of the host
The conquering Scots were there!

And did they twine the laurel-wreath
For those who fought so well?
And did they honour those who lived,
And weep for those who fell?
What meed of thanks was given to them
Let agèd annals tell.
Why should they bring the laurel-wreath—
Why crown the cup with wine?
It was not Frenchman's blood that flowed
So freely on the Rhine--
A stranger band of beggared men
Had done the venturous deed :
The glory was to France alone,
The danger was their meed.
And what cared they for idle thanks
From foreign prince and peer?
What virtue had such honeyed words
The exiled heart to cheer?
What mattered it that men should vaunt
And loud and fondly swear,
That higher feat of chivalry
Was never wrought elsewhere?
They bore within their breasts the grief
That fame can never heal—
The deep, unutterable woe
Which none save exiles feel.
Their hearts were yearning for the land
They ne'er might see again—
For Scotland's high and heathered hills,
For mountain, loch, and glen—
For those who haply lay at rest
Beyond the distant sea,
Beneath the green and daisied turf
Where they would gladly be!

Long years went by. The lonely isle
In Rhine's impetuous flood
Has ta'en another name from those
Who bought it with their blood :
And, though the legend does not live—
For legends lightly die—
The peasant, as he sees the stream
In winter rolling by,
And foaming o'er its channel-bed
Between him and the spot
Won by the warriors of the sword,
Still calls that deep and dangerous ford,
The Passage of the Scot.

MARJORIE DAW.

[Thomas Bailey Aldrich, born at Portsmouth, New Hampshire, 11th November, 1836. An American miscellaneous writer and poet. *Daisy's Necklace; The Ballad of Baby Bell; The Course of True Love; Pampina, and other poems; Out of His Head,* a romance; *The Story of a Bad Boy,* and other prose works, have obtained much popularity. The following story has been translated into French, and published in the *Revue de Deux Mondes,* in which the translator says Mr. Aldrich's "style is lively, and even in his easiest sentences there is a certain acid and savage savour which is agreeable to blasé palates."]

I.

*Dr. Dillon to Edward Delaney, Esq., at
The Pines, near Rye, N.H.*

August 8, 187-.

My dear Sir,—I am happy to assure you
that your anxiety is without reason. Flemming will be confined to the sofa for three or
four weeks, and will have to be careful at first
how he uses his leg. A fracture of this kind
is always a tedious affair. Fortunately the
bone was very skilfully set by the surgeon who
chanced to be in the drug-store where Flemming was brought after his fall, and I apprehend no permanent inconvenience from the
accident. *Flemming is doing perfectly well
physically;* but I must confess that the irritable and morbid state of mind into which he
has fallen causes me a great deal of uneasiness.
He is the last man in the world who ought to
break his leg. You know how impetuous our
friend is ordinarily, what a soul of restlessness
and energy, never content unless he is rushing
at some object, like a sportive bull at a red
shawl; but amiable withal. He is no longer
amiable. His temper has become something
frightful. Miss Fanny Flemming came up
from Newport, where the family are staying
for the summer, to nurse him; but he packed
her off the next morning in tears. He has a
complete set of Balzac's works, twenty-seven
volumes, piled up by his sofa, to throw at
Watkins whenever that exemplary serving-man
appears with his meals. Yesterday I very innocently brought Flemming a small basket of
lemons. You know it was a strip of lemonpeel on the curbstone that caused our friend's
mischance. Well, he no sooner set his eyes
upon these lemons than he fell into such a rage
as I cannot describe adequately. This is only
one of his moods, and the least distressing.
At other times he sits with bowed head regarding his splintered limb, silent, sullen,
despairing. When this fit is on him—and it

sometimes lasts all day—nothing can distract his melancholy. He refuses to eat; does not even read the newspapers; books—except as projectiles for Watkins—have no charms for him. His state is truly pitiable.

Now, if he were a poor man, with a family dependent on his daily labour, this irritability and despondency would be natural enough. But in a young fellow of twenty-four, with plenty of money, and seemingly not a care in the world, the thing is monstrous. If he continues to give way to his vagaries in this manner, he will end by bringing on an inflammation of the fibula. It was the fibula he broke. I am at my wits' end to know what to prescribe for him. I have anæsthetics and lotions, to make people sleep and to soothe pain; but I've no medicine that will make a man have a little common sense. That is beyond my skill, but maybe it is not beyond yours. You are Flemming's intimate friend, his *fidus Achates*. Write to him, write to him frequently, distract his mind, cheer him up, and prevent him from becoming a confirmed case of melancholia. Perhaps he has some important plans disarranged by his present confinement. If he has you will know, and will know how to advise him judiciously. I trust your father finds the change beneficial? I am, my dear sir, with great respect, &c.

II.

Edward Delaney to John Flemming, West 38th Street, New York.

August 9, —.

My dear Jack,—I had a line from Dillon this morning, and was rejoiced to learn that your hurt is not so bad as reported. Like a certain personage you are not so black and blue as you are painted. Dillon will put you on your pins again in two or three weeks, if you will only have patience and follow his counsels. Did you get my note of last Wednesday? I was greatly troubled when I heard of the accident.

I can imagine how tranquil and saintly you are with your leg in a trough! It's deuced awkward, to be sure, just as we had promised ourselves a glorious month together at the seaside; but we must make the best of it. It is unfortunate, too, that my father's health renders it impossible for me to leave him. I think he has much improved; the sea air is his native element; but he still needs my arm to lean upon in his walks, and requires some one more careful than a servant to look after him. I cannot come to you, dear Jack, but I have hours of unemployed time on hand, and I will

write you a whole post-office full of letters if that will divert you. Heaven knows, I haven't anything to write about. It isn't as if we were living at one of the beach houses; then I could do you some character studies, and fill your imagination with hosts of sea-godesses, with their (or somebody else's) raven and blond manes hanging down their shoulders. You should have Aphrodite in morning wrapper, in evening costume, and in her prettiest bathing suit. But we are far from all that here. We have rooms in a farm-house, on a cross-road, two miles from the hotels, and lead the quietest of lives.

I wish I were a novelist. This old house, with its sanded floors and high wainscots, and its narrow windows looking out upon a cluster of pines that turn themselves into æolian-harps every time the wind blows, would be the place in which to write a summer romance. It should be a story with the odours of the forest and the breath of the sea in it. It should be a novel like one of that Russian fellow's—what's his name?—Tourguénieff, Turguenef, Toorguniff, Turgénjew; nobody knows how to spell him. (I think his own mother must be in some doubt about him.) Yet I wonder if even a Liza, or an Alexandra Paulovna could stir the heart of a man who has constant twinges in his leg. I wonder if one of our own Yankee girls of the best type, haughty and *spirituelle*, would be of any comfort to you in your present deplorable condition. If I thought so, I would rush down to the Surf House and catch one for you; or, better still, I would find you one over the way.

Picture to yourself a large white house just across the road, nearly opposite our cottage. It is not a house, but a mansion, built perhaps in the colonial period, with rambling extensions, and gambrel roof, and a wide piazza on three sides—a self-possessed, high-bred piece of architecture, with its nose in the air. It stands back from the road, and has an obsequious retinue of fringed elms and oaks and weeping willows. Sometimes in the morning, and oftener in the afternoon, when the sun has withdrawn from that part of the mansion, a young woman appears on the piazza, with some mysterious Penelope web of embroidery in her hand, or a book. There is a hammock over there—of pine-apple fibre, it looks from here. A hammock is very becoming when one is eighteen, and has gold hair, and dark eyes, and a blue illusion dress looped up after the fashion of a Dresden china shepherdess, and is *chaussée* like a belle of the time of Louis Quatorze. All this splendour goes into that hammock, and sways there like a pond-lily in the golden afternoon. The window of my bedroom looks down on that piazza, and so do I.

But enough of this nonsense, which ill becomes a sedate young attorney taking his vacation with an invalid father. Drop me a line, dear Jack, and tell me how you really are. State your case. Write me a long, quiet letter. If you are violent or abusive I'll take the law to you.

III.

John Flemming to Edward Delaney.

August 11, —.

Your letter, dear Ned, was a god-send. Fancy what a fix I am in; I, who never had a day's sickness since I was born. My left leg weighs three tons. It is embalmed in spices, and smothered in layers of fine linen like a mummy. I can't move. I haven't moved for five thousand years. I'm of the time of Pharaoh.

I lie from morning till night on a lounge staring into the hot street. Everybody is out of town enjoying himself. The brown stone-front houses across the street resemble a row of particularly ugly coffins set up on end. A green mould is settling on the names of the deceased, carved on the silver door-plates. Sardonic spiders have sewed up the key-holes. All is silence and dust and desolation.—I interrupt this a moment, to take a shy at Watkins with the second volume of *César Birotteau.* Missed him! I think I could bring him down with a copy of *Sainte-Beuve*, or the *Dictionnaire Universel*, if I had it. These small Balzac books somehow don't quite fit my hand. But I shall fetch him yet. I've an idea Watkins is tapping the old gentleman's Château Yquem. Duplicate key of the wine-cellar. Hibernian swarries in the front basement. Young Cheops up stairs, snug in his cerements. Watkins glides into my chamber with that colourless, hypocritical face of his drawn out long like an accordion; but I know he grins all the way down stairs, and is glad I have broken my leg. Was not my evil star in the very zenith when I ran up to town to attend that dinner at Delmonico's? I didn't come up altogether for that. It was partly to buy Frank Livingstone's roan mare Margot. And now I shall not be able to sit in the saddle these two months. I'll send the mare down to you at The Pines; is that the name of the place?

Old Dillon fancies that I have something on my mind. He drives me wild with lemons. Lemons for a mind diseased. Nonsense. I am only as restless as the devil under this confinement—a thing I'm not used to. Take a man who has never had so much as a headache or a toothache in his life, strap one of his legs in a section of water-spout, keep him in a room in the city for weeks, with the hot weather turned on, and then expect him to smile, and purr, and be happy! It is preposterous. I can't be cheerful or calm.

Your letter is the first consoling thing I have had since my disaster, a week ago. It really cheered me up for half an hour. Send me a screed, Ned, as often as you can, if you love me. Anything will do. Write me more about that little girl in the hammock. That was very pretty, all that about the Dresden china shepherdess and the pond-lily; the imagery a little mixed perhaps, but very pretty. I didn't suppose you had so much sentimental furniture in your upper story. It shows how one may be familiar for years with the reception-room of his neighbour, and never suspect what is directly under his mansard. I supposed your loft stuffed with dry legal parchments, mortgages, and affidavits; you take down a package of manuscript, and lo! there are lyrics, and sonnets, and canzonettas. You really have a graphic descriptive touch, Edward Delaney, and I suspect you of short love-tales in the magazines.

I shall be a bear until I hear from you again. Tell me all about your pretty *inconnue* across the road. What is her name? Who is she? Who's her father? Where's her mother? Who's her lover? You cannot imagine how this will occupy me. The more trifling the better. My imprisonment has weakened me intellectually to such a degree that I find your epistolary gifts quite considerable. I am passing into my second childhood. In a week or two I shall take to india-rubber rings and prongs of coral. A silver cup with an appropriate inscription would be a delicate attention on your part. In the meantime write!

IV.

Edward Delaney to John Flemming.

August 12, —.

The sick pasha shall be amused. *Bismillah!* he wills it so! If the story-teller becomes prolix and tedious—the bow-string and the sack, and two Nubians to drop him into the Piscataqua! But truly, Jack, I have a hard task. There is literally nothing here, except the little girl over the way. She is swinging in the hammock at this moment. It is to me compensation for many of the ills of life to see her now and then put out a small kid boot, which fits like a glove, and set herself going.

Who is she, and what is her name? Her name is Daw. Only daughter of Mr. Richard W. Daw, ex-colonel and banker. Mother dead. One brother at Harvard; elder brother killed at the battle of Fair Oaks nine years ago. Old, rich family the Daws. This is the homestead, where father and daughter pass eight months of the twelve; the rest of the year in Baltimore and Washington. The New England winter too many for the old gentleman. The daughter is called Marjorie—Marjorie Daw. Sounds odd at first; doesn't it? But after you say it over to yourself half a dozen times you like it. There's a pleasing quaintness to it, something prim and violet-like. Must be a nice sort of girl to be called Marjorie Daw.

I had mine host of The Pines in the witness-box last night, and drew the foregoing testimony from him. He has charge of Mr. Daw's vegetable-garden, and has known the family these thirty years. Of course I shall make the acquaintance of my neighbours before many days. It will be next to impossible for me not to meet Mr. Daw or Miss Daw in some of my walks. The young lady has a favourite path to the sea-beach. I shall intercept her some morning, and touch my hat to her. Then the princess will bend her fair head to me with courteous surprise, not unmixed with haughtiness. Will snub me, in fact. All this for thy sake, O Pasha of the Snapt Axle-tree! . . . How oddly things fall out! Ten minutes ago I was called down to the parlour—you know the kind of parlours in farm-houses on the coast; a sort of amphibious parlour, with sea-shells on the mantel-piece and spruce branches in the chimney-place—where I found my father and Mr. Daw doing the antique polite to each other. He had come to pay his respects to his new neighbours. Mr. Daw is a tall, slim gentleman of about fifty-five, with a florid face, and snow-white mustache and side-whiskers. Looks like Mr. Dombey, or as Mr. Dombey would have looked if he had served a few years in the British army. Mr. Daw was a colonel in the late war, commanding the regiment in which his son was a lieutenant. Plucky old boy, backbone of New Hampshire granite. Before taking his leave the colonel delivered himself of an invitation, as if he were issuing a general order. Miss Daw has a few friends coming at 4 P.M., to play croquet on the lawn (parade-ground), and have tea (cold rations) on the piazza. Will we honour them with our company? (or be sent to the guard-house). My father declines, on the plea of ill-health. My father's son bows with as much suavity as he knows, and accepts.

In my next I shall have something to tell you. I shall have seen the little beauty face to face. I have a presentiment, Jack, that this Daw is a *rara avis!* Keep up your spirits, my boy, until I write you another letter; and send me along word how's your leg.

V.

Edward Delaney to John Flemming.

August 13, —.

The party, my dear Jack, was as dreary as possible. A lieutenant of the navy, the rector of the Episcopal church at Stillwater, and a society swell from Nahant. The lieutenant looked as if he had swallowed a couple of his buttons, and found the bullion rather indigestible; the rector was a pensive youth, of the daffydowndilly sort; and the swell from Nahant was a very weak tidal wave indeed. The women were much better, as they always are; the two Miss Kingsburys of Philadelphia, staying at the Sea-shell House, two bright and engaging girls. But Marjorie Daw!

The company broke up soon after tea, and I remained to smoke a cigar with the colonel on the piazza. It was like seeing a picture to see Miss Marjorie hovering around the old soldier, and doing a hundred gracious little things for him. She brought the cigars and lighted the tapers with her own delicate fingers in the most enchanting fashion. As we sat there she came and went in the summer twilight, and seemed, with her white dress and pale gold hair, like some lovely phantom that had sprung into existence out of the smoke-wreaths. If she had melted into air, like the statue of the lady in the play, I should have been more sorry than surprised.

It was easy to perceive that the old colonel worshipped her, and she him. I think the relation between an elderly father and a daughter just blooming into womanhood the most beautiful possible. There is in it a subtle sentiment that cannot exist in the case of mother and daughter, or that of son and mother. But this is getting into deep water.

I sat with the Daws until half-past ten, and saw the moon rise on the sea. The ocean, that had stretched motionless and black against the horizon, was changed by magic into a broken field of glittering ice. In the far distance the Isles of Shoals loomed up like a group of huge bergs drifting down on us. The polar regions in a June thaw! It was exceedingly fine. What did we talk about? We talked about the weather—and *you!* The weather has been disagreeable for several days past—and so have you. I glided from one topic to the other very naturally. I told my friends of your accident; how it had frustrated all our summer plans, and what our plans were. Then I described you; or, rather, I didn't. I spoke of your amiability; of your patience under this severe affliction; of your touching gratitude when Dillon brings you little presents of fruit; of your tenderness to your sister Fanny, whom you would not allow to stay in town to nurse you, and how you heroically sent her back to Newport, preferring to remain alone with Mary the cook, and your man Watkins, to whom, by the way, you were devotedly attached. If you had been there, Jack, you wouldn't have known yourself. I should have excelled as a criminal lawyer, if I had not turned my attention to a different branch of jurisprudence.

Miss Marjorie asked all manner of leading questions concerning you. It did not occur to me then, but it struck me forcibly afterwards, that she evinced a singular interest in the conversation. When I got back to my room I recalled how eagerly she leaned forward, with her full, snowy throat in strong moonlight, listening to what I said. Positively, I think I made her like you! Miss Daw is a girl whom you would like immensely, I can tell you that. A beauty without affectation; a high and tender nature, if one can read the soul in the face. And the old colonel is a noble character too.

I am glad the Daws are such pleasant people. The Pines is an isolated place, and my resources are few. I fear I should have found life here rather monotonous before long, with no other society than that of my excellent sire. It is true I might have made a target of the defenceless invalid; but I haven't a taste for artillery, moi.

VI.

John Flemming to Edward Delaney.

August 17. —.

For a man who hasn't a taste for artillery, it occurs to me, my friend, you are keeping up a pretty lively fire on my inner works. But go on. Cynicism is a small brass field-piece that eventually bursts and kills the artillery-man.

You may abuse me as much as you like, and I'll not complain; for I don't know what I should do without your letters. They are curing me. I haven't hurled anything at Watkins since last Sunday, partly because I have grown more amiable under your teaching, and partly because Watkins captured my ammunition one night, and carried it off to the library.

He is rapidly losing the habit he had acquired of dodging whenever I rub my ear, or make any slight motion with my right arm. He is still suggestive of the wine-cellar, however. You may break, you may shatter Watkins if you will, but the scent of the Roederer will hang round him still.

Ned, that Miss Daw must be a charming person. I should certainly like her. I like her already. When you spoke in your first letter of seeing a young girl swinging in a hammock under your chamber window, I was somehow strangely drawn to her. I cannot account for it in the least. What you have subsequently written of Miss Daw has strengthened the impression. You seem to be describing a woman I have known in some previous state of existence, or dreamed of in this. Upon my word, if you were to send me her photograph I believe I should recognize her at a glance. Her manner, that listening attitude, her traits of character, as you indicate them, the light hair and the dark eyes, they are all familiar things to me. Asked a lot of questions, did she? Curious about me? That is strange.

You would laugh in your sleeve, you wretched old cynic, if you knew how I lie awake nights, with my gas turned down to a star, thinking of The Pines and the house across the road. How cool it must be down there! I long for the salt smell in the air. I picture the colonel smoking his cheroot on the piazza. I send you and Miss Daw off on afternoon rambles along the beach. Sometimes I let you stroll with her under the elms in the moonlight, for you are great friends by this time, I take it, and see each other every day. I know your ways and your manners! Then I fall into a truculent mood, and would like to destroy somebody. Have you noticed anything in the shape of a lover hanging around the colonial Lares and Penates? Does that lieutenant of the horse-marines, or that young Stillwater parson visit the house much? Not that I am pining for news of them, but any gossip of the kind would be in order. I wonder, Ned, you don't fall in love with Miss Daw. I am ripe to do it myself. Speaking of photographs, couldn't you manage to slip one of her cartes-de-visite from her album—she must have an album, you know—and send it to me? I will return it before it could be missed. That's a good fellow! Did the mare arrive safe and sound? It will be a capital animal this autumn for Central Park.

Oh—my leg? I forgot about my leg. It's better.

VII.

Edward Delaney to John Flemming.

August 20, —.

You are correct in your surmise. I am on the most friendly terms with our neighbours. The colonel and my father smoke their afternoon cigar together in our sitting-room, or on the piazza opposite, and I pass an hour or two of the day or the evening with the daughter. I am more and more struck by the beauty, modesty, and intelligence of Miss Daw.

You ask me why I do not fall in love with her. I will be frank, Jack; I have thought of that. She is young, rich, accomplished, uniting in herself more attractions, mental and personal, than I can recall in any girl of my acquaintance; but she lacks the something that would be necessary to inspire in me that kind of interest. Possessing this unknown quantity, a woman neither beautiful, nor wealthy, nor very young could bring me to her feet. But not Miss Daw. If we were shipwrecked together on an uninhabited island—let me suggest a tropical island, for it costs no more to be picturesque—I would build her a bamboo hut, I would fetch her bread-fruit and cocoanuts, I would fry yams for her, I would lure the ingenuous turtle and make her nourishing soups; but I wouldn't make love to her—not under eighteen months. I would like to have her for a sister, that I might shield her and counsel her, and spend half my income on thread-laces and camel's-hair shawls. (We are off the island now). If such were not my feeling there would still be an obstacle to my loving Miss Daw. A greater misfortune could scarcely befall me than to love her. Flemming, I am about to make a revelation that will astonish you. I may be all wrong in my premises, and consequently in my conclusions; but you shall judge.

That night when I returned to my room after the croquet party at the Daws', and was thinking over the trivial events of the evening, I was suddenly impressed by the air of eager attention with which Miss Daw had followed my account of your accident. I think I mentioned this to you. Well, the next morning as I went to mail my letter, I overtook Miss Daw on the road to Rye, where the post-office is, and accompanied her thither and back, an hour's walk. The conversation again turned on you, and I remarked that inexplicable look of interest which had lighted up her face the previous evening. Since then I have seen Miss Daw perhaps ten times, perhaps oftener, and on each occasion I found that when

I was not speaking of you, or your sister, or some person or place associated with you, I was not holding her attention. She would be absent-minded; her eyes would wander away from me to the sea, or to some distant object in the landscape; her fingers would play with the leaves of a book in a way that convinced me she was not listening. At these moments if I abruptly changed the theme—I did it several times as an experiment—and dropped some remark about my friend Flemming, then the sombre blue eyes would come back to me instantly.

Now, is not this the oddest thing in the world? No, not the oddest. The effect which, you tell me, was produced on you by my casual mention of an unknown girl swinging in a hammock, is certainly as strange. You can conjecture how that passage in your letter of Friday startled me. Is it possible, then, that two people who have never met, and who are hundreds of miles apart, can exert a magnetic influence on each other? I have read of such psychological phenomena, but never credited them. I leave the solution of the problem to you. As for myself, all other things being favourable, it would be impossible for me to fall in love with a woman who listens to me only when I am talking of my friend!

I am not aware that any one is paying marked attention to my fair neighbour. The lieutenant of the navy—he is stationed at Rivermouth—sometimes drops in of an evening, and sometimes the rector from Stillwater; the lieutenant the oftener. He was there last night. I should not be surprised if he had an eye to the heiress; but he is not formidable. Mistress Daw carries a neat little spear of irony, and the honest lieutenant seems to have a particular facility for impaling himself on the point of it. He is not dangerous, I should say; though I have known a woman to satirize a man for years, and marry him after all. Decidedly the lowly rector is not dangerous; yet, again, who has not seen cloth of frieze victorious in the lists where cloth of gold went down?

As to the photograph. There is an exquisite ivorytype of Marjorie in *passe partout*, on the drawing-room mantle-piece. It would be missed at once if taken. I would do anything reasonable for you, Jack; but I've no burning desire to be hauled up before the local justice of the peace on a charge of petty larceny.

P.S.—Inclosed is a spray of mignonette, which I advise you to treat tenderly. Yes, we talked of you again last night as usual. It is becoming a little dreary for me.

VIII.

Edward Delaney to John Flemming.

August 22, —.

Your letter in reply to my last has occupied my thoughts all the morning. I do not know what to think. Do you mean to say that you are seriously half in love with a woman whom you have never seen—with a shadow, a chimera? for what else can Miss Daw be to you? I do not understand it at all. I understand neither you nor her. You are a couple of ethereal beings moving in finer air than I can breathe with my commonplace lungs. Such delicacy of sentiment is something I admire without comprehending. I am bewildered. I am of the earth earthy; and I find myself in the incongruous position of having to do with mere souls, with natures so finely tempered that I run some risk of shattering them in my awkwardness. I am as Caliban among the spirits!

Reflecting on your letter, I am not sure it is wise in me to continue this correspondence. But no, Jack; I do wrong to doubt the good sense that forms the basis of your character. You are deeply interested in Miss Daw; you feel that she is a person whom you may perhaps greatly admire when you know her: at the same time you bear in mind that the chances are ten to five that, when you do come to know her, she will fall far short of your ideal, and you will not care for her in the least. Look at it in this sensible light, and I will hold back nothing from you.

Yesterday afternoon my father and myself rode over to Rivermouth with the Daws. A heavy rain in the morning had cooled the atmosphere and laid the dust. To Rivermouth is a drive of eight miles, along a winding road lined all the way with wild barberry bushes. I never saw anything more brilliant than these bushes, the green of the foliage and the red of the coral berries intensified by the rain. The colonel drove, with my father in front, Miss Daw and I on the back seat. I resolved that for the first five miles your name should not pass my lips. I was amused by the artful attempts she made, at the start, to break through my reticence. Then a silence fell upon her; and then she became suddenly gay. That keenness which I enjoyed so much when it was exercised on the lieutenant was not so satisfactory directed against myself. Miss Daw has great sweetness of disposition, but she can be disagreeable. She is like the young lady in the rhyme, with the curl on her forehead,

" When she is good,
  She is very, very good,
  And when she is bad, she is horrid!"

I kept to my resolution, however; but on the return home I relented, and talked of your mare! Miss Daw is going to try a side-saddle on Margot some morning. The animal is a trifle too light for my weight. By the by, I nearly forgot to say Miss Daw sat for a picture yesterday to a Rivermouth artist. If the negative turns out well, I am to have a copy. So our ends will be accomplished without crime. I wish, though, I could send you the ivorytype in the drawing-room; it is cleverly coloured, and would give you an idea of her hair and eyes, which, of course, the other will not.

No, Jack, the spray of mignonette did not come from me. A man of twenty-eight doesn't inclose flowers in his letters—to another man. But don't attach too much significance to the circumstance. She gives sprays of mignonette to the rector, sprays to the lieutenant. She has even given a rose from her bosom to your slave. It is her jocund nature to scatter flowers, like spring.

If my letters sometimes read disjointedly, you must understand that I never finish one at a sitting, but write at intervals, when the mood is on me.

The mood is not on me now.

IX.

Edward Delaney to John Flemming.

August 23, —.

I have just returned from the strangest interview with Marjorie. She has all but confessed to me her interest in you. But with what modesty and dignity! Her words elude my pen as I attempt to put them on paper; and, indeed, it was not so much what she said as her manner; and that I cannot reproduce. Perhaps it was of a piece with the strangeness of this whole business, that she should tacitly acknowledge to a third party the love she feels for a man she has never beheld! But I have lost, through your aid, the faculty of being surprised. I accept things as people do in dreams. Now that I am again in my room, it all appears like an illusion,—the black masses of shadow under the trees, the fire-flies whirling in Pyrrhic dances among the shrubbery, the sea over there, Marjorie sitting on the hammock!

It is past midnight, and I am too sleepy to write more.

Tuesday Morning.—My father has suddenly taken it into his head to spend a few days at the Shoals. In the meanwhile you will not hear from me. I see Marjorie walking in the garden with the Colonel. I wish I could speak to her alone, but shall probably not have an opportunity before we leave.

X.

Edward Delaney to John Flemming.

August 23, —.

You were passing into your second childhood, were you? Your intellect was so reduced that my epistolary gifts seemed quite considerable to you, did they? I rise superior to the sarcasm in your favour of the 11th instant, when I notice that five days' silence on my part is sufficient to throw you into the depths of despondency.

We returned only this morning from Appledore, that enchanted island,—at four dollars per day. I find on my desk three letters from you! Evidently there is no lingering doubt in *your* mind as to the pleasure I derive from your correspondence. These letters are undated, but in what I take to be the latest are two passages that require my consideration. You will pardon my candour, dear Flemming, but the conviction forces itself upon me that as your leg grows stronger your head becomes weaker. You ask my advice on a certain point. I will give it. In my opinion you could do nothing more unwise than to address a note to Miss Daw, thanking her for the flower. It would, I am sure, offend her delicacy beyond pardon. She knows you only through me; you are to her an abstraction, a figure in a dream—a dream from which the slightest shock would awaken her. Of course, if you inclose a note to me and insist on its delivery, I shall deliver it; but I advise you not to do so.

You say you are able, with the aid of a cane, to walk about your chamber, and that you purpose to come to The Pines the instant Dillon thinks you strong enough to stand the journey. Again I advise you not to. Do you not see that, every hour you remain away, Marjorie's glamour deepens and your influence over her increases? You will ruin everything by precipitancy. Wait until you are entirely recovered; in any case do not come without giving me warning. I fear the effect of your abrupt advent here—under the circumstances.

Miss Daw was evidently glad to see us back again, and gave me both hands in the frankest way. She stopped at the door a moment this afternoon in the carriage; she had been over

to Rivermouth for her pictures. Unluckily the photographer had spilt some acid on the plate, and she was obliged to give him another sitting. I have an impression that something is troubling Marjorie. She had an abstracted air not usual with her. However, it may be only my fancy. . . . . I end this, leaving several things unsaid, to accompany my father on one of those long walks which are now his chief medicine,—and mine!

XI.

Edward Delaney to John Flemming.

August 26, —.

I write in great haste to tell you what has taken place here since my letter of last night. I am in the utmost perplexity. Only one thing is plain,—*you* must not dream of coming to The Pines. Marjorie has told her father everything! I saw her for a few minutes, an hour ago, in the garden; and, as near as I could gather from her confused statement, the facts are these: Lieutenant Bradly—that's the naval officer stationed at Rivermouth—has been paying court to Miss Daw for some time past, but not so much to her liking as to that of the colonel, who it seems is an old friend of the young gentleman's father. Yesterday (I knew she was in some trouble when she drove up to our gate) the colonel spoke to Marjorie of Bradly,—urged his suit, I infer. Marjorie expressed her dislike for the lieutenant with characteristic frankness, and finally confessed to her father—well, I really do not know what she confessed. It must have been the vaguest of confessions, and must have sufficiently puzzled the colonel. At any rate, it exasperated him. I suppose I am implicated in the matter, and that the colonel feels bitterly towards me. I do not see why: I have carried no messages between you and Miss Daw; I have behaved with the greatest discretion. I can find no flaw anywhere in my proceeding. I do not see that anybody has done anything, —except the colonel himself.

It is probable, nevertheless, that the friendly relations between the two houses will be broken off. "A plague o' both your houses," say you. I will keep you informed, as well as I can, of what occurs over the way. We shall remain here until the second week in September. Stay where you are, or at all events, do not dream of joining me. . . . . Colonel Daw is sitting on the piazza looking rather ferocious. I have not seen Marjorie since I parted with her in the garden.

XII.

Edward Delaney to Thomas Dillon, M.D.,
Madison Square, New York.

August 30, —.

My dear Doctor: If you have any influence over Flemming, I beg of you to exert it to prevent his coming to this place at present. There are circumstances, which I will explain to you before long, that make it of the first importance that he should not come into this neighbourhood. His appearance here, I speak advisedly, would be disastrous to him. In urging him to remain in New York, or to go to some inland resort, you will be doing him and me a real service. Of course you will not mention my name in this connection. You know me well enough, my dear doctor, to be assured that, in begging your secret co-operation, I have reasons that will meet your entire approval when they are made plain to you. My father, I am glad to state, has so greatly improved that he can no longer be regarded as an invalid. With great esteem, I am, &c. &c.

XIII.

Edward Delaney to John Flemming.

August 31, —.

Your letter announcing your mad determination to come here has just reached me. I beg of you to reflect a moment. The step would be fatal to your interests and hers. You would furnish just cause for irritation to R. W. D.; and, though he loves Marjorie tenderly, he is capable of going to any lengths if opposed. You would not like, I am convinced, to be the means of causing him to treat *her* with severity. That would be the result of your presence at The Pines at this juncture. Wait and see what happens. Moreover, I understand from Dillon that you are in no condition to take so long a journey. He thinks the air of the coast would be the worst thing possible for you; that you ought to go inland, if anywhere. Be advised by me. Be advised by Dillon.

XIV.

TELEGRAMS.

September 1, —.

1.—*To Edward Delaney.*

Letter received. Dillon be hanged. *I think I ought to be on the ground.*

J. F.

2.—*To John Flemming.*

Stay where you are. You would only complicate matters. Do not move until you hear from me.

E. D.

3.—*To Edward Delaney.*

My being at The Pines could be kept secret. *I must see her.*

J. F.

4.—*To John Flemming.*

Do not think of it. It would be useless. R. W. D. has locked M. in her room. You would not be able to effect an interview.

E. D.

5.—*To Edward Delaney.*

Locked her in her room! That settles the question. I shall leave by the 12·15 express.

J. F.

On the 2d of September, 187—, as the down express due at 3·40 left the station at Hampton, a young man, leaning on the shoulder of a servant whom he addressed as Watkins, stepped from the platform into a hack, and requested to be driven to "The Pines." On arriving at the gate of a modest farmhouse, a few miles from the station, the young man descended with difficulty from the carriage, and, casting a hasty glance across the road, seemed much impressed by some peculiarity in the landscape. Again leaning on the shoulder of the person Watkins, he walked to the door of the farmhouse and inquired for Mr. Edward Delaney. He was informed by the aged man who answered his knock, that Mr. Edward Delaney had gone to Boston the day before, but that Mr. Jonas Delaney was within. This information did not appear satisfactory to the stranger, who inquired if Mr. Edward Delaney had left any message for Mr. John Flemming. There *was* a letter for Mr. Flemming, if he were that person. After a brief absence the aged man reappeared with a letter.

XV.

Edward Delaney to John Flemming.

September 1, —.

I am horror-stricken at what I have done! When I began this correspondence I had no other purpose than to relieve the tedium of your sick-chamber. Dillon told me to cheer you up. I tried to. I thought you entered into the spirit of the thing. I had no idea, until within a few days, that you were taking matters *au sérieux*.

What can I say? I am in sackcloth and ashes. I am a Pariah, a dog of an outcast. I tried to make a little romance to interest you, something soothing and idyllic, and, by Jove! I have done it only too well! My father

107

doesn't know a word of this, so don't jar the
old gentleman any more than you can help.
I fly from the wrath to come—when you arrive!
For O, dear Jack, there isn't any colonial
mansion on the other side of the road, there
isn't any piazza, there isn't any hammock,—
there isn't any Marjorie Daw!!—*Atlantic
Monthly.*

SUNDAY.

[Rev. George Herbert, born at Montgomery Castle,
Wales, 3d April, 1593; died at Bemerton, 1632. He
was the fifth of seven sons, a descendant of the Pem-
broke family, and his elder brother, Edward, who distinguished himself in the camp, the court, and in literature, became Lord Herbert of Cherbury. George was
educated at Westminster and Cambridge, took orders,
and was presented by Charles I. to the living of Bemerton. The immediate cause of his early death was consumption. Izaak Walton in his biography sums up
Herbert's character: "Thus he lived, and thus he died
like a saint, unspotted of the world, full of alms-deeds,
full of humility, and all the examples of a virtuous
life." *The Temple,* Sacred Poems and Private Ejacula-
tions, were first published in 1633. His chief prose
works are: *A Priest to the Temple,* or the Country Parson,
his Character and Rule of Holy Life; and *Jacul P. uden-
tum,* or Outlandish Proverbs, Sentences, &c., selected by
George Herbert.]

O day most calm, most bright,
The fruit of this, the next world's bud,
The indorsement of supreme delight,
Writ by a Friend, and with His blood;
The couch of time; care's balm and bay;
The week were dark, but for thy light:
    Thy torch doth show the way.

The other days and thou
Make up one man; whose face thou art,
Knocking at heaven with thy brow:
The worky-days are the back-part;
The burden of the week lies there,
Making the whole to stoop and bow,
    Till thy release appear.

Man had straight forward gone
To endless death; but thou dost pull
And turn us round to look on One
Whom, if we were not very dull,
We could not choose but look on still;
Since there is no place so alone
    The which He doth not fill.

Sundays the pillars are,
On which heaven's palace arched lies:
The other days fill up the spare
And hollow room with vanities.

They are the fruitful beds and borders
In God's rich garden: that is bare
    Which parts their ranks and orders.

The Sundays of man's life,
Threaded together on time's string,
Make bracelets to adorn the wife
Of the eternal glorious King.
On Sunday heaven's gate stands ope;
Blessings are plentiful and rife,
    More plentiful than hope.

This day my Saviour rose,
And did inclose this light for His:
That, as each beast his manger knows,
Man might not of his fodder miss.
Christ hath took in this piece of ground,
And made a garden there for those
    Who want herbs for their wound.

The rest of our creation
Our great Redeemer did remove
With the same shake, which at His passion
Did the earth and all things with it move.
As Samson bore the doors away,
Christ's hands, though nail'd, wrought our salvation,
    And did unhinge that day.

The brightness of that day
We sullied by our foul offence:
Wherefore that robe we cast away,
Having a new at His expense,
Whose drops of blood paid the full price,
That was required to make us gay,
    And fit for Paradise.

Thou art a day of mirth:
And where the week-days trail on ground,
Thy flight is higher, as thy birth:
O let me take thee at the bound,
Leaping with thee from seven to seven,
Till that we both, being toss'd from earth,
    Fly hand in hand to heaven!

TREES.

BY PROFESSOR WILSON.

Trees are indeed the glory, the beauty, and
the delight of nature. The man who loves
not trees—to look at them—to lie under them
—to climb up them (once more a school-boy)—
would make no bones of murdering Mrs. Jeffs.
In what one imaginable attribute, that it
ought to possess, is a tree, pray, deficient?
Light, shade, shelter, coolness, freshness,
music, all the colours of the rainbow, dew and
dreams dropping through their umbrageous
twilight at eve or morn,—dropping direct,
soft, sweet, soothing, and restorative, from

heaven. Without trees, how in the name of wonder could we have had houses, ships, bridges, easy-chairs, or coffins, or almost any single one of the necessaries, conveniences, or comforts of life? Without trees, one man might have been born with a silver spoon in his mouth, but not another with a wooden ladle.

Tree by itself Tree, "such tents the patriarchs loved,"—Ipse nemus,—"the brotherhood of Trees,"—the Grove, the Coppice, the Wood, the Forest,—dearly, and after a different fashion, do we love you all!—And love you all we shall, while our dim eyes can catch the glimmer, our dull ears the murmur, of the leaves, or our imagination hear at midnight, the far-off swing of old branches groaning in the tempest. Oh! is not Merry also Sylvan England? And has not Scotland, too, her old pine forests, blackening up her Highland mountains? Are not many of her rivered valleys not unadorned with woods,—her braes beautiful with their birken shaws? And does not stately ash or sycamore tower above the kirk-spire in many a quiet glen, overshadowing the humble house of God, "the dial-stone aged and green," and all the deep-sunk, sinking, or upright array of grave-stones, beneath which

"The rude forefathers of the hamlet sleep?"

We have the highest respect for the ghost of Dr. Johnson; yet were we to meet it by moonlight, how should we make it hang its head on the subject of Scottish trees! Look there, you old, blind, blundering blockhead! That Pine Forest is twenty miles square! Many million trees there have at least five hundred arms each, six times as thick as ever your body was, sir, when you were at your very fattest in Bolt Court. As for their trunks—some straight as cathedral pillars—some flung all awry in their strength across cataracts—some without a twig till your eye meets the hawk's nest diminished to a black-bird's, and some overspread, from within a man's height of the mossy sward, with fantastic branches, conc-covered, and green as emerald—what say you, you great, big, lumbering, unweildy ghost you, to trunks like these? And are not the Forests of Scotland the most forgiving that ever were self-sown, to suffer you to flit to and fro, haunting unharmed their ancient umbrage? Yet, Doctor, you were a fine old Tory every inch of you, for all that, my boy; so come glimmering away with you into the gloom after us—don't stumble over the roots—we smell a still at work—and neither you nor I

—shadow nor substance (but, prithee, why so wan, good Doctor? Prithee, why so wan?) can be much the worse, eh, of a caulker of Glenlivat?

Every man of landed property, that lies fairly out of arm's length of a town, whether free or copyhold, be its rental above or below forty shillings a-year, should be a planter. Even an old bachelor, who has no right to become the father of a child, is not only free, but in duty bound to plant a tree. Unless his organ of philoprogenitiveness be small indeed, as he looks at the young tender plants in his own nursery-garden his heart will yearn towards them with all the longing and instinctive fondness of a father. As he beholds them putting forth the tender buds of hope, he will be careful to preserve them from all blight—he will "teach the young idea how to shoot," —and, according to their different natures, he will send them to different places to complete their education, according as they are ultimately intended for the church, the bar, or the navy. The old gentleman will be surprised to see how soon his young plants have grown as tall as himself, even though he should be an extraordinary member of the Six Feet Club. An oak sapling of some five or six springs shall measure with him on his stocking-soles, and a larch considerably younger, laugh to shake its pink cones far over his wig. But they are all dutiful children, never go stravaiging from home after youthful follies; and standing together in beautiful bands, and in majestic masses, they will not suffer the noonday sun to smite their father's head, nor the winds of heaven to "visit his face too roughly."

People are sometimes prevented from planting trees by the slowness of their growth. What a mistake that is! People might just as well be prevented from being wed, because a man-child takes one-and-twenty years to get out of his minority, and a woman-child, except in hot climates, is rarely marriageable before fifteen. Not the least fear in the world, that Tommy and Thomasine and the tree will grow up fast enough—wither at the top—and die! It is a strange fear to feel—a strange complaint to utter—that any one thing in this world, animate or inanimate, is of too slow growth; for the nearer to its perfection, the nearer to its decay.

No man who enjoys good health at fifty, or even sixty, would hesitate, if much in love, to take a wife, on the ground that he could have no hope or chance of seeing his numerous children all grown up into hobbledehoys and Priscilla Tomboys. Get your children first, and let them grow at their own leisure afterwards. In like manner, let no man, Bachelor or Benedict, be his age beyond the limit of conversational confession, fear to lay out a nursery-garden,—to fill it with young seedlings, and thenceforward to keep planting away, up hill and down brae, all the rest of his life.

Besides, in every stage how interesting, both a wood and sap tree, and a flesh and blood child! Look at pretty, ten-year-old, rosy-cheeked, golden-haired Mary, gazing, with all the blue brightness of her eyes, at that large dew-drop, which the sun has let escape unmelted even on into the meridian hours, on the topmost pink-bud, within which the teeming leaf struggles to expand into beauty,—the topmost pink-bud of that little lime-tree, but three winters old and half a spring!—Hark! that is Harry, at home on a holiday, rustling like a roe in the coppice-wood, in search of the nest of the blackbird or mavis; —yet ten years ago that rocky hillside was unplanted, and "that bold boy, so bright and beautiful," unborn. Who, then, be his age what it may, would either linger, "with fond, reluctant, amorous delay," to take unto himself a wife, for the purpose of having children, or to inclose a waste for the purpose of having trees.

At what time of life a human being—man or woman—looks best, it might be hard to say. A virgin of eighteen, straight and tall, bright, blooming, and balmy, seems, to our old eyes, a very beautiful and delightful sight. Inwardly we bless her, and pray that she may be as happy as she is innocent. So, too, is an Oak-tree about the same age, standing by itself, without a twig on its straight, smooth, round, and glossy, silver stem for some feet from the ground, and then branching out into a stately flutter of dark-green leaves; the shape being indistinct in its regular but not formal over-fallings, and over-foldings, and over-hangings, of light and shade. Such an Oak-tree is indeed truly beautiful, with all its tenderness, gracefulness, and delicacy—ay, a delicacy almost seeming to be fragile—as if the cushat, whirring from its concealment, would crush the new spring-shoots, sensitive almost as the gossamer, with which every twig is intertwined. Leaning on our staff, we bless it, and call it even by that very virgin's name; and ever thenceforth behold Louisa lying in its shade. Gentle reader, what it is to be an old, dreamy, visionary, prosing poet!

Let any one who accuses trees of laziness in growing only keep out of sight of them for a few years; and then, returning home to them under cloud of night, all at once open his eyes, of a fine, sunny, summer's morning, and ask them how they have been since he and they mutually murmured farewell! He will not recognize the face or the figure of a single tree. That sycamore, whose top-shoot a cow, you know, browsed off, to the breaking of your heart, some four or five years ago, is now as high as the "riggin" of the cottage, and is murmuring with bees among its blossoms quite like an old tree. What precocity! That wych elm, hide-bound as it seemed of yore, and with only one arm that it could hardly lift from its side, is now a Briareus. Is that the larch you used to hop over?—now almost fit to be a mast of one of the fairy fleet on Windermere! You thought you would never have forgotten the Triangle of the Three Birches, but you stare at them now as if they had dropped from the clouds! And since you think that beech—that round hill of leaves— is not the same shabby shrub you left sticking in the gravel, why call the old gardener hither, and swear him to its identity on the Bible?

Before this confounded gout attacked our toe we were great pedestrians, and used to stalk about all over the banks and braes from sunrising to sunsetting, through all seasons of the year. Few sights used to please us more than that of a new Mansion-house, or Villa, or Cottage ornee, rising up in some sheltered, but open-fronted nook, commanding a view of a few bends of a stream or river winding along old lea, or rich holm ploughed-fields,—sloping uplands, with here and there a farm-house and trees,—and in the distance hill-tops quite clear, and cutting the sky, wreathed with mists, or for a time hidden in clouds. It set the imagination and the heart at work together to look on the young hedgerows and plantations, belts, clumps, and single trees, hurdled in from the nibbling sheep. Ay, some younger brother who, twenty, or thirty, or forty years ago, went abroad to the East, or the West, to push his fortune, has returned to the neighbourhood of his native vale at last, to live and to die among the braes where once, among the yellow broom, the school-boy sported gladsome as any bird. Busy has he been in adorning—perhaps the man who fixes his faith on Price on the Picturesque, would say in disfiguring—the inland haven where he has dropped anchor, and will continue to ride till the vessel of life parts from her moorings, and drifts away on the shoreless sea of eternity. For our own parts, we are not easily offended by any conformation into which trees can be thrown—the bad taste of another must not be suffered to throw us into a bad temper—and as long as the trees are green in their season, and in their season purple, and orange, and yellow, and refrain from murdering each other, to our eye they are pleasant to look upon—to our ear it is music, indeed, to hear them all a-murmur along with the murmuring winds. Hundreds—thousands of such dwellings have, in our time, arisen all over the face of Scotland; and there is room enough, we devoutly trust, and verily believe, for hundreds and thousands more. Of a people's prosperity what pleasanter proof! And, therefore, may all the well-fenced woods make more and more wonderful shoots every year. Beneath and among their shelter, may not a single slate be blown from the blue roof, peering through the trees, on the eyes of distant traveller, as he wheels along on the top of his most gracious majesty's mail-coach;—may the dryads soon wipe away their tears for the death of the children that must, in thinnings, be "wede away;"—and may the rookeries and heronries of Scotland increase in number for the long space of ten thousand revolving years!

Not that we hold it to be a matter of pure indifference how people plant trees. We have an eye for the picturesque, the sublime, and the beautiful, and cannot open it without seeing at once the very spirit of the scene. O ye who have had the happiness to be born among the murmurs of hereditary trees! can ye be blind to the system pursued by that planter—Nature? Nature plants often on a great scale, darkening, far as the telescope can command the umbrage, sides of mountains that are heard roaring still with hundreds of hidden cataracts. And Nature often plants on a small scale, dropping down the stately birk so beautiful, among the sprinkled hazels, by the side of the little waterfall of the wimpling burnie, that stands dishevelling there her tresses to the dew-wind, like a queen's daughter, who hath just issued from the pool of pearls and shines aloft and aloof from her attendant maidens. But man is so proud of his own works that he ceases to regard those of Nature. Why keep poring on that book of plates, purchased at less than half price at a sale, when Nature flutters before your eyes her own folio, which all who run may read; although to study it as it ought to be studied, you must certainly sit down on mossy stump, ledge of an old bridge, stone-wall, stream-bank, or broomy brae, and gaze, and gaze, and gaze, till woods and sky become like your very self, and your very self like them, at once incorporated together and spiritualized. After a few years' such lessons you may become a planter; and under your hands not only shall the desert blossom like the rose, but murmur like the palm, and if "southward through Eden goes a river large," and your name be Adam, what a sceptic not to believe yourself the first of men, your wife the fairest of her daughters Eve, and your policy Paradise!

Blackwood's Magazine.

THE SWAN SONG OF PARSON AVERY.

[John Greenleaf Whittier, born at Haverhill, Massachusetts, 1808. A member of the Society of Friends, and one of the most distinguished of American poets. His early years were occupied in the labours of his father's farm; he then engaged in newspaper work, and distinguished himself as an earnest student, and as an earnest advocate for the abolition of slavery. In 1840 he removed to Amesbury, Massachusetts, where he continues to reside (1873). Numerous editions of his works have been published in America, and several in England; of these the most important are: *Mogg Megone; The Bridal of Pennacook; Legendary Ballads; Voices of Freedom; Songs of Labour; The Chapel of the Hermits; The Panorama; Home Ballads; Poems and Lyrics; In War Time; Snow-Bound; The Tent on the Beach; National Poems; Among the Hills; Miriam; Poems for Public Occasions; The Pennsylvania Pilgrim*: the foregoing works, with the miscellaneous poems, have been issued in one volume complete by Messrs. Osgood & Co., Boston. Dr. Channing wrote: "His poetry bursts from the soul with the fire and energy of an ancient prophet." H. T. Tuckerman says: "He is a true son of New England; and, beneath the calm fraternal bearing of the Quaker, nurses the imaginative ardour of a devotee, both of nature and of humanity."]

When the reaper's task was ended, and the summer wearing late,
Parson Avery sailed from Newbury, with his wife and children eight,
Dropping down the river-harbour in the shallop "Watch and Wait."

Pleasantly lay the clearings in the mellow summer morn,
With the newly-planted orchards dropping their fruits first-born,
And the homesteads like green islands amid a sea of corn.

Broad meadows reached out seaward the tided creeks between,
And hills rolled wave-like inland, with oaks and walnuts green;—
A fairer home, a goodlier land, his eyes had never seen.

Yet away sailed Parson Avery, away where duty led,
And the voice of God seemed calling, to break the living bread
To the souls of fishers starving on the rocks of Marblehead.

All day they sailed: at nightfall the pleasant land-breeze died,
The blackening sky at midnight its starry lights denied,
And far and low the thunder of tempest prophesied!

Blotted out were all the coast-lines, gone were rock, and wood, and sand;
Grimly anxious stood the skipper with the rudder in his hand,
And questioned of the darkness what was sea and what was land.

And the preacher heard his dear ones, nestled round him, weeping sore:
"Never heed, my little children! Christ is walking on before
To the pleasant land of heaven, where the sea shall be no more."

All at once the great cloud parted, like a curtain drawn aside,
To let down the torch of lightning on the terror far and wide;
·And the thunder and the whirlwind together smote the tide.

There was wailing in the shallop, woman's wail and man's despair,
A crash of breaking timbers on the rocks so sharp and bare,
And, through it all, the murmur of Father Avery's prayer.

From his struggle in the darkness with the wild waves and the blast,
On a rock, where every billow broke above him as it passed,
Alone of all his household, the man of God was cast.

There a comrade heard him praying, in the pause of wave and wind:
"All my own have gone before me, and I linger just behind;
Not for life I ask, but only for the rest thy ransomed find!

"In this night of death I challenge the promise of thy word!—
Let me see the great salvation of which mine ears have heard!—
Let me pass from hence forgiven, through the grace of Christ, our Lord!

"In the baptism of these waters wash white my every sin,
And let me follow up to thee my household and my kin!
Open the sea-gate of thy heaven and let me enter in!"

When the Christian sings his death-song, all the listening heavens draw near,
And the angels, leaning over the walls of crystal, hear
How the notes so faint and broken, swell to music in God's ear.

The ear of God was open to his servant's last request;
As the strong wave swept him downward the sweet hymn upward pressed,
And the soul of Father Avery went, singing, to its rest.

There was wailing on the mainland, from the rocks of Marblehead;
In the stricken church of Newbury the notes of prayer were read;
And long, by board and hearthstone, the living mourned the dead.

And still the fishers outbound, or scudding from the squall,
With grave and reverent faces, the ancient tale recall,
When they see the white waves breaking on the Rock of Avery's Fall!

CALEB WILLIAMS.

[William Godwin, born at Wisbeach, Cambridge-shire, 3d March, 1756; died in London, 7th April, 1836. He laboured for five years as a dissenting minister, and then devoted himself to authorship. His political opinions were of the advanced liberal school, and he openly sympathized with the French revolution at a time when it was dangerous to avow such sympathy. He was not prosecuted, however, and his talents as an author won reputation, and obtained for him in his closing years a lucrative appointment in one of the public offices. His works are: *Political Justice; Life of Geoffrey Chaucer; Life of the Earl of Chatham; On Population*, being an answer to the celebrated theory of Malthus; *History of the Commonwealth of England, &c.* His novels are: *Caleb Williams; St. Leon; Mandeville; Cloudesley;* and *Fleetwood, or the New Man of Feeling.* He wrote a tragedy, *Faulkner,* which was hissed off the stage. *Caleb Williams* achieved extensive popularity. Sir T. N. Talfourd wrote of it: "There is no work of fiction which so rivets the attention—no tragedy which exhibits a struggle more sublime, or sufferings more intense than this; yet to produce the effect no complicated machinery is employed."]

[Falkland, a country gentleman of generous disposition but morbidly sensitive to every wind that might tarnish his personal fame, was publicly insulted and struck by a big boorish squire. Falkland in his frenzy of shame killed the man. Two peasants were charged with the murder and hung. Falkland, a prey to keenest remorse, devoted his life to charity, and to the fostering of that good name for which he had sacrificed so much. His secretary, Caleb Williams—who narrates the events—surprised the secret. Then followed persecution on the part of Falkland, and wild efforts on the part of Williams to escape beyond his influence. At length, worn out and despairing, having been in prison and denounced as a thief, Caleb is resolved to bring matters to a crisis.]

All is over. I have carried into execution my meditated attempt. My situation is totally changed. I now sit down to give an account of it. For several weeks after the completion of this dreadful business, my mind was in too tumultuous a state to permit me to write. I think I shall now be able to arrange my thoughts sufficiently for that purpose. How wondrous, how terrible are the events that have intervened since I was last employed in a similar manner! It is no wonder that my thoughts were solemn, and my mind filled with horrible forebodings!

Having formed my resolution, I set out from Harwich for the metropolitan town of the county in which Mr. Falkland resided. Gines (a detective), I well knew, was in my rear.

That was of no consequence to me. He might wonder at the direction I pursued, but he could not tell with what purpose I pursued it. My design was a secret, carefully locked up in my own breast. It was not without a sentiment of terror that I entered a town which had been the scene of my long imprisonment. I proceeded to the house of the chief magistrate the instant I arrived, that I might give no time to my adversary to counterwork my proceeding.

I told him who I was, and that I was come from a distant part of the kingdom for the purpose of rendering him the medium of a charge of murder against my former patron. My name was already familiar to him. He answered, that he could not take cognizance of my deposition; that I was an object of universal execration in that part of the world; and he was determined upon no account to be the vehicle of my depravity.

I warned him to consider well what he was doing. I called upon him for no favour; I only applied to him in the regular exercise of his function. Would he take upon him to say that he had a right at his pleasure to suppress a charge of this complicated nature? I had to accuse Mr. Falkland of repeated murders. The perpetrator knew that I was in possession of the truth upon the subject; and knowing that, I went perpetually in danger of my life from his malice and revenge. I was resolved to go through with the business, if justice were to be obtained from any court in England. Upon what pretence did he refuse my deposition? I was in every respect a competent witness. I was of age to understand the nature of an oath; I was in my perfect senses; I was untarnished by the verdict of any jury, or the sentence of any judge. His private opinion of my character could not alter the law of the land. I demanded to be confronted with Mr. Falkland, and I was well assured I should substantiate the charge to the satisfaction of the whole world. If he did not think proper to apprehend him upon my single testimony, I should be satisfied if he only sent him notice of the charge, and summoned him to appear.

The magistrate, finding me thus resolute, thought proper a little to lower his tone. He no longer absolutely refused to comply with my requisition, but condescended to expostulate with me. He represented to me Mr. Falkland's health, which had for some years been exceedingly indifferent; his having been once already brought to the most solemn examination upon this charge; the diabolical malice in which alone my proceeding must have originated; and the tenfold ruin it would bring down upon my head. To all these representations my answer was short. "I was determined to go on, and would abide the consequences." A summons was at length granted, and notice sent to Mr. Falkland of the charge preferred against him.

Three days elapsed before any further step could be taken in this business. This interval in no degree contributed to tranquillize my mind. The thought of preferring a capital accusation against, and hastening the death of, such a man as Mr. Falkland, was by no means an opiate to reflection. At one time I commended the action, either as just revenge (for the benevolence of my nature was in a great degree turned to gall), or as necessary self-defence, or as that which, in an impartial and philanthropical estimate, included the smallest evil. At another time I was haunted with doubts. But in spite of these variations of sentiment, I uniformly determined to persist! I felt as if impelled by a tide of unconquerable impulse. The consequences were such as might well appal the stoutest heart. Either the ignominious execution of a man whom I had once so deeply venerated, and whom now I sometimes suspected not to be without his claims to veneration; or a confirmation, perhaps an increase, of the calamities I had so long endured. Yet these I preferred to a state of uncertainty. I desired to know the worst; to put an end to the hope, however faint, which had been so long my torment; and, above all, to exhaust and finish the catalogue of expedients that were at my disposition. My mind was worked up to a state little short of frenzy. My body was in a burning fever with the agitation of my thoughts. When I laid my hand upon my bosom or my head, it seemed to scorch them with the fervency of its heat. I could not sit still for a moment. I panted with incessant desire that the dreadful crisis I had so eagerly invoked were come, and were over.

After an interval of three days, I met Mr. Falkland in the presence of the magistrate to whom I had applied upon the subject. I had only two hours' notice to prepare myself; Mr. Falkland seeming as eager as I to have the question brought to a crisis, and laid at rest for ever. I had an opportunity, before the examination, to learn that Mr. Forester was drawn by some business on an excursion to the continent; and that Collins, whose health when I saw him was in a very precarious state, was at this time confined with an alarming illness. His constitution had been wholly broken by his West Indian expedition. The audience

I met at the house of the magistrate consisted of several gentlemen and others selected for the purpose; the plan being, in some respects, as in the former instance, to find a medium between the suspicious air of a private examination, and the indelicacy, as it was styled, of an examination exposed to the remark of every casual spectator.

I can conceive of no shock greater than that I received from the sight of Mr. Falkland. His appearance on the last occasion on which we met had been haggard, ghost-like, and wild, energy in his gestures, and frenzy in his aspect. It was now the appearance of a corpse. He was brought in in a chair, unable to stand, fatigued and almost destroyed by the journey he had just taken. His visage was colourless; his limbs destitute of motion, almost of life. His head reclined upon his bosom, except that now and then he lifted it up, and opened his eyes with a languid glance; immediately after which he sunk back into his former apparent insensibility. He seemed not to have three hours to live. He had kept his chamber for several weeks; but the summons of the magistrate had been delivered to him at his bedside, his orders respecting letters and written papers being so peremptory that no one dared to disobey them. Upon reading the paper he was seized with a very dangerous fit; but as soon as he recovered he insisted upon being conveyed, with all practical expedition, to the place of appointment. Falkland, in the most helpless state, was still Falkland, firm in command, and capable to extort obedience from every one that approached him.

What a sight was this to me! Till the moment that Falkland was presented to my view my breast was steeled to pity. I thought that I had coolly entered into the reason of the case (passion, in a state of solemn and omnipotent vehemence, always appears to be coolness to him in whom it domineers), and that I had determined impartially and justly. I believed that, if Mr. Falkland were permitted to persist in his schemes, we must both of us be completely wretched. I believed that it was in my power, by the resolution I had formed, to throw my share of this wretchedness from me, and that his could scarcely be increased. It appeared therefore to my mind, to be a mere piece of equity and justice, such as an impartial spectator would desire, that one person should be miserable in preference to two; that one person rather than two should be incapacitated from acting his part, and contributing his share to the general welfare. I thought that in this business I had risen superior to personal considerations, and judged with a total neglect of the suggestions of self-regard. It is true, Mr. Falkland was mortal; but, notwithstanding his apparent decay, he might live long. Ought I to submit to waste the best years of my life in my present wretched situation? He had declared that his reputation should be for ever inviolate; this was his ruling passion, the thought that worked his soul to madness. He would probably therefore leave a legacy of persecution, to be received by me from the hands of Gines, or some other villain equally atrocious, when he should himself be no more. Now or never was the time for me to redeem my future life from endless woe.

But all these fine-spun reasonings vanished before the object that was now presented to me. "Shall I trample upon a man thus dreadfully reduced? Shall I point my animosity against one whom the system of nature has brought down to the grave? Shall I poison, with sounds the most intolerable to his ears, the last moments of a man like Falkland? It is impossible. There must have been some dreadful mistake in the train of argument that persuaded me to be the author of this hateful scene. There must have been a better and more magnanimous remedy to the evils under which I groaned."

It was too late: the mistake I had committed was now gone past all power of recall. Here was Falkland, solemnly brought before a magistrate to answer to a charge of murder. Here I stood, having already declared myself the author of the charge, gravely and sacredly pledged to support it. This was my situation; and, thus situated, I was called upon immediately to act. My whole frame shook. I would eagerly have consented that that moment should have been the last of my existence. I however believed that the conduct now most indispensably incumbent on me was to lay the emotions of my soul naked before my hearers. I looked first at Mr. Falkland, and then at the magistrate and attendants, and then at Mr. Falkland again. My voice was suffocated with agony. I began:—

"Why cannot I recall the last four days of my life? How was it possible for me to be so eager, so obstinate, in a purpose so diabolical? Oh, that I had listened to the expostulations of the magistrate that hears me, or submitted to the well-meant despotism of his authority! Hitherto I have been only miserable; henceforth I shall account myself base! Hitherto, though hardly treated by mankind, I stood acquitted at the bar of my own conscience. I had not filled up the measure of my wretchedness!

"Would it were possible for me to retire from this scene without uttering another word! I would brave the consequences — I would submit to any imputation of cowardice, falsehood, and profligacy, rather than add to the weight of misfortune with which Mr. Falkland is overwhelmed. But the situation, and the demands of Mr. Falkland himself, forbid me. He, in compassion for whose fallen state I would willingly forget every interest of my own, would compel me to accuse, that he might enter upon his justification. I will confess every sentiment of my heart.

"No penitence, no anguish, can expiate the folly and the cruelty of this last act I have perpetrated. But Mr. Falkland well knows—I affirm it in his presence—how unwillingly I have proceeded to this extremity. I have reverenced him; he was worthy of reverence: I have loved him; he was endowed with qualities that partook of divine.

"From the first moment I saw him, I conceived the most ardent admiration. He condescended to encourage me; I attached myself to him with the fulness of my affection. He was unhappy; I exerted myself with youthful curiosity to discover the secret of his woe. This was the beginning of misfortune.

"What shall I say?—He was indeed the murderer of Tyrrel; he suffered the Hawkinses to be executed, knowing that they were innocent, and that he alone was guilty. After successive surmises, after various indiscretions on my part, and indications on his, he at length confided to me at full the fatal tale!

"Mr. Falkland! I most solemnly conjure you to recollect yourself! Did I ever prove myself unworthy of your confidence? The secret was a most painful burden to me; it was the extremest folly that led me unthinkingly to gain possession of it; but I would have died a thousand deaths rather than betray it. It was the jealousy of your own thoughts, and the weight that hung upon your mind, that led you to watch my motions, and to conceive alarm from every particle of my conduct.

"You began in confidence; why did you not continue in confidence? The evil that resulted from my original imprudence would then have been comparatively little. You threatened me: did I then betray you? A word from my lips at that time would have freed me from your threats for ever. I bore them for a considerable period, and at last quitted your service, and threw myself a fugitive upon the world in silence. Why did you not suffer me to depart? You brought me back by stratagem and violence, and wantonly accused me of an enormous felony! Did I then mention a syllable of the murder, the secret of which was in my possession? "Where is the man that has suffered more from the injustice of society than I have done? I was accused of a villany that my heart abhorred. I was sent to jail. I will not enumerate the horrors of my prison, the lightest of which would make the heart of humanity shudder. I looked forward to the gallows! Young, ambitious, fond of life, innocent as the child unborn, I looked forward to the gallows! I believed that one word of resolute accusation against my patron would deliver me, yet I was silent; I armed myself with patience, uncertain whether it were better to accuse or to die. Did this show me a man unworthy to be trusted?

"I determined to break out of prison. With infinite difficulty, and repeated miscarriages, I at length effected my purpose. Instantly a proclamation, with a hundred guineas reward, was issued for apprehending me. I was obliged to take shelter among the refuse of mankind, in the midst of a gang of thieves. I encountered the most imminent peril of my life when I entered this retreat, and when I quitted it. Immediately after, I travelled almost the whole length of the kingdom, in poverty and distress, in hourly danger of being re-taken and manacled like a felon. I would have fled my country; I was prevented. I had recourse to various disguises; I was innocent, and yet was compelled to as many arts and subterfuges as could have been entailed on the worst of villains. In London I was as much harassed and as repeatedly alarmed as I had been in my flight through the country. Did all these persecutions persuade me to put an end to my silence? No: I suffered them with patience and submission; I did not make one attempt to retort them upon their author.

"I fell at last into the hands of the miscreants that are nourished with human blood. In this terrible situation I for the first time attempted, by turning informer, to throw the weight from myself. Happily for me, the London magistrate listened to my tale with insolent contempt.

"I soon, and long, repented of my rashness, and rejoiced in my miscarriage.

"I acknowledge that, in various ways, Mr. Falkland showed humanity towards me during this period. He would have prevented my going to prison at first; he contributed towards my subsistence during my detention; he had no share in the pursuit that had been set on foot against me; he at length procured my dis-

charge, when brought forward for trial. But a great part of his forbearance was unknown to me; I supposed him to be my unrelenting pursuer. I could not forget that, whoever heaped calamities on me in the sequel, they all originated in his forged accusation.

"The prosecution against me for felony was now at an end. Why were not my sufferings permitted to terminate then, and I allowed to hide my weary head in some obscure yet tranquil retreat? Had I not sufficiently proved my constancy and fidelity? Would not a compromise in this situation have been most wise and most secure? But the restless and jealous anxiety of Mr. Falkland would not permit him to repose the least atom of confidence. The only compromise that he proposed was that, with my own hand, I should sign myself a villain. I refused this proposal, and have ever since been driven from place to place, deprived of peace, of honest fame, even of bread. For a long time I persisted in the resolution that no emergency should convert me into the assailant. In an evil hour I at last listened to my resentment and impatience, and the hateful mistake into which I fell has produced the present scene.

"I now see that mistake in all its enormity. I am sure that if I had opened my heart to Mr. Falkland, if I had told to him privately the tale that I have now been telling, he could not have resisted my reasonable demand. After all his precautions, he must ultimately have depended upon my forbearance. Could he be sure that, if I were at last worked up to disclose everything I knew, and to enforce it with all the energy I could exert, I should obtain no credit? If he must in every case be at my mercy, in which mode ought he to have sought his safety, in conciliation, or in inexorable cruelty?

"Mr. Falkland is of a noble nature. Yes; in spite of the catastrophe of Tyrrel, of the miserable end of the Hawkinses, and of all that I have myself suffered, I affirm that he has qualities of the most admirable kind. It is therefore impossible that he could have resisted a frank and fervent expostulation, the frankness and the fervour in which the whole soul is poured out. I despaired, while it was yet time to have made the just experiment; but my despair was criminal, was treason against the sovereignty of truth.

"I have told a plain and unadulterated tale. I came hither to curse, but I remain to bless. I came to accuse, but am compelled to applaud. I proclaim to all the world, that Mr. Falkland is a man worthy of affection and kindness, and that I am myself the basest and most odious of mankind! Never will I forgive myself the iniquity of this day. The memory will always haunt me, and embitter every hour of my existence. In thus acting I have been a murderer —a cool, deliberate, unfeeling murderer.—I have said what my accursed precipitation has obliged me to say. Do with me as you please! I ask no favour. Death would be a kindness compared to what I feel!"

Such were the accents dictated by my remorse. I poured them out with uncontrollable impetuosity; for my heart was pierced, and I was compelled to give vent to its anguish. Every one that heard me was petrified with astonishment. Every one that heard me was melted into tears. They could not resist the ardour with which I praised the great qualities of Falkland; they manifested their sympathy in the tokens of my penitence.

How shall I describe the feelings of this unfortunate man? Before I began he seemed sunk and debilitated, incapable of any strenuous impression. When I mentioned the murder I could perceive in him an involuntary shuddering, though it was counteracted partly by the feebleness of his frame, and partly by the energy of his mind. This was an allegation he expected, and he had endeavoured to prepare himself for it. But there was much of what I said which he had had no previous conception. When I expressed the anguish of my mind, he seemed at first startled and alarmed, lest this should be a new expedient to gain credit to my tale. His indignation against me was great for having retained all my resentment towards him thus, as it might be, to the last hour of his existence. It was increased when he discovered me, as he supposed, using a pretence of liberality and sentiment to give new edge to my hostility. But as I went on he could no longer resist. He saw my sincerity; he was penetrated with my grief and compunction. He rose from his seat, supported by the attendants, and—to my infinite astonishment—threw himself into my arms!

"Williams," said he, "you have conquered! I see too late the greatness and elevation of your mind. I confess that it is to my fault and not yours—that it is to the excess of jealousy that was ever burning in my bosom that I owe my ruin. I could have resisted any plan of malicious accusation you might have brought against me. But I see that the artless and manly story you have told has carried conviction to every hearer. All my prospects are concluded. All that I most ardently desired is for ever frustrated. I have spent a life of the basest cruelty to cover one act of

momentary vice, and to protect myself against the prejudices of my species. I stand now completely detected. My name will be consecrated to infamy, while your heroism, your patience, and your virtues will be for ever admired. You have inflicted on me the most fatal of all mischiefs; but I bless the hand that wounds me. And now,"—turning to the magistrate—"and now, do with me as you please. I am prepared to suffer all the vengeance of the law. You cannot inflict on me more than I deserve. You cannot hate me more than I hate myself. I am the most execrable of all villains. I have for many years (I know not how long) dragged on a miserable existence in insupportable pain. I am at last, in recompense for all my labours and my crimes, dismissed from it with the disappointment of my only remaining hope—the destruction of that for the sake of which alone I consented to exist. It was worthy of such a life, that it should continue just long enough to witness this final overthrow. If however you wish to punish me, you must be speedy in your justice; for, as reputation was the blood that warmed my heart, so I feel that death and infamy must seize me together."

I record the praises bestowed on me by Falkland, not because I deserved them, but because they serve to aggravate the baseness of my cruelty. He survived this dreadful scene but three days. I have been his murderer. It was fit that he should praise my patience, who has fallen a victim, life and fame, to my precipitation! It would have been merciful in comparison if I had planted a dagger in his heart. He would have thanked me for my kindness. But, atrocious, execrable wretch that I have been! I wantonly inflicted on him an anguish a thousand times worse than death. Meanwhile I endure the penalty of my crime. His figure is ever in imagination before me. Waking or sleeping, I still behold him. He seems mildly to expostulate with me for my unfeeling behaviour. I live the devoted victim of conscious reproach. Alas! I am the same Caleb Williams that, so short a time ago, boasted that, however great were the calamities I endured, I was still innocent.

Such has been the result of a project I formed for delivering myself from the evil that had so long attended me. I thought that, if Falkland were dead, I should return once again to all that makes life worth possessing. I thought that, if the guilt of Falkland were established, fortune and the world would smile upon my efforts. Both these events are accomplished; and it is now only that I am truly miserable.

GOD'S JUDGMENT ON A BISHOP.

BY ROBERT SOUTHEY.

Here followeth the history of HATTO, Archbishop of Mentz.

It happened in the year 914 that there was an exceeding great famine in Germany, at what time Otho, surnamed the Great, was emperor, and one Hatto, once Abbot of Fulda, was Archbishop of Mentz, of the bishops after Crescens and Crescentius the two-and-thirtieth, of the archbishops after St. Bonifacius the thirteenth. This Hatto, in the time of this great famine aforementioned, when he saw the poor people of the country exceedingly oppressed with famine, assembled a great company of them together into a barn, and, like a most accursed and merciless caitiff, burned up those poor innocent souls, that were so far from doubting any such matter, that they rather hoped to receive some comfort and relief at his hands. The reason that moved the prelate to commit that execrable impiety was, because he thought the famine would the sooner cease if those unprofitable beggars, that consumed more bread than they were worthy to eat, were despatched out of the world. For he said that those poor folks were like to mice, that were good for nothing but to devour corn. But God Almighty, the just avenger of the poor folks' quarrel, did not long suffer this heinous tyranny, this most detestable fact, unpunished. For he mustered up an army of mice against the archbishop, and sent them to persecute him as his furious Alastors, so that they afflicted him both day and night, and would not suffer him to take his rest in any place. Whereupon the prelate, thinking that he should be secure from the injury of mice if he were in a certain tower, that standeth in the Rhine near to the town, betook himself into the said tower as to a safe refuge and sanctuary from his enemies, and locked himself in. But the innumerable troops of mice chased him continually very eagerly, and swam unto him upon the top of the water to execute the just judgment of God, and so at last he was most miserably devoured by those silly creatures; who pursued him with such bitter hostility, that it is recorded they scraped and gnawed his very name from the walls and tapestry wherein it was written, after they had so cruelly devoured his body. Wherefore the tower wherein he was eaten up by the mice is shown to this day, for a perpetual monument to all succeeding ages of the barbarous and inhuman tyranny of this impious prelate, being situate in a little green island in the midst of the Rhine, near to the town of Bing,[1] and is commonly called in the German tongue, the MOWSE-TURN.— CORYAT's *Crudities*, p. 571, 572.

Other authors who record this tale say that the bishop was eaten by rats.

The summer and autumn had been so wet,
That in winter the corn was growing yet;
'Twas a piteous sight to see all around
The grain lie rotting on the ground.

Every day the starving poor
Crowded around Bishop Hatto's door,
For he had a plentiful last-year's store,
And all the neighbourhood could tell,
His granaries were furnish'd well.

[1] *Hodie* Bingen.

At last Bishop Hatto appointed a day,
To quiet the poor without delay;
He bade them to his great barn repair,
And they should have food for the winter there.

Rejoiced such tidings good to hear,
The poor folk flock'd from far and near;
The great barn was full as it could hold
Of women and children, and young and old.

Then when he saw it could hold no more,
Bishop Hatto he made fast the door;
And while for mercy on Christ they call,
He set fire to the barn and burned them all.

"I' faith 'tis an excellent bonfire!" quoth he,
"And the country is greatly obliged to me,
For ridding it in these times forlorn
Of rats that only consume the corn."

So then to his palace returned he,
And he sat down to supper merrily,
And he slept that night like an innocent man,
But Bishop Hatto never slept again.

In the morning as he entered the hall
Where his picture hung against the wall,
A sweat like death all over him came,
For the rats had eaten it out of the frame.

As he look'd there came a man from his farm,
He had a countenance white with alarm,
"My lord, I open'd your granaries this morn,
And the rats had eaten all your corn."

Another came running presently,
And he was as pale as pale could be,
"Fly! my lord bishop, fly," quoth he,
"Ten thousand rats are coming this way,—
The Lord forgive you for yesterday."

"I'll go to my tower on the Rhine," replied he,
"'Tis the safest place in Germany,
The walls are high and the shores are steep,
And the stream is strong and the water deep."

Bishop Hatto fearfully hastened away,
And he cross'd the Rhine without delay,
And reach'd his tower, and barr'd with care
All the windows, doors, and loop holes there.

He laid him down and closed his eyes;—
But soon a scream made him arise,
He started and saw two eyes of flame
On his pillow from whence the screaming came.

He listen'd and look'd;—it was only the cat:
But the bishop he grew more fearful for that,
For she was screaming, mad with fear
At the army of rats that were drawing near.

For they have swum over the river so deep,
And they have climb'd the shores so steep,

And now by thousands up they crawl
To the holes and windows in the wall.

Down on his knees the bishop fell,
And faster and faster his beads did he tell,
As louder and louder drawing near
The saw of their teeth without he could hear

And in at the windows, and in at the door,
And through the walls by thousands they pour,
And down from the ceiling and up through the floor,
From the right and the left, from behind and before,
From within and without, from above and below,
And all at once to the bishop they go.

They have whetted their teeth against the stones,
And now they pick the bishop's bones,
They gnaw'd the flesh from every limb,
For they were sent to do judgment on him.

LADY BETTY'S POCKET-BOOK.

[R. Sullivan, a miscellaneous writer for the annuals and magazines between 1825–35. He was the author of *The Lovers' Quarrels*.]

I passed my five-and-twentieth birthday at Oakenshade. Sweet sentimental age! Dear, deeply-regretted place. Oakenshade is the fairest child of Father Thames, from Gloucestershire to Blackwall. She is the very queen of cottages, for she has fourteen best bed-rooms, and stabling for a squadron. Her trees are the finest in Europe, and her inhabitants the fairest in the world. Her old mistress is the Lady Bountiful of the country, and her young mistresses are its pride. Lady Barbara is black-eyed and hyacinthine, Lady Betty blue-eyed and Madonna-like.

In situations of this kind it is absolutely necessary for a man to fall in love, and in due compliance with the established custom, I fell in love both with Lady Betty and Lady Barbara. Now Barbara was a soft-hearted, high-minded rogue, and pretended, as I thought, not to care for me, that she might not interfere with the interests of her sister; and Betty was a reckless, giddy-witted baggage, who cared for nobody and nothing upon earth, except the delightful occupation of doing what she pleased. Accordingly, we became the Romeo and Juliet of the place, excepting that I never could sigh, and she never could apostrophize. Nevertheless, we loved terribly. Oh, what a time was that! I will just give a sample of a day.—We rose at seven (it was July), and wandered amongst moss roses, velvet lawns, and seques-

tered summer-houses, till the lady-mother summoned us to the breakfast-table. I know not how it was, but the footman on those occasions always found dear Barbara absent on a butterfly chase, gathering flowers, or feeding her pet robin, and Betty and myself on a sweet honeysuckle seat just large enough to hold two, and hidden round a happy corner as snug as a bird's nest. The moment the villain came within hearing, I used to begin, in an audible voice, to discourse upon the beauties of nature, and Betty allowed me to be the best moral philosopher of the age. After breakfast we used to retire to the young ladies' study, in which blest retreat I filled some hundred pages of their albums, whilst Betty looked over my shoulder, and Barbara hammered with all her might upon the grand piano, that we might not be afraid to talk. I was acknowledged to be the prince of poets and riddle-mongers, and in the graphic art I was a prodigy perfectly unrivalled. *Sans doute*, I was a little over-rated. My riddles were so plain, and my metaphors so puzzling—and then my trees were like mountains, and my men were like monkeys. But love had such penetrating optics! Lady Betty could perceive beauties to which the rest of the world were perfectly blind. Then followed our "equestrian exercises." Now Barbara was a good horsewoman, and Betty was a bad one; consequently, Barbara rode a pony, and Betty rode a donkey; consequently, Barbara rode a mile before, and Betty rode a mile behind; and consequently, it was absolutely necessary for me to keep fast hold of Betty's hand, for fear she should tumble off. Thus did we journey through wood and through valley, by flood and by field, through the loveliest and most love-making scenes that ever figured in rhyme or on canvas. The trees never looked so green, the flowers never smelt so sweetly, and the exercise and the fears of her high-mettled palfrey gave my companion a blush which is quite beyond the reach of simile. Of course, we always lost ourselves, and trusted to Barbara to guide us home, which she generally did by the most circuitous routes she could find. At dinner the lady-mother would inquire what had become of us, but none of us could tell where we had been, excepting Barbara.

"Why Betty, my dear, you understood our geography well enough when you were guide to our good old friend, the general!"

Ah, but Betty found it was quite a different thing to be guide to her good young friend, the captain; and her explanation was generally a zigzag sort of performance, which outdid the best riddle of her album. It was the custom of the lady-mother to take a nap after dinner, and having a due regard for her, we always left her to this enjoyment as soon as possible. Sometimes we floated in a little skiff down the broad and tranquil river, which, kindled by the setting sun, moved onward like a stream of fire, tuning our voices to glees and duets, till the nightingales themselves were astonished. Oh, the witchery of bright eyes at sunset and music on the water! Sometimes we stole through the cavernous recesses of the old oak wood, conjuring up fawns and satyrs at every step, and sending Barbara to detect the deceptions, and play at hide and seek with us. At last our mistress the moon would open her eye and warn us home, where, on the little study sofa, we watched her progress, and repeated sweet poesy. Many a time did I long to break the footman's head when he brought the lights and announced the tea. The lady-mother never slept after this, and the business of the day was ended.

Things went on in this way for a week or ten days, and Lady Betty appeared to have less spirits, and a more serious and languid air than heretofore. There was now nothing hoydenish in her behaviour, and instead of the upper lip curling with scorn, the under one was dropping with sentiment. Her voice was not so loud, and fell in a gentler cadence, and the Madonna braid was festooned with a more exquisite grace. When I besought her to let me hear the subject of her thoughts, the little budget was always of so mournful a description, that I could not choose but use my tenderest mode of comforting her. She had, she knew not why, become more serious. She supposed it was because she was growing older, she hoped it was because she was growing better. In fine, she had determined to mend her life, and appointed me master of the ceremonies to her conscience, which, sooth to say, had been in a woful state of anarchy.

I could not, of course, have any doubt that my sweet society had been the cause of this metamorphosis, and I congratulated myself with fervency. She was becoming the very pattern for a wife, and I contemplated in her the partner of my declining years, the soother of my cares, the mother of my children. It was cruel to postpone my declaration, but though I have no Scotch blood in my veins, I was always a little given to caution. Lady Betty had been a sad madcap, and might not this be a mere freak of the moment? Besides there was a charm about the very uncertainty which a declared lover has no idea of, so I de-

termined to observe, and act with deliberation.

Our pastimes continued the same as before, and our interchanges of kindness increased. Amongst other things, Lady Betty signalized me by a purse and pencil case, and in return was troubled with an extreme longing for a lilac and gold pocket-book, in which I was sometimes rash enough to note down my fugitive thoughts. It had been given me by—no matter whom—there was nothing on earth that I would not have sacrificed to Lady Betty. She received it in both her hands, pressed it to her bosom, and promised faithfully that she would pursue the plan I had adopted in it; casting up her delinquencies at the end of the year to see what might be amended.

Alas! the pinnacle of happiness is but a sorry resting-place, from which the chief occupation of mankind is to push one another headlong! Of my own case I have particular reason to complain, for I was precipitated from the midst of my burning, palpitating existence by the veriest blockhead in life. He came upon us like the simoom, devastating every green spot in his progress, and leaving our hearts a blank. In short, he was a spark of quality, who drove four bloods, and cut his own coats. His visage was dangerously dissipated and cadaverous, his figure as taper as a fishing-rod, and his manner had a *je ne sais quoi* of languid impertinence which was a great deal too overwhelming. Altogether, he was a gallant whose incursion would have caused me very considerable uneasiness, had I not felt secure that my mistress was already won.

I shall never forget the bustle which was occasioned by the arrival of this worthy. He was some sort of connection of the lady-mother, thought himself privileged to come without invitation, and declared his intention of remaining till he was tired. He ordered the servants about, and gave directions for his accommodation precisely as if he had been at home, and scarcely deigned to tender his forefinger to the ladies, till he had made himself perfectly comfortable. When I was introduced from the back-ground, from which I had been scowling with indignation and amazement, he regarded my commonplace appearance with careless contempt; made me a bow as cold as if it had come from Lapland, and, in return, received one from the North Pole. I considered that he was usurping all my rights in the establishment; perfect freedom with Betty and Barbara were a violation of my private property, and I even grudged him his jokes with the lady-mother. We were foes from first sight.

Lady Betty saw how the spirit was working within me, and hastened to prevent its effervescence. She gave me one of her overpowering looks, and besought me to assist her in being civil to him; for, in truth, the attentions of common politeness had already completely exhausted her. I was quite charmed with the vexation she felt at his intrusion, and loved her a thousand times better because she detested him. His visit, indeed, had such an effect upon her, that before the day was over she complained to me, in confidence, of being seriously unwell.

From this time the whole tenor of our amusements was revolutionized. Lady Betty's illness was not fancied; she was too weak to ride her donkey, too qualmish to go inside the barouche, which was turned out every day to keep the bloods in wind, and nothing agreed with her delicate health but being mounted on the box beside Lord S——. The evenings passed off as heavily as the mornings. Lady Barbara used to ask me to take the usual stroll with her; and Lady Betty, being afraid to venture upon the damp grass, was again left to the mercy of Lord S——, to whom walking was a low-lifed amusement, for which he had no taste. The lady-mother, as usual, had her sleeping-fits; and when we returned, we invariably found things in disorder. The candles had not been lighted, the tea-things had not been brought in, and Lord S—— had turned sulky with his bottle, and was sitting quietly with Lady Betty. I felt for her more than I can express, and could not, for the life of me, conceive where she picked up patience to be civil to him. She even affected to be delighted with his conversation, and her good breeding was beyond all praise.

With such an example of endurance before me, and the pacific promises which I had made, I could not avoid wearing a benevolent aspect. Indeed, though the enemy had effectually cut off the direct communication of sentiment between us, I was not altogether without my triumphs and secret satisfactions. The general outline which I have given was occasionally intersected with little episodes which were quite charming. For instance, Lady Betty used constantly to employ me upon errands to her mother, who was usually absent in her private room, manufacturing candle and flannel petticoats for the workhouse. When I returned, she would despatch me to her sister, who was requiring my advice upon her drawing, in the study; and thus Lord S—— could not fail to observe the familiar terms we were upon, and that we perfectly understood each other.

What gave me more pleasure than all was, that he must see I had no fears of leaving my liege lady alone with him, which must have galled him to the quick. When she had no other means of showing her devotion to me, she would produce the lilac pocket-book, and pursue the work of amendment which I had suggested to her; indeed, this was done with a regularity which, when I considered her former hair-brained character, I knew could only be sustained by the most ardent attachment. My pride and my passion increased daily.

At last, by a happy reverse of fortune, I was led to look for the termination of my trials. Lord S—— was a personage of too great importance to the nation to be permitted to enjoy his own peace and quiet, and his bilious visage was required to countenance mighty concerns in other parts. His dressing case was packed up, and the barouche was ordered to the door, but poor Lady Betty was still doomed to be a sufferer; she was, somehow or other, hampered with an engagement to ride with him as far as the village, in order to pay a visit for her mother to the charity-school, and I saw her borne off, the most bewitching example of patience and resignation. I did not offer to accompany them, for I thought it would have looked like jealousy; but engaged, in answer to a sweetly-whispered invitation, to meet her in her walk back.

When I returned to the drawing-room, Barbara and the lady-mother were absent on their usual occupations, and I sat down for a moment of happy reflection on the delights which awaited me; my heart was tingling with anticipation, and every thought was poetry. A scrap of paper lay upon the table, and was presently enriched with a sonnet on each side, which I had the vanity to think were quite good enough to be transferred to Lady Betty's most beloved and lilac pocket-book. I raised my eyes, and lo! in the bustle of parting with Lord S——, she had forgotten to deposit it in her desk. What an agreeable surprise it would be for her to find how I had been employed! How fondly would she thank me for such a delicate mode of showing my attention! The sonnets were written in my best hand, and I was about to close the book, when I was struck with the extreme beauty of Lady Betty's caligraphy. Might I venture to peruse a page or so, and enjoy the luxury of knowing her private thoughts of me? Nay, was it not evidently a sweet little finesse to teach me the secrets of her heart, and should I not mortify her exceedingly if I neglected to take advantage of it? This reflection was quite sufficient, and I commenced the chronicle of her innocent cogitations forthwith. It began with noting the day of the month on which I had presented the gift, and stated prettily the plan of improvement which I had suggested. The very first memorandum contained her reasons for loving her dear M——. I pressed the book to my lips, and proceeded to

"REASON THE FIRST.

"A good temper is better in a companion than a great wit. If dear M—— is deficient in the latter it is not his fault, and his excellence in the former makes ample amends."

How! As much as to say I am a good-natured fool. Was there no other construction? No error of the press? None. The context assured me that I was not mistaken.

"REASON THE SECOND.

"Personal beauty is not requisite in a husband; and if he is a little mistaken in his estimate of himself in this respect, it will make him happy, and save me the trouble of labouring for that end."

Conceited and ill-favoured! My head began to swim.

"REASON THE THIRD.

"I have been told that very passionate attachments between married people are productive of much disquietude and jealousy. The temperate regard, therefore, which I feel for dear M—— argues well for the serenity of our lives.—Heigh-ho!"

Furies!

"REASON THE FOURTH.

"I have sometimes doubted whether this temperate regard be really love; but, as pity is next a-kin to love, and I pity him on so many points, I think I cannot be mistaken."

Pity!

"REASON THE FIFTH.

"I pity him, because it is necessary that I should place him on the shelf during Lord S——'s visit, for fear S—— should be discouraged by appearances, and not make the declaration which I have been so long expecting."

Place me on the shelf!!

"REASON THE SIXTH.

"I pity him, because if S—— really comes forward, I shall be obliged to submit poor dear M—— to the mortification of a dismissal."

!!!

"REASON THE SEVENTH.

"I pity him, because he is so extremely kind and obliging in quitting the room whenever his presence becomes troublesome."

!!!!

"REASON THE EIGHTH.

"I pity him, because his great confidence in my affection makes him appear so ridiculous, and because S—— laughs at him."

!!!!!

"REASON THE NINTH.

"I pity him, because, if I do ultimately marry him, S—— will tell everybody that it is only because I could not obtain the barouche and four.—Heigh—heigh-ho."

!!!!!!

"REASON THE TENTH.

"I pity him, because he has so kindly consented to meet me on my return from the charity-school, without once suspecting that I go to give S—— a last opportunity. He is really a very good young man.—Ah, well-a-day!"—

And ah, well-a-day!!!!!!! &c. &c.—Let no man henceforth endeavour to enjoy the luxury of his mistress's secret thoughts.

I closed the book and walked to the window. The river flowed temptingly beneath. Would it be best to drown myself or shoot myself? Or would it be best to take horse after the barouche, and shoot Lord S——? I was puzzled with the alternatives. It was absolutely necessary that *somebody* should be put to death, but my confusion was too great to decide upon the victim.

At this critical juncture of my fate, when I was wavering between the gallows and "a grave where four roads meet," Lady Barbara came dancing in, to request my assistance upon her drawing. She was petrified at my suicidal appearance, and, indeed, seemed in doubt whether the act of immolation had not been already effected. Her fears rushed in crimson to her cheeks, as she inquired the cause of my disorder; and her beauty, and the interesting concern she expressed, cast an entire new light upon me. I would be revenged on Lady Betty in a manner far more cutting than either drowning or shooting. Barbara was the prettiest by far—Barbara was the best by infinity. Sweet, simple, gentle Barbara! How generously had she sacrificed her feelings, and given me up to her sister! How happy was I to have it in my power to reward her for it. *She* now should be the partner of my declining years, the soother of my cares, the mother of my children; and as for Lady Betty, I renounced her. I found that my heart had all along been Barbara's, and I congratulated myself upon being brought to my senses.

The business was soon opened, and we were all eloquence and blushes. I expressed my warm admiration of her self-denial and affection for her sister; hinted at my knowledge of her sentiments for myself; explained every particular of my passion, prospects, and genealogy, fixed upon our place of residence, and allotted her pin-money. It was now Barbara's turn.

"She was confused—she was distressed—she feared—she hoped—she knew not what to say." She paused for composure, and I waited in an ecstasy.

"Why," I exclaimed, "why will you hesitate, my own, my gentle Barbara? Let me not lose one delicious word of this heavenly confession." Barbara regained her courage.

"Indeed, then—indeed, and indeed—I have been engaged to my cousin for more than three years!"

This was a stroke upon which I had never once calculated, and my astonishment was awful. Barbara then was not in love with me after all, and the concern which I had felt for her blighted affections was altogether erroneous! I had made the proposal to be revenged on Lady Betty, and my disappointment had completely turned the tables upon me. Instead of bringing her to shame, I was ashamed of myself, and my mortification made me feel as though she had heaped a new injury upon me. What I said upon the occasion I cannot precisely remember, and if I could, I doubt whether my reader would be able to make head or tail of it. I concluded, however, with my compliments to the lady-mother, and an urgent necessity to decamp. Barbara knew not whether she ought to laugh or to cry. I gave her no time to recover herself, for Betty would be home presently, and it was material to be off before they had an opportunity of comparing notes. In three minutes I was mounted on my horse, and again ruminating on the various advantages of hanging, drowning, and shooting.

I thought I had got clear off; but at the end of the lawn I was fated to encounter the bewitching smile of Lady Betty, on her return from the village. Her words were brimming with tenderness, and her delight to be rid of that odious Lord S—— was beyond measure. It had quite restored her health; she was able to recommence her rides, and would order the donkey to be got ready immediately.

So then, it appeared that the drive to the charity school had not answered the purpose after all, and I was to be the locum tenens of Lady Betty's affections till the arrival of a new acquaintance. I know not whether my constitution is different from that of other people. A pretty face is certainly a terrible criterion of a man's resolution; but for the honour of manhood I contrived for once to be superior to its fascinations. To adhere strictly to truth, I must confess, however humiliating the confession may be, that this dignified behaviour was very materially sustained by the transactions with Lady Barbara, for the consequence of whose communications there was no answering. I declined the donkey ride, looked a most explanatory look of reproach, and declared my necessity of returning to town. Lady Betty was amazed—remonstrated—entreated—looked like an angel—and finally put her handkerchief to her eyes. There was no standing this.

"I go," said I, "I go, because it is proper to quit whenever my presence becomes troublesome—I will not oblige you to put me on the shelf—I will not be too encroaching upon your temperate regard—Heigh—heigh-ho!"

With that I plunged my spurs into my steed, and vanished at full gallop.

It was long before I heard anything more of Oakenshade or its inhabitants. In the middle of the following December I received a piece of wedding-cake from the gentle Barbara, and in the same packet a letter from Lady Betty. She had written instead of mamma, who was troubled with a gouty affection in the hand. She spoke much (and I have no doubt sincerely) of the cruel separation from her sister. Touched feelingly upon the happiness of the time I had spent at Oakenshade, and trusted she might venture to claim a week of me at Christmas. She was truly sorry that she had no inducement to hold out beyond the satisfaction of communicating happiness, which she knew was always a paramount feeling with me. She was all alone, and wretched in the long evenings when mamma went to sleep: and reverted plaintively and prettily to the little study and the ghost stories. As for the lilac pocket-book, she had cast up her follies and misdemeanours, and found the total, even before the end of the year, so full of shame and repentance that she had incontinently thrown it into the fire, trusting to my kindness to give her another with fresh advice. Dear Lady Betty! my resentment was long gone by —I had long felt a conviction that her little follies were blameless, and not at all uncommon;

and I vow, that had her happiness depended upon me, I would have done anything to insure it. I was obliged, however, to send an excuse for the present, for I had only been married a week.

THE INVITATION.

[Cornelius Webbe, miscellaneous writer, and author of *Posthumous Papers of a Person about Town; Lyric Leaves: Glances at Life in City and Suburb;* &c. He was for many years proof-reader of the *Quarterly Review.* "He has feeling and fancy—an eye and a heart for nature."—*Blackwood's Magazine.*]

Mary, when the sun is down,
Steal unnoticed from the town,
Through the dew of daisied green,
Like a shadow dimly seen,
Unto where the lilied-rill
Winds around the woody hill,—
Giving to thy lover's arms,
Truth, and youth, and sacred charms.

When the night doth darken eve,
Thou thy bower mayst safely leave:—
Thou canst have no dread of night,
Having thoughts as pure as light!
Vice may then not be a-bed,
But the wicked have a dread
Of a chaste-eyed maiden's frown,
That keeps ruder passions down.

When the bat hath tired his wing,
And the cricket ceased to sing,
And the sad, sweet nightingale
'Gins to tell her tender tale;
Steal thy path across the green,
Like a shadow dimly seen,
Or a late-returning dove
Winging lonely to her love.

When the first star of the night
Beams with rays of ruddy light,
(Like the lashes of thine eyes
Startling sleep, that sweetly lies
As the bee upon his bed,
Nestling by a blue-bell's head,)
Steal thy way through green and grove,
Silent as the moon doth move.

When the dew is on our feet,
Then the woodland walk is sweet:
When no eye but Heaven's doth see,
Then 'tis sweet with thee to be:
We have passed long hours alone,
Overseen and heard by none;
And may wile a many more,
Till our life, not love, be o'er.

CHANGEABLE CHARLIE:

THE DOMINIE'S TALE.

[Andrew Picken, born in Paisley, 1788; died in London, 23d November, 1833. After various experiences in trade in the West Indies, in Ireland, Glasgow, and Liverpool, he settled in London as a professional author in 1826. His works obtained a fair portion of success, and he was rapidly winning a good position in literature when he was suddenly stricken by apoplexy. He wrote: *Tales and Sketches of the West of Scotland,* in which first appeared, *Mary Ogilvie; The Sectarian, or The Church and the Meeting House,* a novel; *The Dominie's Legacy,* a collection of tales, from which we quote; *Travels and Researches of English Missionaries; The Club Book,* a collection of tales to which G. P. R. James, D. M. Moir, John Galt, Tyrone Power, James Hogg, Allan Cunningham, and William Jerdan contributed; *The Canadas,* compiled from memoranda supplied by Galt; *Waltham,* a romance; and *The Black Watch,* a novel completed shortly before the author's death, and containing the history of the 42d Regiment.]

Really when I come to think on the various fortunes of my pupils after they went from under my charge, I am as much diverted and moved to laughter at the ways and proceedings that were followed out by some, as I am sobered into sorrow at the sad and pathetic fate that befell several others. If I could say conscientiously, that the wisest man always turned to be the happiest or the most fortunate, greatly should I be gratified. But truly, it hath never consisted with the little philosophy that I have gathered in going about the world, to deal much in general rules or specified conclusions; and I have often from my observations been rather tempted to say, with the proverb-making king, that folly is in some cases better than wisdom, and lightness of heart more to be envied than sobriety and sense.

It was in the early part of my life, when I was yet in the apprenticeship of my fortune, that I had the teaching of a pleasant boy, whose name was Charlie Cheap. Charlie's father was a weel-specked witless body, who kept a shop in the largest village near; and having made money by mere want of sense, and selling of the jigs and jags of a country town, was called by the name of John Cheap the Chapman, after the classical story of that personage with which we used to be diverted when we were children: so the old man, seeing indications of genius in his son, sent the lad to me to finish his education.

There was not a better-liked boy in the whole school than Charlie Cheap; for though he never would learn anything effectually, and was the head and ringleader of every trick that was hatched, he had such a laughing happy disposition, and took his very punishment so good-humouredly, that it went to my heart to think of chastising him; and as for the fool's cap and the broom sceptre, they were no punishment to him, for he never seemed better pleased than when he had them on: and when mounted thus on the top of the black stool, he seemed so delighted, and pulled such faces at the rest of the boys, that no mortal flesh could stand to their gravity near him, and my seat of learning was in danger of becoming a perfect hobbleshew of diversion. How to master this was past my power. But Charlie's versatility ended it by his own will, and before he was half learned in his preliminary humanities, his father and he had taken some scheme into their heads, and he was removed from me and sent to the college.

I know not how it was, but for several years I lost sight of Charlie, until I heard that his father was dead, and that he was now a grown man, and was likely to make a great fortune. This news was no surprise to me, for I now began to make the observation, that the greatest fools that I had the honour of preparing for the world most generally became the wealthiest men.

It was one day when on a summer tramp, that entering a decentish town, and looking about at the shop windows, I began to bethink me of the necessity that had befallen upon me, by the tear and wear of the journey, of being at the expense of a new hat, so I entered a magazine of miscellaneous commodities, when who should astonish me in the person of the shopkeeper, but my old pupil, Charlie Cheap. "Merciful me! Charlie," said I, "who would have expected to find you at this trade! I thought you had gone to the college to serve your time for a minister of the gospel."

"Indeed," said Charlie, "that was once the intent, but, in truth, my head got rather confused with the lair and the logic. I had not the least conjugality to the Greek conjugations, and when I came to the Hebrew that is read every word backwards, faith, I could neither read it backwards nor forwards, and fairly stuck, and grew a sticked minister. But I had long begun to see that the minister trade was but a poor business, and that a man might wait for the mustard till the meat was all eaten, and so I just took up a chop like my father before me; and faith, Mr. Dominie, I'm making a fortune."

"Well," said I, "I am really happy to hear it, and I hope, besides that, that you like your employment."

"I'm quite delighted with the chop-keeping, Mr. Balgownie; a very different life from chapping verbs in a cauld college. Besides, I am a respected man in the town; nothing but Mr. Cheap here and Mrs. Cheap there, and ladies coming in at all hours of the day, and bowing and becking to me—and throwing the money to me across the counter;—I would not wonder if they should make me a bailie yet."

"Well, I am really delighted too," said I: "and from my knowledge of bailies, I would not wonder in the least—so good bye, Mr. Cheap. I think this hat looks very well on me."

"Makes you ten years younger, sir—good bye; wish you your health to wear it."

It might be a twelvemonth after that, I was plodding along a country road some ten miles from the forementioned town, when looking over the hedge by my side I saw a team of horses pulling a plough towards me; and my cogitations were disturbed by the yo-ing and yau-ing of the man who followed it. Something struck me that I knew the voice, and when the last of the men came up I discovered, under the plush waistcoat and farmer's bonnet, my old friend Charlie Cheap.

"Soul and conscience!" cried he, thrusting his clay hand through the hedge and grasping mine—"if this is not my old master the dominie!" and truly, he gave me the farmer's gripe, as if my hand had been made of cast metal.

"What are you doing here, Charlie?" said I. "Why are you not minding your shop instead of marching there in the furrows at the plough-tail?"

"Chop," said he, "what chop? Na, na, Dominie, I've gotten a better trade by the hand."

"It cannot be possible, Charlie, that ye've turned farmer?"

"Whether it be possible or no, it is true," said Charlie; "but dinna be standing there whistling through the hedge, but come in by the slap at the corner, and ye shall taste my wife's treacle ale."

"Well really," said I, when I had got down into the farm-house, "this is the most marvellous change."

"No change to speak of," said he; "do ye think I was going to be tied up to haberdrabbery all my days? No, no, I knew I had a genius for farming, the chop-keeping grew flat and unprofitable, a chield from England set up next door to me, so a country customer took a fancy for a town life. I sold him my stock in trade, and he sold me the stock on his farm. He stepped in behind the counter, and I got behind the plough; so here I am, happier than ever; besides, harkie! I am making money fast."

"Are you really? But how do you know that?"

"Can I not count my ten fingers? Have I not figured it on black and white over and over again? There's great profits with management such as mine, that I can assure you, sir."

"But how could you possibly learn farming? That, I believe, is not taught at college."

"Pooh! my friend; I can learn anything. Besides, my wife's mother was a farmer's daughter, and Lizzy herself understands farming already, as if she was reared to it. She makes all the butter, and the children drink all the milk, and we live so happy: birds singing in the morning—cows lowing at night—drinking treacle ale all day; and nothing to do but watch the corn growing. In short, farming is the natural state of man. Adam and Eve were a farmer and his wife, just like me and Lizzy Cheap!"

"But you'll change again shortly, I am afraid, Mr. Cheap!"

"That's impossible, for I've got a nineteen years' lease. I'll grow gray as a farmer. Well, good bye, Dominie. Be sure you give us a call the next time ye pass, and get a drink of our treacle ale."

"Well, really this is the most extraordinary thing," said I to myself, as I walked up the lane from the farm-house. "I shall be curious to ascertain of his going to stick to the farming till he's ruined."

I thought no more of Changeable Charlie for above a year, when, coming towards the same neighbourhood, I resolved to go a short distance out of my way to pay him a visit. My road lay across a clear country stream which winded along a pleasant green valley beneath me; and as I drew near the rustic bridge, my ear caught the lively sound of a waterfall, which murmured from a picturesque spot among opening woods, a little way above the bridge. A little mill-race, with its narrow channel of deep level water, next attracted my notice; and presently after, the regular splash of a water-wheel and the boom of a corn-mill became objects of my meditative observation. The mill looked so quaint and rustic by the stream, the banks were so green and the water so clear, that I was tempted to wander towards it, down from the bridge, just to make the whole a subject of closer observation.

A barefooted girl came forth from the house

and stared in my face, as a Scottish lassie may be supposed to do at a reasonable man. "Can you tell me," said I, willing to make up an excuse for my intrusion, "if this road will lead me to the farm of Longriggs, which is occupied by one Mr. Cheap?" The lassie looked in my face with a thieveless smile, and without answering a word, took a bare-legged race into the mill. Presently, a great lumbering miller came out, like a walking bag of flower from beside the hopper, and I immediately saw he was going to address me.

Never did I see such a snowy man. His miller's hat was inch thick with flour; he whitened the green earth as he walked, the knees of his breeches were loose, and the stockings that hung about his heels would have made a hearty meal for a starving garrison.

"What can the impudent rascal be staring at?" I said, and I began to cast my eyes down on my person, to see if I could find any cause in my own appearance, that the miller and his lassie should thus treat me as a world's wonder.

"Ye were asking I think," he said, "after Charlie Cheap, of the Longriggs?"

"Yes," said I, "but his farm must be some miles from this. Perhaps as you are the miller of the neighbourhood, you can direct me the nearest road to it."

The burley scoundrel first lifted up his eye-winkers, which were clotted with flour, shook out about a pound of it from his bushy whiskers, and then burst into a laugh in my very face as loud as the neighing of a miller's horse.

"Ho, ho, hough!" grinned he, coughing upon me a shower of flour. "Is it possible, Dominie, that ye dinna ken me?" and opening a mouth at least as wide as his own hopper, I began to recognize the exaggerated features of Changeable Charlie.

"Well really," said I, gazing at his grin, and the hills of flour that arose from his cheeks, —"really this beats everything! and so, Charlie, ye're now turned into a miller."

"As sure's a gun!" said he. "Lord bless your soul, Dominie! do you think I could bear to spread dung and turn up dirt all my life? no! I have a soul above that. Besides, your miller is a man in power. He is an aristocrat over the farmers, and with the power has its privileges too, for he takes a multre out of every man's sack, and levies his revenues like a prime minister. No one gets so soon fat as those that live by the labour of others, as you may see; for the landed interest supports me by day, and my water-wheel works for me all night, so if I don't get rich now, the deuce is in it."

"I suppose," said I, following him into the mill, "you are just making a fortune."

"How can I help it?" said he, "making money while I sleep, for I hear the musical click of the hopper in my dreams, and my bairns learn their lessons by the jog of it. I wish every man who has passed a purgatory at college were just as happy as the miller and his wife. Is not that the case, Lizzy?" he added, addressing his better half, who now came forth hung round by children—"as the song goes,"

> "Merry may the maid be that marries the miller,
> For foul day and fair day, he's aye bringing till her—
> His ample hand's in ilk man's pock,
> His mill grinds muckle siller,
> His wife is dressed in silk and lawn,
> For he's aye bringing till her."

"But dear me, Mr. Cheap," said I, "what was it that put you out of the farm, where I thought you were so happy, and making a fortune?"

"I was as happy as a man could be, and making money too, and nothing put me out of the farm, although I was quite glad of the change, but just a penny of fair debt, the which, you know, is a good man's case—and a little argument about the rent. But everything turned out for the best, for Willie Happer, the former miller, just ran awa the same week: I got a dead bargain of the mill, and so I came in to reign in his stead. Am I not a fortunate man?"

"Never was a man so lucky," said I; "but do you really mean to be a waiter on a mill-hopper all your days?"

"As long as wood turns round and water runs; but, Lizzy," he added to his wife, "what are you standing glowering there for, and me like to choke. Gang and fetch us a jug of your best treacle ale."

"It surely cannot be," said I to myself when I had left the mill, "that Changeable Charlie will ever adopt a new profession now, but live and die a miller." I was, however, entirely mistaken in my calculation, as I found before I was two years older, and though I have not time, at this present sitting, to tell the whole of Charlie's story, and have a strong suspicion that my veracity might be put in jeopardy were I to condescend thereto, I am quite ready to take my oath, that after this I found him in not less than five different characters, in all of which he was equally happy and equally certain of making a fortune. Where the mutations of Charlie might have run to, and whether, to speak with a little agreeable stultification, he might not, like another remarkable man, have

exhausted worlds, and then imagined new, it is impossible to predicate, if Fortune had not, in her usual injustice, put an end to his career of change, by leaving his wife Lizzy a considerable legacy.

The last character then that I found Charlie striving to enact, was that of a gentleman—that is, a man who has plenty of money to live upon, and nothing whatever to do. It did not appear, however, that Charlie's happiness was at all improved by this last change; for, besides that, it had taken from him all his private joys, in the *hope* of one day making a fortune, it had raised up a most unexpected enemy, in the shape of old father Time, whom he found it more troublesome and less hopeful to contend with, than all the obstacles that had formerly seemed to stand in his way to the making of an independent fortune.

When the legacy was first showered upon him, however, he seemed as happy under the dispensation as he had been before under any other of his changes. In the hey-day of his joy, he sent for me to witness his felicity, and to give him my advice as to the spending of his money. This invitation I was thoughtless enough to accept, but it was more that I might pick up a little philosophy out of what I should observe, than from any pleasure that I expected, or any good that I was likely to do. When I got to his house I was worried to death by all the fine things I was forced to look at, that had been sent to him from Jamaica, and all that from him and his wife I was forced to hear. I tried to impress him concerning the good that he might do with his money, in reference to many who sorely wanted it; but I found that he had too little feeling himself to understand the feelings of others, and that affliction had never yet driven a nail into his own flesh to open his heart to sympathy. Instead of entering into any rational plans, his wife and he laughed all day at nothing whatever, his children turned the house upside down in their ecstasy at being rich; and, in short, never before had I been so wearied at seeing people happy.

In all this, however, I heard not one single word of thankfulness for this unlooked-for deliverance from constant vicissitude, or one grateful expression to Providence for being so unreasonably kind to this family; while thousands around them struggled incessantly in ill-rewarded industry and unavailing anxiety. So I wound up the story of Changeable Charlie in reflective melancholy; for I had seen so many who would, for any little good fortune, have been most thankful and happy, yet never were

able to attain thereto; and I inclined to the
sombre conclusion, that in this world the wise
and virtuous man was often less fortunate, and
generally less happy, than the fool.

FREELY GIVE.

" Freely ye have received, freely give."—Matthew x. 8.
" It is more blessed to give than to receive."—Acts xx. 35.

Give ! as the morning that flows out of heaven ;
Give ! as the waves when their channel is riven ;
Give ! as the free air and sunshine are given ;
　　Lavishly, utterly, joyfully give :—
Not the waste drops of thy cup overflowing,
Not the faint sparks of thy hearth ever glowing,
Not a pale bud from the June roses blowing ;
　　Give, as He gave thee, who gave thee to live.

Pour out thy love, like the rush of a river,
Wasting its waters, for ever and ever,
Through the burnt sands that reward not the giver ;
　　Silent or songful, thou nearest the sea.
Scatter thy life, as the summer showers pouring !
What if no bird through the pearl-rain is soaring ?
What if no blossom looks upward adoring ?
　　Look to the life that was lavished for thee !

So the wild wind strews its perfumed caresses,
Evil and thankless the desert it blesses,
Bitter the wave that its soft pinion presses,
　　Never it ceaseth to whisper and sing.
What if the hard heart give thorns for thy roses ?
What if on rocks thy tired bosom reposes ?
Sweetest is music with minor keyed closes,
　　Fairest the vines that on ruin will cling.

Almost the day of thy giving is over ;
Ere from the grass dies the bee-haunted clover,
Thou wilt have vanished from friend and from lover ;
　　What shall thy longing avail in the grave ?
Give, as the heart gives, whose fetters are breaking,
Life, love, and hope, all thy dreams and thy waking,
Soon heaven's river thy soul-fever slaking,
　　Thou shalt know God, and the gift that he gave.

THE FOIL.

If we could see below,
The sphere of virtue, and each shining grace,
As plainly as that above doth show ;
This were the better sky, the brighter place.

God hath made stars the foil
To set off virtues ; griefs to set off sinning.
Yet in this wretched world we toil,
As if grief were not foul, nor virtue winning.

　　　　　　　　　　　GEORGE HERBERT.

PLAYS AND PURITANS.

BY CHARLES KINGSLEY.

The Puritans held too exclusively to one pole
of a double truth. They did so, no doubt, in
their hatred of the drama. Their belief that
human relations were, if not exactly sinful,
at least altogether carnal and unspiritual, prevented their conceiving the possibility of any
truly Christian drama, and led them at times
into strange and sad errors, like that New
England ukase of Cotton Mather's, who
punished the woman who should kiss her
infant on the Sabbath-day. Yet their extravagances on this point were but the honest revulsion from other extravagances on the opposite side. If the undistinguishing and immoral
Autotheism of the playwrights, and the luxury
and heathendom of the higher classes, first in
Italy and then in England, were the natural
revolt of the human mind against the Manichæ-
ism of Popish monkery, then the severity and
exclusiveness of Puritanism was a natural and
necessary revolt against that luxury and im-
morality : a protest for man's God-given superiority over nature, against that Naturalism
which threatened to end in sheer brutality.
While Italian prelates have found an apologist
in Mr. Roscoe, and English playwrights in Mr.
Gifford, the old Puritans, who felt and asserted,
however extravagantly, that there was an
eternal law which was above all Borgias and
Machiavels, Stuarts and Fletchers, have surely
a right to a fair trial. If they went too far in
their contempt for humanity, certainly no one
interfered to set them right. The Anglicans
of that time, who held intrinsically the same
anthropologic notions, and yet wanted the
courage and sincerity to carry them out as
honestly, neither could nor would throw any
light upon the controversy : and the only class
who sided with the poor playwrights in asserting that there were more things in man, and
more excuses for man, than were dreamt of in
Prynne's philosophy, were the Jesuit Casuists,
who, by a fatal perverseness, used all their
little knowledge of human nature to the same
undesirable purpose as the playwrights ;
namely, to prove how it was possible to commit every conceivable sinful action without
sinning. No wonder that in an age in which
courtiers and theatre-hunters were turning
Romanists by the dozen, and the priest-ridden
Queen was the chief patroness of the theatre,
the Puritans should have classed players and
Jesuits in the same category, and deduced the

parentage of both alike from the father of lies.

But as for these Puritans having been merely the sour, narrow, inhuman persons they are vulgarly supposed to have been, credat Judæus. There were sour and narrow men enough among them; so there were in the opposite party. No Puritan could have had less poetry in him, less taste, less feeling, than Laud himself. But is there no poetry save words? no drama save that which is presented on the stage? Is this glorious earth, and the souls of living men, mere prose, as long as "carent vate sacro," who will, forsooth, do them the honour to make poetry out of a little of them (and of how little)! by translating them into words, which he himself, just in proportion as he is a good poet, will confess to be clumsy, tawdry, ineffectual? Was there no poetry in these Puritans, because they wrote no poetry? We do not mean now the unwritten tragedy of the battle-psalm and the charge; but simple idyllic poetry and quiet home-drama, love-poetry of the heart and the hearth, and the beauties of everyday human life? Take the most commonplace of them: was Zeal-for-Truth Thoresby, of Thoresby Rise in Deeping Fen, because his father had thought fit to give him an ugly and silly name, the less of a noble lad? Did his name prevent his being six feet high? Were his shoulders the less broad for it, his cheeks the less ruddy for it? He wore his flaxen hair of the same length that every one now wears theirs, instead of letting it hang half-way to his waist in essenced curls; but was he therefore the less of a true Viking's son, bold-hearted as his sea-roving ancestors who won the Danelagh by Canute's side, and settled there on Thoresby Rise, to grow wheat and breed horses, generation succeeding generation in the old moated grange? He carried a Bible in his jack-boot; but did that prevent him, as Oliver rode past him with an approving smile on Naseby-field, thinking himself a very handsome fellow, with his mustache and imperial, and bright-red coat, and cuirass well polished, in spite of many a dint, as he sate his father's great black horse as gracefully and firmly as any long-locked and essenced cavalier in front of him? Or did it prevent him thinking too, for a moment, with a throb of the heart, that sweet Cousin Patience far away at home, could she but see him, might have the same opinion of him as he had of himself? Was he the worse for the thought? He was certainly not the worse for checking it the next instant, with manly shame for letting such "carnal vani-

ties" rise in his heart, while he was "doing the Lord's work" in the teeth of death and hell: but was there no poetry in him then? No poetry in him, five minutes after, as the long rapier swung round his head, redder and redder at every sweep? We are befooled by names. Call him Crusader instead of Roundhead, and he seems at once (granting him only sincerity, which he had, and that of a right awful kind) as complete a knight-errant as ever watched and prayed, ere putting on his spurs, in fantastic Gothic chapel, beneath "storied windows richly dight." Was there no poetry in him, either, half an hour afterwards, as he lay bleeding across the corpse of the gallant horse, waiting for his turn with the surgeon, and fumbled for the Bible in his boot, and tried to hum a psalm, and thought of Cousin Patience, and his father, and his mother, and how they would hear, at least, that he had played the man in Israel that day, and resisted unto blood, striving against sin and the Man of Sin?

And was there no poetry in him, too, as he came wearied along Thoresby dyke, in the quiet autumn eve, home to the house of his forefathers, and saw afar off the knot of tall poplars rising over the broad misty flat, and the one great abele tossing its sheets of silver in the dying gusts, and knew that they stood before his father's door? Who can tell all the pretty child-memories which flitted across his brain at that sight, and made him forget that he was a wounded cripple? There is the dyke where he and his brothers snared the great pike which stole the ducklings—how many years ago? while pretty little Patience stood by trembling, and shrieked at each snap of the brute's wide jaws; and there, down that long dark lode, ruffling with crimson in the sunset breeze, he and his brothers skated home in triumph with Patience when his uncle died. What a day that was! when, in the clear, bright winter noon, they laid the gate upon the ice, and tied the beef-bones under the four corners, and packed little Patience on it.— How pretty she looked, though her eyes were red with weeping, as she peeped out from among the heap of blankets and horse-hides, and how merrily their long fen-runners whistled along the ice-lane, between the high banks of sighing reed, as they towed home their new treasure in triumph, at a pace like the race-horse's, to the dear old home among the poplar trees. And now he was going home to meet her, after a mighty victory, a deliverance from Heaven, second only in his eyes to that Red Sea one. Was there no poetry in his heart at that thought? Did not the glowing sunset, and the reed-beds which it transfigured before him into sheets of golden flame, seem tokens that the glory of God was going before him in his path? Did not the sweet clamour of the wild-fowl, gathering for one rich pæan ere they sank into rest, seem to him as God's bells chiming him home in triumph, with peals sweeter and bolder than those of Lincoln or Peterborough steeple-house? Did not the very lapwing, as she tumbled softly wailing before his path, as she did years ago, seem to welcome the wanderer home in the name of Heaven?

Fair Patience, too, though she was a Puritan, yet did not her cheek flush, her eye grow dim, like any other girl's, as she saw far off the red-coat, like a sliding spark of fire, coming slowly along the strait fen-bank, and fled upstairs into her chamber to pray, half that it might be, half that it might not be he? Was there no happy storm of human tears and human laughter when he entered the courtyard gate? Did not the old dog lick his Puritan hand as lovingly as if it had been a Cavalier's? Did not lads and lasses run out shouting? Did not the old yeoman father hug him, weep over him, hold him at arm's length, and hug him again as heartily as any other John Bull, even though the next moment he called all to kneel down and thank Him who had sent his boy home again, after bestowing on him the grace to bind kings in chains and nobles with links of iron, and contend to death for the faith delivered to the saints? And did not Zeal-for-Truth look about as wistfully for Patience as any other man would have done, longing to see her, yet not daring even to ask for her? And when she came down at last, was she the less lovely in his eyes because she came, not flaunt-ing with bare bosom, in tawdry finery and paint, but shrouded close in coif and pinner, hiding from all the world beauty which was there still, but was meant for one alone, and that only if God willed, in God's good time? And was there no faltering in their voices, no light in their eyes, no trembling pressure of their hands, which said more, and was more, ay, and more beautiful in the sight of Him who made them, than all Herrick's Dianemes, Waller's Saccharissas, flames, darts, posies, love-knots, anagrams, and the rest of the in-sincere cant of the court? What if Zeal-for-Truth had never strung two rhymes together in his life? Did not his heart go for inspiration to a loftier Helicon, when it whispered to itself, "My love, my dove, my undefiled, is but one," than if he had filled pages with son-

nets about Venuses and Cupids, love-sick shep-herds, and cruel nymphs?

And was there no poetry, true idyllic poetry, as of Longfellow's "Evangeline" itself, in that trip round the old farm next morning; when Zeal-for-Truth, after looking over every heifer, and peeping into every sty, would needs canter down by his father's side to the horse-fen, with his arm in a sling; while the partridges whirred up before them, and the lurchers flashed like gray snakes after the hare, and the colts came whinnying round, with staring eyes and streaming manes, and the two chatted on in the same sober business-like English tone, alternately of "The Lord's great dealings" by General Cromwell, the pride of all honest fen-men, and the price of troop-horses at the next Horncastle fair?

Poetry in those old Puritans? Why not? They were men of like passions with ourselves. They loved, they married, they brought up children; they feared, they sinned, they sor-rowed, they fought—they conquered. There was poetry enough in them, be sure, though they acted it like men, instead of singing it like birds.—*Miscellanies.*

THERE'S MAGIC IN THAT LITTLE SONG.

BY REV. J. M'GEORGE.

There's magic in that little song;
  Its simple liquid melody
Can chase the gloom of care away,
  And make grief's phantoms fly.
When gnawing pain around my couch
  Keeps sleepless watch the drear night long,
My brain will cool and calm, if thou
  But sing that little song.

When fortune hides her fickle face,
  When sunshine friends turn cold away,
When first-love's holy vow is broke
  Like foam on ocean spray;
When youth's bright hopes, by gaunt despair,
  Are crushed as by a giant strong,
I will not curse my lot, if thou
  But sing that little song.

There's magic in that little song;
  It soothes each stormy passion down,—
The hopes which bless'd me when a boy
  Again my day-dreams crown.
Sweet visions of departed joys
  Fantastic on my memory throng;
I am a child again when thou
  Dost sing that little song.

GRAVE DOINGS.

[Samuel Warren, D.C.L., Q.C., born in Denbigh-shire, 1807. Educated at the Edinburgh University, at first with a view to the medical profession, but subsequently entered the Inner Temple, and was called to the bar in 1837. He became Recorder of Hull, 1852, and M.P. for Midhurst in 1856, re-elected in the following year, and resigned his seat in 1859, upon being appointed one of the two Masters in Lunacy. He has published a number of legal works, and contributed many miscellaneous articles to *Blackwood's Magazine*. His principal works in fiction are: *The Diary of a Late Physician* (from which we quote); *Ten Thousand a Year; Now and Then:* and *The Lily and the Bee*, an apologue of the Crystal Palace in unrhymed verse. Sir Archibald Alison, in his *History of Europe*, says: "Mr. Warren has taken a lasting place among the imaginative writers."]

My gentle reader—start not at learning that I have been, in my time, a RESURRECTIONIST. Let not this appalling word, this humiliating confession, conjure up in your fancy a throng of vampire-like images and associations, or earn your "Physician's" dismissal from your hearts and hearths. It is your own groundless fears, my fair trembler!—your own superstitious prejudices—that have driven me, and will drive many others of my brethren, to such dreadful doings as those hereafter detailed. Come, come—let us have one word of reason between us on the abstract question—and then for my tale. You expect us to cure you of disease, and yet deny us the only means of learning *how!* You would have us bring you the ore of skill and experience, yet forbid us to break the soil or sink a shaft! Is this fair, *fair* reader? Is this reasonable?

What I am now going to describe was my first and last exploit in the way of body-stealing. It was a grotesque if not a ludicrous scene, and occurred during the period of my "walking the hospitals," as it is called, which occupied the two seasons immediately after my leaving Cambridge. A young and rather interesting female was admitted a patient at the hospital I attended; her case baffled all our skill, and her symptoms even defied diagnosis. *Now*, it seemed an enlargement of the heart—now, an ossification—then this, that, and the other; and at last it was plain we knew nothing at all about the matter—no, not even whether her disorder was organic or functional, primary or symptomatic—or whether it *was* really the heart that was at fault. She received no benefit at all under the fluctuating schemes of treatment we pursued, and at length fell into dying circumstances. As

soon as her friends were apprised of her situation, and had an inkling of our intention to open the body, they insisted on removing her immediately from the hospital, that she might "die at home." In vain did Sir —— and his dressers expostulate vehemently with them, and represent, in exaggerated terms, the imminent peril attending such a step. Her two brothers avowed their apprehension of our designs, and were inflexible in exercising their right of removing their sister. I used all my rhetoric on the occasion, but in vain; and at last said to the young men, "Well, if you are afraid only of our *dissecting* her, we can get hold of her, if we are so disposed, as easily if she die with you as with us."

"Well—we'll *troy* that, measter," replied the elder, while his Herculean fist oscillated somewhat significantly before my eyes. The poor girl was removed accordingly to her father's house, which was at a certain village about five miles from London, and survived her arrival scarcely ten minutes! We soon contrived to receive intelligence of the event; and as I and Sir ——'s two dressers had taken great interest in the case throughout, and felt intense curiosity about the real nature of the disease, we met together and entered into a solemn compact, that, come what might, we would have her body out of the ground. A trusty spy informed us of the time and exact place of the girl's burial; and on expressing to Sir —— our determination about the matter, he patted me on the back, saying, "Ah, my fine fellow!—IF you have SPIRIT enough—dangerous," &c. &c. Was it not skilfully said? The baronet further told us, he felt himself so curious about the matter that if fifty pounds would be of use to us in furthering our purpose, they were at our service. It needed not this, nor a glance at the *éclat* with which the successful issue of the affair would be attended among our fellow-students, to spur our resolves.

The notable scheme was finally adjusted at my rooms in the Borough. M—— and E——, Sir ——'s dressers, and myself, with an experienced "*grab*"—that is to say, a *professional* resurrectionist—were to set off from the Borough about nine o'clock the next evening—which would be the third day after the burial—in a glass coach provided with all "appliances and means to boot." During the day, however, our friend the grab suffered so severely from an overnight's excess as to disappoint us of his invaluable assistance. This unexpected *contretemps* nearly put an end to our project; for the few other grabs we knew were absent on *professional tours!* Luckily, however, I bethought me of a poor Irish porter—a sort of "ne'er-do-weel" hanger-on at the hospital—whom I had several times hired to go on errands. This man I sent for to my rooms, and, in the presence of my two coadjutors, persuaded, threatened, and bothered into acquiescence, promising him half-a-guinea for his evening's work—and as much whisky as he could drink prudently. As Mr. Tip—that was the name he went by—had some personal acquaintance with the sick grab, he succeeded in borrowing his chief tools; with which, in a sack large enough to contain our expected prize, he repaired to my rooms about nine o'clock, while the coach was standing at the door. Our Jehu had received a quiet douceur in addition to the hire of himself and coach. As soon as we had exhibited sundry doses of Irish cordial to our friend Tip —under the effects of which he became quite "bouncible," and *ranted* about the feat he was to take a prominent part in—and equipped ourselves in our worst clothes, and white top-coats, we entered the vehicle—four in number —and drove off. The weather had been exceedingly capricious all the evening—moonlight, rain, thunder, and lightning, fitfully alternating. The only thing we were anxious about was the darkness, to shield us from all possible observation. I must own that, in analyzing the feelings that prompted me to undertake and go through with this affair, the mere love of adventure operated quite as powerfully as the wish to benefit the cause of anatomical science. A midnight expedition to the tombs!—It took our fancy amazingly; and then Sir ——'s cunning hint about the "danger"—and our "spirit!"

The garrulous Tip supplied us with amusement all the way down—rattle, rattle, rattle, incessantly; but as soon as we had arrived at that part of the road where we were to stop, and caught sight of —— church, with its hoary steeple—glistening in the fading moonlight, as though it were standing sentinel over the graves around it, one of which we were going so rudely to violate—Tip's spirits began to falter a little. He said little—and that at intervals. To be very candid with the reader, *none* of us felt over much at our ease. Our expedition began to wear a somewhat hairbrained aspect, and to be environed with formidable contingencies which we had not taken sufficiently into our calculations. What, for instance, if the two stout fellows, the brothers, should be out watching their sister's grave? They were not likely to stand on much cere-

mony with us. And then the manual difficulties! E—— was the only one of us that had ever assisted at the exhumation of a body —and the rest of us were likely to prove but bungling workmen. However, we had gone too far to think of retreating. We none of us *spoke* our suspicions, but the silence that reigned within the coach was tolerably significant. In contemplation, however, of some such contingency, we had put a bottle of brandy in the coach pocket; and before we drew up, had all four of us drunk pretty deeply of it. At length the coach turned down a by-lane to the left, which led directly to the churchyard wall; and after moving a few steps down it, in order to shelter our vehicle from the observation of highway passengers, the coach stopped, and the driver opened the door.

"Come, Tip," said I, "out with you."

"Get out, did you say, sir? To be sure I will—Och! to be sure I will." But there was small show of alacrity in his movements as he descended the steps; for, while I was speaking I was interrupted by the solemn clangour of the church clock announcing the hour of midnight. The sounds seemed to *warn* us against what we were going to do.

"'Tis a cowld night, yer honours," said Tip, in an under tone, as we successively alighted, and stood together, looking up and down the dark lane, to see if anything was stirring but ourselves. "'Tis a cowld night—and—and— and," he stammered.

"Why, you cowardly old scoundrel," grumbled M——, "are you frightened already? What's the matter, eh? Hoist up the bag on your shoulders directly, and lead the way down the lane."

"Och, but yer honours—och! by the mother that bore me, but 'tis a murtherous cruel thing, I'm thinking, to wake the poor cratur from her last sleep." He said this so querulously, that I began to entertain serious apprehensions, after all, of his defection; so I insisted on his taking a little more brandy, by way of bringing him up to par. It was of no use, however. His reluctance increased every moment—and it even dispirited *us.* I verily believe the turning of a straw would have decided us all on jumping into the coach again, and returning home without accomplishing our errand. Too many of the students, however, were apprised of our expedition, for us to think of terminating it so ridiculously. As it were by mutual consent, we stood and paused a few moments, about half-way down the lane. M—— whistled with infinite spirit and distinctness; E—— remarked to me that he always thought a churchyard at midnight was the gloomiest object imaginable;" and I talked about *business*—"soon be over"—"shallow grave"—&c. &c.

"Confound it—what if those two brothers of hers should be there?" said M—— abruptly, making a dead stop, and folding his arms on his breast.

"Powerful fellows, both of them!" muttered E——. We resumed our march—when Tip, our advanced guard—a title he earned by anticipating our steps about three inches—suddenly stood still, let down the bag from his shoulders, elevated both hands in a listening attitude, and exclaimed, "Whisht!—whisht!—By my soul, *what* was that?" We all paused in silence, looking palely at one another—but could hear nothing except the drowsy flutter of a bat wheeling away from us a little overhead.

"Fait—an' wasn't it somebody *spaking* on the far side o' the hedge, I heard?" whispered Tip.

"Poh—stuff, you idiot!" I exclaimed, losing my temper. "Come, M—— and E——, it's high time we had done with all this cowardly nonsense; and if we mean really to *do* anything, we must make haste. 'Tis past twelve—day breaks about four—and it is coming on wet, you see." Several large drops of rain, pattering heavily among the leaves and branches, corroborated my words, by announcing a coming shower, and the air was sultry enough to warrant the expectation of a thunder-storm. We therefore buttoned up our greatcoats to the chin, and hurried on to the churchyard wall, which ran across the bottom of the lane. This wall we had to climb over to get into the churchyard, and it was not a very high one. Here Tip annoyed us again. I told him to lay down his bag, mount the wall, and look over into the yard, to see whether all was clear before us; and, as far as the light would enable him, to look about for a new-made grave. Very reluctantly he complied, and contrived to scramble to the top of the wall. He had hardly time, however, to peer over into the churchyard, when a fluttering streak of lightning flashed over us, followed, in a second or two, by a loud burst of thunder! Tip fell in an instant to the ground, like a cockchafer shaken from an elm-tree, and lay crossing himself, and muttering Paternosters. We could scarcely help laughing at the manner in which he tumbled down, simultaneously with the flash of lightning. "Now, look ye, gintlemen," said he, still squatting on the ground,

"do you mane to give the poor cratur Christian burial, when ye've done wid her? An' will you put her back again as ye found her? 'Case, if you won't, blood an' oons"——

"Hark ye now, Tip," said I sternly, taking out one of a brace of *empty* pistols I had put into my greatcoat pocket, and presenting it to his head, "we have hired you on this business, for the want of a better, you wretched fellow! and if you give us any more of your nonsense, by —— I'll send a bullet through your brain! Do you hear me, Tip?"

"Och, aisy, aisy wid ye! don't murther me! Bad luck to me that I ever cam wid ye! Och, and if iver I live to die, won't I see and bury my ould body out o' the rache of all the doctors in the world? If I don't, divel burn me!" We all laughed aloud at Tip's truly Hibernian expostulation."

"Come, sir, mount! over with you!" said we, helping to push him upwards. "Now, drop this bag on the other side," we continued, giving him the sack that contained our implements. We all three of us then followed, and alighted safely in the churchyard. It poured with rain; and, to enhance the dreariness and horrors of the time and place, flashes of lightning followed in quick succession, shedding a transient awful glare over the scene, revealing the white tombstones, the ivy-grown venerable church, and our own figures, a shivering group, come on an unhallowed errand! I perfectly well recollect the lively feelings of apprehension—"the compunctious visitings of remorse"—which the circumstances called forth in my own breast, and which, I had no doubt, were shared by my companions.

As no time, however, was to be lost, I left the group, for an instant, under the wall, to search out the grave. The accurate instructions I had received enabled me to pitch on the spot with little difficulty; and I returned to my companions, who immediately followed me to the scene of operations. We had no umbrellas, and our greatcoats were saturated with wet; but the brandy we had recently taken did us good service, by exhilarating our spirits, and especially those of Tip. He untied the sack in a twinkling, and shook out the hoes and spades, &c.; and taking one of the latter himself, he commenced digging with such energy, that we had hardly prepared ourselves for work, before he had cleared away nearly the whole of the mound. The rain soon abated, and the lightning ceased for a considerable interval, though thunder was heard occasionally grumbling sullenly in the distance, as if expressing anger at our unholy

doings—at least I felt it so. The pitchy darkness continued, so that we could scarcely see
one another's figures. We worked on in
silence, as fast as our spades could be got into
the ground; taking it in turns, two by two,
as the grave would not admit of more. On—
on—on we worked till we had hollowed out
about three feet of earth. Tip then hastily
joined together a long iron screw or borer,
which he thrust into the ground, for the purpose of ascertaining the depth at which the
coffin yet lay from us. To our vexation, we
found a distance of three feet remained to be
got through. "Sure, and by the soul of St.
Patrick, but we'll not be done by the morning!" said Tip, as he threw down the instrument and resumed his spade. We were all
discouraged. Oh, how earnestly I wished
myself at home, in my snug little bed in the
Borough! How I cursed the Quixotism that
had led me into such an undertaking! I had
no time, however, for reflection, as it was my
turn to relieve one of the diggers; so into the
grave I jumped, and worked away as lustily as
before. While I was thus engaged, a sudden
noise, close to our ears, so startled me, that I
protest I thought I should have dropped down
dead in the grave I was robbing. I and my
fellow-digger let fall our spades, and all four
stood still for a second or two in an ecstasy of
fearful apprehension. We could not see more
than a few inches around us, but heard the
grass trodden by approaching feet! They
proved to be those of an ASS, that was turned
at night into the churchyard, and had gone on
eating his way towards us; and, while we were
standing in mute expectation of what was to
come next, opened on us with an astounding
hee-haw! hee-haw! hee-haw! Even after we
had discovered the ludicrous nature of the interruption, we were too agitated to laugh. The
brute was actually close upon us, and had
given tongue from under poor Tip's elbow,
having approached him from behind, as he
stood leaning on his spade. Tip started suddenly backward against the animal's head, and
fell down. Away sprang the jackass, as much
confounded as Tip, kicking and scampering
like a mad creature among the tombstones,
and hee-hawing incessantly, as if a hundred
devils had got into it for the purpose of dis-
comfiting us. I felt so much fury and fear
lest the noise should lead to our discovery I
could have killed the brute if it had been
within my reach, while Tip stammered, in an
affrightened whisper—"Och, the baste! Och,
the baste! The big black divel of a baste!
The murtherous, thundering"—— and a great

many epithets of the same sort. We gradually
recovered from the agitation which this provoking interruption had occasioned; and Tip,
under the promise of two bottles of whisky as
soon as we arrived safe at home with our prize,
renewed his exertions, and dug with such energy that we soon cleared away the remainder
of the superincumbent earth, and stood upon
the bare lid of the coffin. The grapplers, with
ropes attached to them, were then fixed in the
sides and extremities, and we were in the act
of raising the coffin, when the sound of a
human voice, accompanied with footsteps, fell
on our startled ears. We heard both distinctly,
and crouched down close over the brink of the
grave, awaiting in breathless suspense a cor-
roboration of our fears. After a pause of two
or three minutes, however, finding that the
sounds were not renewed, we began to breathe
freer, persuaded that our ears must have deceived us. Once more we resumed our work,
succeeded in hoisting up the coffin—not without a slip, however, which nearly precipitated
it down again to the bottom, with all four of
us upon it—and depositing it on the grave-
side. Before proceeding to use our screws or
wrenchers, we once more looked and listened,
and listened and looked; but neither seeing
nor hearing anything we set to work, prized
off the lid in a twinkling, and a transient
glimpse of moonlight disclosed to us the
shrouded inmate—all white and damp. I
removed the face-cloth, and unpinned the cap,
while M—— loosed the sleeves from the wrists.
Thus were we engaged, when E——, who had
hold of the feet, ready to lift them out, suddenly let them go—gasped, "Oh, my God!
there they are!" and placed his hand on my
arm. He shook like an aspen leaf. I looked
towards the quarter whither his eyes were
directed, and, sure enough, saw the figure of a
man—if not two—moving stealthily toward
us. "Well, we're discovered, that's clear,"
I whispered as calmly as I could. "We shall
be murdered!" groaned E—— "Lend me
one of the pistols you have with you," said
M—— resolutely; "by ——, I'll have a shot
for my life, however!" As for poor Tip, who
had heard every syllable of this startling
colloquy, and himself seen the approaching
figures, he looked at me in silence, the image
of blank horror! I could have laughed even
then, to see his staring black eyes—his little
cocked ruby-tinted nose—his chattering teeth.
"Hush—hush!" said I, cocking my pistol,
while M—— did the same; for none but myself knew that they were unloaded. To add to
our consternation, the malignant moon with-

drew the small scantling of light she had been doling out to us, and sank beneath a vast cloud, "black as Erebus," but not before we had caught a glimpse of two more figures moving towards us in an opposite direction. "Surrounded!" two of us muttered in the same breath. We all rose to our feet, and stood together, not knowing what to do—unable in the darkness to see one another distinctly. Presently we heard a voice say, in a subdued tone, "Where are they? where? *Sure* I saw them! Oh, there they are. Halloa —halloa!"

That was enough—the signal of our flight. Without an instant's pause, or uttering another syllable, off we sprung, like small-shot from a gun's mouth, all of us in different directions, we knew not whither. I heard the report of a gun—mercy on me! and pelted away, scarcely knowing what I was about, dodging among the graves—now coming full-butt against a plaguy tombstone, then tumbling on the slippery grass—while some one followed close at my heels, panting and puffing, but whether friend or foe I knew not. At length I stumbled against a large tombstone; and, finding it open at the two ends, crept under it, resolved there to abide the issue. At the moment of my ensconcing myself, the sound of the person's footsteps who had followed me suddenly ceased. I heard a splashing sound, then a kicking and scrambling, a faint stifled cry of "Ugh—oh ugh!" and all was still. Doubtless it must be one of my companions, who had been wounded. What could I do, however? I did not know in what direction he lay—the night was pitch-dark—and if I crept from my hiding-place, for all I knew, I might be shot myself. I shall never forget that hour—no, never! There was I, squatting like a tod on the wet grass and weeds, not daring to do more than breathe! Here was a predicament! I could not conjecture how the affair would terminate. Was I to lie where I was till daylight, that then I might step into the arms of my captors? What was become of my companions?—While turning these thoughts in my mind, and wondering that all was so quiet, my ear caught the sound of the splashing of water, apparently at but a yard or two's distance, mingled with the sounds of a half-smothered human voice— "Ugh! ugh! Och, murther! murther! murther!"—another splash—"and isn't it dead, and drowned, and kilt I am"——

Whew! *Tip* in trouble, thought I, not daring to speak. Yes—it was poor Tip, I afterwards found—who had followed at my heels, scampering after me as fast as fright

could drive him, till his career was unexpectedly ended by his tumbling—souse—head over heels, into a newly-opened grave in his path, with more than a foot of water in it. There the poor fellow remained, after recovering from the first shock of his fall, not daring to utter a word for some time, lest he should be discovered—straddling over the water with his toes and elbows stuck into the loose soil on each side, to support him. This was his interesting position, as he subsequently informed me, at the time of uttering the sounds which first attracted my attention. Though not aware of his situation at the time, I was almost choked with laughter as he went on with his soliloquy, somewhat in this strain :—

"Och, Tip, ye ould divel! Don't it sarve ye right, ye fool? Ye villanous ould coffin-robber! Won't ye burn for this hereafter, ye sinner? Ulaloo! When ye are dead yourself, may ye be trated like that poor cratur—and yourself alive to see it! Och, hubbaboo! hubbaboo! Isn't it sure that I'll be drowned, an' then it's kilt I'll be!" A loud splash, and a pause for a few moments, as if he were readjusting his footing—"Och! an' I'm catching my dith of cowld! Fait, an' it's a divel a drop o' the two bottles o' whisky I'll ever see —Och, och, och!"—another splash—"och, an' isn't this uncomfortable! Murther and oons! —if ever I come out of this—sha'n't I be dead before I do?"

"Tip—Tip—Tip!" I whispered in a low tone. There was a dead silence. "Tip, Tip, where are you? What's the matter, eh?" No answer; but he muttered in a low tone to himself—"*Where am I!* by my soul! Isn't it dead, and kilt, and drowned, and murthered I am—that's all!"

"Tip—Tip—Tip!" I repeated, a little louder.

"Tip, indeed! Fait, ye may call, bad-luck to ye—whoever ye are—but it's divel a word I'll be after spaking to ye."

"Tip, you simpleton! It's I—Mr. ——."

In an instant there was a sound of jumping and splashing, as if surprise had made him slip from his standing again, and he called out, "Whoo! whoo! an' is't you, sweet Mr. ——! What is the matter wid ye? Are ye kilt? Where are they all? Have they taken ye away, every mother's son of you?" he asked eagerly, in a breath.

"Why, what are *you* doing, Tip? Where are *you?*"

"Fait, an' it's being *washed* I am, in the feet, and in the queerest *tub* your honour ever saw!" A noise of scuffling, not many yards off, silenced us both in an instant. Presently I distinguished the voice of E——, calling out —"Help, M——!" (my name)—"Where are you?" The noise increased, and seemed nearer than before. I crept from my lurking place, and aided at Tip's resurrection, when both of us hurried towards the spot whence the sound came. By the faint moonlight I could just see the outlines of two figures violently struggling and grappling together. Before I could come up to them both fell down, locked in each other's arms, rolling over each other, grasping one another's collars, gasping and panting as if in mortal struggle. The moon suddenly emerged, and who do you think, reader, was E——'s antagonist? Why, the person whose appearance had so discomfited and affrighted us all—OUR COACHMAN. That worthy individual, alarmed at our protracted stay, had, contrary to our injunctions, left his coach to come and search after us. He it was whom we had seen stealing towards us; his steps—his voice had alarmed us, for he could not see us distinctly enough to discover whether we were his fare or not. He was on the point of whispering my name, it seems—when we must all have understood one another —when lo! we all started off in the manner which has been described; and he himself, not knowing that he was the reason of it, had taken to his heels, and fled for his life! He supposed we had fallen into a sort of ambuscade. He happened to hide himself behind the tombstone next but one to that which sheltered E——. Finding all quiet, he and E——, as if by mutual consent, were groping from their hiding-places, when they unexpectedly fell foul of one another—each too affrighted to speak — and hence the scuffle.

After this satisfactory denouement we all repaired to the grave's mouth, and found the corpse and coffin precisely as we had left them. We were not many moments in taking out the body, stripping it, and thrusting it into the sack we had brought. We then tied the top of the sack, carefully deposited the shroud, &c., in the coffin, re-screwed down the lid— fearful, impious mockery!—and consigned it once more to its resting-place, Tip scattering a handful of earth on the lid, and exclaiming reverently—"An' may the Lord forgive us for what we have done to ye!" The coachman and I then took the body between us to the coach, leaving M——, and E——, and Tip to fill up the grave.

Our troubles were not yet ended, however. Truly it seemed as though Providence were throwing every obstacle in our way. Nothing went right. On reaching the spot where we had left the coach, behold it lay several yards farther in the lane, tilted into the ditch—for the horses, being hungry, and left to themselves, in their anxiety to graze on the verdant bank of the hedge, had contrived to overturn the vehicle in the ditch—and one of the horses was kicking vigorously when we came up—the whole body off the ground—and resting on that of his companion. We had considerable difficulty in righting the coach, as the horses were inclined to be obstreperous. We succeeded, however—deposited our unholy spoil within, turned the horses' heads towards the high-road, and then, after enjoining Jehu to keep his place on the box, I went to see how my companions were getting on. They had nearly completed their task, and told me that "shovelling *in* was surprisingly easier than shovelling *out!*" We took great pains to leave everything as neat, and as nearly resembling what we found it as possible, in order that our visit might not be suspected. We then carried away each our own tools, and hurried as fast as possible to our coach, for the dim twilight had already stolen a march upon us, devoutly thankful that, after so many interruptions, we had succeeded in effecting our object.

It was broad daylight before we reached town, and a wretched coach company we looked, all wearied and dirty—Tip especially, who nevertheless snored in the corner as comfortably as if he had been warm in his bed. I heartily resolved with him, on leaving the coach, that it should be "the devil's own dear self only that should tempt me out again *body-snatching!*"[1]

ALL'S WELL.

The clouds, which rise with thunder slake
   Our thirsty souls with rain;
The blow most dreaded falls to break
   From off our limbs a chain;
And wrongs of man to man but make
   The love of God more plain.
As through the shadowy lens of even
The eye looks farthest into heaven
On gleams of star and depths of blue
The glaring sunshine never knew!

J. G. WHITTIER.

[1] On examining the body, we found that Sir ——'s suspicions were fully verified. It was disease of the heart, but of too complicated a nature to be made intelligible to general readers.

"COME, DINE WITH ME."

[Joseph Hall, born at Bristow Park, Ashby de la Zouch, Leicestershire, 1st July, 1574; died at Higham, near Norwich, 8th September, 1656. Bishop of Exeter and Norwich, successively, and the first English writer of satire. In the prologue to his satires he says :

"I first adventure, follow me who list,
And be the second English satirist."

He also wrote numerous sermons, meditations, and epistles.]

The courteous citizen bade me to his feast,
With hollow words, and overly request:
"Come, will ye dine with me this holyday?"
I yielded, though he hop'd I would say nay :
For had I mayden'd it, as many use:
Loath for to grant, but loather to refuse.
"Alacke, sir, I were loath ; another day,—
I should but trouble you ;—pardon me, if you may."
No pardon should I need ; for, to depart
He gives me leave, and thanks too, in his heart.
Two words for monie, Darbishirian wise ;
(That's one too manie) is a naughtie guise.
Who looks for double biddings to a feast,
May dine at home for an importune guest.
I went, then saw, and found the greate expence ;
The fare and fashions of our citizens.
Oh, Cleoparica ! what wanteth there
For curious cost, and wondrous choice of cheere?
Beefe, that erst Hercules held for finest fare :
Porke for the fat Bœotian, or the hare
For Martial ; fish for the Venetian ;
Goose-liver for the likerous Romane,
Th' Athenian's goate ; quaile, Iolan's cheere ;
The hen for Esculape, and the Parthian deere ;
Grapes for Arcesilas, figs for Plato's mouth,
And chesnuts faire for Amarillis' tooth.
Hadst thou such cheere? wert thou evere there before?
Never.—I thought so : nor come there no more.
Come there no more ; for so meant all that cost :
Never hence take me for thy second host.
For whom he means to make an often guest,
One dish shall serve ; and welcome make the rest.

COMPENSATIONS OF CALAMITY.

BY R. W. EMERSON.

The changes which break up at short intervals the prosperity of men, are advertisements of a nature whose law is growth. Evermore it is the order of nature to grow, and every soul is by this intrinsic necessity quitting its whole system of things, its friends, and home, and laws, and faith, as the shell-fish crawls out of its beautiful but stony case, because it no longer admits of its growth, and slowly forms a new house. In proportion to the vigour of the individual, these revolutions are frequent, until in some happier mind they are incessant, and all worldly relations hang very loosely about

him, becoming, as it were, a transparent fluid membrane through which the form is always seen, and not as in most men an indurated heterogeneous fabric of many dates, and of no settled character, in which the man is imprisoned. Then there can be enlargement, and the man of to-day scarcely recognizes the man of yesterday. And such should be the outward biography of man in time, a putting off of dead circumstances day by day, as he renews his raiment day by day. But to us, in our lapsed estate, resting not advancing, resisting not co-operating with the divine expansion, this growth comes by shocks.

We cannot part with our friends. We cannot let our angels go. We do not see that they only go out, that archangels may come in. We are idolaters of the old. We do not believe in the riches of the soul, in its proper eternity and omnipresence. We do not believe there is any force in to-day to rival or re-create that beautiful yesterday. We linger in the ruins of the old tent, where once we had bread and shelter and organs, nor believe that the spirit can feed, cover, and nerve us again. We cannot again find aught so dear, so sweet, so graceful. But we sit and weep in vain. The voice of the Almighty saith, "Up and onward for evermore !" We cannot stay amid the ruins. Neither will we rely on the new ; and so we walk ever with reverted eyes, like those monsters who look backwards.

And yet the compensations of calamity are made apparent to the understanding also, after long intervals of time. A fever, a mutilation, a cruel disappointment, a loss of wealth, a loss of friends, seems at the moment unpaid loss, and unpayable. But the sure years reveal the deep remedial force that underlies all facts. The death of a dear friend, wife, brother, lover, which seemed nothing but privation, somewhat later assumes the aspect of a guide or genius : for it commonly operates revolutions in our way of life, terminates an epoch of infancy or of youth which was waiting to be closed, breaks up a wonted occupation, or a household, or style of living, and allows the formation of new ones more friendly to the growth of character. It permits or constrains the formation of new acquaintances, and the reception of new influences that prove of the first importance to the next years ; and the man or woman who would have remained a sunny garden flower, with no room for its roots and too much sunshine for its head, by the falling of the walls and the neglect of the gardener, is made the banian of the forest, yielding shade and fruit to wide neighbourhoods of men.

CHORUS OF THANKFUL CHILDREN.

Now thank we all our God,
With heart and hands and voices,
Who wondrous things hath done,
In whom his world rejoices;
Who from our mothers' arms
Hath bless'd us on our way
With countless gifts of love,
And still is ours to-day.

Oh may this bounteous God
Through all our life be near us,
With ever-joyful hearts
And blessed peace to cheer us;
And keep us in his grace,
And guide us when perplex'd,
And free us from all ills
In this world and the next.

All praise and thanks to God
The Father now be given,
The Son, and Him who reigns
With them in highest heaven:
The One eternal God,
Whom earth and heaven adore;
For thus it was, is now,
And shall be evermore!

From the German of MARTIN RINCKART (1636).—
Translation by CATHERINE WINKWORTH.

TITO'S TROUBLES.

[Frederick William Robinson, born in London,
1830. Novelist. His principal works are: *Grandmother's
Money; No Church; Church and Chapel; A Woman's
Ransom; Milly's Hero; Under the Spell; Woodleigh;
Anne Judge, Spinster; For Her Sake; Wrayford's Ward,*
and other Tales (from which we quote); *Slaves of the
Ring;* &c. &c. A review in *Blackwood,* referring to
Church and Chapel, said: "Such novels have a higher
use than the sensations of the moment. If due pains
and care were bestowed upon them, we see no reason
why they should not rank next to biography—works of
more than amusement—contributions towards the history of the inexhaustible yet unchanging race."]

You are all aware that my first school was
not a fashionable academy for young gentlemen. Family reverses, not to mention an
exceedingly large family, prevented my father
from placing me in a high-class, high-priced,
high-pressure seminary, when I arrived at that
objectionable age which necessitated my becoming a nuisance at home to my parents, and
to all my little brothers and sisters. It was
absolutely necessary that I should go somewhere, everybody said; and after much hard
study of advertisements in the daily papers,
and personal inspection by my father of half-
a-hundred establishments, I found myself one
morning settled at Mr. Price's, Belvoir House,
Flatborough-on-the-Sea, an establishment
where boys under fourteen years of age were
educated, boarded, and generally attended to,
for the sum of eight-and-twenty pounds per
annum. This was not a fashionable price, and
it was not, in consequence, a fashionable
school. It was, indeed, rather an unfashion-
able school; the pupils were not highly trained,
and were never "civilly examined," and the
master had not thought of deposing "quarters"
and taking to "terms." There were no extras,
there was not a resident mathematical master,
and the principal himself taught us all the
French he knew, and left the pronunciation a
great deal to our tastes.

Still, looking back, I am disposed to think
that this was a good school—an old-fashioned
school, perhaps, but where the master worked
hard in the midst of his boys, crammed no
particular clique to the detriment of the rest,
and at least did his best—and he was a clever
man in his way—to give us a sound English
education. As a start in a boy's life, possibly
not as a finishing school, Belvoir House was
particularly suitable; and as the situation was
healthy, the terms low, and the master well
known as a man kind to his pupils and interested in his profession, Mr. Price had always
some sixty or seventy boys beneath his care.

Mr. Price was not a rich man; indeed report said that, owing to indiscreet investments
in public companies, he had lost the little that
he had managed to save, before his own large
family—twelve "grown ups" sat down to dinner every day of their lives, and there were
four boys under fourteen in the school itself
—prevented him putting anything more by
for a rainy day.

It was at this school that I met Tito Zalez
—and it is Tito's school-life and strange school-
troubles in which I am about to attempt to
interest you. I suppose that I took readily to
Tito because he arrived at Belvoir House on
the same day as myself, and we both sat in
a waiting-room, on chairs much too high to
allow of our feet touching the ground, staring
sheepishly at one another, whilst our parents
were in solemn conclave with the master in
the drawing-room. I was eleven years of age,
and Tito, I learned afterwards, was ten. I was
a thin, gawky, bullet-headed youth, for my
age; Tito was big and plump, with a dark
skin, black curly hair, a nose that young ladies,
I believe, call "dubby," and two little bead-
like eyes which rolled a great deal in his head,

and somewhat alarmed me after my father had shut me in with him.

Our conversation was disconnected and terse. The following was the dialogue that ensued between us, with an interval of about three minutes and a half before either committed himself to a reply.

"What's your name?"

"Joe Simmons. What's yours?"

"Tito Zalez."

"Oh, is it?"

I thought that it was a very odd name, and that I should not like to have it myself, and that the boys would be very severe upon it presently in the playground, and "chivey" him. After considering the matter in all its details, I told him the result of my deliberations, and he opened his eyes a little wider with amazement and said—

"Do you think so, really?"

I said that I really did.

Another long pause, and just as it struck me that he was going to sleep, and likely to pitch off his chair on to the smallest boy's box that I had ever seen, he said,—

"Where do you come from?"

"Reigate."

Of course I asked him where he came from, and he said London.

He was a very curious boy, or else he was anxious to show off that afternoon, and impress me with his importance, knowing that my questions were simply an echo of his own.

"What's your father?" he said.

"He's in a bank. He scoops money out and in—gold money!"

"Lor!"

"What's your father?"

"He's a gentleman."

"Oh!"

I believe this was all the conversation in which we indulged until my father, and Tito's father, and old Price—we always called him old Price, and intended nothing disrespectful thereby—came in to us again. I looked at Tito's father, and was greatly impressed by him at first sight, and though exceedingly flattered by his notice, secretly wished that he would have stared at me a little less. He was a tall, thin man, with a long gray mustache, and with a face very sallow and wrinkled,—so seamed and knotty a face that it reminded me at once of the carved knob of an eccentric walking-stick which had belonged to my grandfather, and was treasured by my father for old associations sake as well as for its ugliness.

He came to me after he had shaken hands with Mr. Price.

"You and Tito begin life together," he said, with a strong foreign accent, "and will have your way to fight together. Tito is younger than you, and you must not let the big boys bounce—I think you boys call it 'bounce'—over him too much. This little fellow of mine, Master Simmons, has never been away from home before, and so I leave you to take care of him."

I believe that I said, "Thank you, sir;" and after he had shaken hands with me, he took Tito up in his arms, kissed him once or twice, and then marched with his head very erect out of the room, followed, after adieux had been exchanged, by my father. This was my first introduction to Belvoir House, and when Mr. Price had taken a hand of each, and led us into the playground, the ordeal of the great change was completed, and we were at home before the night had fallen on our new world. I do not know that Tito was quite at home, although he had been lively in the playground, and had laughed a little—and a very fat laugh he had too, which made one laugh to hear it—for when we were in "dormitory six," somebody began crying in the night, and the junior usher, who slept in a large crib in the corner, sat up in bed and asked who was making that noise, but getting no answer save muffled sobs and strange effervescent sounds, as of a youth in the agonies of strangulation, he lighted a candle, and came shivering along the line of iron bedsteads until he found Tito, with his mouth full of sheet and blanket, crying all over his clean pillow-case.

"Now then, Zalez, what's the matter?"

"Oh, please, sir, I wa-a-ant to go ho-o-ome."

"Go home?" said the usher, kindly; "why, you've only just come. Besides, see how cross your father would be after all the trouble he has taken!"

"N-n-no, sir, he would-n't. He's too-too-too fo-ond of me."

The usher—Mr. Banstock was his name—sat down and tried to reason with Tito, but with very little effect. He told him that he would soon get used to the change; that he was keeping the other boys awake; that I, Joseph Simmons, from Reigate, was not crying; that Mr. Price would be very cross if he heard him; and that he himself, who was a martyr to rheumatism, would be laid up in the morning if he sat there any longer. But Tito continued to cry, and to make desperate attempts to suffocate himself with the bedding, until Mr. Banstock, as it appeared to me very improperly, promised that he should return home by the first train in the morning.

Tito was calm after that, and stammered forth, by way of apology for his disorderly outburst, that he knew his papa would be glad to see him back, now that his mother had only just gone away, you know, and left him so much alone, sir!

"Gone away—where?" I heard Mr. Banstock ask.

"Why, to heaven, sir, papa says."

Mr. Banstock asked no more questions, but went back to his bed, where I heard him tumbling about restlessly, with all the sleep clean out of him, for half an hour afterwards. Once I heard him say, "Poor little chap!" but when I ventured to look over the bedclothes, and say, "Did you speak, sir?" he told me very sharply to hold my tongue, and that if I did not mind he would give me three cube-roots in the morning. I thought that I did not mind, and that I was very much obliged to him; and I went to sleep at last, wondering whether Mr. Banstock would have to get up early and dig his roots out of the garden, and what possible use they would be to me after he had digged them. However, I did not get my cube-roots the next morning, although I found out all about them before the first quarter was over my head, and did not congratulate myself upon the discovery.

Tito and I were firm friends before the first quarter had expired, for he did not go home in the morning, but had a little talk with Mr. Price in the ante-room again, and came out more composed in mind after the master's gentle reasoning, and very red round the eyelids, like a rabbit. Tito, I may add, was a general favourite after his three months' sojourn at Belvoir House: he was a good-tempered, affectionate boy, not particularly clever at his lessons, and getting into difficulties at times concerning them, but taking the ills that academic flesh is heir to with philosophy, and doing better next time, and making up by perseverance for his want of genius. At the end of three months, Colonel Zalez called. We knew by that time that Tito's father was, or had been, a colonel somewhere, and we felt that he would have greatly obliged the boys of Belvoir House by coming to see his son in full regimentals. I remember that he entered the playground one Saturday afternoon, that Tito suddenly gave a scream of delight, broke a window of the schoolroom with his elbow in his haste to leap down from the sill on which he and I had placed ourselves, and went with a mad plunge at his father's long legs.

Colonel Zalez lifted the boy up in his arms, and kissed him all over his fat face, till some of us certainly burst out laughing; and then he walked up and down the playground for a few minutes, holding Tito's hand, and looking down at him with grave interest. It struck me—it struck two or three of us even—that Colonel Zalez's boots were somewhat down at heel, a fact which was accounted for by young Miles saying that no doubt the colonel had been marching a good bit lately, which we thought immediately he had. He came to us soon after this discovery, and to my surprise and confusion, and to the infinite amusement of my contemporaries, he stooped down and kissed me, tickling me very much with his bristly gray mustache.

"Tito says that you have been very kind to him, Master Simmons," he said, shaking hands with me after his embrace; "I thank you very much, young gentleman."

I should like to have told him not to mention it, but remained red and silent.

"I have asked permission of Mr. Price to take you and Tito for a stroll this afternoon, and to the circus in the evening, if you would like to go with us."

I found my voice then, and my hearty "Thank you," was very conclusive evidence that I should like to go with them very much indeed.

That was a memorable holiday, eclipsing the holiday last week which I had had with my father, who had not asked Tito to join us, as Tito's father had asked me. A holiday marked with a white stone in my calendar of recollections—bright, sunshiny, ineffaceable—which described to the boys afterwards, rendered some of them raving mad with jealousy, and heaped Tito for the next three months with attentions that he could scarcely bear up against, the impression being general that Tito's father had determined to reward munificently all little Tito's friends. We had buns and almond cakes at the pastry-cook's, both in our best clothes; Tito in a new suit of black that his father had brought with him. We went for a sail on the great calm sea before the sun went down; we went back to the pastry-cook's and had tea, with buns and almond cakes; we went for a drive in a hired fly before the horsemanship commenced, and Colonel Zalez lay back and smoked paper cigarettes so furiously that I thought he would set himself on fire before the circus was opened; we went back to the pastry-cook's, and had two bottles of lemonade, and some buns and almond cakes; we attended the performance in the circus and saw wonders upon wonders, and screamed with laughter at the clowns, and thought it was odd—at least

I did—that the dark grim face at which we looked when a good joke was uttered, did not change more frequently; we went back to the pastry-cook's to supper, and had buns and almond cakes, and weak sherry and water as a parting stimulant; and finally we were walking on tiptoe through dormitory six—absent-with-leave fellows—looking down compassionately on boys who had been asleep for hours! It was a great holiday; it was the only one I ever had with Tito. At Christmas, Tito's father came in a hurry to Mr. Price, settled the bill, and then went away again, leaving Tito behind him, after many embraces, and much whispered advice. It began to be understood, after he had departed, that Tito's father was going abroad—going to battle, Tito said, very proudly—and that Tito was to be left at school all through the Christmas holidays. We bade him good-bye, and felt very sorry for him, and my last glimpse of Flatborough-on-the-Sea that "half" was a curve of the embankment, a steep green hill, and Tito jumping about thereon and waving his handkerchief to me.

Next "half" Tito's father did not appear, and Mr. Price began to look anxious when Tito spoke of his papa; but at the beginning of the next quarter, when the midsummer holidays were over, a letter came from abroad that appeared to relieve our master's mind, and that contained a second epistle, which Tito used to read to me and to himself, until it became worn out by constant reference, and by being kept along with his marbles, a pocket-knife, and a pegtop.

It was an English letter, of course, for Tito had been born and bred in England, and had seen no other country; and it was a very kind, fatherly, humorous kind of epistle, full of hope in his return to England before the next quarter was at an end, and of his anticipation of another holiday with his son and his little friend Simmons, if Simmons were still at Belvoir House. I hoped that he would come back soon, and that a circus would be in the town at the time; but the circus came and went away again, and no Colonel Zalez appeared to keep his promise to us.

"He can't be fighting all this time, Tit," I said in mild remonstrance at Tito's father's behaviour; but Tito shook his head, and said he wasn't so sure of it.

The quarter was past, and the second was approaching its termination. Christmas was upon us again; we were talking evermore of the holidays and home. Tito's father was still absent, and Mr. Price regarded Tito very

thoughtfully when the boy said his lessons to him. We went away and left Tito at school —we came back and found Tito there, looking somewhat pale, and his black school suit more than a trifle rusty.

Tito told me confidentially, on my return, that he had received no letter from his father, and that he had heard Mrs. Price say at dinner one day to Mr. Price that she thought it strange, and that Mr. Price had answered that he was inclined to think it rather strange himself, and that he, Tito, was sure that they had been talking about his papa, because they had spoken in whispers, and looked very much at him. I said that it must be fancy, and he tried to agree with me, but hoped that his papa would come to see him soon, for he was out of pocket-money, and his wardrobe was in need of considerable repair. But Colonel Zalez never came, and only Tito his son remained sanguine at last of his return.

I know now, what I did not know in all its details then, that the Prices, père et mère, were becoming very anxious concerning the whereabouts of Tito's father—that two quarters were in arrear, that the extra keep during Tito's holiday was added to the account, and that a third quarter had commenced. I knew afterwards that Mr. Price had written to an out-of-the-way place in Central America, where the colonel had dated his last letter, and that no answer had been returned; that he had written to a British consul and elicited the information that no such person was known within his jurisdiction, and I heard Mr. Price speak once of civil wars and general political confusion, and of the fear that Colonel Zalez had disappeared in a revolutionary vortex for ever.

Lady-day quarter passed, bills were paid, and Tito, waxing shabbier and shabbier, and still wondering why his father never wrote to him, got up every morning with a marvellous confidence in his parent's coming to see him before the day was out. Tito scarcely took into consideration the expense that he was to Mr. Price; he knew nothing of school-bills, and Mr. Price was too tender-hearted a man to show his dissatisfaction to the child himself. Mr. Price was puzzled what to do with him, or how long he was to allow this to last, and he looked more thoughtfully at the small enigma every day, and could not see his way to a solution. One day Mr. Price went to London, to the old town address of Colonel Zalez, and made many inquiries at his last lodgings, I learned afterwards, and returned baffled at all points. Tito's father had paid his bill and disappeared about nine months since, without leaving a clue to his whereabouts. A telegram from abroad had led to his sudden departure, it was elicited, and Colonel Zalez, packing up his boxes, and putting on his boots, probably more down at heel than ever, had departed on his mission, whatever it was, to a foreign state, wherever that might be.

Tito became so very shabby after Lady-day that the master found excuses to leave him at home when the boys went out for their airings or their cricket-matches, and finally, one of our boys spoke positively to a few high words which he had heard exchanged between Mr. and Mrs. Price one evening, with reference to the former's suggestion that he thought he should risk a suit of clothes for Tito.

The high words at all events ended in the suit of clothes being provided for poor Tito, who accompanied us in our walks again, and looked for the tall, sun-burnt, gray-mustached man at the corner of every street we passed.

Midsummer and the holidays came round, Tito was left at school, and Mr. Price's blank look at the unclaimed one assumed by several degrees more stoniness of aspect. Once more the busy hum of school, old pupils and new ones,—and Tito still on the establishment, and Tito's father nowhere. By degrees the story of the boy's forlorn position had found its way amongst the scholars, and Tito was pitied very much by the majority, and laughed at by a few thoughtless ones, who thought it rare fun for a boy to have a father who had run away from him. Tito's position was not an enviable one, but he bore it pretty well, and only fretted to himself a little, and with not half the noise which he had made on the night when he had missed his father for four hours. I was his counsellor and his comforter, and I kept up his hopes at last by strange legends of various fathers and mothers' returns after years of absence from their children, and was continually ransacking story-books for parallel cases to his own.

One day, Mrs. Price and her lord and master began to have a few words again concerning the unfortunate Tito, and Wickers, who was the boots of the school by day, and a page radiant in sugar-loaf buttons at night, came to Tito with the news.

"There's been a jolly row about you, Master Zalez," he said ; "and they've thought it over —only don't you say that I told you, mind— and they think your father is a wenturer, and they're going to send you to the workus."

Tito stared, and finally walked away, keeping from the playground and his playfellows all day. In the evening he came to me when I was deep in geography, and wrestling with "principal towns," and whispered—

"Joe, I want you."

"What is it, Tit?"

"You heard Wickers say that they were going to send me to the workhouse?"

"Yes—but I don't believe it."

"I'm going to ask the master now—come with me."

"Oh, lor!"

"He's at the desk there looking over the 'Themes,' and I want you to hear what he says."

"Very well."

So I left my place at the imminent risk of getting six bad marks for inattention to my lessons, and went with Tito to Mr. Price's desk. I shall never forget the look of astonishment and discomfiture on the master's face when Tito put the question very straightforwardly, and with wonderful composure.

"If you please, sir, is it true that you are going to send me to the workhouse?"

"Bless my soul!—who—who told you that, Tito?"

"I would rather not say who told me, sir —it's all about the school."

"Dear me—how vexing—how very unfortunate! My poor Tito, I should like to speak to you to-morrow morning, about seven. What are you doing out of your place, Simmons?" he asked, catching sight of me at last.

"I came to take care of Tito, sir."

"Six bad marks."

I knew that I should have them, therefore the promulgation of my sentence did not take me very much by surprise. Tito might have made matters worse by getting himself into a scrape and informing Mr. Price that he had asked me to leave my place with him, had not a look from me silenced one who had quite enough troubles of his own. Tito went the next morning to Mr. Price's room, meeting Wickers by the way, who told him that the master and the missus had been "at it" again, and that Mrs. Price was sick of boys whose fathers never paid. Of the particulars of Tito's conference with Mr. Price, these are the principal, as detailed to me by Tito between twelve and two.

It had all been arranged, and Mr. Price broke the news to him in as gentle a manner as he could, and wiped his own eyes once or twice surreptitiously with his pocket-handkerchief. He told Tito that he was not a rich man, that the school was the support of himself and a large family, and that it was beyond his power to keep Tito any longer at his own expense. He had consulted with his solicitor, who had advised him to hand over Tito to the parish authorities of Flatborough, who would pass Tito over to the parish authorities of the district in London where Colonel Zalez had resided for many years. He told Tito that the parish would use every exertion, and take far greater pains to find his father than he could do with a great school on his mind, and that he was taking the best and surest means to put Tito in his father's hands once more. He had no doubt that the parish would treat Tito very well, and that Tito would be very happy; but his auditor having his own opinion on this subject, went away discomfited. His last inquiry was—

"When is this to be, Mr. Price?"

"Oh, not this week," said the master assuringly, "or the next. Not till Michaelmas, at any rate."

Somehow the fate that loomed before Tito became known also to the boys, and was canvassed during play-hours, and generally set down as a "jolly shame," not any of us taking into consideration the ways and means of Mr. Price, and the appetite—always a good one—of Tito Zalez, and the rapid growth upwards and sideways—for Tito kept filling out rapidly—of the unfortunate pupil, who was out of his clothes again before any one knew where he was. Once the bright idea occurred to us of getting up a subscription to pay his arrears amongst ourselves and our parents, but the united contributions only amounting, after all the harass of canvassing, to eight shillings and threepence three farthings, it was thought advisable to return the subscriptions to the Tito fund. The second idea was entirely my own, and consisted in suggesting to my father, in a friendly and persuasive note, that Tito would be worth adopting, being a very nice and amiable boy, whom everybody would like at home. This idea was dashed to the ground by my father's courteous but decisive reply in the negative, and Tito, who had built a little on this letter, said, " Never mind, Joe," and asked whether Michaelmas-day always fell on the 29th of September.

On the twenty-eighth, in the dusky evening, which steals upon us so early at this date, and when the boys were strolling about the playground, waiting for the bell to ring them to tea, Tito suddenly came to me with the bottoms of his trowsers tucked up, and his threadbare jacket buttoned to the chin, in a way that looked like business, and said,

"Good-bye, Joe—I'm off."

"Off!—off where?"

"Hush! don't make a noise; but I can't stand the notion of a workhouse - I'm afraid of it; and—ugh!—the skilley! To-morrow's Michaelmas-day, and I'm going to run away."

"You don't mean it?"

"Yes, I do."

"But what's to become of you?"

"I shall enlist for a drummer, perhaps, or turn farmer's boy, or something. I'm off at once, through the school window, over the washhouse tiles, and so into the back lane."

Tito's sudden resolution took all my breath away; the novelty of the expedition aroused my love of adventure, and regardless of consequences, future hardships, future punishment from the hands of Mr. Price, and the sin of disobedience to my pastor and master, I said—

"I'll go a little way with you, Tit, and come back again before they shut up for the night."

"But how you will catch it!"

"Yes, I know that; but I should not like you to start alone."

"Thank you, Joe; it's very kind of you; but I think you had better stop."

I thought so also, but I went with Tito; and we succeeded in getting from the school by the way which my small friend had ingeniously sketched out. When we were outside the playground wall, and heard the boys' voices welling to our ears from the other side, our hearts sank a little at the boldness of the step, and we hurried on somewhat crestfallen to the sea-shore, and went on by long low-lying sands, knowing that the tide was out, and that we were not likely to meet anybody at that hour to stop us before we reached the King's Gap. This was a cleft in the cliffs, where I was to part with him, and wish him God-speed on his journey. Tito had a bundle with him, in which he had packed a small great-coat, his socks, one shirt, a cricket-ball, a large bag of marbles—the boys were always giving him marbles, by way of token of their respect for him—a few halfpenny prints which he had coloured, and a volume of fairy-tales that his father had given him. The night was soon upon us, and we grew less stout-hearted in the darkness, and were doubtful if the sea might not come up more quickly than we had bargained for, and cut us off from the King's Gap before our tired legs could wade through the deep sand towards it. But we reached the gap in safety, crept past the coast-guard house on the station, and then paused to consider the next step. This was the place of parting : but a look back at the dark country road I had to traverse, and a sudden remembrance of all the

horrible stories I had heard of travellers being
assassinated in lonely districts, and of children
being stripped by gipsies of their clothes, and
turned adrift to die of cold, deterred me from
returning to Belvoir House till daylight. I
said that I would go on with Tito; and Tito, who
had looked dismally in his direction also, said,
"Thank you, Joe," and was evidently grateful
for my company.

We were both becoming very nervous, but
we kept up appearances for a while. We took
the wrong turning, and found ourselves on the
edge of the cliff again. We made a short cut
across a field to "try back" for the roadway,
and lost ourselves completely. We went wandering about meadows and turnip fields in vain
efforts to get off farmers' property, and failed. I
We were frightened almost to death by a white
cow that bellowed suddenly over a hedge at us,
and Tito dropped his bundle in his hurry, and
we had to creep back cautiously for it, but
were never able from that night to set eyes
upon it again. We were overtaken by the rain
—a heavy, steady down-pour, that washed the
last atom of courage from our hearts.

"Joe," said Tito suddenly, "I wish I hadn't
come."

"So do I," I assented; and then, with our
heads very much bent forward, to keep the
rain from our faces, and to allow it more
easily to find its way down the backs of our
necks, we, two foolish miserable hearts, trudged
on, doubtful if we were walking over cross-
country to London, or back again to Flatborough. When it came to thunder and lightning along with the rain, the climax had
arrived, and Tito burst into tears, and wished
that he was in his comfortable workhouse, and
that I was out of trouble; and then the friendly
shelter of an old shed, with the doors off,
suddenly coming across our path, we darted
into it, and huddled together in one corner,
praying for the daylight. How the long night
passed we never knew. We went to sleep at
last, with our arms round each other's neck,
and thought of "The Children in the Wood."
We were scared once more by the white cow,
who came in with stately tread out of the rain
also, and snorted and sniffed about us, and
finally lay down across the doorway, barring
our egress, and pretending to go to sleep.
Tito said that it might take us unawares when
we followed its example. We did not know
that it was a cow till the morning, our impression being that it was a bull of the very mad-
dest description, and one to be especially wary
of, if we set any value on our lives.

Somehow we dozed off to sleep at last,

despite our fears; and when we woke again,
hearing the hum of voices near us, we found
that it was morning, and raining hard still,
and that a red-faced man and a rosy-faced girl
with milk-pails were looking down upon us in
intense astonishment.

"Lawks!" the girl said; "what are you
a-doing here? What boys are you?" I looked
at Tito, and he returned my glance; our
spirits were at zero, and it seemed necessary to
give in.

"We're from Mr. Price's school at Flatborough, and should be glad to get back," said
Tito.

"Flatborough — why, that's fifteen miles
from here," said the farmer's man. "You
don't mean to say that you two little chaps have
been a-playing truant—good gracious!"

But we did mean it; and Tito said that, if
they could put his friend Joe in the right road
for the school, they might drop himself at the
nearest workhouse, when they went that way,
as it was all the same, and he was expected
there; a piece of information which gave our
listeners the impression that we were from the
lunatic asylum five miles off. The farmer was
sent for, and as he knew Belvoir House well,
and was going to Flatborough on business that
morning we were in a fair way towards the end
of our adventure, and its unsatisfactory results.

We drove to the school after a breakfast
which we were not in a fair condition to enjoy;
and Mr. Price, his wife, the assistants, half
the boys, and Wickers, were in the hall to see
our ignominious return.

"You dreadful boys," Mr. Price said;
"what a terrible fright you have given me,
and what a deal of trouble! The county
police are looking everywhere for you. What
made you go away?"

"Please, sir, Tito was afraid of the workhouse," I explained; "and as he did not know
his way to London, I thought that I would
just put him on his road."

"I'll talk to you presently, Simmons," said
Mr. Price, meaningly; and then he turned to
Tito and said—"You need not have been afraid
of Michaelmas-day, Tito, for I had made up
my mind to risk another quarter; but your
anxiety of mind was to a certain extent excusable, and I shall not punish you severely."

I felt a twittering all along my spine, but
said not a word against his manifest partiality.

"And, my boy, I am very happy to relieve
you from a great suspense this morning," said
Mr. Price, laying his hand on Tito's curly
head. "Here is to-day's paper, with a tele-
graphic despatch from Central America."

As he unfolded the paper and pointed to one item of intelligence in the top corner of the right-hand column, I bent forwards with Tito, and read, in large letters, the following news concerning a small state, that at this late stage of my story I need not particularly allude to.

"Great Revolution in ——. Release of Colonel Zalez. His election as President of the Republic."

Tito's troubles were ended from that day. The next mail brought a letter from President Zalez, whose political intrigues had thrown him into prison, and then had placed him at the head of a government, and Mr. Price's account was settled in due course.

I met President Zalez at an hotel in New York, whither he had gone for a holiday, two years ago, and his son Tito was then a bigger fellow than his father. We laughed over Tito's troubles at a princely banquet which the great man gave us, and, as he smoked his paper cigarettes, we reminded him of our first treat together in the little town of Flatborough-on-the-Sea.

"When you were Tito's best friend," he said, holding out his hand to me across the table. "Thank you, Master Simmons!"

I was afraid that he would have kissed me again in his gratitude, but he sat down, sighed as though the cares of government were a little in the way of the peace and rest that he had found in England, leaned back in his chair, and lighted another cigarette.

———

FLORA'S HOROLOGE.

[Mrs. **Charlotte Smith**, born in London, 4th May, 1749; died at Tilford, 28th October, 1806. Novelist and miscellaneous writer; author of *Ethelinde; Celestina; Desmond;* and *The Old Manor House*, which is considered the best of her novels. Robert Chambers said of her works: "The keen satire and observation evinced in her novels do not appear in her verse; but the same powers of description are displayed."]

In every copse and sheltered dell,
    Unveiled to the observant eye,
Are faithful monitors who tell
    How pass the hours and seasons by.

The green-robed children of the spring
    Will mark the periods as they pass,
Mingle with leaves Time's feathered wing,
    And bind with flowers his silent glass.

Mark where transparent waters glide,
    Soft flowing o'er their tranquil bed;
There, cradled on the dimpling tide,
    Nymphæa rests her lovely head.

But conscious of the earliest beam,
    She rises from her humid nest,
And sees, reflected in the stream,
    The virgin whiteness of her breast.

Till the bright day-star to the west
    Declines, in ocean's surge to lave;
Then, folded in her modest vest,
    She slumbers on the rocking wave.

See Hieracium's various tribe,
    Of plumy seed and radiant flowers,
The course of Time their blooms describe,
    And wake or sleep appointed hours.

Broad o'er its imbricated cup
    The goatsbeard spreads its golden rays,
But shuts its cautious petals up,
    Retreating from the nooutide blaze.

Pale as a pensive cloistered nun,
    The Bethlem star her face unveils,
When o'er the mountain peers the sun,
    But shades it from the vesper gales.

Among the loose and arid sands
    The humble arenaria creeps;
Slowly the purple star expands,
    But soon within its calyx sleeps.

And those small bells so lightly rayed
    With young Aurora's rosy hue,
Are to the noontide sun displayed,
    But shut their plaits against the dew.

On upland slopes the shepherds mark
    The hour when, as the dial true,
Cichorium to the towering lark
    Lifts her soft eyes serenely blue.

And thou, "Wee crimson-tipped flower,"
    Gatherest thy fringed mantle round
Thy bosom at the closing hour,
    When night-drops bathe the turfy ground.

Unlike silene, who declines
    The garish noontide's blazing light;
But when the evening crescent shines,
    Gives all her sweetness to the night.

Thus in each flower and simple bell,
    That in our path betrodden lie,
Are sweet remembrancers who tell
    How fast their winged moments fly.

RENSTERN.

[Henry David Inglis, born in Edinburgh, 1795; died in London, 20th March, 1835. He wrote various books of travels in Norway, Sweden, Switzerland, France, Ireland, Spain, &c. His most important works are: *The New Gil Blas*, presenting graphic sketches of life in Spain; *Travels in the Footsteps of Don Quixote*; and *Tales of the Ardennes*, from which our extract is taken. Although an able and industrious author, his life was one of hardship and ill-requited labour.]

Renstern was born to the inheritance of all the lands of Frankenthall. . They extend from Ranstadt in Bavaria as far as Eindort; and he who could walk round them, from morning to his evening meal, would earn it well. Renstern was of an inquiring mind, more given to his studies than to his pleasures; for though his father left him in unrestricted possession at eighteen, he was rarely a partaker in those amusements and pursuits which his youth might have been supposed to incite him to, and which his fortune would have enabled him to follow. Renstern, though a philosopher, was not indifferent to the charms of woman. Philosophy, indeed, generally gave way in the beginning, but in the end it was sure to regain its ascendancy. A fearful inroad, however, was made upon his studies by the charms of Ermance Rosenheim, just growing into woman, the daughter of the Baron Rosenheim, a Bavarian. There may, perhaps, have been lovelier girls than Ermance Rosenheim, but never one more gentle and innocent. She had that, too, which beauty sometimes wants,— that perfect charm of youth and freshness, which seems as if sorrow never could shadow it. Her smile was like the daybreak on an Italian landscape, and the melody of her voice seemed an emanation from the harmony of her soul. Often would Renstern sit down to his metaphysics in the castle of Frankenthall, and remain absorbed in study, till suddenly, the image of Ermance presenting itself, he would close his books, order his horse, and gallop over to Eindort, to press a silky hand, and admire fair tresses. Do not imagine that, because Renstern was a philosopher, he knew not how to woo;—Renstern could say as gallant things as any man in Bavaria; but it was not gallantry he spoke to Ermance. He had an easy task; for he was sincere, and Ermance smiled upon him. It was often late when Renstern returned to Frankenthall; but finding his books lying as if waiting to be read, he would relight his lamp, and plunge into meta-

physics again, and morning would often surprise him at his studies. But this could not last. Renstern married Ermance on his twenty-first birth-day; she was seventeen; and for more than a year he forgot in her arms all his metaphysics and theology. But the dominant passion of the human mind will continue to be dominant. Love is only an episode in a man's life. It cannot occupy his existence. The other sex give up all to the affections, and many of them can live for ever upon their exercise; but they are always deceived. Gentle, kind, affectionate woman! we are too hard-hearted to be your mates: it is true we can love ardently; but it is you alone who know to love constantly. Renstern was again often among his books; and Ermance wondered that he was so often absent from her, and so silent when with her. Renstern still loved Ermance: he mingled in no amusement in which she was not a partaker, nor could he have found any pleasure where she did not share it. He thought he loved her as much as on the day when he led her from the altar in maiden bashfulness and beauty; and if his affection had depended upon her charms and her bashfulness, he would have been right; for Ermance was as lovely and as bashful as ever. But Renstern deceived himself; Ermance could no longer satisfy his existence. Ermance was no metaphysician: he could not talk to her of first causes and future contingents. The marriage state gives rise to many subjects of conversation less elevated than that which precedes it; and it is not wonderful that Renstern should often be silent and thoughtful in her company, since domestic affairs, or even tenderer topics, would cut but a sorry figure in the mind of a man who had just been travelling in the immensity of time and space, and whose mind was occupied with eternal existences, and the nature of a Supreme Intelligence.

Renstern betrayed, indeed, no want of affection, excepting that she had little of his company: his time was divided betwixt study and reverie. Poor Ermance! she was often given up to reverie too; for often did she think of the first months that succeeded her marriage, and often did she recall the words of Renstern, that he had attained the summit of happiness in possessing her. Alas! he spake too truly:—happiness cannot continue at one elevation.

Six months had passed away. One evening said Renstern to Ermance,

"Ermance, there is no reason why we should not live as our fortune and rank entitle us to do. We must enjoy life, my love."

"Do we not, Otto?" replied she. "How would you that we should live?"

"I would carry you to Vienna," replied he; "I would introduce you at court; I would show you the world."

Ermance did not see that living in greater splendour, or being introduced at the court of Vienna, would add to her enjoyment. Her happiest days had been spent at Frankenthall; and if Renstern would be again the Renstern he had once been, she could be as happy as ever. The recollection of those days, however, led her to indulge an undefined hope, that perhaps a change of scene might produce good. Besides, Ermance was too affectionate to oppose anything which Renstern might desire, whatever might be her own wishes. She immediately, therefore, expressed her willingness to go to Vienna.

Their journey might be called a happy one:—Renstern was himself again, and with Ermance former days were renewed. Renstern had an end in view, and all was novelty to Ermance. She was astonished, pleased, and affrighted by turns; she felt all that exhilaration of spirit, and infantine enjoyment, in crossing the boundaries of another kingdom, which every young person experiences when it is the first time it has happened. There is no circumstance in life which draws closer the affections than travelling. In everything that occurs there is a certain degree of common sympathy; and numerous occasions arrive in which the protector must show an interest in the protected. There was nothing to distract Renstern's mind; and the simplicity and astonishment and happiness of Ermance pleased and occupied him. Never had she appeared more charming either. The excitation had restored for a season that tint to her cheek which reminded him of Eindort; and one of the chains which had originally bound Renstern was beauty. Let no one speak lightly of the charm of beauty: it is fragile indeed; and what is not? Are health and youth more durable? and do we despise them? Is the painted flower we gaze upon less perishable? Beauty may be perchance a fatal dowry, and at rare times it may interpret falsely, like the Pontine marshes, which are covered with verdure and flowers; but how beautifully is an angelic soul reflected in celestial features!

Behold the Baron Renstern of Frankenthall and the fair Ermance at the court of Vienna. The manners of Vienna are not those of Ranstadt. There, as in every other capital city, innocence and simplicity are despised,—vice and virtue are judged by the changing verdict of fashion, in place of at the eternal tribunal of truth,—and things can no longer be recognized by their names. Ermance found herself singular in her opinions, and for their correctness she appealed to Renstern; but Renstern saw no distinction betwixt vice and virtue.

The ladies of Vienna are not more virtuous than those of Paris or London. In Paris the spur to intrigue is *éclat*, and therefore there is no concealment. In London, it is the love of it, and therefore there is a great deal of hypocrisy. In Vienna, fashion and inclination conjoin. Judge, then, how much intrigue there must be in Vienna.

Ermance had lost nothing of the beauty which had first captivated Renstern; a slight shade of sadness perhaps added to it, like the *chiaro scuro* which augments the beauty of a *Claude*. She possessed the attraction of novelty, besides, which, if it could not increase the lustre of her charms, had the effect of adding to their *éclat*. It may easily be supposed, therefore, that many were the worshippers of her beauty, and many the suitors for her favour; but it was soon discovered that she loved her husband; a circumstance that had never been imagined. The ladies of Vienna were sufficiently jealous of the beautiful stranger. They were jealous of her charms, and hated her for her virtue. Virtue has perhaps no triumph so great as the hatred of the vicious towards those who practise it; but as Ermance was virtuous and loved her husband, his fall might satisfy jealousy and expiate her faults; and Renstern being rich, and one of the handsomest men of his age, this revenge would neither be devoid of interest nor reward.

Six months of Vienna ruined Renstern. No one in Vienna gave such magnificent entertainments; no one was more distinguished for the splendour of his equipages. These, however, his fortune could have supported; but he gave magnificent presents to his favourites —gambled—and was ruined.

During this period what were the feelings and occupations of Ermance? Alas! sadness had begun to grow to her heart, and had already overcast her brow. Her charms were more touching than ever, though the light of her beauty was gone, like the charm of a southern night, whose beauty testifies to the splendours of the day which preceded it. She had mingled in gaiety without relish, and in society she had found no friend. The flattery she met with disgusted her, and the court that was paid to her fatigued her. She had seen

her husband play deep, and she feared that he
played deeper when she saw him not. Of his
intrigues she knew nothing, and suspected
nothing. She was too innocent to suppose it
possible that her husband would forget his
vows, and plight his faith to others; but she
saw that he too often preferred to hers the
society of others; and she wished that she
possessed their charms, or that she had never
left Frankenthall.

"Ermance," said Renstern to her one
morning, "we must leave Vienna."
Ermance was delighted to hear the intelligence. "I have no desire to remain in
Vienna,". replied she; "I love Frankenthall
better."

"But we shall not go to Frankenthall," said
he; "Frankenthall is no longer mine."

The truth flashed upon Ermance; but her
looks expressed affection and resignation, not
reproach. Renstern was for a moment touched
by her charms and her goodness, and fondly
took her hand, and called her his dear Ermance, and embraced her. It is strange how
mysteriously pain and pleasure are sometimes
mingled. In the moment of learning her
ruin, Ermance tasted a moment of perfect
happiness; and Renstern, in communicating
it, forgot in that moment that he was ruined.
There is a certain point at which the human
mind gathers strength from its calamity; it
grasps, as with giant strength, the very shaft
that pierces; and, in the consciousness of its
power, rises for a time above humanity, and
consequently above that calamity which is
human. But Renstern had told the truth:—
the lands of Frankenthall had passed into
other hands. Renstern, however, like all
gamblers, thought it possible that his fortune
might be regained, and therefore made it a
condition of the sale, that he should have a
power of redeeming his possessions within one
year.

In a few days after this communication,
Renstern and Ermance left Vienna, and retired to the village of Holt in Swabia, in the
neighbourhood of which his uncle resided, who
had offered Renstern a house upon his property. The Comte Font-barre was a man of
immense fortune, of retired habits, and of a
philosophical turn of mind; he had been long
a widower, and his only son had, a few years
before, married contrary to his father's wish,
and gone abroad under his displeasure: but
Font-barre often talked of forgiving him, and
of recalling him, to cheer the evening of his
days. It was impossible that Renstern's uncle
should not disapprove of the conduct which

had brought his nephew to ruin; but he felt
so much interest in Ermance, that he would
not wound her feelings by looking cold upon
her husband; and it may be also, that he was
too happy to have a philosophical companion,
to dwell much upon the cause which brought
about the event.

For some time after Renstern arrived at
Holt he was silent and gloomy, seeming to
enjoy nothing, and to exist without interest.
He had joined in pleasures whose enjoyment
is a fever, but which leaves an apathy and a
void more insupportable than the agonies
which attend it; and he had tasted of unholy
joys, which had left the memory of their intoxication. Renstern, in the village of Holt,
was differently regarded by the world from
Renstern in the castle of Frankenthall; and
he knew not that the world's homage was
sweet, until it was refused to him. One pang,
the severest of all, his principles spared him,—
the consciousness that his misfortunes were
the fruit of his own misconduct. He laid
them at the door of destiny; but he had forgotten to acquire that philosophy, the most
important of all, which teaches man to accommodate himself to the lot which that destiny
shall point out.

Suddenly a change was visible in the manners of Renstern:—he was often more cheerful than he was ever remembered to have been.
He was still sometimes thoughtful, but he was
no longer gloomy or morose; and at times
there was a playfulness in his manner which
reminded Ermance of happier days. It
would have required a deeper discerner of
human character than Ermance, to have discovered that it was like an occasional ripple
upon deep water, which hinders its profundity
from being seen. She was rejoiced at the
change:—she had more of Renstern's company
than she had had since the first year of their
marriage; and though she was somewhat surprised at its suddenness, it was not the less
agreeable on that account, and she fondly
flattered herself that former times were about
to be renewed. She could not, however, help
remarking one circumstance as somewhat extraordinary; it was, that when Renstern was
with his uncle his gaiety was unbounded, and
even unnatural to his character; but that
before and after his visit he was always
thoughtful, gloomy, and absent. The circumstance would have remained unnoticed by
Ermance had it not been that these occasional
reminiscences of former days were painful to her.
They were all that she had now to complain
of; and as her husband's change of manner

had restored to her almost all her former familiarity, she determined to ask the reason.

"Otto," said Ermance one morning, extending to him in sweet confidence her fair hand, "how I rejoice to see your spirits so much improved!" She paused a moment, and then timidly added, "There is now only one occasion on which you are gloomy."

"What is that, my love?" demanded Renstern.

"Before and after visiting your uncle; and you are always so gay when with him."

Before Ermance had finished the sentence, Renstern had risen, and walked across the room; but he immediately returned, and said—

"I am not aware, Ermance, of my being either gay or sad on these occasions; but is it not natural to be gay when with our friends, and sorry when we leave them?"

Ermance asked no further explanation, and hardly thought more of it. It passed rapidly across her mind, indeed, that one ought not to be sad *before* visiting one's friends, and that quitting those whom we are to see next day is hardly a cause for sadness,—but the thought passed away.

About the commencement of Renstern's change of manner, a circumstance occurred which it is necessary to notice. One evening, when Renstern and Ermance were with Font-barre, he addressed his nephew thus:—

"Renstern," said he, "I feel that I can forgive my son; but the overture must come from him. Do you write to your cousin, and say you have reason to think that, if he would ask his father's pardon, it would be granted." Renstern promised; and often since, the good man had expressed his disappointment that there was yet no answer from his son.

It was now ten months since Renstern had left Vienna. He had gone to Ulm on account of some little affair, and returned upon the day which he and Ermance were in the weekly habit of passing with Font-barre.

"Ermance," said he, "I have some business to talk over with my uncle to-day, and I have brought you some baubles from Ulm to amuse you in my absence."

Renstern returned late from his uncle's, and found Ermance reading her prayers. Next morning Font-barre was no more. An early summons informed Renstern of his loss. Being the nearest relation on the spot, he acted as executor; and a will was discovered, by which Font-barre's son was disinherited, and Renstern made heir to his uncle's wealth. Ermance trusted that her lord would be gene-

rous to his cousin,—she was sure he would: but is it to be wondered at, that she was pleased at an event which restored her husband to the rank which she thought him so worthy to hold?

The year was about to expire within which Renstern had the power to redeem his lands. The gold was told out, and Renstern was again lord of Frankenthall.

Do you hear how merrily the bells of Ranstadt are ringing? Children strew flowers on the streets; and the sound of welcome and rejoicing fills the air, as the magnificent equipage drives under the Munich gate. Six horsemen, upon richly-caparisoned Hungarians, ride before, blowing silver trumpets; six horses in magnificent trappings lead rapidly on the chariot, where sit the Baron of Frankenthall and the fair Ermance; and twelve of the chief vassals upon prancing steeds bring up the rear, arrayed in the colours of the house, and bearing its trophies. Sweetly did Ermance smile, and kiss her hand to the people who adored her, as she passed along the streets; and often did the Baron bow in affable dignity.

It was a beautiful May day: the sun looked out joyfully, and the gaiety of external nature seemed to invite happiness to harmonize with it. Never had the abode of Renstern looked more lovely. The trees were covered with leaves and blossoms; the earth was full of flowers, the last of the spring, and the first-born of summer; the perfumes of the hawthorn and the violet mingled together, and made harmony of sweet smells, as the birds made harmony of sounds. Ermance was happy.

There was a great feast that day at Frank-enthall: all Ranstadt and Eindort were invited to partake of it, and many nobles came from far to renew their friendship with its possessor. The feast was loud and joyous, and long after the vassals had retired the hall resounded with the mirth of the nobles; but at length it was past, and all was silent, and Renstern walked forth to taste the cool of the night air. He looked down upon Ranstadt and Eindort: the fires yet blazed on the neighbouring heights, the illuminations were not quite extinct, and the sound of distant mirth occasionally broke upon the silence:—around and above all was calm and still.

It had been intended that Renstern and Ermance should remain a short time at Frank-enthall, and then repair to Vienna. Sad as were Ermance's associations with Vienna, she looked forward to the time with eagerness and joy; for, alas! she was miserable at Franken-thall. Renstern was hardly ever with her, and his presence brought no comfort with it. All day long he would walk or ride over the country, and it was only when day closed that he returned to Frankenthall. When Ermance spoke to him, he seemed hardly to hear her: he was in a state of constant restlessness: the least noise seemed to alarm him; and if at night a knock was heard at the gate, he would start from his chair. He invited the neighbouring gentry to the castle; but they liked not the visit, and seldom came. Renstern, they said, was changed; he seemed absent and uncourtly, and looked upon his guests suspiciously. Sometimes he would drink deep, Ermance the only witness; and then he would laugh loud, and speak of the pleasures of Vienna, and call her his sweet mistress, and declare that life must be enjoyed. Remorse is like a cancer: it eats life away;—the mind becomes a volcano. The flame may burn low; but the fire lives on; and, beneath an outward calmness, there is hell.

All was mystery to Ermance; but she was miserable. How changed was her smile! They came, like unlooked for strangers, to those lips, where, in former days, they lay enamoured, like the golden clouds that worship around the sun. They came suddenly, as if to keep tears down in the fountain of sorrow; they were like sunbeams falling upon thick mists, or like the lamps which illumine a sepulchre. Often would her tears choke the utterance of her prayers; and then she would raise her streaming eyes to heaven, and think of the goodness of God, and the misery of her husband; that misery which, though hidden from her, was no mystery to the Eternal. Often would she wander slowly among the beautiful environs of the castle, to try if the beauty and calmness of nature would communicate tranquillity to her soul. Alas! the charm of nature can soothe that sorrow alone whose pangs would yield to time; but the sorrows which are mingled with uncertainty the calmness of nature cannot still. Sometimes she was on the point of telling her misery to Renstern,—of throwing herself into his arms, and asking leave to console him: but his looks were forbidding, and she feared to learn evil. At last the misery of uncertainty triumphed over her diffidence and her fears.

"Otto," said she, fearfully and with a trembling voice, "when we drove through Ranstadt I thought we should be happy at Frankenthall."

Renstern made no reply; but she could no longer hide her wretchedness and her tears: she threw herself upon her husband's neck, and sobbed bitterly. Renstern did not repulse her.

"Ermance," said he, "my kind one, I shall be less gloomy to-morrow, and then you will be happier."

The morrow came, and Ermance perceived a change in his manner: he remained at Frankenthall all day, and spoke more, and looked with more kindness upon her than she had remembered for a long time.

It was the evening, and they were sitting together, and alone; a bright fire blazed on the hearth, and Ermance felt that a ray of hope and happiness had entered her heart.

"Ermance," said Renstern to her, "I will tell you a story. There was once a Silesian, and this Silesian was an atheist. You know, Ermance, what an atheist is?"

"Yes," replied she, "but I do not wish to hear a story about atheists."

"This Silesian," continued he, "inherited great possessions; but they passed from him, no matter how. The Silesian had a rich relative, who had an only son; but the son was in a foreign land; and what do you think the Silesian did?"

"I know not," said Ermance.

"Nay, but guess," said he; "the sequel is the best of it."

"Indeed I cannot; but look less wildly, Otto."

"He forged a will in his own favour, and poisoned his uncle."

"His uncle, did you say!" interrupted Ermance.

"I know not," continued he; "his relative; but it matters not: the Silesian recovered his lands, and he thought he should then enjoy himself."

"Enjoy himself!" interrupted Ermance: "how could a murderer hope to enjoy himself?"

"But I have told you," continued Renstern, "that the Silesian was an atheist. He knew that the deed could not be discovered in this world; and as he did not believe in any other, he thought he had nothing to fear."

"He had his conscience to fear," said Ermance.

"I know not," continued Renstern; "but the Silesian was deceived. He became the slave of fear, and he knew not of what, but yet he was miserable. He was afraid to look around him, lest he should see his uncle; his fear was foolish, for he knew his uncle could not rise from his grave. He heard for ever a silent talking in the air—a horrid silence, which was not silence. The most

common things became in his eyes objects of
terror; even the implements of household use
took, in his imagination, shapes of hideous
deformity, which he dared not look upon.
The least noise would alarm him."

Ermance trembled: the traits of resemblance
had produced no suspicion:—still the resemblance affrighted her; and an undefined horror
thrilled through her.

"Renstern, Otto," said she, "finish this
dreadful tale."

"Presently," continued he. "The Silesian
dreaded his sleeping hours the most; and he
tried to keep himself awake. His dreams!—
but they were too dreadful to tell you. He
thought of requesting his wife to awake him
when he slept."

"Alas! he had a wife then?" said Ermance.

"He had," continued Renstern; "but she
knew nothing of his deeds until the day when
he poisoned himself."

"Alas! his poor wife!" said Ermance.

"The Silesian found existence insupportable; and he knew that death would terminate his misery. It might be in the evening, about this time, that the Silesian entered
the room where his wife was, after he had
drunk poison, and he said he would tell her
the story of a Bavarian who—"

Renstern stopped—death was upon his cheek
—his eyes closed.

"Mercy!" cried Ermance,—and she sprung
to him. But death kept his prey. He was
buried at the old churchyard of Ranstadt,
and Ermance lived a life of sorrow, loved and
lamented by all, and said daily masses for the
soul of Renstern.

FANCY IN NUBIBUS,
OR THE POET IN THE CLOUDS.

O! it is pleasant, with a heart at ease,
Just after sunset, or by moonlight skies,
To make the shifting clouds be what you please,
Or let the easily-persuaded eyes
Own each quaint likeness issuing from the mould
Of a friend's fancy; or, with head bent low
And cheek aslant, see rivers flow of gold
'Twixt crimson banks; and then a traveller go
From mount to mount through Cloudland, gorgeous
    land!
Or list'ning to the tide, with closed sight,
Be that blind bard who, on the Chian strand
By those deep sounds possess'd, with inward light
Beheld the Iliad and the Odyssey
Rise to the swelling of the voiceful sea.

S. T. COLERIDGE.

THE NIGHTINGALE'S COMPLAINT.
BY SHAKSPEARE.

As it fell upon a day,
In the merry month of May,
Sitting in a pleasant shade
Which a grove of myrtles made,
Beasts did leap, and birds did sing,
Trees did grow, and plants did spring:
Everything did banish moan,
Save the nightingale alone:
She, poor bird, as all forlorn,
Lean'd her breast up-till a thorn,
And there sung the dolefull'st ditty,
That to hear it was great pity:
Fie, fie, fie, now would she cry,
Teru, Teru, by and by:

That to hear her so complain,
Scarce I could from tears refrain;
For her griefs, so lively shown,
Made me think upon mine own.
Ah! (thought I) thou mourn'st in vain;
None take pity on thy pain:
Senseless trees, they cannot hear thee;
Ruthless beasts, they will not cheer thee;
King Pandion, he is dead;
All thy friends are lapp'd in lead:
All thy fellow-birds do sing,
Careless of thy sorrowing.
Even so, poor bird, like thee,
None alive will pity me.

Whilst as fickle fortune smil'd,
Thou and I were both beguil'd.
Every one that flatters thee
Is no friend in misery.
Words are easy like the wind;
Faithful friends are hard to find.
Every man will be thy friend,
Whilst thou hast wherewith to spend;
But if store of crowns be scant,
No man will supply thy want;
If that one be prodigal,
Bountiful they will him call;
And with such like flattering,
"Pity but he were a king."

If he be addict to vice,
Quickly him they will entice;
If to women he be bent,
They have him at commandement;
But if fortune once do frown,
Then farewell his great renown:
They that fawn'd on him before,
Use his company no more.
He that is thy friend indeed,
He will help thee in thy need;

If thou sorrow, he will weep;
If thou wake, he cannot sleep:
Thus of every grief in heart
He with thee doth bear the part.
These are certain signs to know
Faithful friend from flattering foe.

HOUSE-HUNTING.

BY ALARIC A. WATTS.

Next to the election of a lady as "a companion for life," there is, perhaps, nothing on earth so perplexing as the choice of a house. The requisites admitted, by universal consent, to be indispensable both for the comfort and convenience of persons of even moderate ambition, are of so multiform and diverse a nature, that it is next to impossible to find them united in any one tenement (however eligible it may appear on a first "view") under the canopy of heaven. It is in vain that you fortify your memory with all the *desiderata* which the most experienced House-hunter may have it in his power to suggest for your information; for, although the eligibilities turn out to be ever so numerous and important, there is always some little piddling nuisance to weaken and impair the freshness of a "first impression"—some objection which, to borrow the language of the law, is sure to be "fatal," and to overturn all our plans of colonization. Sometimes, indeed, the point is "reserved" for the opinion of that most righteous of all "judges," a discreet wife: but one trifling evil *in posse*, in such cases at least, is uniformly allowed to counterbalance a whole host of conveniences *in esse*.

Now, as I have the good fortune to be united to a woman who is allowed by all her neighbours to be one of the best managers in the country, and whose opinion on every question of domestic economy is (according to her own belief) infallible, it will readily be believed that the vexations and disappointments which I have been called upon to endure, in the course of my various changes of domicile, have been such as no ordinary foresight could have averted. Blessed with an adviser of surpassing clearness of perception, I must inevitably have escaped all inconvenience, had not my perplexities been of a very peculiar character.—But I am anticipating the disclosure of my miseries.

Some few months ago, a maiden aunt of my wife, from whom we had, in reality, no reasonable expectations (although my penetrating spouse has repeatedly declared, that she should not be *surprised* if aunt Grizzy were to leave us something comfortable), died, and bequeathed us two thousand pounds in the three per. cents. This God-send, for such indeed it was to us, occasioned a good deal of discussion in our little circle. The point in debate was not whether we wanted such an accession to our fortune—for it was admitted, *nem. con.* that nothing could have been more seasonable —but to what purposes it should be applied? After repeated deliberations, it was proposed by my daughter Monimia (a lively girl of sixteen), and seconded by her mother, that we should straightway remove to a larger and more commodious residence. They both affected to feel convinced, that the difference of rent between a small and what they were pleased to term a *respectable* house, would be more than compensated for by the increased convenience to papa, for whose fatiguing walks to and from town they had just then begun to feel the most poignant concern. Independently of this, and other weighty reasons which I was not prepared to controvert, the dearness of all the necessaries of life at our distance from the great city, and the impossibility of passing a social evening with a friend, or of witnessing a new play, or a new opera, without a most grievous taxation in the shape of coach-hire (not to mention the shoe-leather destroyed, and dresses dilapidated in wading through suburban mire), were all thrown into the scale; no wonder, therefore, that it should have kicked the beam in the twinkling of an eye. To say the truth, although I affected to object to our removal, I was by no means inclined to oppose it *à l'outrance.* So far from it, indeed, that I had a strong inclination to locate in a more agreeable neighbourhood myself, and was only restrained from giving expression to my sentiments by the apprehension, that my too ready acquiescence might produce an unfavourable alteration in my wife's opinions; who, notwithstanding that she is possessed of innumerable good qualities, is not without the common failing of her sex. Perhaps, too, I was the more anxious that the matter should appear to originate solely with herself, as I was well assured that if it did not turn out quite so favourably as we anticipated, she would lay the whole burden of the failure entirely at my door:—for, although I am allowed a very limited share in the credit of any new scheme that may happen to be successful in its results, of which I am the author, I am pretty secure of bearing the full brunt of the odium, should it chance to miscarry.

The question of expediency having been decided in the affirmative, the next point for consideration was, when we should carry our intentions into effect, and where we should choose a "place of rest" better suited to the improved state of our finances and the increased importance of our station in society, than the hovel (for such Monimia was pleased to entitle it) in which we had been vegetating for so many years. This was a knotty point, and one upon which we found it extremely difficult to agree. I intimated my preference to the east end of London, on account of its proximity to my place of business; but my wife and daughter were excruciated at the idea.

"Surely, papa," expostulated Monimia, "you would never think of settling within the sound of Bow bells! We had better remain where we are, than migrate to so vastly ungenteel a neighbourhood. We have only four rooms and a half that are habitable, in our present residence, it is true—but then we have a string of excellent excuses always at hand for whatever inconveniences we may sustain, in the extraordinary salubrity of the air; our proximity to an excellent friend Lady Dashwood (who, by the way, had only done us the honour of calling upon us once, and then merely to shelter herself from a shower of rain, which had overtaken her before she could reach her own lodge-gate); the great facility of conveyance to and from the metropolis, &c. &c. The East—my gracious! I see mamma is ready to expire at the thought! If it come to that, we shall certainly be exhibited along with Mr. Deputy Dip, of the Ward of Farringdon Without, in some future lucubration of the Smiths."

Here my wife took up the strain: "Beside, my dear, there's our Monimia is just verging into womanhood, and must be introduced. She is older, and a far greater proficient on the harp than Dr. Tympanum's daughter, who was brought out a year ago. What advantages, in the way of society, shall we be able to afford her, if we take up our abode in the purlieus of all that is odious and disagreeable? Only reflect now, 'Mrs. and Miss ——, one door from the pump, at Aldgate,' when read upon a card. For any sake, my love, abandon the idea of immolating our gentility at the shrine of vulgar mercantile convenience! What think you of some nice street out of Portland Place? or leading to either Portman, Cavendish, or Grosvenor Squares? or—"

She would have proceeded with her enumeration, but I cut her short by reminding her that the rent and taxes of a house in any one of the fashionable situations for which she appeared to have imbibed so peculiar a predilection, would amount to something more than our entire annual income,—a consideration worthy the attention of matter-of-fact people addicted to the plebeian practice of eating and drinking. This poser appeared to startle her not a little; and as it was an argument which no ingenuity could controvert, she made a virtue of necessity, and like a good housewife, as she is, admitted the importance of the objection with all imaginable deference and good humour. It was, however, mutually agreed, that there must be a number of quiet streets in the west end (for on this point she continued inexorable), in which it might not be difficult to meet with a habitation suited both to our means and our ambition. It was accordingly resolved, that we should devote a certain portion of every day of the ensuing week to various peregrinations of discovery. The lease of our Cottage Ornee had, to be sure, two years to run; but we entertained no doubt whatever of letting it at a few days' notice.

Determined not to proceed precipitately or unadvisedly in the matter, we consumed nearly the whole of Sunday (a breach of propriety to which the pious reader will no doubt refer all our subsequent mishaps) in concocting and digesting a series of questions for our guidance in House-hunting, which would, we fondly imagined, secure us from the possibility of mischance. In this memorandum we fancied we had glanced at every "particular" to which it could be necessary to advert in taking a house. It was as follows:—

I. The annual rent; and whether there be an after-clap in the shape of a premium?

II. The amount of taxes—for some parishes are rated lower than others; and whether the preceding tenant will be disposed to produce his receipts for the same, up to the period of his departure,—parish officers not being particular as to whether the taxes have been incurred by you or your predecessor, provided there be enough of your furniture on the premises to satisfy their claims?

III. The character of the said predecessor? For if he have left the neighbourhood in debt, you will stand a fair chance of being cheated by your trades-people, to make amends for his defalcations.

IV. Do the chimneys smoke?

V. Has the house an offensive breath? In other words—are the sewers and cesspools adequate to the purposes for which they were excavated?

VI. What quantity of old iron, brass cocks, and leaden mains is to be foisted upon you, under the denomination of "fixtures?" and whether you are to take them at a *fair* valuation—which means twice as much as you are ever likely to get for them again ;—or at your landlord's own estimate—which is sure to be half as much again as they cost at first hand?

VII. Whether the floors and walls are given to cold perspirations? And, above all, whether a boat will be necessary, at certain periods of the year, to enable your servants to navigate your kitchen and cellars?

VIII. Whether the house is in good and tenantable repair?

With this document reduced to black and white, and tucked into one of my gloves, in order that we might be able to refer to it at a moment's notice, did my wife, my daughter, and myself, commence our first day's peregrinations. Not a single empty house, from about the scale we considered likely to suit us, to the town mansion of the peer, did we suffer to escape our observation. To paraphrase a passage in Scott's admirable translation of Burger's "Leonora,"—

Tramp-tramp along the path we sped,
Splash-splash across the road !

Wherever we saw a placard, containing the words "This house to be let—Inquire within," thither did we forthwith direct our steps. It was in vain that I reminded my companions that many of the edifices into which they seemed bent upon penetrating, were obviously too large and too expensive for our means ; they would persist in tramping through them, in order to see "what kind of places they were." "Beside, my dear," my wife would sometimes exclaim, "who knows but we *may*, some day or other, want such a house !" Our first day's expedition afforded us a tolerable insight into the mysteries of House-hunting : and what with ascending and descending stairs, and exploring cellars and servants' offices, we found ourselves pretty considerably fatigued before we reached home.

To attempt to give anything like a detailed account of our adventures would be to fill a volume. Some persons were most obsequious in their civilities ; others, surveying us with a degree of scrutiny which seemed by no means unmingled with suspicion, demanded (before we had passed the threshold of their doors) if we *really* considered the house *likely to suit us.* Mr. A. was at breakfast, and could not be disturbed ! Mrs. B. had no objection to our viewing her sitting-rooms, but the bed-chambers (the black-holes of her establishment),

were in a state of confusion, which rendered it impossible that we could be allowed to inspect them ! Mrs. C. had the chimney-sweepers in her kitchen ! (it was just then under water, and might have impressed us with an ugly prejudice against the general comfort of the tenement) so that we were not allowed to penetrate lower than her dining-room. Mrs. D. was at dinner ; and wondered how people could expect to obtain admittance at so unseasonable an hour. Here, the landlord had put a capricious rent of twice its real value upon his house, and had taken an oath that it should rot to the foundation before he would let it for less. There, an officer's lady, whose husband was with our army in India (in what regiment it might be difficult to ascertain), wished to dispose of her lease and furniture, in order that she might join her spouse? In one place, the house had grown too large for the family— in another, the family had grown too large for the house ! Under any other circumstances, the party would not have vacated it for the world. At this place we were informed, that Mr. E.'s sole reason for leaving his residence was, that he wished to retire into the country ; —at the other, that the increase of Mr. F.'s professional avocations would not admit of his living at so great a distance from the Inns of Court. In no single instance was any motive assigned, which could possibly invalidate the supposed eligibility of the tenement. Our queries (which, whenever there appeared to be the slightest chance of our suiting ourselves, were always at our fingers' ends) were answered, for the most part, satisfactorily. Where a servant or charwoman had the care of a house, the common reply to our various inquiries was, "Yes, ma'am ; for aught I have *heard* to the contrary !" and "No, ma'am ; not as I *know* of." For all the more important particulars, however, we were, in such cases, usually referred to "my master," or, "the gentleman as puts me in ;"—living some six or seven English miles from the scene of action.

At first we found it difficult to account for the extraordinary candour of the people who had the letting of houses for agents and upholsterers ; for, however fervent they were in their general recommendations of the premises, they had always some little candid communication to make at our second visit, which was sure to save us the trouble of calling again : "It was true that the chimneys *did* smoke a little, and the kitchens were shocking damp." While we were yet green in our vocation we considered ourselves bound, in common gratitude, to present our informant with a shilling, as a premium for her timely intimation; but we soon found that it was the common trick of the profession. The Mrs. Candid in question had house rent-free, and so much a week for taking care of the premises, to say nothing of an odd shilling every now and then for telling the whole truth, and sometimes a little more than the truth! Where is the starving and homeless wretch who would have been proof against such a temptation?

But I shall not fatigue my reader with *minutiæ*. It is sufficient for all useful purposes to remark, that after six days' peregrinations, just as we were about to make up our minds that such a domicile as we were in search of—like happiness—was not to be met with in this world, our attention was attracted by a placard in the window of a genteel-looking house, in —— Street, —— Square: and although it did certainly appear a cut above our means, we determined (on my wife's favourite principle) to take a peep at it. We accordingly knocked at the door, and were ushered into the drawing-room, where we were informed that "Mrs. Varnish" would wait upon us without delay. In the meantime, we had leisure to survey the apartment. My wife and daughter were in ecstasies. If the rent *should* prove at all moderate, it was just the very thing we wanted.—We were here interrupted by the *entrée* of a smart, smirking lady of a "certain age," who, tripping across the room with more than fairy lightness, addressed me with, "I fear, sir, you will be disappointed, if you have called respecting the house, as it is, I have reason to believe, already let. Indeed, the rent is so *extremely* low, considering its size and conveniences, that I might have parted with it half a dozen times over, had I been less fastidious than I am."

This rent was, she then informed us, one hundred pounds per annum (twenty pounds beyond the limit I had prescribed as our ultimatum); and there were a few fixtures—better, she declared, than new; including her carpets and curtains, which, as they were planned to the rooms, it would be "a thousand pities to disturb." Here my daughter manifested considerable impatience to know if the house was *really* let; and Mrs. Varnish (all complaisance as she was) rang the bell, to catechise her servant (who had of course her cue), as to whether Mr. Fitzroy Wilmington had sent his definitive answer that morning or not;—when it turned out that he had not, but that he considered the matter as all but settled, and would call and make the final arrangements in person at two o'clock. Mrs. V. expressed great satisfaction that she had it still in her power to oblige us, as the house seemed to suit us so entirely. She must, however, beg to show the two ladies through her sleeping apartments before she could allow us to form any decision.

On their return, they appeared to have made the most of their time, for they had grown as intimate as if they had known each other a dozen years. "What a delightful woman!" whispered Monimia, aside, to me. I nodded my assent; for, in truth, Mrs. V. did appear to me to be a most fascinating creature. She was all delicacy and disinterestedness! She even offered to give us a day for consideration; but this my wife declared would be taking an unfair advantage of her generosity, considering her situation with respect to Mr. Fitzroy Wilmington. We accordingly brought the matter to an issue upon the spot. To save the trouble and expense of appraisement, Mrs. V. proposed to take 20 per cent. off the cost price of her fixtures, &c. She had spent a vast deal of money on ornamental repairs, but for this she should charge nothing; neither would she require a premium, notwithstanding the extraordinary cheapness and eligibility of the house. In short, she was a paragon of a landlady; and we seemed mutually charmed with each other, until we got fairly in,—and then—but I must make short work of a long story.

It is quite true, that Mrs. Varnish had guaranteed us, in her memorandum of agreement, against any of the nuisances referred to in the schedule I have already presented to my readers; but, gracious goodness! we had to encounter horrors without number, which nothing short of the wisdom of Solomon would have enabled us to avert.

Imprimis.—The house had the dry-rot; and although it was impossible to prove that it was not in "tenantable repair" when we took it, it was equally so to affirm with truth that it might not, some day or other, suddenly tumble about our ears. To add to our confusion, our tenure was a "repairing lease."

Secondly.—Our opposite neighbour kept a private mad-house; and although his patients were not quite so turbulent as some of Mr. Warburton's maniacs, they were sufficiently so to be extremely troublesome, on summer evenings more especially. Several of them, too, had an ugly trick of grinning, showing their teeth, and otherwise distorting their features, at the windows, to such a degree. that we could not occupy our front rooms in the daytime, without the risk of being horrified by their demoniacal gesticulations.

Thirdly.—Our next-door neighbour, on the right hand, was no other than our worthy friend Dr. Tympanum, the professor of music; a circumstance which, however auspicious it appeared when we first heard of it, turned out in the event to be a most intolerable nuisance. My good neighbour (whose eminence in his art had been rewarded by a musical diploma) had begun to teach upon the Logerian system, just three days after we were fairly housed. My readers are no doubt aware of the slender texture of a single-brick London party-wall! His classes commenced at eight o'clock in the morning, and continued (with the exception of an hour's intermission for dinner) until eight in the evening. Merciful Heaven! I thought all the devils in Pandemonium had broken loose, and were conspiring to torment me. Strum! strum! strum!—crash! crash! crash!—from no less than twenty pair of hands, from morning to night!

Fourthly.—To escape the annoyance,—at least partially, for to flee from it wholly was impossible—I resolved to make a study of my back drawing-room; but here another evil awaited me. The rear of my house looked directly upon the yard of a "Statuary Mason," who had no less than two brace of desperadoes employed constantly in sawing blocks of marble into slabs. No powers of the pen could do justice to a quartetto of such performers. Suffice it to say, that it quite eclipsed the most violent *crescendos* of Dr. Tympanum's concerts.

Fifthly.—My house had been built with green wood. The consequence of which was, that there was not a door that had not shrunk beyond the reach of the latch-bolt; so that we could only keep them closed by setting chairs or tables against them; to say nothing of the windows, which admitted the breezes of heaven in all directions. As to the flooring, it was one continued series of *crevasses*, or abysses, through which the wind rushed with such amazing impetuosity, that it was impossible for a lady to walk over any part of the room uncovered by the carpet, without having her petticoats puffed up like an air balloon. I once read (I think it was in the *Morning Post*) of a respectable old lady who was carried up to a second-floor window in the Strand, by means of the wind and her tenacious adherence to her umbrella; and after what I have seen of the operation of the same element in my own house, I can believe anything of it.

Sixthly.—My left-hand neighbour was a good enough sort of a man, of quiet habits and highly respectable character; but a nuisance

of the most overwhelming description notwithstanding. He was a wholesale wax and tallow chandler, and what with his "Melting Days" and "Evenings in Grease" (for his warehouse is directly contiguous to the premises of my friend "The Statuary Mason") well nigh stunk me into a consumption. Nay, the bare mention of his name, at this distance of time, is equivalent to a dose of emetic tartar.

Seventhly.—But no!——I can stand it no longer. My fire is out—my candle is expiring —and I am almost frozen to an icicle. I have a score more evils yet to enumerate. Pandora found Hope at the bottom of her budget, but I fear I have no such luck. However, *au revoir*, my dear reader; for I have groans without number still to pour into thy kindly-sympathizing ear.—*Scenes of Life and Shades of Character.*

SERIOUS COUNSEL.

[Sir John Davies, born at Chisgrove, Wiltshire, 1570; died in London, 7th December, 1626. He was a lawyer, judge, and a poet. *The Immortality of the Soul* (from which we quote) is his principal poem. He also wrote *Hymns to Astræa*—a series of adulatory acrostics to Queen Elizabeth—and *The Orchestra*, an explanation of the antiquity and excellence of dancing.]

O ignorant poor man! what dost thou bear
  Lock'd up within the casket of thy breast?
What jewels, and what riches hast thou there?
  What heav'nly treasure in so weak a chest?

Look in thy Soul, and thou shalt beauties find,
  Like those which drown'd Narcissus in the flood;
Honour and pleasure both are in my mind,
  And all that in the world is counted good.

Think of her worth, and think that God did mean,
  This worthy mind should worthy things embrace:
Blot not her beauties with thy thoughts unclean,
  Nor her dishonour with thy passion base.

Kill not her quick'ning pow'r with surfeitings:
  Mar not her sense with sensuality:
Cast not her wit on idle things:
  Make not her free-will slave to vanity.

And when thou think'st of her eternity,
  Think not that death against her nature is:
Think it a birth: and when thou go'st to die,
  Sing like a swan, as if thou went'st to bliss.

And thou, my Soul, which turn'st with curious eye,
  To view the beams of thine own form divine,
Know, that thou canst know nothing perfectly,
  While thou art clouded with this flesh of mine.

Take heed of over weening, and compare
Thy peacock's feet with thy gay peacock's train:
Study the best and highest things that are,
But of thyself an humble thought retain.

Cast down thyself, and only strive to raise
The glory of thy Maker's sacred name:
Use all thy pow'rs, that blessed pow'r to praise,
Which gives thee pow'r to be, and use the same.

CAPTURING A WHALE.

BY J. FENIMORE COOPER.

The cockswain cast a cool glance at the crests of foam that were breaking over the tops of the billows, within a few yards of where their boat was riding, and called aloud to his men—

"Pull a stroke or two; away with her into dark water."

The drop of the oars resembled the movements of a nice machine, and the light boat skimmed along the water like a duck, that approaches to the very brink of some imminent danger, and then avoids it at the most critical moment, apparently without an effort. While this necessary movement was making, Barnstable arose, and surveyed the cliffs with keen eyes, and then, turning once more in disappointment from his search, he said—

"Pull more from the land, and let her run down, at an easy stroke, to the schooner. Keep a look-out at the cliffs, boys; it is possible that they are stowed in some of the holes in the rocks, for it's no daylight business they are on."

The order was promptly obeyed, and they had glided along for near a mile in this manner, in the most profound silence, when suddenly the stillness was broken by a heavy rush of air and a dash of water, seemingly at no great distance from them.

"By Heaven! Tom," cried Barnstable, starting, "there is the blow of a whale."

"Ay, ay, sir," returned the cockswain, with undisturbed composure; "here is his spout, not half a mile to seaward; the easterly gale has driven the creater to leeward, and he begins to find himself in shoal water. He's been sleeping, while he should have been working to windward!"

"The fellow takes it cooly, too! he's in no hurry to get an offing."

"I rather conclude, sir," said the cockswain, rolling over his tobacco in his mouth very composedly, while his little sunken eyes began to twinkle with pleasure at the sight, "the

gentleman has lost his reckoning, and don't know which way to head, to take himself back into blue water."

"'Tis a fin-back!" exclaimed the lieutenant; "he will soon make head-way, and be off."

"No, sir, 'tis a right whale," answered Tom; "I saw his spout; he threw up a pair as pretty rainbows as a Christian would wish to look at. He's a raal oil-but, that fellow!"

Barnstable laughed, turned himself away from the tempting sight, and tried to look at the cliffs; and then unconsciously bent his eyes again on the sluggish animal, who was throwing his huge carcass at times for many feet from the water, in idle gambols. The temptation for sport, and the recollection of his early habits, at length prevailed over his anxiety in behalf of his friends, and the young officer inquired of his cockswain—

"Is there any whale-line in the boat to make fast to that harpoon which you bear about with you in fair weather or foul?"

"I never trust the boat from the schooner without part of a shot, sir," returned the cockswain; "there is something natural in the sight of a tub to my old eyes."

Barnstable looked at his watch, and again at the cliffs, when he exclaimed in joyous tones—

"Give strong way, my hearties! There seems nothing better to be done; let us have a stroke of a harpoon at that impudent rascal."

The men shouted spontaneously, and the old cockswain suffered his solemn visage to relax into a small laugh, while the whale-boat sprang forward like a courser for the goal. During the few minutes they were pulling towards their game, long Tom arose from his crouching attitude in the stern sheets, and transferred his huge frame to the bows of the boat, where he made such preparation to strike the whale as the occasion required. The tub, containing about half of a whale-line, was placed at the feet of Barnstable, who had been preparing an oar to steer with, in place of the rudder, which was unshipped in order that, if necessary, the boat might be whirled round when not advancing.

Their approach was utterly unnoticed by the monster of the deep, who continued to amuse himself with throwing the water in two circular spouts high into the air, occasionally flourishing the broad flukes of his tail with graceful but terrific force, until the hardy seamen were within a few hundred feet of him, when he suddenly cast his head downwards, and, without an apparent effort, reared his immense body for many feet above the water, waving his tail violently, and producing a whizzing noise, that sounded like the rushing of winds. The cockswain stood erect, poising his harpoon ready for the blow; but, when he beheld the creature assume this formidable attitude, he waved his hand to his commander, who instantly signed to his men to cease rowing. In this situation the sportsmen rested a few moments, while the whale struck several blows on the water in rapid succession, the noise of which re-echoed along the cliffs like the hollow report of so many cannon. After this wanton exhibition of his terrible strength, the monster sunk again into his native element, and slowly disappeared from the eyes of his pursuers.

"Which way did he head, Tom?" cried Barnstable, the moment the whale was out of sight.

"Pretty much up and down, sir," returned the cockswain, whose eye was gradually brightened with the excitement of the sport; "he'll soon run his nose against the bottom, if he stands long on that course, and will be glad to get another snuff of pure air; send her a few fathoms to starboard, sir, and I promise we shall not be out of his track."

The conjecture of the experienced old seaman proved true, for in a few minutes the water broke near them, and another spout was cast into the air, when the huge animal rushed half his length in the same direction, and fell on the sea with a turbulence and foam equal to that which is produced by the launching of a vessel, for the first time, into its proper element. After this evolution, the whale rolled heavily, and seemed to rest from further efforts. His slightest movements were closely watched by Barnstable and his cockswain, and, when he was in a state of comparative rest, the former gave a signal to his crew to ply their oars once more. A few long and vigorous strokes sent the boat directly up to the broadside of the whale, with its bows pointing towards one of the fins, which was at times, as the animal yielded sluggishly to the action of the waves, exposed to view. The cockswain poised his harpoon with much precision, and then darted it from him with a violence that buried the iron in the body of their foe. The instant the blow was made, long Tom shouted with singular earnestness—

"Starn all!"

"Stern all!" echoed Barnstable; when the obedient seamen, by united efforts, forced the boat in a backward direction, beyond the reach of any blow from their formidable antagonist. The alarmed animal, however, meditated no

such resistance; ignorant of his power, and of the insignificance of his enemies, he sought refuge in flight. One moment of stupid surprise succeeded the entrance of the iron, when he cast his huge tail into the air with a violence that threw the sea around him into increased commotion, and then disappeared, with the quickness of lightning, amid a cloud of foam.

"Snub him!" shouted Barnstable; "hold on, Tom; he rises already."

"Ay, ay, sir," replied the composed cockswain, seizing the line, which was running out of the boat with a velocity that rendered such a manoeuvre rather hazardous, and causing it to yield more gradually round the large loggerhead that was placed in the bows of the boat for that purpose. Presently the line stretched forward, and, rising to the surface with tremulous vibrations, it indicated the direction in which the animal might be expected to reappear. Barnstable had cast the bows of the boat towards that point, before the terrified and wounded victim rose once more to the surface, whose time was, however, no longer wasted in his sports, but who cast the waters aside as he forced his way, with prodigious velocity, along their surface. The boat was dragged violently in his wake, and cut through the billows with a terrific rapidity, that at moments appeared to bury the slight fabric in the ocean. When long Tom beheld his victim throwing his spouts on high again, he pointed with exultation to the jetting fluid, which was streaked with the deep red of blood, and cried—

"Ay, I've touched the fellow's life. It must be more than two foot of blubber that stops my iron from reaching the life of any whale that ever sculled the ocean!"

"I believe you have saved yourself the trouble of using the bayonet you have rigged for a lance," said his commander, who entered into the sport with all the ardour of one whose youth had been chiefly passed in such pursuits; "feel your line, Master Coffin; can we haul alongside of our enemy? I like not the course he is steering, as he tows us from the schooner."

"'Tis the creater's way, sir," said the cockswain; "you know they need the air in their nostrils when they run, the same as a man: but lay hold, boys, and let us haul up to him."

The seamen now seized their whale-line, and slowly drew their boat to within a few feet of the tail of the fish, whose progress became sensibly less rapid, as he grew weak with the loss of blood. In a few minutes he stopped running, and appeared to roll uneasily on the water, as if suffering the agony of death.

"Shall we pull in and finish him, Tom?" cried Barnstable; "a few sets from your bayonet would do it."

The cockswain stood examining his game with cool discretion, and replied to this interrogatory—

"No, sir, no—he's going into his flurry; there's no occasion for disgracing ourselves by using a soldier's weapon in taking a whale. Starn off, sir, starn off! the creater's in his flurry!"

The warning of the prudent cockswain was promptly obeyed, and the boat cautiously drew off to a distance, leaving to the animal a clear space while under its dying agonies. From a state of perfect rest, the terrible monster threw its tail on high as when in sport, but its blows were trebled in rapidity and violence, till all was hid from view by a pyramid of foam, that was deeply dyed with blood. The roarings of the fish were like the bellowings of a herd of bulls, and, to one who was ignorant of the fact, it would have appeared as if a thousand monsters were engaged in deadly combat behind the bloody mist that obstructed the view. Gradually these effects subsided, and, when the discoloured water again settled down to the long and regular swell of the ocean, the fish was seen exhausted, and yielding passively to its fate. As life departed, the enormous black mass rolled to one side, and when the white and glistening skin of the belly became apparent, the seamen well knew that their victory was achieved.

VIRTUE.

Sweet day, so cool, so calm, so bright,
The bridal of the earth and sky,
The dew shall weep thy fall to-night:
    For thou must die.

Sweet rose, whose hue angry and brave
Bids the rash gazer wipe his eye,
Thy root is ever in its grave,
    And thou must die.

Sweet spring, full of sweet days and roses,
A box where sweets compacted lie,
My music shows ye have your closes,
    And all must die.

Only a sweet and virtuous soul,
Like season'd timber, never gives;
But though the whole world turn to coal,
    Then chiefly lives.

           GEORGE HERBERT.

BEAUTY'S PRAYER.

[Mrs. Frances Sargent Osgood, born in Boston, U.S., 1812; died in New York, 12th May, 1850. A favourite American poet; author of the *Casket of Fate*; *A Wreath of Wild Flowers from New England*; and editor of several volumes of poetry —"Grace of expression, and delicacy of moral feeling pervade all she ever wrote."—*Sarah J. Hale.*]

Round great Jove his lightning shone,
  Rolled the universe before him,
Stars, for gems, lit up his throne,
  Clouds, for banners, floated o'er him.

With her tresses all untied,
  Touched with gleams of golden glory,
Beauty came, and blushed, and sighed,
  While she told her piteous story.

"Hear! oh, Jupiter! thy child:
  Right my wrong, if thou dost love me!
Beast, and bird, and savage wild,
  All are placed in power above me.

"Each his weapon thou hast given,
  Each the strength and skill to wield it:
Why bestow, Supreme in heaven!
  Bloom on me with naught to shield it?

"Even the rose—the wild-wood rose,
  Fair and frail as I, thy daughter,
Safely yields to soft repose,
  With her lifeguard thorns about her."

As she spake in music wild,
  Tears within her blue eyes glistened:
Yet her red lip dimpling smiled,
  For the god benignly listened.

"Child of Heaven!" he kindly said,
  "Try the weapons Nature gave thee;
And if danger near thee tread,
  Proudly trust to them to save thee.

"Lance and talon, thorn and spear:
  Thou art armed with triple power,
In that blush, and smile, and tear!
  Fearless go, my fragile flower.

"Yet dost thou, with all thy charms,
  Still for something more beseech me?—
Skill to use thy magic arms?
  Ask of Love—and Love will teach thee?"

MILLY LANCE.

[Dutton Cook, born in London, 1831. Novelist. *Paul Foster's Daughter; A Prodigal Son; The Trials of the Tredgolds; Leo; Sir Felix Foy, Baronet; Hobson's Choice; Over Head and Ears; Dr. Muspratt's Patient,* and other Tales (from which we quote); and *Art in England,* a Series of Essays and Studies, are his principal works. Mr. Cook's stories display the genius of pathos and humour in a remarkable degree.]

CHAPTER I.

Dr. Dendy was not good-looking. He might even have been called ugly, but that there is an excellent precept impressed on all well-eared-for minds in their nursery stage of formation, to the effect that no one may be so offensively described, except it be a certain notorious personage whom it will not be necessary to name. Let us say, therefore, that Dr. Dendy was plain.

He was a physician in large practice. Jocose people said of him that, in the course of his professional career he had had occasion to thrust so many guineas into his pockets that eventually the gold coin, carried so much about his person, had got into his own circulation, and affected the colour of his skin. Certainly his complexion was deeply tinged with yellow. He was very bald, with a narrow festoon of iron-gray hair at the back of his head. His small, neat, wiry figure was always clothed in black—his coat being invariably buttoned tightly across his chest. He was of middle age, perhaps a little better; which expression, as applied to age, is generally understood to signify a little worse, or older. He lived in a grand, gaunt, murky house in Harley Street, seldom setting foot in more than two rooms in it, however—his library and his bedroom. He was the author of an admired Treatise on the Pathology of the Heart, to which work he was constantly adding annotations and commentaries, with a view to completely exhausting and settling the subject. When he was able to devote a little more time to it, his book, he was satisfied, would be the only authority on the heart—physiologically and pathologically considered.

But his time was very much occupied. He saw patients at his own house almost before he had swallowed his breakfast; later in the day, he saw other patients at their own homes; he was one of the physicians to St. Lazarus Hospital, and gave lectures on Materia Medica, course after course, to the students of that excellent institution; he was a Fellow, or a Member, of all sorts of scientific societies, and on certain days in the week he attended the boards of various Assurance companies, examined papers, and passed or rejected lives proposed for insurance. He was hard-working and prosperous. Few men in the profession, it was said, made so large an income. Go to what part of the town you would, you seemed to be for ever encountering Dr. Dendy's two-horse carriage rattling along at a great pace, going to or from patients and the accompanying golden fees.

When the doctor started in the morning, he gave his coachman a list of the places he was to drive to. In this list the coachman had known entered now for some months a certain house in Calthorpe Street. You called it Calthorpe Street, Russell Square, if you were desirous of consulting the predilections of its inhabitants; if you were heedless in that respect, you spoke of it with perhaps greater accuracy as Calthorpe Street, Gray's Inn Road. Dr. Dendy always appeared to prefer the first-mentioned designation.

The coachman treated himself to a furtive smile whenever he read Calthorpe Street in his list. The doctor had a patient there, of course. But then, as the coachman noted, his master went there oftener and stayed there longer than anywhere else. Of course the patient might be in a more deplorable state, might stand more in need of protracted visits from a medical adviser than any other of Dr. Dendy's patients; but the coachman was inclined to think that such was not the case.

On the first floor of the house in Calthorpe Street visited by Dr. Dendy, there lodged one Captain Lance, a retired Indian officer, and his only child, Miss Milly Lance. Captain Lance was in feeble health from a distressing asthma, and from other infirmities of a painful nature. He did not bear his sufferings patiently; was, indeed, very peevish and petulant and hard to please; exhibited all the selfishness and want of consideration which a long course of ill-health is apt to develop in almost any one, however great may have been his original stock of equanimity and good-nature. But Captain Lance had not begun with much excellence of temper; and now, a confirmed invalid, it may be said of him that he had no temper at all, except of the very worst sort. He was attended, however, with a ceaseless solicitude, an untiring affection, by his daughter Milly, a slim, fair girl of eighteen or so, not very remarkable-looking, beyond that she possessed a profusion of glossy brown hair, and a pair of large, luminous, dove-like eyes.

No wonder she was pale. She was always by the side or within call of her invalid father. She was hardly ever permitted to stir from his sick room. It was dull, tiring work. "Don't go, Milly," he would say, sharply; "I may want you; there's no knowing." She could only escape when he dozed: his asthma lulled for a while by anodynes. Awake, he would have her ever near him, waiting on him, slaving for him, nursing him. Now and then he would upbraid her bitterly for some fancied neglect of him, the poor child with a twitching face patiently standing by him the while, replying only by her tears, her caresses, and her increased exertions for his comfort. Then he would make her the audience of his repinings, tell over and over again the story of his sufferings, bursting out occasionally into passionate lamentations over his broken health and ruined fortunes. What could she say? What could she do? It was tiring, cruel work for poor Milly Lance.

The Captain was poor. The fact was too often harped on and groaned over for Milly not to be conscious enough of it.

Yet it must be said that Dr. Dendy had made no inroads on the sick officer's straitened means.

"No, my dear," he said to Milly, on his first visit, putting from him with a smile the proffered fee, "it musn't be. We doctors have all our crotchets. Each of us has his free list. One enters clergymen upon it; another, authors; a third, artists. For my part, I never take a fee from a soldier I should be ashamed to do it. My father was a soldier, and served in India, as your father has served; only he was more fortunate. He was a general of division when he died. Don't let us hear any more talk about fees. It musn't be thought of for a moment."

"Oh, Dr. Dendy, how good of you! But you'll come and see him again?" Milly said, timidly thankful, yet alarmed. Would so great a man as the physician be content to continue labouring without his due reward?

"My dear, I shall come again and again, as often as possible, till between us we've made poor papa quite well again."

This was on the occasion of Dr. Dendy's first visit to Calthorpe Street. Milly's gratitude seemed to know no bounds. And then, thanks to Providence and the doctor's remedies, her invalid's health had certainly mended of late. He had not scolded her for nearly three days, and for about a quarter of an hour he had been almost cheerful. Indeed, she had reason to be grateful.

CHAPTER II

The doctor left Milly Lance with a fluttering sensation about his heart, such as he had taken no account, made no mention of whatever, in his famous treatise upon that organ. He returned to Calthorpe Street often. He alleged that it was very necessary for him to watch closely the effect of his prescriptions upon his patient. And each time that he saw Milly Lance—and he now felt a curious desire to see her as frequently as possible—he experienced a return of that strange fluttering sensation in the cardiac region. He was not alarmed at it; he did not think it was disease; and if it was, he didn't care, for it was not at all disagreeable. Indeed, he liked it. Professionally, he was inclined to regard it as a new development of action—quite healthy in its nature.

For the first time he felt the chosen pursuits of his life not sufficiently attractive or absorbing. Thoughts of a new kind broke in upon his studies, disturbed his practice, interrupted the flow and harmony of his lectures. His great house seemed to him very dreary, his existence very desolate. "Who would nurse and tend me," he asked himself, "if I were to fall ill like that poor Captain Lance?" Yet he dismissed the reflections suggested by that inquiry as selfish and unworthy. "No," he said, "I couldn't wish to chain a fair young creature like that to my side only to be my nurse and my servant. If I fall ill —which Heaven forbid!—I must have a paid attendant from the hospital; that will be quite good enough for me. It isn't for such a reason I should wish to make her mine."

For it had come to that. He wished to make Milly Lance his wife.

It was love that was so restless in his heart —playing as many pranks with him as "that shrewd and knavish sprite called Robin Goodfellow" among "maidens of the villagery," housewives and night wanderers. At least, he surmised that love was the disturbing cause of his heart's pulsing. He had had no experience of the sort of thing before; but still he thought he could hardly be mistaken. His disorder must arise from what people generally called Love.

It got to be more than he could bear at last. So he plucked up courage, and in an old-fashioned formal way he spoke to Captain Lance on the subject, and besought permission to address himself to Miss Lance. And he named a very handsome sum which he proposed to settle on his future wife—if he might regard Miss Lance in that light.

"It shall make no difference to you, captain," he said in conclusion, with an adroit consideration for his patient's selfishness. "There's plenty of room in my house. You must pitch your tent there. You shan't be deprived of your nurse. And your medical attendant will be on the spot always. We'll soon make you your old self again."

"I congratulate you, Milly," Captain Lance said presently to his daughter, the doctor having taken his departure. "You'll accept him, of course. He's ill-looking enough, but he can't help that, and one gets accustomed to ill looks. I don't think him nearly so plain as I first thought him. And he's old; he can't help that either, and he'll the sooner make you his widow. And he's rich, Milly; very rich. Thank goodness, we shall have done with this infernal poverty! You'll accept him at once?"

"You wish it, papa?"

Her face was very white, and there was a sort of choke in her throat as she spoke.

"Of course I do," he answered sharply. "You must be a fool to ask. You don't expect such another chance, do you? And there's no one else in the way. You don't love any one else?"

"No," she answered faintly.

"I congratulate you. You'll be a happy woman. You'll have more money than you'll know what to do with. The luck's turned at last. Give me a glass of wine, and I'll drink your health and his."

She obeyed; then stooped to kiss him, by way of thanks for his good wishes. Soon she made an excuse to quit the room. She did not want him to see how fast the tears were streaming down her face.

The doctor received a favourable answer to his suit. Milly only pleaded in a faint voice, with a frightened look on her face, that there might be no hurry—that time might be allowed her—because—because she so wanted her father's health to improve before she left him, if only for a day.

"Certainly, certainly," said the elated doctor. "Your will is my law," he added, gallantly; but, at the same time, he thought she need not have seemed quite so much scared at him. Then, not a little embarrassed at so unaccustomed a performance, he kissed her on the forehead. It was hard to say which was the more blushing and confused, the kisser or the kissed.

CHAPTER III

After this the doctor was more than ever at the captain's lodgings in Calthorpe Street. His care for his patient was unremitting. Captain Lance mended—slowly, but certainly.

The doctor's coachman treated himself to more and more smiles of a furtive sort, especially when the doctor persuaded Milly now and then to take a drive, and accompany him on a round of professional calls; she remaining in the carriage, of course, while he saw his patients, wrote prescriptions, and fingered pulses and fees. The coachman even ventured to confide to a few favoured intimates his opinion that there would, before long, be a "young missus" presiding over the establishment in Harley Street.

Dr. Dendy was very happy. Perhaps he wished, now and then, that Milly would look a little less grave; but then he consoled himself with the reflection that it was best so.

"It would be too absurd, at my time of life, to marry a romping, giggling girl. I have no right to expect from her extravagant affection. I must work for her love and earn it. In that way I shall surely gain it at last; at present it is a little too like gratitude. But time will change that—time and my own great affection for her. Dear little Milly!"

He was himself a staid, forbearing, rather stately lover. In such wise he surely recommended himself to Milly, and obtained a ready grant of all her regard and esteem. For her love he was content to wait, and labour, and hope.

Like most men of great mental activity, the doctor was always very busy with his fingers. His abundant vitality demonstrated itself in a certain restlessness of body and limb. As he talked he liked to curl up a string, or fold up a pipelight, or snip paper with a pair of scissors. He toyed with Milly's tapes and cottons, let loose her needles from their case, stuck pins into her pin-cushion in curious forms and patterns. One day as he sat by her in a playful mood (Captain Lance being asleep in an adjoining room), he turned her workbox over bodily, strewing its contents all about the table.

He took up a carved ivory card-case, and examined it curiously.

"That was a present from Hong-Kong. Is it not beautifully cut?" Milly demanded.

There was a flush upon her cheek as she spoke. He had opened the card-case, which was deemed, perhaps, too good for use; indeed,

Milly had few friends upon whom to call and leave cards, and her case contained none; but a photograph fell out.

"That is my cousin, Mark Lance. He it was who sent me the card-case. He represents a mercantile house at Hong-Kong." Her voice trembled a little as she volunteered this explanation.

"Has he been out there long?" the doctor asked, quietly.

"He came home two years ago. He went out first of all quite as a boy."

"A very good-looking young fellow."

The doctor closed the card-case. He next took up a small, carefully tied-up packet.

"Those are Mark's letters," said Milly, rather breathlessly. "He generally writes about every other mail. Of late, however, he has not been so regular. I thought we should have heard from him last week; but no letter came."

The doctor looked thoughtful. Had not something like a sigh escaped her as she said that no letter had come? Did she, then, long so very much to have tidings of her cousin? He turned the letters over and over, poising them in his hand.

"I see they are addressed to you, Milly," he said. There was further inquiry in the expression of his face.

"Would you like to read them?" she asked, simply. "Mark writes very amusing letters. He gives such a capital account of his life at Hong-Kong. I think it would amuse you to read it."

"No, thank you, Milly." And he pressed her hand tenderly, as he gave her back the letters. For a moment he had doubted her; but he dismissed his doubts. Still he could not repress a feeling of jealousy in regard to this cousin of Milly's—this Mark Lance. It was a comfort to reflect, however, that Hong-Kong was a very long way off.

CHAPTER IV.

In the course of a few days there was another visitor calling in Calthorpe Street. Mark Lance had arrived from Hong-Kong. He had written no letter, it appeared, because he was coming in person.

Dr. Dendy, attending his patient with customary punctuality, found the young man in the drawing-room, and recognized him at once. Only, the doctor was not especially pleased to discover the photograph hardly did Mr. Mark Lance justice. He was, in truth, far handsomer than he appeared in his carte de visite—a tall, broad, muscular gentleman, with a

sunburnt skin, bright, unflinching, blue eyes, and a very white and perfect set of teeth.

Milly seemed nervous and ill at ease, avoided her cousin's gaze, answered him monosyllabically. He had brought with him all sorts of presents for her—shawls, scarfs, fans, feathers, paintings, Oriental curiosities, and valuable knick-knackery. She hardly looked at these treasures, however; could with difficulty return her cousin common words of thanksgiving. She was at pains to avoid conversing with him—sought excuses for quitting him. He surveyed her with surprised eyes. "Was this Milly?" he was asking himself. And he felt wronged and hurt.

Dr. Dendy cast searching glances at the cousins.

"I must go now," said Mark, abruptly. "I have business at the ship's agents in the city."

"I suppose we shall see you again soon?" Milly asked, in faint tones, looking away from him as she spoke.

"I suppose so," he answered, carelessly.

"I'm going your way into the city—to the Ostrich Insurance Office, in Cornhill," said Dr. Dendy to the young man. "Let me give you a lift in my brougham; you'll find I go faster than most cabs."

They went away together.

"I'm a madman and a fool, that's what I am!" said Mark Lance, impetuously, as he sat in the doctor's carriage.

"How so?"

"I can't, of course, expect you to understand or sympathize with a lover's miserable imbecilities," the young man went on. "You have never loved as I have. You don't know what love is, as I know it."

"Perhaps not—perhaps not," said the doctor, with perfect composure.

"I must speak out," cried Mark. "I must tell some one—any one—what I suffer, or I shall go mad! Do you know why I came home so suddenly? Because I loved that girl; because I was sick and dying for love of her; because I couldn't bear to live longer away from her; because it seemed to me that, at all costs, I must set eyes on her again; speak to her of my love for her, whole and true and tender as it is, and entreat her to give me some portion of her love in return. I have been mastered by my love; it has possessed me—it possesses me now, absolutely. To what end? What good has come of it all? You saw how she treated me. She shrinks from, loathes, despises me. I have come home for that!"

"You have loved her long?"

"I have loved her all my life. As a child and a schoolboy I loved her—years, years ago. I used to long, while we were playing together, that some wild beast might spring upon her, so that I might destroy it, and save her or perish for her. I would have done anything for her even then. Any mad task she set me I strove to execute. I was delighted to peril life or limb in her cause. Any mischief that she did, I took the blame of, ever. I have been horsewhipped for her many a time. What did I care for the pain, so long as Milly came afterwards to comfort me and dry my tears? What suffering would not yield to a kiss from her, a smile, or a kindly word? But I am a fool to complain—I gave her my heart for a plaything. She has put it from her now with the rest of her playthings ruined and broken —quite done with. I had no right to expect she would do otherwise."

"She knew of your love?"

"How could she not know of it? Yet I was wrong, perhaps, not to speak out. I ought to have put it plainly before her. No; she does not know of my love. I have never dared to speak openly to her concerning it. I was too poor when I came home before—or, rather, I wanted to be richer, and so in some sort worthy of her, before I spoke to her. I thought she cared for me then a little. But that is all over now. Her love for me, if she ever felt any, has quite died out of her heart now. It is hard, very hard to bear. I have toiled only for her; I am rich now. Even her father, my uncle, he is an exacting gentleman enough—but even he would own that I am now rich enough to think of marrying even his daughter. And now it seems it is too late. What have I go by my toils, my long waiting, my forbearance? Nothing. A great gulf has opened between Milly and me, I know not how or why. I have lost all hope of her. I am the most miserable fellow on this earth."

And Mark Lance covered his face with his hands.

"I am, I know, a fool, a weak fool, to talk like this," he said, presently recovering himself. "What must you think of me? What are my sorrows to you? What can you care for a lover's troubles, and longings, and despair? What is my heart to you? What can you know or care about it? Nothing, of course not; nothing."

"Nothing, of course not," the doctor echoed, mechanically. "No; I know nothing of the human heart."

CHAPTER V.

From the city Dr. Dendy, having parted with Mark Lance, returned to Calthorpe Street. As he entered the drawing-room with the cautious and noiseless tread of a man well used to sick chambers and acutely sensitive patients, he heard a faint moaning sound.

Milly Lance, with tearful eyes, was reading over once again her cousin's letters—was contemplating once more the photograph contained in the ivory card-case. She started, with a half scream, as she found the doctor at her side.

"Forgive me!" she cried, in an agonized voice. "I—I am going to burn them." And then, hardly knowing what she did, she seemed to be trying to fall on her knees at the doctor's feet. He raised her up with tenderness.

"Calm yourself, Milly," he said.

She made an effort to throw the letters into the fire-place, but her courage or her strength failed her, and she burst into a passionate flood of tears.

"Have mercy," she moaned; "have mercy."

"You are ill, Milly," he said, gently. "Don't be afraid of me, my dear. I wouldn't wrong you or pain you for the world. Calm yourself; dry your eyes. Come, that's better. But what a pulse! Give me a sheet of note-paper. I must write you a prescription at once. Mind, you must obey my instructions to the letter." He scribbled a few lines. "Read that, Milly," he said.

She glanced at the paper, expecting to find the usual unintelligible medical hieroglyphics. She started. To her amazement, she found she could understand the prescription—it was written in English, being the first and last prescription which Dr. Dendy in the whole course of his professional career had written out of the Latin tongue.

It ran something in this wise—

R. Take cousin Mark to church with you as soon as possible, and make him your husband. God bless you.
(Signed)　　　JOHN DENDY, M.D.

How her heart beat!

"But does he love me?"

"You know he does. And you love him. Tell him so when he comes this evening. You needn't speak; only let him read it in your eyes."

"And my father?"

"He shall give his consent. I'll take care of that."

With a cry of joy, she threw herself into his arms. She could not speak her thanks, but this action of hers was sufficiently explicit.

He kissed her on the forehead. She put up her lips to him; but he didn't, or wouldn't, or couldn't see what she meant.

He went away sighing, very grave in aspect, and yet lightened and comforted by the thought that he had acted rightly.

"Perhaps I shall be able to finish that book of mine now," he said, gravely. "It's time it was done. One thing—I know more about it than I did. It's but a poor, weak, troublesome organ, after all, the heart. And its ache is very hard to bear. I don't believe there's any certain cure for that in the whole range of the pharmacopœia."

Poor Dr. Dendy looked very miserable. "This won't do," he said, presently. "I must prescribe for myself. Hard work; that's my best medicine. It cures a good many complaints. At any rate, it prevents the patient having time to think about them."

THE BLIND LINNET.

BY ROBERT BUCHANAN.

The sempstress's linnet sings
    At the window opposite me;—
It feels the sun on its wings,
    Though it cannot see.
Can a bird have thoughts? May be.

The sempstress is sitting,
    High o'er the humming street,
The little blind linnet is flitting
    Between the sun and her seat.
All day long
    She stitches wearily there,
And I know she is not young,
    And I know she is not fair;
For I watch her head bent down
    Throughout the dreary day,
And the thin meek hair o' brown
    Is threaded with silver gray;
And now and then, with a start
    At the fluttering of her heart,
She lifts her eyes to the bird,
    And I see in the dreary place
The gleam of a thin white face,
    And my heart is stirr'd.

Loud and long
    The linnet pipes his song!
For he cannot see
    The smoky street all round,
But loud in the sun sings he,
    Though he hears the murmurous sound;
For his poor, blind eyeballs blink,
    While the yellow sunlights fall,
And he thinks (if a bird can think)
    He hears a waterfall,

Or the broad and beautiful river
    Washing fields of corn,
Flowing for ever
    Through the woods where he was born;
And his voice grows stronger,
    While he thinks that he is there,
And louder and longer
    Falls his song on the dusky air.
And oft, in the gloaming still,
    Perhaps (for who can tell?)
The musk and the muskatel,
    That grow on the window sill,
Cheat him with their smell.

But the sempstress can see
    How dark things be;
How black through the town
    The stream is flowing;
And tears fall down
    Upon her sewing.
So at times she tries,
    When her trouble is stirr'd,
To close her eyes,
    And be blind like the bird.
And then, for a minute,
    As sweet things seem,
As to the linnet
    Piping in his dream!
For she feels on her brow
    The sunlight glowing,
And hears nought now
    But a river flowing—
A broad and beautiful river,
    Washing fields of corn,
Flowing for ever
    Through the woods where she was born
And a wild bird winging
    Over her head, and singing!
And she can smell
    The musk and the muskatel
That beside her grow,
    And, unaware,
She murmurs an old air
    That she used to know!

London Poems.

CONTENT.

Would you be free? 'Tis your chief wish, you say;
Come on, I'll show thee, friend, the certain way:
If to no feasts abroad thou lov'st to go,
While bounteous God does bread at home bestow;
If thou the goodness of thy clothes dost prize
By thine own use and not by others' eyes;
If (only safe from weathers) thou canst dwell
In a small house, but a convenient shell;
If thou without a sigh, or golden wish,
Canst look upon thy beechen bowl and dish:
If in thy mind such power and greatness be,
The Persian king's a slave compared with thee.

ABRAHAM COWLEY (from Martial).

DAVID SWAN.—A FANTASY.

BY NATHANIEL HAWTHORNE.

We can be but partially acquainted even with the events which actually influence our course through life and our final destiny. There are innumerable other events, if such they may be called, which come close upon us, yet pass away without actual results, or even betraying their near approach by the reflection of any light or shadow across our minds. Could we know all the vicissitudes of our fortunes, life would be too full of hope and fear, exultation or disappointment, to afford us a single hour of true serenity. This idea may be illustrated by a page from the secret history of David Swan.

We have nothing to do with David until we find him, at the age of twenty, on the high road from his native place to the city of Boston, where his uncle, a small dealer in the grocery line, was to take him behind the counter. Be it enough to say, that he was a native of New Hampshire, born of respectable parents, and had received an ordinary school education, with a classic finish by a year at Gilmanton academy. After journeying on foot from sunrise till nearly noon of a summer's day, his weariness and the increasing heat determined him to sit down in the first convenient shade, and await the coming up of the stage-coach. As if planted on purpose for him, there soon appeared a little tuft of maples with a delightful recess in the midst, and such a fresh bubbling spring that it seemed never to have sparkled for any wayfarer but David Swan. Virgin or not, he kissed it with his thirsty lips, and then flung himself along the brink, pillowing his head upon some shirts and a pair of pantaloons, tied up in a striped cotton handkerchief. The sunbeams could not reach him; the dust did not yet rise from the road after the heavy rain of yesterday; and his grassy lair suited the young man better than a bed of down. The spring murmured drowsily beside him; the branches waved dreamily across the blue sky overhead; and a deep sleep, perchance hiding dreams within its depths, fell upon David Swan. But we are to relate events which he did not dream of.

While he lay sound asleep in the shade other people were wide awake, and passed to and fro, afoot, on horseback, and in all sorts of vehicles, along the sunny road by his bedchamber. Some looked neither to the right hand nor the left, and knew not that he was there; some merely granted that way, without admitting the slumberer among their busy thoughts; some laughed to see how soundly he slept; and several, whose hearts were brimming full of scorn, ejected their venomous superfluity on David Swan. A middle-aged widow, when nobody else was near, thrust her head a little way into the recess, and vowed that the young fellow looked charming in his sleep. A temperance lecturer saw him, and wrought poor David into the texture of his evening's discourse, as an awful instance of dead drunkenness by the roadside. But censure, praise, merriment, scorn and indifference were all one, or rather all nothing, to David Swan.

He had slept only a few moments when a brown carriage, drawn by a handsome pair of horses, bowled easily along, and was brought to a standstill nearly in front of David's resting-place. A linch-pin had fallen out and permitted one of the wheels to slide off. The damage was slight, and occasioned merely a momentary alarm to an elderly merchant and his wife, who were returning to Boston in the carriage. While the coachman and a servant were replacing the wheel, the lady and gentleman sheltered themselves beneath the maple trees, and there espied the bubbling fountain and David Swan asleep beside it. Impressed with the awe which the humblest sleeper usually sheds around him, the merchant trod as lightly as the gout would allow; and his spouse took good heed not to rustle her silk gown lest David should start up all of a sudden.

"How soundly he sleeps!" whispered the old gentleman. "From what a depth he draws that easy breath! Such sleep as that brought on without an opiate would be worth more to me than half my income; for it would suppose health and an untroubled mind."

"And youth besides," said the lady. "Healthy and quiet age does not sleep thus. Our slumber is no more like his than our wakefulness."

The longer they looked the more did this elderly couple feel interested in the unknown youth, to whom the wayside and the maple shade were as a secret chamber, with the rich gloom of damask curtains brooding over him. Perceiving that a stray sunbeam glimmered down his face, the lady contrived to twist a branch aside so as to intercept it. And having done this little act of kindness, she began to feel like a mother to him.

"Providence seems to have laid him here," whispered she to her husband, "and to have brought us hither to find him, after our disappointment in our cousin's son. Methinks I can see a likeness to our departed Henry. Shall we awaken him?"

"To what purpose?" said the merchant, hesitating. "We know nothing of the youth's character."

"That open countenance!" replied his wife, in the same hushed voice, yet earnestly. "This innocent sleep!"

While these whispers were passing the sleeper's heart did not throb, nor his breath become agitated, nor his features betray the least token of interest. Yet fortune was bending over him, just ready to let fall a burden of gold. The old merchant had lost his only son, and had no heir to his wealth except a distant relative, with whose conduct he was dissatisfied. In such cases people sometimes do stranger things than to act the magician, and awaken a young man to splendour who fell asleep in poverty.

"Shall we not awaken him?" repeated the lady, persuasively.

"The coach is ready, sir," said the servant behind.

The old couple started, reddened, and hurried away, mutually wondering that they should ever have dreamed of doing anything so very ridiculous. The merchant threw himself back in the carriage, and occupied his mind with the plan of a magnificent asylum for unfortunate men of business. Meanwhile David Swan enjoyed his nap.

The carriage could not have gone above a mile or two, when a pretty young girl came along, with a tripping pace, which showed precisely how her little heart was dancing in her bosom. Perhaps it was this merry kind of motion that caused—is there any harm in saying it?—her garter to slip its knot. Conscious that the silken girth, if silk it were, was relaxing its hold, she turned aside into the shelter of the maple trees, and there found a young man asleep by the spring. Blushing as red as any rose that she should have intruded into a gentleman's bed-chamber, and for such a purpose too, she was about to make her escape on tiptoe. But there was peril near the sleeper. A monster of a bee had been wandering overhead—buzz, buzz, buzz—now among the leaves, now flashing through the strips of sunshine, and now lost in the dark shade, till finally he appeared to be settling on the eyelid of David Swan. The sting of a bee is sometimes deadly. As free-hearted as she was innocent, the girl attacked the intruder with her handkerchief, brushed him soundly, and drove him from beneath the maple shade.

How sweet a picture! This good deed accomplished, with quickened breath and a deeper blush, she stole a glance at the youthful stranger, for whom she had been battling with a dragon in the air.

"He is handsome!" thought she, and blushed redder yet.

How could it be that no dream of bliss grew so strong within him that, shattered by its very strength, it should part asunder and allow him to perceive the girl among its phantoms? Why, at least, did no smile of welcome brighten upon his face? She was come, the maid whose soul, according to the old and beautiful idea, had been severed from his own, and whom, in all his vague but passionate desires, he yearned to meet. Her only could he love with perfect love—him only could she receive into the depths of her heart—and now her image was faintly blushing in the fountain by his side; should it pass away, its happy lustre would never gleam upon his life again.

"How sound he sleeps!" murmured the girl.

She departed, but did not trip along the road so lightly as when she came.

Now this girl's father was a thriving country merchant in the neighbourhood, and happened at that identical time to be looking out for just such a young man as David Swan. Had David formed a wayside acquaintance with the daughter, he would have become the father's clerk, and all else in natural succession. So here again had good fortune—the best of fortunes—stolen so near that her garments brushed against him; and he knew nothing of the matter.

The girl was hardly out of sight when two men turned aside beneath the maple shade. Both had dark faces, set off by cloth caps, which were drawn down aslant over their brows. Their dresses were shabby, yet had a certain smartness. These were a couple of rascals, who got their living by whatever the devil sent them, and now, in the interim of other business, had staked the joint profits of their next piece of villany on a game of cards, which was to have been decided here under the trees. But finding David asleep by the spring, one of the rogues whispered to his fellow—

"Hist!—Do you see that bundle under his head?"

The other villain nodded, winked, and leered.

"I'll bet you a horn of brandy," said the first, "that the chap has either a pocket-book or a snug little hoard of small change stowed away amongst his shirts. And if not there, we shall find it in his pantaloons' pocket."

"But how if he wakes?" said the other. His companion thrust aside his waistcoat, pointed to the handle of a dirk, and nodded. "So be it!" muttered the second villain.

They approached the unconscious David, and, while one pointed the dagger toward his heart, the other began to search the bundle beneath his head. Their two faces, grim, wrinkled, and ghastly with guilt and fear, 'ent over their victim, looking horrible enough to be mistaken for fiends should he suddenly awake. Nay, had the villains glanced aside into the spring, even they would hardly have known themselves as reflected there. But David Swan had never worn a more tranquil aspect, even when asleep on his mother's breast.

"I must take away the bundle," whispered one. "If he stirs I'll strike," muttered the other.

But at this moment a dog, scenting along the ground, came in beneath the maple trees, and gazed alternately at each of these wicked men and then at the quiet sleeper. He then lapped out of the fountain.

"Pshaw!" said one villain. "We can do nothing now. The dog's master must be close behind."

"Let's take a drink and be off," said the other.

The man with the dagger thrust back the weapon into his bosom and drew forth a pocket pistol, but not of that kind which kills by a single discharge. It was a flask of liquor, with a block tin tumbler screwed upon the mouth. Each drank a comfortable dram and left the spot, with so many jests and such laughter at their unaccomplished wickedness that they might be said to have gone on their way rejoicing. In a few hours they had forgotten the whole affair, nor once imagined that the recording angel had written down the crime of murder against their souls in letters as durable as eternity. As for David Swan, he still slept quietly, neither conscious of the shadow of death when it hung over him nor of the glow of renewed life when that shadow was withdrawn.

He slept, but no longer so quietly as at first. An hour's repose had snatched from his elastic frame the weariness with which many hours of toil had burdened it. Now he stirred—now moved his lips, without a sound—now talked, in an inward tone, to the noonday spectres of his dream. But a noise of wheels came rattling louder and louder along the road, until it dashed through the dispersing mist of David's slumber—and there was the stage-coach. He started up, with all his ideas about him.

"Halloo, driver!—Take a passenger?" shouted he.

"Room on top!" answered the driver.

Up mounted David, and bowled away merrily toward Boston, without so much as a parting glance at that fountain of dreamlike vicissitude. He knew not that a phantom of Wealth had thrown a golden hue upon its waters—nor that one of Love had sighed softly through their murmur--nor that one of Death had threatened to crimson them with his blood—all in the brief hour since he lay down to sleep. Sleeping or waking, we hear not the airy footsteps of the strange things that almost happen. Does it not argue a superintending Providence that, while viewless and unexpected events thrust themselves continually athwart our path, there should still be regularity enough in mortal life to render foresight even partially available.—*Thrice-Told Tales.*

THE WELL OF LOCH MAREE.[1]
BY J. G. WHITTIER.

Calm on the breast of Loch Maree
   A little isle reposes;
A shadow woven of the oak
   And willow o'er it closes.

Within, a Druid's mound is seen,
   Set round with stony warders;
A fountain, gushing through the turf,
   Flows o'er its grassy borders.

And whoso bathes therein his brow,
   With care or madness burning,
Feels once again his healthful thought
   And sense of peace returning.

O restless heart and fevered brain,
   Unquiet and unstable,
That holy well of Loch Maree
   Is more than idle fable!

Life's changes vex, its discords stun,
   Its glaring sunshine blindeth,
And blest is he who on his way
   That fount of healing findeth!

The shadows of a humbled will
   And contrite heart are o'er it;
Go read its legend—"TRUST IN GOD"—
   On Faith's white stones before it.

---

[1] Pennant, in his *Voyage to the Hebrides*, describes the holy well of Loch Maree, the waters of which were supposed to effect a miraculous cure of melancholy, trouble, and insanity.

REPLY TO A LETTER INCLOSING A LOCK OF HAIR.

[Frederick Locker, born at Greenwich Hospital, 1821. Poet. He belongs to an old Kentish family; his father was a civil commissioner of Greenwich Hospital, and his grandfather was Captain W. Locker, R.N., under whom Lord Nelson and Lord Collingwood served. His works are: Lyra Elegantiarum and London Lyrics (Strahan & Co.) The latter volume, which has gone through many editions, has won for the author the laureateship amongst writers of vers de société. "Mr. Locker seems most deservedly characterized by two epithets which no one dreams of applying to Prior, and we think must be denied to Praed—earnest and tender. He is so well furnished at all points that only by comparison is any deficiency perceptible, and when perceived it will be disregarded, in view of his higher excellences." —Contemporary Review.]

> "'My darling wants to see you soon,'—
> I bless the little maid, and thank her;
> To do her bidding night and noon
> I draw on Hope—Love's kindest banker!"
> Old MSS.

Yes, you were false, and though I'm free,
  I still would be the slave of yore;
Then join'd our years were thirty-three,
  And now—yes now I'm thirty-four.
And though you were not learnèd—well,
  I was not anxious you should grow so;—
I trembled once beneath her spell
  Whose spelling was extremely so-so!

Bright season! why will memory
  Still haunt the path our rambles took,—
The sparrow's nest that made you cry,
  The lilies captured in the brook?
I'd lifted you from side to side,
  (You seem'd as light as that poor sparrow;)
I know who wish'd it twice as wide,
  I think you thought it rather narrow.

Time was, indeed a little while,
  My pony could your heart compel;
And once, beside the meadow-stile,
  I thought you loved me just as well;
I'd kiss'd your cheek; in sweet surprise
  Your troubled gaze said plainly, "Should
      he?"
But doubt soon fled those daisy eyes,—
  " He could not wish to vex me, could he?"

The brightest eyes are soonest sad,
  But your fair cheek, so lightly sway'd,
Could ripple into dimples glad,
  For O, my stars, what mirth we made!
The brightest tears are soonest dried,
  But your young love and dole were stable;
You wept when dear old Rover died,
  You wept—and dress'd your dolls in sable.

As year succeeds to year, the more
  Imperfect life's fruition seems;
Our dreams, as baseless as of yore,
  Are not the same enchanting dreams.
The girls I love now vote me slow--
  How dull the boys who once seem'd witty!
Perhaps I'm getting old—I know
  I'm still romantic—more's the pity!

A vain regret! To few, perchance,
  Unknown, and profitless to all:
The wisely-gay, as years advance,
  Are gaily-wise. Whate'er befall,
We'll laugh at folly, whether seen
  Beneath a chimney or a steeple;
At yours, at mine—our own, I mean,
  As well as that of other people.

I'm fond of fun, the mental dew
  Where wit, and truth, and ruth are blent,
And yet I've known a prig or two,
  Who, wanting all, were all content.
To say I hate such dismal men
  Might be esteem'd a strong assertion;
If I've blue devils now and then,
  I make them dance for my diversion.

And here's your letter debonair.
  "My friend, my dear old friend of yore,"
And is this curl your daughter's hair?
  I've seen the Titian tint before.
Are we the pair that used to pass
  Long days beneath the chestnut shady!
You then were such a pretty lass!
  I'm told you're now as fair a lady.

I've laugh'd to hide the tear I shed,
  As when the Jester's bosom swells,
And mournfully he shakes his head,
  We hear the jingle of his bells.
A jesting vein your poet vex'd,
  And this poor rhyme, the Fates determine,
Without a parson or a text,
  Has proved a rather prosy sermon.

A BUTTERFLY ON A CHILD'S GRAVE.

A butterfly bask'd on a baby's grave,
  Where a lily had chanced to grow:
"Why art thou here, with thy gaudy dye,
When she of the blue and sparkling eye
  Must sleep in the churchyard low?"

Then it lightly soar'd through the sunny air.
  And spoke from its shining track:
"I was a worm till I won my wings,
And she whom thou mourn'st like a seraph sings:
  Wouldst thou call the blest one back?"

MRS. LYDIA HUNTLEY SIGOURNEY.

ELIZABETH LATIMER.

[Nathaniel Parker Willis, born in Portland, Maine,
20th January, 1806; died at Idlewild, on the Hudson,
20th January, 1867. Poet, journalist, and miscellaneous
writer. He travelled much in Europe. His chief works
are: *Melanie, Lady Jane*, and other poems; *Pencillings
by the Way; Inklings of Adventure; Romance of Travel*,
comprising Tales of Five Lands: *People I have Met*, or
Pictures of Society and People of Mark; *A Health-trip
to the Tropics; Out-doors at Idlewild; Paul Fane*, or
Parts of a Life else Untold: a Novel; &c. "As a writer
of 'sketches' properly so called, Mr. Willis is unequalled.
Sketches—especially of society—are his forte, and they
are so for no other reason than that they afford him the
best opportunity of introducing the personal Willis—
or more distinctly because this species of composition is
most susceptible of impression from his personal character."—*Edgar A. Poe.*]

Elizabeth Latimer, at twenty-four, found
herself in possession of an accomplished mind,
a memory stored with reading of the best kind,
and a judgment accustomed to exercise itself
from its earliest development; and this, with a
graceful person and a countenance of great
sweetness and intelligence, was pretty nearly
all that Elizabeth possessed. She had been
for many years the only daughter of a merchant,
who, though he did not draw his resources from
all the ends of the earth, yet possessed enough
for the indulgence of luxury. The indications
of talent which he very early discovered in the
young Elizabeth, determined him to bestow on
her an education that would save her from
adding to the number of those precocious
geniuses who, from a misapplication of their
powers, become unfit either for the daily concerns of life, or to hold a place among those
who are gradually procuring indulgence and
respect for female intellect. With this view
he engaged a gentleman who had been a
classmate of his, and who had devoted himself
to literature, to take up his abode with him
and assist him in cultivating his daughter's
mind.

"You will easily understand," he wrote to
Mr. Elliot, "with what different eyes I look
upon this subject from those with which I regarded it twenty years ago. To have mind
enough to love and obey me, and, withal,
think me supremely wise, was quite mind
enough in a wife, but I am willing to pay it
greater respect since I find it in my darling
Elizabeth. As I am as anxious about her
moral as her intellectual education, I dread
lest, being an only child and surrounded by all
that will tend to her gratification, she may
form habits of selfishness, against which no

warnings, no precepts will avail. A companion
of her own age would secure her from this risk,
and I can think of no one so well suited, on all
accounts, to be brought up with my little girl
as your own Marianne. I need not assure you
how entirely like my own daughter she shall
be considered."

We will not detail the progress of Elizabeth's
studies. They were such as opened her young
mind to all that was lovely in virtue and lofty
and excellent in intellect. She lived principally
in the country, in a small but intelligent
circle, sufficiently enlightened to save them
from the dominion of a gossiping spirit, yet not
so learned as to allow her to acquire anything
like a pedantic one.

The tranquillity of their own house had received a startling shock when Elizabeth was
about fifteen, by Mr. Latimer's bringing home
a second wife, very little more than her own
age, but of entirely different temper, habits,
and tastes. It was then that Mr. Latimer
perceived that he had done wisely in giving to
Elizabeth habits by which she could abstract
her thoughts from the jarrings of a step-mother,
jealous of her, of her gentle friend Marianne,
of Mr. Elliot, of everything that her husband
loved. But their school of trial did not last
long. Mrs. Latimer only lived to present her
husband with a son, and expired, leaving all
the family with just such sensations as one
feels on awaking from an uncomfortable dream,
and Elizabeth and her father heaved a sigh of
relief as they inwardly responded "Amen!" to
the clergyman of the village who came to pay
them a visit of consolation.

When Elizabeth entered into society, she
carried with her many warnings from her father
to avoid the display of acquirements which
were not common to all. She listened, determined to profit by his advice, though she felt
there was some injustice in laying this embargo
upon wit and learning.

"Why," thought she, "should Miss C——
be permitted, nay, solicited, to display her
playing and singing, both excellent enough to
excite envy, while all the powers that I possess
must be so sedulously concealed? However,
as there is no reasoning to any purpose on this
apparent inconsistency, I will try to resemble
the greater part of the world I am going to
mingle with;" and in imagination she behaved
with perfect discretion, occupied only in veiling the mistakes of the ignorant, in drawing
out the talents of the timid, nicely discriminat-
ing when and with whom to talk seriously or
lightly, and gliding through society with all
the tact which only a knowledge of the world,

gained by one's own experience and much practice in that world, can give.

But poor Elizabeth found herself sadly at a loss when she encountered a bewildering number of new faces, whose ready smiles and pliancy of expression concealed all that was passing in the heart. She felt it as impossible to catch the light tone of those around her, to talk of nothing, to express rapture and enthusiasm where she felt only indifference, as it would have been for one of the gay circle to have shone forth as an improvisatrice. Being perfectly unaffected and simple, she took refuge in silence; but her speaking countenance often betrayed the listlessness she felt, and as the silence of persons who are known or supposed to be able to talk well, is looked upon with an invidious eye, she felt a degree of restraint, whether she spoke or not, which prevented her ever taking much pleasure in the amusements of the world. But there were some whom she did please, and that in no moderate degree. The cultivated and intelligent found a charm in her manner that they recollected with pleasure long after she had retired from society. Elizabeth lost her friend Marianne, who married an English gentleman and accompanied him to England. Mr. Elliot was persuaded to join them, and Mr. Latimer found his household reduced to a small number. But his mind seemed too much occupied to miss his companions, and, to Elizabeth's grief, she discovered that her father was bent upon making a fortune for his son Louis. In vain she urged that Louis would never want, and the possession of wealth might only check exertion by depriving him of a stimulus to industry. She represented to him the risk he ran by engaging so deeply in speculations, none of which had hitherto been successful; but Mr. Latimer had the gambling fit so strong upon him, that he looked forward to seeing his ships riding the ocean laden with the treasures of the Asiatic islands, and realizing the wildest dreams of his avarice. Elizabeth deplored this for his own and for Louis' sake. She saw how the fluctuations of hope and despair, the pangs of suspense and repeated disappointments, preyed upon her father's health and spirits, and she anticipated for Louis and herself the loss of all they had considered their own.

But these fears were transient. We seldom reflect long, amid the enjoyments of affluence, upon their precarious nature. She retired from the world and devoted herself to her father and to the education of Louis, whom she loved with all a mother's tenderness. He was indeed a sweet and gentle child, fond only of books and sedentary amusements, and Elizabeth's time passed away as happily as time passed in the exercise of duty usually does. She was often uneasy, often tormented by vague fears of future poverty and distress, but these were only clouds that overshadowed her at times. Her horizon generally was bright; but the blow anticipated fell upon her at last. Mr. Latimer had ventured the remains of his fortune in a speculation which was to enrich Louis and his posterity for ever.

After many months' suspense the news reached Mr. Latimer that he was ruined. He did not long survive it, and his son and daughter found themselves friendless and poor. A few hundred dollars was all that could be collected for them, nor had they any claims upon others. They had but few family friends, and Elizabeth's was not a spirit to brook dependence. Poverty at first sight is not so frightful as when it comes near enough to lay its cold, griping fingers on us; and in the present excited state of her feelings the prospect of maintaining herself did not appear as difficult as she afterwards proved it. Her idea of submission to the will of Heaven was not confined to subduing a murmur, when death has removed by a stroke the desire of our eyes. She had been accustomed to exercise it in all the disappointments and sorrows of her life; for who, at twenty-four, has not tasted of the bitterness of the waters of life? A few passages of her letter to Marianne will show how schooled her mind had been, by being early taught of Heaven.

"You know, dearest Marianne, your excellent father often cautioned us against trusting to our perceptions of Heaven's justice. With him we were accustomed to trace in the records of history the hand of Infinite Wisdom guiding all things onward to some great end, that should vindicate his ways to future ages. Ah! how easy it is for the thoughtful mind to pursue this truth through events that have passed away! how much easier than to acknowledge it when our idols have been overthrown! We are personal only in those things which can do us no good. Let me now lay those lessons to heart, and follow the obvious track which Providence has marked out for me. It seems very plain—I must support myself and the darling object of my lost parent's love. The manner of doing this is very embarrassing. My mind is full of energy, but where to bestow it costs me days and nights of anxious thought."

Mr. Latimer had insisted, some months before his death, that Louis should be placed at a large public school. Elizabeth had consented to his plan with readiness, though it grieved her to part with the little companion whose quickness enabled him to catch with facility everything she taught him; but she was aware that a public school is indispensable towards acquiring manly habits, and that independence of ridicule, which are necessary to all who walk the world, however retired be the path they choose.

It was evening, and she was alone when she took possession of two small rooms in ——— Street. Dull and dreary was the aspect of everything. The window of the little sitting-room was close to a high stone wall, nor were light and beauty shut out from that entrance only. From her chamber window nothing could be discerned but a long range of warehouses. There was not even the sight or sound of labour to cheer the prospect.

"A cobbler or a blacksmith would enliven the scene," thought Elizabeth, "but I hope I shall not stay here long."

Her first attempt to escape from her new dwelling was a letter to a lady with whom she had long been intimate. Her plan was to open a school, and she solicited Mrs. Graham's assistance, or rather patronage, without taking into consideration how little that lady had to bestow. She answered Elizabeth kindly, explaining to her that her influence was confined to five or six families, none of whom had it in their power to engage for their children an instructress whose accomplishments would entitle her to a higher salary than is given to those who teach the elementary parts of education.

Over this first disappointment Elizabeth did not long weep. Keeping a school is a very depressing prospect, and she felt almost relieved by Mrs. Graham's letter.

Her next application was to a lady who was desirous of procuring a governess for her daughters—one of those ladies whose *beau ideal* of a governess is that of a being with every talent and every virtue under heaven, combined with a degree of humility that will endure every insult that narrow minds bestow upon the unfortunate. Mrs. S—— gave her a week's suspense, then found her way into Elizabeth's parlour one morning, with a "How d'ye do, Miss Latimer—for I suppose that's you. I believe I've made you wait for an answer, but I've been so beset. People are so anxious to get to me, as if I could take a hundred. But, before we go any further, we must settle one thing—you're a musician, of course?"

The colour that had been deepening on Elizabeth's cheeks became crimson as she faintly answered,

"No, madam."

"No! gracious goodness! what could you be thinking of when you offered yourself as governess? Such a salary as I give, and pay a music master besides!"

"Then reduce the salary," Elizabeth began, but Mrs. S—— stopped her—

"What! and get a master for the girls! What's that to the purpose. You ought to be able to superintend their practising. Well, that sets the matter at rest. Good morning, ma'am," and Mrs. S—— made her exit as abruptly as her entrance, leaving Elizabeth a foretaste of what she afterwards suffered from other applications and other disappointments.

One lady objected to her because she could not teach velvet painting. It was in vain Elizabeth, who liked the mild tones of this amateur in footstools and sofa covers, urged the superiority of the higher branches of painting. "That might do for artists," said the lady, and Elizabeth took her leave. Another expected her to teach embroidery and shoe-making to six daughters; but the most fatal bar to her success was the .ant of a knowledge of music.

After many failures she relinquished the hope of obtaining a situation, and turned her thoughts to her last resource. She determined, with a heavy heart, to offer her services as a translator to a publisher whom she had often heard spoken of as a man of taste and liberality. Translating is a fatiguing and inglorious task, but she had no alternative. While she was hesitating whether to address him by letter or apply to him in person, Mr. Warren was announced. Elizabeth knew him well, for he had been a frequent visitor at Mr. Latimer's. He was remarkable only for his extreme dulness, and his desire of being thought a man of genius and learning. He picked up scraps from pocket-books and newspapers, and wearied his friends by commonplace remarks, uttered in a tone of oracular wisdom. His address to Elizabeth was hesitating and confused. He was usually wont to speak with a deliberateness that fell upon the ear like the strokes of a hammer, but now he spoke with a rapidity that made him quite unintelligible. With an uneasy looking about as if he dreaded being overheard, at last he abruptly asked her if money had been her object in wishing to procure a situation as governess.

"Certainly," said Elizabeth; "what else could induce me to undertake such an office?"

He muttered something about his sorrow at her wanting it and his wish to serve her, then opened his business; prefaced, however, by desiring a promise of secrecy. Elizabeth, inwardly provoked at his solemn foppery, promised all he required, and he then informed his impatient auditress, that several of his literary friends were about to establish a critical journal, in which all the best talents of the city were to be displayed—" and you will not be surprised," said he, " to hear, that much is expected from me, particularly in the department of the belles-lettres. I hope you are not surprised," he continued, as he saw the astonishment painted on Elizabeth's countenance.

" No, I am never surprised at people's expectations, and I am sure Mr. Warren will not disappoint those formed by his well-judging friends ; but, pray, proceed."

" Everybody says to me, ' Warren! now is your time. This is the opportunity for you to show your critical acumen. Seize the moment, Warren! and give us something that will be read a hundred years hence.' I am pressed on all sides, and I begin to feel that I really ought, in justice to myself, to do something to keep up the credit of this journal."

" He is mad," thought Elizabeth, "or has been in the hands of some dexterous quizzer;" and she sighed as she thought that he could have nothing to say that could interest her, for she had at first hoped that he might bring her occupation. However, Warren went on:—

" My health, you know, is delicate, and my avocations very numerous ; and from various causes I am afraid I shall not be able to write until the spring; but, in the meantime, my dear Miss Latimer, I will make use of your pen. Our minds—I say it without flattery, believe me—our minds are somewhat of the same order, allowing for the difference of sex and education. Now, all I ask of you is this: just give me, from time to time, a critique upon some modern writer, and now and then we will review an old one. I leave the choice of subjects to you; of course you will have the advantage of my additions and corrections. Well, what say you? Does the scheme appear feasible? However, I see you are taken by surprise? An hour's reflection will be necessary. Good morning. This evening you shall see me again."

" He has made me laugh, at least," said Elizabeth, after an impatient " pshaw!" " I always thought him a fool, but never expected such an excess of folly from him; but it will cure me of attempting to set bounds to the folly of a foolish man."

Elizabeth did not, at first, give his plan a second thought. The idea of being joined with Warren in a work which she knew would be conducted by men of learning and science,

was absurd in the last degree, and she began her letter to the publisher, but her reluctance to undertake this laborious kind of occupation increased every moment. She threw down her pen and abandoned herself to despondency. Then, in spite of herself, Warren's plan recurred to her. It was not as ridiculous as she had thought. There had been, she recollected, instances of starving authors in a garret, while the indolent or empty were building up a reputation upon their labours. Besides, Warren would not be the first fool who had thrust himself into the place of wiser men. They are to be found everywhere—in the halls of legislators, in the cabinet of ministers. They have had their followers and their eulogists, and we have only to look behind the scenes to exclaim with Oxenstiern, *Quam parva sapientia regitur mundus!* At all events it would not be Warren, but herself who would write, and though she doubted her own capacity for the task, still she wished to try. It offered a means of accomplishing her grand object, keeping Louis at school, and it had the charm of privacy, for, since her unsuccessful attempts to escape from her gloomy closets, she had shrunk into them with a feeling more allied to love than to distaste

By the time Warren returned Elizabeth had so balanced the advantages of his scheme against its objections, as to give him the assent he expected. His presence revived the ridiculous ideas that his proposal had at first suggested. The tone of his voice was expressive of extreme dulness, and there was a stupidity about him that completely oppressed Elizabeth. She began to be ashamed of acceding to his plan, doubting, indeed, if any production, supposed to be his, would obtain a reading from the editor. However, a short time would decide her fate, and she resolved to make the experiment. She inquired beforehand what was to be the compensation for her trouble. He named the probable sum.

" You rate intellectual labour very low," said she, " but no wonder. However, that, four or five times repeated, will be enough for my purpose. You are aware that you must furnish me with books. I must have a great many authorities to bring to the field. A man like you will be expected to be very accurate."

He professed himself willing to be guided by her in everything, begged her to try and catch his style, and urged her over and over to exert herself to the utmost, before he relieved her of his presence.

Elizabeth began her task with great animation, but she soon found it more difficult than she had anticipated. Her mind was full, yet she was puzzled and distressed. She wanted the habit of writing, which alone, according to Lord Bacon, insures correctness. She found great difficulty in arranging and condensing her ideas, and preserving a degree of order, without which even the writings of the learned and brilliant appear a chaotic mass. She had to weigh well all she said, lest she should be guilty of error or presumption. Her subject was a comparison between the writers of the reign of Anne and the present day. It was not without some timidity that she expressed opinions opposed to the prevailing cant which raves about the march of mind. Physical science is in its glory, and philosophy has made such magnificent presents to the arts, that knowledge is carried with winged speed from the college to the cottage; but mind, alas! must have its limits, must obey the law, which says, "So far shalt thou come and no farther."

Though Elizabeth wrote with facility, she was obliged to refer to so many authorities, to correct and strike out so many redundancies, that she sat up a great part of the night previous to the latest day on which Warren was to call for her little essay. It was finished at last, and she committed it to its trial with a beating heart.

Great was the astonishment of the editor when Warren presented himself in his library with a manuscript of an imposing size in his hand. Greater still at sight of the subject; and it rose to its highest pitch after reading the first few sentences. He knew little of Warren, but he had always heard his name used as a synonym with dulness, and he was betrayed into abruptly exclaiming,

"Mr. Warren! I had no idea—I mean I did not expect—Mr. Warren, is this yours?"

The blush of guilt flew to poor Warren's face, but Mr. Leslie hastened to apologize. "Leave it with me for an hour or two," said he, "and you shall hear from me to-morrow."

As soon as Warren received what gave him a delight which he felt in the same degree with Harpagon—that of "touching something"—he hastened in a transport of generosity to divide it with Elizabeth. It was more than she had hoped for, and the consciousness of possessing the means of contributing to her own support, gave an exhilaration to her spirits to which she had long been a stranger. She walked to the school where Louis was making a progress that repaid her for parting with him, and paid, with a thrill of delight, the first-fruits of her industry to his master.

Dr. B——'s seminary was a mile out of town, and the fresh air of the country, the song of the birds, the very sight of the sky, made her heart glow again with hope and peace. She had something to look forward to. Louis would one day reward her toils. She should one day recount to him how, for his sake, she had conquered the indolence and love of leisure which she foresaw would be a stumbling-block in his way. To see Louis kindling at the tale of her difficulties and promising to repay them all, to hear him spoken of with distinction, and to witness his happiness and success in life, now formed her daily reveries. Her pen often fell from her hand while indulging in these dreams. Dreams they were indeed.

She continued to supply Warren with materials for the fame he was acquiring, though there were times when Mr. Leslie strongly doubted his positive assertions that he was the author of the manuscripts. There was a taste, an elegance in their style, and a sensibility that he felt never came from the coarse mind of Warren. However, he had no means of elucidating the point, and gave it up, hoping that accident might one day or other expose the deception.

In the meantime Warren, who began to find the sums he received from Mr. Leslie extremely convenient for his own purposes, began to reduce Elizabeth's share to a third, and then a fourth of the whole. "She cannot want much," he argued with his conscience, "living in those little garrets. I don't see how she can possibly spend five dollars in six months, and always plainly dressed too. I really think I give her more than enough. I dare say she can manage a little to great advantage."

People who are extravagant on themselves are often wonderfully ingenious in devising plans of economy for others. Elizabeth was surprised at this falling off; but, in the simplicity of her heart, she never suspected him of such a pitiless fraud.

"I have overrated my own productions," said she, "and yet I certainly think I have improved. I have studied the rules of good writing; I read with a deeper spirit of observation; it is strange my pieces should appear of less value to the publishers in proportion as they seem to me more spirited and better finished. Perhaps they are thought studied. I myself find a sameness in them."

Among the many causes she was attributing her diminished resources to, the true one never occurred to her. She knew, of course, from

Warren's imposing on Mr. Leslie and the public that he was not a man of much principle. Indeed, a fool cannot have strict principles. He cannot distinguish sufficiently between right and wrong; but, in the broad path of honesty, she thought he might find his way.

A year passed on, and she found that she had just enough to defray Louis' school expenses, and nothing to lay by towards sending him to college. Her health, too, was impaired by constant application, and her spirits crushed by the unvaried sameness of her employment. Sweet is the sleep of the labouring man; but it must be that labour which feels the breath of heaven fan the brow—alternate motion and rest. But when, after a whole day has been passed in mental exercise, the fevered head is laid upon its pillow, and the stretched and burning eyelids refuse to close: when the glare of white paper, or interminable rows of letters dance before the throbbing eyeballs, and one idea haunts the brain till its repetition becomes maddening—these are the pains and penalties of mind that make us wish to have been born among those whose hands alone are employed to procure their daily bread. Elizabeth had been accustomed to study and reflection, but there is something very different between study in a large and airy chamber where light and shade are pleasantly blended, when the first sensations of fatigue may be dissipated by exercise or conversation, and leaning incessantly over a flat, low table, by the side of a little window where light is struggling with darkness. She felt her health languish, her head ached incessantly, but still she went on for several months, indulging herself now and then with a walk to Dr. B——'s, and an evening spent at Mrs. Graham's. This lady had often a little circle of friends around her, whose society would have been of service to Elizabeth's spirits, but she shrunk from company, and, with an irritability peculiar to the unfortunate, who feel lonely, neglected, and unappreciated, often repulsed those who wished to be kind to her.

"My temper is growing savage," said she, one evening, while she was putting on her hat to go to her friends; "I believe I answered that kind and lovely-looking woman who spoke so sweetly to me the last time I was at Mrs. Graham's, with a canine growl. But, alas! I felt a horrid kind of envy at seeing a creature so happy and apparently so beloved by every one present. Her happiness did not seem to be put on for the occasion, but the abiding expression of her face, and while I was contrasting her situation with mine, to hear her speak to me with that easy, confiding tone of voice that came from a heart at ease—oh! she would have forgiven me if she had seen the wretchedness of mine!" and Elizabeth sat down and wept in penitence at having given way to such feelings.

She hoped to meet Mrs. Leslie again, and was disappointed to find Mrs. Graham alone. She dared not speak of Mrs. Leslie, for she felt her voice falter as she thought of her. Yet she tried to induce Mrs. Graham to begin the subject. But as she was drawing a portrait of gentleness and beauty which made her friend exclaim, "Why, one would think you were acquainted with Mrs. Leslie," Mr. Graham came in, and after expressing his pleasure at seeing Elizabeth, whose absence from his little parties had pained him, he turned to Mrs. Graham and asked her if she had any idea to whom she was indebted for the pleasure of her morning's reading.

"No," said she; "I am glad you remind me of it, for I thought of Elizabeth while I was reading. It is," she continued, turning to her friend, "a very well-written essay upon simplicity, real and affected; and contrasts the strong, manly simplicity of Crabbe with the childish, unmeaning prattle of Wordsworth, in almost the same words which I have heard you make use of in arguing with Marianne."

Elizabeth trembled. She suspected Mr. Graham alluded to her, but he went on.

"I would ask you to guess the author, but I should be weary of seeing you puzzled. Know, then, that Warren—Philip Augustus Warren—is the principal contributor to Mr. Leslie's journal."

"Now, I am not surprised," said his wife, "for it is impossible to make me believe such a tale. You forget we both know Warren, and know that he is ignorant as well as dull. I question much if he knows what poetry is, unless he attaches some idea of rhyme to it."

"I thought so myself, but listen. This morning I was talking with Mr. Leslie, who was in his library, where, to my surprise, I found Warren taking down books and turning over leaves with quite the air of an author. Something was said about the miseries of authors:—'They are no longer pecuniary miseries,' said Leslie. 'The times are changed since Dryden wrote prologues for two guineas a piece.' Here Warren turned briskly round, exclaiming, 'Two guineas! bless me! times are changed. Why, Mr. Leslie, I receive more than triple that sum for some of my humble contributions to your journal.' I looked at Leslie with as much amazement as if I had heard him proclaim himself the Emperor of China; but Leslie did not look surprised, he only said, 'Very true.' I waited a long time for Warren to go away, that I might understand this mystery, and at length I learned that he regularly carries Mr. Leslie every month a paper for his magazine. He pointed them out to me in some of the numbers, and I assure you they were the same I have frequently heard you admire."

"Even now," said Mrs. Graham, "I do not believe it. He is vain as well as foolish, and he has either stolen those pieces, or hired some one to write them."

"That is what I hinted to Leslie; but he told me that he had once offended Warren by expressing his own doubts on the subject, and that his assurances of their being his were so positive that he felt he had no right to accuse him of falsehood till he had proved it. One thing that disgusted me in Warren was his counting up the money he had received, and muttering every now and then, "Dryden wrote prologues for two guineas! Why, I have made two hundred dollars in the last six months." That entirely convinced me that he is speculating in the talents of some one he keeps concealed."

It is impossible to describe Elizabeth's indignation at learning how she had been deceived. She did not hesitate a moment how to act. Warren was to call the next morning for some manuscripts that she had ready for him, and she determined to speak to him of the baseness of his conduct, and break with him at once. But there is something in the mere presence of a fool that blunts our most eloquent reproaches. It would be absurd, she thought, to talk to him of defrauding the orphan; it will be enough to tell him he has acted dishonestly, and that I will no longer "lend him my pen."

Warren turned pale at her stern inquiry whether he had fulfilled his promise of giving her whatever he should receive from the editor. He solemnly declared that he had done so, but Elizabeth stopped him short by repeating, word for word, the conversation that had passed in Mr. Leslie's library.

"Now, Mr. Warren, after this it is impossible that I can continue to give up time and health for you. You know the object of my labour; you know my anxiety to procure for Louis the advantages of a good education, and you have enriched yourself at my expense. Find somewhere else a pen that will be at your service; mine writes not another word for you."

It was in vain Warren entreated, promised, swore. He even knelt to conjure her to retract. He offered to refund, to pay most liberally; but she was inexorable, and he was obliged to depart, cursing his own folly for boasting of making more by his pen than Dryden by his prologues.

And now what was to become of Elizabeth? She thought of sending her papers to Mr. Leslie, but that would instantly betray Warren, and she had promised him to be silent. She was strongly tempted, but resisted. "He has behaved ill to me, certainly," said she, "but I must not, on that account, forget my own principles. It is the spirit of retaliation that makes dishonesty travel on like a snowball. I must not think of such redress; but what am I to do? The Grahams have already proved their inability to assist me. However, 'God tempers the wind to the shorn lamb,'"—and, hurrying to her room, Elizabeth put on her bonnet and set out for the publisher to offer herself as a translator.

The courteousness of her reception encouraged her, but he looked dubious as to the success of her plan. "Translations did not take," he said, "at present—almost everybody read French, and the best novels were already translated."

"But," said Elizabeth, hurriedly, "I do not confine myself to French or to novels. I know several languages, and have the habit of writing. Let me undertake any work that you will risk the publication of; and if you are not satisfied I will give it up."

For several minutes she waited in suspense while he knit his brows, tapped upon the table, and gave evident signs of hesitation. At length he said, "Well, madam, there is a work of Herder's that you may try."

"May try!" Elizabeth rose, then sat down again. At last, summoning all her fortitude, she said, "My object is neither amusement nor reputation, sir. I simply write for my support, and came to know if you would give me occupation, with a moderate compensation."

Mr. C—— was touched by the look of pain and weariness on her countenance, and agreed immediately to give her a hundred dollars for an elegant translation. The sum sounded magnificent, and she retraced her steps with a lightened heart.

But her task proved tedious and difficult. The extreme attention it required fatigued her mind. There were subjects for verbal criticism that required a great deal of thought, and, in the present state of her health, thought and study completely overpowered her. Eighteen months of seclusion and application, uncheered by success, and rendered still more painful by the privations to which poverty is liable, had destroyed the vigour of her mind, and injured a frame that had never been robust. There were times when she felt such a dying away of her mental powers that she feared her faculties were leaving her. She sought to revive her sinking spirits by going oftener to Mrs. Graham's, and by frequent walks to Dr. B——'s, but the exertion now became a toil, and panting for breath she would sit on a bank at some distance from the school, hoping that chance or sport might lead her darling in that direction. One evening he did discover her, and rushing into her arms reproached her for her long absence.

"You must ask leave to come and see me, Louis. This walk is not a short one, you know, and I am apt to be tired."

Louis looked at her and attempted to speak, but turned his head away and burst into tears. Elizabeth soothingly inquired into his distress, and found that he wished to be taken from school. Oh! do not deny me, dearest Elizabeth. It is for me you look so thin and pale. Instead of living in comfort, you are spending all you have upon me. Now take me from school and bind me to some trade. Don't look so shocked! I have been reading the *Life of Franklin*, and if he, from being an apprentice to a printer, rose to be such a great man, why should I despair? Do, dear sister, bind me to a printer. It is the best trade—at least, the most agreeable trade I can think of, and some years hence I may repay all your goodness."

"Louis—Louis—dear, generous boy! do not pain me by such language. You can requite me better by applying to your studies, than by trying the uncertainty of rising from obscurity into eminence. You forget Dr. Franklin had a wonderful mind, and lived in times to draw forth powerful energies. The probability is, dear Louis, that if you are a printer at fifteen, you will still be a printer at thirty; but another time we will speak of this. The sun is setting and I have far to walk."

It was with feeble steps she regained her dwelling, and, with a reluctant pen, resumed her task, which became daily more difficult. Her headaches were so frequent and so intense that she frequently spent whole days in correcting the mistakes of the preceding ones. The very attitude necessary for writing gave her pain, but she felt that she could not stop, and some days after the time appointed by Mr. C—— she walked with a beating heart to his house with her translation. She was shown into a parlour at the back of the book-shop, where she sat absorbed in her own feelings, unconscious that she had drawn the attention of a gentleman who entered some moments after her, and who stood gazing with painful interest upon her anxious and excited countenance, which he was sure he had seen before, but could not recollect when or where. And, indeed, Elizabeth was changed since he had seen her last. The calm, high, meditative brow was now contracted by pain, and care had dug caves for those once placid eyes. She sat leaning her head upon her wasted hand, lost in her own anxious thoughts till Mr. C—— came in.

"Ah! you have brought the translation. However, I have changed my mind since you were here last." Elizabeth, who had learned to anticipate injustice, lost all self-command, and clasping her hands, burst into a passion of tears. "Nay, do not suppose," said Mr. C——, distressed at his own abruptness, "that I have forgotten our agreement. I have no idea of depriving you of the price of your labours."

He unlocked a desk and took out bills which he put into her hand, saying, "I only meant to tell you that I have deferred the publication of this work for a few months, as there are so many new books in the press."

Elizabeth hardly heard him. All she thought of was to be at home and alone. Yet still the future occurred to her. She offered her address to Mr. C——, saying in a voice of hopelessness, "Should you have occasion to employ any one in the drudgery of literature, in copying, correcting"——she paused, feeling as if she were soliciting charity. The card dropped from her fingers and she hurried away.

Mr. Leslie, for it was he who had been an unobserved spectator of Elizabeth's distress, took up the manuscript that lay on the table.

"A singular young person, that," said the bookseller; "I must try and find her some employment. Yet I cannot understand how such an elegant and accomplished woman should be in such extreme distress. But what astonishes you?" for, as soon as Leslie had cast his eyes on the handwriting, he recognized that of Warren's manuscripts.

Everything was the same—the folding of the paper, the very silk with which it was fastened. There could be no doubt as to her being the charming writer he had so long wished to discover. "Latimer!" he exclaimed; "surely this must be the daughter of him who was involved in the ruin of B—— and T——."

Upon making inquiries Mr. Leslie found that she who was now struggling with poverty and neglect had once been among the favourites of fortune. He described to his wife the scene in Mr. C——'s parlour, and she readily joined with him in the wish to serve Elizabeth. But it was too late to serve or save. She had returned to her lodgings, and throwing herself upon her bed, gave way to utter despondency. A low fever had been for sometime hanging about her, and she now lay down, expecting to rise no more. Oh! that sinking of the heart, when, after struggling with ill fortune, we find ourselves at the very spot from which we set out, like the shipwrecked wretch who, after buffeting the waves through a long night of darkness, sees himself at morning in the midst of a shoreless ocean, with hope and strength exhausted.

Elizabeth had not moved from the spot where she had first thrown herself, when her landlady announced Mr. Leslie. His name excited no emotion. She rose mechanically, and went down. Leslie had been examining the books which crowded her little apartment, and everything he saw convinced him that he was right in his suspicions. He delicately stated to her his discovery, and expressed a wish to remove her to a station where her talents might procure for her competency and respect. The words sounded like mockery to Elizabeth. Her mind was in that state of abandonment and depression that, had the honours and riches of the world been within her grasp, she would not have extended her hand.

Mr. Leslie proceeded to offer her the superintendence of the education of six young ladies, all of that age when a desire to learn saves the teacher an infinity of trouble. She was about to decline, but the thought of Louis roused her. She lifted her languid head, and attempted to thank Mr. Leslie.

"Yet give me a short interval of rest before I begin any new employment. It will be but short, for now I feel as if the prospect of accomplishing the first wish of my heart will give me new life and spirits. It is not to contribute to my own necessities that I have struggled with misfortune, but I have a brother dependent upon me—a boy of such uncommon abilities, that I feel it would be neglecting one of Heaven's best gifts were I to repress them by devoting him to an employment better suited to his circumstances."

"This indeed," thought Leslie, "is woman's love! This is woman's pure, self-sacrificing spirit! That which has supported the sage in his dungeon, the martyr at the stake, and many a misnamed hero, is not wanting here. She is satisfied with her motive, looking forward to a reward so uncertain as the promise of talent in boyhood, a promise as deceitful as the winds or waters."

He left Elizabeth with excited hopes, that prevented her from feeling for some hours the fever that was preying upon her. But the hour of reaction came. All night the wild images of delirium danced before her tortured eyes, and on the morrow, when Mrs. Leslie called to invite her to her house, Elizabeth's ear was deaf to the soft voice that tried to awaken consciousness.

As soon as she was well enough to bear removal, Mrs. Leslie carried her into the country, where the sight of the green hills and slopes made her feel as if she could again brush the dew from their summits; but even Nature—beautiful Nature—once so beloved, and, during her long, gloomy hours in —— Street, so anxiously pined after, failed to restore elasticity to her step. It was autumn—a season she had always loved better even than

———"The music and the bloom
And all the mighty ravishment of spring."

But now, those softly shaded days, which once filled her heart with a pensiveness that she would not have exchanged for mirth, gave a chill to her frame as though the season had been December.

Elizabeth felt that her race was run; but the heart, where despondency had long made its cheerless abode, was now soothed by the new and welcome feelings of gratitude and love.

Mrs. Leslie was one of those benevolent beings who seize upon our affections as their right. The heart gave itself up to her with perfect confidence. The greatest sceptic as to the existence of virtue could not look upon her open, candid countenance without feeling staggered, nor witness the happiness she diffused around her, by the influence of a heavenly disposition upon the daily events of life, without feeling that the source from whence they flowed was pure. One felt in her presence that something good was near, yet there was no parade of goodness about Mrs. Leslie—not obvious, not obtrusive, and only seen—

------"In all those graceful acts,
Those thousand decencies that daily flow
From all her words and actions."

"Look, dear Elizabeth," said she to her languid, pale companion, as they were returning from an excursion to some of the beautiful villages on the Connecticut; "Look! that is Mount Holyoke. He overlooks my native village. I hope the time is not far off when we shall climb his rugged sides together."

Elizabeth shook her head. "Do not deceive me. I feel that ere long I shall be in the presence of God. And yet I cannot say I die without regret, for I am yet young, and youth, even though oppressed with care, shrinks back at sight of the grave. Yet, as I feel drawing nearer to it, much of the fear that it once excited subsides, and perhaps before my last hour comes, I may cease to think even on Louis. Poor Louis! if I could have lived a few years longer—but God's will be done!"

Mrs. Leslie wept. She understood how dreadful was the uncertainty of Elizabeth's mind as to Louis, and she lost no time in consulting her husband about removing the only weight from her heart. He willingly agreed to her benevolent proposal, and that very evening Elizabeth was made happy by his assuring her that Louis should receive the same advantages of education as his own son. She could only weep and press their hands. "My generous friends! may his future life thank you! may he rise up with your own and call you blessed!"

Elizabeth lingered only a month longer. The Leslies would not part with her, and their attachment grew stronger as the object of it was fading before their eyes. There were times when all her delightful powers seemed renewed; when the treasures of her memory and imagination charmed away the winter evening; but the flushed cheek and glittering eye warned them that the lamp of life was burning fast away.

One evening she left the drawing-room earlier than usual. Mrs. Leslie saw with alarm the extreme paleness of her countenance, and after a brief interval followed her to her chamber. She paused a minute at the door, for Elizabeth had sunk on her knees at the foot of the bed. One arm hung by her side; her head had fallen on the other, which she had flung across the bed. Mrs. Leslie trembled as she saw her motionless, then rushed forward—but the hand she grasped was icy cold. The spirit had quitted its earthly tabernacle for ever.— *The Legendary.*

VIEW FROM A HALTING-PLACE. [1]

A stretch of bleak December heath,
  And one lone being o'er it wending
After his shadow, which but tells him
  The sun is fast descending;—
A very cheering piece of news
  To one with travel bending, —
And many a mile between him plac'd
  And any hope of ending.

The small birds wander here and there –
  And yonder goes a falcon floating
Along the rough rocks by the stream,—
  Each nook and cranny noting
Where haply some unlucky wretch
  May harbour, little woting
That such a visitor is near,
  On his destruction doating.

The crowding mountains far away
  Look very cold and melancholy
Beneath their snow locks—while the wind
  Scarce brings the rushing volley
Of their hoar cataracts, which rave
  For aye, like sprites unholy—
All things, in short, have bid a truce
  To aught of mirth or folly.

The cattle seem in musing mood,
  To gaze on distance, with slow-winking
And languid eyes:—one almost knows
  They cannot but be thinking
Of summer with its shiny days,
  And grass with dew-drops twinking,
And wild bees from the fragrant flowers
  The honey-treasure drinking.

The clouds are marble—like above—
  So also is the gray ground under—
The heron on the marsh stone stands
  Lost in a dreamy wonder
Why such a thing as ice should keep
  The fish and him asunder,—
And fears that old dame Nature now
  Has got into a blunder.

So this is Highland winter—well
  He has a solemn air about him
Among these desert plains and steeps,—
  And rules it sternly, I don't doubt him—
That's right:—fire—candles—and the tea-cups,
  And *Blackwood*—who could do without him?
Sweet "May-day"—"Cottages"—and "Birds;"
  If winter ventures here, we'll rout him.

---

[1] Rev. Thomas Brydson, died about 1856. Whilst labouring as minister of Kilmalcolm he contributed in prose and verse to various periodicals. The above is from his volume entitled *Pictures of the Past.*

THE SHIP-BUILDERS.

BY J. G. WHITTIER.

The sky is ruddy in the east,
  The earth is gray below,
And, spectral in the river-mist,
  The ship's white timbers show.
Then let the sounds of measured stroke
  And grating saw begin;
The broad-axe to the gnarléd oak,
  The mallet to the pin!

Hark!—roars the bellows, blast on blast,
  The sooty smithy jars,
And fire-sparks, rising far and fast,
  Are fading with the stars.
All day for us the smith shall stand
  Beside that flashing forge;
All day for us his heavy hand
  The groaning anvil scourge.

From far-off hills, the panting team
  For us is toiling near;
For us the raftsmen down the stream
  Their island barges steer.
Rings out for us the axe-man's stroke
  In forests old and still,—
For us the century-circled oak
  Falls crashing down his hill.

Up!—up!—in nobler toil than ours
  No craftsmen bear a part:
We make of Nature's giant powers
  The slaves of human Art.
Lay rib to rib and beam to beam,
  And drive the treenails free;
Nor faithless joint nor yawning seam
  Shall tempt the searching sea!

Where'er the keel of our good ship
  The sea's rough field shall plough,—
Where'er her tossing spars shall drip
  With salt-spray caught below,—
That ship must heed her master's beck,
  Her helm obey his hand,
And seamen tread her reeling deck
  As if they trod the land.

Her oaken ribs the vulture-beak
  Of Northern ice may peel;
The sunken rock and coral peak
  May grate along her keel;
And know we well the painted shell
  We give to wind and wave,
Must float, the sailor's citadel,
  Or sink, the sailor's grave!

Ho!—strike away the bars and blocks,
  And set the good ship free!
Why lingers on these dusty rocks
  The young bride of the sea?

Look! how she moves adown the grooves,
  In graceful beauty now!
How lowly on the breast she loves
  Sinks down her virgin prow!

God bless her! wheresoe'er the breeze
  Her snowy wing shall fan,
Aside the frozen Hebrides,
  Or sultry Hindostan!
Where'er, in mart or on the main,
  With peaceful flag unfurled,
She helps to wind the silken chain
  Of commerce round the world!

Speed on the ship!—But let her bear
  No merchandise of sin,
No groaning cargo of despair
  Her roomy hold within;
No Lethean drug for Eastern lands,
  Nor poison-draught for ours;
But honest fruits of toiling hands
  And Nature's sun and showers.

Be hers the Prairie's golden grain,
  The Desert's golden sand,
The clustered fruits of sunny Spain,
  The spice of Morning-land!
Her pathway on the open main
  May blessings follow free,
And glad hearts welcome back again
  Her white sails from the sea!
          —*Songs of Labour.*

THE WAR-TRUMPET.

BY MRS. HEMANS.

The trumpet's voice hath roused the land,
  Light up the beacon-pyre!
A hundred hills have seen the brand
  And waved the sign of fire!
A hundred banners to the breeze
  Their gorgeous folds have cast,
And, hark! was that the sound of seas?
  A king to war went past!

The chief is arming in his hall,
  The peasant by his hearth;
The mourner hears the thrilling call,
  And rises from the earth!
The mother on her first-born son
  Looks with a boding eye;—
They come not back, though all be won,
  Whose young hearts leap so high.

The bard hath ceased his song, and bound
  The falchion to his side;
E'en for the marriage altar crowned,
  The lover quits his bride!
And all this haste, and change, and fear,
  By *earthly* clarion spread!
How will it be when kingdoms hear
  The blast that wakes the dead?

DYSPEPSY.

"O cookery! cookery! that kills more than weapons, guns, wars, or poisons, and would destroy all, but that physic helps to make away some." - ANTHONY BREWER.

Ye who flatter yourselves that indolence and luxury are compatible with the enjoyment of health and hilarity of spirits, that the acquisition of the means of happiness is to be happy, and that the habitual pampering of the senses is not for ever paid for by the depression of the immortal soul, listen to my story, and be wise.

People talk of the mischiefs of drinking; invent remedies and preventives, and institute societies, as if eating was not ten times more pernicious. There are a hundred die of eating to one that dies of drinking. But gluttony is the vice of gentlemen, and gentlemanly vices require neither remedies, preventives, nor societies.

It was my good fortune, as the world would call it, to meet with a young man of capital, who wanted a partner skilled in the business to which I had been trained. We accordingly entered into partnership, and our business proved exceedingly profitable. In a few years I had more money than I required for my wants. And with the necessity for exertion ceased the inclination. When a man has been toiling for years to get rich, and dreaming all the while that riches will add to his enjoyments, he must try and realize his dreams after his exertions have been crowned with success. I had proposed to myself a life of ease and luxury as the reward of all my labours. Accordingly, finding myself sufficiently wealthy, I retired from the firm as an active partner, continuing, however, my name to the connection, and receiving a share of the profits, in return for the use of my capital.

I am now my own master, said I, as I shook the dust of the counting-house from my feet. I can do as I please, and go where I please. Now a man that has but one thing to do, and one place to go to, can never be in the predicament of the animal between two bundles of hay; nor puzzled to death in the midst of conflicting temptations. At first I thought of going to Europe; but before I could make up my mind the packet had sailed, and before another was ready I had altered my mind. Next I decided for the Springs; then for the Branch; then for Schooley's Mountain; and then, in succession, for every other "resort of

beauty and fashion" in these United States. In conclusion, I went to none of them. I made but two excursions; one to the Fireplace, to catch trout, where I caught an ague; and the other to Sing Sing, to see the new state prison, where I missed the ague and caught a bilious fever. Thus the summer had passed away, and I may say I did nothing but eat. That is an enjoyment in which both ease and luxury are combined, and my indisposition had left behind a most voracious appetite. Towards the latter end of autumn I began to feel, I can scarcely tell how. I slept all the evening, and lay awake all the night; or if I fell asleep, always dreamed I was suffocating between two feather-beds. I was plagued worse than poor Pharaoh. I had aches of all sorts; stiff-necks, pains in the shoulders, sides, back, loins, head, breast; in short, there never was a man so capriciously used by certain inexplicable, unaccountable infirmities as I was. I dare say I had often felt the same pains before without thinking of them, because I was too busy to mind trifles; for it is a truth which my experience has since verified, that the most ordinary evils of life are intolerable without the stimulus of some active pursuit to draw us from their perpetual contemplation. What was very singular, I never lost my appetite all this time, but ate more plentifully than ever. Indeed eating was almost the only amusement I had ever since I became a man of pleasure; and it was only while eating that I lost the sense of those innumerable pains that tormented me at other times.

I went to a physician, who gave me directions as to the various modes of treatment in these cases. "You are dyspeptic," said he, "and you must either eat less, exercise more, take physic, or be sick." As to eating less, that was out of the question. What is the use of being rich unless a man can eat as much as he likes? As to exercise, what is the use of being rich if a man can't be as lazy as he pleases? The alternative lay between being sick and taking physic, and I chose the latter. The physician shook his head and smiled; but it is not the doctor's business to discourage the taking of physic, and he prescribed accordingly. I took medicines, I ate more than ever; and what quite discouraged me, I grew worse and worse. I sent for the doctor again. "You have tried physic in vain; suppose you try exercise on horseback," said he.

I bought a horse, cantered away every morning like a hero, and ate more than ever; for what was the use of exercise except to give one impunity in eating? I never worked half so hard when I was an apprentice, and not worth a groat, as I did now I was a gentleman of ease and luxury. It was necessary, the doctor said, that the horse should be a hard trotter; and accordingly I bought one that trotted so hard, that he actually broke the paving-stones in Broadway, and struck fire at every step. O reader! gentle reader, if thou art of Christian bowels, pity me. I was dislocated in every joint, and sometimes envied St. Barnabas his gridiron. But I will confess that the remedy proved not a little efficacious; and it is my firm opinion that, had I persevered, I should have been cured in time, had I not taken up a mistaken notion, that a man who exercised a great deal might safely eat a great deal. Accordingly I ate by the mile, and every mile I rode furnished an apology for a further indulgence of appetite. The exercise and the eating being thus balanced, I remained just where I was before.

I sent for the physician again. "You have tried medicine and exercise, suppose you try a regimen. Continue the exercise; eat somewhat less; confine yourself to plain food, plainly dressed; abstain from rich sauces, all sorts of spices, pastes, confectionaries, and puddings, particularly plum-puddings, and generally every kind of luxury, and drink only a glass or two of wine."

"Why, zounds! doctor, I might as well be a poor man at once. Why, what is the use of being rich if I can't eat and drink, and do just as I like? Besides, I am particularly fond of sauces, spices, and plum-puddings."

"Why, so you may, do as you like," replied he, smiling. "You have your choice between Dyspepsy and all these good things."

The doctor left me to take my choice, and after great and manifold doubts, resolutions, and retractions, I decided on trying the effects of this most nauseating remedy. I practised the most rigid self-denial; tasted a little of this, a very little of that, a morsel of the other, and ate moderately of everything on the table; cheating myself occasionally by tasting slily a bit of confectionary, or a slice of plum-pudding. Now and then, indeed, when I felt better than usual, I indulged more freely, as indeed I had a right to do; for what is the use of starving at one time, except to enable one's self to indulge at another? The physician came one day to dine with me at my boarding-house, the most famous eating place in the whole city, and the most capital establishment for Dyspepsy. He came, he said, on purpose to see how I followed his prescription. I was extremely abstinent that day, only eating a mouthful of everything now and then. The doctor, I observed, played a glorious knife and fork, and seemed particularly fond of rich sauces, spices, paste, and plum-pudding.

"Well, doctor," said I, after the rest of the company had retired, "am not I a hero—a perfect anchorite?"

"My dear sir," said he, "I took the trouble to count every mouthful. You have eaten twice as much as an ordinary labourer, and tasted of everything on the table."

"But only tasted, doctor; while you—you—gave me a most edifying example! Faith, you displayed a most bitter antipathy to pies, custards, rich sauces, and most especially plum-pudding!"

"My dear Ambler," said the doctor, "you are to follow my prescriptions, not my example. But, by the way, that was delightful wine, that last bottle—Bingham, or Marston, ey!"

I took the hint, and sent for another bottle, which we discussed equally between us, glass for glass. I felt so well I sent for another, and we discussed that too. "My dear fellow," said the doctor, who by this time saw double, "my dear friend, mind, don't forget my prescription: no sauces, no paste, no plum-pudding, and above all, no wine. Adieu! I am going to a consultation."

That night I suffered martyrdom; nightmare, dreams, and visions of horror. A grinning villain came, and seizing me by the toe exclaimed, "I am Gout; I come to avenge the innocent calves who have suffered in forced meat-balls, and mock-turtle, for your gratification." Another blear-eyed, sneering rogue gave me a box on the ear, that stung through every nerve, crying out, "I am Catarrh, come to take satisfaction for the wine you drank yesterday." While a third, more hideous than the other two, a miserable, cadaverous, long-faced fiend, came up, touching me into a thousand various pains, and crying in a hollow, despairing voice, "I am Dyspepsy, come to punish you for the gluttony of yesterday." I awoke next morning in all the horrors of indigestion and acidity, which lasted several days, during which time I made divers excellent resolutions, forswearing wine, particularly old wine, most devoutly.

This time, however, I had one consolation. The doctor and not I was to blame. It was he that led me into excesses for which I was now paying the penalty. I felt quite indignant. "I'll let him know," said I, "that I am my own master, and not to be forced to drink against my inclination." So I discharged the doctor who set me such a bad example, and called in three more, being pretty well assured that I should now hear all sides of the question.

But it would not do, though I continued my system of abstinence, and only barely tasted a little of everything; at the same time compromising matters with my conscience by drinking twelve half-glasses of wine instead of six whole ones. The doctors, on the whole, did me more harm than good. My spirits began to sink; for I considered that I had now tried all remedies, and that my case was hopeless. The fear of death, swelled into a gigantic and disproportioned magnitude of evil, came upon me. I never heard of a person dying of a disease, let it be what it would, that I did not make that the bugbear of my imagination, and feel all the symptoms appropriate to it. Thus I had by turns all the diseases under the sun; sometimes separately, sometimes all together. The sound of a church bell conjured up the most gloomy associations, and the sight of a churchyard withered every feeling of hilarity in my bosom; in short, there were moments of my life when I could fully comprehend the paradox of a human being seeking death as a relief from its perpetual apprehension.

It is one of the most melancholy features of the disease under which I laboured, that it creates a most disproportioned apprehension of death—a vague and horrible exaggeration, if possible ten times worse than the reality. In most other disorders the pain of the body supersedes that of the mind; in this the mind predominates over the body, and the sense of apprehension of the future swallows up the present entirely. This was the case with me; and often have I welcomed an acute fit of rheumatism, or colic, as a present cure for anticipated evils. I had another enemy to contend with, and that was the want of sympathy. People laughed at my complaints, when they saw me eat my meals with so good an appetite; for the world seldom gives a man credit for ailing when he can eat his allowance; nor is it easy to persuade the vulgar that there is such a disease as appetite. Besides, a man who is always complaining and never seeming to grow worse, is enough to tire the patience of Job, much more of such friends as Job had and most afflicted people are blessed with. My mind was in a perpetual state of fluctuation. One day I threw all my phials, and boxes, and doses into the street, determined to take no more physic; and the next, perhaps, sent for some more, and renewed my potions. I had lost by this time all confidence in physicians, but still continued to believe in physic.

For a while white mustard seed was a treasure to me, and such was my firm reliance on its wonderful virtues, that I actually indulged myself in a few extra glasses, and a few extra luxuries, on the credit of its prospective operation. I read all the guides to health, and all the lectures of Dr. Abernethy. In short I took every means but the only proper ones to effect a cure. I proportioned my eating and other indulgences to my faith in the workings of my favourite panacea. When I took a dose of physic, I considered myself as fairly entitled to take a small liberty the day after; and when I rode or walked farther than usual, I made the old wine, and the sauces, and plum-pudding pay for it. It was thus that I managed to keep myself in a perfect equilibrium, and, like another Penelope, undid in the afternoon the work of the morning. I found, after all, nothing did me so much good as laughing; but, alas! what was there for me to laugh at in this world!

The summer of my second year of ease and luxury I was advised to go to the Springs, where all the doctors send those patients who get out of patience at not being cured in a reasonable time. Here I found several companions in affliction, and was mightily comforted to learn that some of them had been in their present state almost a score of years, without ever dying at all. We talked over our infirmities, and I found there was a wonderful family resemblance in them all, for not one of us could give a tolerable account of his symptoms. One was bilious, another rheumatic, a third was nervous, and a fourth was all these put together.

"Why don't you exercise in the open air?" said I, to this last martyr, one day.

"I catch cold, and that brings on my rheumatism."

"In the house then?"

"It makes me nervous."

"Why don't you sit still?"

"It makes me bilious."

I thank my stars, thought I, here is a man to grow happy upon; he is worse off than myself. He became my favourite companion; and no one can tell how much better I felt in his society.

We formed a select coterie, and managed to sit next each other at meals, where we discussed the subject of digestion. We were all blessed with excellent appetites, and particularly fond of the things that did not agree with us.

"Really, Mr. Butterfield, you are eating the very worst thing on the table."

"I know it, my dear sir, but I am so fond of it."

"My good friend, Mr. Creamwell, how can you taste that hot bread?"

"My dear sir, don't you see I only eat the crust."

"Let me advise you not to try that green corn, Mr. Ambler. It is the worst thing in the world for dyspeptic people."

"I know it, my dear Abstract, but I always take good care to chew before I swallow it."

Thus we went on discussing and eating, and I particularly noticed that every one ate what he preferred, because the fact was, he was so particularly fond of that particular dish he could not help indulging in it sometimes. However we talked a great deal on the subject of diet, and not a man of us but believed himself a pattern of abstinence. I continued my custom of riding every fair day, and occasionally met a fat lady fagging along on a little fat pony, with a fat servant behind her. One day when it was excessively hot I could not help asking her how she could think of riding out in the broiling sun. "Oh, sir, I've got the dyspepsy." I happened to see her at dinner that day, and did not wonder at it.

I passed my time rather pleasantly here with my companions in misfortune. We exchanged notes, compared our infirmities, and gave a full and true history of their rise, progress, and present state, always leaving out the eating. By degrees I became versed in the history of each. One gentleman's diseases were so provokingly contrasted, that what was good for one was bad for the other. Being one day interrogated on the subject, he began:—" I was born in the lap of—" here he yawned pathetically, "and I shall die in the arms of—" here he gave another great yawn, "but really, gentlemen, I feel so nervous, and bilious, and rheumatic this morning—I am sure the wind is easterly—pray excuse me—some other time." So saying, he yawned once more, and went to see which way the wind blew.

My readers, if they are such readers as alone I address myself to, in looking back on the progress of whatever wisdom and experience time and opportunity may have bestowed on them, will have observed that a particular branch of knowledge, or a special conviction of the understanding, will often baffle our pursuit for a long while. We grope in the dark—we lose ourselves—and lose sight of the object of our pursuit—yet still we are gaining upon it unknown and imperceptibly to ourselves. The light is hidden, though just at hand, and finally all at once bursts upon us,

illuminates the mind, and brings with it the full, perfect perception. Thus was it with me. I had read all the most approved books, to come at the mystery of a man being always sick and always hungry; and I had taken all the steps, save one, which they recommended, either as cures or palliatives. I was still in the dark, but I was approaching the light. The history of my complaining friends at once put me upon the right path. I saw in them what I could not see in myself.

On comparing their autobiographies I could not but perceive a family likeness in all. They had commenced the world with active ardent pursuits before them, and were all too busy as well as too poor in their youth to become gluttons; and again they had each, without exception, attained at mid age the means of enjoying a life of luxury and ease. They had arrived at stations in which they could enjoy both, without the necessity of exertion either of body or mind, and they did enjoy them. But they wanted something still—they wanted a hobby-horse, a stimulant of some kind or other, sufficiently ardent to carry their minds along without dragging on the ground, and wearing them out with the labour of nothingness.

Next to the necessity for exertion, is a hobby—a pursuit of some kind or other, something to awake the sleeping mind, if it be only to get up and play puss in a corner. I know a worthy gentleman who has kept off ennui, and its twin sister Dyspepsy, by a habit of going every day round all the docks, counting the vessels, and reading the names on the stern. Another distances the foul fiend, which is as lazy as a pampered house-dog, by walking up one street and down another, examining all the new houses that are building, counting the number of rooms, closets, and pantries, and noting divers other particulars. But in my opinion the wisest of all my friends was a wealthy idler, who was fast sinking into the embraces of the besetting fiend of the age. He all at once bethought himself of altering his dinner hour, and afterwards went about telling it to all his friends. Let not the dingy moralists, who send out their decrees for the acquisition of happiness from the depths of darkness, and know no more of the world than a ground mole, turn up their noses at these my especial friends. Did they know what they ought to know before they set themselves up as teachers; did they only know that when men have made their fortunes by industry and economy, when they have paid their debt to society in useful and honourable pursuits, there comes a time when the bow must be unstrung, when amusements, or at least light occupations, become indispensable, and trifles assume the importance, because they exercise the influence of weighty circumstances on our happiness. It is then that he who can find out an innocent mode of living, and innocent sources of amusement, which interfere with no one's happiness and contribute to his own—which keep his mind from preying on itself, and his body healthy, is better entitled to the honours of philosophy than inexperienced people are aware.

What would have been the effect of the new light which had thus broke in upon me, whether habit would have yielded to conviction, or whether, as is generally the case with old offenders, I should have continued to act against my better reason, I know not. Happily, as I now know, I was not left to decide for myself; fortune took the affair in her own hands. I one morning received a letter apprising me of the failure of our house, and the probable ruin it would bring upon myself. That very day I set out for the city.

Arriving in town, I plunged into a sea of troubles. The younger partner of our house, being in a hurry to grow rich, had encouraged a habit of speculating with, unfortunately for us all, produced a pernicious habit of gambling in schemes of vast magnitude. Having thrown doublets two or three times in succession, he did not, like a wise calculator, conclude that his luck must be nearly exhausted, and retire from the game with his winnings. He doubled again, and lost all. I will not fatigue my readers with the details of a bankruptcy of this kind. It will be sufficient to say, that I took the business directly in hand; nearly deranged my head in arranging my affairs, and by dint of extraordinary industry, and I will say extraordinary integrity, managed to do what only three men before me in similar circumstances had ever done in this city, since the landing of Hendrick Hudson. I paid the debts of the firm to the last farthing, leaving myself nothing but a good name, a good conscience, and a large farm in the very centre of the Highlands. I worked every day in the business like a hero, and took no care what I should eat or what I should drink. My mind was fully occupied, and I was perpetually running about, or engaged in my affairs at the counting-house.

I went to pay off my last and greatest debt to my last creditor, a hard-featured, hard-working, gigantic Scotsman, who had the reputation of being a most inflexible dealer. When all was settled he said,

"Mr. Ambler, of course you mean to begin business again. Remember that my credit, ay, sir, my purse is at your service. You have gained my confidence."

"I thank you, Mr. Hardup," replied I, "warmly, sincerely, for I know you are sincere in your offers. But I mean to retire into the country with what I have saved from the wreck of my fortune. I am tired of business, and too poor to be idle. I have a farm in the mountains, which, I thank God, is mine; for my creditors are all paid. You, sir, are the last."

"Very well, very well," replied Mr. Hardup, stumping about as was his custom, "but is your farm stocked, and all that?"

I was obliged to answer in the negative. It was almost in a state of nature. Mr. Hardup said nothing more, and I bade him farewell with a feeling of indignation at his dry inquiries. The next day I received the following note, inclosing a cheque for a sum which I shall not mention:—

Sir,—You must have something to stock your farm. Pay the inclosed when you are able. I shall come and see you one of these days, when you are settled. Send me neither receipt nor thanks for the money. There is more where that came from. You have gained my confidence, I repeat again; and no man ever gained that without I hope being the better for it, sooner or later.—Your friend and servant,

ALEXANDER HARDUP.

P. S. Get up early in the morning, see to matters yourself; and never buy anything dear except a good name.—A. H.

A worthy man was this Mr. Hardup; and I shall never, while I live, again judge of anybody by the expression of the face, or the common report of the world.

It was in the spring of the year that I bade adieu to the city, and went to take possession of my farm, where I arrived just when the sun was gilding the mountain tops with his retreating rays, as he sunk behind the equally high hills on the opposite side of the river. The scene indeed was beautiful to look at, but by no means encouraging to a man who was going to sit down here and labour for a livelihood. I was received by an old man and his wife, who had occupied my farm a long time at a very moderate rent. The aspect of the house was melancholy. Broken windows, broken chairs, and a broken table. But there was plenty of fresh air, and I slept that night on a straw bed, and studied astronomy through the holes in the roof. The dead silence too that reigned in this lonely retreat, contrasted

with the ceaseless racket of the town, to
which I had been so long accustomed, had a
mournful effect on my spirits, and disposed
my mind to gloomy thoughts of the future.
The fatigue of my journey, however, at last
overpowered me, and I fell asleep with the
certainty of waking next morning with some
terrible malady, arising from my exposed situation. It is a singular fact, that I slept that
night more sweetly than I had done ever since
I determined upon the enjoyment of a life of
luxury and ease; and what is equally singular,
I waked early in the morning without either
a sore throat, a swelled face, or a rheumatic
headache. I am certain of this, for I felt my
throat, shook my head to hear if it cracked,
and looked in a bit of glass to see if my face
retained its true proportions. I confess I was
rather disappointed. "But never mind,"
thought I, "I shall certainly pay for it to-
morrow."

The morrow came, however, and I was again
disappointed. I was sure it would come next
day. But wonderful as it may seem, I thought
I felt better than when I had slept on a feather-
bed, and in a warm room. I began to be encouraged, and by degrees became reconciled to the
enormity of sleeping on a straw bed, in a room
where the air was playing about in zephyrs,
without catching cold. My reader, if he chance
to be in the enjoyment of ease and luxury, will
shrink with horror from my dinners, which
consisted of a piece of salt pork and potatoes
for the first course, and some bread and butter,
or bread and milk for the dessert. At first I
was certain the pork would produce indigestion;
but I suppose, as there was nothing particularly inviting in it, I did not eat enough to do
me any harm, for I certainly felt as light as a
feather after my meals, and instead of dozing
away an hour in a chair, was ready for exercise
at a minute's warning.

The old couple welcomed me to my "nice
place," and were exceedingly eloquent in praise
of my nice, comfortable house, the nice pork,
the bread and butter, and the milk, all equally
"nice." By degrees I began to be infected
with their unaffected content, and sometimes
actually caught myself enjoying the scanty
comforts before me. I did not reason on the
matter, and cudgel myself into an unwilling
submission to necessity; but I benefited by
the example of the honest old couple, without
reasoning at all about it. Reason and precept are a sort of pedagogues, that at best but
bring about a grumbling acquiescence; but
example comes in the shape of a gentle guide,
himself pursuing the right way, and not

commanding us to follow but beckoning on us
with smiles.

I confess, when I looked around on my
domain, I despaired of ever bringing it into
order, beauty, or productiveness. I knew not
the magic of labour and perseverance; nor did
I dream that the fields around me, which seemed
only fruitful in rocks and stones, could ever be
made to wave in golden grain or green meadows. The only spot of all my extensive estate
that seemed susceptible of improvement was
about twenty acres that lay directly before my
door, between two shelving rocky mountains,
and through which ran a little brook of clear
spring water. But even this was so sprinkled
with rocks which had rolled down from the
neighbouring hills, that it was sufficiently dis-
couraging to a man who had for several years
worn spatterdashes, because he shrunk from
pulling on his boots. I spent a month nearly
in pondering on what I should first undertake,
and ended in despairing to undertake anything.

One day I was leaning over the bars at the
entrance to my house, when a tall raw-boned
figure, with hardly an ounce of flesh to his
complement, came riding along, on a horse as
hardy and raw-boned as himself. He stopped
at the bars, and bade me good morning. In
justice to myself I must say, that though
proud enough in all conscience, I am not one
of those churls who, because they have a better
coat on their backs, which by the way often
belongs to the tailor, think themselves entitled
to receive the honest salute of an honest man
with coldness or contempt.

"Good morning, good morning," said the
tall man on the tall horse, and "Good morning, good morning," replied I, repeating the
salutation twice, not to be outdone in courtesy.

"I believe you don't know me," said he,
after a short pause, which, short as it was,
proved the longest he ever afterwards made in
his conversations with me. "I believe you
don't know me. My name is Lightly, and I
am your next neighbour over the mountain
yonder."

"And my name is Ambler," said I, "and I
am heartily glad to have you for a neighbour.
Won't you alight?"

"Why, I don't care if I do; it was partly
my business to come and have a talk with you."

Mr. Lightly accordingly dismounted, and
fastening his horse under a tree, to protect him
from the sun, which was waxing hot, followed
me into the house. After taking something,
he looked about, first at one mountain, then
at another, and at length began, "A rough
country this you've got into, Mr. Ambler."

"Very," replied I, "so rough that I am afraid I shall never make any part of it smooth."

"No?" said Mr. Lightly, "why not?"

"Look at the trees."

"You must cut them down."

"Look at the rocks."

"You must grub them up, they'll make excellent stone walls."

"Doubtless, if I had the people who piled Ossa on Pelion to assist me." Mr. Lightly had never read the history of the great rebellion of the giants, and rather stared at me. "But," added I, "do you really think I can make anything out of these mountains?"

"Do I?" said he, "only come over and see me to-morrow, and I will give you proof of it; but no, now I think of it, not to-morrow, the day after: I am going to walk to Poughkeepsie to-morrow, and sha'n't be back till sundown."

"Poughkeepsie!" cried I, "and back again in one day: why 'tis sixty miles; you mean you'll be back the day after to-morrow evening."

"No I don't: I mean to-morrow evening, God willing; but my days are much longer than yours."

"I should think so; you mean to make the sun stand still, like Joshua."

"No, I don't; though my name is Joshua. I mean to be up at the first crowing of an old cock, that never sleeps after three in the morning, in summer."

"But you've got a horse, why don't you ride?"

"O, that would take me two days; and I can't well spare the time. I never ride when I'm in a hurry."

So saying, Mr. Lightly, after taking my promise to come over the day after to-morrow, took his departure, leaving me to ponder on the vast improbability of a man walking to Poughkeepsie and back again in one day. If he does, thought I, I shall begin to believe in the seven-league boots.

The next morning but one, accordingly, my old man guided me by a winding path to the summit of the mountain, and pointing to a comfortable looking house, surrounded by a large barn, and other out-houses, standing in the midst of green meadows and cultivated fields, told me that was the place to which I was going. As I paused awhile to contemplate the little rural landscape, I could not help wishing that it had pleased Providence to cast my lot where the rocks were so scarce, and the meadows so green. Lightly saw me at the top of the hill, and making some half-a-dozen long

strides with his long legs, met me more than half way up the mountain side.

"Good morning, good morning," said he, repeating it twice, for I soon found he was very fond of talking, and often repeated the same thing to keep himself going. I returned his salutation, adding, "I see you have got back."

"O yes; but not quite so soon as I calculated. I went about four miles out of my way, to bring home my old woman's yarn from the manufactory, and it was almost dark before I got home."

During his brief dialogue he had shot ahead of me two or three times. "You are no great walker, I see," said Mr. Lightly.

"Why, no; I don't think I could walk sixty-eight miles a-day, in the month of June, without being a little tired."

"There's nothing like trying," said he.

"I don't think I shall try," thought I.

My new friend, Mr. Lightly, kept me with him all day, showing me what he had done in the course of eight or ten years, and describing his farm as it was when he first purchased it, for little or nothing. We came to a beautiful meadow, which I could not help admiring, and wishing I had such a one on my farm. "You have a much finer one," said Lightly.

"Where? I never saw it."

"Directly before your door."

"That! why it is paved with rocks."

"Well, and so was this."

"What has become of them all?"

"There they are," pointing to the wall which surrounded the meadow.

The wall seemed a work of the Cyclops, for it was literally rocks piled on rocks. I inquired how he got these rocks one upon the other, as I did not see any machinery. "We had no machines but such as these," holding out his hard, bony hands, and baring part of his arms, that were nothing but twisted sinews.

"But you did not dig these rocks out of the ground, and pile them up here yourself, surely."

"No, no; not quite that either. I have six boys, who assisted me. You shall see them; they will be home from work presently."

"Fine boys' work! faith I should like to see them."

"Yonder they come," said Mr. Lightly.

I followed the direction of his eye, and beheld coming down the hill, afar off, what I took for six giants, striding onward with intent to devour us at one meal. As they advanced towards me my apprehensions subsided, for I saw in their open countenances, and clear blue eyes, indubitable tokens of harmlessness and good nature. I never saw such men before: and here in the mountains, out of the sphere of those artificial distinctions which level in some measure all physical disparities, I could not help feeling a sort of qualm of inferiority. In the crowded city, and amid the conflicts of civilized society, the mind predominates; but here my business was to cut down trees and remove rocks, and the man best qualified for these was the great man for my money. After seeing these "boys," I did not so much wonder at the miracles they had achieved. The whole farm, in fact, exhibited proofs of the wonders which may be wrought by a few strong arms, animated and impelled by as many stout hearts.

"You see what we have done," said Lightly, "why can't you do the same?"

"My good sir, I am neither a giant myself, nor have I any sons that are giants."

"Well, well," said he, "I will tell you what was partly my reason—what was partly my reason for asking you over to see me. My youngest boy—step out, Ahasuerus—my youngest boy is just married, and as our hive is pretty full, it is necessary that he should swarm out with his wife, who is a good, hearty, industrious girl, that will be excellent help for your old woman. You can't get on at first without some hard work, and you will not be able to work yourself for some time very hard; you will want such a boy as mine to break the way a little smooth for you."

I caught at the proposal instantly: we were not long in coming to terms, and in three days the new married couple, the boy and the girl, were established at my house. "She don't know anything about housekeeping," said my old woman. "You shall teach her," said I, and she went about her work perfectly content. "He is a mere boy," quoth my old man, "what can he know of farming?" "He will learn it of you," said I, and the old man felt as proud as a peacock.

My Polyphemus with two eyes set to work without delay under the direction of my old man, who talked a great deal, and did nothing; and who, after having given his opinion, was content to follow that of the other. I was busy, too, looking on, running about, doing little or nothing; but taking an interest, and sympathizing with the lusty labours of the young giant Ahasuerus to such a degree that I have often actually fallen into a violent perspiration at seeing him raise a large stone. Thus I got a great deal of the benefit of hard work without actually fatiguing myself. By degrees I came to work a little myself; and when I did

not work, I gave my advice, and saw the others work. One day—it was the crisis of my life—one day Ahasuerus and the old man were attempting to raise a rock out of the ground by means of a lever, but their weight was not sufficient. They tried several times, but in vain; whereat the spirit came upon me, and, seizing the far end of the lever, I hung upon it with all my might, kicking most manfully all the while. The rock yielded to our united exertions, and rolled out of the ground. It was my victory. "We should not have got it out without you," said Ahasuerus. "It was all your doing," quoth the old man.

But, to tell you the honest truth, I quaked in the midst of my triumph, lest this unheard-of exertion might have injured a blood-vessel, or strained some of the vital parts. That night I thought, somehow or other, I felt rather faintish and languid. But it may be I was only a little sleepy; for I fell asleep in five minutes, and did not wake till sunrise. It was some time before I could persuade myself I was quite well; but being unable fairly to detect anything to the contrary, I arose and walked forth into the freshness of the morning, and my spirit laughed in concert with the sprightly insects and chirping birds.

After this I became bolder and bolder, until finally, animated by the example of the great Ahasuerus, I one day laid hold of a rock and rolled it fairly out of its bed. I was astonished at this feat; I had no idea that I could make the least exertion, without suffering for it severely in some way or other. I never could do it before, and what is the reason I can do it now? thought I; I certainly used to feel very faint, on occasion of sometimes drawing a hard cork out of a bottle. My new monitor, experience, whispered me that this was nothing but apprehension, which, when it becomes a habit, and gains a certain mastery over the mind, produces a sensation allied to faintness. It embarrasses the pulsation, and that occasions a feeling of swooning. The mental causes the physical sensation. I was never so happy in my whole life as when I received this lesson of experience. I was no longer afraid of dying off-hand of the exertion of drawing a cork.

Thus we went on during the summer. The salt pork relished wonderfully; the bread and milk became a delicious dessert; and the rocks daily vanished from the meadow, like magic.

Winter came, and having a vast forest of wood, some of which was decaying, and the remainder had reached its full maturity, I determined to have it cut down and sold to pay my debt to the old Scotsman. With the assistance of one or two others Ahasuerus performed wonders in the woods, as he had done among the rocks. I forget how many loads he sent to market, but it produced enough to pay my old friend, and then I stood upon the proudest eminence an unambitious man can attain—I owed no man a penny, and I could live without running in debt. This is a great and solid happiness, not sufficiently appreciated at this time. People who know no better are apt to think that winter in the country is one long series of dead uniformity, and that there is no enjoyment away from the fireside. But they are widely mistaken; nature everywhere presents a succession of varieties, and those of winter are not the least beautiful.

I did not spend my winter idly, but went out every day to see my wood-cutters. In order to give some interest to my walks, I purchased a gun, procured a brace of fox-hounds, and in time became a mighty hunter. No man of sentiment has ever heard the "deep-mouthed hound," saluting the clear frosty morning with sonorous and far-sounding challenges, without feeling its inspiration, in the silence of the mountains. I found their society, and that of my gun, delightful, though truth obliges me to confess, that I seldom got anything but exercise and a keen appetite in my sporting rambles. Almost the first extensive excursion I made, being intent on following the hounds, I unluckily fell through the ice into a small pond, which the melting of the first snows had formed into a little valley. I got completely wet from head to foot and I was some miles from home. The whole way I suffered the horrible anticipation of diseases without number—rheumatism, consumption, catarrh, sore throat, inflammation of the chest, and a hundred others. In short, I gave myself up for gone; and was in such a hurry to get home and settle my affairs, that I arrived there in a perfect glow. I lost no time in changing my dress, and it being now evening, went directly to bed, expecting next morning to find myself as stiff as a poker. At first I fell into a profuse perspiration, and then into a sound sleep, which lasted till morning. I can hardly believe it myself at this moment; I awoke as well as ever I was in my life, and never felt any ill effects from my accident. After this I defied the whole college of physicians, nay, all the colleges put together. I considered myself another Achilles, invulnerable even at the heel, and now cared no more for the weather than a grizzly bear, or a seeker of the north-west passage.

Thus passed my first winter. In the spring I paid my debt to Hardup with the produ t of my wood. In the summer he came to see me. "I would not come before, for fear you would think it was to dun you," said he. He has repeated his visit every summer for the last seven years, and assures me every time, that were he not Hardup he would be Ambler. It would be tedious to detail the progress I made, and the wonders achieved by Ahasuerus, from the period in which I first took possession of my estate to that in which I am now writing. Great as they were, they bear no comparison with those I have undergone. My farm is now a little Eden among the high hills, whose rugged aspects only add richness and beauty to the cultivated fields. I have saved enough to add two wings to my old house, and to put it in good repair, besides building a barn and other out-houses. Every year I execute some little improvements, just to keep up the excitement of novelty, and prevent me from thinking too much of myself. Every fair day in spring, summer, and autumn, it is my custom to climb a part of the mountain, which overlooks my little domain, and affords a full view of its green or golden inclosures.

It lies at the head of a long narrow vale, skirted on either side by rough, rocky, steep mountains, clothed with vast forests of every growth. My house is on a little round knoll, just on the edge of the meadow I spoke of at my first arrival here, and which now has not a single stone above its surface. The clear spring brook which meanders through it, and is full of trout, forms the head of a little river, which, gathering as it proceeds onward the tribute of the hills, waxes larger as it goes, and appears, at different points far down the valley, coursing its bright way to the Hudson. On either side of the valley, among rocks and woods, is sometimes seen a cultivated field or two, with a house, and a few cattle: but, with this exception, there is a perfect and beautiful contrast between the bosom and the sides of the valley. The former is all softness, verdure, and fertility, the latter is stately forests, or naked sublimity. In a clear day, and a north-west wind, I can see the junction of the little stream, of which, as being the proprietor of its parent spring, I consider myself the father, with the majestic Hudson. I wish the reader, that is, if he is a clever man, or what is still better, a clever and pretty lady, would come and see my farm next summer.

Were mankind aware of the total inability of wealth to confer content, or to make ease and leisure delightful, they would perchance seek it with less avidity, and fewer sacrifices of that integrity which is a far more essential ingredient in human happiness than the gold for which it is so often sacrificed. My history may afford a useful example to those whose situations entail on them the necessity of labour and economy, by teaching them the impossibility of reconciling a life of luxury and ease with the enjoyment of jocund spirits, lusty health, and rational happiness.

"But what has become of your DYSPEPSY all this time?" the reader will ask.

Well! I had forgot that entirely!

———

SAY, SWEET CAROL! WHO ARE THEY?

BY JOANNA BAILLIE.

Say, sweet Carol! who are they
Who cheerly greet the rising day?
Little birds in leafy bower;
Swallows twitt'ring on the tower;
Larks upon the light air borne;
Hunters roused with shrilly horn;
The woodman whistling on his way;
The new-waked child at early play,
Who barefoot prints the dewy green,
Winking to the sunny sheen;
And the meek maid, who binds her yellow hair,
And blithely doth her daily task prepare.

Say, sweet Carol! who are they
Who welcome in the evening gray?
The housewife trim and merry lout,
Who sit the blazing fire about;
The sage a-conning o'er his book;
The tired wight in rushy nook,
Who, half asleep, but faintly hears
The gossip's tale hum in his ears;
The loosen'd steed in grassy stall;
The Thanes feasting in the hall;
But most of all, the maid of cheerful soul,
Who fills her peaceful warrior's flowing bowl.

———

THE BANK NOTE.

BY MRS. AMELIA OPIE.[1]

"Are you returning immediately to Worcester?" said Lady Leslie, a widow residing near that city, to a young officer who was paying her a morning visit.

"I am; can I do anything for you there?"

"Yes; you can do me a great kindness.

My confidential servant, Baynes, is gone out for the day and night; and I do not like to trust my new footman, of whom I know nothing, to put this letter in the post-office, as it contains a fifty-pound note."

"Indeed! that is a large sum to trust to the post."

"Yes; but I am told it is the safest conveyance. It is, however, quite necessary that a person whom I can trust should put the letter in the box."

"Certainly," replied Captain Freeland. Then, with an air that showed he considered himself as a person to be trusted, he deposited the letter in safety in his pocket-book, and took leave; promising he would return to dinner the next day, which was Saturday.

On his road Freeland met some of his brother-officers, who were going to pass the day and night at Great Malvern; and as they earnestly pressed him to accompany them, he wholly forgot the letter intrusted to his care; and, having despatched his servant to Worcester for his sac de nuit[2] and other things, he turned back with his companions, and passed the rest of the day in that sauntering but amusing idleness, that dolce far niente[3] which may be reckoned comparatively virtuous, if it leads to the forgetfulness of little duties only, and is not attended by the positive infringement of greater ones. But in not putting this important letter into the post, as he had engaged to do, Freeland violated a real duty; and he might have put it in at Malvern, had not the rencounter with his brother-officers banished the commission given him entirely from his thoughts. Nor did he remember it till, as they rode through the village the next morning on their way to Worcester, they met Lady Leslie walking in the road.

At sight of her Freeland recollected, with shame and confusion, that he had not fulfilled the charge committed to him; and fain would he have passed her unobserved; for, as she was a woman of high fashion, great talents, and some severity, he was afraid that his negligence, if avowed, would not only cause him to forfeit her favour, but expose him to her powerful sarcasm.

To avoid being recognized was, however, impossible; and as soon as Lady Leslie saw him, she exclaimed, "Oh! Captain Freeland, I am so glad to see you! I have been quite uneasy concerning my letter since I gave it to your care; for it was of such consequence! Did you put it into the post yesterday?"

---

[1] From Illustrations of Lying in all its Branches.   [2] Night bag.   [3] Sweet doing nothing.

"Certainly," replied Freeland, hastily, and in the hurry of the moment, "certainly. How could you, dear madam, doubt my obedience to your commands?"

"Thank you! thank you!" cried she, "How you have relieved my mind!"

He had so; but he had painfully burdened his own. To be sure, it was only a white lie —the lie of fear. Still he was not used to utter falsehood: and he felt the meanness and degradation of this. He had yet to learn that it was mischievous also, and that none can presume to say where the consequences of the most apparently trivial lie will end. As soon as Freeland parted with Lady Leslie, he bade his friends farewell, and, putting spur to his horse, scarcely slackened his pace till he had reached a general post-office, and deposited the letter in safety.

"Now then," thought he, "I hope I shall be able to return and dine with Lady Leslie, without shrinking from her penetrating eye."

He found her, when he arrived, very pensive and absent; so much so, that she felt it necessary to apologize to her guests, informing them that Mary Benson, an old servant of hers, who was very dear to her, was seriously ill, and painfully circumstanced; and that she feared she had not done her duty by her.

"To tell you the truth, Captain Freeland," said she, speaking to him in a low voice, "I blame myself for not having sent for my confidential servant, who was not very far off, and despatched him with the money, instead of trusting it to the post."

"It would have been better to have done so, certainly!" replied Freeland, deeply blushing.

"Yes; for the poor woman, to whom I sent it, is not only herself on the point of being confined, but she has a sick husband, unable to be moved; and as, but owing to no fault of his, he is on the point of bankruptcy, his cruel landlord has declared that, if they do not pay their rent by to-morrow, he will turn them out into the street, and seize the very bed they lie on! However, as you put the letter into the post yesterday, they must get the fifty pound note to-day, else they could not; for there is no delivery of letters in London on a Sunday, you know."

"True, very true," replied Freeland, in a tone which he vainly tried to render steady.

"Therefore," continued Lady Leslie, "if you had told me when we met that the letter was not gone, I should have recalled Baynes, and sent him off by the mail to London; and then he would have reached Somerstown, where the Bensons live, in good time;—but now,

though I own it would be a comfort to me to send him, for fear of accident, I could not get him back again soon enough; therefore, I must let things take their chance; and, as letters seldom miscarry, the only danger is that the note may be taken out."

She might have talked an hour without answer or interruption, for Freeland was too much shocked, too much conscience-stricken to reply; as he found that he had not only told a falsehood, but that, if he had had moral courage enough to tell the truth, the mischievous negligence of which he had been guilty could have been repaired; but now, as Lady Leslie said, it was too late!

But while Lady Leslie became talkative, and able to perform her duties to her friends after she had thus unburdened her mind to Freeland, he grew every minute more absent and more taciturn: and, though he could not eat with appetite, he threw down, rather than drank, repeated glasses of hock and champagne, to enable him to rally his spirits; but in vain. A naturally ingenuous and generous nature cannot shake off the first compunctious visitings, of conscience for having committed an unworthy action, and having also been the means of injury to another. All on a sudden, however, his countenance brightened: and as soon as the ladies left the table he started up, left his compliments and excuses with Lady Leslie's nephew, who presided at dinner, said he had a pressing call to Worcester; and, when there, as the London mail was gone, he threw himself into a post-chaise, and set off for Somerstown, which Lady Leslie had named as the residence of Mary Benson.

"At least," said Freeland to himself with a lightened heart, "I shall now have the satisfaction of doing all I can to repair my fault."

But, owing to the delay occasioned by want of horses and by finding the ostlers at the inns in bed, he did not reach London and the place of his destination till the wretched family had been dislodged; while the unhappy wife was weeping, not only over the disgrace of being so removed, and for her own and her husband's increased illness in consequence of it, but from the agonizing suspicion that the mistress and friend, whom she had so long loved and relied upon, had disregarded the tale of her sorrows, and had refused to relieve her necessities!

Freeland soon found a conductor to the mean lodging in which the Bensons had obtained shelter; for they were well known, and their hard fate was generally pitied. But it was some time before he could speak, as he stood by their bedside—he was choked with painful emotion at first, with pleasing emotions afterwards—for his conscience smote him for the pain he had occasioned, and applauded him for the pleasure which he came to bestow.

"I come," said he at length, while the sufferers waited in almost angry wonder to hear his reason for thus intruding on them, "I come to tell you, from your kind friend Lady Leslie"—

"Then she has not forgotten me!" screamed out the poor woman, almost gasping for breath.

"No, to be sure not:—she could not forget you; she was incapable. . . ." here his voice wholly failed him. "Thank Heaven!" cried she, tears trickling down her pale cheek. "I can bear anything now; for that was the bitterest part of all!"

"My good woman," said Freeland, "it was owing to a mistake:—pshaw! no, it was owing to my fault, that you did not receive a fifty pound note by the post yesterday."

"Fifty pounds!" cried the poor man, wringing his hands, "why, that would have more than paid all we owed; and I could have gone on with my business, and our lives would not have been risked, nor our character disgraced!"

Freeland now turned away, unable to say a word more; but, recovering himself, he again drew near them, and, throwing his purse to the agitated speaker, said, "There! get well! only get well! and whatever you want shall be yours! or I shall never lose this horrible choking again while I live!"

Freeland took a walk after this scene, and with hasty, rapid strides, the painful choking being his companion very often during the course of it, for he was haunted by the image of those whom he had disgraced; and he could not help remembering that, however blamable his negligence might be, it was nothing, either in sinfulness or mischief, to the lie told to conceal it, and that, but for that lie of fear, the effects of his negligence might have been repaired in time.

But he was resolved that he would not leave Somerstown till he had seen these poor people settled in a good lodging. He therefore hired a conveyance for them, and superintended their removal that evening to apartments full of every necessary comfort.

"My good friends," said he, "I cannot recall the mortification and disgrace which you have endured through my fault; but I trust that you will have gained in the end, by leaving a cruel landlord who had no pity for your unmerited poverty.—Lady Leslie's note will, I trust, reach you to-morrow;—but if not, I will make up the loss; therefore be easy, and

when I go away, may I have the comfort of knowing that your removal has done you no harm!"

He then, but not till then, had courage to write to Lady Leslie and tell her the whole truth, concluding his letter thus:—

"If your interesting protegés have not suffered in their health, I shall not regret what has happened, because I trust that it will be a lesson to me through life, and teach me never to tell even the most apparently trivial white lie again. How unimportant this violation of truth appeared to me at the moment! and how sufficiently motived! as it was to avoid falling in your estimation: but it was, you see, overruled for evil;—and agony of mind, disgrace, and perhaps risk of life, were the consequences of it to innocent individuals, not to mention my own pangs—the pangs of an upbraiding conscience. But forgive me, my dear Lady Leslie. Now, however, I trust that this evil, so deeply repented of, will be blessed to us all; but it will be long before I forgive myself."

Lady Leslie was delighted with this candid letter, though grieved by its painful details, while she viewed with approbation the amends which her young friend had made, and his modest disregard of his own exertions.

The note arrived in safety; and Freeland left the afflicted couple better in health, and quite happy in mind, as his bounty and Lady Leslie's had left them nothing to desire in a pecuniary point of view.

When Lady Leslie and he met, she praised his virtue, while she blamed his fault; and they fortified each other in the wise and moral resolution, never to violate truth again, even on the slightest occasion; as a lie, when told, however unimportant it may at the time appear, is like an arrow shot over a house, whose course is unseen, and may be unintentionally the cause to some one of agony or death.

REVENGE OF INJURIES.

[Lady Elizabeth Carew, lived in the reign of James I. She wrote a tragedy, *Marian, the Fair Queen of Jewry*, 1613, in which the following lines occur.]

The fairest action of our human life
Is scorning to revenge an injury;
For who forgives without a further strife,
His adversary's heart to him doth tie.
And 'tis a firmer conquest truly said,
To win the heart, than overthrow the head.

If we a worthy enemy do find,
  To yield to worth it must be nobly done;
But if of baser metal be his mind,
  In base revenge there is no honour won.
Who would a worthy courage overthrow,
And who would wrestle with a worthless foe?

We say our hearts are great, and cannot yield;
  Because they cannot yield, it proves them poor:
Great hearts are task'd beyond their power, but seld
The weakest lion will the loudest roar.
Truth's school for certain doth this same allow,
High-heartedness doth sometimes teach to how.

A noble heart doth teach a virtuous scorn:
  To scorn to owe a duty over long;
To scorn to be for benefits forborne:
  To scorn to lie, to scorn to do a wrong:
To scorn to bear an injury in mind;
To scorn a free-born heart slave-like to bind.

But if for wrongs we needs revenge must have,
  Then be our vengeance of the noblest kind;
Do we his body from our fury save,
  And let our hate prevail against our mind?
What can 'gainst him a greater vengeance be,
Than make his foe more worthy far than he?

BARON MUNCHAUSEN.

[Rudolph Erich Raspe, born in Germany about 1736; died at Mucross, Ireland, 1794. The real authorship of the amusing burlesque of the *Travels of Baron Munchausen* has been only recently discovered. Baron Friederich von Munchausen, of Bodenweder, Hanover, was the original of the character. He had seen some service, and on his retirement was addicted to the chase, good cheer, and story-telling of the most extravagant sort. Raspe, gifted with much talent, a member of various learned societies, and sometime a professor in Cassel, but a man of lax principles, wrote out his friend's stories, exaggerating them, and adding to them, as his fancy inspired him, and published them first in England. Munchausen's travels became popular, and their authorship was attributed to various well-known writers. Raspe died in a state of destitution. The following will serve as an example of his extravagant humour.]

We sailed from Amsterdam with despatches from their High Mightinesses, the States of Holland. The only circumstance which happened on our voyage worth relating, was the wonderful effects of a storm, which had torn up by the roots a great number of trees of enormous bulk and height, in an island where we lay at anchor to take in wood and water; some of these trees weighed many tons, yet they were carried by the wind so amazingly high, that they appeared like the feathers of small birds floating in the air, for they were at least five miles above the earth. However, as soon as the storm subsided, they all fell perpendicularly into their respective places, and took root again, except the largest, which happened, when it was blown into the air, to have a man and his wife, a very honest old couple, upon its branches, gathering cucumbers (in this part of the globe that useful vegetable grows upon trees): the weight of this couple, as the tree descended, overbalanced the trunk, and brought it down in a horizontal position: it fell upon the chief man of the island, and killed him on the spot; he had quitted his house in the storm, under an apprehension of its falling upon him, and was returning through his own garden when this fortunate accident happened. The word fortunate here requires some explanation. This chief was a man of a very avaricious and oppressive disposition, and though he had no family, the natives of the island were half-starved by his oppressive and infamous impositions.

The very goods which he had thus taken from them were spoiling in his stores, while the poor wretches from whom they were plundered were pining in poverty. Though the destruction of this tyrant was accidental, the people chose the cucumber gatherers for their governors, as a mark of their gratitude for destroying, though accidentally, their late tyrant.

After we had repaired the damages we sustained in this remarkable storm, and taken leave of the new governor and his lady, we sailed with a fair wind for the object of our voyage.

In about six weeks we arrived at Ceylon, where we were received with great marks of friendship and true politeness. The following singular adventure may not prove unentertaining.

After we had resided at Ceylon about a fortnight, I accompanied one of the governor's brothers on a shooting party. He was a strong athletic man, and being used to that climate (for he had resided there some years), he bore the violent heat of the sun much better than I could; in our excursion he had made a considerable progress through a thick wood when I was only at the entrance.

Near the banks of a large piece of water, which had engaged my attention, I thought I heard a rustling noise behind; on turning about, I was almost petrified (as who would not?) at the sight of a lion, which was evidently approaching with an intention of satisfying his appetite with my poor carcass, and that without asking my consent. What was to be done in this horrible dilemma? I had not even a moment for reflection; my piece was only charged with swan-shot, and I had no other about me: however, though I could have no idea of killing such an animal with that weak kind of ammunition, yet I had some hopes of frightening him by the report, and perhaps of wounding him also. I immediately let fly, without waiting till he was within reach; and the report did but enrage him, for he now quickened his pace, and seemed to approach me full speed: I attempted to escape, but that only added (if an addition could be made) to my distress; for the moment I turned about, I found a large crocodile with his mouth extended almost ready to receive me: on my right hand was the piece of water before mentioned, and on my left a deep precipice, said to have, as I have since learned, a receptacle at the bottom for venomous creatures; in short, I gave myself up as lost, for the lion was now upon his hind legs, just in the act of seizing me: I fell involuntarily to the ground with fear, and, as it afterwards appeared, he sprang over me. I lay some time in a situation which no language can describe, expecting to feel his teeth or talons in some part of me every moment: after waiting in this prostrate situation a few seconds, I heard a violent but unusual noise, differing from any sound that had ever before assailed my ears; nor is it at all to be wondered at, when I inform you from whence it proceeded; after listening for some time, I ventured to raise my head and look around, when, to my unspeakable joy, I perceived the lion had, by the eagerness with which he sprang at me, jumped forward as I fell, into the crocodile's mouth! which, as before observed, was wide open; the head of the one stuck in the throat of the other; and they were struggling to extricate themselves; I fortunately recollected my couteau-de-chasse, which was by my side; with this instrument I severed the lion's head at one blow, and the body fell at my feet! I then, with the but-end of my fowling-piece, rammed the head farther into the throat of the crocodile, and destroyed him by suffocation, for he could neither gorge nor eject it.

Soon after I had thus gained a complete victory over my two powerful adversaries, my companion arrived in search of me; for, finding I did not follow him into the wood, he returned, apprehending I had lost my way or met with some accident.

After mutual congratulations, we measured the crocodile, which was just forty feet in length.

As soon as we had related this extraordinary adventure to the governor, he sent a waggon and servants, who brought home the two carcasses. The lion's skin was properly preserved with its hair on; after which it was made into tobacco-pouches, and presented by me, upon our return to Holland, to the burgomasters, who, in return, requested my acceptance of a thousand ducats.

The skin of the crocodile was stuffed in the usual manner, and makes a capital article in their public museum at Amsterdam, where the exhibitor relates the whole story to each spectator, with such additions as he thinks proper: some of his variations are rather extravagant; one of them is, that the lion jumped quite through the crocodile, and was making his escape when, as soon as his head appeared, Monsieur the Great Baron (as he is pleased to call me) cut it off, and three feet of the crocodile's tail along with it; nay, so little attention has this fellow to the truth, that he sometimes adds, as soon as the crocodile missed his tail he turned about, snatched the couteau-de-chasse out of Monsieur's hand, and swallowed it with such eagerness that it pierced his heart, and killed him immediately!

The little regard which this impudent knave has to veracity, makes me sometimes apprehensive that my *real facts* may fall under suspicion, by being found in company with his confounded inventions.

***

THE WORLD.

BY GEORGE HERBERT.

Love built a stately house; where Fortune came :
And spinning fancies she was heard to say,
That her fine cobwebs did support the frame,
Whereas they were supported by the same :
But Wisdom quickly swept them all away.

Then Pleasure came, who, liking not the fashion.
Began to make balconies, terraces,
Till she had weaken'd all by alteration :
But reverend laws, and many a proclamation
Reformed all at length with menaces.

Thou enter'd Sin, and with that sycamore,
Whose leaves first shelter'd man from drought and dew,
Working and winding slily evermore,
The inward walls and summers cleft and tore :
But Grace shored these, and cut that as it grew.

Then Sin combined with Death in a firm band,
To raze the building to the very floor :
Which they effected, none could them withstand ;
But Love and Grace took Glory by the hand,
And built a braver palace than before.

SWORD AND SHUTTLE.

MY OLD NURSE'S STORY OF SOME FRENCH REFUGEES.

[Thomas Archer, born in London, 1830. Novelist and miscellaneous writer. His principal works are: *Madame Prudence; Wayfe Summers; Strange Work; A Fool's Paradise; The Pauper, the Thief, and the Convict*, a Book on Crime and Poverty; *The Terrible Sights of London; The Frogs' Parish Clerk; The Boys' Book of Trades; The History of France*, from the Accession of Louis Philippe to the Close of the German Occupation; and he has edited a family edition of Richardson's *Pamela*. One critic says: "Mr. Archer's style is easy and unaffected, placing before the reader pictures of the vice and misery that surround us, often with a striking minuteness of detail, but never with anything approaching to coarseness."]

PART I.

Ah, my dear, these are almost the only things I can remember now. It's just the way with an old woman like me, that all that happened years and years ago comes out clear as yesterday, and the things of yesterday go backward and backward till we forget them altogether. Age makes a solitude of its own, just as youth does—both of 'em are waiting for company—only one is to be taken to it and the other sent to it.

I wonder ——! but there, what signifies wondering; you want to hear something of the old French folks, and particularly of your great uncle's family—the Du Boissons—and what they were like. Well then, figure to yourself this:—

It is a long low room, with leaden casements that swing open, and look out first on a row of blue and white flower-pots all along the sill, and then between the leaves and flowers—a complete window-blind in themselves—upon a garden all laid out with such gaudy blooms, that every bed, round or square, or cut into odd shapes, looks like a separate nosegay. It has been raining; and now the sun is out again, and the perfume of mignonette and clove pink, narcissus, rose, and verbena goes up to heaven along with the incense of sweet thyme, basil, and knotted marjoram. For it is a French garden, dear, and a corner of it is kept for pot-herbs and salads—chervil and sorrel, and if not for garlic, at any rate for shallots.

It is a French garden, and there are two Frenchmen sitting together in the little arbour at the end of it—an arbour formed by an elder tree drooping over a little rustic wood-work that shelters a bench.

Those two men are the elder Du Boisson and the pastor Duchesne.

I said the elder Du Boisson, and he is old indeed now. Peeping at him, as I used to do as a child, over the privet hedge that divided our gardens, I have often thought he must have wonderful stories to tell of the dreadful times in France when men, women, and children were scarred with sword, and set alight like torches, and yet not suffered to leave France, under pain of fresh tortures if they were arrested on the way. This old man had escaped through great dangers, but his wife had died of grief and terror, and only he and his one son reached England, leaving house and lands behind. His estates were at St. Ambroix in the south of France, which will account for his coming at once to London and joining the colony of our emigrés that had settled in Spitalfields; for St. Ambroix is a silk district, and the elder Du Boisson knew some of the weavers here very well, and also some of the noblemen, who, having no trade, because they were high-born, learned of their wives to make pillow-lace, and wrought at Coventry and other places. As I have said, Du Boisson, father and son, came to Spitalfields; and behold, in thirty years they were there still, for the son had grown into a middle-aged, stout, rosy, dark-eyed gentleman, gay with the sprightly jollity of our countrymen of those times, and married to a comely wife—your relation, dear—of the old families who came over from Rouen and the north, in the early troubles, after the bishops and the Bourbon had broken faith with God and man.

It was just beyond Spitalfields, and close to the pleasant fields and hedgerows of Bethnal Green that our houses stood. Ah! these places were pretty and countrified then. Once pass the great frowning tower of London, and the old artillery-ground where the train-bands and soldiers used to practise, and you were close to St. Mary's 'Spital, and among the tall houses with great upper-rooms and wide casements, where caged-birds sang in answer to the click of the loom and the swift whistle of the flying shuttle. The Spitalfields silks were the most sought after in those days, dear, and many a weaver wore gold pieces or crowns instead of buttons to his flapped coat or his embroidered waistcoat. The Du Boissons had not reached England penniless, and they were money-making people—thrifty as the old Huguenot gentry knew how to be—thrifty and industrious. When the son married he had not left off working at his trade. There was a loom in the upper-room of the house still, but the younger Du Boisson had several other looms elsewhere, and a journeyman hard at work at every one of them making figured-silk and velvet. Little Hugo slept in the shadow of that loom at the house in Bethnal Green. He worked there in the day, for he was to be taught his trade—his father would have it so, and he slept there at night. The likeness of that boy to his grandfather was something wonderful. The same keen, severely-cut face, the same firm mouth and chin. Except that he has his mother's fair skin and pleading eye, he would look much more than his fourteen years on this afternoon that his grandfather and le Pasteur Duchesne sit talking so earnestly in the summer-house. For it is Hugo's birth-day, and therefore a household holiday; the loom is silent; the boy himself has gone out to spend the crown-piece that made a part of his morning present. His father and mother are both sitting in the lower room—she a fair woman, beautiful still, and with that serene look that so well accords with her dainty lace-cap, the fine snow-white tucker which covers her shapely throat, and the sleeves that show off the whiteness of her taper fingers as they move swiftly in embroidering a waistcoat, which is to be finished as a gift to her boy before he comes in to their early tea.

Somehow everybody who saw Madame Du Boisson sitting in her pretty parlour, associated her with the delicate china which was set out on mahogany shelves in a recess of the wall, and with the charming figures of brocaded lovers surrounded by flowers, and holding candle-sconces in their hands, which adorned the mantel-piece. There were many such pretty nick-nacks about, with flowers and sweet-herbs in china vases and bowls, just in the old French way. The elder Du Boisson's flute and the fiddle of the younger hung on the wall, and a spinette in the corner of the room was open, with some written music on the desk in front of it. For madame could play and sing prettily. Some of the ornaments of their home, and a good stock of clothes and linen, was nearly all the dowry she brought to her husband, though she came of one of the old families, and on her mother's side belonged to the French nobility. Her husband thought her face fortune enough, and her sweet placid temper all the dower a man need ask. He thinks so now, as he leans back a little in his chair and blows away the light wreath of smoke from his pipe that he may see the better. A handsome crisp-haired, dark-eyed, ruddy man—almost more English than French in his ways—a man contented to leave the dead past to bury its

dead, although he has still a deep, solemn memory of his mother, and of the old home in the "Gard," whence she fled to die before she could reach a place of refuge—contented to be what he is—a master weaver with a good home about him, a sweet wife, and a boy whom he hopes to make his "right-hand man" in three or four years more. Ah, that boy! how little he is like his father. The grandfather sees that often, as he sits in his elbow-chair and shoots furtive, almost eager, and yet rather troubled glances at the lad. The mother sees it too, and, strangely enough, divines much of what may come of it. I said strangely—but madame was of the old old Protestants, people who had insight, my dear, and who kept to the old names and the old ways, and had a sword for the enemies of France, as the wicked rulers of their nation found to their cost more than once.

"Yes, Louis," she says, taking up their conversation as she took up a thread, "I have watched the dear child often, and he will grow into it. Only the other day I heard him say to his grandfather, "Grandpere, if the persecutions should cease and we could claim our own, you will take me with you?"

"And what did my father say?"

"He laughed, and then there came that flash into his eyes, Louis, and he put the boy back a little and said, 'Why, we might have to choose again between our Christianity or our property, my dear child ; instead of persecutors who stab and burn in the name of the church and of religion, we may yet hear of those who rob and murder in the name of reason and of universal brotherhood. At present we Protestants are kept out of legal registers, and are not suffered to make wills. The time may shortly come when law itself will be abolished, and all property be confiscated.'"

"Hum! he knows a few things, that father of mine," says the husband with a serious look. "That is from the pastor. Duchesne has information. You know that he has only returned from Paris but these three days, my love?"

"I did not know. He is here to-day, though, with our father. They have secrets, those two; but there can be no bad secrets in which the pastor takes part?"

"I think I know their secret," replies the husband, laughing again and lighting a fresh pipe.

"Is it about the property, Louis?"

"Yes; I think so."

"Does our father wish you to try to reclaim it?"

"It would be useless as well as dangerous."

"Would you, if the persecutions were to cease?"

"No."

"Why not, my dear?"

"First, because it would be more trouble than it is worth. Secondly, because some child or other is now growing up in possession of it. Thirdly, because I am now less French than English, and have founded another property here, where it is safe, even though it be small."

He looks round with beaming eyes which rested on his wife. A tear falls on the embroidery at which she is working.

"Thou art right, dear Louis," she says presently, "and yet, for the sake of our boy and the old race ——"

The husband looks at her a moment and then breaks into a gay laugh.

"What has become of our races, Madeleine?" he says presently. "Thou art now of mine, and of mine Hugo (why did Duchesne persuade thee to choose that name?) is the last. It would be better for the lad to begin a new family of his own here, than to go to fight a barren suit and be pulled down either by the wolves that slaked their thirst for blood in the service of the debauchee of Le Parc aux Cerfs, or by the rabble which, as my father says ——"

"Oh! you too, then, are in the secrets of the Pastor Duchesne?" interrupts his wife.

"Well, only a little; but as we love our boy, dear wife, let us keep to the known. Besides, who can tell whether there may not be ——"

"Hush!" says madame, raising a warning finger, "here he comes;" and Hugo runs in and throws his arms round his mother's neck.

"Child, what is that thou hast bought? Foolish boy, what is the use of a sword in a country where we are safe?"

"What, don't you want mamma?" replies the lad with heightened colour: "this is grandpapa's present of the day. He has just buckled it round me himself as I came through the garden. 'There, my dear grandson,' he said, 'that was the sword that my grandfather, and now I place it on you. Beware how you ever disgrace it. As you cannot wear it, place it somewhere where you may look at it sometimes.' May I hang it up over my bed, papa?"

"You may, my dear lad; but—I don't want to weaken your pleasure, Hugo—it is by the spindle rather than the sword that the Du Boissons have done best, and in England the former is justly regarded as the nobler implement. Remember, 'those who use the sword

shall perish by it.' The history of the country I have left may teach us the truth of that saying."

The boy looks very earnestly at his father's grave but still smiling face.

"Don't you mean any longer to be a Frenchman then, papa?" he says presently.

"Faith, I can't help that, Hugo. We talk in French, at any rate whenever your grandfather is present, and we cook and live in the French fashion still, but still I am an Englishman."

"And you would not go back to France to live, even if you could get your own?"

"See here, my lad," says Du Boisson, drawing the boy to him, "we shall never get back our house and lands at St. Ambroix; and even if we could, they would not be worth the holding, for the troubles are not over yet, nor will be till —— But there, it is your birth-day, and I will not trouble even your dreams; but take off the sword to-morrow, and don't go out with it, lest the draw-boys and the apprentices should laugh at you, and you should be tempted to try its temper through losing your own."

The elder Du Boisson and Pastor Duchesne continued talking in the summer-house. Their conference was long and earnest, for the pastor had but just returned from one of those swift and sudden journeys to France which he seemed to make periodically.

The old man had by his side, on a table which was fixed in front of the bench, a large carved oaken box, and from this he took a bundle of papers and parchments.

"Here are the title-deeds, Duchesne; here the letters-patent, the leases, the everything—saved with what property we could carry, on that terrible night when I turned my back on the home that I had loved—and—and—on the strange grave that held ——"

The pastor placed his hand on the old man's arm.

"The grave holds nothing," he said, in a voice peculiarly low and sweet. "Heaven holds a saint the more, earth not a sacred memory—hardly a sacred presence—the less. As to these papers (taking them in his hand), I accept the trust, and will be faithful to it. But again I say, with all my soul, Louis is right. You and I, old friend, have fought the battle and want to be fighting it yet. But we shall have to bow before the sword of the Lord; and he alone knows what shape that fiery weapon will take, that France may have her proud-flesh cut away and be left bleeding, but with blood unpoisoned. Give me the papers. Should I live till times when the king, who is weakly virtuous, can undo the deeds of the strongly vicious, I will give the lad your message and show them to him, if he still craves for the old château of Le Platane, and thinks to found the seigneury afresh. I tell you plainly, though, that I believe all seigneury is at an end—that you and I, and those who have hoped to find work to do for the good cause, will see France nearly perish, and ruin come upon the men who, in casting us and ours out from the land, flung away those whose influence might have saved them from the swift destruction that they merit."

"You say you have been to Gard, and actually seen my old house of Le Platane? Who is the usurper—who the robber that now despoils my garden and eats the ripe fruit from the orchard?" asked the old man gloomily.

"No usurper is there yet, my friend," said the pastor gently. "The faithful Corneille, the son of your old steward, and the playmate of Louis, holds house and land yet. The apples hung ripe upon the trees, the grapes upon the vines; and still, like many of us, the faithful fellow hopes to see the day when the refugees may return. He has done some slight service to his department, I hear, but he is still hesitating. I gathered from what he said that he thinks the title-deeds were stolen, perhaps burned. I could have undeceived him, but wanted your permission; so he and his son and daughter live there yet, as it were, on sufferance. Lucky for him, perhaps, that he had influence with the other party, who left him there in charge. As it is, you remember Pithon?"

"What, the drunken foreman of the tan-pits?"

"Yes. He is a second cousin of Corneille, and has an evil eye. He too has a son—a worthy pair. Corneille suspects that the elder Pithon conducted the dragoons to your house that fatal night. He is dead. The son takes up his hatred with the malignity of a Vendetta. Already he accuses Corneille of being a Protestant in disguise, and swears to denounce him."

"You can come and go, Duchesne, and yet are unhurt."

"Yes, but I know where my friends are, and pass quickly, and not without danger. I must go, old friend; a fire consumes me sometimes, calm and impassive as I may seem. I left France before you, and as a young man, the chosen pastor of a people who loved and trusted me. Wolves ravened amidst my flock, and I was spattered with the blood of those who stood around me, sword in hand, to fight for life and liberty. I came here—blessed coun-

try! asylum for freedom of religion! and again I am the Pastor Duchesne. See my little chapel, built as you know from money subscribed by those who had left much behind them for truth's sake. I look around and feel that I have grown almost into a green old age, with many brethren and sisters, many children round me. I am pastor, friend, schoolmaster, and move serenely amidst our band of emigrants, loving and beloved; and yet—and yet——"

"Yes, I know," said old Du Boisson, with a kind of spasm, wringing his friend's hand.

"I don't often confess—it is not a Protestant ordinance," said the pastor, growing pale and calm again; "but friend, let us pray to be delivered from faithlessness, from the awful delusion that anything other than His strength will be sufficient for us. Let us pray, too, that it may be made perfect in weakness."

So saying Pastor Duchesne rose, carefully buttoned the packet of papers and parchments into his capacious pocket, and the two men walked towards the house.

PART II.

Now, my dear, figure to yourself also this:—A low, flat country, straggling out into a kind of broken waste, intersected here and there with factories, tan-pits, and clumps of wood. Still further in the distance, fields and country roads, the latter leading occasionally over bridges spanning a stream. Further again, a long house of white stone, with a queer gabled roof, and a courtyard in front, reached by clanging iron gates; and behind, level with offices, kitchens, and out-houses, a broad terrace with a stone balcony, overlooking a flower-garden, which leads by various paths to orchards, meadows, and farm-buildings.

The house has been known as, and is still called by the name of Le Platane, a title taken from a great plane-tree which still rears its dusty and somewhat drooping head in front of the entrance-gate. One limb of the tree is bare, and seems to have been blasted with fire. For ten years in the history of the house a fragment of tarred rope hung to this fork of the plane-tree. A Protestant had been hung there, covered with pitch, and lighted. The hand that set the flame to the pitch was that of Jules Pithon, foreman of one of the tanneries; the hand that cut down the body was that of Jean Corneille, who, from being steward at Le Platane, had kept about the place after its master had fled to England, and the furniture and effects had been stolen or destroyed

by a mob set on by bishops and royalist robbers. Then, finding that nobody returned to
the bare walls and the gardens, he moved a
few effects into the building; and having certain letters from the suffragan which might
be his authority in case of inquiries, settled
down in the mansion, not its master, but its
tenant, paying only tithe and tax, and living
less in fear of church questions than of Pithon.

Pithon had vainly wooed a young girl who
was the personal attendant of Madame Du
Boisson, but she chose to marry the steward,
who was then no more than assistant at the
silk factory at Ambroix. What the jealous
rage of Pithon, who was a drunkard, with the
voice of a boar and the face of a satyr, might
have had to do with the misfortune that had
overtaken Le Platane cannot now be told, but
it is certain that he continued his enmity
after Corneille and the wife, who had borne
him two children, were dead. That enmity was
handed down to Pithon's son; so that though the
younger Corneille, himself now a widower with
one little girl, kept house in a sad, lonely way,
with his sister to supply the place of a mother
to his child, the present foreman of the tanneries, who was by far below him in social position, spoke always of Le Platane with a sneer,
and of its tenant with a bitter hatred, which was
the more remarkable as he had sworn to his
intimates that for the sister, Sara Corneille,
he, Pithon, would have his skin converted into
shoe-leather at any moment.

Not that she had ever spoken to the man.
She, a modest, shy, rather melancholy, pretty
woman, had seen his shock-head sometimes as
she passed the Golden Bear not far from the
suburb at St. Ambroix; had noted an alarming expression in his eyes as he turned on the
bench in front of the door, and took his pipe
out of his mouth to stare after her; but even
her brother Jean knew little or nothing of
the younger Pithon. His father's enemy being
dead, and times having altered a little, there
was so much less to fear, that he was now only
disturbed by wondering whether any of the old
master's family would venture to return.

It is three years since the Pastor Duchesne,
appearing suddenly at Le Platane, brought
Corneille intelligence of the death of the elder Du
Boisson, his father's old master. The younger
was still alive he heard—alive and happy—
with a charming lady, and a son the very
image of the old race, and now not far from
twenty years old.

Three years had passed since then, and yet
he was only tenant of Le Platane, to the mas-

ters of which he had been faithful—to them,
and the promise made to his father on his
death-bed. Now, however, something should
be done. The title-deeds had never been found.
Closet and panel, garret and cellar, had been
searched and sounded in vain. They were
doubtless either burned, as many others had
been, or had been taken away with some old
piece of furniture and lost to that day.

At any rate, now was the time to seek some
better title to the house that he had held so
long; if not for himself, might he not obtain
some kind of warrant for the family. That
merciful prince, Louis XVI., would have no
dragonnading under his royal sanction. He
had already given his Protestants the right to
registration of marriage and certificate of death,
and since that time men had believed that the
persecutions were at an end.

Corneille had some friends about the court,
and after long deliberation and many provisions
for the safety of his sister and his child, he
drew up a document setting forth his wishes,
to be framed into a petition to royalty or an
appeal to some person in power, and started
for Paris.

PART III.

Hugo Du Boisson had grown into a man,
and the sword that his grandfather had hung
to his shoulder on his fourteenth birth-day was
still on its hook at the head of his bed in the
old house, but it was now a souvenir of the
dead.

The Pastor Duchesne was in France on one
of those excursions which he continued to take
thither, though he was now more than seventy
years old. A wonderful man that good pastor.
I remember him so well—tall, slim, and upright
as a youth, with a bright eye and an unblemished skin, his long hair, black streaked with
silver, hanging down upon his smooth cheek—
a man of whom one longed to learn the secret
of health, the rule of diet. I have heard him tell
it. "Eat what you can get, but eat little. Drink
what you need, which is not much." He made
tisane of herbs according to the old French
way—beverages and medicines in one. His
friend, Louis Du Boisson, would have none of
them, but took French wine or English beer,
and watered both.

He is taking wine on the day I speak of—
wine that he has fetched from a little cellar
under the house, and has opened with his own
hand.

Madame is still sitting opposite to him.
Hugo—slender, handsome, and, from his pale

complexion and straight features, a contrast to
his father's apple cheek and jolly figure—waits
for the toast. Their glasses are filled, and as
they clink them together the mother looks
lovingly on her handsome boy.

"'Tis your birth-day, dear son," she says,
"long life and happiness to you?"

The father clasps the son's hand. "What a
joy to be together still when so many of our
poor French people are even yet parting from
home and all that they love," he says. "Hugo,
do you still dream of seeking our old house,
and of claiming the barren right to call its
rotting timbers yours?"

"Forgive me if I say yes," says the young
man, "though all I hold dear are under this
roof. I feel as though I should not fulfil a
trust till I had tried to do what you could not
do, father—to restore Le Platane to our family.
Grandfather expected it of me, though he said
no word. I saw it often in his face. I knew
it six years ago when he gave me that old
sword. I guess that he has left some message
for me with the pastor, for I saw him hand
him a packet in the garden on that very
day, and ——"

"Do you know what that packet was, my
boy?" said the father. "I will tell you. It
held the title-deeds and conveyance of house
and land, which, having left, I felt would
never become mine, so I abdicate. I will tell
you what the message was also, for this is the
day when you should know it, and Duchesne,
who ought to be the first to break it to you—
Duchesne ——"

"Here he is," said a calm mellow voice, and
the pastor lifted the outer latch by pulling the
bobbin that held it, and walked into the room.
He had spoken through the window, for it was
summer time again.

There was much questioning, for he had but
just returned from France, "where things
look promising," he said, "if the king do but
hold. At any rate, now is the time for my
pupil here to decide whether or not he will
look at his inheritance and try to win it back;
though, mind, I do not counsel it. You have
converted me, Louis," he added. "Those
who hold it have the better claim after all
these years—Corneille's sister and his mother-
less child." Hugo was silent for a minute.

"By making it ours we could better make it
theirs," he said presently. "Will you give
me my grandfather's message, pastor?"

"The message is here," said Duchesne, as
he handed him a sheet of paper containing six
lines.

It said:—"If your father and mother con-

sent, and you still desire to see the inheritance
that should be yours, wait for the occasion
when you may visit it in safety. Should Corneille still live, he will admit you. Should you
have the courage, you may take possession.
By vast good fortune you may hold it. Tell
your father there may yet be a trade in silk at
St. Ambroix, when looms are again silent in
Spitalfields."

"Yes, I know," said M. Du Boisson sadly,
when Hugo read this to him. "My dear father
was the soul of honour, and kept no secret from
me. Go, my boy, if you have a mind. You
will not stay, if I know your heart."

On the morning of the third day after Jean
Corneille left St. Ambroix for Paris, it was
observed that Pithon was not at work. For
some days past there had been one or other of
the men absent from the tanneries, and the
nailers had struck their labour, letting the
forges go out, and standing about in groups or
drinking at the wretched little wine shops in
the suburbs.

A band of stunted, miserable-looking fellows
with wild looks, people who lived in stone huts
and fed on chestnuts, had come down from the
mountains towards Lozere. Evidently there
was something strange going forward.

One evening little Elizabeth Corneille, who
had been out to the fowl-house to see if her
speckled hen was sitting, came running in to
Mademoiselle Corneille with a scared face.

"Oh, my aunt!" she cried, as she hid her
head in her apron, "there are men in the
wood with faces like toads, and with red caps
on their heads. They laugh and gnash their
teeth, and they come this way;" and the frightened child crept to her aunt's side and cowered
there, trembling. At the same time there was
a knocking at the back-door leading to the
terrace, and presently angry voices were heard
in altercation.

Mademoiselle Corneille was one of those fair,
plaintive-looking women who know little of
fear all the time that they appear so much
afraid. She would probably be in some terror
if a wasp buzzed about her face, but she was
always ready for a great emergency. That was
so much the better now that she opened the
window leading on to the balcony, and was
confronted by Pithon, who had forced his way
past the cow-boy and the two kitchen servants.

Elizabeth still clung to her aunt's apron.
Pithon looked down at her with an ugly scowl.

"Send in the brat," he said; "I want to
speak to you."

He was, for him, quite fashionably dressed,

in a broad-skirted blue-coat, and pantaloons of dirty white nankeen. His neck was enveloped in a huge neckcloth, on his head was a cocked hat adorned with an enormous tricolour rosette, and a huge sabre clanked at his heel.

"What is your pleasure here?" asked mademoiselle, "and who are you?"

Pithon frowned.

"You ask who am I," he said, between his teeth, "I who have followed you with my eyes as a wolf—nay, I won't call myself a wolf either—I can be a lamb, as you will find. Your hand could tame me at any minute, and it is your hand that I want. I, Pithon, chief of my circle in the coming rights of men, I who love you, come to-day a lamb, beware how you turn me into a wolf."

"Pithon!" she exclaimed in a tone of horror. The name had been to her all that was vile; and now the son of the man who was her father's enemy stood before her, and in tones of half drunken frenzy demanded that she should leave the house and go with him to Paris. There was something so monstrous in the proposition, that she would have laughed but for the danger in which she stood. Still among the trees on the left she could see a number of men wearing red caps, and armed with axes, pikes, and muskets. What did it all mean?

"Do you not know that even if you were to compel me, the law would punish you; that once in Paris, where my brother has friends, you would be held accountable, as you will be here, if you do not leave this house; that I have but to summon aid even now and denounce you?"

"Bah!" grinned Pithon, "that's all over. There is no law but that of the people, no prisons for the patriots who hold Paris and have cracked the Bastille itself like a nut. As to your brother, he was alive when I last saw him; whether he lives to-morrow depends upon yourself."

"So you think to frighten a woman, do you, brave man?" retorted mademoiselle, indignantly.

In another moment she had sprung to a wooden stair leading to a small round tower whence hung a rope. With a vigorous pull she set the bell in the tower ringing, and its loud clang resounded in the sultry air.

"Bah! who dare aid you?" shouted Pithon hoarsely. "Come down or I will dash out the brains of this young rook!" and he seized the little Elizabeth, holding her up in his arms.

Only for a moment though. A swift, light step sounded in the garden, a tall figure darted

on to the balcony, a crashing blow from a heavy cane struck Pithon senseless over the balustrade; and mademoiselle, looking down, saw the Pastor Duchesne standing there, and by his side a younger man, who held the child in his arms. This young man was Hugo Du Boisson. He had come at a strange time to claim his inheritance. In the courtyard in front a score or so of honest men, Protestants of the district, had come with their pastor to witness, if need were, the acceptance of the rightful owner of Le Platane by Corneille. As the bell rung its noisy summons, they came running round by the stables.

Before they had reached the balcony the pastor checked them by a warning gesture, and went down into the garden. In a minute or so, Pithon, who showed some signs of reviving, was gagged, and securely bound with leathern thongs from the old coach-house, wherein he was locked till he might recover. The men in red caps had heard the summons of the bell, and so had some of the people far away in the village. There were old folks there yet who remembered that clang when it was the tocsin summoning Protestant gentlemen to buckle on their swords. A crowd of men and women were coming towards the house in front. The knot of insurgents who were waiting for Pithon came running to the garden-wall, over which they climbed, one or two muskets being discharged as those who held them scrambled through the thicket.

"Shall we arm and defend the house, pastor?" asked one of Duchesne's body-guard. "There are but a score of these fellows, and the reformation has not yet reached St. Ambroix. These are not patriots, they are robbers."

"Keep them parleying for one minute," he said hastily. "There is no safety for the woman and the child here. The cup of the iniquity of kings is full, and France has begun to wade in blood which will be soon knee-deep."

In a moment he had taken the child from Hugo, and, followed by mademoiselle, entered the house.

"There is no safety for you here," he said quickly, "for more of these ruffians may be upon us before night. Let me know what can be saved in a few words, and then put some bread and wine in a basket and follow me, just as you are—or stay—put on a servant's white cap and coarse shawl, and bring the child with you as she is."

There was no time to question. In less than ten minutes she was by his side, he going down into the cellars, and the child following in wonder.

"Are we to hide here in the cellars?" she said.

"No," replied the pastor, as he came to a great baulk of timber, or what had once been the wine-cellar, "follow me."

He knew that house better than she or her brother. With a vigorous push the timber yielded a little, and a bolt was shot. It was a heavy door, and led to a passage underground.

Stooping and groping his way, the pastor led them on for a hundred yards or so, till they saw light glimm‑... rock just before...

"This should... his shoulder to a... ed a foot or so, b... pile of loose shale...

"Now, in six... he kissed the ch... hands, "squeeze... find yourselves i... yond the old ch... the right and go... bank; you have... old Gregoire's ho... ferryman, and tr... you after dark, i... ger will bring y... from me, and te... spoke he held up his watch... through the ope... again to‑ wards the passag...

The insurgent... balcony, the Pro... itself, both side... tions, when a str... along the open ro... of many men, th... the crunching o... wild cries.

Pastor Duches... heard it as he emerge... from the house again, after having stumbled along the subterranean passage.

"Listen! it is a regiment of soldiers," said Hugo, seizing his hand.

"Not so; it is a body of insurgents," replied the old man after a pause. "The wolves are coming now in packs."

The sounds reached the ears of Pithon's men, and with a wild shout they hurried towards the road.

"Now is the time," said Duchesne, and beckoning Hugo to follow him, he went through the house, snapping up here and there an article of jewelry, a watch, or any portable thing of value. There were very few of such things.

Meantime the uproar on the road grew louder.

"My friends, resistance will be useless without arms, and in face of a savage mob with fire and sword. Farewell! let each of you take care of his own safety."

"And you, pastor?"

"I shall take care of mine and of this boy's better than if I had you. Adieu!" and he bent his head in prayer.

Every head was bent also, and the men went slowly out, scattering over the fields by the backway.

...louder, a wild mob of ...shame to say, were some ...along the road with cries and ...naked, smeared with dirt, and ...with all kinds of weapons, but almost ...were wearing red... they howled the ...terrible... There were no ...en carried some‑ ...stopped, and two ...or th... leaders, called ...for sil... our ceased, the ...lness... head calm was in ...sult... loud tipped with ...will join... ...a mess... Is this... One of the leaders. ...he comes... "This is the house," replied a fellow who ...As he seemed to be lieutenant of Pithon's band. ...ed them... This is the... zen." ...put... sign," shouted a ...a wretch... ron, girded with ...a lon... ge‑hammer over ...his... en plenty of such ...the... are effective." ...ound the bearers ...of the band... in the leathern ...apron... his waist and ...flung a... sted limb of the ...great pl... a sharp jerk, a ...nd a man's dead body swung there—the body of Jean Corneille.

"We couldn't save him even if we'd been so minded," shouted the leader. "He went where the intendant Foulon and Berthier, his son-in-law, grinned their last, as pike-heads. All's one!"

"Pithon! Pithon! where's Pithon? Come, comrade, let us have no private affairs to interfere with business. Come!"

The Pastor Duchesne and Hugo had seen the horrid spectacle and heard the words that accompanied it. The insurgents were preparing to fire and sack the house. The old man drew his companion away, and both descended to the cellar. When they emerged into the open air and looked back, a terrible storm had broken; a peal of thunder shook Le

Platane, and the great plane-tree creaked as a vivid flash lighted its ghastly burden. They hurried forward, anxious for the safety of mademoiselle and little Elizabeth, who were out in the storm.

"Well, Hugo, my dear lad, never mind; I have set ten more looms going since you left us. Thank Heaven you are safely back, my boy. Alas, poor France! Duchesne is no more fit to be trusted, and yet we should be glad you went, for here are two dear souls saved alive—though, fancy little Elise coming over in a hamper on board that fishing-smack. They thought it was full of a great goose, didn't they, my child?" and the elder Du Boisson lifted the little emigrant on his knee.

For a time mademoiselle and her little niece lived with this dear family; but soon Elise must learn something, and so became a pupil at that school of La Providence which the refugees founded in the early troubles. As to mademoiselle, she was married in less than two years, for she was a Protestant, though her brother had remained a Catholic. Not till they had grown well used to their asylum did the pastor tell aunt and niece of the dreadful death of Jean Corneille, and by that time Louis Du Boisson and his wife had found a daughter in Elizabeth—Elizabeth a brother in Hugo—well, no, not quite a brother either, for one day when she came home from her studies, an armful of books in a blue bag over her shoulder, her great lustrous eyes full of intelligence, her hair falling in ringlets that blew about her like a fine silken veil, Hugo found out the secret of his heart and of hers. On the old bench of the old garden they plighted their troth, and Hugo's father only laughed when he heard of it, saying, he knew long ago what it must come to.

Madame was a little cold. She came of the noblesse, you see, and then Jean Corneille was but a steward; but who could look at Elise without loving her? Not such a gentle creature as Madeleine Du Boisson. Thus the story ends, dear, as all stories should end; but yet there is a word still to say.

The Pastor Duchesne, ninety years old, is sitting on that very same bench in the old gay garden at Bethnal Green. Louis Du Boisson sits beside him, stouter, rosier, older, and with his crisp dark hair turning white. Madame, more than ever like that fine Sèvres china, stands snipping the withered leaves from a bush of blush-roses.

In the suburbs of the town of St. Ambroix a lady and gentleman alight from a carriage

at the sign of the "Golden Bear," and stand at the door to ask a question of the landlord.

"I see no signs of the place," says the gentleman; "it cannot have sunk into the earth. Surely it must have been burned on that terrible night, though the pastor says no. You were too little to remember where it stood, dear. We will inquire."

"What! Le Platane?" says the landlord, with open eyes. "Why, over yonder, where the barrack is being built. It was a mere ruin for ever so long, and then came the restoration, and then the hundred days—that was when it was burned—what the democrats left, the reactionists finished. Vive le Roi!"

"And of one Pithon, does anybody know what became of him?"

"What Pithon? He—ah, yes—as he had helped others to a pinch, so he himself sneezed in the sack."

The bloody footsteps of the revolution had overtaken the enemy of Jean Corneille.

"Son and daughter," said Louis Du Boisson, as he sat in his little parlour a week afterwards, "I have bought for you the house I spoke of in Essex. Call it Le Platane if you like, but I wouldn't. The name's unlucky, and we are all English now."

GERTY'S GLOVE.

BY FREDERICK LOCKER.

" Elle avait au bout de ses manches,
Une paire de mains si blanches!"

Slips of a kid-skin deftly sewn,
A scent as through her garden blown,
The tender hue that clothes her dove,
All these, and this is Gerty's glove.

A glove but lately dofft, for look—
It keeps the happy shape it took
Warm from her touch! What gave the glow?
And where's the mould that shaped it so?

It clasp'd the hand, so pure, so sleek,
Where Gerty rests a pensive cheek,
The hand that when the light wind stirs,
Reproves those laughing locks of hers.

You fingers four, you little thumb!
Were I but you, in days to come
I'd clasp, and kiss, and keep her—go!
And tell her that I told you so.
—*London Lyrics.*

BEHIND THE SCENES AT SEVILLE.

[Henry Blackburn, born at Portsmouth, 15th February, 1830. Traveller, journalist, and sometime editor of *London Society*. In 1871 he received an appointment in the civil service commission. His works are *Life in Algeria; Travelling in Spain; The Pyrenees*, illustrated by Gustave Doré; *Artists and Arabs; Normandy Picturesque; Art in the Mountains*, the Story of the Passion Play in Bavaria; *The Harz Mountains*, &c. He seizes the most picturesque characteristics of life and scenery, and reproduces them admirably with pen and pencil.]

The curtain has gone down at last—Don Alphonso has touched the last note on his guitar, and the dark-eyed prima donna, with the gigantic false roses in her hair, has heaved her last sigh from the casement above. Jealous lovers in false wigs and black conspirators all have sheathed their pasteboard daggers for the night, and the stage is clear for the ballet, or what our good friend the impresario, who has French proclivities, calls a *pantomime d'amour*.

It is Christmas-time at Seville, and the people who never do any work to speak of, now take holiday, and disport themselves in most rampant fashion. Every day and every night there has been some grand *foncion*, something to see, to do, or to suffer. We are fairly "weary of the world," of the Seville world of saints' days, high-masses, miraculous cures, cock-fights, bull-fights, cachuchas, and fandangos. But to-night is a special festival, and we have promised our host, Don Pedro, who manages matters theatrical in Seville, that we will come to see his daughter dance the bolero. There was nothing new in seeing the "bolero," the *baile nacional* of Spain. Had we not seen it the day after we arrived in the city, as performed in the second-floor-back of a dark street, by two or three painted and powdered señoritas, whose especial business it was to exhibit to strangers the manners and customs of their country? had we not paid five francs each to sit for an hour in a crowded room, choked with dust, and deafened with the clash of castanets; and had we not had black mail levied upon us by those painted eyes, and our purses emptied, as one of the customs of Spain? Had we not, after a few weeks' sojourn, seen through the folly of these things, and gone boldly with a great English painter (one no longer amongst us, who lived and worked at Seville, and brought home to England more of the living power of Murillo and Velasquez than any artist of his time) over the bridge to that most racketty and disreputable suburb, Triana, on the banks of the Guadalquivir, to see and study with a painter's eye the grace and beauty of

the bolero as danced by wild gipsy kings and queens, who live here in picturesque poverty, whose life in youth is to dance and to sing? Had we not seen the population of a whole suburb of Granada come out to join in passionate joy and sorrow, as expressed in motion by one or two skilled performers dancing to the monotonous twang of a cracked guitar? We had seen all this, and we had begun to understand how truly dancing in Spain was a part of the nation's existence; but we had not yet seen the audience of a theatre under its influence. The great charm of the Spanish theatre, according to Ford, is the national dance—matchless, unequalled, and inimitable—only to be performed by Andalucians. It is the essence, the *sauce piquant* of the night's entertainment. However languid the house, however laughable the tragedy, or serious the comedy, the sound of the castanet awakens the most listless; the sharp, spirit-stirring click is heard behind the scenes, the effect is instantaneous—it silences the tongues of countless women—*on n'écoute que le ballet!*

The little theatre in Seville—where opera and ballet seem as much *de rigueur* as at the Haymarket Opera House in London when Grisi and Cerito were presiding stars—is full to the ceiling to-night, with a noisy, clamorous crowd, who cannot help smoking surreptitiously during the performance, and whose consumption of glasses of water is marvellous to behold. Looking through the curtain which divides us so slightly from the rows of señoritas in dark veils (some so close that we could whisper to them from our hiding-place), this seething mass of humanity looks dangerous in its excitability and, considering the small space into which they are crowded and the sparks and little waves of smoke that curl up here and there, it is a positive relief to see so much cold water distributed amongst them.

But there the orchestra is tuning up, and the signal is given to clear the stage. As we stand at the wings, Don Pedro comes proudly forward with his daughter, a little bright-eyed girl of fifteen, dressed, not in ordinary ballet costume, with skirts ungracefully short and scanty, but in the natural, national dress of Andalucia, familiar to everyone in pictures, but especially charming here, both in colour and character, as a contrast to the tinsel and artificiality of the modern stage. She wore a high comb and black lace veil, with a bright red camellia in her hair, and held in her hand a fan, the whole armour of battle of a southern coquette. Her face glowed with pleasure and delight, her bare arms were not whitened, her face was not powdered, her little feet and ankles were shapely, and not overstrained or made angular under the ballet-master's hand. Such was Perea Nena in the bloom of youth. Who that has seen her in Paris or London during the last few years will remember her triumphant *début* in a *pantomime d'amour?*

Soon the curtain rises to a scene of an orange-garden, lighted up with coloured lamps. There is a terrace, a lake, and the full moon is shining down. As the curtain disappears above our heads the close, hot air comes into our faces, and the impatient sounds of a hundred tongues. Nena trembles a little as she stands waiting by the side, tapping her feet to the click of the irresistible castanets; but at the signal she is ready, and tripping past us, all sparkles and smiles, faces the audience, who greet her with a shout of welcome. Spirit-stirring dance-music, now slow, now fast, but not as strictly in time as we are accustomed to hear it, comes from below the footlights; a little posturing, hesitating, coquetting, and most graceful and indescribably eloquent swaying of the arms and limbs, and then the Nena glides through the orange-groves, flitting and flying, the little feet twinkling to the music, following its passages apparently without method, but in perfect time, and with such *abandon*, grace, and enjoyment as we never see on any other stage. Tripping from flower to flower, now floating apparently half in air, now settling on a green bank, the Spanish butterfly imparts the fulness of her grace and joy to the excited audience, who had seen all this a hundred times before! Strange contrast to a grand *ballet d'action*, with its army of trained warriors in muslin, crowding together behind the scenes, and forming in wonderfully-disciplined groups before a listless audience at Her Majesty's Opera in London. Here all is quiet on the stage, and the excitement and enthusiasm come spontaneously from the audience. Thus they watch with eager eyes and half-held breath the Spirit of the Dance, as she flits before them with her black tresses flying in the wind: when there enters upon the scene Don Juan—young, handsome, gallant, glittering with silver buttons and lace—the model caballero. He steals softly to the Nena—a kiss, surprise, flight down the orange-groves, rapid movement in the orchestra, silence and suspense with the audience, and soon the pair appear again under the trees. Then pantomimic love-making, stirring music, passionate declaration, adoration, expressed in a dance in which there were few steps but more meaning and intensity

than could be described in any words, or conceived by a northern people. The eye especially is delighted with the picturesque beauty of the two young figures, the harmonious colouring of their dresses, the rich red embroidery on velvet, the sparkle of gold lace and silver filigree, without a suspicion of tinsel or stage sham. There they stand together, entrancing and bewitching all beholders.

"Beautiful expression of joy, youth, hope, and fervour!" says one eye-witness; "beautiful similitude and pantomime of love!" Suddenly they disappear from the stage, and as suddenly dart forward from opposite sides, like separated lovers, who after long search, have found each other again; no thought, apparently, of spectators, no care for the world before the curtain; *their* world is with each other. Their happiness is contagious; it is a delight to watch them together, and the audience is now so sympathetic, so entranced, that what immediately follows comes as a shock—a general calamity. What is the matter—a misunderstanding? The music stops suddenly, the pair hesitate in the middle of what we should call a most graceful *pas de deux*, in which the arms and hands had, strange to say, taken more part than the feet. They expostulate, they are silent, all but their eloquent eyes. A pause of agonizing suspense, and their world of love stands still! Then pantomime of explanation, expostulation, quick music, the angry rattle of castanets; trip, trip, and away they glide from one another and the world, now one of general confusion and despair, both before and behind the curtain. Are we dreaming? Can it be possible, looking out from our hiding-place on the stage, that we can see tears in those faded señoritas' eyes, and at least a hundred people with a shade of sorrow over their hardened faces, because the sun has set for a moment on two young lives? This is the mystery of the dance of Spain, which no words can describe, and no ballet-master in Paris or Vienna can understand. But stay—here comes the Nena upon the stage alone; there is an expression of sorrow and repentance in her face, and the end can be imagined. Soft music and a delicately-touched guitar, a clear voice through the orange-groves, a lover on his knees by her side, reconciliation, rapture, music in quick time—music such as only comes from stringed instruments under nervous hands—and then a dance of joy that brings happiness to all hearts.

And how does it all end? With loud and universal calls before the curtain, and enormous false bouquets hurled by friends from dark boxes? Not at all; this would spoil everything. The happiness of the lovers now complete, they go hand in hand together up the stage, where the moon is shining over a lake; they take a boat, and glide away from our sight under the silver moon. It is poetical to the end, with just one touch of contrast to heighten the effect. As the curtain rolls slowly down, shutting off the noise and the heated air, there peeps out from the side scenes the grim, mocking visage of Mephistopheles, attired in diabolical red for some after-burlesque. Whether the audience sees him, or is intended to see him, we cannot tell, but so ends the *pantomime d'amour*. In half an hour the audience has dispersed, and we are threading the silent streets of Seville; a real moon is lighting up the Giralda, and the fountains are sparkling under the old Moorish walls.

Does the Perea Nena, we wonder, dancing now to a fashionable, crowded opera-house, ever recall the triumph of the little girl of fifteen summers, and that passionate audience which she conquered with her eyes? Does the "first lady" of the ballet, the envied centre of a hundred ballet-girls—gliding down the centre of the stage on pasteboard toes, or swung aloft between rows of gas jets and painted clouds of heaven—ever achieve a triumph like this?

But the dance—the Bolero, the reader may ask; what is it? For we have not really described it at all. It is, in one word, the poetry of motion, and the language of the eyes. It is one of the *cosas d'Espana;* it is oriental in its origin, and it has entranced men and women for four thousand years. But the fire is dying out before over-civilization, and one of its embers flickers for a moment—where, my good friend Don Pedro? In the pages of the *Casquet of Literature.—Christmas No. of London Society*, 1871.

THE ROBIN.

BY J. G. WHITTIER.

My old Welch neighbour over the way
Crept slowly out in the sun of spring,
Pushed from her ears the locks of gray,
And listened to hear the robin sing.

Her grandson, playing at marbles, stopped,
And, cruel in sport as boys will be,
Tossed a stone at the bird, who hopped
From bough to bough in the apple-tree.

"Nay!" said the grandmother; "have you not heard,
My poor, bad boy! of the fiery pit,
And how, drop by drop, this merciful bird
Carries the water that quenches it?

"He brings cool dew in his little bill,
And lets it fall on the souls of sin:
You can see the mark on his red breast still
Of fires that scorch as he drops it in.

"My poor Bron rhuddyn! my breast-burned bird,
Singing so sweetly from limb to limb,
Very dear to the heart of Our Lord
Is he who pities the lost like Him!"

"Amen!" I said to the beautiful myth;
"Sing, bird of God, in my heart as well:
Each good thought is a drop wherewith
To cool and lessen the fires of hell.

"Prayers of love like rain-drops fall,
Tears of pity are cooling dew,
And dear to the heart of Our Lord are all
Who suffer like Him in the good they do!"

WHEESHT!

[Robert Chambers, LL.D., born in Peebles, 10th July, 1802; died at St. Andrews, 17th March, 1871. He was intended for the ministry, but family misfortunes compelled him at an early age to begin business in Edinburgh as a bookseller. His elder brother, William, was engaged in the same trade, and the two afterwards united to establish the firm of W. & R. Chambers. In their capacities as authors, editors and publishers, the brothers Chambers have earned a distinguished place in the history of literature in the present century. *The Memoir of Robert Chambers, with A utobiographic Reminiscences of William Chambers*, is a valuable and interesting work, which shows what talent and industry may achieve. Dr. Robert Chambers produced over seventy volumes, exclusive of detached papers; the more important of his works are: *Traditions of Edinburgh; The Popular Rhymes of Scotland; Histories of the Scottish Rebellions; Dictionary of Eminent Scotsmen; A Cyclopædia of English Literature; Life and Works of Burns; Domestic Annals of Scotland; Life of Smollett; Ancient Sea-margins; The Book of Days*, &c. &c. Of the brothers the *Dublin University Magazine* said they were "both of them men of remarkable native power, both of them trained to habits of business and punctuality, both of them upheld in all their dealings by strict prudence and conscientiousness, and both of them practised, according to their different aims and tendencies, in literary labour."]

Genius of Silence! whose step, as thou walkest over the earth, falls as lightly as the descending snow-flake, invest me with thy mantle of down, and provide me with a quill of softest plume, while I attempt to recount all the properties and associations of thy shibboleth—WHEESHT!

Everybody must have more or less acquaintance with a provokingly quiet set of people, who constantly look and move as if they were saying wheesht!—a velvet-footed race, with smooth, goodly faces, who eat, drink, walk, and sleep—perhaps snore too—below their breath, and would not for the world be guilty of what they call making a fuss. This set of people are always very anxious that things should be managed in a prudent, quiet, unostentatious way. If they were going to have a ride in a coach—supposing they could bear the rattle of such a thing—they would have it drawn up six doors off.

> "———lest folk
> Should say that they were proud."

They keep the doors within their house always well oiled, and the pulleys of their windows in the best state of repair, so that none of them may ever be guilty of a single creak or rattle. Their clothes are always very trim about their persons,—or, to use a Scottish phrase, clappit; no superfluous skirts—no majestic train—not so much as a useless lappel, if it can be avoided; because such things tend to make a fuss—might even happen to pull down something that would make a crash, or a clash, or a dash, or a splash, or something else in ash. When they rise to leave a room, it is perceptible that they are sedulous to glide away as smoothly, and noiselessly, and unobservedly, as possible: they are evidently much put about that they cannot devolve through the key-hole, so as to save the fluster of opening the door. "We must learn to walk circumspectly. We must make no stir. Let us take things coolly. Let us do everything with decency and propriety. Allow no room for evil tongues. As well not give people occasion to speak. We'll do very well in our own quiet way. WHEESHT!" As these people move along, they keep a clear look-out on all hands, afraid to come in contact with anything; and they evidently would feel much convenienced, if Providence would see fit to furnish them with antennæ like the spider, or whiskers like the cat, so that they might be admonished beforehand of the chance of being disturbed by any little object. If they saw a nut-shell in the way, they would go about to avoid treading upon it. "Bad boys, to throw their nut-shells down in the way!" If you were to come up behind one of them in the street, and, conceiving him to be one of your

own hearty hail-fellow-well-met kind of acquaintances, give him a sound slap on the shoulder, and ask him how he did, you would see him start like a Laputan philosopher under the influence of the flapper, and perhaps next moment faint, sink, and die away upon the street, unknelled, uncoffined, and unknown, unless an address card happened to be found in his pocket. But see one trysted with an obstreperous bottle of small ale, with which he is going to regale you as you drop in, some warm, thirsty forenoon, at his country box. He brings in the bottle in his arms, nursing it all the way as carefully as he would a new-born babe. He sets about the business of driving in the screw with all the solemnity, and silence, and decorum with which a Druid could have set about the sacrifice of a human being. The stopper is recusant—it requires more exertion than he can at any time think of making, for this violent gesture is equivalent to noise. It has to be transferred to your own less scrupulous care. You make the cork fly in a moment, and see what a water-spout of foam! The quietist is paralyzed with the loudness of the report, and the fizzing, cheeping, squeaking, spirting, and squirting which the liquor makes, as you vainly endeavour to repress it with your hand. The echoes of the house, that have slumbered for months, are roused by your calls for relays of tumblers, wherein to receive the seemingly endless effusion of froth. And after puzzling and noozling your way to the bottom of half-a-dozen of these tumblers, in the vain quest of a mouthful, you leave the unhappy quietist in agony for the evening—his ears rent with your jocund remarks on the small ale, and all the rest of his senses shattered, and torn, and disgusted with the scene of ravage which you have been the innocent means of introducing into his parlour. It must be remarked that these velvet people scarcely detest anything so much as a hearty laugh. They mark a cachinnator as a man to be avoided. Of men whom they have every other reason to regard with esteem, they will remark—"Yes, he is very good—a very estimable man: but don't you think he has a rather boisterous way of laughing?" Your quietist never laughs, even at the most amusing incident or witticism: he only treats you to a soft noiseless smile. In their conversation, they appear as if they were at some pains to avoid using the harsh consonants, such as r and s: they indulge chiefly in liquids and vowels, and do a great deal with such monosyllabic interjections, as ah, eh, ay, oh, &c. They often speak upon a respiration, instead of an aspiration, as if their words made

less noise when bound inwards than outwards:
they seem as if they wished to swallow their
very language, upon the same principal as a
manufactory consuming its own smoke, so
that it might never more give any trouble, or
create any fuss in the world. Sometimes, in
company, they escape the horror of making a
noise with their tongues altogether. They sit
in a composed manner, perhaps looking into
the fire, and only signify their appreciation of
what you are saying to them by occasional
inarticulate sounds within their closed lips, or
by a motion of the head to one side, or by a
mere transient glance of the eye. This is what
they call having a little quiet conversation;
and when the parties rise, it is always observable that they display an appearance of vast
edification.

These men of aspirate existence are often
found in possession of small public dignities,
such as that of provost, bailie, or town-clerk
in some country burgh. Nothing can be done
by such people—no step can be taken, till
they have thoroughly ascertained that it is to
have a perfectly good appearance, and that
there is no back-come or negative influence
which may derange it. "Wheesht! just let
us keep a *calm sough*. We must proceed de-
cently. We must walk with circumspection.
That business about the Port-brae—I'll just
take occasion some night to ca' in by John
Richie's, and hear what *he* says about it, and
if he doesna seem to hae ony objection, we'll
see what may be done. In the meantime, ye
may throw yersell in Mr. ——'s way, and hear
his breath. We canna be ower cautious.
Dinna gang anes eerand. That would look
ower *set-like* on the business. We'll see about
it a', by and by; ay, we'll see about it; just
be canny for awhile; wheesht!"

Or perhaps it is—"That business about the
clerkship to the buird: my son John, he's a
weel-doing lad. Mr. Jamieson, his late master,
just looked upon him as the apple o' his ee.
He used to say he could take a voyage to
Cheena, and hae an easy mind a' the time, for
he was sure that John wad hae everything
richt when he cam back. Served a regular
apprenticeship to a double-you-ess. Though
it's mysel that says't, there canna be a candi-
date better qualifeed. For my ain part, I'm
an auld servant o' the toon. In that business,
ye ken, o' the brig, I was never aff my feet—
lost a gude deal o' my ain business by negleck
—and ye ken as weel as ony body hoo muckle
fyke I've ha'en wi' the Puir's House, I've just
been considering whether John has ony chance.
We're anxious to soond our way afore we gang

ony farther; for we wadna like to pit in for't
and no get it after a'. Ye'll hae a vote?
[Here the person addressed intimates many
friendly wishes, but is not inclined to give a
distinct pledge.] Ou na—we canna expek
that, ye ken. It wad neither be richt o' me
to ask it, nor for you to gie't. The toon's interest, abune a' things! But I just ca'd to let
ye ken hoo things stude. I'm by na means
anxious for the place to John. But some o'
oor freends wad hae us to come forrit, and we
did na like that they should ha' been at sae
muckle trouble on oor account, and we fa'
back after a'. In the meantime, ye'll say
naething till ye hear frae me. We're gaun
to be very cautious. We'll *feel* our way—
Wheesht!"

Even to the humblest individuals connected
with corporations this system of quietness extends. There is always a kind of valet or *man*
of the corporation's body, who hands about the
circulars which call the members together,
attends to the decoring, as Caleb Balderstone
would call it, of the hall of assembly, and lives
in a den hard by, where he "keeps the keys."
This man is always found to be a most decided
votary of the idea of *wheesht*. He goes noiseless about the place, like a puff of Old Town
smoke, and seems absolutely oppressed with a
sense of the decency with which it is necessary
to conduct "corporation business." Yea, he
cannot pronounce the very word "corporation,"
without that sinking of the voice and interjec-
tional reverence of manner with which certain
words of a really sacred nature are properly
uttered in ordinary discourse. He looks upon
"the corporation" as the greatest of all public
bodies; if the government itself be greater, it
is only greater in another way. And the
deacon, in his opinion—oh, no man can equal
the deacon. "The corporation is very rich.
We support twenty-three dekeyed members
and eleven widows, and *we* ha'e a richt to put
five callants into the Orphan Hospital. We've
our chairter frae James the Sixth; and our record—we've a grand record. It has the Catholic oath at the beginning,—"By my paint of
Paradise"—that ilk member swears to, when
he enters. If you wad be very quiet about it,
ye micht gang up stairs and see't. Mak' nae
noise, now. Wheesht!"

There is a kindred set of men, who act in
something like the same capacity to places of
worship—old decent men—squires of the
church's body, who come in, as avant-couriers
of the minister, to lay down his Bible on the
desk, and who evidently are at a great deal of
trouble in keeping up a tremendously grave

and important aspect, appropriate to their duties. These old men appear in large entailed black coats, which have been in the family for ages, and the skirts of which sweep solemnly by, almost like the mainsheet of a seventy-four. Such persons might be the very door-keepers of the Court of Silence—the high-priests of the idea of *wheesht.* They are immensely impressed with a sense of the greatness of the minister, though, perhaps, he is in reality no conflagrator of the Thames; and their whole form and impression breathes of the solemnity of "the vestry." Anything that an elder says is to them law; and if the minister were to address himself to them, they would feel the honour so deeply, that they would not know what they were about all the rest of the day. When they appear within the body of the church they do not, of course, say anything; but it is evident that they mean a great deal by their anti-disturbance aspect. "Children, be all quiet; public worship is just about to commence; it behoves all people to show an outward decency in the house of God. I could give ye a word mysel'; but I leave it to the minister. All I shall say is—*Wheesht!*"[1]

Then there is a set of equally peaceable old men, who, in the country, act as elders, and stand every Sunday, with a peculiarly morti-fied and speechless aspect, beside the plate which receives the oblations of the congrega-tion—"grave and reverend seignors," fixed as statues, with their hands thrust into the oppo-site cuffs of their spencers, and downcast faces that would not smile for untold gold. The boys, and even older people, are almost afraid to pass them, they are so awfully solemn. In one respect they are a kind of fuglemen. The countenances of the worshippers in passing catch from them the contagion of decorum, and instead of the easy, this-world expression

which they sported a few minutes ago, while talking in the churchyard upon such terrene subjects as crops and markets, display in their pews a gravity appropriate to the place, but which could scarcely have been otherwise assumed. In fact, these old grave men, if planted in the entrance to the cave of Tropho-nius, would have been sufficient to account for the miracle. During the first prayer they are seen to enter the body of the church, and plant themselves in a seat under the pulpit, with a quietness and solemnity that would not be amiss among the special jurors of Rhada-manthus. If you visit one in his own residence, some evening during the week, you find him sitting in a small lonely room, with a large Bible open before him, into which, as you enter, he quietly thrusts his spectacles for a mark. You almost tremble to disturb so fine a picture of religious contemplation. When he speaks, you find that he has a deep, guttural voice, broken and softened into something in-expressibly smooth and gentle; a constant *susurrus* of wheesht! If you converse regard-ing books, you find that, of all secular compo-sitions, he likes Hervey's Meditations, and what he calls *Strum's* Reflections. The sub-dued tone of these works harmonizes finely with the tranquil pulsations of his soul and heart. On a Sunday afternoon, when the slight bustle which the dismissal of the con-gregation has made upon the street is all hush-ed down into the soft and melancholy calm which ever rests that day upon the rural towns of Scotland, if you drop quietly in upon him, you find him sitting in his back room, in the midst of his family, with a stream of rich light from the setting sun falling upon his quiet gray head, and a large Bible displaying its brighter treasures before him. He is read-ing a chapter to his children in the low, mur-muring voice peculiar to him. The whole scene is one of piquant noiselessness and repose; the children, admirably trained, are all as quiet as doves, and, besides his own voice, there is no sound to be heard, excepting, perhaps, the soft occasional wail of the wind, or the equivocal lull of the distant waterfall. Should one of the young people betray but the slightest mark of restlessness, a glance from the old man, *over the top of the spectacles,* stills it in an instant. There is something in the scene that seems to say,—"Children, let us all be meek and gentle of spirit—let us all be reverent, and lowly, and quiet; let us sit amidst the stillness of the evening hour, and offer up the silent vespers of a grateful and devout spirit—be every worldly and profane

---

[1] Personages of this kind abound in the streets of Edinburgh during the hour between ten and eleven on Sunday forenoons, when they are all going to their respective places of worship. One of them was observ-ed gliding gently along Prince's Street one forenoon, in company with some other "decent people," to whom he was evidently making a few quiet, solemn remarks upon the subject of things in general, with, perhaps, a particular reference to the gaudy show of fine new houses and elegantly dressed people, whom he saw around him. He was just overheard to make one ob-servation; but it was most characteristic of the quiet tribe to which he belonged: "Sirs," said he with a philosophical glance from side to side, "*there's nae reality in naething now!*"

This world is but a fleeting show
For man's illusion given.

thought banished—be ye holy and calm—wheesht!"

There is a set of the generation of quietists, who are ever and anon coming up to you in the street with a curious *entre-nous* expression of phiz, as if, like a grief-laden ghost, they were possessed of some secret which they could not bring themselves to divulge. Now, for my part, I have no curiosity after secrets. I would rather want the best of them than be at the trouble of recollecting to keep them to myself. Yet these people do often seize me by the button, and attempt to work off "a great secret" upon me, in their quiet way, dribble by dribble, notwithstanding all I can do to the contrary. "Have you heard of anything within the last few days? Anything about ——? I heard it whispered last night, but I could not believe it. It was talked of to-day, however, I know, in the Parliament House. And Guthry, I'm told, knows all about it. For God's sake, however, speak loundly about it; and don't say I told you. It's a very delicate business. Wheesht!" And so, after a thousand insinuations, by whisper, wink, shrug, and smile, they quit button, and leave you weltering in astonishment, unable to make out, for the life of you, what all this means; nay, perhaps, so completely do you feel bamboozled by the tide of new and imperfect ideas which has been let loose upon you, that you scarcely know that you are walking on the earth for five minutes after. You feel ravished away, as it were, into middle air, *caput ferit alta sidera*—not with elation, but with botheration of spirit. Your imagination toils and pants after their meaning through the great abyss of space; and you hardly feel the pressure of the real world around you for the afternoon.

Then there is a set of people, of the quieter sex—good neighbours, mothers of families—who, when there is any sickness in your own house, and the mistress of the house herself is not very well able to take care of it, rush in unbidden, apparently upon the same instinct which brings birds of prey to fields of battle, and immediately begin to assume a strange kind of unauthorized directorate, as if they had been all their lives as familiar with the scene as yourself. These kind persons leave their own houses to Providence, all selfish considerations being abandoned for the time at the call of what they term distress. On coming home to dinner, totally unwitting of the trouble which has befallen the family in your absence, you are surprised *in limine*, at the very door-step, by meeting a quiet-looking oldish woman in her stocking-soles, who comes

forward, holding up her hand, after the manner of a judge administering an oath, and only pronounces the single emphatic word—wheesht! You are beckoned in a most mysterious manner into a side-room, and told to be very quiet, for —— has just fallen into a sleep, which the doctor expects to do a great deal of good, and there must, upon no account, be any disturbance. Though the bedroom of the patient is so far away that no voice, however loud, could reach it, this high-priestess of silence still speaks thirty degrees below the zero of articulation, the sense of the necessity of quiet being so weighty upon her mind, that she totally forgets the state of the case in this particular instance, and even, perhaps, if she were removed to the distance of several miles, would still fear to give her words full utterance. You soon find this discreet old lady in full possession of your house, invested with the management of the keys, arbitress of all matters connected with the children's frocks, and sole autocrat of the bread and butter. If you live in any of the streets of the New Town, where hardly a cart or carriage is to be heard from morning till night, you immediately find the street in front of the door strewed with tanners' bark, to deafen the sound of those rarely-occurring annoyances. Of course, if you live in the Old Town, where carts and carriages are incessant, the patient is understood to have nerves accordingly, and no bark is required. Suppose the case to be one where the mistress of the house herself is indisposed: for some time you find your consequence as master entirely absorbed; you are a mere subordinate where once you were principal; the attentions of all the servants, and also of the discreet lady, are all engrossed by the patient; and you come into, and go out of the house, without ever being heeded or regarded; unless, perhaps, when you happen to make a very *leetle* noise, and then a troop of harpies, with the discreet lady at their head, fly upon you, with open mouth and uplifted hands, and all the gesticulation and expression which might properly accompany an outburst of indignant remonstrance, but which, in this case, is a kind of dumb thunder, ending all in the awful monosyllable — wheesht! Then, there is an oiling of doors, and a throng of women going through the house in their stockings, or at most in what are called *carpet shoes*, and a whispering and breathing of wheesht! for many days, till at last, through very contagion, you yourself become as timid as a titmouse, and almost forget the sound of your own voice. Then the mysterious old woman, how beautifully she manages everything! Her out-goings and her in-comings are all most becoming and composed. The flame which you see her occasionally sending over a plateful of brandy for the sick-room, is not more gently lambent than her own pace. You see her a few yards off addressing herself to some underling, and, although you hear not a whisper nor a breath, except, perhaps, the ever interjected *wheesht*, to your surprise her language appears to be comprehended by the person spoken to, and lo and behold it is immediately acted upon. The very children, albeit unaccustomed to the reign of silence, are overborne and dashed down by the awful influence of the everlasting *wheesht*, and are observed crawling, like so many kittens, through a suite of apartments, where they crst performed gallopades of the most outrageous description. If you happen to take a peep into the sick-chamber, you see the mysterious woman standing over the bed, with the air and gestures of an inspired Pythoness, pointing to distant bottles and boxes, and doing everything, speech excepted, to make herself understood. If the wrong bottle or box be touched by the servant, she writhes her whole body and countenance in an agony of dumb negation; but, when the right one is pounced upon at last, she suddenly relaxes into approval, and her agonies cease. Suppose that the patient at last "departs," the stillness of the household is not remitted, in consideration of there being no longer any one to be disturbed. It rather becomes more deep and solemn than ever. There is still the same carpet-shoeing as before —the same ejaculating of *wheesht*. The house begins to look like an absolute sepulchre, and the mysterious woman, like some marble and unspeaking cherub, planted to guard it. She takes a leading hand in the melancholy duties paid to the dead, and is always able to recommend a person who makes grave-clothes—Mrs. So-and-so—living in some close in the Old Town, first stair, fifth door up. She can even do something in the way of mournings for the survivors; the children will require this, and the servants that; so much crape for this one's hat; so much black ribbon for that one's bonnet. Even after all these matters have been arranged by her friendly intervention, she does not yet depart. She must see after the wine and cake at the funeral, and take care that everything is managed with decency, and, above all things, *quietly*. At last, when all is over, she soofs out at the door, with a strange rustle of silk, as if she were saying, and saying for the last farewell time, the oft-repeated shibboleth of her kind—WHEESHT!

AN INTERLUDE.

[Algernon Charles Swinburne, born in London, 5th April, 1837. Poet. He is a son of Admiral Charles Henry Swinburne. He studied at Baliol College, Oxford; afterwards visited Florence, and enjoyed the society of Walter Savage Landor. His works are: *The Queen Mother* and *Rosamond*, two plays; *Atalanta in Calydon*, a tragedy; *Chastelard*, a tragedy; *Poems and Ballads* (from which we quote); *Siena; A Song of Italy; Songs before Sunrise; Bothwell; Poems and Ballads*, 2d Series (1878); &c. He has written various prose essays, the most notable of which is that on William Blake, the artist and poet. "He is gifted with no small portion of the all-important divine fire, without which no man can hope to achieve poetic success; he possesses considerable powers of description, a keen eye for natural scenery, and a copious vocabulary of rich yet simple English."—*Times.*]

In the greenest growth of the Maytime,
  I rode where the woods were wet,
Between the dawn and the daytime;
  The spring was glad that we met.

There was something the season wanted,
  Though the ways and the woods smelt sweet;
The breath at your lips that panted,
  The pulse of the grass at your feet.

You came, and the sun came after,
  And the green grew golden above;
And the flag-flowers lightened with laughter,
  And the meadow-sweet shook with love.

Your feet in the full-grown grasses
  Moved soft as a weak wind blows;
You passed me as April passes,
  With face made out of a rose.

By the stream where the stems were slender,
  Your bright foot paused at the sedge;
It might be to watch the tender
  Light leaves in the springtime hedge.

On boughs that the sweet month blanches
  With flowery frost of May:
It might be a bird in the branches,
  It might be a thorn in the way.

I waited to watch you linger
  With foot drawn back from the dew,
Till a sunbeam straight like a finger
  Struck sharp through the leaves at you.

And a bird overhead sang *Follow*,
  And a bird to the right sang *Here;*
And the arch of the leaves was hollow,
  And the meaning of May was clear.

I saw where the sun's hand pointed,
  I knew what the bird's note said;
By the dawn and the dewfall anointed,
  You were queen by the gold on your head.

As the glimpse of a burnt-out ember
  Recalls a regret of the sun,
I remember, forget, and remember
  What Love saw done and undone.

I remember the way we parted,
  The day and the way we met;
You hoped we were both broken-hearted,
  And knew we should both forget.

And May with her world in flower
  Seemed still to murmur and smile
As you murmured and smiled for an hour;
  I saw you turn at the stile.

A hand like a white wood-blossom
  You lifted, and waved, and passed,
With head hung down to the bosom,
  And pale, as it seemed, at last.

And the best and the worst of this is
  That neither is most to blame
If you've forgotten my kisses
  And I've forgotten your name.

THE MINING CURATE.

[John Carne was the author of *Letters in the East*;
*Recollections of Travels in Syria and Palestine; Lives of
Eminent Missionaries,* &c., and he was a frequent contributor to the annuals of forty years ago. His works
are distinguished by graphic and faithful descriptions
of places and people.]

A wide and a wild parish is that of Calartha.
Its aspect is strange and unusual; for the
mines with which it abounds are situated on
the brink of precipices, and even carried out
into the sea. The edifices attached to them
are seen fixed on isolated rocks, in the midst
of the wave; while the rich produce drawn
from the bowels of the deep, far beneath, is
conveyed, with singular ingenuity, over the
lofty cliffs that tower behind. If any one is
satiated with luxuriant scenery (and it will
sometimes satiate); if he would exchange
groves, meadows, and fertile fields, for some
new aspect of the ever-varied and impressive
face of nature, let him come to this territory.
The miner thrives, so does the farmer who
lives in the few cultivated and romantic valleys; the fisherman, also, plies his trade with
great success off the coast; but the clergyman
has scarcely enough to keep body and soul
together. Notwithstanding the numerous
population of the parish, he has only forty
pounds a year. Now the man who, at the
time of our acquaintance with the affairs of
Calartha, was the appointed religious in-

structor of its inhabitants, was, in every respect, admirably suited to his office. His form
was spare and fitted for activity; his features
aquiline, and his large gray eye for ever restless. Had he doffed the cassock and assumed
the broad-brimmed hat and the coarse woollen
jacket and trousers of the miner, and descended
every day into the earth, he would have found
there a better return for his labour than the
marble hearts of his parishioners were disposed
to give him. But then his profession made
him a gentleman; he had received a good education, and had lived, for some time at least,
among scholars and men of taste—having
been maintained at the university by one of
the foundation societies, who often send there
candidates for holy orders. Poor man! from
the moment he set his foot in Calartha his
daily and nightly study seemed to be, how to
supply the wants of nature in a comfortable
and sufficient manner: it would be profane to
say luxurious—for what had he to do with
luxury? He was acutely sensible he had
nothing to do with it.

Men's minds soon grow submissive to their
situations! and after a vain and ineffectual
struggle of a few weeks to keep up appearances,
to vie in many things with his neighbours, to
be thought to have a decent table, to be seen
to wear a decent dress—he gave it up in despair, just in time to save himself from total
ruin. It may be said that a bachelor, in so
distant a province, where there was no competition to enhance the price of a single article,
need not be ruined, with economy, even on
forty pounds a year; but the curate had a
mother and sister to maintain; and they took
a little house on the slope of a hill, and lived
together in it. How they lived, how they
lodged, what they ate and drank—are mysteries that have never yet been sufficiently
explained.

Now, the curate was no economist; had the
money found its way entire into his hands it
would have all melted away like the mists on
one of the neighbouring hills. He would often
give, and wished always to give, to the poor;
he loved, but not to excess, a cheerful glass;
and sometimes would cast his eye on his threadbare coat, with a determined purpose to have a
new one. All these indulgences would quickly
have made frightful invasions on the income,
if the mother and sister had not received the
quarterly ten pounds with an eager grasp, and
watched over its little, gradual ebbings with a
lynx eye and iron hand. The money had as
well been at the bottom of the tin shaft in the
vale below for any indulgence it brought to

him who toiled for it. It was in vain that the son sometimes appealed to the parent in moving terms, when, returned from a hot and dusty walk in the midst of summer, he begged hard for a few shillings.

"James," said the old lady, "remember the dignity of the cloth. Would you lower yourself by drinking, may be, more than you can bear? Go and finish the discourse you've been writing, bit by bit, all the week: 'tis a beautiful piece o' writing, and there's no doubt the squire will ask you to dinner after hearin' of it."

The son looked down at the sound of dignity of the cloth: both his elbows were struggling through the time-worn vestment; yet he rose with a sigh, took down his manuscript, drew the table near the window, and was soon plunged in the very depths of his subject.

It might be thought that the imagination would freeze, and the power of composition be arrested by the hourly pressure of petty sacrifices and denials—the uncertainty, when he rose in the morning, whether any sufficient refection would be that day given to the outward man; but it did not seem so, at least his public discourses were oftentimes very good, and even eloquent, and had evidently been the work of care and time. One reason of this perhaps was, that Sunday was his day of triumph, and he felt it to be so. After sinking, in temporal things, below his parishioners during the whole of the week; after pining for comforts which they enjoyed to the full—he found himself on this day elevated above them—was their instructor, their pastor, looked on by them as a man of learning and of power. He was far better adorned, also, than on week-days: the gown left by his predecessor was in very good condition, and his appearance, on the whole, was respectable and impressive. Then, after the service, the hand was held out more freely and respectfully; the squire stopped in the aisle, and the rich farmer without the door, to exchange kind and friendly words with him; and an invitation to dinner, from some one or another, sometimes followed. There was a singular difference in all his demeanour, and tone, and bearing, on this day: his look was no longer restless and depressed, nor his attitude stooping, nor his air soft and cringing; he spoke fast and free, sat at the friendly table as a gentleman should, and thought no more of his forty pounds a year. The privations of the whole week rendered the now loaded board an exquisite luxury. Perhaps, for his own peace, he had better never have sat there; for, on his return at night, he was beset with the fruitless remarks and desires of his mother and sister, who were hardly ever asked out on these occasions; and during the ensuing week the daily and frugal meal was often embittered with their repinings.

To entertain a friend in his own house was a thing that never entered his head; had he dared to make the attempt, he might as well have faced two hungry harpies, as met the looks and words of his rigid relatives. He was often to be seen of an evening seated in the little window-seat, overlooking the road; and there he feasted his eyes on the joyous groups that returned from the market of the neighbouring town, where they had ate and drunk, and were now returning, in the fulness of their hearts, to a comfortable home, to their own warm hearth. And then a knot of farmers would jog merrily by, talking in loud voices of the current prices, the coming harvests, and of their own well-stored barns and yards.

"And why should so great a gulf be fixed between the pastor and his flock?" was a question he might well ask himself. Even when twilight had spread its dimness over dwelling and path, the form of the curate might still be seen seated there: for candle-light was spared, with infinite care and skill, within the walls; and not till the middle of November was any fire allowed. So he loved to linger over the last gleams of light, rather than turn to the void of his cheerless habitation. To defend himself from the increasing cold, he used to put on his ancient and rusty great-coat, and fold it tightly round him. The want of light was supplied from the public-house of the village, which was directly opposite, and only a few yards distant; for, the rooms being as usual profusely lighted, a partial glare was received from them through the windows of the curate's apartment. But this was more to his annoyance than his comfort. Much has been said of the torments of Tantalus; but as much, and with equal justice, might be said of the sufferings of this thirsty, poor, and much desiring man, who sat from hour to hour in a partial gloom, in which all the senses are more vividly awake, listening to the ringing of glasses, and the calls, continually repeated, for more supplies of some refreshing beverage, of new and old ale, and even wine. Often he retired to rest with a spirit tried to the very core. Alas! it needs not a guilty conscience to embitter life; salt tears will stream down blameless cheeks.

Thus passed away two or three years; when one morning saw him summoned to a different scene—to attend one of his parishioners, whose dwelling was at some distance. The man was dying, and over his bed bent a form and face that the eye would hardly look for within such walls: his condition in life was only that of a peasant, yet the daughter, who was his only child, was, in all opinions, the loveliest girl in the parish. Often, with surprise, had the curate marked her beauty from the pulpit; and in his few visits to the cottage he had entered into conversation with her, and found, by the words that fell gently from her lips, that she had treasured his sermons in her memory and heart — the sweetest flattery, perhaps, that a woman can pay to a youthful minister.

He thought little of these things at this moment, however, but drew nigh to the side of his parishioner, and spoke to him in earnest and heartfelt tones: the man raised his hand in token of satisfaction, and seemed to devour every word he heard; but his eye, on which the world was now closing, was not lifted to heaven, but bent on the girl who hung over him. She was to be an orphan; and it seemed to be more than he could bear: he strove to man his spirit and call faith to his aid. But it might not be; the dread reality of the moment would not yield to the hope of future protection, which the minister strove to inculcate. The parishioner, a man of strong but untutored mind, listened in seeming calmness for some time; but when death drew near, he struggled against the stern summons, laid one hand firmly on his daughter's form, and when he felt that hand loose its hold, he turned his glazing eye on his pastor, and said,

"Man, if there's a love stronger than death, 'tis that for a desolate daughter: watch over mine, if you hope for mercy, for she is an orphan."

The tears of the girl did not fall alone; for the feelings of the curate were moved to the uttermost. Deaths and funerals had, from habit, become to him familiar things, but a death like this assailed every avenue of his heart and memory; the sun was yet rising, and his red beams fell through the cottage window on the face of the dead, whose thin hand was still extended towards his child, as if he miserably mocked the king of terrors; and on the features of that child was utter friendlessness. The minister stood with folded arms on the other side of the bed: his earnest aspect and compressed lips showed him to be no passionless spectator: he bent forward, and taking the trembling hand of the girl, led her from the apartment. He hastened to his home; and thither the scene followed him, the dying charge still thrilling in his ear. On the next Sunday his eye wandered unconsciously to the people

who entered: and when the orphan girl came in her mourning, the looks of the whole congregation were instantly turned on her; for utter desolation ever commands interest and pity. A stronger feeling was excited in the curate's mind as he often sought the cottage and gazed on her beauty, and loved it. But what had he to do with love, when poverty, like an armed man, stood in his path, and sternly warned the resistless stranger away? Could he for a moment think of introducing another to share the small pittance of his household? If he did, the delusive hope flitted in a moment away, like a cloud from the bosom of the rocky hill on which his dwelling stood; yet in spite of fate he continued to love, and, in the meantime, exerted all his little influence in the parish to improve the condition of the orphan.

Thus passed away a year, at the end of which a change came over his fortunes, a sudden and a great change. An old sister of his mother's died and left to her nephew the property which had been the reward of a whole life of griping and saving. They were all at their scanty breakfast when a letter, with a black seal, was delivered: the son took and opened it; a sudden light came to his eyes that had long been a stranger there, and a deep flush passed over his cheek; for it was the letter containing the account of the bequest. The strong emotions that seized every one were some time in subsiding. There was now a delightful certainty that poverty would dwell with them no more: life had never brought an hour so elevating, they shed tears, and then they laughed loud and long, in the fulness of their hearts; for the bequest amounted to nearly a thousand pounds. As it was all left to the son, he had, of course, the entire disposal of every farthing; and while the mother and sister naturally wished to surround their little household with comforts and enjoyments, and extend their consequence among the neighbours, he was occupied with different thoughts. The use he made of the money affords an instance of the strange waywardness of the human heart. He no sooner received the sum than the insatiable desire of increasing it, like a demon, entered his heart. The strong and sudden novelty of the event had its share, perhaps, in this: to a man to whom the command of a few shillings at a time had been an object of desire, the possession of so much wealth was exquisite.

But there was a deeper cause also, and one of longer standing. The extensive parish of which he was the curate offered a beautiful and enticing field of speculation, in which any sum, vast or minute, might be quickly employed. The soil was in many parts covered with mines, whose piles of ore, worthless as well as valuable, were strewed over the surface. The curate had often fallen in company with the miners, who formed, indeed, no small part of his parishioners, and the shrewdness and intelligence of these men had not failed to interest him. Then he had loved to linger, during his various walks, on the brink of these tempting scenes, to survey the various and valuable produce, and to watch the iron-bound vessel that rose every moment to the surface and poured its fresh treasures from the deep caverns of the earth. It had never entered his mind that he could partake in the mighty adventure, that he could ever blend his own destiny with that of the mine that spread around; but now the face of things was altered, and he resolved to adventure boldly and skilfully the property that had been left him. It was in vain that his parent, and Rachel, his sister, implored him to pause ere he committed so perilous and fearful a deed—for they never could survive, they said, the loss of this treasure: the nature of the man was changed; and there never was a more striking proof of the sudden influence of money on a disposition hitherto untried by it. He returned brief and stern answers to the mother before whom his voice had formerly been subdued and submissive; looked her full in the face, and met her glance of authority with one of equal command. The unhappy woman sank into a chair, wrung her hands, and said that a curse would come on the money thus awfully risked.

But there was another and more youthful eye and tone that he dared not thus to meet. In the evening he hastened to the cottage where the daughter of the peasant still lived: his feelings were delightful as he entered; and he grasped her hand fervently, and looked long and earnestly in her lovely face. His own features were full of pride mingled with tenderness; for he felt that she was his own; and, to his ardent imagination there seemed something exquisite in rescuing her from desertion, and executing the trust of her dying father: for poverty had crushed hitherto the spirit of the curate, and shrouded everything that was noble and generous in it. The girl spoke low and passionately, and there was hope in her voice and eye, as she wished him joy of his good fortune; for she had begun to love the kind-hearted minister, who had been a faithful friend in her distress. By his unceasing efforts he had procured her the situation of lady's-maid in the town at about twenty miles'

distance, and she was to depart in a few days. "Then you would not wish me to go now," she asked, "now that the world smiles upon you; you would rather, perhaps, that I should stay here?" He returned no answer. "It is a place of pride," she resumed, "and of command; and my father's cottage will be far dearer to me than that lady's house."

He turned to the small window, through which the moonlight was shining beautifully, and she saw that his face was pale and agitated. Mistaking the cause, the colour rushed to her own cheek, and she said something about his despising her now he was rich: he started at the words, and pressed her to his heart, that throbbed with anguish. He had known enough of the delusions of the human spirit in the various scenes of suffering, sorrow, and death, that this extensive parish offered, to be aware that his own was now miserably led captive.

"Mary," he said, "the bitterness of parting will be hard to bear: we might now be married, I know, and be happy; but—but I am not rich, as you say—not rich enough to live in comfort: no, my love, I wish to surround you with enjoyments, with affluence, that all thoughts of poverty may be chased from our dwelling, as chaff before the wind."

And then he told her of the purpose he had formed and matured, of laying out the property in a flourishing mine in the neighbourhood, where, in the course of a year, there was a certain prospect of its being doubled.

As he spoke on the tempting theme his eye flashed, his voice rose, and his gestures were impassioned. The girl gazed in surprise and sorrow, and thought of the gentle tone, the happy smile, the look full of hope and affection, with which he had been wont to enter her dwelling. It was clear that she must part from her home and its wild and loved scenes, from which she had never wandered before; for till his golden expectations were accomplished, as he admitted, the day of their union could not come, and he would be, in fact, as poor and dependent as ever. Her tears fell fast at the thought, and a warning conviction seemed to rush over her mind. She knelt before him, and, clasping his hand in her own, blessed him for all the care and tenderness with which he had watched over her orphan state, and besought him not to cast away the only prospect that might ever be of their union—not to love gold better than her love; and then she pointed to the chamber in which her father died. The curate's spirit was severely tried: the look, the action, the sorrow of the kneeling girl were almost irresistible, and he felt them to be so; the struggle was violent: but pride, a new sensation, at last came to his aid. "Why will you not," he said, "be guided by my advice? Have I not in everything sought your welfare? and you blame me because I seek to make our home a more wealthy one! Bear this absence of a few months with patience, and then I will come and bring you to our home."

She rose, and spoke not another word of complaint or sorrow; and soon after he parted from her kindly as ever, and sought his own dwelling on the hill. On the following day she left her home, and went to the distant town.

And now the curate knew no rest night or day. He was not long in deciding in what adventure to place his money; and yet the moments of suspense ere he came to that decision were beautiful. He traversed the whole neighbourhood every day with rapid and eager steps, canvassed with his own eyes the bearings and value of every enterprise. But how different were his air and tone! No longer bending and dependent, but firm, elevated, and clear. And many attentions and civilities were paid him; for, as the precise amount of the bequest was not known, people began to imagine it much greater than it was.

At last he fixed upon a very flourishing, or rather promising, copper mine, that had not been discovered more than twelve months; and here he embarked the whole of his property. The moment he had done this, a devouring thirst and gnawing anxiety seized on his soul: the traveller, dying in the desert, does not long more intensely for the cooling water, than the curate did for the gains that were so soon to flow from his adventure. Religion; the sermons and prayers of the Sabbath; the visiting of the sick; the comforting of the dying—all these were light as the autumn leaf, compared to the beloved, the glowing, the golden speculation. He was thin before, but now he wasted to a shadow. Murmurings began to rise in the parish at his neglect and insensibility; several people, who lived at the distance of many miles, in their last moments had longed for the sacrament, and seemed to linger on life's fading shore, unwilling to leave it without that consolation: yet it never came. But the misery or happiness of others was now become quite indifferent to him: he rose with the earliest light, quitted the house before either of its inmates was stirring, and repaired, over the moor, to the scene of the distant mine. The living object of his attachment he visited once or twice in the distant town, and told her

with a sparkling eye of his ardent hopes; but no lover ever hung with more fondness over the untimely grave of his mistress than the curate did, morn and eve, over the black heaps that rose at his feet, in which he felt his own fate involved. He sat beside them, took the moist stones in his hand; minutely, darkly, distinctly traced were the veins of the rich mineral; and then he retraced the path to his dwelling, and sat down silent and abstracted. The puny income, that had so long been his sole resource, he now thought of with perfect contempt. "Ten pounds a quarter!—he had not the slightest· intention of retaining his cure beyond the time when the returns of the mine began to pour in." And these returns really seemed, for a short time, about to realize his most sanguine anticipations:· a small vein of valuable copper was cut into; the shares rose greatly in price; and his own, for which he had given nearly a thousand pounds, might now be sold for fifteen hundred. A few months before the receipt of this sum would have been felt to be the greatest blessing that ever fell to man; but now the prospect of the future was so glorious, that he received the tempting offer with no small scorn, observing, "that he should be a fool to part with what would soon gain him many thousands."

Could a man whose every thought and imagination were thus deliciously occupied, attend earnestly to the poor, cold, rugged realities that called every moment for his exertions? It is a painful and a bitter thing, however, when our enjoyments depend wholly on the uncertain chances of each coming day and hour: the reports from the mine beneath were not always favourable; there were some moments when the vein of copper began to be less productive, at others a total extinction was threatened. The curate gazed on the countenances of the miners, just ascended from the scene of toil, with a lynx and scrutinizing eye, that said, ere the tone could utter, "Oh say that my hopes still live!" But death came at last, and the curate felt the barbed arrow in his soul. Not the extinction of being—that, perhaps, had been mercy; but the withering for ever of every happy and every golden hope. After a few weeks of thrilling suspense and joy the vein of ore failed utterly: other parts of the ground were explored, and excavations made in every direction, but all in vain; and in a few months the whole speculation fell through. The legacy was entirely gone, and not the slightest addition had been made to the real comforts and enjoyments of the possessors. The miserable man now allowed the truth of this, and the words of his mother fell awfully on his ear: they were fierce, unsparing, and ceaseless; and he listened to them in silence, but not in calmness. There was a voice that would have brought comfort, that he loved to hear; but it was afar, and he had long been a stranger to its sweet tones; for, during the fever of speculation, he had neglected the orphan girl, and had lately heard that she had gone to a more distant residence.

Nearly twelve months passed away: the curate's mind, that had borne calmly the long pressure of real poverty, could not support the fearful blow that cut off his expectations: a deep despondency grew on his spirits daily, and the care of his parish seemed to be a heavy burden. It was strange, but his thoughts still hovered around the scene of his ruin. One evening he had wandered thither, and was seated on one of the scattered heaps that attested with what avidity riches had been sought: it was an evening in autumn, and the rays of the sun, setting in the sea, that was full in view, were thrown on the waste spot. The stones, containing a portion of the rich mineral, gleamed with a golden hue, as the fading beams rested on them, as if in mockery of the hopes of the wretched man who sat there. But he needed no illusions of fancy to swell the sum of real anguish: thought after thought coursed wildly through his brain, and in them were despair, remorse, and blasted love. Raising his eyes from the barren soil, he saw a female advancing slowly over the moor, as if her steps were turned to the neighbouring village. The path led through the ruined mine, and as the stranger drew near to the despairing curate she paused, and the eyes of each were fastened intensely on the other. It was Mary, the object of his affection, of whom he had often thought with self-reproach, and a longing desire to see her again. And now she stood before him. He who has bent beneath misery and desertion can tell how welcome are the returning glance and form of those who love us. The curate clasped his hands fervently, and a deep flush came to his wasted features.

"Mary," he said, "you are come to comfort me: I thought you would not forget or forsake me."

The girl stood silent for a few moments; but it was not the silence of a full heart. She was deeply changed: the look of simplicity and candour had given place to one of haughtiness; the spirit, too, it was evident, had been affected by the scenes of dissipation and splendour in which she had resided.

"James," she said, "I am come, but not to be your wife—that hour is past; and as to forsaken, you never came to see me for many months, till I thought you had forgot me."

He spoke in sincere and glowing words of his bright and prolonged hopes, and how they had wholly occupied his mind; and of former moments of her destitution, and his fidelity. Still she listened coldly: he knelt before her, and gazed on her beauty, in agony at the conviction that it never could be his; and then he told of the hour of her father's death, and how, in that last moment, she had been given to his care. She turned pale, and seemed to be struggling with remembrances.

"Mr. Collins," she said at last, "it is of no use to talk of this now; I cannot feel as I did then: remember the time when I kneeled before you, and prayed with tears that I might not leave my home, and that you would prefer my love to the love of gold. You would not, and now it is gone from you: not because of the ruin you have met with, but in the places where I have dwelt, other feelings, and prouder ones, have been nurtured. Farewell, my kind and generous protector, may every blessing attend you! but—but I never can be your wife."

She turned from the spot with a quickened step: he gazed after her retreating figure as long as it remained in sight, and then he turned to the solitude of his own heart.

"Is that my Mary?" he said, with a miserable smile, "the dear devoted girl that I watched over when her father died? Surely she was to be my wife, my beautiful wife! and was to comfort me in my misery." He would have sat down once more on the glittering pile beside him; but a sudden thought crossed his brain, and he started from the spot as if a serpent had stung him: he clenched his hand fiercely, and gnashed his teeth:—"There, there," he said, wildly, "was my ruin; my love, my fortune, all my joy on earth, and hope in heaven, were sold for these accursed heaps. I sold my bride, with all her tenderness and beauty, for these detested stones— ha! ha!—that now mock me like so many fiends."

The night had set in darkly ere he went to his wretched home; his spirit was utterly crushed, and his frame soon sank also. Before long he was unable, as well as unfit, to attend to his ministerial duties; and his numerous flock saw with pity that their pastor's career, it was probable, would soon draw to a close. Six months had not passed when the girl he loved, and whose attachment was the last silver cord to which he had clung, was married to

a young farmer in the neighbourhood. Even
had she been faithful, what prospect remained
to the curate of supporting a wife on the miserable pittance to which the loss of his bequest
reduced him? But his feelings were embittered
by the knowledge that she had brought a small
portion to her husband, which was bequeathed to
her by the will of the lady whom she had served.
Another curate also was found to supply the wide
parish of Calartha; but the people, in kindness,
continued to allow their former minister his
poor salary, from the conviction, perhaps, that
he would soon cease to be a burden to them.
He still loved, when his failing strength permitted, to walk out into the wild paths that
had so long been familiar to him; and his feet,
it was observed, though they sometimes fainted
by the way, seemed to wander mechanically to
the scene of his dazzling hopes and of his ruin;
and there he would stay for hours, grasping,
at times with a trembling hand, some stray
stones, richly veined with the mineral, while
his hollow eye and attenuated form showed that
poverty and wealth would soon be alike indifferent to him. One day he had been absent
from his home much longer than usual, and
his mother and sister went forth to trace his
steps to the well-known scene, and found him
reclined peacefully there; but the flitting remains of strength had been exhausted beneath
the heat of the day. They called on his name,
and bade him come to his home: but he heard
them no more; for life was extinct, and it
seemed, from the expression of his features,
that he had welcomed death.

———

I DO CONFESS THOU ART SAE FAIR.

BY ROBERT BURNS.

I do confess thou art sae fair,
    I wad been o'er the lugs in love,
Had I not found the slightest prayer
    That lips could speak thy heart could move.
I do confess thee sweet, but find
    Thou art sae thriftless o' thy sweets,
Thy favours are the silly wind,
    That kisses ilka thing it meets.

See yonder rose-bud, rich in dew,
    Amang its native briers sae coy:
How sune it tines its scent and hue,
    When pu'd and worn a common toy!
Sic fate, ere lang, shall thee betide,
    Though thou may gaily bloom awhile;
Yet soon thou shalt be thrown aside,
    Like any common weed and vile.

INFANTINE INQUIRIES.

BY JAMES PENNYCOOK BROWN.

"Tell me, O mother! when I grow old,
Will my hair, which my sisters say is like gold,
Grow gray as the old man's, weak and poor,
Who asked for alms at our pillared door?
Will I look as sad, will I speak as slow
As he, when he told us his tale of woe?
Will my hands then shake, and my eyes be dim?
Tell me, O mother! will I grow like him?

"He said—but I knew not what he meant—
That his aged heart with sorrow was rent.
He spoke of the grave as a place of rest,
Where the weary sleep in peace, and are bless'd;
And he told how his kindred there were laid,
And the friends with whom in his youth he played;
And tears from the eyes of the old man fell,
And my sisters wept as they heard his tale!

"He spoke of a home where, in childhood's glee,
He chased from the wild flowers the singing bee;
And followed afar, with a heart as light
As its sparkling wings, the butterfly's flight;
And pulled young flowers, where they grew 'neath the
    beams
Of the sun's fair light, by his own blue streams;—
Yet he left all these, through the earth to roam!
Why, O mother! did he leave his home?"

"Calm thy young thoughts, my own fair child!
The fancies of youth in age are beguiled;—
Though pale grow thy cheeks, and thy hair turn gray,
Time cannot steal the soul's youth away!
There's a land of which thou hast heard me speak,
Where age never wrinkles the dweller's cheek;
But in joy they live, fair boy! like thee—
It was there that the old man longed to be!

"For he knew that those with whom he had played,
In his heart's young joy, 'neath their cottage shade—
Whose love he shared, when their songs and mirth
Brightened the gloom of this sinful earth—
Whose names from our world had passed away,
As flowers in the breath of an autumn day—
He knew that they, with all suffering done,
Encircled the throne of the Holy One!

"Though ours be a pillared and lofty home,
Where Want with his pale train never may come,
Oh! scorn not the poor with the scorner's jest,
Who seek in the shade of our hall to rest;
For He who hath made them poor may soon
Darken the sky of our glowing noon,
And leave us with woe, in the world's bleak wild!
Oh! soften the griefs of the poor, my child!"
                      Poetical Ephemera.

THE STOLEN SHEEP.

BY JOHN BANIM.

The Irish plague, called typhus fever, raged in its terrors. In almost every third cabin there was a corpse daily. In every one, without an exception, there was what had made the corpse—hunger. It need not be added that there was poverty too. The poor could not bury their dead. From mixed motives of self-protection, terror, and benevolence, those in easier circumstances exerted themselves to administer relief in different ways. Money was subscribed—(then came England's munificent donation—God prosper her for it!)—wholesome food, or food as wholesome as a bad season permitted, was provided; and men of respectability, bracing their minds to avert the danger that threatened themselves, by boldly facing it, entered the infected house, where death reigned almost alone, and took measures to cleanse and purify the close-cribbed air, and the rough, bare walls. Before proceeding to our story let us be permitted to mention some general marks of Irish virtue, which, under those circumstances, we personally noticed. In poverty, in abject misery, and at a short and fearful notice, the poor man died like a Christian. He gave vent to none of the poor man's complaints or invectives against the rich man who had neglected him, or who he might have supposed had done so, till it was too late. Except for a glance—and, doubtless a little inward pang while he glanced—at the starving, and perhaps infected wife, or child, or old parent as helpless as the child,—he blessed God, and died. The appearance of a comforter at his wretched bedside, even when he knew comfort to be useless, made his heart grateful, and his spasmed lips eloquent in thanks. In cases of indescribable misery—some members of his family lying lifeless before his eyes, or else some dying,—stretched upon damp and unclean straw, on an earthen floor, without cordial for his lips, or potatoes to point out to a crying infant,—often we have heard him whisper to himself (and to another who heard him!), "The Lord giveth, and the Lord taketh away, blessed be the name of the Lord." Such men need not always make bad neighbours.

In the early progress of the fever, before the more affluent roused themselves to avert its career, let us cross the threshold of an individual peasant. His young wife lies dead; his second child is dying at her side; he has just sunk into a corner himself, under the first stun of disease, long resisted. The only persons of his family who have escaped contagion, and are likely to escape it, are his old father, who sits weeping feebly upon the hob, and his first-born, a boy of three or four years, who, standing between the old man's knees, cries also for food.

We visit the young peasant's abode some time after. He has not sunk under "the sickness." He is fast regaining his strength, even without proper nourishment; he can creep out of doors, and sit in the sun. But in the expression of his sallow and emaciated face there is no joy for his escape from the grave, as he sits there alone, silent and brooding. His father and his surviving child are still hungry—more hungry, indeed, and more helpless than ever; for the neighbours who had relieved the family with a potato and a mug of sour milk are now stricken down themselves, and want assistance to a much greater extent than they can give it.

"I wish Mr. Evans was in the place," cogitated Michaul Carroll; "a body could spake fornent him, and not spake for nothin', for all that he's an Englishman; and I don't like the thoughts o' goin' up to the house to the steward's face—it wouldn't turn kind to a body. May be he'd soon come home to us, the master himself."

Another fortnight elapsed. Michaul's hope proved vain. Mr. Evans was still in London; though a regular resident on his small Irish estate since it had come into his possession, business unfortunately—and he would have said so himself—now kept him an unusually long time absent. Thus disappointed, Michaul overcame his repugnance to appear before the "hard" steward. He only asked for work, however. There was none to be had. He turned his slow and still feeble feet into the adjacent town. It was market-day, and he took up his place among a crowd of other claimants for agricultural employment, shouldering a spade, as did each of his companions. Many farmers came to the well-known "stannin," and hired men at his right and at his left, but no one addressed Michaul. Once or twice, indeed, touched perhaps by his sidelong looks of beseeching misery, a farmer stopped a moment before him, and glanced over his figure; but his worn and almost shaking limbs giving little promise of present vigour in the working field, worldly prudence soon conquered the humane feeling which started up towards him in the man's heart, and, with a choking in his throat, poor Michaul saw the arbiter of his fate pass on.

He walked homeward without having broken his fast that day. "Bud, *musha*, what's the harm o' that," he said to himself; "only here's the ould father, an' *her* pet boy, the weenock, without a pyatee either. Well *asthore*, if they can't have the pyatees, they must have betther food—that's all;—ay—" he muttered, clenching his hands at his sides, and imprecating fearfully in Irish—"an' so they must."

He left his house again, and walked a good way to beg a few potatoes. He did not come back quite empty-handed. His father and his child had a meal. He ate but a few himself; and when he was about to lie down in his corner for the night, he said to the old man, across the room—

"Don't be a-crying to-night, father, you and the child, there; bud sleep well, and ye'll have the good break'ast afore ye in the mornin'."

"The good break'ast, *ma-bauchal?*[1] a-then, an' where 'ill id come from?"

"A body promised it to me, father.

"*Avich!* Michaul, an' sure its fun your making of us now, at any rate. Bud, the good night, *a chorra,*[2] an' my blessin' on your head, Michaul; an' if we keep trust in the good God, an' ax his blessin', too, mornin' an' evenin', gettin' up an' lyin' down, He'll be a friend to us at last: that was always an' ever my word to you, poor boy, since you was at the years o' your own weenock, now fast asleep at my side; an' it's my word to you now, *ma-bauchal;* an' you won't forget id; and there's one sayin' the same to you, out o' heaven, this night—herself, an' her little angel-in-glory by the hand, Michaul *a-vourneen.*"

Having thus spoken in the fervent and rather exaggerated, though every-day, words of pious allusion of the Irish poor man, old Carroll soon dropped asleep, with his arms round his little grandson, both overcome by an unusually abundant meal. In the middle of the night he was awakened by a stealthy noise. Without moving, he cast his eyes round the cabin. A small window, through which the moon broke brilliantly, was open. He called to his son, but received no answer. He called again and again: all remained silent. He arose, and crept to the corner where Michaul had lain down. It was empty. He looked out through the window into the moonlight. The figure of a man appeared at a distance, just about to enter a pasture-field belonging to Mr. Evans.

The old man leaned his back against the wall of the cabin, trembling with sudden and terrible misgivings. With him, the language

of virtue, which we have heard him utter, was not cant. In early prosperity, in subsequent misfortunes, and in his late and present excess of wretchedness, he had never swerved in practice from the spirit of his own exhortations to honesty before men, and love for, and dependence upon God, which, as he has truly said, he had constantly addressed to his son since his earliest childhood. And hitherto that son had, indeed, walked by his precepts, further assisted by a regular observance of the duties of his religion. Was he now about to turn into another path? to bring shame on his father in his old age? to put a stain on their family and their name, "the name that a rogue or a bould woman never bore?" continued old Carroll, indulging in some of the pride and egotism for which an Irish peasant is, under his circumstances, remarkable. And then came the thought of the personal peril incurred by Michaul; and his agitation, incurred by the feebleness of age, nearly overpowered him.

He was sitting on the floor, shivering like one in an ague-fit, when he heard steps outside the house. He listened, and they ceased: but the familiar noise of an old barn-door creaking on its crazy hinges came on his ear. It was now day-dawn. He dressed himself; stole out cautiously; peeped into the barn through a chink of the door, and all he had feared met full confirmation. There, indeed, sat Michaul, busily and earnestly engaged, with a frowning brow and a haggard face, in quartering the animal he had stolen from Mr. Evan's field.

The sight sickened the father—the blood on his son's hands, and all. He was barely able to keep himself from falling. A fear, if not a dislike, of the unhappy culprit also came upon him. His unconscious impulse was to re-enter their cabin unperceived, without speaking a word; he succeeded in doing so; and then he fastened the door again, and undressed, and resumed his place beside his innocent grandson.

About an hour afterwards Michaul came in cautiously through the still open window, and also undressed and reclined on his straw after glancing towards his father's bed, who pretended to be asleep. At the usual time for arising old Carroll saw him suddenly jump up and prepare to go abroad. He spoke to him, leaning on his elbow.

"And what *holly*[3] is on you now, *ma-bauchal?*"

"Going for the good break'ast I promised you, father dear.

---

[1] My boy.   [2] Term of endearment.   [3] What are you about?

" An' who's the good Christhin 'll give id to us, Michaul?"

"Oh, you'll know that soon, father: now, a good-bye:"—he hurried to the door.

" A good-bye then, Michaul; bud tell me what's that on your hand?"

"No—nothin'," stammered Michaul, changing colour, as he hastily examined the hand himself; "nothin' is on id: what could there be?" (nor was there, for he had very carefully removed all evidence of guilt from his person; and the father's question was asked upon grounds distinct from anything he then saw).

" Well avich, an' sure I didn't say anything was on it wrong; or anything to make you look so square, an' spake so sthrange to your father, this mornin';—only I'll ax you, Michaul, over agin, who has took such a sudd'n likin' to us, to send us the good break'ast?—an' answer me sthraight, Michaul—what is id to be, that you call it so good?"

" The good mate, father:"—he was again passing the threshold.

"Stop!" cried his father; "stop an' turn fornent me. Mate?—the good mate?—What 'ud bring mate into our poor house, Michaul? Tell me, I bid you again an' again, who is to give id to you?"

" Why, as I said afore, father, a body that——"

" A body that thieved id, Michaul Carroll!" added the old man, as his son hesitated, walking close up to the culprit; "a body that thieved id, an' no other body. Don't think to blind me, Michaul. I am ould, to be sure; but sense enough is left in me to look round among the neighbours, in my own mind, an' know that none of 'em that has the will has the power to send us the mate for our break'ast, in an honest way. An' I don't say, outright, that you had the same thought wid me, when you consented to take it from a thief—I don't mean to say that you'd go to turn a thief's receiver, at this hour o' your life, an' afther growin' up from a boy to a man widout bringin' a spot o' shame on yourself, or on your wee-nock, or on one of us. No; I won't say that. Your heart was scalded, Michaul, an' your mind was darkened, for a start; an' the thought o' getting comfort for the ould father, an' for the little son, made you consent in a hurry, widout lookin' well afore you, or widout look-in' up to your good God."

" Father, father, let me alone! don't spake them words to me," interrupted Michaul, sitting on a stool, and spreading his large and hard hands over his face.

" Well thin, an' I won't, avich; I won't;—

nothin' to throuble you sure: I didn't mean id;—only this, a-vourneen, don't bring a mouthful o' the bad, unlucky victuals into this cabin, the pyatees, the wild berries o' the bush, the wild roots o' the arth, will be sweeter to us, Michaul; the hunger itself will be sweeter; an' when we give God thanks afther our poor meal, or afther no meal at all, our hearts will be lighter, and our hopes for to-morrow sthronger, avich-ma-chree, than if we faisted on the fat o' the land, but couldn't ax a blessin' on our faist."

" Well thin, I won't either, father; I won't: —an' sure you have your way now. I'll only go out a little while from you—to beg; or else, as you say, to root down in the ground, with my nails, like a baste-brute, for our break'ast."

" My vourneen you are, Michaul, an' my blessin' on your head; yes, to be sure avich, beg, an' I'll beg wid you—sorrow a shame is in that:—No; but a good deed, Michaul, when it's done to keep us honest. So come; we'll go among the Christhins together. Only, before we go, Michaul, my own dear son, tell me—tell one thing."

" What, father?" Michaul began to suspect.

" Never be afraid to tell me, Michaul Carroll, ma-bauchal? I won't—I can't be angry wid you now. You are sorry; an' your Father in heaven forgives you, an' so do I. But you know, avich, there would be danger in quitting the place widout hiding every scrap of anything that could tell on us."

" Tell on us! What can tell on us?" demanded Michaul; "what's in the place to tell on us?"

"Nothin' in the cabin, I know, Michaul; but——have you left nothing in the way, out there?" whispered the old man, pointing towards the barn.

" Out there? Where? What? What do you mean at all, now father? Sure you know it's your ownsef has kep me from as much as laying a hand on it."

" Ay, to-day-mornin'; bud you laid a hand on it last night, avich, an' so——"

" Curp-an-duoul!" imprecated Michaul— "this is too bad, at any rate; no I didn't— last night—let me alone I bid you, father."

"Come back again, Michaul," commanded old Carroll, as the son once more hurried to the door: and his words were instantly obeyed. Michaul, after a glance abroad, and a start, which the old man did not notice, paced to the middle of the floor, hanging his head and saying in a low voice—" Hushth now, father —it's time."

"No Michaul, I will not hushth; an' it's not time; come out with me to the barn."

"Hushth!" repeated Michaul, whispering sharply: he had glanced sideways to the square patch of strong morning sunlight on the ground of the cabin, defined there by the shape of the open door, and saw it intruded upon by the shadow of a man's bust leaning forward in an earnest posture.

"Is it in your mind to go back into your sin, Michaul, an' tell me you were not in the barn at daybreak the mornin'?" asked his father, still unconscious of a reason for silence.

"Arrah, hushth, ould man!" Michaul made a hasty sign towards the door, but was disregarded.

"I saw you in id," pursued old Carroll, sternly: "ay, and at your work in id, too."

"What's that you're sayin', ould Peery Carrol!" demanded a well-known voice.

"Enough to hang his son," whispered Michaul to his father, as Mr. Evans' land-steward, followed by his herdsman and two policemen, entered the cabin. In a few minutes afterwards the policemen had in charge the dismembered carcass of the sheep, dug up out of the floor of the barn, and were escorting Michaul, handcuffed, to the county jail, in the vicinity of the next town. They could find no trace of the animal's skin, though they sought attentively for it; and this seemed to disappoint them and the steward a good deal.

From the moment that they entered the cabin, till their departure, old Carroll did not speak a word. Without knowing it, as it seemed, he sat down on his straw bed, and remained staring stupidly around him, or at one or another of his visitors. When Michaul was about to leave the wretched abode, he paced quickly towards his father, and holding out his ironed hands, and turning his cheek for a kiss, said, smiling miserably—"God be wid you, father, dear." Still the old man was silent, and the prisoner and all his attendants passed out on the road. But it was then the agony of old Carroll assumed a distinctness. Uttering a fearful cry, he snatched up his still sleeping grandson, ran with the boy in his arms till he overtook Michaul; and, kneeling down before him in the dust, said—"I ax pardon o' you avich—won't you tell me I have id afore you go? an' here, I've brought little Peery for you to kiss; you forgot him, a-vour-neen."

"No, father, I didn't," answered Michaul, as he stooped to kiss the child; "an' get up, father, get up; my hands are not my own, or I wouldn't let you do that afore your son."

Get up, there's nothin' for you to throuble yourself about; that is, I mean, I have nothin' to forgive you: no, but everything to be thankful for an' to love you for; you were always an' ever the good father to me; an'——" The many strong and bitter feelings which till now he had almost perfectly kept in, found full vent, and poor Michaul could not go on. The parting from his father, however, so different from what it had promised to be, comforted him. The old man held him in his arms, and wept on his neck. They were separated with difficulty.

Peery Carroll, sitting on the road-side after he lost sight of the prisoner, and holding his screaming grandson on his knees, thought the cup of his trials was full. By his imprudence he had fixed the proof of guilt on his own child; that reflection was enough for him, and he could indulge it only generally. But he was yet to conceive distinctly in what dilemma he had involved himself as well as Michaul. The policemen came back to compel his appearance before the magistrate; and when the little child had been disposed of in a neighbouring cabin, he understood, to his consternation and horror, that he was to be the chief witness against the sheep-stealer. Mr. Evans' steward knew well the meaning of the words he had overheard him say in the cabin, and that if compelled to swear all he was aware of, no doubt would exist of the criminality of Michaul, in the eyes of a jury. "'Tis a sthrange thing to ax a father to do," muttered Peery more than once, as he proceeded to the magistrate's; "it's a very sthrange thing."

The magistrate proved to be a humane man. Notwithstanding the zeal of the steward and the policemen, he committed Michaul for trial, without continuing to press the hesitating and bewildered old Peery into any detailed evidence; his nature seemed to rise against the task, and he said to the steward—"I have enough of facts for making out a committal; if you think the father will be necessary on the trial, subpœna him."

The steward objected that Peery would abscond, and demanded to have him bound over to prosecute, on two sureties, solvent and respectable. The magistrate assented; Perry could name no bail; and consequently he also was marched to prison, though prohibited from holding the least intercourse with Michaul.

The assizes soon came on. Michaul was arraigned; and, during his plea of "not guilty," his father appeared, unseen by him, in the jailer's custody, at the back of the dock, or rather in an inner dock. The trial excited a keen and painful interest in the court, the bar, the jury-box, and the crowds of spectators. It was universally known that a son had stolen a sheep, partly to feed a starving father; and that out of the mouth of that father it was now sought to condemn him. "What will the old man do?" was the general question which ran through the assembly: and while few of the lower orders could contemplate the possibility of his swearing to the truth, many of their betters scarcely hesitated to make out for him a case of natural necessity to swear falsely.

The trial began. The first witness, the herdsman, proved the loss of the sheep, and the finding the dismembered carcass in the old barn. The policemen and the steward followed to the same effect, and the latter added the allusions which he had heard the father make to the son, upon the morning of the arrest of the latter. The steward went down from the table. There was a pause, and complete silence, which the attorney for the prosecution broke by saying to the crier deliberately,

"Call Peery Carroll."

"Here, sir," immediately answered Peery, as the jailer led him by a side door, out of the back dock to the table. The prisoner started round; but the new witness against him had passed for an instant into the crowd.

The next instant old Peery was seen ascending the table, assisted by the jailer and by many other commiserating hands, near him. Every glance fixed on his face. The barristers looked wistfully up from their seats round the table; the judge put a glass to his eye and seemed to study his features attentively. Among the audience there ran a low but expressive murmur of pity and interest.

Though much emaciated by confinement, anguish, and suspense, Peery's cheeks had a flush, and his weak blue eyes glittered. The half-gaping expression of his parched and haggard lips was miserable to see. And yet he did not tremble much, nor appear so confounded as upon the day of his visit to the magistrate. The moment he stood upright on the table he turned himself fully to the judge, without a glance towards the dock.

"Sit down, sit down, poor man," said the judge.

"Thanks to you, my lord, I will," answered Peery, "only, first I'd ax you to let me kneel, for a little start;" and he accordingly did kneel, and after bowing his head, and forming the sign of the cross on his forehead, he looked up, and said—"My Judge in heaven above, 'tis you I pray to keep me to my duty, afore my earthly judge, this day:—amen;"—and then repeating the sign of the cross, he seated himself.

The examination of the witness commenced, and humanely proceeded as follows—(the counsel for the prosecution taking no notice of the superfluity of Peery's answers).

"Do you know Michaul, or Michael, Carroll, the prisoner at the bar?"

"Afore that night, sir, I believed I knew him well; every thought of his mind, every bit of the heart in his body: afore that night no living creatur could throw a word at Michaul Carroll, or say he ever forgot his father's renown, or his love of his good God;—an' sure the people are afther telling you by this time, how it come about that night—an' you, my lord,—an' ye, gintlemen,—an' all good Christians that hear me;—here I am to help to hang him—my own boy, and my only one—but, for all that, gintlemen, ye ought to think of it; 'twas for the weenock and the ould father that he done it;—indeed, an'deed, we hadn't a pyatee in the place; an' the sickness was among us, a start afore; it took the wife from him, and another babby; an' id had himself down a week or so beforehand; an' all that day he was looking for work, but couldn't get a hand's turn to do; an' that's the way it was; not a mouthful for me an' little Peery; an' more betoken, he grew sorry for id, in the mornin', an' promised me not to touch a scrap of what was in the barn,—ay, long afore the steward and the peelers came on us,—but was willin' to go among the neighbours an' beg our breakfast, along wid myself, from door to door, sooner than touch it."

"It is my painful duty," resumed the barrister, when Peery would at length cease,— "to ask you for closer information. You saw Michael Carroll in the barn, that night?—"

"Musha—The Lord pity him and me—I did sir."

"Doing what?"—

"The sheep between his hands," answered Peery, dropping his head, and speaking almost inaudibly.

"I must still give you pain, I fear;—stand up; take the crier's rod; and if you see Michael Carroll in court, lay it on his head."

"Och, musha, musha, sir, don't ax me to do that!" pleaded Peery, rising, wringing his hands, and for the first time weeping—" och, don't, my lord, don't, and may your own judgment be favourable, the last day."

"I am sorry to command you to do it, witness, but you must take the rod," answered the judge, bending his head close to his notes, to hide his own tears; and at the same time many a veteran barrister rested his forehead on the edge of the table. In the body of the court were heard sobs.

"Michaul, avich! Michaul, a corra-ma-chree!" exclaimed Peery, when at length he took the rod, and faced round to his son,— "is id your father they make to do it, ma-bau-chal?"

"My father does what is right," answered Michaul, in Irish. The judge immediately asked to have his words translated; and when he learned their import, regarded the prisoner with satisfaction.

"We rest here, my lord," said the counsel, with the air of a man freed from a painful task.

The judge instantly turned to the jury-box. "Gentlemen of the jury. That the prisoner at the bar stole the sheep in question there can be no shade of moral doubt. But you have a peculiar case to consider. A son steals a sheep that his own famishing father and his own famishing son may have food. His aged parent is compelled to give evidence against him here for the act. The old man virtuously tells the truth, and the whole truth, before you and me. He sacrifices his natural feelings—and we have seen that they are lively—to his honesty, and to his religious sense of the sacred obligations of an oath. Gentlemen, I will pause to observe, that the old man's conduct is strikingly exemplary, and even noble. It teaches all of us a lesson. Gentlemen, it is not within the province of a judge to censure the rigour of the proceedings which have sent him before us. But I venture to anticipate your pleasure that, notwithstanding all the evidence given, you will be enabled to acquit that old man's son, the prisoner at the bar. I have said there cannot be the shade of a moral doubt that he has stolen the sheep, and I repeat the words. But, gentlemen, there is a legal doubt, to the full benefit of which he is entitled. The sheep has not been identified. The herdsman could not venture to identify it (and it would have been strange if he could) from the dismembered limbs found in the barn. To his mark on its skin, indeed, he might have positively spoken; but no skin has been discovered. Therefore, according to the evidence, and you have sworn to decide by that alone, the prisoner is entitled to your acquittal. Possibly, now that the prosecutor sees the case in its full bearing, he may be pleased with this result."

While the jury, in evident satisfaction, prepared to return their verdict, Mr. Evans,

who had but a moment before returned home, entered the court, and becoming aware of the concluding words of the judge, expressed his sorrow aloud that the prosecution had ever been undertaken; that circumstances had kept him uninformed of it, though it had gone on in his name; and he begged leave to assure his lordship that it would be his future effort to keep Michaul Carroll in his former path of honesty, by finding him honest and ample employment, and, as far as in him lay, to reward the virtue of the old father.

While Peery Carroll was laughing and crying in a breath, in the arms of his delivered son, a subscription, commenced by the bar, was mounting into a considerable sum for his advantage.

GARDEN GOSSIP.

ACCOUNTING FOR THE COOLNESS BETWEEN
THE LILY AND VIOLET.

"I will tell you a secret," the honey-bee said
To a violet drooping her dew-laden head;
"The lily's in love! for she listened last night,
While her sisters all slept in the holy moonlight,
To a zephyr that just had been rocking the rose,
Where, hidden, I hearkened in seeming repose.

"I would not betray her to any but you,
But the secret is safe with a spirit so true—
It will rest in your bosom in silence profound."
The violet bent her blue eye to the ground;
A tear and a smile in her loving look lay,
While the light-winged gossip went whirring away.

"I will tell you a secret," the honey-bee said,
And the young lily lifted her beautiful head—
"The violet thinks, with her timid blue eye,
To pass for a blossom enchantingly shy;
But for all her sweet manners, so modest and pure,
She gossips with every gay bird that sings to her.

"Now let me advise you, sweet flower, as a friend,
Oh, ne'er to such beings your confidence lend;
It grieves me to see one, all guileless like you,
Thus wronging a spirit so trustful and true:
But not for the world, love, my secret betray!"
And the little light gossip went buzzing away.

A blush in the lily's cheek trembled and fled:
"I'm sorry he told me," she tenderly said;
"If I mayn't trust the violet, pure as she seems,
I must fold in my own heart my beautiful dreams."
Was the mischief well managed? fair lady is't true?
Did the light garden gossip take lessons of you?
                                    Mrs. F. S. Osgood.

EARLY SCOTTISH POETRY.

[William Hickling Prescott, born at Salem, Massachusetts, 4th May, 1706; died 28th January, 1859. Critic and historian. He studied at Harvard College with the intention of adopting the legal profession, in which his father was already distinguished; but an accident deprived him of the sight of one eye and seriously affected that of the other. He devoted himself to letters, and despite many physical inconveniences produced a series of historical works, which take rank amongst the first of their class. *History of the Reign of Ferdinand and Isabella; The Catholic; History of the Conquest of Mexico, and the Life of the Conqueror Hernando Cortez; The Conquest of Peru; Philip the Second of Spain*, which was to have extended to five volumes, but soon after the publication of the third the author died; *Critical and Historical Essays* contributed to the *North American Review* (London: Routledge). Sir Archibald Alison said: "Mr. Prescott was by far the first historian of America; and he may justly be assigned a place beside the very greatest of modern Europe."]

The peculiarities of early Scottish poetry may also be referred, in a great degree, to the political relations of the nation, which for many centuries was distracted by all the rancorous dissensions incident to the ill-balanced fabric of feudal government. The frequent and long regencies, always unfavourable to civil concord, multiplied the sources of jealousy, and armed with new powers the facetious aristocracy. In the absence of legitimate authority each baron sought to fortify himself by the increased number of his retainers, who, in their turn, willingly attached themselves to the fortunes of a chief who secured to them plunder and protection. Hence a system of clanship was organized, more perfect and more durable than has existed in any other country, which is not entirely effaced at the present day. To the nobles who garrisoned the marches still greater military powers were necessarily delegated for purposes of state defence; and the names of Home, Douglas, and Buccleuch make a far more frequent and important figure in national history than that of the reigning sovereign. Hence private feuds were inflamed and vindicated by national antipathies, and a pretext of patriotism was never wanting to justify perpetual hostility. Hence the scene of the old ballads was laid chiefly on the borders, and hence the minstrels of the "North Countrie" obtained such pre-eminence over their musical brethren.

The odious passion of revenge, which seems adapted by nature to the ardent temperaments of the South, but which even there has been mitigated by the spirit of Christianity, glowed with fierce heat in the bosoms of those northern savages. An offence to the meanest individual was espoused by his whole clan, and was expiated not by the blood of the offender only, but by that of his whole kindred. The sack of a peaceful castle, and the slaughter of its sleeping inhabitants, seem to have been as familiar occurrences to these Border heroes as the lifting of a drove of cattle, and attended with as little compunction. The following pious invocation, uttered on the eve of an approaching foray, may show the acuteness of their moral sensibility:—

> "He that ordained us to be born
> Send us mair meat for the morn,
> Come by right or come by wrang,
> Christ, let us not fast owre lang,
> But blithely spend what's gaily got,—
> Ride, Rowland, hough 's i' the pot."

When superstition usurps the place of religion there will be little morality among the people. The only law they knew was the command of their chief; and the only one he admitted was his sword. "By what right," said a Scottish prince to a marauding Douglas, "do you hold these lands?" "By that of my sword," he answered.

From these causes the early Scottish poetry is deeply tinged with a gloomy ferocity, and abounds in details of cool, deliberate cruelty. It is true that this is frequently set off, as in the fine old ballads of *Chevy Chase* and *Auld Maitland*, by such deeds of rude but heroic gallantry as, in the words of Sydney, "stir the soul like the sound of a trumpet." But, on the whole, although the scene of the oldest ballads is pitched as late as the fourteenth century, the manners they exhibit are not much superior, in point of refinement and humanity, to those of our own North American savages.

From wanton or vindictive cruelty, especially when exercised on the defenceless or the innocent, the cultivated mind naturally shrinks with horror and disgust. But it was long ere the stern hearts of our English ancestors yielded to the soft impulses of mercy and benevolence. The reigns of the Norman dynasty are written in characters of fire and blood. As late as the conclusion of the fourteenth century we find the Black Prince, "flower of English knighthood," as Froissart styles him, superintending the butchery of three thousand unresisting captives, men, women, and children, who vainly clung to him for mercy. The general usage of surrendering as hostages their wives and children, whose members were mutilated or lives sacrificed on the least infraction of their engagements, is a still better evidence of the universal barbarism of the so much lauded age of chivalry.

Another trait in the old Scotch poetry, and of a very opposite nature from that we have been describing, is its occasional sensibility; touches of genuine pathos are found scattered among the cold, appalling passions of the age, like the flowers which, in Switzerland, are said to bloom alongside the avalanche. No state of society is so rude as to extinguish the spark of natural affection; tenderness for our offspring is but a more enlarged selfishness, perfectly compatible with the utmost ferocity towards others. Hence scenes of parental and filial attachment are to be met with in these poems, which cannot be read without emotion. The passion of love appears to have been a favourite study with the ancient English writers; and by none, in any language we have read, is it managed with so much art and feeling as by the dramatic writers of Queen Elizabeth's day. The Scottish minstrels, with less art, seem to be entitled to the praise of possessing an equal share of tenderness. In the Spanish ballad love glows with the fierce ardour of a tropical sun. The amorous serenader celebrates the beauties of his Zayda (the name which, from its frequency, would seem to be a general title for a Spanish mistress) in all the florid hyperbole of oriental gallantry, or, as a disappointed lover, wanders along the banks of the Guadalete, imprecating curses on her head, and vengeance on his devoted rival. The calm dejection and tender melancholy which are diffused over the Scottish love-songs are far more affecting than all this turbulence of passion. The sensibility which, even in a rude age, seems to have characterized the Scottish maiden, was doubtless nourished by the solemn complexion of the scenery by which she was surrounded, by the sympathies continually awakened for her lover in his career of peril and adventure, and by the facilities afforded her for brooding over her misfortunes in the silence of rural solitude.

To similar physical causes may be principally referred those superstitions which are so liberally diffused over the poetry of Scotland down to the present day. The tendency of wild, solitary districts, darkened with mountains and extensive forests, to raise in the mind ideas of solemn, preternatural awe, has been noticed from the earliest ages. "Where is a lofty and deeply shaded grove," writes Seneca in one of his epistles, "filled with venerable trees, whose interlacing boughs shut out the face of heaven, the grandeur of the wood, the silence of the place, the shade so dense and

uniform, infuse into the breast the notion of a divinity;" and thus the speculative fancy of the ancients, always ready to supply the apparent void of nature, garrisoned each grove, fountain, or grotto with some local and tutelary genius. These sylvan deities, clothed with corporeal figures, and endowed with mortal appetites, were brought near to the level of humanity. But the Christian revelation, which assures us of another world, is the "evidence of things unseen;" and while it dissipates the gross and sensible creations of classic mythology, raises our conceptions to the spiritual and the infinite. In our eager thirst for communication with the world of spirits we naturally imagine it can only be through the medium of spirits like themselves; and in the vulgar creed these apparitions never come from the abodes of the blessed, but from the tomb, where they are supposed to await the period of a final and universal resurrection, and whence they are allowed to "revisit the glimpses of the moon," for penance or some other inscrutable purpose. Hence the gloomy, undefined character of the modern apparition is much more appalling than the sensual and social personifications of antiquity.

The natural phenomena of a wild uncultivated country greatly conspire to promote the illusions of the fancy. The power of clouds to reflect, to distort, and to magnify objects is well known; and on this principle many of the preternatural appearances in the German mountains and the Scottish Highlands, whose lofty summits and unreclaimed valleys are shrouded in clouds and exhalations, have been ingeniously and philosophically explained. The solitary peasant, as the shades of evening close around him, witnesses with dismay the gathering phantoms, and, hurrying home, retails his adventures with due amplification. What is easily believed is easily seen, and the marvellous incident is soon placed beyond dispute by a multitude of testimonies. The appetite, once excited, is keen in detecting other visions and prognostics, which as speedily circulate through the channels of rustic tradition, until in time each glen and solitary heath has its unearthly visitants, each family its omen or boding spectre; and superstition, systematized into a science, is expounded by indoctrinated wizards and gifted seers.

In addition to these fancies, common, though in a less degree, to other nations, the inhabitants of the North have inherited a more material mythology, which has survived the elegant fictions of Greece and Rome, either because it was not deemed of sufficient importance to provoke the arm of the church, or because it was too nearly accommodated to the moral constitution of the people to be thus easily eradicated. The character of a mythology is always intimately connected with that of the scenery and climate in which it is invented. Thus the graceful Nymphs and Naiads of Greece; the Peris of Persia, who are said to live in the colours of the rainbow, and on the odours of flowers; the Fairies of England, who in airy circles " dance their ringlets to the whistling wind," have the frail gossamer forms and delicate functions congenial with the beautiful countries which they inhabit; while the Elves, Bogles, Brownies, and Kelpies, which seem to have legitimately descended, in ancient Highland verse, from the Scandinavian Dvergar, Nisser, &c., are of a stunted and malignant aspect, and are celebrated for nothing better than maiming cattle, bewildering the benighted traveller, and conjuring out the souls of new-born infants. Within the memory of the present generation very well authenticated anecdotes of these ghostly kidnappers have been circulated and greedily credited in the Scottish Highlands. But the sunshine of civilization is rapidly dispelling the lingering mists of superstition. The spirits of darkness love not the cheerful haunts of men; and the bustling activity of an increasing, industrious population allows brief space for the fears or inventions of fancy.

The fierce aspect of the Scottish ballad was mitigated under the general tranquillity which followed the accession of James to the united crowns of England and Scotland; and the northern muse might have caught some of the inspiration which fired her southern sister at this remarkable epoch, had not the fatal prejudices of her sovereign in favour of an English or even a Latin idiom diverted his ancient subjects from the cultivation of their own. As it was, Drummond of Hawthornden, whose melodious and melancholy strains, however, are to be enrolled among English verse, is the most eminent name which adorns the scanty annals of this reign. The civil and religious broils, which, by the sharp concussion they gave to the English intellect during the remainder of this unhappy century, seemed to have forced out every latent spark of genius, served only to discourage the less polished muse of the North. The austerity of the reformers chilled the sweet flow of social song, and the only verse in vogue was a kind of rude satire, sometimes pointed at the licentiousness of the Roman clergy, and sometimes at the formal affectation of the Puritans, but which,

from the coarseness of the execution, and the transitory interest of its topics, has for the most part been consigned to a decent oblivion.

The Revolution in 1688, and the subsequent union of the two kingdoms, by the permanent assurance they gave of civil and religious liberty, and lastly, the establishment of parochial schools about the same period, by that wide diffusion of intelligence among the lower orders which has elevated them above every other European peasantry, had a most sensible influence on the moral and intellectual progress of the nation. Improvements in art and agriculture were introduced; the circle of ideas was expanded, and the feelings liberalized by a free communication with their southern neighbours; and religion, resigning much of her austerity, lent a prudent sanction to the hilarity of social intercourse. Popular poetry naturally reflects the habits and prevailing sentiments of a nation. The ancient notes of the border trumpet were exchanged for the cheerful sounds of rustic revelry; and the sensibility which used to be exhausted on subjects of acute but painful interest, now celebrated the temperate pleasures of domestic happiness, and rational though romantic love.

The rustic glee which had put such mettle into the compositions of James I. and V., those royal poets of the commonalty, as they have been aptly styled, was again renewed; ancient songs, purified from their original vices of sentiment or diction, were revived; new ones were accommodated to ancient melodies; and a revolution was gradually effected in Scottish verse, which experienced little variation during the remainder of the eighteenth century. The existence of a national music is essential to the entire success of lyrical poetry. It may be said, indeed, to give wings to song, which, in spite of its imperfections, is thus borne along, from one extremity of the nation to the other, with a rapidity denied to many a nobler composition.

Thus allied, verse not only represents the present, but the past; and while it invites us to repose or to honourable action, its tones speak of joys which are gone, or wake in us the recollections of ancient glory.

TRUE GREATNESS.

Ambition's goal—the love of praise,
A fever in the mind doth raise;
Renown contemn'd more greatness shows,
Than glory's self, when sought, bestows.
JOSEPH SCALIGER.

MAY.

BY N. P. WILLIS.

Oh, the merry May has pleasant hours,
And dreamily they glide,
As if they floated like the leaves
Upon a silver tide;
The trees are full of crimson buds,
And the woods are full of birds,
And the waters flow to music,
Like a tune with pleasant words.

The verdure of the meadow-land
Is creeping to the hills,
The sweet, blue-bosom'd violets
Are blowing by the rills;
The lilac has a load of balm
For every wind that stirs,
And the larch stands green and beautiful
Amid the sombre firs.

There's perfume upon every wind—
Music in every tree—
Dews for the moisture-loving flowers—
Sweets for the sucking bee:
The sick come forth for the healing South,
The young are gathering flowers;
And life is a tale of poetry,
That is told by golden hours.

It must be a true philosophy,
That the spirit when set free
Still lingers about its olden home,
In the flower and the tree,
For the pulse is stirr'd as with voices heard
In the depth of the shady grove,
And while lonely we stray through the fields away,
The heart seems answering love.

LOST LOVE.

BY JOAQUIN MILLER.

Thatch of palm and a cover of clover,
Breath of balm in a field of brown;
The clouds blew up and the birds flew over,
And I looked upward, but who looked down?

Who was true in the test that tried us?
Who was it mocked? Who now may mourn
The loss of a love that a cross denied us.
With folded hands and a heart forlorn?

God forgive when the fair forget us!
The worth of a smile, the weight of a tear,
Why, who can measure? The fates beset us—
We laugh a moment, we mourn a year.

THE GUINEAMAN.

[Michael Scott, born in Glasgow, 30th October, 1789; died there, 7th November, 1835. Author of two of the most powerful and attractive sea novels which have been yet written, namely *Tom Cringle's Log* and *The Cruise of the Midge*. He was for several years engaged in business in Jamaica, and the numerous visits he was obliged to pay to the various islands of the Spanish Main supplied him with the knowledge of West Indian society and sea life which he afterwards turned to such good account. The stories first appeared in *Blackwood's Magazine*. The following incident occurs during the first cruise of the *Wave*, which was also Tom Cringle's first command. He had on board with him several friends, who, although only guests, thoroughly enter into the spirit of the action with the slaveship. Tom Cringle writes:—]

I expected the breeze would have freshened as the day broke, but I was disappointed; it fell, towards six o'clock, nearly calm. Come, thought I, we may as well go to breakfast; and my guests and I forthwith set down to our morning meal. Soon after, the wind died away altogether—and "out sweeps" was the word; but I soon saw we had no chance with the chase at this game, and as to attacking him (the slaver) with the boats, it was entirely out of the question; neither could I, in the prospect of a battle, afford to murder the people by pulling all day under a roasting sun, against one who could man his sweeps with relays of slaves, without one of his crew putting a finger to them; so I reluctantly laid them in, and there I stood looking at him the whole forenoon, as he gradually drew ahead of us. At length I piped to dinner, and the men having finished theirs, were again on deck; but the calm still continued; and seeing no chance of it freshening, about four in the afternoon we sat down to ours in the cabin. There was little said; my friends, although brave and resolute men, were naturally happy to see the brig creeping away from us, as fighting could only bring them danger; and my own feelings were of that mixed quality, that while I determined to do all I could to bring him to action, it would not have broken my heart had he escaped. We had scarcely finished dinner, however, when the rushing of the water past the run of the little vessel, and the steadiness with which she skimmed along, showed that the light air had freshened.

Presently Tailtackle came down. "The breeze has set down, sir; the strange sail has got it strong to windward, and brings it along with him cheerily."

"Beat to quarters, then, Tailtackle; all hands stand by to shorten sail. How is she standing?"

"Right down for us, sir.

I went on deck, and there was the Guineaman about two miles to windward, evidently cleared for action, with her decks crowded with men, bowling along steadily under her single-reefed topsails.

I saw all clear. Wagtail and Gelid had followed me on deck, and were now busy with their black servants inspecting the muskets. But Bang still remained in the cabin. I went down. He was gobbling his last plantain, and forking up along with it most respectable slices of cheese, when I entered.

I had seen before I left the deck that an action was now unavoidable, and judging from the disparity of force, I had my own doubts as to the issue. I need scarcely say that I was greatly excited. It was my first command: my future standing in the service depended on my conduct *now*—and, God help me, I was all this while a mere lad, not more than twenty-one years old. A strange indescribable feeling had come over me, and an irresistible desire to disburden my mind to the excellent man before me. I sat down.

"Hey day," quoth Bang, as he laid down his coffee-cup; "why, Tom, what ails you? You look deuced pale, my boy."

"Up all night, sir, and bothered all day," said I; "wearied enough I can tell you."

I felt a strong tremor pervade my whole frame at this moment; and I was impelled to speak by some unknown impulse, which I could not account for nor analyze.

"Mr. Bang, you are the only friend whom I could count on in these countries; you know all about me and mine, and, I believe, would willingly do a kind action to my father's son."

"What are you at, Tom, my dear boy? come to the point, man."

"I will. I am distressed beyond measure at having led you and your excellent friends, Wagtail and Gelid, into this danger; but I could not help it, and I have satisfied my conscience on that point; so I have only to entreat that you will stay below, and not unnecessarily expose yourselves. And if I should fall—may I take this liberty, my dear sir," and I involuntarily took his hand—"if I should fall, and *I doubt if I shall ever see the sun set again,* as we are fearfully overmatched——"

Bang struck in—

"Why, if our friend be too big—why not be off then? Pull foot, man, eh?—Havannah under your lee?"

"A thousand reasons against it, my dear sir. I am a young man and a young officer; my character is to *make* in the service—No,

no, it is impossible—an older and more tried hand might have bore up, but I must fight it out. If any stray shot carries me off, my dear sir, will you take"—Mary, I would have said, but I could not pronounce her name for the soul of me—"will you take charge of *her* miniature, and say I died as I have"—a choking lump rose in my throat, and I could not proceed for a second; "and will you send my writing-desk to my poor mother, there are letters in"—the lump grew bigger, the hot tears streamed from my eyes in torrents. I trembled like an aspen leaf, and grasping my excellent friend's hand more firmly, I sunk down on my knees in a passion of tears, and wept like a woman, while I fervently prayed to that great God in whose almighty hand I stood, that I might that day do my duty as an English seaman. Bang knelt by me. Presently the passion was quelled. I rose, and so did he.

"Before you, my dear sir, I am not ashamed to have ——"

"Don't mention it, my good boy, don't mention it; neither of us, as the old general said, will fight a bit the worse."

I looked at him. "Do you then mean to fight?" said I.

"To be sure I do—why not? I have no wife," he did not say he had no children— "Fight? To be sure I do."

"Another gun, sir," said Tailtackle, through the open skylight. Now all was bustle, and we hastened on deck. Our antagonist was a large brig, three hundred tons at the least, a long low vessel, painted black, out and in, and her sides round as an apple, with immensely square yards. She was apparently full of men. The sun was getting low, and she was coming down fast on us, on the verge of the dark blue water of the sea breeze. I could make out ten ports and nine guns of a side. I inwardly prayed they might not be long ones, but I was not a little startled to see through the glass that there were crowds of naked negroes at quarters, and on the forecastle and poop. That she was a contraband Guineaman I had already made up my mind to believe; and that she had some fifty hands of a crew, I also considered likely: but that her captain should have resorted to such a perilous measure, perilous to themselves as well as to us, as arming the captive slaves, was quite unexpected, and not a little alarming, as it evinced his determination to make the most desperate resistance.

Tailtackle was standing beside me at this time, with his jacket off, his cutlass girded on his thigh, and the belt drawn very tight. All the rest of the crew were armed in a similar fashion; the small-arm men with muskets in their hands, and the rest at quarters at the guns; while the pikes were cast loose from the spars round which they had been stopped, with tubs of wadding, and boxes of grape, all ready ranged, and everything clear for action.

"Mr. Tailtackle," said I, "you are gunner here, and should be in the magazine. Cast off that cutlass; it is not your province to lead the boarders." The poor fellow blushed, having, in the excitement of the moment, forgotten that he was anything more than captain of the *Firebrand's* maintop.

"Mr. Timotheus," said Bang, "have you one of these bodkins to spare?"

Timothy laughed. "Certainly, sir; but *you* don't mean to head the boarders, do you?"

"Who knows, now since I have learned to walk on this dancing cork of a craft?" rejoined Aaron with a grim smile, while he pulled off his coat, braced on his cutlass, and tied a large red cotton shawl round his head. He then took off his neckerchief and fastened it round his waist, as tight as he could draw.

"Strange that all men in peril—on the uneasiness, like," said he, "should always gird themselves as tightly as they can."

The slaver was now within musket-shot, when he put his helm to port, with the view of passing under our stern. To prevent being raked, we had to luff up sharp in the wind, and fire a broadside. I noticed the white splinters glance from his black wales; and a sharp yell rung in our ears, followed by a long melancholy howl.

"We have pinned some of the poor blacks," said Tailtackle, who still lingered on the deck; small space for remark, for the slaver again fired his broadside at us, with the same cool precision as before.

"Down with the helm, and let her come round," said I; "that will do—master, run across his stern—out sweeps forward, and keep her there—get the other carronade over to leeward—that is it—now, blaze away while he is becalmed—fire, small-arm men, and take good aim."

We were now right across his stern, with the spanker boom within ten yards of us; and although he worked his two stern-chasers with great determination, and poured whole showers of musketry from his rigging, and poop, and cabin-windows, yet, from the cleverness with which our sweeps were pulled, and the accuracy with which we were kept in our position, right athwart his stern, our fire, both from the cannon and musketry, the former loaded with

round and grape, was telling, I could see, with fearful effect.

Crash—"There, my lads, down goes his maintopmast—pepper him well while they are blinded and confused among the wreck. Fire away—there goes the peak, shot away cleverly, close by the throat. Don't cease firing, although his flag be down—it was none of his doing. . There, my lads, there he has it again; you have shot away the weather foretopsail sheet, and he cannot get from under you."

Two men at this moment lay out on his larboard foreyardarm, apparently with the intention of splicing the sheet, and getting the clew of the foretopsail once more down to the yard; if they had succeeded in this, the vessel would again have fetched way, and drawn out from under our fire. Mr. Bang and Paul Gelid had all this time been firing with murderous precision, from where they had ensconced themselves under the shelter of the larboard bulwark, close to the tafferel, with their three black servants in the cabin loading the six muskets, and little Wagtail, who was no great shot, sitting on the deck, handing them up and down.

"Now, Mr. Bang," cried I, "for the love of Heaven,"—and may Heaven forgive me for the ill-placed exclamation—"mark these two men—down with them!"

Bang turned towards me with all the coolness in the world—"What, those chaps on the end of the long stick?"

"Yes—yes" (I here spoke of the larboard foreyardarm), "yes, down with them."

He lifted his piece as steadily as if he had really been duck-shooting.

"I say, Gelid, my lad, take you the inner-most."

"Ah!" quoth Paul. They fired—and down dropped both men, and squattered for a moment in the water, like wounded waterfowl, and then sank for ever, leaving two small puddles of blood on the surface.

"Now, master," shouted I, "put the helm up and lay him alongside—there—stand by with the grapplings—one round the backstay —the other through the chainplate there—so —you have it." As we ranged under his counter—"Mainchains are your chance, men —boarders, follow me." And in the enthusiasm of the moment I jumped into the slaver's main channel, followed by twenty-eight men. We were in the act of getting over the netting when the enemy rallied, and fired a volley of small arms, which sent four out of the twenty-eight to their account, and wounded three more. We gained the quarterdeck, where the

Spanish captain and about forty of his crew showed a determined front, cutlass and pistol in hand—we charged them—they stood their ground. Tailtackle (who, the moment he heard the boarders called, had jumped out of the magazine, and followed me) at a blow clove the Spanish captain to the chin; the lieutenant, or second in command, was my bird, and I had disabled him by a sabre-cut on the sword-arm, when he drew his pistol, and shot me through the left shoulder. I felt no pain, but a sharp pinch, and then a cold sensation, as if water had been poured down my neck.

Jigmaree was close by me with a boarding-pike, and our fellows were fighting with all the gallantry inherent in British sailors. For a moment the battle was poised in equal scales. At length our antagonist gave way, when about fifteen of the slaves, naked barbarians, who had been ranged with muskets in their hands on the forecastle, suddenly jumped down into the waist with a yell, and came to the rescue of the Spanish part of the crew.

I thought we were lost. Our people, all but Tailtackle, poor Handlead, and Jigmaree, held back. The Spaniards rallied, and fought with renewed courage, and it was now, not for glory, but for dear life, as all retreat was cut off by the parting of the grapplings and warps that had lashed the schooner alongside of the slaver, for the Wave had by this time forged ahead, and lay across the brig's bows, in place of being on our quarter, with her foremast jammed against the slaver's bowsprit, whose spritsail-yard crossed our deck between the masts. We could not therefore retreat to our own vessel if we had wished it, as the Spaniards had possession of the waist and forecastle; all at once, however, a discharge of round and grape crashed through the bridleport of the brig, and swept off three of the black auxiliaries before mentioned, and wounded as many more, and the next moment an unexpected ally appeared on the field. When we boarded, the Wave had been left with only Peter Mangrove; the five dockyard negroes; Pearl, one of the captain's gigs, the handsome black already introduced on the scene; poor little Reefpoint, who was badly hurt; Aaron Bang, Paul Gelid, and Wagtail. But this Pearl without price, at the very moment of time when I thought the game was up, jumped on deck through the bowport, cutlass in hand, followed by the five black carpenters and Peter Mangrove, after whom appeared no less a personage than Aaron Bang himself and the three blackamoor valets, armed with boarding-pikes. Bang flourished his cutlass for an instant.

"Now, Pearl, my darling, shout to them in Coromantee—shout;" and forthwith the black quartermaster sung out, "Coromantee Sheik Cocoloo, kockernony populorum fiz," which, as I afterwards learned, being interpreted, is, "Behold the Sultan Cocoloo, the great ostrich, with a feather in his tail like a palm branch; fight for him, you sons of female dogs." In an instant the black Spanish auxiliaries sided with Pearl, and Bang, and the negroes, and joined in charging the white Spaniards, who were speedily driven down the main hatchway, leaving one-half of their number dead or badly wounded on the blood-slippery deck. But they still made a desperate defence by firing up the hatchway. I hailed them to surrender.

"Zounds!" cried Jigmaree, "there's the clink of hammers; they are knocking off the fetters of the slaves."

"If you let the blacks loose," I sung out in Spanish, "by the Heaven above us, I will blow you up, although I should go with you! Hold your hands, Spaniards! Mind what you do, madmen!"

"On with the hatches, men," shouted Tailtackle.

They had been thrown overboard, or put out of the way, they could nowhere be seen. The firing from below continued.

"Cast loose that carronade there; clap in a canister of grape—so—now run it forward, and fire down the hatchway." It was done, and taking effect amongst the pent-up slaves, such a yell arose—O God! O God!—I never can forget it. Still the maniacs continued firing up the hatchway.

"Load and fire again." My people were now furious, and fought more like incarnate fiends broke loose from hell than human beings.

"Run the gun up to the hatchway once more." They ran the carronade so furiously forward, that the coaming or ledge was split off, and down went the gun, carriage and all, with a crash into the hold. Presently smoke appeared rising up the fore-hatchway.

"They have set fire to the brig; overboard! —regain the schooner, or we shall all be blown into the air like peels of onions!" sung out little Jigmaree.

But where was the Wave? She had broke away, and was now a cable's length ahead, apparently fast leaving us, with Paul Gelid and Wagtail, and poor little Reefpoint, who, badly wounded as he was, had left his hammock, and come on deck in the emergency, making signs of their inability to cut away the halyards;

and the tiller being shot away, the schooner had become utterly unmanageable.

"Up, and let fall the foresail, men—down with the foretack—cheerily now—get way on the brig, and overhaul the *Wave* promptly, or we are lost," cried I. It was done with all the coolness of desperate men. I took the helm, and presently we were once more alongside of our own vessel. Time we were so, for about one hundred and fifty of the slaves, whose shackles had been knocked off, now scrambled up the fore-hatchway, and we had only time to jump overboard when they made a rush aft; and no doubt, exhausted as we were, they would have massacred us on the spot, frantic and furious as they had become from the murderous fire of grape that had been directed down the hatchway.

But the fire was quicker than they. The smouldering smoke, that was rising like a pillar of cloud from the fore-hatchway, was now streaked with tongues of red flame, which, licking the masts and spars, ran up and caught the sails and rigging. In an instant the fire spread to every part of the gear aloft, while the other element, the sea, was also striving for the mastery in the destruction of the doomed vessel; for our shot, or the fall of the carronade into the hold, had started some of the bottom planks, and she was fast settling down by the head. We could hear the water rushing in like a mill-stream. The fire increased—her guns went off as they became heated—she gave a sudden heel—and while five hundred human beings, pent up in her noisome hold, split the heavens with their piercing death-yells, down she went with a heavy lurch, head foremost, right in the wake of the setting sun, whose level rays made the thick dun wreaths that burst from her as she disappeared glow with the hue of the amethyst; and while the whirling clouds, gilded by his dying radiance, curled up into the blue sky in rolling masses, growing thinner and thinner, until they vanished away, even like the wreck whereout they arose,—and the circling eddies created by her sinking no longer sparkled and flashed in the red light,—and the stilled waters where she had gone down, as if oil had been cast on them, were spread out like polished silver, shining like a mirror, while all around was dark blue ripple,—a puff of fat black smoke, denser than any we had yet seen, suddenly emerged, with a loud gurgling noise, from out the deep bosom of the calmed sea, and rose like a balloon, rolling slowly upwards, until it reached a little way above our mast-heads, where it melted and spread out into a dark pall, that overhung the scene of death, as if the incense of such a horrible and polluted sacrifice could not ascend into the pure heaven, but had been again crushed back upon our devoted heads, as a palpable manifestation of the wrath of *Him* who hath said—"Thou shalt not kill."

For a few moments all was silent as the grave, and I felt as if the air had become too thick for breathing, while I looked up like another Cain.

Presently, about one hundred and fifty of the slaves, *men, women,* and *children,* who had been drawn down by the vortex, rose amidst numberless pieces of smoking wreck to the surface of the sea; the strongest yelling like fiends in their despair, while the weaker, the women, and the helpless gasping little ones, were choking, and gurgling, and sinking all around. Yea, the small thin expiring cry of the innocent sucking infant torn from its sinking mother's breast, as she held it for a brief moment above the waters, which had already for ever closed over herself, was there. But we could not perceive one single individual of her white crew; like desperate men, they had all gone down with the brig. We picked up about one half of the miserable Africans, and —my pen trembles as I write it—fell necessity compelled us to fire on the remainder, as it was utterly impossible for us to take them on board. Oh that I could erase such a scene for ever from my memory! One incident I cannot help relating. We had saved a woman, a handsome, clear-skinned girl of about sixteen years of age. She was very faint when we got her in, and was lying with her head over a port-sill, when a strong athletic young negro swam to the part of the schooner where she was. She held down her hand to him; he was in the act of grasping it, when he was shot through the heart from above. She instantly jumped overboard, and, clasping him in her arms, they sank, and disappeared together. "Oh, woman, whatever may be the colour of your skin, your heart is of one only!" said Aaron.

Soon all was quiet; a wounded black here and there was shrieking in his great agony, and struggling for a moment before he sank into his watery grave for ever; a few pieces of wreck were floating and sparkling on the surface of the deep in the blood-red sunbeams, which streamed in a flood of glorious light on the bloody deck, shattered hull, and torn sails and rigging of the *Wave,* and on the dead bodies and mangled limbs of those who had fallen; while some heavy scattering drops of rain fell sparkling from a passing cloud, as if

Nature had wept in pity over the dismal scene; or as if they had been blessed tears, shed by an angel in his heavenward course, as he hovered for a moment and looked down in pity on the fantastic tricks played by the worm of a day—by weak man, in his little moment of power and ferocity. I said something—ill and hastily. Aaron was close beside me, sitting on a carronade slide, while the surgeon was dressing a pike wound in his neck. He looked up solemnly in my face, and then pointed to the blessed luminary, that was now sinking in the sea and blazing up into the resplendent heavens—"Cringle, for shame—for shame—your impatience is blasphemous. Remember this morning—and thank *Him*"—here he looked up and crossed himself—"thank Him who, while he has called poor Mr. Handlead and so many brave fellows to their last awful reckoning, has mercifully brought *us* to the end of this fearful day;—oh, thank Him, Tom, *that you have seen the sun set once more!*"

MY NATIVE VALE.

BY ALLAN CUNNINGHAM.

My native vale, my native vale! In visions and in dreams
I see your towers and trees, and hear the music of your streams;
I feel the fragrance of the thorn where lovers loved to meet;
I walk upon thy hills and see thee slumbering at their feet.
In every knoll I see a friend, in every tree a brother,
And clasp thy breast, as I would clasp the bosom of my mother.

There stands the tottering tower I climb'd, and won the falcon's brood;
There flows the stream I've trysted through, when it was wild in flood.
There is the fairy glen—the pools I mused in youth among,
The very nook where first I pour'd forth unconsider'd song:
And stood with gladness in my heart, and bright hope on my brow—
Ah! I had other visions then than I have visions now.

I went into my native vale—alas! what did I see?
At every door strange faces, where glad looks once welcomed me;
The sunshine faded on the hills, the music left the brooks,
The song of its unnumber'd larks was as the voice of rooks;
The plough had been in all my haunts, the axe had touch'd the grove;
And death had follow'd—there was nought remain'd for me to love.

My native vale, farewell! farewell!—my father, on thy hearth
The light extinguish'd—and thy roof no longer rings with mirth;
There sits a stranger on thy chair; and they are dead and gone
Who charm'd my early life—all—all sleep 'neath the churchyard stone:
There's nought moves save yon red round moon, nought lives but that pure river,
That lived when I was young—all—all are gone, and gone for ever!

Keir with thy pasture mountains green, Drumlanrig with thy towers,
Curse with thy lily banks and braes, and Blackwood with thy bowers,
And fair Dalswinton with thy walks of scented thorn and holly,
Where some had toil'd the day, and shared the night 'tween sense and folly,--
Farewell, farewell, your flowers will glad the bird, and feed the bee,
And charm ten thousand hearts, although no more they'll gladden me.

I stood within my native vales, fast by the river brink,
And saw the long and yellow corn 'neath shining sickles sink;
I heard the fair-hair'd maidens wake songs of thy latter day;
And joy'd to see the bandsmen smile, albeit their locks were gray:
I thought on mine own musings—when men shook their tresses hoary,
And said, "Alas!" and named my name, "thou art no heir of glory!"

MELROSE ABBEY.

BY ROBERT CHAMBERS.

Upon the southern bank of the Tweed stand the ruins of the celebrated abbey of Melrose, surrounded by the little village of the same name. The ruins of this ancient monastery, or rather of the church connected with it (for the domestic buildings are entirely gone), afford the finest specimen of Gothic architecture and Gothic sculpture of which this country can boast. By singular good fortune Melrose is also one of the most entire, as it is the most beautiful, of all the ecclesiastical ruins scattered throughout this Reformed land. To say that it is beautiful is to say nothing. It is exquisitely—splendidly lovely. It is an object possessed of infinite grace and unmeasurable charm; it is fine in its general aspect and in its minutest details; it is a study—a glory. The beauty of Melrose, however, is not a healthful ordinary beauty:

> So coldly sweet, so deadly fair,
> We start, for soul is wanting there.
> *Its* is the loveliness in death,
> That parts not quite with parting breath;
> But beauty with that fearful bloom,
> That hue which haunts it to the tomb.

Its is not the beauty of summer, but the melancholy grace of autumn ; not the beauty of a blooming bride, but that of a pining and death-stricken maiden. It is not that this is a thing of perfect splendour that we admire it, but because it is a fragment which only represents or shadows forth a matchless whole which *has been*, and whose merits we are, from this shattered specimen, completely disposed to allow.

Melrose Abbey was first built by David I. in the year 1136, dedicated to St. Mary, and devoted to the use of a body of Cistercian monks. The church, which alone remains, measures 287 feet in length, and 157 at the greatest breadth. It is built in the most ornate style of the Gothic architecture, and therefore decorated with an infinite variety of sculptures, most of which are exquisitely fine. While the western extremity of the building is entirely ruined and removed, the eastern and more important parts are fortunately in a state of tolerable preservation; in particular, the oriel window, and that which surmounts the south door, both alike admirable, are almost entire. It is also matter of great thankfulness that a good many of the shapely pillars for the sup-

port of the roof are still extant. It is to these objects that the attention of travellers is chiefly directed.

It is not to the zeal of Reformers alone that the desecration of our best old religious buildings is to be attributed. The enthusiasm of individuals in more recent times has sometimes done that which the Reformers left undone ; as is testified by a notorious circumstance told by the person who shows Melrose. On the eastern window of the church there were formerly thirteen effigies, supposed to represent our Saviour and his apostles.[1] These, harmless and beautiful as they were, happened to provoke the wrath of a canting weaver in Gattonside, who, in a moment of inspired zeal, went up one night by means of a ladder, and with a hammer and chisel knocked off the heads and limbs of the figures. Next morning he made no scruple to publish the transaction, observing with a great deal of exultation to every person whom he met, that he had "fairly stumpet thae vile paipist dirt *now!*" The people sometimes catch up a remarkable word when uttered on a remarkable occasion by one of their number, and turn the utterer into ridicule by attaching it to him as a nickname ; and it is some consolation to think that this monster was therefore treated with the sobriquet of "Stumpie," and of course carried it about with him to his grave.

It would require a distinct volume to do justice to the infinite details of Melrose Abbey; for the whole is built in a style of such elaborate ornament, that almost every foot-breadth has its beauty, and every beauty is worthy of notice. I shall content myself with merely adding the description which Sir Walter Scott has given of it in his *Lay of the Last Minstrel:—*

> If thou wouldst view fair Melrose aright,
> Go visit it by the pale moonlight;
> For the gay beams of lightsome day
> Gild but to flout the ruins gray.
> When the broken arches are dark in night,
> And each shafted oriel glimmers white;
> When the cold light's uncertain shower
> Streams on the ruin'd central tower;
> When buttress and buttress, alternately,
> Seem framed of ebon and ivory;
> When silver edges the imagery,
> And the scrolls that teach thee to live and die ;
> When distant Tweed is heard to rave,
> And the howlet to hoot o'er the dead man's grave,

---

[1] In the drawing of Melrose Abbey in Slezer's *Theatrum Scotiæ*, the niches are all filled with statues. Slezer took his drawings early in the reign of King William.

Then go—but go alone the while—
Then view St. David's ruined pile;
And, home returning, soothly swear,
Was never scene so sad and fair.

. . . . . .

By a steel-clench'd postern door,
They enter'd now the chancel tall;
The darken'd roof rose high aloof
On pillars, lofty, light, and small;
The key-stone, that lock'd each ribbed aisle,
Was a fleur-de-lys or a quatre-feuille;
The corbells[1] were carved grotesque and grim;
And the pillars, with cluster'd shafts so trim,
With base and capital furnish'd around,
Seem'd bundles of lances which garlands had bound.

. . . .

The moon on the east oriel shone,
Through slender shafts of shapely stone,
By foliaged tracery combined;
Thou wouldst have thought some fairy's hand
'Twixt poplars straight the osier wand
In many a freakish knot had twined;
Then framed a spell, when the work was done,
And changed the willow-wreaths to stone.

At the time of the Reformation the inmates of this abbey shared in the general reproach of sensuality and irregularity thrown upon the Romish churchmen, as is testified by a ballad then popular, which contained the following verse:—

The monks of Melrose made gude kail
On Fridays, when they fasted;
Nor wanted they gude beef and ale
As lang as their neighbours' lasted.

Whatever might be the sensuality of the monks of Melrose, it is certain that some of their power was sometimes matter of real inconvenience to the public. The abbot had such an extensive jurisdiction, and the privileges of girth and sanctuary interfered so much with the execution of justice, that James V. is said to have once acted as baron baillie, in order to punish those malefactors in the character of the abbot's deputy, whom his own sovereign power, and that of the laws, were unable to reach otherwise. But whatever may be thought of this, there can be no doubt that the protection extended to criminals by the religious was a true blessing in the main, at a time when the law could neither inflict punishment nor protect a criminal from the rash and unmeasured retribution of those whom he had offended.

After the Reformation a brother of the Earl of Morton became commendator of the abbey,

and out of the ruins built himself a house, which may still be seen about fifty yards to the north-east of the church. The regality soon after passed into the hands of Lord Binning, an eminent lawyer, ancestor to the Earl of Haddington: and about the middle of last century the whole became the property of the Buccleuch family.[2]

——————

THE RIVER.

[Caroline Anne Bowles (Mrs. Southey), born at Buckland, Hants, 6th December, 1787; died 20th July, 1854. She was a daughter of Captain Charles Bowles, and her poetical gifts were early manifested, although for many years she continued to publish her poems anonymously. In 1839 she married Robert Southey, the poet-laureate. Her principal works are: *Ellen Fitzarthur*, a metrical tale; *The Widow's Tale*, and other Poems; *Solitary Hours; Chapters on Churchyards* (her only prose work); *The Birthday; Tales of the Factories*, &c. "Mrs. Southey is the Cowper of our modern poetesses. She has much of that great writer's humour, fondness for rural life, melancholy pathos, and moral satire."—*H. N. Coleridge.*]

River! River! little River!
  Bright you sparkle on your way,
O'er the yellow pebbles dancing,
Through the flowers and foliage glancing,
  Like a child at play.

River! River! swelling River!
  On you rush o'er rough and smooth—
Louder, faster, brawling, leaping
Over rocks, by rose-banks sweeping,
  Like impetuous youth.

River! River! brimming River!
  Broad and deep and *still* as Time,
Seeming *still*—yet still in motion,
Tending onward to the ocean,
  Just like mortal prime.

River! River! rapid River!
  Swifter now you slip away;
Swift and silent as an arrow,
Through a channel dark and narrow,
  Like life's closing day.

River! River! headlong River!
  Down you dash into the sea;
Sea, that line hath never sounded,
Sea, that voyage hath never rounded,
  Like eternity.

———————————————

[1] Corbells, the projections from which the arches spring, usually cut in a fantastic face or mask.

VOL. V.

[2] The late George M. Kemp, the celebrated architect of the Scott Monument in Edinburgh, made a drawing of Melrose Abbey, showing the edifice as it is supposed to have appeared when in its perfect condition. This drawing (now in possession of the publishers of the *Casquet*) represents a building of rare beauty.

TOBY WILT.

[Dr. Moritz Erdmann Engel, born at Plauen, 1764;
died there 1836. He was professor of philosophy and
town's deacon of his native place, and was the author
of *Moral Tales; Mottoes for Youth,* &c. &c.]

One of the chief ornaments of a little provincial town, his native place, flourished Mr.
Toby Wilt. At no period had he evinced a
desire to travel, and never, on any occasion,
exceeded his prescribed limits round the adjacent hamlets. In spite of this, however he
knew more of the world than many who had
travelled a great deal farther, and some who
had expended the best part of their fortune on
a fashionable trip to Paris or Italy. He was
possessed of a rich fund of little anecdotes of
the most useful class, which he had obtained
by observation, and retailed for his own and
his friends' edification. And though these
showed no great stretch of genius or invention,
they possessed considerable practical merit, and
were, for the most part, remarkable for coming
before company coupled together, always two
and two.

Among his acquaintance was a careful young
gentleman of the name of Till, a great admirer
of Mr. Toby Wilt for his known prudence and
stock of observations. On one occasion he
ventured to express his high opinion of them,
to which his old friend replied in his stuttering
style, " Ha! hem?—what, do you indeed think
me such a wiseacre, then?"

" Why, all the world says so, Mr. Wilt; and
I should be glad to become your pupil."

" Would you so, young man? Nothing more
easy. If you really wish to be a prudent
youth, in fact, you have only to study the
conduct and deportment of fools."

" In what manner do you mean?"

" What manner! by trying to act differently,
to be sure."

" May I beg an anecdote, or example, for
the sake of illustration?"

" I believe I can accommodate you with one,
Mr. Till. When I was a young man, there
resided in this town a Mr. Veit, an old
mathematician, rather a meagre and morose
sort of personage. I used often to see him
walking about, muttering to himself as he
went along, and never stopping to salute any
of his neighbours and acquaintance; much
less would he look them in the face and converse with them; being always too earnestly
engaged in solving the problem of his own
perfections. Now what do you suppose, Mr.

Till, that people were in the habit of saying
of him?"

" Most probably that he was a very shrewd,
wise old gentleman," said Mr. Till.

" No; you are somewhat on the wrong side;
they called him an old fool. So, so! I used
to think within myself—for this sort of title,
however general, was not at all to my taste—
I must take care how I imitate my old friend
Mr. Veit. I see that will never do; one must
not appear to be too full of one's self. Perhaps
it is not well-bred, at all events, to go muttering with one's self; I see we must be more
sociable, and talk a little to our neighbours.
Let me hear your notion on the subject, Mr.
Till; did I judge rightly?"

" Oh, indisputably; I think you were in the
right."

" Nay, I am not so sure of that; not exactly
so, as you will find. For we had another
genius, a finical kind of personage, and a
dancing-master, the very converse of the old
postulating mathematician; and yet he did
not please, though he used to stare in everybody's face as he skipped along. He was glad
to talk to every one who would listen to him,
as long as their patience lasted. Well, Mr.
Till, and what do you suppose people used to
say of *him?*"

" Most likely they would call him a wild,
merry sort of fellow; somewhat of a bore
withal."

" There you are not so very wide of the
mark, Mr. Till; for they called him a fool.
You see he won the same title by a very opposite kind of merit. Here's for us! I thought
to myself; this is odd enough. What must
one do? how in the world must one contrive
to win the reputation of a wise man? It is
plain one must take neither Mr. Veit nor Mr.
Slight for our model. No: first of all, Mr. Till,
you must look persons full in the face, and salute them like the dancing-master, and then you
must have your eyes upon yourself, and reflect
seriously, talk with your neighbours, like
Mr. Slight, and think of your own affairs
afterwards, like Mr. Veit. That was my mode
of arguing, Mr. Till. I compounded the gentleman, sir: people called me a prudent, long-
headed fellow; and this is the whole of the
mystery."

On another occasion our prudent citizen
received a visit from a young merchant of the
name of Flau. He, too, came to consult;
and, after making some wry faces, he began
to lament the extent of his losses and misfortunes.

" Well," replied old Wilt, giving him a tap

on the shoulder, "and what does all this amount to?"

"You must be on the alert, sir, and pursue fortune more diligently. She is a shy bird; and you must be on the look-out like a sportsman."

"So I have, my dear sir, this long time past, but all to no purpose. One unlucky blow followed another, till I was fairly tripped up by the heels. For the future, I shall fold my arms, and rest quietly at home."

"In that you are wrong again, young gentleman; you must be on the look-out, I tell you; you need only to have a care how you carry your head."

"How I carry my head!" repeated Mr. Flau; "what do you mean, Mr. Wilt, by that?"

"Only what I say; you must have a care how you carry your head, and the rest will follow of course. Let me explain how. When my left-hand neighbour was employed in building his new house, the whole street was paved with bricks and beams and rubbish, not very pleasant to pass over. Now one day, who should happen to be going that way but our worthy mayor Mr. Trick, then a young fashionable alderman. He always carried his head high, and thus he came skipping along, with his arms dangling by his side, and his nose elevated towards the clouds; yet the next moment he found himself sprawling upon the ground; he had contrived to trip up his own heels, to break one of his legs, and obtain the advantage of limping to the end of his days, as you may often see. Do you take? do you comprehend me, Mr. Flau?"

"Perhaps you allude to the old proverb, 'Take heed not to carry your head too high.'"

"To be sure, but you must likewise contrive not to carry it too low; faults on both sides! If you have borne it too high, don't bear it now too low; you comprehend me? and you will do yet.

"Not long afterwards Mr. Schale, the poet, was passing the same dangerous way, Mr. Flau. He was, perhaps, spouting verses, or brooding over his *res angustæ domi*—I know not which; but he came jogging forwards with a woeful aspect, 'eyes bent on earth,' and a stooping, slouching gait, as if he would be glad to lower himself into the ground, sir. Well! he walked over one of the ropes; smack it went, and one of the great beams came tumbling about his ears from the scaffolding above. But he was too miserable a dog to be killed; he unluckily escaped; but was so terrified and nervous, poor devil, with the shock, that he fainted away,

fell sick, and was confined to his garret for several weeks.

"Do you comprehend my meaning yet, Mr. Flau? How would you carry your head when you passed?"

"I! I would keep it in just equilibrium, to be sure."

"True; we must not cast our eye too ambitiously towards the clouds, nor fix it too demurely upon the ground. Whether we look above, around, or before us, Mr. Flau, let us do it in a calm, becoming sort of manner, and then we shall get on in the world, and no accidents will be likely to befall us. Let us preserve our equanimity: you comprehend me? Good morning, Mr. Flau."

On a third occasion a certain Mr. Wills waited upon his friend Mr. Wilt, for the purpose of borrowing a sum of money to complete some little speculation he had in hand.

"It is quite a prudent step; very sure," he said to old Mr. Wilt, "though I am sensible it is not one of your lucrative speculations; but, as it happens to come very *apropos*, I should like to turn it to account, and make the most of it."

Old Wilt did not much relish this style of salutation, and seeing whither it would lead—

"Pray, my dear Mr. Wills," inquired he, "how much money, do you think, will serve your turn?"

"It is nothing much of a sum, a mere trifle; some hundred dollars will suffice."

"So! if it be no more, I will directly comply with your request. Indeed, to show how much I have your interest at heart, I will also present you with something else, which, between ourselves, is worth more than a thousand dollars."

"Ah! pray explain yourself, my dear Mr. Wilt."

"Nay! it is only a short story; but it will serve our turn. In my younger days, I had rather an eccentric kind of man for my neighbour, a Mr. Grell. He had continually a certain cant phrase at his tongue's end, which at last proved his ruin."

"You surprise me! I should like to know it."

"You shall. When any of his acquaintance used casually to accost him, observing, 'Well, Grell, how does business go on; how much did you clear by the last bargain?' 'Pshaw!' he would say, 'a mere trifle—some fifty dollars or so, but what of that?' Then again when he was asked: 'Well, Grell, how much are you minus by the last bankruptcy?' 'Pshaw!' he would answer, 'it is not worth speaking of; a mere trifle, some five per cent.' Now, though

Grell was a warm man in his day, I can assure you, this cursed foolish phrase of his brought him to ruin. He was at length compelled to decamp, sir, bag and baggage."

"What was the sum, Mr. Wills, which you stated?"

"I think I requested the loan of one hundred dollars."

"Exactly so; but my memory is growing treacherous. Well, Mr. Wills, but I had another neighbour, one Mr. Tomms, a corn-dealer. By means of another sort of saying did that man build the fine mansion you see yonder, with all its offices and warehouses to boot, sir. What say you?"

"I say it is very strange indeed, Mr. Wilt: I have a great curiosity to hear this second phrase."

"You shall, Mr. Wills. Why, when his friends accosted him, 'Well, Mr. Tomms, how does business proceed? what cleared you by your last concern?' 'A good round sum —a hundred, that I did!' was his invariable answer, at the same time you might see that he was in high glee. When they perceived on the other hand that he was low, very low in spirits, they would inquire: 'What is the matter, Mr. Tomms? how much have you lost?' 'No joke indeed! a good round sum; some fifty dollars, I assure you.' Now this man began his career with a very small capital; but, as I told you before, he has built that large house with all its offices, I say, and warehouses round it. Now, Mr. Wills, which of these two phrases seems best suited to your taste?"

"Why the last of them, Mr. Wilt, of course."

"Yet," replied old Wilt, "this Mr. Tomms does not quite suit me. He had the knack of saying a good round sum, to be sure, even when he was paying his poor-rates or his taxes. Then, I think, he ought to have employed, like a humane and loyal man, the saying of my other neighbour—'a mere trifle, nothing worth speaking of.' The truth is, Mr. Wills, that as they were both my near neighbours, I carefully preserved both their phrases, and apply them according to the circumstances of time and place; sometimes speaking like Mr. Grell, and at others like Mr. Tomms."

"Not so with me," cried Mr. Wills; "I admire Mr. Tomms' phrase; I do from my soul, sir."

"What was your demand—the sum you have occasion for, Mr. Wills?"

"A good round sum of money—one hundred dollars: no trifle, my dear Mr. Wilt!"

"There you talk like a man of sense—a very prudent man, Mr. Wills: you have really

learned your monied catechism very well. Your answer was quite correct. Had you come to request really only a small trifle, I might perhaps have listened to you; but, as you observe it is a good round sum, allow me to pause. I wish you a good morning, Mr. Wills."—But, having thus amused himself, old Mr. Wilt lent him the sum of money.

THE HOURS.

BY THOMAS ATKINSON.

Hours—minutes—moments are the smaller coin
That make the sum of even the richest life:
But yet there are no misers of their hoards,
Nor usance reckoned in the mart upon them;
Still they are priceless !—

Nay, Pallet, paint not thus the hours,—
Young urchins, weaving wreaths of flowers;
Hiding in the buds of roses,
Where the folding pink-leaf closes,
Peeping from the sunflower's stem,
Or a beauty's garment hem !
No!—rather, Limner, make them lurk,
Busy at their blanching work,
Withering wrinkles in the cheek,—
Every hour before, more sleek;—
In the dimples—'neath the lid
Of the eye;—or show them slid
Sly among the auburn tresses,
Like a falcon bound with jesses,
Turning them to silvery gray;
Scattering snow tints in their play !
Oh ! the hours are crabbed creatures,
Still at war with beauty's features !—
                              —The Chameleon.

WITHIN AND WITHOUT.

Poor soul, the centre of my sinful earth,
Fool'd by those rebel powers that thee array,
Why dost thou pine within, and suffer dearth,
Painting thy outward walls so costly gay?
Why so large cost, having so short a lease,
Dost thou upon thy fading mansion spend?
Shall worms, inheritors of this excess,
Eat up thy charge? Is this thy body's end?
Then, soul, live thou upon thy servant's loss,
And let that pine to aggravate thy store;
Buy terms divine in selling hours of dross;
Within be fed, without be rich no more:
    So shalt thou feed on death, that feeds on men.
    And, death once dead, there's no more dying then.
                              SHAKSPEARE.

GERMAN LITERATURE.

[Thomas Carlyle, born at Ecclefechan, Dumfries shire, 1795. Historian, biographer, and essayist. He studied at the Edinburgh University with a view to the ministry, but afterwards resolved to devote himself to literature. In 1823 he contributed articles upon "Montesquieu," "Montaigne," "Nelson," and the "Two Pitts" to Brewster's *Edinburgh Encyclopædia*, and various critical papers to the *Edinburgh Review*. These were soon followed by a translation of *Legendre's Geometry* with an "Essay on Proportion," a translation of Goethe's *Wilhelm Meister*, and the *Life of Schiller*. In the course of years—years of earnest labour, which have had an important influence upon modern thought, although the influence was at first somewhat slow of growth—Mr Carlyle produced: *Sartor Resartus*, the Life and Opinions of Herr Teufelsdröckh; *The French Revolution* ("No work of greater genius, either historical or poetical, has been produced in this country for many years"—*Westminster Review*); *Chartism; Hero Worship; Oliver Cromwell's Letters and Speeches; Latter-day Pamphlets; Past and Present; Life of John Stirling; Life of Frederick the Great;* and a collection in seven volumes of his *Critical and Miscellaneous Essays*.[1] One of the many services Mr. Carlyle has rendered to the present century has been the revelation of the importance and value of German literature.]

Taste, if it mean anything but a paltry connoisseurship, must mean a general suscep tibility to truth and nobleness; a sense to discern, and a heart to love and reverence all beauty, order, goodness, wheresoever or in whatsoever forms and accompaniments they are to be seen. This surely implies, as its chief condition, not any given external rank or situation, but a finely-gifted mind, purified into harmony with itself, into keenness and justness of vision; above all, kindled into love and generous admiration. Is culture of this sort found exclusively among the higher ranks? We believe it proceeds less from without than within, in every rank. The charms of Nature, the majesty of Man, the infinite loveliness of Truth and Virtue, are not hidden from the eye of the poor; but from the eye of the vain, the corrupted and self-seeking, be he poor or rich. In old ages, the humble Minstrel, a mendicant, and lord of nothing but his harp and his own free soul, had intimations of those glories, while to the proud Baron in his barbaric halls they were unknown. Nor is there still any aristocratic monopoly of judgment more than of genius: for as to that *Science of Negation* which is taught peculiarly by men of professed elegance, we confess we hold it rather cheap. It is a necessary, but decidedly a subordinate

accomplishment; nay, if it be rated at the highest, it becomes a ruinous vice. This is an old truth; yet ever needing new application and enforcement. Let us know what to love, and we shall know also what to reject; what to affirm, and we shall know also what to deny: but it is dangerous to *begin* with denial, and fatal to end with it. To deny is easy; nothing is sooner learned or more generally practised: as matters go, we need no man of polish to teach it; but rather, if possible, a hundred men of wisdom to show us its limits, and teach us its reverse.

Such is our hypothesis of the case; how stands it with the facts? Are the fineness and truth of sense manifested by the artist found, in most instances, to be proportionate to his wealth and elevation of acquaintance? Are they found to have any perceptible relation either with the one or the other? We imagine not. Whose taste in painting, for instance, is truer and finer than Claude Lorraine's? And was not he a poor colour-grinder; outwardly the meanest of menials? Where, again, we might ask, lay Shakspeare's rent-roll; and what generous peer took him by the hand and unfolded to him the "open secret" of the Universe; teaching him that this was beautiful, and that not so? Was he not a peasant by birth, and by fortune something lower; and was it not thought much, even in the height of his reputation, that Southampton allowed him equal patronage with the zanies, jugglers, and bearwards of the time? Yet compare his taste, even as it respects the negative side of things; for, in regard to the positive and far higher side, it admits no comparison with any other mortal's,—compare it, for instance, with the taste of Beaumont and Fletcher, his contemporaries, men of rank and education, and of fine genius like himself. Tried even by the nice, fastidious, and in great part false and artificial delicacy of modern times, how stands it with the two parties; with the gay triumphant men of fashion, and the poor vagrant linkboy? Does the latter sin against, we shall not say taste, but etiquette, as the former do? For one line, for one word, which some Chesterfield might wish blotted from the first, are there not in the others whole pages and scenes which, with palpitating heart, he would hurry into deepest night? This too, observe, respects not their genius, but their culture; not their appropriation of beauties, but their rejection of deformities, by supposition the grand and peculiar result of high breeding! Surely, in such instances, even that humble supposition is ill borne out.

---

[1] Chapman & Hall publish various editions of these works: the "People's Edition" is admirable in every respect.

The truth of the matter seems to be, that with the culture of a genuine poet, thinker or other artist, the influence of rank has no exclusive or even special concern. For men of action, for senators, public speakers, political writers, the case may be different; but of such we speak not at present. Neither do we speak of imitators, and the crowd of mediocre men, to whom fashionable life sometimes gives an external inoffensiveness, often compensated by a frigid malignity of character. We speak of men who, from amid the perplexed and conflicting elements of their everyday existence, are to form themselves into harmony and wisdom, and show forth the same wisdom to others that exist along with them. To such a man, high life, as it is called, will be a province of human life, but nothing more. He will study to deal with it as he deals with all forms of mortal being; to do it justice, and to draw instruction from it: but his light will come from a loftier region, or he wanders for ever in darkness; dwindles into a man of *vers de société*, or attains at best to be a Walpole or a Caylus. Still less can we think that he is to be viewed as a hireling; that his excellence will be regulated by his pay. "Sufficiently provided for from within, he has need of little from without;" food and raiment, and an unviolated home, will be given him in the rudest land; and with these, while the kind earth is round him, and the everlasting heaven is over him, the world has little more that it can give. Is he poor? So also were Homer and Socrates; so was Samuel Johnson; so was John Milton. Shall we reproach him with his poverty, and infer that, because he is poor, he must likewise be worthless? God forbid that the time should ever come when he too shall esteem riches the synonym of good! The spirit of Mammon has a wide empire; but it cannot, and must not, be worshipped in the Holy of Holies. Nay, does not the heart of every genuine disciple of literature, however mean his sphere, instinctively deny this principle, as applicable either to himself or another? Is it not rather true, as D'Alembert has said, that for every man of letters, who deserves that name, the motto and the watchword will be FREEDOM, TRUTH, and even this same POVERTY; that if he fear the last, the two first can never be made sure to him?

We have stated these things, to bring the question somewhat nearer its real basis; not for the sake of the Germans, who nowise need the admission of them. The German authors are not poor; neither are they excluded from association with the wealthy and well-born.

On the contrary, we scruple not to say that in both these respects they are considerably better situated than our own. Their booksellers, it is true, cannot pay as ours do; yet, there as here, a man lives by his writings; and, to compare *Jördens* with *Johnson* and *D'Israeli*, somewhat better there than here. No case like our own noble Otway's has met us in their biographies; Boyces and Chattertons are much rarer in German than in English history. But farther, and what is far more important: From the number of universities, libraries, collections of art, museums, and other literary or scientific institutions of a public or private nature, we question whether the chance which a meritorious man of letters has before him, of obtaining some permanent appointment, some independent civic existence, is not a hundred to one in favour of the German, compared with the Englishman. This is a weighty item, and indeed the weightiest of all; for it will be granted that, for the votary of literature, the relation of entire dependence on the merchants of literature is, at best, and however liberal the terms, a highly questionable one. It tempts him daily and hourly to sink from an artist into a manufacturer; nay, so precarious, fluctuating, and everyway unsatisfactory must his civic and economic concerns become, that too many of his class cannot even attain the praise of common honesty as manufacturers. There is, no doubt, a spirit of martyrdom, as we have asserted, which can sustain this too: but few indeed have the spirit of martyrs; and that state of matters is the safest which requires it least. The German authors, moreover, to their credit be it spoken, seem to set less store by wealth than many of ours. There have been prudent, quiet men among them, who actually appeared not to want more wealth; whom wealth could not tempt either to this hand or that, from their preappointed aims. Neither must we think so hardly of the German nobility as to believe them insensible to genius, or of opinion that a patent from the Lion King is so superior to "a patent direct from Almighty God." A fair proportion of the German authors are themselves men of rank: we mention only, as of our own time, and notable in other respects, the two Stolbergs and Novalis. Let us not be unjust to this class of persons. It is a poor error to figure them as wrapt up in ceremonial stateliness, avoiding the most gifted man of a lower station; and, for their own supercilious triviality, themselves avoided by all truly gifted men. On the whole, we should change our notion of the German nobleman: that ancient, thirsty, thick-headed, sixteen-quartered Baron, who still hovers in our minds, never did exist in such perfection, and is now as extinct as our own Squire Western. His descendant is a man of other culture, other aims and other habits. We question whether there is an aristocracy in Europe which, taken as a whole, both in a public and private capacity, more honours art and literature, and does more both in public and private to encourage them. Excluded from society! What, we would ask, was Wieland's, Schiller's, Herder's, Johannes Müller's society? Has not Goethe, by birth a Frankfort burgher, been, since his twenty-sixth year, the companion, not of nobles but of princes, and for half his life a minister of state? And is not this man, unrivalled in so many far deeper qualities, known also and felt to be unrivalled in nobleness of breeding and bearing; fit not to learn of princes in this respect, but by the example of his daily life to teach them?

We hear much of the munificent spirit displayed among the better classes in England; their high estimation of the arts, and generous patronage of the artist. We rejoice to hear it; we hope it is true, and will become truer and truer. We hope that a great change has taken place among these classes since the time when Bishop Burnet could write of them, "They are for the most part the *worst* instructed and the *least* knowing of any of their rank I ever went among!" Nevertheless, let us arrogate to ourselves no exclusive praise in this particular. Other nations can appreciate the arts, and cherish their cultivators, as well as we. Nay, while learning from us in many other matters, we suspect the Germans might even teach us somewhat in regard to this. At all events, the pity which certain of our authors express for the civil condition of their brethren in that country is, from such a quarter, a superfluous feeling. Nowhere, let us rest assured, is genius more devoutly honoured than there, by all ranks of men, from peasants and burghers up to legislators and kings. It was but last year that the Diet of the Empire passed an act in favour of one individual poet: the Final Edition of Goethe's Works was guaranteed to be protected against commercial injury in every State of Germany; and special assurances to that effect were sent him, in the kindest terms, from all the authorities there assembled, some of them the highest in his country or in Europe. Nay, even while we write, are not the newspapers recording a visit from the Sovereign of Bavaria in person to the same venerable man?—a mere cere-

mony perhaps, but one which almost recalls to us the era of the antique Sages and the Grecian Kings.

This hypothesis, therefore, it would seem, is not supported by facts, and so returns to its original elements. The causes it alleges are impossible: but, what is still more fatal, the effect it proposes to account for has, in reality, no existence. We venture to deny that the Germans are defective in taste; even as a nation, as a public, taking one thing with another, we imagine they may stand comparison with any of their neighbours; as writers, as critics, they may decidedly court it. True, there is a mass of dulness, awkwardness, and false susceptibility in the lower regions of their literature: but is not bad taste endemical in such regions of every literature under the sun? Pure Stupidity, indeed, is of a quiet nature, and content to be merely stupid. But seldom do we find it pure; seldom unadulterated with some tincture of ambition, which drives it into new and strange metamorphoses. Here it has assumed a contemptuous trenchant air, intended to represent superior tact, and a sort of all-wisdom; there a truculent atrabilious scowl, which is to stand for passionate strength: now we have an outpouring of tumid fervour; now a fruitless, asthmatic hunting after wit and humour. Grave or gay, enthusiastic or derisive, admiring or despising, the dull man would be something which he is not and cannot be. Shall we confess that, of these two common extremes, we reckon the German error considerably the more harmless, and, in our day, by far the more curable? Of unwise admiration much may be hoped, for much good is really in it: but unwise contempt is itself a negation; nothing comes of it, for it is nothing.

To judge of a national taste, however, we must raise our view from its transitory modes to its perennial models; from the mass of vulgar writers, who blaze out and are extinguished with the popular delusion which they flatter, to those few who are admitted to shine with a pure and lasting lustre; to whom, by common consent, the eyes of the people are turned, as to its loadstars and celestial luminaries. Among German writers of this stamp, we would ask any candid reader of them, let him be of what country or creed he might, whether bad taste struck him as a prevailing characteristic. Was Wieland's taste uncultivated? Taste, we should say, and taste of the very species which a disciple of the Negative School would call the highest, formed the great object of his life; the perfection he unweariedly endeavoured after, and, more than any other perfection, has attained. The most fastidious Frenchman might read him, with admiration of his merely French qualities. And is not Klopstock, with his clear enthusiasm, his azure purity, and heavenly if still somewhat cold and lunar light, a man of taste? His *Messias* reminds us oftener of no other poets than of Virgil and Racine. But it is to Lessing that an Englishman would turn with readiest affection. We cannot but wonder that more of this man is not known among us; or that the knowledge of him has not done more to remove such misconceptions. Among all the writers of the eighteenth century, we will not except even Diderot and David Hume, there is not one of a more compact and rigid intellectual structure; who more distinctly knows what he is aiming at, or with more gracefulness, vigour, and precision sets it forth to his readers. He thinks with the clearness and piercing sharpness of the most expert logician; but a genial fire pervades him, a wit, a heartiness, a general richness and fineness of nature, to which most logicians are strangers. He is a sceptic in many things, but the noblest of sceptics; a mild, manly, half-careless enthusiasm struggles through his indignant unbelief; he stands before us like a toilworn but unwearied and heroic champion, earning not the conquest but the battle; as indeed himself admits to us, that "it is not the finding of truth, but the honest search for it, that profits." We confess we should be entirely at a loss for the literary creed of that man who reckoned Lessing other than a thoroughly cultivated writer; nay, entitled to rank, in this particular, with the most distinguished writers of any existing nation. As a poet, as a critic, philosopher, or controversialist, his style will be found precisely such as we of England are accustomed to admire most; brief, nervous, vivid; yet quiet, without glitter or antithesis; idiomatic, pure without purism; transparent, yet full of character and reflex hues of meaning. "Every sentence," says Horn, and justly, "is like a phalanx;" not a word wrong placed, not a word that could be spared; and it forms itself so calmly and lightly, and stands in its completeness so gay, yet so impregnable! As a poet he contemptuously denied himself all merit; but his readers have not taken him at his word: here too a similar felicity of style attends him; his plays, his *Minna von Barnhelm*, his *Emilie Galotti*, his *Nathan der Weise*, have a genuine and graceful poetic life; yet no works known to us in any language are purer from exaggeration, or any appearance of

falsehood. They are pictures, we might say, painted not in colours, but in crayons; yet a strange attraction lies in them; for the figures are grouped into the finest attitudes, and true and spirit-speaking in every line. It is with his style chiefly that we have to do here; yet we must add, that the matter of his works is not less meritorious. His Criticism and philosophic or religious Scepticism were of a higher mood than had yet been heard in Europe, still more in Germany: his *Dramaturgie* first exploded the pretensions of the French theatre, and, with irresistible conviction, made Shakspeare known to his countrymen; preparing the way for a brighter era in their literature, the chief men of which still thankfully look back to Lessing as their patriarch. His *Laocoon*, with its deep glances into the philosophy of Art, his *Dialogues of Freemasons*, a work of far higher import than its title indicates, may yet teach many things to most of us, which we know not, and ought to know.

With Lessing and Klopstock might be joined, in this respect, nearly every one, we do not say of their distinguished, but even of their tolerated contemporaries. The two Jacobis, known more or less in all countries, are little known here, if they are accused of wanting literary taste. These are men, whether as thinkers or poets, to be regarded and admired for their mild and lofty wisdom, the devoutness, the benignity and calm grandeur of their philosophical views. In such, it were strange if among so many high merits, this lower one of a just and elegant style, which is indeed their natural and even necessary product, had been wanting. We recommend the elder Jacobi no less for his clearness than for his depth; of the younger, it may be enough in this point of view to say that the chief praisers of his earlier poetry were the French. Neither are Hamann and Mendelsohn, who could meditate deep thoughts, defective in the power of uttering them with propriety. The *Phædon* of the latter, in its chaste precision and simplicity of style, may almost remind us of Xenophon: Socrates, to our mind, has spoken in no modern language so like Socrates, as here, by the lips of this wise and cultivated Jew.[1]

---

[1] The history of Mendelsohn is interesting in itself, and full of encouragement to all lovers of self-improvement. At thirteen he was a wandering Jewish beggar, without health, without home, almost without a language—for the jargon of broken Hebrew and provincial German which he spoke could scarcely be called one. At middle age he could write this *Phædon*, was a man of wealth and breeding, and ranked among the teachers of his age. Like Pope, he abode by his original creed,

Among the poets and more popular writers of the time, the case is the same: Utz, Gellert, Cramer, Ramler, Kleist, Hagedorn, Rabener, Gleim, and a multitude of lesser men, whatever excellences they might want, certainly are not chargeable with bad taste. Nay, perhaps of all writers they are the least chargeable with it: a certain clear, light, unaffected elegance, of a higher nature than French elegance, it might be, yet to the exclusion of all very deep or genial qualities, was the excellence they strove after, and, for the most part, in a fair measure attained. They resemble English writers of the same, or perhaps an earlier period, more than any other foreigners: apart from Pope, whose influence is visible enough, Beattie, Logan, Wilkie, Glover, unknown perhaps to any of them, might otherwise have almost seemed their models. Goldsmith also would rank among them; perhaps in regard to true poetic genius, at their head, for none of them has left us a *Vicar of Wakefield;* though, in regard to judgment, knowledge, general talent, his place would scarcely be so high.

The same thing holds in general, and with fewer drawbacks, of the somewhat later and more energetic race, denominated the *Göttingen School;* in contradistinction from the Saxon, to which Rabener, Cramer, and Gellert directly belonged, and most of those others indirectly. Hölty, Bürger, the two Stolbergs, are men whom Bossu might measure with his scales and compasses as strictly as he pleased. Of Herder, Schiller, Goethe, we speak not here: they are men of another stature and form of movement, whom Bossu's scale and compasses could not measure without difficulty, or rather not at all. To say that such men wrote with taste of this sort were saying little; for this forms not the apex, but the basis, in their conception of style; a quality not to be paraded as an excellence, but to be understood as indispensable,

as there by necessity and like a thing of course.

In truth, for it must be spoken out, our opponents are widely astray in this matter; so widely that their views of it are not only dim and perplexed, but altogether imaginary and delusive. It is proposed to school the Germans in the Alphabet of taste; and the Germans are already busied with their Accidence! Far from being behind other nations in the practice or science of Criticism, it is a fact, for which we fearlessly refer to all competent judges, that they are distinctly and even considerably in advance. We state what is already known to a great part of Europe to be true. Criticism has assumed a new form in Germany; it proceeds on other principles, and proposes to itself a higher aim. The grand question is not now a question concerning the qualities of diction, the coherence of metaphors, the fitness of sentiments, the general logical truth, in a work of art, as it was some half-century ago among most critics; neither is it a question mainly of a psychological sort, to be answered by discovering and delineating the peculiar nature of the poet from his poetry, as is usual with the best of our own critics at present: but it is, not indeed exclusively, but inclusively of those two other questions, properly and ultimately a question on the essence and peculiar life of the poetry itself. The first of these questions, as we see it answered, for instance, in the criticisms of Johnson and Kames, relates, strictly speaking, to the *garment* of poetry; the second, indeed, to its *body* and material existence, a much higher point; but only the last to its *soul* and spiritual existence, by which alone can the body, in its movements and phases, be *informed* with significance and rational life. The problem is not now to determine by what mechanism Addison composed sentences and struck out similitudes; but by what far finer and more mysterious mechanism Shakspeare organized his dramas, and gave life and individuality to his Ariel and his Hamlet. Wherein lies that life; how have they attained that shape and individuality? Whence comes that empyrean fire which irradiates their whole being, and pierces, at least in starry gleams, like a diviner thing, into all hearts? Are these dramas of his not veri-similar only, but true; nay, truer than reality itself, since the essence of unmixed reality is bodied forth in them under more expressive symbols! What is this unity of theirs; and can our deeper inspection discern it to be indivisible, and existing by necessity, because each work springs, as it were, from the general elements of all

though often solicited to change it: indeed, the grand problem of his life was to better the inward and outward condition of his own ill-fated people; for whom he actually accomplished much benefit. He was a mild, shrewd, and worthy man; and might well love *Phædon* and Socrates, for his own character was Socratic. He was a friend of Lessing's: indeed, a pupil; for Lessing, having accidentally met him at chess, recognized the spirit that lay struggling under such incumbrances, and generously undertook to help him. By teaching the poor Jew a little Greek, he disenchanted him from the Talmud and the Rabbins. The two were afterwards co-labourers in Nicolai's *Deutsche Bibliothek,* the first German *Review* of any character; which, however, in the hands of Nicolai himself, it subsequently lost. Mendelsohn's works have mostly been translated into French.

Thought, and grows up therefrom into form and expansion by its own growth? Not only who was the poet, and how did he compose; but what and how was the poem, and why was it a poem and not rhymed eloquence, creation and not figured passion? These are the questions for the critic. Criticism stands like an interpreter between the inspired and the uninspired; between the prophet and those who hear the melody of his words, and catch some glimpse of their material meaning, but understand not their deeper import. She pretends to open for us this deeper import; to clear our sense that it may discern the pure brightness of this eternal Beauty, and recognize it as heavenly, under all forms where it looks forth, and reject, as of the earth earthy, all forms, be their material splendour what it may, where no gleaming of that other shines through.

This is the task of Criticism as the Germans understand it. And how do they accomplish this task? By a vague declamation clothed in gorgeous mystic phraseology? By vehement tumultuous anthems to the poet and his poetry; by epithets and laudatory similitudes drawn from Tartarus and Elysium, and all intermediate terrors and glories; whereby, in truth, it is rendered clear both that the poet is an extremely great poet, and also that the critic's allotment of understanding, overflowed by these Pythian raptures, has unhappily melted into deliquium? Nowise in this manner do the Germans proceed: but by rigorous scientific inquiry; by appeal to principles which, whether correct or not, have been deduced patiently, and by long investigation, from the highest and calmest regions of Philosophy. For this finer portion of their Criticism is now also embodied in systems; and standing, so far as these reach, coherent, distinct, and methodical, no less than, on their much shallower foundation, the systems of Boileau and Blair. That this new Criticism is a complete, much more a certain science, we are far from meaning to affirm: the *æsthetic* theories of Kant, Herder, Schiller, Goethe, Richter, vary in external aspect, according to the varied habits of the individual; and can at best only be regarded as approximations to the truth, or modifications of it; each critic representing it as it harmonizes more or less perfectly with the other intellectual persuasions of his own mind, and of different classes of minds that resemble his. Nor can we here undertake to inquire what degree of such approximation to the truth there is in each or all of these writers; or in Tieck and the two Schlegels, who, especially the latter, have laboured so meritoriously in

reconciling these various opinions; and so successfully in impressing and diffusing the best spirit of them, first in their own country, and now also in several others. Thus much, however, we will say: That we reckon the mere circumstance of such a science being in existence, a ground of the highest consideration, and worthy the best attention of all inquiring men. For we should err widely if we thought that this new tendency of critical science pertains to Germany alone. It is a European tendency, and springs from the general condition of intellect in Europe. We ourselves have all, for the last thirty years, more or less distinctly felt the necessity of such a science: witness the neglect into which our Blairs and Bossus have silently fallen; our increased and increasing admiration, not only of Shakspeare, but of all his contemporaries, and of all who breathe any portion of his spirit; our controversy whether Pope was a poet; and so much vague effort on the part of our best critics everywhere to express some still unexpressed idea concerning the nature of true poetry; as if they felt in their hearts that a pure glory, nay a divineness, belonged to it, for which they had as yet no name and no intellectual form. But in Italy too, in France itself, the same thing is visible. Their grand controversy, so hotly urged, between the *Classicists* and *Romanticists*, in which the Schlegels are assumed, much too loosely, on all hands, as the patrons and generalissimos of the latter, shows us sufficiently what spirit is at work in that long-stagnant literature. Doubtless this turbid fermentation of the elements will at length settle into clearness, both there and here, as in Germany it has already in a great measure done; and perhaps a more serene and genial poetic day is everywhere to be expected with some confidence. How much the example of the Germans may have to teach us in this particular needs no farther exposition.

The authors and first promulgators of this new critical doctrine were at one time contemptuously named the *New School;* nor was it till after a war of all the few good heads in the nation with all the many bad ones had ended as such wars must ever do,[1] that these

---

[1] It began in Schiller's *Musenalmanach* for 1797. The *Xenien* (a series of philosophic epigrams jointly by Schiller and Goethe) descended there unexpectedly, like a flood of ethereal fire, on the German literary world: quickening all that was noble into new life, but visiting the ancient empire of Dulness with astonishment and unknown pangs. The agitation was extreme; scarcely since the age of Luther has there been such stir and

critical principles were generally adopted; and their assertors found to be no *School*, or new heretical Sect, but the ancient primitive Catholic communion, of which all sects that had any living light in them were but members and subordinate modes. It is, indeed, the most sacred article of this creed to preach and practise universal tolerance. Every literature of the world has been cultivated by the Germans; and to every literature they have studied to give due honour. Shakspeare and Homer, no doubt, occupy alone the loftiest station in the poetical Olympus; but there is space in it for all true Singers out of every age and clime. Ferdusi and the primeval Mythologists of Hindostan live in brotherly union with the Troubadours and ancient Storytellers of the West. The wayward mystic gloom of Calderon, the lurid fire of Dante, the auroral light of Tasso, the clear icy glitter of Racine, all are acknowledged and reverenced; nay, in the celestial forecourt an abode has been appointed for the Gressets and Delilles, that no spark of inspiration, no tone of mental music, might remain unrecognized. The Germans study foreign nations in a spirit which deserves to be oftener imitated. It is their honest endeavour to understand each, with its own peculiarities, in its own special manner of existing: not that they may praise it, or censure it, or attempt to alter it, but simply that they may see this manner of existing as the nation itself sees it, and so participate in whatever worth or beauty it has brought into being. Of all literatures, accordingly, the German has the best as well as the most translations; men like Goethe, Schiller, Wieland, Schlegel, Tieck, have not disdained this task. Of Shakspeare there are three entire versions admitted to be good; and we know not how many partial, or considered as bad. In their criticisms of him, we ourselves have long ago admitted that no such clear judgment or hearty appreciation of his merits had ever been exhibited by any critic of our own.

To attempt stating in separate aphorisms the doctrines of this new poetical system, would, in such space as is now allowed us, be to insure them of misapprehension. The science of Criticism, as the Germans practise it, is no study of an hour; for it springs from

the depths of thought, and remotely or immediately connects itself with the subtlest problems of all philosophy. One characteristic of it we may state, the obvious parent of many others. Poetic beauty, in its pure essence, is not, by this theory, as by all our theories, from Hume's to Alison's, derived from anything external, or of merely intellectual origin; not from association, or any reflex or reminiscence of mere sensations; nor from natural love, either of imitation, of similarity in dissimilarity, of excitement by contrast, or of seeing difficulties overcome. On the contrary, it is assumed as underived; not borrowing its existence from such sources, but as lending to most of these their significance and principal charm for the mind. It dwells and is born in the inmost Spirit of Man, united to all love of Virtue, to all true belief in God; or rather, it is one with this love and this belief, another phase of the same highest principle in the mysterious infinitude of the human Soul. To apprehend this beauty of poetry, in its full and purest brightness, is not easy, but difficult; thousands on thousands eagerly read poems, and attain not the smallest taste of it; yet to all uncorrupted hearts, some effulgences of this heavenly glory are here and there revealed; and to apprehend it clearly and wholly, to acquire and maintain a sense and heart that sees and worships it, is the last perfection of all humane culture. With mere readers for amusement, therefore, this criticism has, and can have, nothing to do; these find their amusement in less or greater measure, and the nature of Poetry remains for ever hidden from them in deepest concealment. On all hands, there is no truce given to the hypothesis that the ultimate object of the poet is to please. Sensation, even of the finest and most rapturous sort, is not the end, but the means. Art is to be loved, not because of its effects, but because of itself; not because it is useful for spiritual pleasure, or even for moral culture, but because it is Art, and the highest in man, and the soul of all beauty. To inquire after its *utility* would be like inquiring after the *utility* of a God, or, what to the Germans would sound stranger than it does to us, the *utility* of Virtue and Religion. On these particulars, the authenticity of which we might verify, not so much by citation of individual passages, as by reference to the scope and spirit of whole treatises, we must for the present leave our readers to their own reflections. Might we advise them, it would be to inquire farther, and, if possible, to see the matter with their own eyes.

strife in the intellect of Germany; indeed, scarcely since that age has there been a controversy, if we consider its ultimate bearings on the best and noblest interests of mankind, so important as this, which, for the time, seemed only to turn on metaphysical subtleties, and matters of mere elegance. Its farther applications became apparent by degrees.

THE PERFECT LOVER.

(Sir John Suckling, born at Whitton, Middlesex, 1608; died in France, 1641. Poet and soldier in the troublous days of Charles I. He was educated at Cambridge. His works are: *The Session of the Poets; Aglaura*, a tragi-comedy; *The Discontented Colonel*, and *A Sad One*, tragedies; *The Goblins*, a comedy; *An Account of Religion by Reason;* the *Ballad on a Wedding;* &c. "The grace and elegance of his songs and ballads are inimitable."—*George Ellis.*)

Honest lover whosoever,
If in all thy love there ever
Was one wav'ring thought, if thy flame
Were not still even, still the same:
    Know this,
      Thou lov'st amiss,
    And to love true,
Thou must begin again, and love anew.

If, when she appears i' th' room,
Thou dost not quake, and art struck dumb;
And in striving this to cover
Dost not speak thy words twice over:
    Know this,
      Thou lov'st amiss,
    And to love true,
Thou must begin again, and love anew.

If fondly thou dost not mistake,
And all defects for graces take,
Persuad'st thyself that jests are broken,
When she has little or nothing spoken:
    Know this,
      Thou lov'st amiss,
    And to love true,
Thou must begin again, and love anew.

If when thou appear'st to be within,
Thou let'st not men ask and ask again;
And when thou answer'st, if it be
To what was ask'd thee properly:
    Know this,
      Thou lov'st amiss,
    And to love true,
Thou must begin again, and love anew.

If when thy stomach calls to eat,
Thou cut'st not fingers 'stead of meat;
And with much gazing on her face
Dost not rise hungry from the place:
    Know this,
      Thou lov'st amiss,
    And to love true,
Thou must begin again, and love anew.

If by this thou dost discover
That thou art no perfect lover,
And desiring to love true,
Thou dost begin to love anew:
    Know this,
      Thou lov'st amiss,
    And to love true,
Thou must begin again, and love anew.

A HIGHLAND GLEN.

BY PROFESSOR WILSON.

To whom belongs this valley fair,
That sleeps beneath the filmy air,
  Even like a living thing?
Silent—as infant at the breast—
Save a still sound that speaks of rest,
  That streamlet's murmuring!

The heavens appear to love this vale;
Here clouds with unseen motion sail,
  Or 'mid the silence lie!
By that blue arch this beauteous earth
'Mid evening's hour of dewy mirth
  Seems bound unto the sky.

Oh! that this lovely vale were mine—
Then from glad youth to calm decline
  My years would gently glide;
Hope would rejoice in endless dreams,
And Memory's oft-returning gleams
  By peace be sanctified.

There would unto my soul be given,
From presence of that gracious Heaven,
  A piety sublime;
And thoughts would come of mystic mood,
To make, in this deep solitude,
  Eternity of time!

And did I ask to whom belonged
This vale?—I feel that I have wronged
  Nature's most gracious soul!
She spreads her glories o'er the earth,
And all her children from their birth
  Are joint heirs of the whole!

Yea! long as Nature's humblest child
Hath kept her temple undefiled
  By sinful sacrifice,
Earth's fairest scenes are all his own,
He is a monarch, and his throne
  Is built amid the skies.

ON A FADED VIOLET.

The odour from the flower is gone,
  Which like thy kisses breathed on me;
The colour from the flower is flown,
  Which glowed of thee, and only thee.

A shrivelled, lifeless, vacant form,
  It lies on my abandoned breast,
And mocks the heart which yet is warm,
  With cold and silent rest.

I weep—my tears revive it not!
  I sigh—it breathes no more on me!
Its mute and uncomplaining lot
  Is such as mine should be.
              P. B. SHELLEY.

THE INVENTOR.

[Erckmann-Chatrian, the compound name of two French authors. Emile Erckmann, born at Phalsbourg, in the department of the Meurthe, 20th May, 1822. Alexandre Chatrian, born at Soldatenthal, Meurthe, 18th December, 1826. In conjunction, and under the name of Erckmann-Chatrian, the two friends have produced numerous tales and plays, which were for some time supposed to proceed from one pen. *The Illustrious Doctor Mathéus* was the first work which obtained popularity, and since then the authors have written the following amongst other novels:—*The Conscript of 1813; Madame Thérèse; The Invasion; Waterloo; A Man of the People; The War; The Blockade* (of Phalsbourg); *History of a Peasant; Master Daniel Rock; Tales of the Rhine Borders; Friend Fritz; The Story of the Plébicite; The Polish Jew*, a play, &c. &c. Their works are distinguished by faithful and vivid portraiture of rural life and manners; and sometimes by a kind of weird fancy playing with scientific possibilities.]

On the twenty-ninth day of July, 1835, Kasper Bœck, a shepherd of the village of Hirchwiller, his large felt hat hanging upon his shoulders, his canvas wallet hanging by his side, and followed by his great yellow-pawed dog, presented himself about nine o'clock in the evening at the house of the Burgomaster Petrousse, who had just finished supper, and was helping himself to a glass of kirschenwasser to aid his digestion.

The Burgomaster was a tall thin man, and wore on his lip a large grizzly moustache. He had, in former days, served in the army of the Archduke Charles; and, while possessed of a good-natured disposition, he ruled the village of Hirchwiller with a wag of his finger and a nod of his head.

"Burgomaster!" cried the shepherd in a state of excitement; but Petrousse, without waiting to hear him further, frowned and said—

"Kasper Bœck, begin by taking off your hat; send out your dog, and then speak plainly without spluttering, in order that I may understand you."

Whereupon the Burgomaster, standing near the table, quietly emptied his glass, and sucked the fringe of his great moustache with an air of indifference.

Kasper sent out his dog and returned, cap in hand.

"Now," said Petrousse, seeing the shepherd somewhat composed, "tell me what has happened."

"It happens that the ghost has appeared again in the ruins of Geirstein!"

"Ah! I doubt that very much. Have you seen it, Kasper?"

"That I have, Burgomaster, very plainly."

"What was it like?"

"It looked like a little man."

"Good."

Then the old soldier, unhooking his gun from above the door, slung it over his shoulder and addressed the shepherd,

"Go and tell the constable to meet me directly in the little lane of the hollies," said he. "Your ghost is likely to prove some vagabond rascal; but if it should turn out to be only a fox, I'll make its skin into a cap with long ears for you."

So saying the Burgomaster strode out, followed humbly by Kasper Bœck.

The weather was charming. Whilst the shepherd hastened to knock at the door of the constable, Petrousse ensconced himself in a grove of elders which skirted the back of the old village church. Two minutes later Kasper and Hans Gœrner, his short sword dangling by his side, joined the Burgomaster at a sharp trot. The three advanced towards the ruins of Geirstein.

These ruins, situated at about twenty minutes' walk from the village, appeared insignificant enough, consisting of several fragments of a broken-down wall, some four or six feet in height, which made themselves barely visible amidst the brushwood. Archæologists called them the aqueducts of Seranus, the Roman camp of Holderloch, or the vestiges of Theodoric, according to their fancy. The only remarkable feature about these ruins was the flight of stairs of a cavern cut in the rock. Contrary to most winding stairs, instead of the concentric circles contracting at every downward sweep, the spiral of this hollow increased in width in such a manner that the bottom of the hollow became three times as large as the outlet.

Could this be a caprice of architecture? or what other strange cause determined so odd a structure? It is a matter which need concern us little; sufficient for the present is the fact, that in the cavern might be heard that vague murmur which any one may hear by applying the hollow of a shell to his ear: you could hear also the step of the wayfarer upon the gravel, the sighing of the breeze, the rustling of the leaves, and even the conversation of the passersby.

The three travellers ascended the little footpath which lay between the vines and the cabbage-gardens of Hirchwiller.

"I can see nothing," broke forth the Burgomaster, turning up his nose mockingly.

"Nor I either," Hans chimed in, imitating the tone of his superior.

"Oh, it is in the hole," muttered the shepherd.

"We shall see, we shall see," the Burgomaster replied confidently. And after this fashion in about a quarter of an hour they reached the mouth of the cavern.

I have said that the night was clear, bright, and perfectly calm. The moon, as far as the eye could reach, lit with bluish tints one of those nocturnal landscapes clothed with silvery trees, the shadows of which upon the ground seem traced in the firm dark lines of a pencil. The heath and the broom in blossom perfumed the breeze with an odour sharpened by the night air; and the frogs of a neighbouring marsh croaking their hoarse strains broke from time to time the silence of the night.

But all these appearances escaped the attention of our worthy rustics; they thought only of laying hands upon the ghost.

Arriving at the cavern mouth the three halted and listened. Then they looked into the darkness: nothing could be seen, nothing stirred.

"Confound it," exclaimed the Burgomaster, "we have forgotten to bring a bit of candle with us. Get down the stair, Kasper, you know the way better than I do; I will follow you."

At this proposal the shepherd recoiled hastily. If he had followed his own inclination the poor fellow would have taken to his heels: his piteous looks caused the Burgomaster to fall into fits of laughter.

"Very well then, Hans, since Kasper is afraid to descend, you must lead the way."

"But—but, good Burgomaster," expostulated the constable, "you know there are some of the steps awanting. We run the risk of breaking our necks."

"Then send on your dog, Kasper," continued the Burgomaster.

The shepherd called his dog; he showed him the stairs, he urged him forward, but the dog no more than the men inclined to make the venture.

At this moment a brilliant idea occurred to Hans.

"Ha! Mister Petrousse," he exclaimed, "suppose you fire a shot into the cave?"

"By my faith," cried the Burgomaster, "you are right. We shall see clearly at any rate."

And without hesitating the bold man approached the staircase holding his gun. But by reason of the acoustic effects which have been already pointed out, the ghost, the vagabond, or whatever it was occupied the cavern, heard all that had passed. The idea of receiving the report of a gun did not seem to suit his tastes, for in a small shrill voice he cried—

"Hold! do not fire! I ascend to you!"

Then the three besiegers regarded each other, subduing their laughter, and the Burgomaster again bending over the hollow shouted in rude tone—

"Make haste, rascal, or I fire!"

He shouldered his gun. The click of the lock seemed to hasten the ascent of the mysterious individual, and several stones, detached in his haste, were heard to roll to the bottom. Nevertheless, more than a minute elapsed before any one appeared, the cavern being at least sixty feet in depth.

What could engage that man in the midst of such darkness? Surely he must be some great criminal! Thus thought at least the Burgomaster and his attendants.

At length a vague form emerged from the shade. Then slowly, step by step, a little lean red-haired man, four and a half feet in height, his complexion sallow, his eye sparkling like a magpie's, his hair in disorder, and his clothes in tatters, issued from the cavern crying—

"By what right, wretches, do you come to disturb my studies?"

This authoritative speech was not at all in keeping with the dress and figure of the little fellow, so the Burgomaster replied indignantly:—

"Make haste to prove yourself an honest man, you wretched imp, or I shall begin by giving you a thrashing."

"A thrashing!" cried the manikin, dancing with rage and drawing himself up under the nose of the Burgomaster.

"Yes, a thrashing," replied Petrousse, who, nevertheless, could not help admiring the courage of the dwarf, "if you do not reply in a satisfactory manner to the questions I am about to put to you. I am the Burgomaster of Hirchwiller; here is the constable, the shepherd, and his dog; we are stronger than you, observe; be wise, therefore, and tell me peaceably what you are, what you do here, and why you do not appear in the light of day. After that we shall see what is to be done with you."

"All that does not concern you," replied the little man in his harsh voice; "I will not answer you."

"In that case then, forward, march!" the Burgomaster responded, seizing him by the neck, "you shall take up your quarters in prison."

The little fellow struggled and twisted like

a weasel: he even attempted to bite, and the dog was already manifesting designs upon his calves, when, thoroughly exhausted, he said, not without a certain dignity:—

"Release me sir, I yield to force; I shall follow you."

The Burgomaster, not wanting in courtesy, became more calm in turn.

"You promise me that," said he.

"I promise you."

"That is well: walk then in front of us."

And this is how, on the night of the twenty-ninth of July, 1835, the Burgomaster of Hirchwiller effected the capture of a little red-haired man, issuing from the ruins of Geirstein.

On reaching the village the constable ran to seek the key of the prison, and the captive was shut in under double lock.

The next day, towards nine o'clock, Hans Gœrner, having received orders to lead the prisoner to the court-house in order to submit him to a new interrogation, betook himself with four stout fellows to the cell. They opened the door, full of curiosity to see the ghost, but what was their surprise to see him hanging by his cravat to the railing of the skylight window. Without delay they set off to the house of the Burgomaster, to apprise him of the event.

The justice of peace and the doctor of Hirchwiller drew up in legal form a deposition of the witnesses of the catastrophe; then they buried the unknown one in a neighbouring clover-field, and so the matter ended.

But about three weeks after these events I went to see my cousin Petrousse, of whom I happened to be the nearest relative and heir, circumstances which maintained between us an attachment of the closest kind. We were dining together and talking of various subjects, in the course of which he related to me the preceding history, just as I have reported it.

"It is strange, cousin," said I to him, "very strange! and you have no other trace of that mysterious being?"

"None."

"You have learned nothing which can give you a hint of his intentions?"

"Absolutely nothing, Christian."

"But what could he be doing in the cave? what could be the object of his life?"

The Burgomaster shrugged his shoulders, refilled our glasses, and replied—

"Your health, cousin."

"And yours."

We remained silent for some minutes. It was impossible for me to be satisfied with the sudden termination of this adventure, and in spite of myself I fell into a dreamy melancholy, thinking of the sad fate of certain men who appear and disappear in the world like the flowers of the field, without leaving behind them the least remembrance or the least regret.

"Cousin," I at length inquired, "how far may it be from here to the ruins of Geirstein?"

"Twenty minutes' walk at farthest. Why do you ask?"

"Just that I wish to see them."

"You know that to-day we have a meeting of the council, and that I cannot accompany you."

"Oh! I replied, "I shall easily find them myself."

"That is unnecessary," he said, "Hans will show you the way; he has nothing better to do." And my cousin, having tapped upon his glass, called his servant and said—

"Katel, go seek Hans Gœrner; let him make haste; it is now two o'clock, and I must be going."

The domestic departed, and Hans arrived without delay. He received instructions to conduct me to the ruins, and, whilst the Burgomaster proceeded leisurely to the council chamber, we mounted the brow of the hill. Hans Gœrner pointed out to me with his hand the remains of the aqueduct. At this moment the rocky edge of the plateau, the blue mountains of Hundsrück, the sadly dilapidated walls covered with sombre ivy, the clang of the village bell calling the worthies of Hirchwiller to council, the panting constable clinging to the brushwood, all produced within me a sad and sombre impression I could hardly account for, unless it might be the history of the poor suicide casting a shadow on the horizon.

The staircase of the cavern appeared to me extremely curious, its spiral form elegant. The rough shrubs springing from the fissures at almost every step, and the desolate aspect of the place, accorded with my sadness.

We descended, and soon the luminous point of the opening above, which appeared to become more and more narrow, taking the form of a star with diverging rays, alone lent us its pale light.

On reaching the bottom of the cave it was a wondrous sight which the whole flight of steps presented, lighted from above and casting their shadows with a marvellous regularity. I now heard the resonance Petrousse had spoken of to me; the immense granite shell had as many echoes as stones.

"Has any one descended here since the little

man was discovered?" I inquired of Hans Gœrner.

"No, sir, the peasants are afraid; they imagine that the ghost has gone back again. No one ventures into the Screech-owl's Ear."

"Do they call this the Screech-owl's Ear?"

"Yes."

"It resembles that closely," said I lifting my eyes. "This vault reversed forms the concha or outer part, underneath the stairs we have the tympanic cavity, and the windings of the staircase represent the cochlea, the labyrinth, and the vestibule of the ear. Here, then, is the cause of the murmur which is heard: we are at the base of a colossal ear."

"It is very likely," replied Hans, who seemed to understand nothing of my observations.

We prepared to ascend, and I had already mounted a few steps when I felt something crumble under my foot. Bending down to see what it might be, I perceived at the same time a white object before me, which proved to be a tattered sheet of paper. As for the hard substance which had been broken, I recognized in it a kind of glazed brown stone jug.

"Oh, ho!" I cried, "this may throw some light upon the Burgomaster's story," and I rejoined Hans Gœrner, who already awaited me at the mouth of the cavern.

"Now sir," he said to me, "where do you wish to go?"

"In the first place," said I, "let us rest a little: we shall consider presently."

I sat down upon a stone, while Hans cast his falcon eye round about the village in search of plunderers in the gardens, if any such could be discovered.

I examined carefully the stone vase, of which only a fragment remained. That fragment presented the form of the mouth of a trumpet lined with down. Its use I could not make out. I then read the fragment of the letter, which was written in a steady flowing hand. I have transcribed it word for word. It seems to form a continuation of another portion of the sheet, which I have since sought for unsuccessfully in and about the ruins.

. . . .

"My micracoustic cornet has therefore the double advantage of multiplying infinitely the intensity of sounds, and of introducing into the ear nothing which will in the least annoy the observer. You could hardly credit, my dear master, the delight which one experiences in distinguishing the thousand imperceptible noises which, in the beautiful summer days, combine to form one immense hum. The bee

has his song, like the nightingale; the wasp is the linnet of the mosses; the grasshopper the twittering swallow of the tall grass; the gnat resembles the wren in the same degree; its voice is only a sigh, but that sigh is melodious.

"This discovery, from a philosophic point of view, which makes us share in the life universal, surpasses in importance all that I am able to say of it.

"After so much suffering, privation, and weariness, how glorious it is to gather in at last the reward of our labours. With what thankfulness the soul lifts itself towards the divine Author of these microscopic worlds, the magnificence of which has been revealed to us! What are now the long hours of anguish, of hunger, of scorn, which formerly overwhelmed us? Nothing, my dear master, nothing! Tears of gratitude moisten our eyes. We are proud of having bought by suffering new joys for humanity and of having contributed to its elevation. But however vast, however admirable may be these first results of my micracoustic cornet, its advantages do not stop there. There are others more positive, more material, so to speak, and which are demonstrable by figures.

"Just as the telescope enables us to discover myriads of worlds accomplishing their harmonious revolutions in space, so does my micracoustic cornet carry the sense of hearing beyond the bounds of the possible. Thus, sir, I do not stop at the circulation of the blood and the humours of the living body. You may hear them rush along with the impetuosity of cataracts, you may perceive them with a distinctness that would astonish you. The least irregularity in the pulse, the slightest obstacle in its course, strikes you, and produces the effect of a rock against which are dashed the waters of a torrent!

"This is unquestionably an immense gain in the development of our physiological and pathological knowledge, but it is not on this point I insist.

"On applying your ear, sir, to the ground, you can hear the hot mineral waters springing up at immense depths; you can estimate their volume, their currents, their obstacles. Do you desire to go further? Descend into a subterranean vault so constructed as to collect a considerable quantity of appreciable sounds; then at night, when all sleep, and nothing disturbs the interior sounds of our globe, listen!

"My dear master, all that I can say at this moment—for in the midst of my deep misery, of my privations, and often indeed of my despair, there is left for me only a few lucid moments in which I can pursue my geological observations—all it is possible for me to tell you is, that the bubbling of flaming lava and the uproar of elements in ebullition is something awful and sublime, and which can only be compared to the feelings of the astronomer sounding with his glass the depths of space and infinitude. Nevertheless I must confess to you, that these experiences have need of being further studied and classified in methodic manner, in order to draw from them reliable conclusions. Also, as soon as you have deigned, my dear and worthy master, to forward to me at Newstadt the small sum I have asked of you to meet my pressing wants, we shall come to an understanding, with the view of establishing three subterranean observatories—one in the valley of Catane, the other in Iceland, and the third in one of the valleys of Capac-Uren, of Songay, or of Cayembe-Uren, the deepest in the Cordilleras, and consequently . . .

.   .   .   .   .   .

Here the letter ended! My hands fell by my sides, I was stupified. Had I been reading the ravings of a madman or the realized inspirations of a genius? What could one say? What could one think? This miserable man living at the bottom of a pit, dying with hunger, had been perhaps one of those chosen ones whom the Supreme Being sends upon the earth to enlighten future generations. This man had hung himself in disgust. His prayer had not been responded to, although he asked only a morsel of bread in exchange for his discovery. It was a horrible thought. Long I remained there, lost in reverie and thanking Heaven for not having willed to make of me a leading man in the community of martyrs. At length Hans Gœrner, seeing me with eyes fixed and mouth agape, ventured to touch me on the shoulder.

"Sir," said he, "it grows late; the Burgomaster by this time will have returned from the council."

"Ah! you are right," I exclaimed, crumpling the paper in my hand; "let us go."

We descended the bank. My cousin met us on the threshold, a smile upon his face.

"Well, friend Christian! you have found nothing of the simpleton who hung himself?"

"No."

"I thought as much," continued the Burgomaster. "He was doubtless some lunatic escaped from Stefansfeld or other madhouse. By my faith, he did well to hang himself. When one is good for nothing, that is the wisest thing he can do."—*From the French, by* JOHN CHALMERS, M. D.

ON THE PICTURE OF "A CHILD TIRED OF PLAY."

BY N. P. WILLIS.

Tired of play! Tired of play!
What hast thou done this livelong day?
The birds are silent, and so is the bee;
The sun is creeping up steeple and tree;
The doves have flown to the sheltering eaves,
And the nests are dark with the drooping leaves;
Twilight gathers, and day is done—
How hast thou spent it—restless one?

Playing? But what hast thou done beside
To tell thy mother at eventide?
What promise of morn is left unbroken?
What kind word to thy playmate spoken?
Whom hast thou pitied, and whom forgiven?
How with thy faults has duty striven?
What hast thou learn'd by field and hill,
By greenwood path, and by singing rill?

There will come an eve to a longer day,
That will find thee tired—but not of play!
And thou wilt lean, as thou leanest now,
With drooping limbs and aching brow,
And wish the shadows would faster creep,
And long to go to thy quiet sleep.
Well were it then if thine aching brow
Were as free from sin and shame as now!
Well for thee, if thy lip could tell
A tale like this, of a day spent well.
If thine open hand hath relieved distress—
If thy pity hath sprung to wretchedness—
If thou hast forgiven the sore offence,
And humbled thy heart with penitence—
If Nature's voices have spoken to thee
With her holy meanings eloquently—
If every creature hath won thy love,
From the creeping worm to the brooding dove—
If never a sad, low spoken word
Hath pled with thy human heart unheard—
Then, when the night steals on, as now,
It will bring relief to thine aching brow,
And, with joy and peace at the thought of rest,
Thou wilt sink to sleep on thy mother's breast.

———

THE ROSE.

The rose, alas! thy guardian hand
    Saved yesterday from dying,
Pale, wan, and wither'd from its stem,
    Is now in ruins lying:
But the fond flower, to show she still
    Was grateful e'en in death,
Her blushes to thy cheek bequeathed,
    Her perfume to thy breath.

SIR THOMAS E. CROFT.

A MATCH.

BY ALGERNON CHARLES SWINBURNE.

If love were what the rose is,
    And I were like the leaf,
Our lives would grow together
In sad or singing weather,
Blown fields or flowerful closes,
    Green pleasure or gray grief;
If love were what the rose is,
    And I were like the leaf.

If I were what the words are,
    And love were like the tune,
With double sound and single
Delight our lips would mingle,
With kisses glad as birds are
    That get sweet rain at noon;
If I were what the words are
    And love were like the tune.

If you were life, my darling,
    And I your love were death,
We'd shine and snow together
Ere March made sweet the weather
With daffodil and starling
    And hours of fruitful breath;
If you were life, my darling,
    And I your love were death.

If you were thrall to sorrow,
    And I were page to joy,
We'd play for lives and seasons
With loving looks and treasons
And tears of night and morrow
    And laughs of maid and boy;
If you were thrall to sorrow,
    And I were page to joy.

If you were April's lady,
    And I were lord in May,
We'd throw with leaves for hours
And draw for days with flowers,
Till day like night were shady
    And night were bright like day;
If you were April's lady,
    And I were lord in May.

If you were queen of pleasure,
    And I were king of pain,
We'd hunt down love together,
Pluck out his flying-feather,
And teach his feet a measure,
    And find his mouth a rein;
If you were queen of pleasure,
    And I were king of pain.

THE GREAT FIRE OF LONDON.

[John Evelyn, born at Wotton, Surrey, 31st October, 1620; died 27th February, 1705-6 He saw much of the court of Charles II., but retained his character of an upright and studious gentleman. He wrote numerous works, chiefly on social and scientific subjects, but his *Diary* (from which our extract is taken) and his *Sylva*, or a Discourse of Forest Trees, are the only ones which have kept their place in general estimation. Of his other works it will suffice to mention: *Fumifugium*, or the Inconvenience of the Air and Smoke of London Dissipated; *Tyrannus*, or the Mode, in a Discourse of Sumptuary Laws; *Sculptura*, or the History and Art of Chalcography and Engraving on Copper; *Terra*, a Philosophical Discourse of the Earth; *Mundus Muliebris*, or the Ladies' Dressing-room Unlocked and her Toilette Spread,—a burlesque; *Numismata*, a Discourse of Medals, Ancient and Modern, &c. "His life, which was extended to eighty-six years, was a course of inquiry, study, curiosity, instruction, and benevolence." —*Horace Walpole.*]

1666.   2 Sept.   This fatal night about ten, began that deplorable fire neere Fish Streete in London.

3.   I had public prayers at home.   The fire continuing, after dinner I took coach with my wife and sonn and went to the Bank side in Southwark, where we beheld the dismal spectacle, the whole City in dreadfull flames neare the water side; all the houses from the Bridge, all Thames Street, and upwards towards Cheapeside, downe to the Three Cranes, were now consum'd: and so returned exceeding astonished what would become of the rest.

The fire having continu'd all this night (if I may call that night which was light as day for ten miles round about, after a dreadfull manner) when conspiring with a fierce Eastern wind in a very drie season; I went on foote to the same place, and saw the whole South part of the City burning from Cheapeside to the Thames, and all along Cornehill (for it likewise kindl'd back against the wind, as well as forward), Tower Streete, Fen-church Streete, Gracious Streete, and so along to Bainard's Castle, and was now taking hold of St. Paule's Church, to which the scaffolds contributed exceedingly.   The conflagration was so universal, and the people so astonish'd, that from the beginning, I know not by what despondency or fate, they hardly stirr'd to quench it, so that there was nothing heard or seene but crying out and lamentation, running about like distracted creatures, without at all attempting to save even their goods; such a strange consternation there was upon them, so as it burned both in breadth and length, the Churches,

Public Halls, Exchange, Hospitals, Monuments, and ornaments, leaping after a prodigious manner from house to house and streete to streete, at greate distances one from the other: for the heate with a long set of faire and warme weather had even ignited the aire and prepar'd the materials to conceive the fire, which devour'd after an incredible manner houses, furniture, and every thing. Here we saw the Thames cover'd with goods floating, all the barges and boates laden with what some had time and courage to save, as, on the other, the carts, &c. carrying out to the fields, which for many miles were strew'd with moveables of all sorts, and tents erecting to shelter both people and what goods they could get away. Oh the miserable and calamitous spectacle! such as happly the world had not seene the like since the foundation of it, nor be outdon till the universal conflagration of it. All the skie was of a fiery aspect, like the top of a burning oven, and the light seene above 40 miles round about for many nights. God grant mine eyes may never behold the like, who now saw above 10,000 houses all in one flame; the noise and cracking and thunder of the impetuous flames, the shreiking of women and children, the hurry of people, the fall of Towers, Houses and Churches, was like an hideous storme, and the aire all about so hot and inflam'd that at the last one was not able to approch it, so that they were forc'd to stand still and let the flames burn on, which they did for neere two miles in length and one in bredth. The clowds also of smoke were dismall, and reach'd upon computation neer 56 miles in length. Thus I left it this afternoone burning, a resemblance of Sodom, or the last day. It forcibly call'd to my mind that passage *non enim hic habemus stabilem civitatem:* the ruines resembling the picture of Troy. London was, but is no more! Thus I returned home.

Sept. 4. The burning still rages, and it was now gotten as far as the Inner Temple; all Fleet Streete, the Old Bailey, Ludgate Hill, Warwick Lane, Newgate, Paules Chaine, Watling Streete, now flaming, and most of it reduc'd to ashes; the stones of Paules flew like granados, the mealting lead running downe the streetes in a streame, and the very pavements glowing with fiery rednesse, so as no horse nor man was able to tread on them, and the demolition had stopp'd all the passages, so that no help could be applied. The Eastern wind still more impetuously driving the flames forward. Nothing but the Almighty power of God was able to stop them, for vaine was the help of man.

5. It crossed towards Whitehall; but oh,

the confusion there was then at that Court! It pleas'd his Majesty to command me among the rest to looke after the quenching of Fetter Lane end, to preserve if possible that part of Holborn, whilst the rest of the gentlemen tooke their several posts, some at one part, some at another (for now they began to bestir themselves, and not till now, who hitherto had stood as men intoxicated, with their hands acrosse), and began to consider that nothing was likely to put a stop but the blowing up of so many houses as might make a wider gap than any had yet ben made by the ordinary method of pulling them downe with engines; this some stout seamen propos'd early enough to have sav'd nearly the whole Citty, but this some tenacious and avaritious men, aldermen, &c. would not permit, because their houses must have ben of the first. It was therefore now commanded to be practic'd, and my concerne being particularly for the Hospital of St. Bartholomew neere Smithfield, where I had my wounded and sick men, made me the more diligent to promote it; nor was my care for the Savoy lesse. It now pleas'd God by abating the wind, and by the industrie of the people, when almost all was lost, infusing a new spirit into them, that the furie of it began sensibly to abate about noone, so as it came no farther than the Temple Westward, nor than the entrance of Smithfield North: but continu'd all this day and night so impetuous toward Cripple-gate and the Tower as made us all despaire; it also brake out againe in the Temple, but the courage of the multitude persisting, and many houses being blown up, such gaps and desolations were soone made, as with the former three days consumption, the back fire did not so vehemently urge upon the rest as formerly. There was yet no standing neere the burning and glowing ruines by neere a furlongs space.

The coale and wood wharfes and magazines of oyle, rosin, &c. did infinite mischeife, so as the invective which a little before I had dedicated to his Majesty and publish'd,[1] giving warning what might probably be the issue of suffering those shops to be in the Citty, was look'd on as a prophecy.

The poore inhabitants were dispers'd about St. George's Fields, and Moorefields, as far as Highgate, and severall miles in circle, some under tents, some under miserable hutts and hovells, many without a rag or any necessary utensills, bed or board, who from delicatenesse, riches, and easy accomodations in stately and

---

[1] The *Fumifugium.*

well furnish'd houses, were now reduced to extreamest misery and poverty.

In this calamitous condition I return'd with a sad heart to my house, blessing and adoring the distinguishing mercy of God to me and mine, who, in the midst of all this ruine was like Lot, in my little Zoar, were safe and sound.

Sept. 6, Thursday. I represented to his Majesty the case of the French prisoners at war in my custodie, and besought him that there might be still the same care of watching at all places contiguous to unseised houses. It is not indeede imaginable how extraordinary the vigilance and activity of the King and the Duke was, even labouring in person, and being present to command, order, reward, or encourage workmen, by which he shewed his affection to his people and gained theirs. Having then dispos'd of some under cure at the Savoy, I return'd to White-hall, where I din'd at Mr. Offley's,[1] the groome porter, who was my relation.

7. I went this morning on foote from White-hall as far as London Bridge, thro' the late Fleete Street, Ludgate Hill, by St. Paules, Cheapeside, Exchange, Bishopsgate, Aldersgate, and out to Moorefields, thence thro' Cornehill, &c. with extraordinary difficulty, clambering over heaps of yet smoking rubbish, and frequently mistaking where I was. The ground under my feete so hot, that it even burnt the soles of my shoes. In the mean time his Majesty got to the Tower by water, to demolish the houses about the graff, which being built intirely about it, had they taken fire and attack'd the White Tower where the magazine of powder lay, would undoubtedly not only have beaten downe and destroyed all the bridge, but sunke and torne the vessells in the river, and render'd the demolition beyond all expression for several miles about the countrey.

At my returne I was infinitely concern'd to find that goodly Church St. Paules now a sad ruine, and that beautifull portico (for structure comparable to any in Europe, as not long before repair'd by the late King) now rent in pieces, flakes of vast stone split asunder, and nothing remaining intire but the inscription in the architrave, shewing by whom it was built, which had not one letter of it defac'd. It was astonishing to see what immense stones the heate had in a manner calcin'd, so that all

the ornaments, columnes, freezes, capitals, and projectures of massie Portland stone flew off, even to the very roofe, where a sheet of lead covering a great space (no lesse than 6 akers by measure) was totally mealted ; the ruines of the vaulted roofe falling broke into St. Faith's, which being fill'd with the magazines of bookes belonging to the Stationers, and carried thither for safety, they were all consum'd, burning for a weeke following. It is also observable that the lead over the altar at the East end was untouch'd, and among the divers monuments, the body of one Bishop remain'd intire. Thus lay in ashes that most venerable Church, one of the most antient pieces of early piety in the Christian world, besides neere 100 more. The lead, yron worke, bells, plate, &c. mealted; the exquisitely wrought Mercers Chapell, the sumptuous Exchange, the august fabriq of Christ Church, all the rest of the Companies Halls, splendid buildings, arches, enteries, all in dust; the fountaines dried up and ruin'd, whilst the very waters remain'd boiling; the voragos of subterranean cellars, wells, and dungeons, formerely warehouses, still burning in stench and darke clowds of smoke, so that in five or six miles traversing about, I did not see one loade of timber unconsum'd, nor many stones but what were calcin'd white as snow. The people who now walk'd about the ruines appear'd like men in some dismal desart, or rather in some greate Citty laid waste by a cruel enemy; to which was added the stench that came from some poore creatures bodies, beds, and other combustible goods. Sir Tho. Gressham's statue, tho' fallen from its nich in the Royal Exchange, remain'd intire, when all those of the Kings since the Conquest were broken to pieces; also the standard in Cornehill, and Q. Elizabeth's effigies, with some armes on Ludgate, continued with but little detriment, whilst the vast yron chaines of the Citty streetes, hinges, barrs and gates of prisons, were many of them mealted and reduced to cinders by the vehement heate. Nor was I yet able to passe through any of the narrower streetes, but kept the widest; the ground and aire, smoake and fiery vapour, continu'd so intense that my haire was almost sing'd, and my feete unsufferably surbated. The bie lanes and narrower streetes were quite fill'd up with rubbish, nor could one have possibly knowne where he was, but by the ruines of some Church or Hall, that had some remarkable tower or pinnacle remaining. I then went towards Islington and Highgate, where one might have scene 200,000 people of all ranks and degrees dispers'd and lying along

---

[1] Dr. Offley was rector of Abinger, and donor of farms to Okewood Chapel in the parish of Wotton, in the patronage of the Evelyn family.

by their heapes of what they could save from the fire, deploring their losse, and tho' ready to perish for hunger and destitution, yet not asking one pennie for reliefe, which to me appear'd a stranger sight than any I had yet beheld. His Majesty and Council indeed tooke all imaginable care for their reliefe by proclamation for the country to come in and refresh them with provisions. In the midst of all this calamity and confusion, there was, I know not how, an alarme begun that the French and Dutch, with whom we were now in hostility, were not onely landed, but even entering the Citty. There was in truth some days before greate suspicion of those two nations joyning; and now, that they had ben the occasion of firing the towne. This report did so terrifie, that on a suddaine there was such an uproare and tumult that they ran from their goods, and taking what weapons they could come at, they could not be stopp'd from falling on some of those nations whom they casually met, without sense or reason. The clamour and peril grew so excessive that it made the whole Court amaz'd, and they did with infinite paines and greate difficulty reduce and appease the people, sending troops of soldiers and guards to cause them to retire into the fields againe, where they were watch'd all this night. I left them pretty quiet, and came home sufficiently weary and broken. Their spirits thus a little calmed, and the affright abated, they now began to repaire into the suburbs about the Citty, where such as had friends or opportunity got shelter for the present, to which his Majesty's Proclamation also invited them.

Still the plague continuing in our parish, I could not without danger adventure to our church.

10. I went againe to the ruines, for it was now no longer a Citty.

13 Sept. I presented his Majesty with a survey of the ruines, and a plot for a new Citty, with a discourse on it; whereupon after dinner his Majesty sent for me into the Queen's bed-chamber, her Majesty and the Duke onely being present; they examin'd each particular, and discours'd on them for neere an houre, seeming to be extreamely pleas'd with what I had so early thought on. The Queene was now in her cavalier riding habite, hat and feather, and horseman's coate, going out to take the aire.

16. I went to Greenewich Church, where Mr. Plume preached very well from this text: 'Seeing therefore all these things must be dissolved,' &c. taking occasion from the late unparalell'd conflagration to remind us how we ought to walke more holyly in all manner of conversation.

27. Dined at Sir Wm. D'Oylie's with that worthy gent. Sir John Holland of Suffolke.

10 Oct. This day was order'd a generall fast thro' the Nation, to humble us on the late dreadfull conflagration, added to the plague and warr, the most dismall judgments that could be inflicted, but which indeede we highly deserv'd for our prodigious ingratitude, burning lusts, dissolute Court, profane and abominable lives, under such dispensations of God's continu'd favour in restoring Church, Prince, and People from our late intestine calamities, of which we were altogether unmindfull, even to astonishment. This made me resolve to go to our parish assemblie, where our Doctor preached on the 19 Luke 41, piously applying it to the occasion. After which was a collection for the distress'd loosers in the late fire.

LOVE'S EYES.

O me, what eyes hath love put in my head,
Which have no correspondence with true sight!
Or, if they have, where is my judgment fled,
That censures falsely what they see aright?
If that be fair whereon my false eyes dote,
What means the world to say it is not so?
If it be not, then love doth well denote
Love's eye is not so true as all men's "No."
How can it? O, how can Love's eye be true,
That is so vex'd with watching and with tears?
No marvel then, though I mistake my view;
The sun itself sees not till heaven clears.
    O cunning Love! with tears thou keep'st me blind,
    Lest eyes well-seeing thy foul faults should find.
                              SHAKSPEARE.

THE SEA CAVE.

Hardly we breathe, although the air be free.
How massively doth awful nature pile
The living rock, like some cathedral aisle,
Sacred to silence and the solemn sea!
How that clear pool lies sleeping tranquilly,
And under its glassed surface seems to smile,
With many hues, a mimic grove the while,
Of foliage submarine—shrub, flower, and tree!
Beautiful scene! and fitted to allure
The printless footsteps of some sea-born maid;
Who here, with her green tresses disarrayed,
'Mid the clear bath, unfearing and secure,
May sport, at noontide in the caverned shade,
Cold as the shadow, as the waters pure.
                              THOMAS DOUBLEDAY.

NEW YEAR NUMBERS.

[William Sawyer, born at Brighton, 26th July, 1828. Poet and novelist. He was early connected with literature as a contributor to the magazines; in 1846 he published *Stray Leaves*, and in 1849 *Thought and Reverie*, two volumes of poems. In 1867 appeared his *Ten Miles from Town*, and in 1872 his *Legend of Phyllis*—an exquisite new reading of an old story—which established his reputation as a poet. He has also written a number of novels, which have appeared anonymously. Of *Ten Miles from Town*, Dr. Westland Marston said: "It is long since I have enjoyed, in modern works, pictures so charming, so individual, so earnestly and so conscientiously wrought out as those this book presents; or listened to strains of feeling so high and pure, and so finished in point of execution." Grace, fancy, music, and tender thought distinguish his poems.]

Trust Him that is thy God, and have no fear:
His eyelids ache not with the drowse of sleep,
He cannot tire, and how should He forget?

Self-centred in His own eternity,
He that is All is cause and law of all;
Alike in orb and atom infinite.

The worlds He soweth broadcast with His hand,
As o'er the glebe the sower soweth seed,
Till with His glory all the heavens are sown.

Yet perfect from His shaping fingers sent
The rain-drop glitters populous with life;
And in a jewelled surcoat wheels the gnat.

Behold the yearly miracle of Spring!
The pinky nipples of the budding leaves
Break in a night, and lo, the wood is green!

Art thou more bare than is the winter wood,
Or less esteemed of Him who gives thee joy
In the first rustle of the April leaves?

And if thy prime be gone and thou lament,
"The leaves are falling and the fruit is done!"
Yet shrink not from the winter of thy days.

See where the cruel winds have swept the trees
And all are branching bare against the night,
There, in the barren spaces, hang the stars.

So when the leafage of thy days is past,
And life is desolate, repine thou not,—
God can give thee the stars of heaven for fruit!

Nor fear thou death. God's law is gain in loss:
Growth and decay obey a common law,
The starry blossom and the seed are one.

Think! Thou wert born and fashioned for a world
Assorted to thy needs and thy delights,
And wherein thou hast dwelt and had content.

Not of thy strength nor cunning didst thou come,
Into the fief and heritage of life;
And shall all fail thee in thy going hence?

Thou art not of thyself a thing alone,
But of the earth which shaped and nourisheth
And is thy vital warmth and fount of life.

Its mountains are thy brothers, and its woods,
Its seas have lent thee, and its affluent winds
Spare thee thy being for a little space.

All things have part in thee as thou in all
Hast thine own part; thy soul its part in God,
And all enduring, shalt not thou endure?

The salt foam of the sea upon thy lips,
The blown sand of the desert in thy face,
Shall these outlast the ages and not thou?

The star shines and the cloud slips from its face
Each to its function, moving to one law;
And both imperishable, cloud and star.

Content thyself and comfort thee in this;
In God's design is neither best nor worst,
To Him the greater is not nor the less.

The All of all embraces gain and loss,
His steadfast and his fleeting are as one,
And of His ordered change is ordered good.

In Him love bounds the infinite of might,
And He who giveth both to live and die
Is equal Lord of Life and Lord of Death.

THE WIDOW'S MITE.

BY FREDERICK LOCKER.

A widow, she had only one!
A puny and decrepit son;
  But, day and night,
Though fretful oft, and weak and small,
A loving child, he was her all—
  The widow's mite.

The widow's mite—ay, so sustain'd,
She battled onward, nor complain'd
  Tho' friends were fewer:
And while she toil'd for daily fare,
A little crutch upon the stair
  Was music to her.

I saw her then,—and now I see
That, though resign'd and cheerful, she
  Has sorrow'd much:
She has, HE gave it tenderly,
Much faith; and, carefully laid by,
  A little crutch.

1856.   —*London Lyrics.*

SOCIETY IN LAST CENTURY.

[Frances Burney (Madame D'Arblay), born at Lynn Regis, Norfolk, 13th June, 1752; died at Bath, 6th January, 1840. She was the second daughter of Dr. Charles Burney, the author of the *History of Music*, and was for five years one of the keepers of the robes to Queen Charlotte. She had many opportunities of studying society and manners, and her works show that she did not neglect them. Her most notable productions are: *Evelina*, or the History of a Young Lady's Introduction to the World (from which we quote); *Cecilia*, or the Memoirs of an Heiress; *Camilla*, or a Picture of Youth; *The Wanderer*, or Female Difficulties; and the *Memoirs* of her father Dr. Burney. Her diary, published after her death, contains several valuable sketches of society towards the close of the last century. Dr. Johnson said: "Miss Burney is a real wonder. What she is, she is intuitively." Macaulay thought that "Miss Burney did for the English novel what Jeremy Collier did for the English drama. She first showed that a tale might be written in which both the fashionable and the vulgar life of London might be exhibited with great force, and with broad comic humour, and which yet should not contain a single line inconsistent with rigid morality."]

[The characters in the following scenes are:—Mrs. Beaumont, the hostess of the party; Lady Louisa, sister of Lord Orville, affected and vain, and betrothed to Lord Merton, a dissipated man about town, pretending to be reformed; Mr. Coverley, a sporting gentleman; Mr. Lovel, a fop; Mrs. Selwyn, a shrewd sarcastic lady in charge of Evelina, the heroine, who is a beautiful and unsophisticated girl, now betrothed to Lord Orville, a gentleman of sense and position; Captain Mirvan, a retired seaman, rough, and given to practical jokes; Maria, his daughter. Evelina writes:—]

The charming city of Bath answered all my expectations. The Crescent, the prospect from it, and the elegant symmetry of the Circus, delighted me. The Parades, I own, rather disappointed me; one of them is scarce preferable to some of the best paved streets in London: and the other, though it affords a beautiful prospect, a charming view of Prior-Park and of the Avon, yet wanted something in *itself* of more striking elegance than a mere broad pavement, to satisfy the ideas I had formed of it.

At the pump-room I was amazed at the public exhibition of the ladies in the bath; it is true, their heads are covered with bonnets; but the very idea of being seen in such a situation, by whoever pleases to look, is indelicate.

"'Fore George," said the captain, looking into the bath, "this would be a most excellent place for old Madame French to dance a fandango in! By jingo, I wouldn't wish for better sport than to swing her round this here pond!"

"She would be very much obliged to you," said Lord Orville, "for so extraordinary a mark of your favour."

"Why, to let you know," answered the captain, "she hit my fancy mightily; I never took so much to an old tabby before."

"Really now," cried Mr. Lovel, looking also into the bath, "I must confess it is, to me, very incomprehensible why the ladies choose that frightful unbecoming dress to bathe in! I have often pondered very seriously upon the subject, but could never hit upon the reason."

"Well, I declare," said Lady Louisa, "I should like of all things to set something new a-going; I always hated bathing, because one can get no pretty dress for it! Now do, there's a good creature, try to help me to something."

"Who, me!—O dear ma'am," said he, simpering, "I can't pretend to assist a person of your ladyship's taste; besides, I have not the least head for fashions—I really don't think I ever invented above three in my life! but I never had the least turn for dress,—never any notion of fancy or elegance."

"O fie, Mr. Lovel! how can you talk so?—don't we all know that you lead the *ton* in the *beau monde*? I declare, I think you dress better than anybody."

"O dear, ma'am, you confuse me to the last degree! *I* dress well!—I protest I don't think I'm ever fit to be seen!—I'm often shocked to death to think what a figure I go. If your ladyship will believe me, I was full half an hour this morning thinking what I should put on!"

"Odds my life," cried the captain, "I wish I'd been near you!—I warrant I'd have quickened your motions a little. Half an hour thinking what you'd put on! and who the deuce do you think cares the snuff of a candle whether you've anything on or not?"

"O pray, captain," cried Mrs. Selwyn, "don't be angry with the gentleman for *thinking*, whatever be the cause, for I assure you he makes no common practice of offending in that way."

"Really, ma'am, you're prodigiously kind," said Mr. Lovel, angrily.

"Pray now," said the captain, "did you ever get a ducking in that there place yourself?"

"A ducking, sir!" repeated Mr. Lovel: "I protest I think that's rather an odd term!—but if you mean a *bathing*, it is an honour I have had many times."

"And pray, if a body may be so bold, what do you do with that frizzle-frize top of your own? Why, I'll lay you what you will, there is fat and grease enough on your crown to buoy you up, if you were to go in head downwards."

"And I don't know," cried Mrs. Selwyn, "but that might be the easiest way: for I'm sure it would be the lightest."

"For the matter of that there," said the captain, "you must make him a soldier before you can tell which is lightest, head or heels. Howsomever, I'd lay ten pounds to a shilling I could whisk him so dexterously over into the pool, that he should light plump upon his foretop and turn round like a tetotum."

"Done!" cried Lord Merton; "I take your odds."

"Will you?" returned he; "why then, 'fore George, I'd do it as soon as say Jack Robinson."

"He, he!" faintly laughed Mr. Lovel, as he moved abruptly from the window; "'pon honour, this is pleasant enough; but I don't see what right anybody has to lay wagers about one without one's consent."

"There, Lovel, you are out," cried Mr. Coverley; "any man may lay what wager about you he will; your consent is nothing to the purpose: he may lay that your nose is sky-blue if he pleases."

"Ay," said Mrs. Selwyn, "or that your mind is more adorned than your person;—or any absurdity whatsoever."

"I protest," said Mr. Lovel, "I think it's a very disagreeable privilege, and I must beg that nobody may take such a liberty with *me.*"

"Like enough you may," cried the captain; "but what's that to the purpose? Suppose I've a mind to lay that you've never a tooth in your head—pray, how will you hinder me?"

"You'll allow me, at least, sir, to take the liberty of asking how you'll *prove* it?"

"How?—why, by knocking them all down your throat."

"Knocking them all down my throat, sir!" repeated Mr. Lovel, with a look of horror; "I protest I never heard anything so shocking in my life! And I must beg leave to observe, that no wager, in my opinion, could justify such a barbarous action."

Here Lord Orville interfered, and hurried us to our carriages.

We returned in the same order we came. Mrs. Beaumont invited all the party to dinner, and has been so obliging as to beg Miss Mirvan may continue at her house during her stay. The captain will lodge at the Wells.

The first half-hour after our return was de-

voted to hearing Mr. Lovel's apologies for dining in his riding-dress.

Mrs. Beaumont then, addressing herself to Miss Mirvan and me, inquired how we liked Bath.

"I hope," said Mr. Lovel, "the ladies do not call this seeing Bath."

"No!—what should ail 'em?" cried the captain; "do you suppose they put their eyes in their pockets?"

"No, sir; but I fancy you will find no person—that is, no person of any condition—call going about a few places in a morning *seeing Bath.*"

"Mayhap, then," said the literal captain, "you think we should see it better by going about at midnight?"

"No, sir, no," said Mr. Lovel, with a super cilious smile, "I perceive you don't understand me;—*we* should never call it *seeing Bath* without going at the right season."

"Why, what a plague then," demanded he, "can you only see at one season of the year?" Mr. Lovel again smiled; but seemed superior to making any answer.

"The Bath amusements," said Lord Orville, "have a sameness in them, which, after a short time, renders them rather insipid; but the greatest objection that can be made to the place is the encouragement it gives to gamesters."

"Why, I hope, my lord, you would not think of abolishing *gaming,*" cried Lord Merton; "'tis the very *zest* of life! Devil take me if I could live without it."

"I am sorry for it," said Lord Orville, gravely, and looking at Lady Louisa.

"Your lordship is no judge of this subject," continued the other; "but if once we could get you to a gaming-table, you'd never be happy away from it."

"I hope, my lord," cried Lady Louisa, "that nobody *here* ever occasions your quitting it."

"Your ladyship," said Lord Merton, recollecting himself, "has power to make me quite anything."

"Except *herself,*" said Mr. Coverley. "Egad, my lord, I think I've helped you out there!"

"You men of wit, Jack," answered his lordship, "are always ready; for my part, I don't pretend to any talents that way."

"Really, my lord?" asked the sarcastic Mrs. Selwyn: "well, that is wonderful, considering success would be so much in your power."

"Pray, ma'am," said Mr. Lovel to Lady Louisa, "has your ladyship heard the news?"

"News!—what news?"

"Why, the report circulating at the Wells concerning a certain person."

"O Lord, no: pray tell me what it is?"

"O no, ma'am, I beg your la'ship will excuse me; 'tis a profound secret, and I would not have mentioned it, if I had not thought you knew it."

"Lord, now, how can you be so monstrous? I declare, now, you're a provoking creature! But come, I know you'll tell me;—won't you, now?"

"Your la'ship knows I am but too happy to obey you; but, 'pon honour, I can't speak a word if you won't all promise me the most inviolable secrecy."

"I wish you'd wait for that from me," said the captain, "and I'll give you my word you'd be dumb for one while. Secrecy, quoth-a!— 'Fore George, I wonder you a'n't ashamed to mention such a word when you talk of telling it to a woman. Though, for the matter of that, I'd as lief blab it to the whole sex at once as to go for to tell it to such a thing as you."

"Such a thing as me, sir!" said Mr. Lovel, letting fall his knife and fork, and looking very important; "I really have not the honour to understand your expression."

"It's all one for that," said the captain; "you may have it explained whenever you like it."

"'Pon honour, sir," returned Mr. Lovel, "I must take the liberty to tell you, that I should be extremely offended, but that I suppose it to be some sea-phrase; and therefore I'll let it pass without further notice."

Lord Orville, then, to change the discourse, asked Miss Mirvan, if she should spend the ensuing winter in London.

"No, to be sure," said the captain; "what should she for? she saw all that was to be seen before."

"Is London, then," said Mr. Lovel, smiling at Lady Louisa, "only to be regarded as a sight?"

"Why, pray, Mr. Wiseacre, how are you pleased for to regard it yourself?—Answer me to that."

"O sir, my opinion, I fancy, you would hardly find intelligible. I don't understand sea-phrases enough to define it to your comprehension. Does not your la'ship think the task would be rather difficult?"

"O Lord, yes," cried Lady Louisa; "I declare I'd as soon teach my parrot to talk Welsh."

"Ha! ha! ha! admirable!—'Pon honour, your la'ship's quite in luck to-day; but that, indeed, your la'ship is every day. Though,

to be sure, it is but candid to acknowledge, that the gentlemen of the ocean have a set of ideas, as well as a dialect, so opposite to ours, that it is by no means surprising they should regard London as a mere show, that may be seen by being looked at. Ha! ha! ha!"

"Ha! ha!" echoed Lady Louisa: "Well, I declare you are the drollest creature."

"He! he! 'Pon honour, I can't help laughing at the conceit of seeing London in a few weeks!"

"And what a plague should hinder you?" cried the captain; "do you want to spend a day in every street?"

Here again Lady Louisa and Mr. Lovel interchanged smiles.

"Why, I warrant you, if I had the showing it, I'd haul you from St. James's to Wapping the very first morning."

The smiles were now, with added contempt, repeated; which the captain observing, looked very fiercely at Mr. Lovel, and said, "Hark'ee, my spark, none of your grinning!—'tis a lingo I don't understand; and if you give me any more of it, I shall go near to lend you a box o' the ear."

"I protest, sir," said Mr. Lovel, turning extremely pale, "I think it's taking a very particular liberty with a person, to talk to one in such a style as this!"

"It's like you may," returned the captain: "but give a good gulp, and I'll warrant you'll swallow it." Then calling for a glass of ale, with a very provoking and significant nod, he drank to his easy digestion.

Mr. Lovel made no answer, but looked extremely sullen; and soon after, we left the gentlemen to themselves.

At tea-time we were joined by all the gentlemen but Captain Mirvan, who went to the hotel where he was to sleep, and made his daughter accompany him, to separate her trumpery, as he called it, from his clothes.

As soon as they were gone, Mr. Lovel, who still appeared extremely sulky, said, "I protest I never saw such a vulgar, abusive fellow in my life as that captain: 'pon honour, I believe he came here for no purpose in the world but to pick a quarrel: however, for my part, I vow I won't humour him."

"I declare," cried Lady Louisa, "he put me in a monstrous fright;—I never heard anybody talk so shocking in my life!"

"I think," said Mrs. Selwyn, with great solemnity, "he threatened to box your ears, Mr. Lovel:—did not he?"

"Really, ma'am," said Mr. Lovel, colouring, "if one was to mind everything those low kind of people say, one should never be at rest for one impertinence or other; so I think the best way is to be above taking any notice of them."

"What!" said Mrs. Selwyn, with the same gravity, "and so receive the blow in silence?"

During this discourse I heard the captain's chaise stop at the door, and ran downstairs to meet Maria. She was alone, and told me that her father, who, she was sure, had some scheme in agitation against Mr. Lovel, had sent her on before him. We continued in the parlour till his return, and were joined by Lord Orville, who begged me not to insist on a patience so unnatural, as submitting to be excluded our society. And let me, my dear sir, with a grateful heart let me own, I never before passed half an hour in such perfect felicity.

I believe we were all sorry when the captain returned; yet his inward satisfaction, from however different a cause, did not seem inferior to what ours had been. He chucked Maria under the chin, rubbed his hands, and was scarce able to contain the fulness of his glee. We all attended him to the drawing-room; where, having composed his countenance, without any previous attention to Mrs. Beaumont, he marched up to Mr. Lovel, and abruptly said, "Pray, have you e'er a brother in these here parts?"

"Me, sir? No, thank Heaven, I'm free from all encumbrances of that sort."

"Well," cried the captain, "I met a person just now so like you, I could have sworn he had been your twin-brother."

"It would have been a most singular pleasure to me," said Mr. Lovel, "if I also could have seen him: for, really, I have not the least notion what sort of person I am, and I have a prodigious curiosity to know."

Just then the captain's servant, opening the door, said, "A little gentleman below desires to see one Mr. Lovel."

"Beg him to walk up stairs," said Mrs. Beaumont. "But, pray, what is the reason William is out of the way?"

The man shut the door without any answer.

"I can't imagine who it is," said Mr. Lovel. "I recollect no little gentleman of my acquaintance now at Bristol,—except indeed the Marquis of Charlton;—but I don't much fancy it can be him. Let me see, who else is there so very little?"

A confused noise among the servants now drew all eyes towards the door: the impatient captain hastened to open it; and then clapping his hands, called out, "'Fore George,

'tis the same person I took for your relation."

And then, to the utter astonishment of everybody but himself, he hauled into the room a monkey, full dressed, and extravagantly à la mode!

The dismay of the company was almost general. Poor Mr. Lovel seemed thunderstruck with indignation and surprise: Lady Louisa began a scream, which for some time was incessant; Miss Mirvan and I jumped involuntarily upon the seats of our chairs; Mrs. Beaumont herself followed our example; Lord Orville placed himself before me as a guard; and Mrs. Selwyn, Lord Merton, and Mr. Coverley, burst into a loud, immoderate, ungovernable fit of laughter, in which they were joined by the captain, till, unable to support himself, he rolled on the floor.

The first voice which made its way through this general noise was that of Lady Louisa, which her fright and screaming rendered extremely shrill. "Take it away!" cried she, "take the monster away;—I shall faint, I shall faint, if you don't!"

Mr. Lovel, irritated beyond endurance, angrily demanded of the captain what he meant.

"Mean?" cried the captain, as soon as he was able to speak; "why only to show you in your proper colours." Then, rising and pointing to the monkey, "Why, now, ladies and gentlemen, I'll be judged by you all!—Did you ever see anything more like? —Odds my life, if it wasn't for this here tail, you wouldn't know one from t'other."

"Sir," cried Mr. Lovel, stamping, "I shall take a time to make you feel my wrath."

"Come now," continued the regardless captain, "just for the fun's sake, doff your coat and waistcoat, and swop with Monsieur Grinagain here; and I'll warrant you'll not know yourself which is which."

"Not know myself from a monkey!—I assure you, sir, I'm not to be used in this manner, and I won't bear it, curse me if I will!"

"Why, hey-day!" cried the captain, "what, is master in a passion?—Well, don't be angry —come, he sha'n't hurt you;—here, shake a paw with him:—why, he'll do you no harm, man!—come, kiss and be friends!"

"Who, I?" cried Mr. Lovel, almost mad with vexation; "as I'm a living creature, I would not touch him for a thousand worlds!"

"Send him a challenge," cried Mr. Coverley, "and I'll be your second."

"Ay, do," said the captain, and I'll be second

to my friend Monsieur Clapperclaw here. Come to it at once!—tooth and nail!"

"Heaven forbid!" cried Mr. Lovel, retreating, "I would sooner trust my person with a mad bull!"

"I don't like the looks of him myself," said Lord Merton, "for he grins most horribly."

"O, I'm frightened out of my senses!" cried Lady Louisa: "take him away, or I shall die!"

"Captain," said Lord Orville, "the ladies are alarmed; and I must beg you would send the monkey away."

"Why, where can be the mighty harm of one monkey more than another?" answered the captain: "howsomever if it's agreeable to the ladies, suppose we turn them out together?"

"What do you mean by that, sir?" cried Mr. Lovel, lifting up his cane.

"What do you mean?" cried the captain, fiercely: "be so good as to down with your cane."

Poor Mr. Lovel, too much intimidated to stand his ground, yet too much enraged to submit, turned hastily round, and, forgetful of consequences, vented his passion by giving a furious blow to the monkey.

The creature, darting forwards, sprung instantly upon him: and clinging round his neck, fastened his teeth to one of his ears.

I was really sorry for the poor man; who, though an egregious fop, had committed no offence that merited such chastisement.

It was impossible now to distinguish whose screams were loudest, those of Mr. Lovel or of the terrified Lady Louisa, who, I believe, thought her own turn was approaching: but the unrelenting captain roared with joy.

Not so Lord Orville: ever humane, generous, and benevolent, he quitted his charge, who he saw was wholly out of danger, and seizing the monkey by the collar, made him loosen the ear; and then, with a sudden swing, flung him out of the room, and shut the door.

Poor Mr. Lovel, almost fainting with terror, sunk upon the floor, crying out, "O, I shall die, I shall die! O, I'm bit to death!"

"Captain Mirvan," said Mrs. Beaumont, with no little indignation, "I must own I don't perceive the wit of this action; and I am sorry to have such cruelty practised in my house."

"Why, Lord, ma'am," said the captain, when his rapture abated sufficiently for speech, "how could I tell they'd fall out so?—By jingo, I brought him to be a messmate for t'other."

"Egad," said Mr. Coverley, "I would not have been served so for a thousand pounds."

"Why, then, there's the odds of it," said the captain; "for you see he is served so for nothing. But come," turning to Mr. Lovel, "be of good heart; all may end well yet, and you and monseer Longtail be as good friends as ever."

"I'm surprised, Mrs. Beaumont," cried Mr. Lovel, starting up, "that you can suffer a person under your roof to be treated so inhumanly."

"What argufies so many words?" said the unfeeling captain; "it is but a slit of the ear; it only looks as if you had been in the pillory."

"Very true," added Mrs. Selwyn; "and who knows but it may acquire you the credit of being an antiministerial writer?"

"I protest," cried Mr. Lovel, looking ruefully at his dress, "my new riding-suit's all over blood!"

"Ha, ha, ha!" cried the captain, "see what comes of studying for an hour what you shall put on!"

Mr. Lovel then walked to the glass; and looking at the place, exclaimed, "O Heaven, what a monstrous wound! my ear will never be fit to be seen again!"

"Why then," said the captain, "you must hide it;—'tis but wearing a wig."

"A wig!" repeated the affrighted Mr. Lovel; "I wear a wig?—No, not if you would give me a thousand pounds an hour!"

"I declare," said Lady Louisa, "I never heard such a shocking proposal in my life!"

Lord Orville then, seeing no prospect that the altercation would cease, proposed to the captain to walk. He assented; and having given Mr. Lovel a nod of exultation, accompanied his lordship down stairs.

"'Pon honour," said Mr. Lovel, the moment the door was shut, "that fellow is the greatest brute in nature! he ought not to be admitted into a civilized society."

"Lovel," said Mr. Coverley, affecting to whisper, "you must certainly pink him: you must not put up with such an affront."

"Sir," said Mr. Lovel, "with any common person I should not deliberate an instant; but really with a fellow who has done nothing but fight all his life, 'pon honour, sir, I can't think of it!"

"Lovel," said Lord Merton, in the same voice, "you must call him to account."

"Every man," said he, pettishly, "is the best judge of his own affairs; and I don't ask the honour of any person's advice."

"Egad, Lovel," said Mr. Coverley, "you're in for it!—you can't possibly be off!"

"Sir," cried he, very impatiently, "upon any proper occasion, I should be as ready to show my courage as anybody; but as to fighting for such a trifle as this—I protest I should blush to think of it!"

"A trifle!" cried Mrs. Selwyn; "good Heaven! and have you made this astonishing riot about a *trifle?*"

"Ma'am," answered the poor wretch in great confusion, "I did not know at first but that my cheek might have been bit; but as 'tis no worse, why, it does not a great deal signify. Mrs. Beaumont, I have the honour to wish you a good evening; I'm sure my carriage must be waiting." And then, very abruptly, he left the room.

What a commotion has this mischief-loving captain raised! Were I to remain here long, even the society of my dear Maria could scarce compensate for the disturbances which he excites.

ON SIGHT OF A LADY'S FACE IN THE WATER.

[Thomas Carew, born 1589; died 1639. He belonged to a Gloucestershire family of distinction; educated at Oxford, and became gentleman of the privy chamber and sewer in ordinary to Charles I. He wrote elegant lyrics, and a masque entitled *Cœlum Britannicum*, once ascribed to Sir William Davenant. "He deservedly ranks among the earliest of those who gave a cultivated grace to our lyrical strains."—*Campbell.*]

Stand still, you floods, do not deface
    That image which you bear:
So votaries, from every place,
    To you shall altars rear.

No winds but lover's sighs blow here,
    To trouble these glad streams,
On which no star from any sphere
    Did ever dart such beams.

To crystal then in haste congeal,
    Lest you should lose your bliss;
And to my cruel fair reveal,
    How cold, how hard she is.

But if the envious Nymphs shall fear
    Their beauties will be scorn'd,
And hire the ruder winds to tear
    That face which you adorn'd;

Then rage and foam amain, that we
    Their malice may despise;
And from your froth we soon shall see
    A second Venus rise.

CŒUR DE LION IN PALESTINE.

[Edward Gibbon, born at Putney, Surrey, 27th April, 1737; died in London, 15th January, 1794. Author of *The Decline and Fall of the Roman Empire*; *The History of the Crusades*; *An Essay on the Study of Literature*, and an *Autobiography*. His great History was first projected in October, 1764, and was completed on the 27th June, 1787, at Lausanne, where a large portion of it was written and where the author spent much of his life. Gibbon is said to have received £6000 for the whole work.]

Philip Augustus and Richard I. are the only kings of France and England who (A.D. 1191–92) have fought under the same banners; but the holy service in which they were enlisted was incessantly disturbed by their national jealousy; and the two factions which they protected in Palestine were more averse to each other than to the common enemy. In the eyes of the orientals the French monarch was superior in dignity and power, and in the emperor's absence the Latins revered him as their temporal chief. His exploits were not adequate to his fame. Philip was brave, but the statesman predominated in his character; he was soon weary of sacrificing his health and interest on a barren coast. The surrender of Acre became the signal of his departure; nor could he justify this unpopular desertion by leaving the Duke of Burgundy, with 500 knights and 10,000 foot, for the service of the Holy Land. The King of England, though inferior in dignity, surpassed his rival in wealth and military renown; and if heroism be confined to brutal and ferocious valour, Richard Plantagenet will stand high among the heroes of the age. The memory of Cœur de Lion, of the lion-hearted prince, was long dear and glorious to his English subjects, and at the distance of sixty years it was celebrated in proverbial sayings by the grandsons of the Turks and Saracens, against whom he had fought. His tremendous name was employed by the Syrian mothers to silence their infants; and if a horse suddenly started from the way, his rider was wont to exclaim, "Dost thou think King Richard is in that bush?" His cruelty to the Mohammedans was the effect of temper and zeal; but I cannot believe that a soldier so free and fearless in the use of his lance would have descended to whet a dagger against his valiant brother Conrad of Montferrat, who was slain at Tyre by some secret assassins. After the surrender of Acre and the departure of Philip, the King of England led the Crusaders to the recovery of the sea-coast; and the cities of Cæsarea and Jaffa were added to the fragments of the Kingdom of Lusignan. A march of 100 miles from Acre to Ascalon was a great and perpetual battle of eleven days. In the disorder of his troops Saladin remained on the field with seventeen guards without lowering his standard or suspending the sound of his brazen kettle-drum. He again rallied and renewed the charge, and his preachers or heralds called aloud on the *unitarians* manfully to stand up against the Christian idolaters. But the progress of these idolaters was irresistible; and it was only by demolishing the walls and buildings of Ascalon that the sultan could prevent them from occupying an important fortress on the confines of Egypt. During a severe winter the armies slept; but in the spring the Franks advanced within a day's march of Jerusalem, under the leading standard of the English king, and his active spirit intercepted a convoy or caravan of 7000 camels. Saladin had fixed his station in the holy city, but the city was struck with consternation and discord. He fasted, he prayed, he preached, he offered to share the dangers of the siege; but his Mamalukes, who remembered the fate of their companions at Acre, pressed the sultan with loyal or seditious clamours to reserve *his* person and *their* courage for the future defence of the religion and empire. The Moslems were delivered by the sudden, or, as they deemed, the miraculous retreat of the Christians; and the laurels of Richard were blasted by the prudence or envy of his companions. The hero, ascending an hill and veiling his face, exclaimed with an indignant voice, "Those who are unwilling to rescue are unworthy to view the sepulchre of Christ!" After his return to Acre, on the news that Jaffa was surprised by the sultan, he sailed with some merchant vessels, and leaped foremost on the beach. The castle was relieved by his presence, and 60,000 Turks and Saracens fled before his arms. The discovery of his weakness provoked them to return in the morning, and they found him carelessly encamped before the gates with only seventeen knights and 300 archers. Without counting their numbers he sustained their charge; and we learn from the evidence of his enemies that the King of England, grasping his lance, rode furiously along their front from the right to the left wing without meeting an adversary who dared to encounter his career. Am I writing the history of Orlando or Amadis? During these hostilities a languid and tedious negotiation between the Franks and Moslems was started, and continued, and broken, and again resumed, and again broken. Some

acts of royal courtesy, the gift of snow and fruit, the exchange of Norway hawks and Arabian horses, softened the asperity of religious war. From the vicissitudes of success the monarchs might learn to suspect that Heaven was neutral in the quarrel; nor, after the trial of each other, could either hope for a decisive victory. The health both of Richard and Saladin appeared to be in a declining state, and they respectively suffered the evils of distant and domestic warfare. Plantagenet was impatient to punish a perfidious rival who had invaded Normandy in his absence; and the indefatigable sultan was subdued by the cries of the people, who was the victim, and of the soldiers, who were the instruments of his martial zeal. The first demands of the King of England were the restitution of Jerusalem, Palestine, and the true cross; and he firmly declared that himself and his brother pilgrims would end their lives in the pious labour rather than return to Europe with ignominy and remorse. But the conscience of Saladin refused, without some weighty compensation, to restore the idols or promote the idolatry of the Christians. He asserted with equal firmness his religious and civil claim to the sovereignty of Palestine; descanted on the importance and sanctity of Jerusalem; and rejected all terms of the establishment or partition of the Latins. The marriage which Richard proposed of his sister with the sultan's brother was defeated by the difference of faith. A personal interview was declined by Saladin, who alleged their mutual ignorance of each other's language; and the negotiation was managed with much art and delay by their interpreters and envoys. The final agreement (A.D. 1192, Sept.) was equally disapproved by the zealots of both parties, by the Roman pontiff, and the Caliph of Bagdad. It was stipulated that Jerusalem and the holy sepulchre should be open, without tribute or vexation, to the pilgrimage of the Latin Christians; that after the demolition of Ascalon they should inclusively possess the sea-coast from Jaffa to Tyre; that the Count of Tripoli and the Prince of Antioch should be compromised in the truce; and that, during three years and three months, all hostilities should cease. The principal chiefs of the two armies swore to the observance of the treaty, but the monarchs were satisfied with giving their word and their right hand: and the royal majesty was excused from an oath, which always implies some suspicion of falsehood and dishonour. Richard embarked for Europe to seek a long captivity and a premature grave; and the space of a few months (A.D. 1193,

March 4) concluded the life and glories of Saladin. The orientals describe his edifying death, which happened at Damascus; but they seem ignorant of the equal distribution of his alms among the three religions, or of the display of a shroud instead of a standard, to admonish the East of the instability of human greatness. The unity of empire was dissolved by his death; his sons were oppressed by the stronger arm of their uncle Saphadin; the hostile interests of the sultans of Egypt, Damascus, and Aleppo were again revived; and the Franks or Latins stood, and breathed, and hoped in their fortresses along the Syrian coast.

TO INDOLENCE.

[Dr. Thomas Brown, born at Kirkcudbright, 9th January, 1778; died in London, 1820. His first poems were issued in two volumes in 1804; his *Paradise of Coquettes* in 1814; *The War Fiend*, 1816; *The Wanderer in Norway; Agnes; Emily*, and other Poems, 1818. In 1808-9 he became the assistant, and subsequently the successor, of Dugald Stewart in the chair of moral philosophy in the Edinburgh University.]

Come to my bower,
Nymph of the softly sleeping eye!
Come where I lie,
Safe from the sun, and mock his feeble power.
The beams, that thro' the foliage stray,
But with thy quivering glance shall play,
And, while its veil they close,
Woo the sweet languor to more sweet repose.

Not Silence weaves
Her waveless gossamer around;
—The pause of sound
Would tempt too wakeful fancy—But the leaves,
Scarce fann'd by Zephyr's lightest wing,
Shall such faint fluttering murmurs fling
As, lost by fits and caught,
May fill at once and lull the listless thought.

Where evening sips
Sweet fragrance for her dews unseen,
There let me lean,
Couch'd on soft roses, o'er thy softer lips,
And watch their breathings number'd all
By thy slow bosom's rise and fall,—
Till tired I sink, oppress'd
With the sweet toil, and slumber on thy breast!

No dream shall rise
Of morrow's weary strife and care:
Enough, if there
A moment's joy the moment's thought supplies;
Her softest, gentlest visions shed,
Calm Pleasure floating o'er our head,
Shall pause in smiles above:—
Rest even our waking, even our sleep all love.

THE AUTOCRAT OF THE BREAKFAST TABLE.

[Oliver Wendell Holmes, M.D., born at Cambridge, Massachusetts, 29th August, 1809. Professor of anatomy first in Dartmouth College, and afterwards in Harvard University. He has written a number of valuable works on medical subjects, but he is best known to the general public as a poet and humourist. *Poetry*, a Metrical Essay; *Terpsichore: Urania*, a Rhymed Lesson; and *Astraea*, the Balance of Illusions, are amongst his more important productions in verse: *Elsie Venner*, a novel; and *The Guardian Angel* have been also widely appreciated. *The Autocrat of the Breakfast Table*, a series of gossiping discourses supposed to be delivered at the breakfast table of a boarding-house, by its humour, pathos, and epigrammatic expression of shrewd observation, has obtained great popularity. It has been followed by two not less successful, although similar works: *The Professor at the Breakfast Table*, and *The Poet at the Breakfast Table*.]

CONVERSATION.

This business of conversation is a very serious matter. There are men that it weakens one to talk with an hour more than a day's fasting would do. Mark this that I am going to say, for it is as good as a working professional man's advice, and costs you nothing: It is better to lose a pint of blood from your veins than to have a nerve tapped. Nobody measures your nervous force as it runs away, nor bandages your brain and marrow after the operation.

There are men of *esprit* who are excessively exhausting to some people. They are the talkers who have what may be called *jerky* minds. Their thoughts do not run in the natural order of sequence. They say very bright things on all possible subjects, but their zigzags rack you to death. After a jolting half-hour with one of these jerky companions, talking with a dull friend affords great relief. It is like taking the cat in your lap after holding a squirrel.

What a comfort a dull but kindly person is, to be sure, at times! A ground-glass shade over a gas-lamp does not bring more solace to our dazzled eyes than such a one to our minds.

CONCEITED PEOPLE.

"So you admire conceited people, do you?" said the young lady who has come to the city to be finished off for—the duties of life.

I am afraid you do not study logic at your school, my dear. It does not follow that I wish to be pickled in brine because I like a salt-water plunge at Nahant. I say that conceit is just as natural a thing to human minds as a centre is to a circle. But little-minded people's thoughts move in such small circles that five minutes' conversation gives you an arc long enough to determine their whole curve. An arc in the movement of a large intellect does not sensibly differ from a straight line. Even if it have the third vowel as its centre, it does not soon betray it. The highest thought, that is, is the most seemingly impersonal; it does not obviously imply any individual centre.

Audacious self-esteem, with good ground for it, is always imposing. What resplendent beauty that must have been which could have authorized Phryne to "peel" in the way she did! What fine speeches are those two: "*Non omnis moriar*," and "I have taken all knowledge to be my province!" Even in common people, conceit has the virtue of making them cheerful; the man who thinks his wife, his baby, his house, his horse, his dog, and himself severally unequalled, is almost sure to be a good-humoured person, though liable to be tedious at times.

SELF-MADE MEN.

Self-made men? Well, yes. Of course everybody likes and respects self-made men. It is a great deal better to be made in that way than not to be made at all. Are any of you younger people old enough to remember that Irishman's house on the marsh at Cambridgeport, which house he built from drain to chimney-top with his own hands? It took him a good many years to build it, and one could see that it was a little out of plumb, and a little wavy in outline, and a little queer and uncertain in general aspect. A regular hand could certainly have built a better house; but it was a very good house for a "self-made" carpenter's house, and people praised it, and said how remarkably well the Irishman had succeeded. They never thought of praising the fine blocks of houses a little farther on.

Your self-made man, whittled into shape with his own jack-knife, deserves more credit, if that is all, than the regular engine-turned article, shaped by the most approved pattern, and French-polished by society and travel. But as to saying that one is every way the equal of the other, that is another matter. The right of strict social discrimination of all things and persons, according to their merits, native or acquired, is one of the most precious republican privileges. I take the liberty to exercise it when I say that, *other things being*

equal, in most relations of life I prefer a man of family.

A PARADOX.

It is not easy, at the best, for two persons talking together to make the most of each other's thoughts, there are so many of them.

[The company looked as if they wanted an explanation.]

When John and Thomas, for instance, are talking together, it is natural enough that among the six there should be more or less confusion and misapprehension.

[Our landlady turned pale;—no doubt she thought there was a screw loose in my intellects,—and that involved the probable loss of a boarder. A severe-looking person, who wears a Spanish cloak and a sad cheek, fluted by the passions of the melodrama, whom I understand to be the professional ruffian of the neighbouring theatre, alluded, with a certain lifting of the brow, drawing down of the corners of the mouth, and somewhat rasping *voce di petto*, to Falstaff's nine men in buckram. Everybody looked up. I believe the old gentleman opposite was afraid I should seize the carving-knife; at any rate, he slid it to one side, as it were carelessly.]

I think, I said, I can make it plain to Benjamin Franklin here, that there are at least six personalities distinctly to be recognized as taking part in that dialogue between John and Thomas.

Three Johns.
{
1. The real John; known only to his Maker.
2. John's ideal John; never the real one, and often very unlike him.
3. Thomas's ideal John; never the real John, nor John's John, but often very unlike either.
}

Three Thomases.
{
1. The real Thomas.
2. Thomas's ideal Thomas.
3. John's ideal Thomas.
}

Only one of the three Johns is taxed; only one can be weighed on a platform-balance; but the other two are just as important in the conversation. Let us suppose the real John to be old, dull, and ill-looking. But as the Higher Powers have not conferred on men the gift of seeing themselves in the true light, John very possibly conceives himself to be youthful, witty, and fascinating, and talks from the point of view of this ideal. Thomas, again, believes him to be an artful rogue, we will say; therefore he *is*, so far as Thomas's attitude in the conversation is concerned, an artful rogue, though really simple and stupid. The same conditions apply to the three Thomases. It follows, that, until a man can be found who knows himself as his Maker knows him, or who sees himself as others see him, there must be at least six persons engaged in every dialogue between two. Of these, the least important, philosophically speaking, is the one that we have called the real person. No wonder two disputants often get angry, when there are six of them talking and listening all at the same time.

[A very unphilosophical application of the above remarks was made by a young fellow, answering to the name of John, who sits near me at table. A certain basket of peaches—a rare vegetable, little known to boarding-houses —was on its way to me *via* this unlettered Johannes. He appropriated the three that remained in the basket, remarking that there was just one apiece for him. I convinced him that his practical inference was hasty and illogical, but in the mean time he had eaten the peaches.]

CYCLES OF THOUGHT.

Just as we find a mathematical rule at the bottom of many of the bodily movements, just so thought may be supposed to have its regular cycles. Such or such a thought comes round periodically, in its turn. Accidental suggestions, however, so far interfere with the regular cycles, that we may find them practically beyond our power of recognition. Take all this for what it is worth, but at any rate you will agree that there are certain particular thoughts that do not come up once a day, nor once a week, but that a year would hardly go round without your having them pass through your mind. Here is one which comes up at intervals in this way. Some one speaks of it, and there is an instant and eager smile of assent in the listener or listeners. Yes, indeed; they have often been struck by it.

All at once a conviction flashes through us that we have been in the same precise circumstances as at the present instant, once or many times before.

Oh, dear, yes!—said one of the company— everybody has had that feeling.

The landlady didn't know anything about such notions; it was an idea in folks' heads, she expected.

The schoolmistress said, in a hesitating sort of way, that she knew the feeling well, and didn't like to experience it; it made her think she was a ghost, sometimes.

The young fellow whom they call John said he knew all about it; he had just lighted a cheroot the other day, when a tremendous con-

viction all at once came over him that he had done just that same thing ever so many times before. I looked severely at him, and his countenance immediately fell—*on the side toward me;* I cannot answer for the other, for he can wink and laugh with either half of his face without the other half's knowing it. I have noticed—I went on to say—the following circumstances connected with these sudden impressions. First, that the condition which seems to be the duplicate of a former one is often very trivial—one that might have presented itself a hundred times. Secondly, that the impression is very evanescent, and that it is rarely, if ever, recalled by any voluntary effort, at least after any time has elapsed. Thirdly, that there is a disinclination to record the circumstances, and a sense of incapacity to reproduce the state of mind in words. Fourthly, I have often felt that the duplicate condition had not only occurred once before, but that it was familiar, and, as it seemed, habitual. Lastly, I have had the same convictions in my dreams.

How do I account for it? Why, there are several ways that I can mention, and you may take your choice. The first is that which the young lady hinted at—that these flashes are sudden recollections of a previous existence. I don't believe that; for I remember a poor student I used to know told me he had such a conviction one day when he was blacking his boots, and I can't think he had ever lived in another world where they use Day and Martin.

Some think that Dr. Wigan's doctrine of the brain's being a double organ, its hemispheres working together like the two eyes, accounts for it. One of the hemispheres hangs fire, they suppose, and the small interval between the perceptions of the nimble and the sluggish half seems an indefinitely long period, and therefore the second perception appears to be the copy of another, ever so old. But even allowing the centre of perception to be double, I can see no good reason for supposing this indefinite lengthening of the time, nor any analogy that bears it out. It seems to me most likely that the coincidence of circumstances is very partial, but that we take this partial resemblance for identity, as we occasionally do resemblances of persons. A momentary posture of circumstances is so far like some preceding one that we accept it as exactly the same, just as we accost a stranger occasionally, mistaking him for a friend. The apparent similarity may be owing perhaps quite as much to the mental state at the time, as to the outward circumstances.

THE RACE OF LIFE.

Nothing strikes one more, in the race of life, than to see how many give out in the first half of the course. "Commencement day" always reminds me of the start for the "Derby," when the beautiful high-bred three-year-olds of the season are brought up for trial. That day is the start, and life is the race. Here we are at Cambridge, and a class is just "graduating." Poor Harry! he was to have been there too, but he has paid forfeit; step out here into the grass back of the church; ah! there it is:—

> " HUNC LAPIDEM POSUERUNT
>   SOCII MŒRENTES."

But this is the start, and here they are,—coats bright as silk, and manes as smooth as *eau lustrale* can make them. Some of the best of the colts are pranced round, a few minutes each, to show their paces. What is that old gentleman crying about? and the old lady by him, and the three girls, what are they all covering their eyes for? Oh, that is *their* colt which has just been trotted upon the stage. Do they really think those little thin legs can do any thing in such a slashing sweepstakes as is coming off in these next forty years? Oh, this terrible gift of second-sight that comes to some of us when we begin to look through the silver rings of the *arcus senilis!*

Ten years gone. First turn in the race. A few broken down; two or three bolted. Several show in advance of the ruck. *Cassock*, a black colt, seems to be ahead of the rest; those black colts commonly get the start, I have noticed, of the others, in the first quarter. *Meteor* has pulled up.

Twenty years. Second corner turned. *Cassock* has dropped from the front, and *Judex*, an iron-gray, has the lead. But look! how they have thinned out! Down flat,—five,—six,—how many? They lie still enough! they will not get up again in this race, be very sure! And the rest of them, what a "tailing off!" Anybody can see who is going to win,—perhaps.

Thirty years. Third corner turned. *Dives*, bright sorrel, ridden by the fellow in a yellow jacket, begins to make play fast; is getting to be the favourite with many. But who is that other one that has been lengthening his stride from the first, and now shows close up to the front? Don't you remember the quiet brown colt *Asteroid*, with the star in his forehead? That is he; he is one of the sort that lasts;

look out for him! The black "colt," as we used to call him, is in the background, taking it easily in a gentle trot. There is one they used to call the *Filly*, on account of a certain feminine air he had; well up, you see; the Filly is not to be despised, my boy!

Forty years. More dropping off,—but places much as before.

Fifty years. Race over. All that are on the course are coming in at a walk; no more running. Who is ahead? Ahead? What! and the winning-post a slab of white or gray stone standing out from that turf where there is no more jockeying or straining for victory! Well, the world marks their places in its betting-book; but be sure that these matter very little, if they have run as well as they knew how!

OLD AGE.

As to *giving up*, because the Almanac or the Family Bible says that it is about time to do it, I have no intention of doing any such thing. I grant you that I burn less carbon than some years ago. I see people of my standing really good for nothing,—decrepit, effete, *la lèvre inférieure déjà pendante*, with what little life they have left mainly concentrated in their epigastrium. But as the disease of old age is epidemic, endemic, and sporadic, and every body that lives long enough is sure to catch it, I am going to say, for the encouragement of such as need it, how I treat the malady in my own case.

First. As I feel that, when I have any thing to do, there is less time for it than when I was younger, I find that I give my attention more thoroughly, and use my time more economically, than ever before; so that I can learn any thing twice as easily as in my earlier days. I am not, therefore, afraid to attack a new study. I took up a difficult language a very few years ago with good success, and think of mathematics and metaphysics by and by.

Secondly. I have opened my eyes to a good many neglected privileges and pleasures within my reach, and requiring only a little courage to enjoy them. You may well suppose it pleased me to find that old Cato was thinking of learning to play the fiddle, when I had deliberately taken it up in my old age, and satisfied myself that I could get much comfort, if not much music, out of it.

Thirdly. I have found that some of those active exercises, which are commonly thought to belong to young folks only, may be enjoyed at a much later period.

117

BRAINS.

Our brains are seventy-year clocks. The Angel of Life winds them up once for all, then closes the case, and gives the key into the hand of the Angel of the Resurrection. Tic-tac! tic-tac! go the wheels of thought; our will cannot stop them; they cannot stop themselves; sleep cannot still them; madness only makes them go faster; death alone can break into the case, and, seizing the ever-swinging pendulum, which we call the heart, silence at last the clicking of the terrible escapement we have carried so long beneath our wrinkled foreheads.

If we could only get at them, as we lie on our pillows and count the dead beats of thought after thought and image after image jarring through the over-tired organ! Will nobody block those wheels, uncouple that pinion, cut the string that holds those weights, blow up the infernal machine with gunpowder? What a passion comes over us sometimes for silence and rest!—that this dreadful mechanism, un-winding the endless tapestry of time, embroid-ered with spectral figures of life and death, could have but one brief holiday! Who can wonder that men swing themselves off from beams in hempen lassos?—that they jump off from parapets into the swift and gurgling waters beneath?—that they take counsel of the grim friend who has but to utter his one peremptory monosyllable, and the restless ma-chine is shivered as a vase that is dashed upon a marble floor? Under that building which we pass every day there are strong dungeons, where neither hook, nor bar, nor bed-cord, nor drinking vessel from which a sharp frag-ment may be shattered, shall by any chance be seen. There is nothing for it, when the brain is on fire with the whirling of its wheels, but to spring against the stone wall and silence them with one crash. Ah, they remembered that,—the kind city fathers,—and the walls are nicely padded, so that one can take such exercise as he likes without damaging himself on the very plain but serviceable upholstery. If anybody would only contrive some kind of a lever that one could thrust in among the works of this horrid automaton and check them, or alter their rate of going, what would the world give for the discovery?—

From half a dime to a dime, according to the style of the place and the quality of the liquor,—said the young fellow whom they call John.

You speak trivially, but not unwisely,—I

said. Unless the will maintain a certain con-trol over these movements, which it cannot stop, but can to some extent regulate, men are very apt to try to get at the machine by some indirect system of leverage or other. They clap on the brakes by means of opium; they change the maddening monotony of the rhythm by means of fermented liquors. It is because the brain is locked up, and we cannot touch its movement directly, that we thrust these coarse tools in through any crevice by which they may reach the interior, and so alter its rate of going for a while, and at last spoil the machine.

SCOTTISH BALLAD.[1]

It was a' for our rightfu' king
  We left fair Scotland's strand;
It was a' for our rightfu' king
  We e'er saw Irish land, my dear,
  We e'er saw Irish land.

Now all is done that man can do,
  And all is done in vain;
My love and native land, fareweel,
  For I maun cross the main, my dear,
  For I maun cross the main.

I turn'd me right and round about
  Upon the Irish shore,
An' ga'e my bridle-reins a shake,
  With "Adieu for evermore, my dear,"
  With "Adieu for evermore."

The sodger frae the war returns,
  The sailor frae the main;
But I hae parted frae my love,
  Never to meet again, my dear,
  Never to meet again.

When day is gane an' night is come,
  An' a' folk bound in sleep,
O think on him that's far awa',
  The lee-lang night, an' weep, my dear,
  The lee-lang night. an' weep.

A THÓUGHT.

Though far away,
Though ruthless time have scatter'd memory's dream;
Some scenes can ne'er decay,
But rest where all is change, like islands on a stream.
          REV. THOMAS BRYDSON.

[1] The author of this ballad is said to be Captain Ogilvie of the house of Inverquharity, who accompanied the deposed James II. to Ireland and France.

HUGH SUTHERLAND'S PANSIES.

[Robert Buchanan, born at Caverswall, Staffordshire, 18th August, 1841. Educated in Glasgow, where his father, the late Robert Buchanan, was editor and proprietor of several newspapers. As early as 1859, Mr. Buchanan had published two volumes of verse, *Lyrics*, and *Mary*, and other poems. His first important work was *Undertones*, first issued in 1862. It was followed by *Idyls and Legends of Inverburn; London Poems; Danish Ballads* (a series of admirable translations); *Wayside Posies; Napoleon Fallen*, a lyrical drama; *The Land of Lorne*, descriptive sketches; *The Drama of Kings; The Fleshly School of Poetry*, an attack on Swinburne and D. G. Rossetti; &c. Anonymously he has published much in prose and verse, fiction, essays and plays. With singular versatility of genius he unites rare powers of poetic expression.]

The aged Minister of Inverburn,
A mild heart hidden under features stern,
Leans in the sunshine on the garden pale,
Pensive, yet happy, as he tells this tale,—
And he who listens sees the garden lie
Blue as a little patch of fallen sky.

"The lily minds me of a maiden brow,"
Hugh Sutherland would say; "the marigold
Is full and sunny like her yellow hair,
The full-blown rose her lips with sweetness tipt;
But if you seek a likeness to her eye—
Go to the pansy, friend, and find it there!"
"Ay, leeze me on the pansies!" Hugh would say—
Hugh Sutherland, the weaver—he who dwelt
Here in the white-wash'd cot you fancy so—
Who knew the learnèd names of all the flowers,
And recognized the lily, tho' its head
Rose in a ditch of dull Latinity!

Pansies? You praise the ones that grow to-day
Here in the garden: had you seen the place
When Sutherland was living! Here they grew,
From blue to deeper blue, in midst of each
A golden dazzle like a glimmering star,
Each broader, bigger, than a silver crown;
While here the weaver sat, his labour done,
Watching his azure pets and rearing them,
Until they seem'd to know his step and touch,
And stir beneath his smile like living things!
The very sunshine loved them, and would lie
Here happy, coming early, lingering late,
Because they were so fair.

. Hugh Sutherland
Was country-bred—I knew him from the time
When on a bed of pain he lost a limb,
And rose at last, a lame and sickly lad,
Apprenticed to the loom—a peevish lad,
Mooning among the shadows by himself.
Among these shadows, with the privilege
Of one who loved his flock, I sought him out,
And gently as I could I won his heart;
And then, tho' he was young and I was old,

We soon grew friends. He told his griefs to me,
His joys, his troubles, and I help'd him on;
Yet sought in vain to drive away the cloud
Deep pain had left upon his sickly cheek,
And lure him from the shades that deepen'd it.
Then Heaven took the task upon itself,
And sent an angel down among the flowers!
Almost before I knew the work was done,
I found him settled in this hut and ben,
Where, with an eye that brighten'd, he had found
The sunshine loved his garden, and begun
To rear his pansies.

Sutherland was poor,
Rude, and untutor'd; peevish, too, when first
The angel in his garden found him out;
But pansy-growing made his heart within
Blow fresh and fragrant. When he came to share
This cottage with a brother of the craft,
Only some poor and sickly bunches bloom'd,
Vagrant, though fair, among the garden-plots;
And idly, carelessly, he water'd these,
Spread them and train'd them, till they grew and
  grew
In size and beauty, and the angel thrust
Its bright arms upward thro' the bright'ning sod,
And clung around the sickly gardener's heart.
Then Sutherland grew calmer, and the cloud
Was fading from his face. Well, by and by,
The country people saw and praised the flowers,
And what at first had been an idle joy
Became a sober serious work for fame.
Next, being won to send a bunch for show,
He won a prize—a sixth or seventh rate,
And slowly gath'ring courage, rested not
Till he had won the highest prize of all.
Here in the sunshine and the shade he toil'd
Early and late in joy, and, by and by,
Rose high in fame; for not a botanist,
A lover of the flowers, poor man or rich,
Came to the village, but the people said,
"Go down the lane to Weaver Sutherland's,
And see his pansies!"

Thus the summers pass'd,
And Sutherland grew gentler, happier;
The angel God had sent him clung to him:
There grew a rapturous sadness in his tone
When he was gladdest, like the dewiness
That moistens pansies when they bloom the best;
And in his face there dawn'd a gentle light,
Like that which softly clings about a flow'r,
And makes you love it. Yet his heart was glad,
More for the pansies' sakes than for his own:
His eye was like a father's, moist and bright,
When they were praised; and, as I said, they seem'd
To make themselves as beauteous as they could,
Smiling to please him. Blessings on the flowers!
They were his children! Father never loved
His little darlings more, or for their sakes
Fretted so dumbly! Father never bent
More tenderly above his little ones,

In the still watches of the night, when sleep
Breathes balm upon their eyelids! Night and day
Poor Hugh was careful for the gentle things
Whose presence brought a sunshine to the place
Where sickness dwelt : this one was weak and small,
And needed watching like a sickly child ;
This one so beauteous, that it shamed its mates
And made him angry with its beauteousness.
"I cannot rest!" cried Hughie with a smile,
"I scarcely snatch a moment to myself—
They plague me so!" Part fun, part earnest, this:
He loved the pansies better than he knew.
Ev'n in the shadow of his weaving room
They haunted him and brighten'd on his soul:
Daily while busy working at the loom
The humming-humming seem'd a melody
To which the pansies sweetly grew and grew—
A leaf unrolling soft to every note,
A change of colours with the change of sound ;
And walking to the door to rest himself,
Still with the humming-humming in his ears,
He saw the flowers and heard a melody
They made in growing. Pleasure such as this,
So exquisite, so lonely, might have pass'd
Into the shadowy restlessness of yore ;
But wholesome human contact saved him here,
And kept him fresh and meek. The people came
To stir him with their praise, and he would show
The medals and the prizes he had got—
As proud and happy as a child who gains
A prize in school.

        The angel still remain'd
In winter, when the garden-plots were bare,
And deep winds piloted the shriven snow:
He saw its gleaming in the cottage fire,
While, with a book of botany on his knee,
He sat and hunger'd for the breath of spring.
The angel of the flowers was with him still !
Here beds of roses sweeten'd all the page;
Here lilies whiter than the fallen snow
Crept gleaming softly from the printed lines;
Here dewy violets sparkled till the book
Dazzled his eyes with rays of misty blue ;
And here, amid a page of Latin names,
All the sweet Scottish flowers together grew
With fragrance of the summer.

        Hugh and I
Were still fast friends, and still I help'd him on ;
And often in the pleasant summer-time,
The service over, on the Sabbath-day,
I join'd him in the garden, where we sat
And chatted in the sun. But all at once
It came upon me that the gardener's hand
Had grown less diligent ; for tho' 'twas June
The garden that had been the village pride
Look'd but the shadow of its former self;
And ere a week was out I saw in church
Two samples fairer far than any blown
In Hughie's garden—blooming brighter far

In sweeter soil. What wonder that a man,
Loving the pansies as the weaver did—
A skilful judge, moreover—should admire
Sweet Mary Moffat's sparkling pansy-eyes?

      The truth was out. The weaver play'd the game
(I christen'd it in sport that very day)
Of "Love among the Pansies !" As he spoke,
Telling me all, I saw upon his face
The peevish cloud that it had worn in youth;
I cheer'd him as I could, and bade him hope :
"You both are poor, but, Sutherland, God's flowers
Are poor as well!" He brighten'd as I spoke,
And answer'd, "It is settled ! I have kept
The secret till the last, lest 'nay' should come
And spoil it all ; but 'ay' has come instead,
And all the help we wait for is your own!"

    Even here, I think, his angel clung to him.
The fairies of his garden haunted him
With similes and sympathies that made
His likes and dislikes, though he knew it not.
Beauty he loved if it was meek and mild,
And like his pansies tender ev'n to tears ;
And so he chose a maiden pure and low,
Who, like his garden pets, had love to spare,
Sunshine to cast upon his pallid cheek,
And yet a tender clinging thing, too weak
To bloom uncared for and unsmiled upon.

    Soon Sutherland and she he loved were one,—
And bonnily a moon of honey gleam'd
At night among the flowers! Amid the spring
That follow'd, blossom'd with the other buds
A tiny maiden with her mother's eyes.
The little garden was itself again,
The sunshine sparkled on the azure beds;
The angel Heaven had sent to save a soul
Stole from the blooms and took an infant shape ;
And, wild with pleasure, seeing how the flowers
Had given her their choicest lights and shades,
The father bore his baby to the font
And had her christen'd PANSY.

         After that,
Poor Hugh was happy as the days were long,
Divided in his cares for all his pets,
And proudest of the one he loved the best.
The summer found him merry as a king,
Dancing the little one upon his knee,
Here in the garden, while the plots around
Gleam'd in the sun, and seem'd as glad as he.

    But moons of honey wane, and summer suns
Of wedlock set to bring the autumn in!
Hugh Sutherland, with wife and child to feed,
Wrought sore to gain his pittance in a world
His pansies made so fair. Came Poverty
With haggard eyes to dwell within the house;
When first she saw the garden she was glad,
And, seated on the threshold, smiled and span,
But times grew harder, bread was scarce as gold,

A shadow fell on Pansy and the flowers;
And when the strife was sorest, Hugh received
An office - lighter work and higher pay—
To take a foreman's place in Edinglass.
'Twas hard, 'twas hard, to leave the little place
He loved so dearly; but the weaver look'd
At Mary, saw the sorrow in her face,
And gave consent,—happy at heart to think
His dear ones would not want. To Edinglass
They went, and settled. Thro' the winter hours
Bravely the weaver toil'd; his wife and child
Were happy, he was heartsome—tho' his taste
Was grassy lowlands and the caller air.

The cottage here remain'd untenanted,
The angel of the flowers forsook the place,
The sunshine faded, and the pansies died.

Two summers pass'd; and still in Edinglass
The weaver toil'd, and ever when I went
Into the city, to his house I hied—
A welcome guest. Now first, I saw a change
Had come to Sutherland: for he was pale
And peevish, had a venom on his tongue,
And hung the under-lip like one that doubts.
Part of the truth I heard, and part I saw—
But knew too late, when all the ill was done!
At first, poor Hugh had shrunk from making friends,
And pored among his books of botany;
And later, in the dull dark nights he sat,
A dismal book upon his knee, and read:
A book no longer full of leaves and flowers,
That glimmer'd on the soul's sweet consciousness.
Yet seem'd to fill the eye,—a dismal book,—
Big-sounding Latin, English dull and dark,
And not a breath of summer in it all.
The sunshine perish'd in the city's smoke,
The pansies grew no more to comfort him,
And he began to spend his nights with those
Who waste their substance in the public-house:
The flowers had lent a sparkle to his talk,
Which pleased the muddled wits of idle men.
Sought after, treated, liked by one and all,
He took to drinking; and at last lay down
Stupid and senseless on a rainy night,
And ere he waken'd caught the flaming fire,
Which gleams to white heat on the face, and burns
Clear crimson in the lungs.

But it was long
Ere any knew poor Hughie's plight; and, ere
He saw his danger, on the mother's breast
Lay Pansy withering; tho' the dewy breath
Of spring was floating like a misty rain
Down from the mountains. Then the tiny flower
Folded its leaves in silence, and the sleep
That dwells in winter on the pansy-beds
Fell on the weaver's house. At that sad hour
I enter'd, scarcely welcomed with a word
Of greeting: by the hearth the woman sat

Weeping full sore, her apron o'er a face
Haggard with midnight watching, while the man
Cover'd his bloodshot eyes and cursed himself.
Then leaning o'er, my hand on his, I said—
"She could not bear the smoke of cities, Hugh!
God to His Garden has transplanted her,
Where summer dwells for ever, and the air
Is fresh and pure!" But Hughie did not speak,
I saw full plainly that he blamed himself;
And ere the day was out he bent above
His little sleeping flower, and wept, and said:
"Ay, sir! she wither'd, wither'd like the rest,
Neglected!" and I saw his heart was full.
When Pansy slept beneath the churchyard grass
Poor Hughie's angel had return'd to Heaven,
And all his heart was dark. His ways grew strange
Peevish, and sullen; often he would sit
And drink alone; the wife and he grew cold,
And harsh to one another; till at last
A stern physician put an end to all,
And told him he must die.

No bitter cry,
No sound of wailing rose within the house
After the doctor spoke, but Mary mourn'd
In silence, Hughie smoked his pipe and set
His teeth together, at the ingleside.
Days pass'd; the only token of a change
Was Hughie's face—the peevish cloud of care
Seem'd melting to a tender gentleness.
After a time, the wife forgot her grief,
Or could at times forget it, in the care
Her husband's sickness brought. I went to them
As often as I could, for Sutherland
Was dear to me, and dearer for his sin
Weak as he was he did his best to toil,
But it was weary work! By slow degrees,
When May was breathing on the sickly bunch
Of mignonette upon the window-sill,
I saw his smile was softly wearing round
To what it used to be, when here he sat
Rearing his flowers; altho' his brow at times
Grew cloudy, and he gnaw'd his under lip.
At last I found him seated by the hearth,
Trying to read: I led his mind to themes
Of old langsyne, and saw his eyes grow dim:
"O sir," he cried, "I cannot, cannot rest!
Something I long for, and I know not what,
Torments me night and day!" I saw it all,
And sparkling with the brilliance of the thought,
Look'd in his eyes and caught his hand, and cried,
"Hugh, it's the pansies! Spring has come again.
The sunshine breathes its gold upon the air,
And threads it through the petals of the flowers,
Yet have you linger in the dark!" I ceased,
And watch'd him. Then he trembled as he said,
"I see it now, for as I read the book,
The lines and words, the Latin seem'd to blur,
And they peep'd thro'." He smiled, like one ashamed,
Adding in a low voice, "I long to see
The pansies ere I die!"

What heart of stone
Could throb on coldly, sir, at words like those?
Not mine, not mine! Within a week poor Hugh
Had left the smoke of Edinglass behind,
And felt the wind that runs along the lanes,
Spreading a carpet of the grass and flowers
For June the sunny-hair'd to walk upon.
In the old cottage here he dwelt again:
The place was wilder than it once had been,
But buds were blowing green around about,
And with the glad return of Sutherland
The angel of the flowers came back again.
The end was near, and Hugh was wearied out,
And like a flower was closing up his leaves
Under the dropping of the gloaming dews.

And daily, in the summer afternoon,
I found him seated on the threshold there,
Watching his flowers, and all the place, I thought,
Brighten'd when he was nigh. Now first I talk'd
Of heavenly hopes unto him, and I knew
The angel help'd me. On the day he died
The pain had put its shadow on his face,
And words of doubt were on his tremulous lips:
"Ah, Hughie, life is easy!" I exclaim'd,
"Easier, better, than we know ourselves:
'Tis pansy-growing on a mighty scale,
And God above us is the gardener.
The fairest win the prizes, that is just,
But all the flowers are dear to God the Lord:
The Gardener loves them all, He loves them all!"
He saw the sunshine on the pansy-beds
And brighten'd. Then by slow degrees he grew
Cheerful and meek as dying man could be,
And as I spoke there came from far-away
The faint sweet melody of Sabbath bells.
And "Hugh," I said, "if God the Gardener
Neglected those he rears as you have done
Your pansies and your Pansy, it were ill
For we who blossom in His garden. Night
And morning He is busy at His work.
He smiles to give us sunshine, and we live:
He stoops to pluck us softly, and our hearts
Tremble to see the darkness, knowing not
It is the shadow He, in stooping, casts.
He pluckt your Pansy so, and it was well.
But, Hugh, though some be beautiful and grand,
Some sickly, like yourself, and mean and poor,
He loves them all, the Gardener loves them all!"
Then later, when no longer he could sit
Out on the threshold, and the end was near,
We set a plate of pansies by his bed
To cheer him. "He is coming near," I said;
"Great is the garden, but the Gardener
Is coming to the corner where you bloom
So sickly!" And he smiled, and moan'd, "I hear!"
And sank upon his pillow wearily.
His hollow eyes no longer bore the light,
The darkness gather'd round him as I said,
"The Gardener is standing at your side,
His shade is on you, and you cannot see:

O Lord, that lovest both the strong and weak,
Pluck him and wear him!" Even as I pray'd,
I felt the shadow there and hid my face;
But when I look'd again the flower was pluck'd,
The shadow gone: the sunshine thro' the blind
Gleam'd faintly, and the widow'd woman wept.

ROSE SONG.

BY WILLIAM SAWYER.

Sunny breadths of roses,
    Roses white and red,
Rosy bud and rose leaf
    From the blossom shed!
Goes my darling flying
    All the garden through,
Laughing she eludes me,
    Laughing I pursue.

Now to pluck the rose-bud,
    Now to pluck the rose,
(Hand a sweeter blossom)
    Stopping as she goes:
What but this contents her,
    Laughing in her flight?
Pelting with the red rose,
    Pelting with the white.

Roses round me flying,
    Roses in my hair,
I to snatch them trying,—
    Darling, have a care!
Lips are so like flowers,
    I might snatch at those
Redder than the rose leaves,
    Sweeter than the rose.
                —*Legend of Phyllis*

TO ENGLAND.

Happy is England! I could be content
    To see no other verdure than its own;
    To feel no other breezes than are blown
Through its tall woods with high romances blent:
Yet do I sometimes feel a languishment
    For skies Italian, and an inward groan
    To sit upon an Alp as on a throne,
And half forget what world or worldling meant.
Happy is England! sweet her artless daughters;
    Enough their simple loveliness for me,
    Enough their whitest arms in silence clinging:
Yet do I often warmly burn to see
Beauties of deeper glance, and hear their singing,
And float with them about the summer waters!

                JOHN KEATS.

THE LEGEND OF THE DEVIL'S DYKE,

AS RELATED BY MASTER CISBURY OLDFIRLE, SCHOOLMASTER OF POYNINGS.

[William Harrison Ainsworth, born in Manchester, 1805, Novelist. He studied law, but before he had attained his majority he published *Sir John Chiverton*, a romance which obtained the favour of Sir Walter Scott. Soon afterwards Mr. Ainsworth devoted himself entirely to literature; he became editor of *Bentley's Miscellany* on the retirement of Dickens in 1840; he also edited *Colburn's New Monthly*, and the magazine which bore his own name in the title. His chief works are: *Rookwood; Crichton; Guy Fawkes; The Tower of London; Old St. Paul's; Windsor Castle; The Miser's Daughter; Lancashire Witches; The Flitch of Bacon; The Star Chamber; The Constable of the Tower; Mervyn Clitheroe; Ovingdean Grange*, a romance of the times of the Commonwealth (from which we quote); *John Law, the Projector; Hilary St. Ives; Myddleton Pomfret*, &c. &c. He has also written a number of poems, amongst which are *Ballads, Romantic, Fantastical, and Humorous;* and *The Combat of the Thirty*, a Breton legend. Cheap editions of his works are issued by Routledge and Sons.]

The wondrous event I am about to detail happened in the time of the good Saint Cuthman of Steyning, in this county—a holy man, who, from his extraordinary piety and austerity, was believed to be endowed with supernatural power. Many miracles are attributed to him, some of which occurred long before his canonization. While yet a boy, and employed in tending his father's sheep on the downs, in order to pursue his devotional exercises undisturbed, he was wont to trace a large circle round the flock with his crook, beyond which none of them could stray, neither could any enemy approach them. Moreover, the good saint could punish the scoffer, as well as bless and sustain the lowly and the well-doer. Derided by certain blasphemous haymakers for carrying his palsied mother in a barrow—no better means of conveyance being at hand at the time—he brought down a heavy shower upon their heads, rendering their labour of no account; and thenceforward, whenever grass was cut and dried within that meadow, rain would fall upon it, and turn it to litter. Such was holy Cuthman—a man, you will perceive, whom it was necessary to treat with the respect due to his exalted virtues.

At a later period of the saint's life, when his aged mother had gone from him, when he had built a wooden church with his own hands at Steyning—wherein, in the fulness of time, he was interred—and when his reputation for sanctity and austerity had greatly increased, causing him to be equally reverenced and dreaded—dreaded, I mean, by evil-doers, to whom he was especially obnoxious—the holy man walked forth one afternoon in early autumn, wholly unattended, across the downs; his purpose being to visit a recluse named Sister Ursula, who dwelt in a solitary cell on the summit of a hill adjoining Poynings, and whom he had been told was sick, and desirous of being shriven by him. Now Saint Cuthman had his staff in his hand, without which he never journeyed abroad, and he walked on until he reached the eminence for which he was bound. On the brow of this hill in former times the heathen invaders of the land had made a camp, vestiges of which may still be discerned. But it was not with these memorials of a by-gone and benighted people that Saint Cuthman concerned himself. If he thought about the framers of those mighty earthworks at all, it was with thanksgiving that they had been swept away, and had given place to a generation to whom the purer and brighter light of the gospel was vouchsafed.

Thus communing with himself, it may be, holy Cuthman reached the northern boundary of the rampart surrounding the old Roman camp, and cast his eyes over the vast weald of Sussex, displayed before him like a map. The contemplation of this fair and fertile district filled his soul with gladness; but what chiefly rejoiced him was to note how the edifices reared for worship had multiplied since he first looked upon the extensive plain. He strove to count the numerous churches scattered about, but soon gave up the attempt—he might as well have tried to number the trees. But the difficulty he experienced increased his satisfaction, inasmuch as it proved to him that true religion had taken deep root in the land. And he gave glory and praise accordingly, where glory and praise are due.

Scarcely were his audibly-uttered thanksgivings ended when he became aware that some one stood nigh him, and turning his head, he beheld a tall man of singularly swarthy complexion, haughty mien, and eyes that seemed to burn like coals of fire. The habiliments of this mysterious and sinister-looking personage were of blood-red hue, and though their richness and the egret in his velvet cap betokened princely rank, he bore the implements of a common labourer, namely, a pickaxe and a shovel. No sound had proclaimed the stranger's approach, and his appearance was as sudden and startling as if he had risen from the earth. As Saint Cuthman regarded him with the aversion inspired by the sight of a venomous and deadly snake, yet wholly without fear, he knew that he was in the presence of the Author of Ill. "Comest thou to tempt me, accursed one?" the holy man sternly demanded. "If so, learn that I am proof against thy wiles. Depart from me, or I will summon good spirits that shall cast thee hence."

"Thou canst not do so," the inauspicious-looking stranger replied, laughing derisively. "I am master here. Altars have been reared to strange gods upon this hill, and sacrifices made to them,—nay, I myself have been worshipped as Dis, and the blood of black bulls has been poured out upon the ground in mine honour. Therefore the hill is mine, and thou thyself art an intruder upon it, and deservest to be cast down headlong into the plain. Yet will I spare thee——"

"Thou darest not so much as injure a hair of my head, Sathanas," interrupted the saint in a menacing voice, and raising his staff as he spoke. "Approach! and lightnings shall blast thee."

"I tell thee I have no design to harm thee," returned the fiend, with a look that showed he would willingly have rent the holy man in pieces. "But give heed to what I am about to say. Vainly hast thou essayed to count the churches in the Sussex weald, and thou hast glorified Heaven because of the number of the worshippers gathered within those fanes. Now mark me, thou servant of God! Thou hast taken a farewell look of that plain, so thickly studded with structures pleasing in thy sight, but an abomination to me. Before to-morrow morn that vast district, far as thine eye can stretch, even to the foot of yon distant Surrey hills—the whole Weald of Sussex, with its many churches, its churchmen, and its congregations, shall be whelmed beneath the sea."

"Thou mockest me," returned Saint Cuthman, contemptuously: "but I know thee to be the Father of Lies."

"Disbelieve me if I fail in my task—not till then," said the fiend. "With the implements which I hold in my hand I will cut such a dyke through this hill, and through the hills lying between it and Hove, as shall let in the waters of the deep, so that all dwelling within yonder plain shall be drowned by them."

"And thinkest thou thy evil work will be permitted?" cried the saint, shaking his head.

"Thou, at least, canst not prevent it," rejoined the fiend, with a bitter laugh. "I will take my chance of other hindrance."

The holy man appeared for a moment troubled, but his confidence was presently restored.

"Thou deceivest thyself," he said. "The task thou proposest to execute is beyond thy power."

"Beyond my power!" exclaimed the demon. "It is a trifle in comparison with what I can achieve. I have had a hand in many wonderful works, some of which are recognized as mine, though I have not got credit for a tithe of those I have performed. Devil's bridges are common enough, methinks, in mountainous gorges—devil's towers are by no means rare in old castles. Most of the camps upon these downs were planned and executed by me—the very rampart upon which we stand being partly my work. The first Cæsar has got the credit of many of my performances, and he is welcome to it. He is not the only man who has worn laurels belonging by right to others. Saint as thou art, it is meet thou give the devil his due. Do so, and thou must needs praise his industry."

"Thy industry in evil-doing is unquestionable," rejoined the saint. "But good work is out of thy power. Thou darest not affirm that thou hast had any hand in the erection of temples and holy piles."

"Ask thy compeers, Saint Dunstan and Saint Augustine—they will tell thee differently. But I disdain to boast. I have certainly had no hand in thy ugly little wooden church at Steyning."

"And thy present feat is to be performed before to-morrow, thou sayest?" demanded the saint, highly offended at this uncalled-for allusion to his own favourite structure.

"Between sunset and sunrise, most saintly sir."

"That is but a short time for so mighty a task," said the holy man, in an incredulous tone. "Bethink thee, a September night is not a long night?"

"The shortest night is long enough for me," the fiend replied. "If the dawn comes and finds my work incomplete, thou shalt be at liberty to deride me."

"I shall never treat thee otherwise than with scorn," the saint rejoined. "But thou hast said it, and I hold thee to thy word. Between sunset and sunrise thy task must be done. If thou failest, from whatever cause, thy evil scheme shall be for ever abandoned."

"Be it so! I am content," the fiend rejoined. "But I shall not fail," he added, with a fearful laugh. "Come hither at sunset, and thou wilt see me commence my work. Thou mayst tarry nigh me, if thou wilt, till it be done."

"Heaven forfend that it should be done!" ejaculated the saint, casting his eyes upwards.

When he looked up again towards the spot where the Evil One had stood, he could no more perceive him.

"No!" exclaimed the good saint, allowing his gaze to wander over the smiling and far-stretching weald, "I cannot believe that I am taking farewell of this lovely plain. I cannot for an instant believe that its destruction will be permitted. Its people have not sinned, but have incurred the hatred of the arch-fiend solely because of their piety and zeal. It shall be my business to defeat his hateful design."

The holy man turned away, and quitting the camp, proceeded in an easterly direction over the hill until he came to a small stone structure, standing near a gray old thorn-tree, on an acclivity covered with gorse and heather. The occupant of this solitary cell belonged to a priory of Benedictine nuns, situated at Leominster, near Arundel, and attached to the Abbey of Almenesches in Normandy. Sister Ursula Braose had retired to this lonesome spot in order to pass the whole of her time in devotion, and had acquired a reputation for sanctity and asceticism scarcely inferior to that of holy Cuthman himself. She was a daughter of the noble house of Braose of Bramber Castle. Once a week the purveyor of the priory at Leominster brought her a scanty supply of provisions (for the poor soul needed but little), and it was from him that Saint Cuthman had heard of her illness, and of her desire to be shriven by him.

He found the recluse occupied in her devotions. She was kneeling before an ivory crucifix fastened against the wall of her cell, and was so absorbed as to be entirely unconscious of the saint's approach. He did not make his presence known to her till she had done. Sister Ursula Braose had once been remarkable for beauty, but years, the austere life she had led, and the frequent and severe penances she had undergone, had obliterated all traces of loveliness from her features. She was old and wrinkled now; her hair white as snow, and her fingers thin as those of a skeleton. She was clothed in a loose black robe, with a cincture of cord round her waist. Reverentially saluting the holy man, she prayed him to be seated upon a stool, which, with another small seat hewn out of stone, a stone table, and a straw pallet, formed the entire furniture of her cell. An iron lamp hung by a chain from the roof. On the table were placed a missal written on vellum, an hour-glass, and a small taper.

After inquiring as to her ailments, and expressing his satisfaction that she felt somewhat better, Saint Cuthman said, "Are you still fasting, sister? I know you are wont only to break bread and drink water after the hour of vespers."

"Since yestere'en nothing has passed my lips, holy father," the recluse replied.

"It is well," said the saint. "The prohibition I am about to lay upon you—painful to any other unaccustomed to severe mortification of the flesh—will by you be scarcely accounted a penance. I enjoin you to refrain from all refreshment of the body, whether by food or rest, until to-morrow morning. Think you you can promise compliance with the order?"

"Do I think it, holy father?" Sister Ursula cried. "If Heaven will spare me so long, I am sure of it. I was in hopes," she added, almost with a look of disappointment, "that you were about to enjoin me some severe discipline such as my sinfulness merits, and I pray you to add sharp flagellations, or other wholesome correction of the flesh, to your mandate."

"Nay," rejoined the saint, smiling at the recluse's zeal; "the scourge is unneeded. You have no heavy offence, I am well assured, on your conscience. But keep strict vigil throughout the night, and suffer not sleep to weigh down your eyelids for a moment, or you may be exposed to temptation and danger. The arch-fiend himself will be abroad."

"I will spend the livelong night in prayer," said Sister Ursula, trembling.

"Fear nothing," returned the saint; "the Prince of Darkness has other business on hand, and will not trouble you. He will be engaged in a terrible work, but, with Heaven's aid, good sister, yours shall be the hand to confound him."

"Mine!" exclaimed the recluse, seeking by her looks for an explanation from the holy man.

"When the sun hath gone down," rejoined Saint Cuthman, "which will be about the seventh hour, turn this hour-glass, and let the sand run out six times—six times, do you mark, good sister? That will bring you to the first hour after midnight. Kneel then before yon crucifix, and pray fervently that the dark designs of him who took our Saviour to the top of the high mountain, and showed him all the kingdoms of the world in a moment, may be defeated. Next light this taper, which I will presently consecrate; set it within the bars of that little grated window looking towards the east; and pray that its glimmer may be as the first gray light of dawn. Again I say, do you mark me, sister?"

"Not a word uttered by you, holy father, but hath sank deep in my breast," she replied. "Your instructions shall be scrupulously obeyed."

"Nothing evil shall cross this threshold during the night," pursued the saint. "I will guard it as in the days of my youth I guarded my father's flocks on the hills. Light not your lamp, but only the taper, as I have bidden you; and stir not forth on any threat or summons, for such will only be a snare to injure you; and let not your heart quail because of the frightful sounds you may hear. Though the earth should quake beneath your feet, and this solid hill tremble to its foundations, yet shall not a stone of your cell be removed, neither shall any harm befall you."

The saint then took up the taper, and blessed it in these terms:—"*Domine Jesu Christi, fili Dei vivi, benedic candelam istam supplicationibus nostris: infunde in, Domine, per virtutem sanctæ crucis benedictionem cælestem; ut quibuscumque locis accensa, sive posita fuerit, discedant principes tenebrarum, et contremiscant, et fugiunt pavidi cum omnibus ministris suis ab habitationibus illis: nec præsumant amplius inquietare, aut molestare servientes tibi omnipotenti Deo.*"

After going through certain other ceremonials, which it is needless to describe, the saint sat down, and addressing Sister Ursula, declared his readiness to shrive her.

The recluse then knelt down before him, and inclining her head so as to conceal her features, said she had one secret within her breast which she had never revealed to her confessor—one sin upon her soul of which she had never been able to repent.

After duly reproving her, the saint told her to make clean her breast by confession, declaring she would then be able to repent.

Thus exhorted, Sister Ursula replied, in accents half suffocated by irrepressible emotion: "My secret is, that I loved you—you, holy father—when I was young. My unrepented sin is that I have never been able to banish that love from my heart."

"Alas! sister," rejoined the holy man, trembling in spite of himself, "we have been equally unhappy. In days long gone by I could not behold unmoved the charms of the fair and noble Lady Ursula Braose. But I conquered the passion, and repented that I had ever indulged it. Thou must do likewise. The struggle may be hard, but strength will be given thee for it. Hast thou aught more to confess?"

And the poor recluse, who shed abundance of tears, replying in the negative, the saint gave her absolution, saying that the penance he had already enjoined was sufficient, and that ere the morrow her breast would be free from its load. Struck by her looks, which were those of one not long for this world, he told her that if her sickness should prove mortal, dirges and trentals should be said for the repose of her soul.

The recluse thanked him, and after a while became composed and even cheerful.

Saint Cuthman tarried in the cell, discoursing with her upon the glorious prospects of futurity, and carefully avoiding any reference to the past, until, from the door of the little structure, which opened toward the west, he beheld the sun sink into the sea. Telling the good sister that a thousand lives depended upon her vigilance, he gave her his benediction and departed, never more to behold her alive.

As he took his way towards the north-eastern boundary of the ancient encampment, a noise resembling thunder smote his ear, and the ground shook so violently beneath his feet that he could scarcely stand, but reeled to and fro, as if his brain—his! whose lips no drink stronger than water had ever passed—had been assailed by the fumes of wine. Nevertheless he went on, and after a while reached the lofty headland overlooking Poynings.

Here, as he expected, he beheld the arch-fiend at work. The infernal excavator had already made a great breach into the down, and enormous fragments of chalk and flint-stones rolled down with a terrific crash like that caused by an avalanche amidst the Alps. Every stroke of his terrible pickaxe shook the hill to its centre. No one who was not sustained by supernatural power could have stood firmly upon the quaking headland. But Saint Cuthman, planting his staff upon the ground, remained unmoved—the only human witness of the astounding scene. The fiend's proportions had now become colossal, and he looked like one of that giant race whom poets of heathendom tell us warred against Jove. His garb was suited to his task, and resembled that of a miner. His brawny and hirsute arms were bared to the shoulder, and the curled goat's-horns were visible on his uncovered head. His implements had become enormous as himself, and the broadest and heaviest anchor-fluke ever forged was as nought to the curved iron head of his pickaxe. Each stroke plunged fathom-deep into the ground, and tore up huge boulder-like masses of chalk, the smallest of which might have loaded a wain.

The fiend worked away with might and main, and the concussion produced by his tremendous strokes was incessant and terrible, echoing far over the weald like the rattling of a dreadful thunderstorm.

But the sand ran out, and Sister Ursula turned her glass for the first time.

Suddenly the fiend stopped, and clapped his hand to his side, as if in pain. "A sharp stitch!" quoth he. "My side tingles as if pricked by a thousand pins. The sensation is by no means pleasant—but 'twill soon pass." Then perceiving the saint watching him, he called out derisively, "Aha! art thou there, thou saintly man? What thinkest thou now of the chance of escape for thy friends in the weald? Thou art a judge of such matters, I doubt not. Is my dyke broad enough and profound enough, thinkest thou—or shall I widen it and deepen it yet more?" And the chasm resounded with his mocking laughter.

"Thou art but a slovenly workman after all," remarked Saint Cuthman. "The sides of thy dyke are rough and uneven, and want levelling. A mortal labourer would be shrewdly reprimanded if he left them in such an untidy condition."

"No mortal labourer could make such a trench," cried the fiend. "However, it shall never be said that I am a slovenly workman." Whereupon he seized his spade, and proceeded to level the banks of the dyke, carefully removing all roughness and irregularity.

"Will that satisfy thy precise notions?" he called out when he had done.

"I cannot deny that it looks better," returned the holy man, glad to think that another hour had passed — for a soft touch falling upon his brow made him aware that at this moment Sister Ursula had turned the hour-glass for the second time.

A sharp sudden pain smote the fiend, and made him roar out lustily, "Another stitch, and worse than the first! But it shall not hinder my task."

Again he fell to work. Again the hill was shaken to its base. Again mighty masses of chalk were hurled into the valley, crushing everything upon which they descended. Again the strokes of the pickaxe echoed throughout the weald.

It was now dark. But the fiery breath of the demon sufficed to light him in his task. He toiled away with right good-will, for the devil can work hard enough, I promise you, if the task be to his mind. All at once he suspended his labour. The hour-glass had been turned for the third time.

"What is the matter with thee?" demanded the saint.

"I know not," replied the writhing fiend. "A sudden attack of cramp in the arms and legs, I fancy. I must have caught cold on these windy downs. I will do a little lighter work till the fit passes off." Upon this he took up the shovel, and began to trim the sides of the dyke as before.

While he was thus engaged the further end of the chasm closed up, so that when he took up the pickaxe once more he had all his work to do again. This caused him to snort and roar like a mad bull; and so much flame and smoke issued from his mouth and nostrils, that the bottom of the dyke resembled the bed of a volcano.

Sister Ursula then turned the glass for the fourth time. Hereupon an enormous mass of breccia, or gold-stone, as the common folk call it, which the fiend had dislodged, rolled down upon his foot and crushed it. This so enraged him that he sent the fragment of gold-stone whizzing over the hills to Hove. What with rubbing his bruised foot and roaring, a quarter of an hour elapsed before he could resume his work.

The fifth turning of the glass gave him such pains in the back, that for some minutes he was completely disabled.

"An attack of lumbago!" he cried. "I seem liable to all mortal ailments to-night."

"Thou hadst better desist," said the saint. "The next attack may cripple thee for all time."

"I am all right again!" shouted the demon. "It was but a passing seizure, like those that have gone before it. Thou shalt now see what I can do."

And he began to ply his pickaxe with greater energy than ever, toiling on without intermission, filling the chasm with flame from his fiery nostrils, and producing the effect of a continuous thunderstorm over the weald. Thus he wrought on, I say, uninterruptedly for the space of another hour. Sister Ursula then turned the glass for the last time.

The fiend was suddenly checked, but not this time by pains in the limbs or prostration of strength. He had struck the pickaxe so deeply into the chalk that he could not remove it. He strained every nerve to pluck it forth, but it continued firmly embedded; and the helve, which was thick as the mainmast of a ship, and of toughest oak, broke in his grasp.

While he was roaring like an infuriated lion

with rage and mortification, Saint Cuthman called out to him to come forth.

"Wherefore should I come forth?" the fiend cried. "Thou thinkest I am baffled; but thou art mistaken. I will dig out my axe-head presently, and my shovel will furnish me with a new handle."

"Cease, if thou canst, for a short space, to breathe forth flame and smoke; and look towards the east," cried the saint.

"There is a glimmer of light in the sky in that quarter!" exclaimed the demon, holding his breath; "but dawn cannot be come already."

"The streak of light grows rapidly wider and brighter," said the saint. "The shades of night are fleeing fast away. The larks are beginning to rise and carol forth their matin hymns on the downs. The rooks are cawing amid the trees of the park beneath us. The cattle are lowing in the meads—and hark! dost thou not hear the cocks crowing in the adjacent village of Poynings?"

"Cocks crowing at Poynings!" yelled the fiend. "It must be the dawn. But the sun shall not behold my discomfiture."

"Hide thy head in darkness, accursed being!" exclaimed the saint, raising his staff. "Hence with thee! and return not to this hill. The dwellers within the Sussex Weald are saved from thy malice, and may henceforth worship without fear. Get thee hence! I say."

Abashed by the awful looks of the saint, the demon fled. Howling with rage, like a wild beast robbed of its prey, he ran to the northern boundary of the rampart surrounding the camp, where the marks of his gigantic feet may still be seen indelibly impressed on the sod. Then springing off, and unfolding his sable pinions, he soared over the weald, alighting on Leith Hill.

Just as he took flight Sister Ursula's taper went out. Instant darkness fell upon the hill, and Night resumed her former sway. The village cocks ceased crowing, the larks paused in their songs and dropped to the ground like stones, the rooks returned to roost, and the lowing herds became silent.

Saint Cuthman had to make a considerable circuit to reach Sister Ursula's cell, a deep gulf having been placed between it and the headland on which he had taken his stand. On arriving at the little structure he found that the recluse's troubles were over. Her loving heart had for ever ceased to beat. Her failing strength had sufficed to turn the hour-glass for the last time, and just as the consecrated taper expired she passed away. In

death she still retained the attitude of prayer, her clasped hands being raised heavenwards.

"*Suspice Domine, preces nostras pro animâ famulæ tuæ; ut si quæ ei maculæ de terrenis contagiis adhæserunt, remissionis tuæ misericordia deleantur!*" ejaculated the holy man.

"She could not have had a better ending. May my own be like it! She shall have sepulture in my mother's grave at Steyning. And masses and trentals, according to my promise, shall be said for the repose of her soul. Peace be with her!" And he went on his way.

Thus was the demon banished by Saint Cuthman from that hill overlooking the fair Sussex Weald, and the people of the plain ever after prayed in peace. But the devil's handiwork, the unfinished dyke, exists to this day. Though I never heard that his pickaxe had been found.

LOVE'S PHILOSOPHY.

The fountains mingle with the river,
　And the rivers with the ocean;
The winds of heaven mix for ever
　With a sweet emotion;
Nothing in the world is single;
All things by a law divine
In one another's being mingle;—
　Why not I with thine?

See, the mountains kiss high heaven,
　And the waves clasp one another;
No sister flower would be forgiven
　If it disdained its brother;
And the sunlight clasps the earth,
　And the moonbeams kiss the sea;—
What are all these kissings worth,
　If thou kiss not me?

　　　　　　　　　　　P. B. SHELLEY.

THE FAMILY PICTURE.

With work in hand, perchance some fairy cap
To deck the little stranger yet to come;
One rosy boy struggling to mount her lap—
The eldest studious, with a book or map—
Her timid girl beside, with a faint bloom,
Conning some tale—while, with no gentle tap,
Yon chubby urchin beats his mimic drum,
Nor heeds the doubtful frown her eyes assume.
So sits the mother! with her fondest smile
Regarding her sweet little ones the while.
And he, the happy man! to whom belong
These treasures, feels their living charm beguile
All mortal cares, and eyes the prattling throng
With rapture-rising heart, and a thanksgiving tongue!

　　　　　　　SIR AUBREY DE VERE HUNT.

THE ANNUITY.

[George Outram, born at Glasgow, 25th March, 1805; died there, 1856. He was called to the bar in 1827; became part proprietor and editor of the *Glasgow Herald*, and wrote a number of humorous and satirical verses. A collection of his poems is published by Blackwood.]

I gaed to spend a week in Fife—
An unco week it proved to be—
For there I met a waesome wife
Lamentin' her viduity.
Her grief brak out ane fierce and fell,
I thought her heart wad burst the shell:
And—I was ane left to mysel'—
I sell't her an annuity.

The bargain lookit fair eneugh—
She just was turn'd saxty-three—
I couldna guess'd she'd prove sae teugh
By human ingenuity.
But years have come, and years have gane,
And there she's yet as stieve's a stane—
The limmer's growin' young again,
Since she got her annuity.

She's crined awa' to bane and skin;
But that it seems is naught to me.
She's like to live—although she's in
The last stage of tenuity.
She munches wi' her wizen'd gums,
An' stumps about on legs o' thrums,
But comes as sure as Christmas comes—
To ca' for her annuity.

I read the tables drawn wi' care
For an Insurance Company:
Her chance o' life was stated there
Wi' perfect perspicuity.
But tables here, or tables there,
She's lived ten years beyond her share,
An's like to live a dozen mair,
To ca' for her annuity.

Last Yule she had a fearfu' hoast—
I thought a kink might set me free—
I led her out, 'mang snaw and frost,
Wi' constant assiduity.
But deil may care! the blast gaed by,
And miss'd the auld anatomy;
It just cost me a tooth, forbye
Discharging her annuity.

If there's a sough of cholera,
Or typhus—wha sae gleg as she!
She buys up baths, and drugs an a',
In siccan superfluity!
She doesna need—she's fever-proof:
The pest walk'd o'er her very roof—
She tauld me sae—and then her loof
Held out for her annuity.

Ae day she fell—her arm she brak—
A compound fracture as could be;
Nae leech the cure wad undertak,
Whate'er was the gratuity.
It's cured!—she handles't like a flail—
It does as weel in bits as hale;
But I'm a broken man mysel'
Wi' her and her annuity.

Her broozled flesh and broken banes
Are weel as flesh and banes can be;
She bents the taeds that live in stanes
And fatten in vacuity.
They die when they're exposed to air—
They canna thole the atmosphere;
But her!—expose her onywhere,
She lives for her annuity.

If mortal means could nick her thread
Sma' crime it wad appear to me:
Ca't murder, or ca't homicide,
I'd justify't—and do it tae.
But how to fell a wither'd wife
That's carved out o' the tree o' life!
The timmer limmer daurs the knife
To settle her annuity.

I'd try a shot; but whar's the mark?
Her vital parts are hid frae me;
Her back-bane wanders through her sark,
In an unkenn'd cork-screwity.
She's palsified, and shakes her head
Sae fast about, ye scarce can see't:
It's past the power o' steel or lead
To settle her annuity.

She might be drown'd: but go she'll not
Within a mile o' loch or sea;
Or hang'd—if cord could grip a throat
O' siccan exiguity.
It's fitter far to hang the rope—
It draws out like a telescope:
'Twad tak a dreadfu' length o' drop
To settle her annuity.

Will puzion do't?—It has been tried.
But be't in hash or fricassee,
That's just the dish she can't abide,
Whatever kind o' *gout* it hae.
It's needless to assail her doubts:
She gangs by instinct, like the brutes,
And only eats an' drinks what suits
Hersel' and her annuity.

The Bible says the age o' man
Threescore and ten perchance may be.
She's ninety-four.—Let them wha can
Explain the incongruity.
She should hae lived afore the flood;
She's come o' patriarchal blood;
She's some auld pagan mummified,
Alive for her annuity.

She's been embalm'd inside and out;
She's sauted to the last degree;
There's pickle in her very snout,
Sae caper-like and cruety.
Lot's wife was fresh compared to her:
They've kyanized the useless knir—(witch);
She canna decompose—nae mair
Than her accurs'd annuity.

The water-drap wears out the rock,
As this eternal jaud wears me.
I could withstand the single shock,
But not the continuity.
It's pay me here, and pay me there,
And pay me, pay me, evermair;
I'll gang demented wi' despair—
I'm *charged* for her annuity.

ON DECISION OF CHARACTER.

[Rev. John Foster, born in Yorkshire, 1770; died at Stapleton, 15th October, 1843. He officiated for some time as a Baptist minister, but his latter years were chiefly occupied in literary pursuits. His reputation rests mainly upon his essays: *On a Man's writing Memoirs of Himself; On Decision of Character; The Application of the Epithet Romantic; Evangelical Religion;*—these were written in the form of a series of letters to a friend; *Evils of Popular Ignorance; Lectures,* &c. "Mr. Foster's essays are full of ingenuity and original remarks; the style of them is at once terse and elegant."—*Dr. Dibdin.*]

A person of undecisive character wonders how all the embarrassments in the world happened to meet exactly in *his* way, to place him just in that one situation for which he is peculiarly unadapted, but in which he is also willing to think no other man could have acted with facility or confidence. Incapable of setting up a firm purpose on the basis of things as they are, he is often employed in vain speculations on some different supposable state of things, which would have saved him from all this perplexity and irresolution. He thinks what a determined course he could have pursued *if* his talents, his health, his age, had been different; if he had been acquainted with some one person sooner; if his friends were, in this or the other point, different from what they are; or if fortune had showered her favours on him. And he gives himself as much license to complain as if all these advantages had been among the rights of his nativity, but refused, by a malignant or capricious fate, to his life. Thus he is occupied, instead of marking with a vigilant eye, and seizing with a strong hand, all the possibilities of his actual situation.
A man without decision can never be said to belong to himself; since, if he dared to

assert that he did, the puny force of some cause, about as powerful as you would have supposed, as a spider, may make a seizure of the hapless boaster the very next moment, and contemptuously exhibit the futility of the determinations by which he was to have proved 'the independence of his understanding and his will. He belongs to whatever can make capture of him; and one thing after another vindicates its right to him, by arresting him while he is trying to go on; as twigs and chips floating near the edge of a river are intercepted by every weed, and whirled in every little eddy. Having concluded on a design, he may pledge himself to accomplish it—*if* the hundred diversities of feeling which may come within the week will let him. His character precluding all foresight of his conduct, he may sit and wonder what form and direction his views and actions are destined to take to-morrow; as a farmer has often to acknowledge that next day's proceedings are at the disposal of its winds and clouds. This man's notions and determinations always depend very much on other human beings; and what chance for consistency and stability while the persons with whom he may converse or transact are so various? This very evening he may talk with a man whose sentiments will melt away the present form and outline of his purposes, however firm and defined he may have fancied them to be. A succession of persons whose faculties were stronger than his own might, in spite of his irresolute reaction, take him and dispose of him as they pleased. Such infirmity of spirit practically confesses him made for subjection, and he passes, like a slave, from owner to owner. Sometimes indeed it happens that a person so constituted falls into the train, and under the permanent ascendency, of some one stronger mind, which thus becomes through life the oracle and guide, and gives the inferior a steady will and plan. This, when the governing spirit is wise and virtuous, is a fortunate relief to the feeling, and an advantage gained to the utility of the subordinate and, as it were, appended mind.
The regulation of every man's plan must greatly depend on the course of events, which come in an order not to be foreseen or prevented. But in accommodating the plans of conduct to the train of events, the difference between two men may be no less than that, in the one instance the man is subservient to the events, and in the other the events are made subservient to the man. Some men seem to have been taken along by a succession of events, and, as it were, handed forward in

helpless passiveness from one to another, having no determined principle in their own characters by which they could constrain those events to serve a design formed antecedently to them, or apparently in defiance of them. The events seized them as a neutral material, not they the events. Others, advancing through life with an internal invincible determination, have seemed to make the train of circumstances, whatever they were, conduce as much to their chief design as if they had, by some directing interposition, been brought about on purpose. It is wonderful how even the casualties of life seem to bow to a spirit that will not bow to them, and yield to subserve a design which they may, in their first apparent tendency, threaten to frustrate.

You may have known such examples, though they are comparatively not numerous. You may have seen a man of this vigorous character in a state of indecision concerning some affair in which it was necessary for him to determine, because it was necessary for him to act. But in this case his manner would assure you that he would not remain long undecided; you would wonder if you found him still balancing and hesitating the next day. If he explained his thoughts you would perceive that their clear process, evidently at each effort gaining something toward the result, must certainly reach it ere long. The deliberation of such a mind is a very different thing from the fluctuation of one whose second thinking only upsets the first, and whose third confounds both. To *know how* to obtain a determination is one of the first requisites and indications of a rationally decisive character.

When the decision was arrived at, and a plan of action approved, you would feel an assurance that something would absolutely be done. It is characteristic of such a mind to think for effect, and the pleasure of escaping from temporary doubt gives an additional impulse to the force with which it is carried into action. The man will not re-examine his conclusions with endless repetition, and he will not be delayed long by consulting other persons after he had ceased to consult himself. He cannot bear to sit still among unexecuted decisions and unattempted projects. We wait to hear of his achievements, and are confident we shall not wait long. The possibility or the means may not be obvious to us, but we know that everything will be attempted, and that a spirit of such determined will is like a river, which, in whatever manner it is obstructed, will make its way somewhere. It must have cost Cæsar many anxious hours of deliberation

before he decided to pass the Rubicon, but it is probable he suffered but few to elapse between the decision and the execution. And any one of his friends who should have been apprised of his determination, and understood his character, would have smiled contemptuously to hear it insinuated that though Cæsar had resolved, Cæsar would not dare; or that though he might cross the Rubicon, whose opposite banks presented to him no hostile legions, he might come to other rivers which he would not cross; or that either rivers, or any other obstacle, would deter him from prosecuting his determination from this ominous commencement to its very last consequence.

One signal advantage possessed by a mind of this character is that its passions are not wasted. The whole measure of passion of which any one, with important transactions before him, is capable, is not more than enough to supply interest and energy for the required practical exertions; therefore as little as possible of this costly flame should be expended in a way that does not augment the force of action. But nothing can less contribute, or be more destructive to vigour of action, than protracted anxious fluctuation, through resolutions adopted, rejected, resumed, suspended; while yet nothing causes a greater expense of feeling. The heart is fretted and exhausted by being subjected to an alternation of contrary excitements, with the ultimate mortifying consciousness of their contributing to no end. The long-wavering deliberation, whether to perform some bold action of difficult virtue, has often cost more to feeling than the action itself, or a series of such actions, would have cost; with the great disadvantage too of not being relieved by any of that invigoration which the man in action finds in the activity itself, that spirit created to renovate the energy which the action is expending. When the passions are not consumed among dubious musings and abortive resolutions, their utmost value and use can be secured by throwing all their animating force into effective operation.

Another advantage of this character is that it exempts from a great deal of interference and obstructive annoyance which an irresolute man may be almost sure to encounter. Weakness in every form tempts arrogance, and a man may be allowed to wish for a kind of character with which stupidity and impertinence may not make so free. When a firm decisive spirit is recognized, it is curious to see how the space clears around a man, and leaves him room and freedom. The disposition to interrogate, dictate, or banter preserves a respectful and politic distance, judging it not unwise to keep the peace with a person of so much energy. A conviction that he understands, and that he wills with extraordinary force, silences the conceit that intended to perplex or instruct him, and intimidates the malice that was disposed to attack him. There is a feeling, as in respect to fate, that the decrees of so inflexible a spirit *must* be right, or that at least they *will* be accomplished.

But not only will he secure the freedom of acting for himself: he will obtain also by degrees the coincidence of those in whose company he is to transact the business of life. If the manners of such a man be free from arrogance, and he can qualify his firmness with a moderate degree of insinuation; and if his measures have partly lost the appearance of being the dictates of his will, under the wider and softer sanction of some experience that they are reasonable, both competition and fear will be laid to sleep, and his will may acquire an unresisted ascendency over many who will be pleased to fall into the mechanism of a system which they find makes them more successful and happy than they could have been amidst the anxiety of adjusting plans and expedients of their own, and the consequences of often adjusting them ill. I have known several parents, both fathers and mothers, whose management of their families has answered this description, and has displayed a striking example of the facile complacency with which a number of persons, of different ages and dispositions, will yield to the decisions of a firm mind, acting on an equitable and enlightened system.

The last resource of this character is hard inflexible pertinacity, on which it may be allowed to rest its strength after finding it can be effectual in none of its milder forms. I remember admiring an instance of this kind in a firm, sagacious, and estimable old man whom I well knew, and who has long-been dead. Being on a jury in a trial of life and death, he was satisfied of the innocence of the prisoner; the other eleven were of the opposite opinion. But he was resolved the man should not be condemned; and as the first effort for preventing it, very properly made application to the *minds* of his associates, spending several hours in labouring to convince them. But he found he made no impression, while he was exhausting the strength which it was necessary to reserve for another mode of operation. He then calmly told them that it should now be a trial who could endure confinement and famine the longest, and that they might be quite assured he would sooner die than release them at

the expense of the prisoner's life. In this situation they spent about twenty-four hours; when at length all acceded to his verdict of acquittal. It is not necessary to amplify on the indispensable importance of this quality in order to the accomplishment of anything eminently good. We instantly see that every path to signal excellence is so obstructed and beset that none but a spirit so qualified can pass.

––––––––

"IN MAIDEN MEDITATION."

[Thomas Haynes Bayly, born near Bath, 1797 ; died 1839. Educated at Oxford, and intended for the church. He wrote thirty-six pieces for the stage, several novels —*Aylmers; Kindness in Women,* &c.,—and numerous songs. As a song-writer, he was most prolific and most popular: *The Soldier's Tear* (one of four lyrics published under the title of *Songs of a Soldier's Story,* and the only one of them worth remembering), *We Met—'twas in a Crowd,* and a few others, are still well known. D. M. Moir said of him: "He possessed a playful fancy, a practised ear, a refined taste, and a sentiment which ranged pleasantly from the fanciful to the pathetic."]

What is her thought? may we not guess
What those eloquent eyes express?
May we not read in her tranquil cheek
All that her musical voice could speak?

What is her thought? sits she alone,
Watching the path of the absent one,
Eager to welcome him home again,
From the ocean-storm or the battle-plain!
If it be so, how blest is he,
The treasured thought of her memory!

Upon her knees, at dawn of day,
For him she fervently will pray;
And, when her midnight lamp grows dim,
Again her prayer will be for him.

What is her thought? of former days?
Of childhood's bright and flowery ways?
Of ardent hopes untimely cross'd,
And early friends too early lost?

No, in that calm and lovely face
Nothing of sadness can we trace,
For self-reproach is the canker-worm
That wears away the beauteous form.

When the first wild storm of grief is spent,
There are tranquil days for the innocent ;
She hath assuaged, while in prayer she knelt,
The keenest wound that her heart hath felt.

What is her thought? of the time to come?
Of a cheerful hearth, of a happy home?
Of love unchanging? of a friend
Whose fond affection ne'er will end?
What is her thought?—whatever it be,
May thoughts as pure be in store for me!

ADVENTURES OF A CAVALIER.

[Daniel De Foe, born in London, 1661; died there, 24th April, 1731. He was the son of a butcher in St. Giles, Cripplegate, and was educated with a view to the Presbyterian ministry. He became a soldier (as an adherent to Monmouth), a hosier, a tile-maker, and a woollen merchant in succession. His political and satirical pamphlets—*Essay on Projects; The True-Born Englishman* (verse); and *The Shortest Way with the Dissenters*—earned for him reputation and imprisonment. He was employed as a government agent in the negotiations for the Union between Scotland and England, which supplied him with the materials for his history of that event. But his raillery and satire were misunderstood, imprisonment and fines impoverished him, slander harassed him, and he was stricken with apoplexy whilst writing his defence in 1715—*An Appeal to Honour and Justice, though it be of his Worst Enemies*, being a True Account of his Conduct in Public Affairs. He recovered his health, and thinking that it would be more to his advantage to attempt to amuse the public than to reform it, he produced *Robinson Crusoe*. The success was immediate and enduring. It was followed by *The Life and Piracies of Captain Singleton; The Adventures of Roxana; The Life of Colonel Juck; The History of Duncan Campbell; Moll Flanders; A Journal of the Plague in 1665; Religious Courtship; The Political History of the Devil, and a System of Magic; A Relation of the Apparition of one Mrs. Veal* (written to sell a heavy book, *Drelincourt on Death*); *A Tour through England and Scotland; A Plan of the English Commerce; Giving Alms no Charity*; and *The Memoirs of a Cavalier*, during the Civil Wars in England, from which we quote the Cavalier's adventures in escaping from the battle of Marston Moor. De Foe is said to have produced 210 books and pamphlets, and in all he was excellent. He is acknowledged to be one of the master spirits of English literature.]

I had but very coarse treatment in this fight; for, returning with the prince from the pursuit of the right wing, and finding all lost, I halted with some other officers to consider what to do. At first we were for making our retreat in a body, and might have done so well enough if we had known what had happened before we saw ourselves in the middle of the enemy; for Sir Thomas Fairfax, who had got together his scattered troops, and joined by some of the left wing, knowing who we were, charged us with great fury. It was not a time to think of anything but getting away, or dying upon the spot. The prince kept on in the front; and Sir Thomas Fairfax, by this charge, cut off about three regiments of us from our body; but bending his main strength at the prince, left us, as it were, behind him in the middle of the field of battle. We took this for the only opportunity we could have to get off; and joining together, we made across the place of battle in as good order as we could, with our carabines presented. In this posture we passed

by several bodies of the enemy's foot, who stood with their pikes charged to keep us off; but they had no occasion, for we had no design to meddle with them, but to get from them. Thus we made a swift march, and thought ourselves pretty secure; but our work was not done yet, for on a sudden we saw ourselves under a necessity of fighting our way through a great body of Manchester's horse, who came galloping upon us over the moor. They had, as we suppose, been pursuing some of our broken troops which were fled before, and seeing us, they gave us a home charge. We received them as well as we could, but pushed to get through them, which at last we did with a considerable loss to them. However, we lost so many men, either killed or separated from us (for all could not follow the same way), that of our three regiments, we could not be above 400 horse together when we got quite clear, and these were mixed men, some of one troop and regiment, some of another. Not that I believe many of us were killed in the last attack, for we had plainly the better of the enemy; but our design being to get off, some shifted for themselves one way, and some another, in the best manner they could, and as their several fortunes guided them. Four hundred more of this body, as I afterwards understood, having broke through the enemy's body another way, kept together, and got into Pontefract Castle; and 300 more made northward and to Skipton, where the prince afterwards fetched them off.

These few of us that were left together, with whom I was, being now pretty clear of pursuit, halted, and began to inquire who and what we were, and what we should do; and, on a short debate, I proposed we should make to the first garrison of the king's that we could recover, and that we should keep together, lest the country people should insult us upon the roads. With this resolution we pushed on westward for Lancashire; but our misfortunes were not yet at an end. We travelled very hard, and got to a village upon the river Wharf, near Wetherby. At Wetherby there was a bridge, but we understood that a party from Leeds had secured the town and the post, in order to stop the fleeing Cavaliers, and that it would be very hard to get through there, though, as we understood afterwards, there were no soldiers there but a guard of the townsmen. In this pickle we consulted what course to take. To stay where we were till morning, we all concluded would not be safe. Some advised to take the stream with our horses; but the river, which is deep, and the current strong, seemed to bid us have a care what we did of that kind, especially in the night. We resolved therefore to refresh ourselves and our horses, which indeed is more than we did, and go on till we might come to a ford or bridge, where we might get over. Some guides we had, but they either were foolish or false; for after we had rid eight or nine miles, they plunged us into a river at a place they called a ford, but it was a very ill one, for most of our horses swam, and seven or eight were lost, but we saved the men. However, we got all over.

We made bold, with our first convenience, to trespass upon the country for a few horses where we could find them, to remount our men whose horses were drowned, and continued our march. But being obliged to refresh ourselves at a small village on the edge of Bramham Moor, we found the country alarmed by our taking some horses; and we were no sooner got on horseback in the morning, and entering on the moor, but we understood we were pursued by some troops of horse. There was no remedy but we must pass this moor; and though our horses were exceedingly tired, yet we pressed on upon a round trot, and recovered an inclosed country on the other side, where we halted. And here, necessity putting us upon it, we were obliged to look out for more horses, for several of our men were dismounted, and others' horses disabled by carrying double, those who lost their horses getting up behind them; but we were supplied by our enemies against their will.

The enemy followed us over the moor, and we having a woody inclosed country about us where we were, I observed by their moving they had lost sight of us; upon which I proposed concealing ourselves till we might judge of their numbers. We did so; and lying close in a wood, they passed hastily by us without skirting or searching the wood, which was what on another occasion they would not have done. I found they were not above 150 horse, and considering that to let them go before us would be to alarm the country and stop our design, I thought, since we might be able to deal with them, we should not meet with a better place for it, and told the rest of our officers my mind, which all our party presently (for we had not time for a long debate) agreed to. Immediately upon this I caused two men to fire their pistols in the wood at two different places, as far asunder as I could. This I did to give them an alarm and amuse them: for being in the lane, they would otherwise have got through before we had been ready, and I resolved to engage them there as soon as it

was possible. After this alarm we rushed out of the wood with about a hundred horse, and charged them on the flank in a broad lane, the wood being on their right. Our passage into the lane being narrow, gave us some difficulty in our getting out; but the charge did our work, for the enemy, thinking we had been a mile or two before, had not the least thoughts of this onset till they heard us in the wood, and then they who were before could not come back. We broke into the lane just in the middle of them, and by that means divided them; and facing to the left, charged the rear. First our dismounted men, which were near fifty, lined the edge of the wood, and fired with their carabines upon those which were before so warmly, that they put them into a great disorder. Meanwhile fifty more of our horse from the further part of the wood showed themselves in the lane upon their front. This put them of the foremost party into a great perplexity, and they began to face about to fall upon us who were engaged in the rear; but their facing about in a lane where there was no room to wheel (and one who understands the manner of wheeling a troop of horse must imagine), put them into a great disorder. Our party in the head of the lane taking the advantage of this mistake of the enemy, charged in upon them, and routed them entirely. Some found means to break into the inclosures on the other side of the lane, and get away. About thirty were killed, and about twenty-five made prisoners, and forty very good horses were taken; all this while not a man of ours was lost, and not above seven or eight wounded. Those in the rear behaved themselves better, for they stood our charge with a great deal of resolution, and all we could do could not break them; but at last our men, who had fired on foot through the hedges at the other party, coming to do the like here, there was no standing it any longer. The rear of them faced about, and retreated out of the lane, and drew up in the open field to receive and rally their fellows. We killed about seventeen of them, and followed them to the end of the lane, but had no mind to have any more fighting than needs must; our condition at that time not making it proper, the towns round us being all in the enemy's hands, and the country but indifferently pleased with us. However, we stood facing them till they thought fit to march away. Thus we were supplied with horses enough to remount our men, and pursued our first design of getting into Lancashire. As for our prisoners, we let them off on foot.

But the country being by this time alarmed, and the rout of our army everywhere known, we foresaw abundance of difficulties before us; we were not strong enough to venture into any great towns, and we were too many to be concealed in small ones. Upon this we resolved to halt in a great wood, about three miles beyond the place where we had the last skirmish, and sent out scouts to discover the country, and learn what they could, either of the enemy or of our friends.

Anybody may suppose we had but indifferent quarters here, either for ourselves or for our horses; but, however, we made shift to lie here two days and one night. In the interim I took upon me, with two more, to go to Leeds to learn some news. We were disguised like country ploughmen; the clothes we got at a farmer's house, which for that particular occasion we plundered; and I cannot say no blood was shed in a manner too rash, and which I could not have done at another time; but our case was desperate, and the people too surly, and shot at us out of the window, wounded one man, and shot a horse, which we counted as great a loss to us as a man, for our safety depended upon our horses. Here we got clothes of all sorts, enough for both sexes; and thus, dressing myself up a la paisant, with a white cap on my head, and a fork on my shoulder, and one of my comrades in the farmer's wife's russet gown and petticoat, like a woman; the other with an old crutch like a lame man, and all mounted on such horses as we had taken the day before from the country, away we go to Leeds by three several ways, and agreed to meet upon the bridge. My pretended countrywoman acted her part to the life, though the party was a gentleman of good quality of the Earl of Worcester's family; and the cripple did as well as he; but I thought myself very awkward in my dress, which made me very shy, especially among the soldiers. We passed their sentinels and guards at Leeds unobserved, and put up our horses at several houses in the town, from whence we went up and down to make our remarks. My cripple was the fittest to go among the soldiers, because there was less danger of being pressed. There he informed himself of the matters of war, particularly that the enemy sat down again to the siege of York; that flying parties were in pursuit of the Cavaliers; and there he heard that 500 horse of the Lord Manchester's men had followed a party of Cavaliers over Bramham Moor; and that, entering a lane, the Cavaliers, who were 1000 strong, fell upon them, and killed them all but about fifty. This, though

it was a lie, was very pleasant to us to hear, knowing it was our party because of the other part of the story, which was thus: that the Cavaliers had taken possession of such a wood, where they rallied all the troops of their flying army; that they had plundered the country as they came, taking all the good horses they could get; that they had plundered Goodman Thompson's house, which was the farmer I mentioned, and killed man, woman, and child; and that they were about 2000 strong.

My other friend in woman's clothes got among the good wives at an inn, where she set up her horse, and there she heard the same sad and dreadful tidings; and that this party was so strong, none of the neighbouring garrisons durst stir out, but that they had sent expresses to York for a party of horse to come to their assistance.

I walked up and down the town, but fancied myself so ill disguised, and so easy to be known, that I cared not to talk with anybody. We met at the bridge exactly at our time, and compared our intelligence, found it answered our end of coming, and that we had nothing to do but to get back to our men; but my cripple told me he would not stir till he bought some victuals: so away he hops with his crutch, and buys four or five great pieces of bacon, as many of hung beef, and two or three loaves; and borrowing a sack at the inn (which I suppose he never restored), he loads his horse, and getting a large leather bottle, he filled that of aqua vitæ instead of small beer; my woman comrade did the like. I was uneasy in my mind, and took no care but to get out of the town. However, we all came off well enough; but it was well for me that I had no provisions with me, as you will hear presently. We came, as I said, into the town by several ways, and so we went out; but about three miles from the town we met again exactly where we had agreed. I being about a quarter of a mile from the rest, I met three country fellows on horseback: one had a long pole on his shoulder, another a fork, the third no weapon at all that I saw. I gave them the road very orderly, being habited like one of their brethren; but one of them stopping short at me, and looking earnestly, calls out, "Hark thee, friend," says he, in a broad north-country tone, "whar hast thou thilk horse?" I must confess I was in the utmost confusion at the question, neither being able to answer the question, nor to speak in his tone; so I made as if I did not hear him, and went on. "Na, but ye's not gang soa," says the boor, and comes up to me, and takes hold of the horse's bridle to stop me; at which, vexed at heart that I could not tell how to talk to him, I reached him a great knock on the pate with my fork, and fetched him off his horse, and then began to mend my pace. The other clowns, though it seems they knew not what the fellow wanted, pursued me; and finding they had better heels than I, I saw there was no remedy but to make use of my hands, and faced about. The first that came up with me was he that had no weapons, so I thought I might parley with him; and speaking as country-like as I could, I asked him what he wanted? "Thou'st knaw that soon," says Yorkshire, "and I'se but come at thee." "Then keep awa', man," said I, "or I'se brain thee." By this time the third man came up, and the parley ended; for he gave me no words, but laid at me with his long pole, and that with such fury that I began to be doubtful of him. I was loathe to shoot the fellow, though I had pistols under my gray frock, as well for that the noise of a pistol might bring more people in, the village being in our rear, and also because I could not imagine what the fellow meant or would have; but at last, finding he would be too many for me with that long weapon, and a hardy strong fellow, I threw myself off my horse, and running in with him, stabbed my fork into his horse; the horse being wounded, staggered awhile and then fell down, and the booby had not the sense to get down in time, but fell with him; upon which, giving him a knock or two with my fork, I secured him. The other by this time had furnished himself with a great stick out of a hedge, and before I was disengaged from the last fellow, gave me two such blows that if the last had not missed my head and hit me on the shoulder, I had ended the fight and my life together. It was time to look about me now, for this was a madman; I defended myself with my fork, but it would not do. At last, in short, I was forced to pistol him, and get on horseback again, and with all the speed I could make, get away to the wood to our men.

If my two fellow spies had not been behind, I had never known what was the meaning of this quarrel of the three countrymen; but my cripple had all the particulars, for he being behind us, as I have already observed, when he came up to the first fellow, who began the fray, he found him beginning to come to himself. So he gets off, and pretends to help him, and sets him upon his breach, and being a very merry fellow, talked to him: "Well, and what's the matter now?" says he to him. "Ah,

wae's me," says the fellow, "I'se killed!" "Not quite, mon," says the cripple. "O that's a fause thief," says he; and thus they parleyed. My cripple got him on his feet, and gave him a dram of his aqua vitæ bottle, and made much of him, in order to know what was the occasion of the quarrel. Our disguised woman pitied the fellow too, and together they set him up again upon his horse, and then he told them that that fellow was got upon one of his brother's horses who lived at Wetherby. They said the Cavaliers stole him, but it was like such rogues; no mischief could be done in the country but it was the poor Cavaliers must bear the blame, and the like; and thus they jogged on till they came to the place where the other two lay. The first fellow they assisted as they had done the other, and gave him a dram out of the leather bottle; but the last fellow was past their care, so they came away. For when they understood that it was my horse they claimed, they began to be afraid that their own horses might be known too, and then they had been betrayed in a worse pickle than I, and must have been forced to have done some mischief or other to have got away.

I had sent out two troopers to fetch them off if there was any occasion; but their stay was not long, and the two troopers saw them at a distance coming towards us, so they returned.

I had enough of going for a spy, and my companions had enough of staying in the wood; for other intelligences agreed with ours, and all concurred in this, that it was time to be going. However, this use we made of it, that while the country thought us so strong, we were in the less danger of being attacked, though in the more of being observed; but all this while we heard nothing of our friends till the next day. We then heard Prince Rupert, with about 1000 horse, was at Skipton, and from thence marched away to Westmoreland.

We concluded now we had two or three days' time good; for, since messengers were sent to York for a party to suppress us, we must have at least two days' march of them, and therefore all concluded we were to make the best of our way. Early in the morning, therefore, we decamped from those dull quarters; and as we marched through a village, we found the people very civil to us, and the woman cried out, "God bless them; it is a pity the Roundheads should make such work with such brave men," and the like. Finding we were among our friends, we resolved to halt a little and refresh ourselves; and indeed the people were very kind to us, gave us victuals and drink, and took care of our horses. It happened to be my lot to stop at a house where the good woman took a great deal of pains to provide for us; but I observed the good man walked about with a cap upon his head, and very much out of order. I took no great notice of it, being very sleepy, and having asked my landlady to let me have a bed, I lay down and slept heartily. When I waked I found my landlord on another bed groaning very heavily.

When I came down stairs I found my cripple talking with my landlady. He was now out of his disguise, but we called him cripple still; and the other who put on the woman's clothes we called Goody Thompson. As soon as he saw me he called me out. "Do you know," says he, "the man of the house you are quartered in?" "No, not I," says I. "No, so I believe, nor they you," says he. "If they did, the goodwife would not have made you a posset, and fetched a white loaf for you." "What do you mean?" says I. "Have you seen the man?" says he. "Seen him?" says I, "yes, and heard him too. The man is sick, and groans so heavily," says I, "that I could not lie upon the bed any longer for him." "Why, this is the poor man," says he, "that you knocked down with your fork yesterday; and I have had all the story out yonder at the next door." I confess it grieved me to have been forced to treat one so roughly who was one of our friends; but to make some amends, we contrived to give the poor man his brother's horse; and my cripple told him a formal story, that he believed the horse was taken away from the fellow by some of our men; and if he knew him again, if it was his friend's horse he should have him. The man came down upon the news, and I caused six or seven horses, which were taken at the same time, to be shown him. He immediately chose the right; so I gave him the horse, and we pretended a great deal of sorrow for the man's hurt, and that we had not knocked the fellow on the head as well as took away the horse. The man was so overjoyed at the revenge he thought was taken on the fellow, that we heard him groan no more. We ventured to stay all day at this town, and the next night; and got guides to lead us to Blackstone Edge, a ridge of mountains which parts this side of Yorkshire from Lancashire. Early in the morning we marched, and kept our scouts very carefully out every way, who brought us no news for this day. We kept on all night, and made our horses do penance for that little rest they had, and the next morning we passed the hills and got into Lancashire, to a town called

Littleborough, and from thence to Rochdale, a little market-town. And now we thought ourselves safe as to the pursuit of enemies from the side of York, our design was to get to Bolton, but all the county was full of the enemy in flying parties; and how to get to Bolton we knew not. At last we resolved to send a messenger to Bolton; but he came back and told us he had, with lurking and hiding, tried all the ways that he thought possible, but to no purpose, for he could not get into the town. We sent another, and he never returned; and some time afterward we understood he was taken by the enemy. At last one got into the town, but brought us word they were tired out with constant alarms, had been straitly blocked up, and every day expected a siege, and therefore advised us either to go northward, where Prince Rupert and the Lord Goring ranged at liberty, or to get over Warrington Bridge, and so secure our retreat to Chester. This double direction divided our opinions: I was for getting into Chester, both to recruit myself with horses and with money, both which I wanted, and to get refreshment, which we all wanted; but the major part of our men were for the north. First, they said, there was their general, and it was their duty to the cause, and the king's interest obliged us to go where we could do best service; and there were their friends, and every man might hear some news of his own regiment, for we belonged to several regiments; besides, all the towns to the left of us were possessed by Sir William Brereton; Warrington and Northwich garrisoned by the enemy, and a strong party at Manchester; so that it was very likely we should be beaten and dispersed before we could get to Chester. These reasons, and especially the last, determined us for the north, and we had resolved to march the next morning, when other intelligence brought us to more speedy resolutions. We kept our scouts continually abroad to bring us intelligence of the enemy, whom we expected on our backs, and also to keep an eye upon the country; for as we lived upon them something at large, they were ready enough to do us any ill turn as it lay in their power.

The first messenger that came to us was from our friends at Bolton, to inform us that they were preparing at Manchester to attack us. One of our parties had been as far as Stockport, on the edge of Cheshire, and was pursued by a party of the enemy, but got off by the help of the night. Thus all things looking black to the south, we had resolved to march northward in the morning, when one of our scouts from the side of Manchester assured us Sir Thomas Middleton, with some of the Parliament forces and the country troops, making above 1200 men, were on their march to attack us, and would certainly beat up our quarters that night. Upon this advice we resolved to be gone; and getting all things in readiness, we began to march about two hours before night; and having gotten a trusty fellow for a guide—a fellow that we found was a friend to our side—he put a project into my head which saved us all for that time, and that was to give out in the village that we were marched back to Yorkshire, resolving to get into Pontefract Castle; and accordingly he leads us out of the town the same way we came in; and taking a boy with him, he sends the boy back just at night, and bade him say he saw us go up the hills at Blackstone Edge; and it happened very well, for this party were so sure of us that they had placed 400 men on the road to the northward to intercept our retreat that way, and had left no way for us, as they thought, to get away, but back again.

About ten o'clock at night they assaulted our quarters, but found we were gone; and being informed which way, they followed upon the spur, and travelling all night, being moonlight, they found themselves the next day about fifteen miles east, just out of our way; for we had, by the help of our guide, turned short at the foot of the hills, and through blind untrodden paths, and with difficulty enough, by noon the next day had reached almost twenty-five miles north, near a town called Clithero. Here we halted in the open field, and sent out our people to see how things were in the country. This part of the country, almost unpassable, and walled round with hills, was indifferent quiet; and we got some refreshment for ourselves, but very little horsemeat, and so went on; but we had not marched far before we found ourselves discovered; and the 400 horse sent to lie in wait for us as before, having understood which way we went, followed us hard; and, by letters to some of their friends at Preston, we found we were beset again. Our guide began now to be out of his knowledge, and our scouts brought us word the enemy's horse was posted before us; and we knew they were in our rear. In this exigence we resolved to divide our small body, and so amusing them, at least one might get off, if the other miscarried. I took about eighty horse with me, among which were all that I had of my own regiment, amounting to about thirty-two, and took the hills towards Yorkshire. Here we met with such unpassable

hills, vast moors, rocks, and stony ways, as lamed all our horses and tired our men; and sometimes I was ready to think we should never be able to get over them, till our horses falling, and jack-boots being but indifferent things to travel in, we might be starved before we should find any road or towns, for guide we had none but a boy who knew but little, and would cry when we asked him any questions. I believe neither men nor horses ever passed in some places where we went, and for twenty hours we saw not a town nor a house, excepting sometimes from the top of the mountains, at a vast distance. I am persuaded we might have encamped here, if we had had provisions, till the war had been over, and have met with no disturbance; and I have often wondered since how we got into such horrible places, as much as how we got out. That which was worse to us than all the rest was, that we knew not where we were going, nor what part of the country we should come into when we came out of those desolate crags. At last, after a terrible fatigue, we began to see the western parts of Yorkshire, some few villages, and the country at a distance looked a little like England; for I thought before it looked like old Brennus hill, which the Grisons call the grandfather of the Alps. We got some relief in the villages, which indeed some of us had so much need of that they were hardly able to sit their horses, and others were forced to help them off, they were so faint. I never felt so much of the power of hunger in my life, for having not eaten in thirty hours, I was as ravenous as a hound; and if I had had a piece of horseflesh, I believe I should not have had patience to have stayed dressing it, but have fallen upon it raw, and have eaten it as greedily as a Tartar.

However, I ate very cautiously, having often seen the danger of men's eating heartily after long fasting. Our next care was to inquire our way. Halifax, they told us, was on our right; there we durst not think of going. Skipton was before us, and there we knew not how it was; for a body of 3000 horse, sent out by the enemy in pursuit of Prince Rupert, had been there but two days before, and the country people could not tell us whether they were gone or no; and Manchester's horse, which were sent out after our party, were then at Halifax in quest of us, and afterwards marched into Cheshire. In this distress we would have hired a guide, but none of the country people would go with us, for the Roundheads would hang them, they said, when they came there. Upon this I called a fellow to me: "Hark ye, friend," says I, "dost thee know the way so as to bring us into Westmoreland, and not keep the great road from York?" "Ay, marry," says he, "I ken the ways weel enou." "And you would go and guide us," said I, "but that you are afraid the Roundheads will hang you?" "Indeed would I," says the fellow. "Why then," says I, "thou hadst as good be hanged by a Roundhead as a Cavalier; for if thou wilt not go, I'll hang thee just now." "Na, and ye serve me soa," says the fellow, "I'se ene gang with ye; for I care not for hanging; and ye'll get me a good horse, I'se gang and be one of ye, for I'll nere come heame more." This pleased us still better; and we mounted the fellow, for three of our men died that night with the extreme fatigue of the last service.

Next morning, when our new trooper was mounted and clothed, we hardly knew him; and this fellow led us by such ways, such wildernesses, and yet with such prudence, keeping the hills to the left that we might have the villages to refresh ourselves, that without him we had certainly either perished in those mountains, or fallen into the enemy's hands. We passed the great road from York so critically as to time, that from one of the hills he showed us a party of the enemy's horse, who were then marching into Westmoreland. We lay still that day, finding we were not discovered by them; and our guide proved the best scout that we could have had, for he would go out ten miles at a time, and bring us in all the news of the country. Here he brought us word that York was surrendered upon articles, and that Newcastle, which had been surprised by the king's party, was besieged by another army of Scots, advanced to help their brethren.

Along the edges of those vast mountains we passed, with the help of our guide, till we came into the forest of Swale: and finding ourselves perfectly concealed here—for no soldier had ever been here all the war, nor perhaps would not if it had lasted seven years—we thought we wanted a few days' rest, at least for our horses: so we resolved to halt, and while we did so we made some disguises, and sent out some spies into the country; but as here were no great towns nor no post-road, we got very little intelligence. We rested four days, and then marched again: and indeed, having no great stock of money about us, and not very free of that we had, four days was enough for those poor places to be able to maintain us.

We thought ourselves pretty secure now; but our chief care was how to get over those terrible mountains; for having passed the great

road that leads from York to Lancaster, the crags, the farther northward we looked, looked still the worse, and our business was all on the other side. Our guide told us he would bring us out if we would have patience, which we were obliged to, and kept on this slow march till he brought us to Stanhope, in the county of Durham, where some of Goring's horse and two regiments of foot had their quarters. This was nineteen days from the battle of Marston Moor. The prince, who was then at Kendal in Westmoreland, and who had given me over as lost, when he had news of our arrival sent an express to me to meet him at Appleby. I went thither accordingly, and gave him an account of our journey; and there I heard the short history of the other part of our men, whom we parted from in Lancashire. They made the best of their way north. They had two resolute gentlemen who commanded; and being so closely pursued by the enemy that they found themselves under the necessity of fighting, they halted and faced about, expecting the charge. The boldness of the action made the officer who led the enemy's horse (which it seems were the county horse only) afraid of them; which they perceiving, taking the advantage of his fears, bravely advance and charge them; and though they were above 200 horse, they routed them, killed about thirty or forty, got some horses and some money, and pushed on their march night and day; but coming near Lancaster, they were so waylaid and pursued that they agreed to separate, and shift every man for himself. Many of them fell into the enemy's hands, some were killed attempting to pass through the river Lune, some went back again, six or seven got to Bolton, and about eighteen got safe to Prince Rupert.

HOAR-FROST.

What dream of beauty ever equall'd this!
What hands from Faeryland have sallied forth,
With snowy foliage from the abundant North,
With imagery from the realms of bliss!
What visions of my boyhood do I miss
That here are not restored! All splendours pure,
All loveliness, all graces that allure;
Shapes that amaze; a paradise that is,
Yet was not,—will not in few moments be:
Glory from nakedness, that playfully
Mimics with passing life each summer hoon;
Clothing the ground--replenishing the tree;
Weaving arch, bower, and delicate festoon;
Still as a dream,—and like a dream to flee!

WILLIAM HOWITT.

THE VOICE OF SPRING.

[Mrs. Felicia Dorothea Hemans, born in Liverpool, 25th September, 1794; died in Dublin, 12th May, 1835. She began to write verses before she was nine years of age, and her first volume of poems, *Early Blossoms*, appeared in 1808. Four years afterwards she became the wife of Captain Hemans, from whom she separated about the period of the birth of her fifth son. Her principal works are: *England and Spain, or Valour and Patriotism; The Domestic Affections; Restoration of the Works of Art in Italy; Modern Greece; Wallace and Bruce: Tales and Historic Scenes; Vespers of Palermo*, a tragedy; *The Sceptic; The Forest Sanctuary; Records of Women; Hymns for Childhood; Scenes and Hymns of Life*, &c. She also contributed to the *Edinburgh Review*, and edited and compiled many miscellaneous volumes. Sir Archibald Alison said: "Mrs. Hemans was imbued with the very soul of lyric poetry; she only required to have written a little less to have been one of the greatest in that branch that England ever produced." In the *Noctes* the Shepherd says: "It's no in that woman's power, sir, to write ill; for when a feeling heart and a fine genius forgather in the bosom o' a young matron, every line o' poetry is like a sad or cheerful smile frae her een, and every poem, whatever be the subject, in as sense a picture o' hersel' – sae that a' she writes has an affecting and an endearing mannerism and moralism about it, that inspires the thochtful reader to say in to himsel'—that's Mrs. Hemans."]

I come, I come! ye have call'd me long,
I come o'er the mountains with light and song!
Ye may trace my step o'er the wakening earth,
By the winds which tell of the violet's birth,
By the primrose-stars in the shadowy grass,
By the green leaves opening as I pass.

I have breathed on the South, and the chestnut flowers
By thousands have burst from the forest bowers;
And the ancient graves, and the fallen fanes,
Are veil'd with wreaths on Italian plains.
—But it is not for me, in my hour of bloom,
To speak of the ruin or the tomb!

I have pass'd o'er the hills of the stormy North,
And the larch has hung all his tassels forth,
The fisher is out on the sunny sea,
And the rein-deer bounds through the pasture free,
And the pine has a fringe of softer green,
And the moss looks bright where my step has been.

I have sent through the wood-paths a gentle sigh,
And call'd out each voice of the deep blue sky,
From the night-birds' lay through the starry time,
In the groves of the soft Hesperian clime,
To the swan's wild note by the Iceland lakes,
When the dark fir-bough into verdure breaks.

From the streams and founts I have loosed the chain;
They are sweeping on to the silvery main,

They are flashing down from the mountain-brows,
They are flinging spray on the forest boughs,
They are bursting fresh from their sparry caves,
And the earth resounds with the joy of waves.

Come forth, O ye children of gladness, come!
Where the violets lie may be now your home.
Ye of the rose-cheek and dew-bright eye,
And the bounding footstep, to meet me fly,
With the lyre, and the wreath, and the joyous lay,
Come forth to the sunshine, I may not stay!

Away from the dwellings of care-worn men,
The waters are sparkling in wood and glen,
Away from the chamber and dusky hearth,
The young leaves are dancing in breezy mirth,
Their light stems thrill to the wild-wood strains,
And youth is abroad in my green domains.

But ye!—ye are changed since ye met me last;
A shade of earth has been round you cast!
There is that come over your brow and eye
Which speaks of a world where the flowers must die!
Ye smile!—but your smile hath a dimness yet—
—O! what have ye look'd on since last we met?

Ye are changed, ye are changed!—and I see not here
All whom I saw in the vanish'd year!
There were graceful heads, with their ringlets bright,
Which toss'd in the breeze with a play of light;
There were eyes, in whose glistening laughter lay
No faint remembrance of dull decay.

There were steps that flew o'er the cowslip's head,
As if for a banquet all earth were spread;
There were voices that rung through the sapphire sky,
And had not a sound of mortality!
—Are they gone?—is their mirth from the green hills
pass'd?
—Ye have look'd on death since ye met me last!

I know whence the shadow comes o'er ye now,
Ye have strewn the dust on the sunny brow!
Ye have given the lovely to the earth's embrace,
She hath taken the fairest of Beauty's race!
With their laughing eyes and their festal crown,
They are gone from amongst you in silence down.

They are gone from amongst you, the bright and fair,
Ye have lost the gleam of their shining hair!
—But I know of a world where there falls no blight,
I shall find them there, with their eyes of light!
Where Death 'midst the blooms of the morn may dwell,
I tarry no longer,—farewell, farewell!

The summer is hastening, on soft winds borne,
Ye may press the grape, ye may bind the corn!
For me, I depart to a brighter shore,
Ye are mark'd by care, ye are mine no more.
I go where the loved who have left you dwell,
And the flowers are not Death's;—fare ye well! farewell!

A GENTLEMAN.

[Henry Brooke, born at Rantavan, Ireland, 1706; died 1783. He was the son of an Irish clergyman; and as a poet, dramatist, and novelist obtained a large measure of popular favour during his life. The patronage of Pope and Swift helped him to that popularity. Besides occasional poems, he wrote thirteen tragedies, of which the most successful were *Gustavus Vasa* and the *Earl of Essex*. His novel, *The Fool of Quality, or the History of Henry, Earl of Moreland*, was held in high esteem, and contains passages of merit. A new edition of this work, with biographical preface by Charles Kingsley, was issued in 1872. (Macmillan & Co.)]

There is no term in our language more common than that of "Gentleman;" and whenever it is heard, all agree in the general idea of a man some way elevated above the vulgar. Yet perhaps no two living are precisely agreed respecting the qualities they think requisite for constituting this character. When we hear the epithets of a "fine Gentleman," "a pretty Gentleman," "much of a Gentleman," "Gentlemanlike," "something of a Gentleman," "nothing of a Gentleman," and so forth; all these different appellations must intend a peculiarity annexed to the ideas of those who express them; though no two of them, as I said, may agree in the constituent qualities of the character they have formed in their own mind. There have been ladies who deemed a bag-wig, tasselled waistcoat, new-fashioned snuff-box, and a sword-knot, very capital ingredients in the composition of—a Gentleman. A certain easy impudence acquired by low people, by casually being conversant in high life, has passed a man current through many companies for—a Gentleman. In the country, a laced hat and long whip makes—a Gentleman. In taverns and some other places, he who is the most of a bully, is the most of—a Gentleman. With heralds, every Esquire is, indisputably,—a Gentleman. And the highwayman, in his manner of taking your purse; and your friend, in his manner of deceiving your wife, may, however, be allowed to have—much of the Gentleman. Plato, among the philosophers, was "the most of a man of fashion;" and therefore allowed, at the court of Syracuse, to be—the most of a Gentleman. But seriously, I apprehend that this character is pretty much upon the modern. In all ancient or dead languages we have no term, any way adequate, whereby we may express it. In the habits, manners, and characters of old Sparta and old Rome, we find an antipathy to all the elements of modern gentility. Among those rude and unpolished people, you read of philosophers, of orators, patriots, heroes, and demigods; but you never hear of any character so elegant as that of—a pretty Gentleman.

When those nations, however, became refined into what their ancestors would have called corruption; when luxury introduced, and fashion gave a sanction to certain sciences, which Cynics would have branded with the ill-mannered appellations of debauchery, drunkenness, whoredom, gambling, cheating, lying, &c., the practitioners assumed the new title of Gentlemen, till such Gentlemen became as plenteous as stars in the milky-way, and lost distinction merely by the confluence of their lustre. Wherefore as the said qualities were found to be of ready acquisition, and of easy descent to the populace from their betters, ambition judged it necessary to add further marks and criterions for severing the general herd from the nobler species — of Gentlemen.

Accordingly, if the commonalty were observed to have a propensity to religion, their superiors affected a disdain of such vulgar prejudices; and a freedom that cast off the restraints of morality, and a courage that spurned at the fear of a God, were accounted the distinguishing characteristics—of a Gentleman.

If the populace, as in China, were industrious and ingenious, the grandees, by the length of their nails and the cramping of their limbs, gave evidence that true dignity was above labour and utility, and that to be born to no end was the prerogative—of a Gentleman.

If the common sort, by their conduct, declared a respect for the institutions of civil society and good government, their betters despise such pusillanimous conformity, and the magistrates pay becoming regard to the distinction, and allow of the superior liberties and privileges—of a Gentleman.

If the lower set show a sense of common honesty and common order, those who would figure in the world think it incumbent to demonstrate that complaisance to inferiors, common manners, common equity, or anything common, is quite beneath the attention or sphere—of a Gentleman.

Now, as underlings are ever ambitious of imitating and usurping the manners of their superiors; and as this state of mortality is incident to perpetual change and revolution: it may happen, that when the populace, by encroaching on the province of gentility, have arrived to their *ne plus ultra* of insolence, debauchery, irreligion, &c., the gentry, in order to be again distinguished, may assume the station that their inferiors had forsaken, and, however ridiculous the supposition may appear at present, humanity, equity, utility, complaisance, and piety may in time come to be the distinguishing characteristics—of a Gentleman.

It appears that the most general idea which people have formed of a Gentleman is that of a person of fortune above the vulgar, and embellished by manners that are fashionable in high life. In this case, fortune and fashion are the two constituent ingredients in the composition of modern Gentlemen; for whatever the fashion may be, whether moral or immoral, for or against reason, right or wrong, it is equally the duty of a Gentleman to conform. And yet I apprehend, that true gentility is altogether independent of fortune or fashion, of time, customs, or opinions of any kind. The very same qualities that constituted a Gentleman in the first age of the world, are permanently, invariably, and indispensably necessary to the constitution of the same character to the end of time.

Hector was the finest Gentleman of whom we read in history, and Don Quixote the finest Gentleman we read of in romance; as was instanced from the tenor of their principles and actions.

Some time after the battle of Cressy, Edward III. of England, and Edward the Black Prince, the more than heir of his father's renown, pressed John, king of France to indulge them with the pleasure of his company at London. John was desirous of embracing the invitation, and accordingly laid the proposal before his parliament at Paris. The parliament objected that the invitation had been made with an insidious design of seizing his person, thereby to make the cheaper and easier acquisition of the crown, to which Edward at that time pretended. But John replied, with some warmth, that he was confident his brother Edward, and more especially his young cousin, were too much of the GENTLEMAN to treat him in that manner. He did not say too much of the king, of the hero, or of the saint, but too much of the GENTLEMAN to be guilty of any baseness.

The sequel verified this opinion. At the battle of Poictiers King John was made prisoner, and soon after conducted by the Black Prince to England. The prince entered London in triumph, amid the throng and acclamations of millions of the people. But then this rather appeared to be the triumph of the

French king than that of his conqueror. John was seated on a proud steed, royally robed, and attended by a numerous and gorgeous train of the British nobility; while his conqueror endeavoured, as much as possible, to disappear, and rode by his side in plain attire, and degradingly seated on a little Irish hobby.

As Aristotle and the Critics derived their rules, for epic poetry and the sublime, from a poem which Homer had written long before the rules were formed, or laws established for the purpose: thus, from the demeanour and innate principles of particular Gentlemen, art has borrowed and instituted the many modes of behaviour which the world has adopted, under the title of good manners.

One quality of a Gentleman is that of charity to the poor; and this is delicately instanced in the account which Don Quixote gives, to his fast friend Sancho Pancha, of the valorous but yet more pious knight-errant Saint Martin. On a day, said the Don, Saint Martin met a poor man half naked, and taking his cloak from his shoulders, he divided and gave him the one half. Now, tell me at what time of the year this happened? Was I a witness? quoth Sancho; how the vengeance should I know in what year or what time of the year it happened? Hadst thou, Sancho, rejoined the knight, anything within thee of the sentiment of Saint Martin, thou must assuredly have known that this happened in winter; for had it been summer, Saint Martin would have given the whole cloak.

Another characteristic of the true Gentleman is a delicacy of behaviour toward that sex whom nature has entitled to the protection, and consequently entitled to the tenderness, of man.

The same Gentleman-errant, entering into a wood on a summer's evening, found himself entangled among nets of green thread, that here and there hung from tree to tree; and conceiving it some matter of purposed conjuration, pushed valorously forward, to break through the enchantment. Hereupon some beautiful shepherdesses interposed with a cry, and besought him to spare the implements of their innocent recreation. The knight, surprised and charmed by the vision, replied,—Fair creatures! my province is to protect, not to injure; to seek all means of service, but never of offence, more especially to any of your sex and apparent excellences. Your pretty nets take up but a small piece of favoured ground; but, did they inclose the world, I would seek out new worlds, whereby I might win a passage, rather than break them.

Two very lovely but shamefaced girls had a cause of some consequence depending at Westminster, that indispensably required their personal appearance. They were relations of Sir Joseph Jeckel, and on this tremendous occasion requested his company and countenance at the court. Sir Joseph attended accordingly; and the cause being opened, the judge demanded whether he was to entitle those ladies by the denomination of spinsters? No, my lord, said Sir Joseph; they are lilies of the valley, they toil not, neither do they spin, yet you see that no monarch, in all his glory, was ever arrayed like one of these.

Another very peculiar characteristic of a Gentleman, is the giving place, and yielding to all with whom he has to do. Of this we have a shining and affecting instance in Abraham, perhaps the most accomplished character that may be found in history, whether sacred or profane. A contention had arisen between the herdsmen of Abraham and the herdsmen of his nephew Lot, respecting the propriety of the pasture of the lands wherein they dwelled, that could now scarce contain the abundance of their cattle. And those servants, as is universally the case, had respectively endeavoured to kindle and inflame their masters with their own passions. When Abraham, in consequence of this, perceived that the countenance of Lot began to change toward him, he called, and generously expostulated with him as followeth: "Let there be no strife, I pray thee, between me and thee, or between my herdsmen and thy herdsmen; for we be brethren. If it be thy desire to separate thyself from me, is not the whole land before thee? If thou wilt take the left hand, then will I go to the right; or if thou depart to the right hand, then I will go to the left."

Another capital quality of the true Gentleman is, that of feeling himself concerned and interested in others. Never was there so benevolent, so affecting, so pathetic a piece of oratory exhibited upon earth, as that of Abraham's pleading with God for averting the judgments that then impended over Sodom. But the matter is already so generally celebrated, that I am constrained to refer my reader to the passage at full; since the smallest abridgment must deduct from its beauties, and that nothing can be added to the excellences thereof.

Honour, again, is said, in Scripture, peculiarly to distinguish the character of a Gentleman; where it is written of Sechem, the son of Hamor, "that he was more honourable than all the house of his father." This young prince, giving way to the violence of his passion, had dishonourably deflowered Dinah the daughter of Jacob. But his affections and soul cleaved to the party whom he had injured. He set no limit to his offers for repairing the wrong. Ask me, he said to her kindred, "ask me never so much dowry and gift, and I will give according as ye shall say unto me; but give me the damsel to wife."

From hence it may be inferred, that human excellence, or human amiableness, doth not so much consist in a freedom from frailty, as in our recovery from lapses, our detestation of our own transgressions, and our desire of atoning, by all possible means, the injuries we have done and the offences we have given. Herein therefore may consist the very singular distinction which the great apostle makes between his estimation of a just and of a good man. "For a just or righteous man," says he, "one would grudge to die; but for a good man one would even dare to die." Here the just man is supposed to adhere strictly to the rule of right or equity, and to exact from others the same measure that he is satisfied to mete; but the good man, though occasionally he may fall short of justice, has, properly speaking, no measure to his benevolence, his general propensity is to give more than the due. The just man condemns, and is desirous of punishing the transgressors of the line prescribed to himself; but the good man, in the sense of his own falls and failings, gives latitude, indulgence, and pardon to others; he judges, he condemns no one save himself. The just man is a stream that deviates not, to the right or left, from its appointed channel, neither is swelled by the flood of passion above its banks: but the heart of the good man, the man of honour, the Gentleman, is as a lamp lighted by the breath of God, and none save God himself can set limits to the efflux or irradiations thereof.

Again, the Gentleman never envies any superior excellence, but grows himself more excellent by being the admirer, promoter, and lover thereof. Saul said to his son Jonathan, "Thou son of the perverse, rebellious woman, do not I know that thou hast chosen the son of Jesse to thine own confusion? For as long as the son of Jesse liveth upon the ground, thou shalt not be established, nor thy kingdom: wherefore send and fetch him unto me, for he shall surely die."—Here every interesting motive that can possibly be conceived to have an influence on man united to urge Jonathan to the destruction of David; he would thereby have obeyed his king, and pacified a father who was enraged against him. He would thereby have removed the only luminary that then eclipsed the brightness of his own achievments. And he saw, as his father said, that the death of David alone could establish the kingdom in himself and his posterity. But all those considerations were of no avail to make Jonathan swerve from honour, to slacken the bands of his faith, or cool the warmth of his friendship. O Jonathan! the sacrifice which thou then madest to virtue was incomparably more illustrious in the sight of God and his angels, than all the subsequent glories to which David attained. What a crown was thine, "Jonathan, when thou wast slain in thine high places!"

Saul of Tarsus had been a man of bigotry, blood, and violence; making havoc, and breathing out threatenings and slaughter against all who were not of his own sect and persuasion. But, when the spirit of that INFANT, who laid himself in the manger of human flesh, came upon him, he acquired a new heart and a new nature; and he offered himself a willing subject to all the sufferings and persecutions which he had brought upon others.

Saul, from that time, exemplified in his own person all those qualities of the Gentleman which he afterwards specifies in his celebrated description of that charity, which, as he says, alone endureth for ever. When Festus cried, with a loud voice, "Paul, thou art beside thyself, much learning doth make thee mad;" Paul stretched the hand, and answered, "I am not mad, most noble Festus, but speak forth the words of truth and soberness. For the king knoweth of these things, before whom also I speak freely; for I am persuaded that none of these things are hidden from him. King Agrippa, believest thou the prophets? I know that thou believest." Then Agrippa said unto Paul, "Almost thou persuadest me to be a Christian." And Paul said, "I would to God, that not only thou, but also all that hear me this day, were not only almost, but altogether, such as I am,—except these bonds." Here, with what an inimitable elegance did this man, in his own person, at once sum up the orator, the saint, and the Gentleman!

From these instances, my friend, you must have seen that the character, or rather quality of a GENTLEMAN, does not, in any degree, depend on fashion or mode, on station or opinion; neither changes with customs, climates, or ages. But as the Spirit of God can alone inspire it into man; so it is, as God is, the same yesterday, to-day, and for ever.

THE TROOPER'S DEFENCE.

BY WILLIAM SAWYER.

Do I plead guilty to it? Yes, I do;
For I have never lied, and shall not now;
But give me a dog's leave to say a word
Touching what happened, and the why and how.

The night-guard went their rounds that night at one;
My post was in the lower dungeon range,
Down level with the moat, all slime and ooze
And damp; but there, 'tis fit we change and change,

We sentinels. Besides, 'twas in a sort
The place of honour, or of trust, we'll say;
For in the cell there with the mortised door
The young boy-lord, guilty of treason, lay.

Well, with my partisan I'd tramped an hour
Down in the dark there—just a lantern hung
By the wet wall—when close at hand I heard
My own name spoken by a woman's tongue.

My hair was like to lift my morion up,
For the keep's haunted; but I turned, to see
A woman like a ghost—face white, all white,
Ready to drop, and not a yard from me.

How she had come there God in heaven knows.
However, long before my tongue I'd found,
She tore out of her hair the white pearls, big
As pigeon's eggs, then dropt upon the ground.

"One word!" she said, "only one word with him;
He dies to-morrow! See, my pearls I give,
My bracelets too"—she slipt them from her arms—
"One word, and I will bless you while I live!

"Your face is stern. O, but one word, one word!"
With my big hand I set her on her feet;
But she clung to me, would not be thrust off,
Still pleading in a bird's voice, soft and sweet.

"Only one word with him!" that was her plea;
One word; he would be dead at break of day!
She wept till all her pretty face was wet,
And my heart melted; yea, she had her way.

They spake together. Did I hear? Not I;
Best ask me if I took her bribes. Well, there,
You know the rest—know how yon Judas-spy,
Yon starveling cur, crawled down the winding stair;

And how he caught the bird fast in the cage,
And made report of me with eager breath
For breach of duty. Right; it was a breach,
And that means, in our soldier-fashion, death!

Well, I can face it. only give me leave
To slit the weasand of yon craven hound,
Yon Judas-spy there, and I'd fall content,
Aye, as I'd fall to sleep upon the ground.

LADY CORISANDE.

[Benjamin Disraeli, D.C.L., Earl of Beaconsfield, born in London, 21st December, 1805. He is the eldest son of the late Isaac Disraeli, author of *The Curiosities of Literature*, &c., and has won the highest distinction as a statesman and novelist. His works are: *Vivian Grey* (1826); *Voyage of Captain Popanilla; The Young Duke; England and France; Alroy*, the Wondrous Tale; and *The Rise of Iskander; Contarini Fleming; The Revolutionary Epic*, a poem (1834); *The Crisis Examined; Vindication of the English Constitution; Letters of Runnymede; Henrietta Temple; Venetia; Alcaros*, a tragedy; *Coningsby*, or the New Generation; *Sibyl*, or the New Nation; *Ixion; Tancred*, or the New Crusade; *Lord George Bentinck*, a Political Biography; and *Lothair* (1870)—from which we quote. In 1837 Mr. Disraeli was returned to Parliament by the Maidstone constituency; by that of Shrewsbury in 1841, and by the electors of the county of Buckingham in 1847. He has served the state as chancellor of the exchequer and as prime minister. In 1874 Mr. Disraeli again became First Lord. In 1876 he carried through Parliament the bill adding to the Queen's titles, "Empress of India." At the close of the same session he retired from the Commons, and entered the Upper House as the Earl of Beaconsfield. His novels faithfully reflect his views of life, philosophy, and politics. Lothair is a young nobleman of unbounded wealth, and the novel is occupied with his adventures from his entrance into the world till his final escape from the schemes of Jesuits and Romanists to win him to their creed, and his settlement in life with the beautiful, accomplished, and Protestant Lady Corisande.[1]]

One's life changes in a moment. Half a month ago Lothair, without an acquaintance, was meditating his return to Oxford. Now he seemed to know everybody who was anybody. His table was overflowing with invitations to all the fine houses in town. First came the routs and the balls; then, when he had been presented to the husbands, came the dinners. His kind friends the Duchess and Lady St. Jerome were the fairies who had worked this sudden scene of enchantment. A single word from them, and London was at Lothair's feet.

He liked it amazingly. He quite forgot the conclusion at which he had arrived respecting society a year ago, drawn from his vast experience of the single party which he had then attended. Feelings are different when you know a great many persons, and every person is trying to please you; above all, when there are individuals whom you want to meet,

and whom, if you do not meet, you become restless.

Town was beginning to blaze. Brougham whirled and bright barouches glanced, troops of social cavalry cantered and caracolled in morning rides, and the bells of prancing ponies, lashed by delicate hands, gingled in the laughing air. There were stoppages in Bond Street, which seems to cap the climax of civilization, after crowded clubs and swarming parks.

But the great event of the season was the presentation of Lady Corisande. Truly our bright maiden of Brentham woke and found herself famous. There are families whom everybody praises, and families who are treated in a different way. Either will do; all the sons and daughters of the first succeed, all the sons and daughters of the last are encouraged in perverseness by the prophetic determination of society. Half a dozen married sisters, who were the delight and ornament of their circles, in the case of Lady Corisande were good precursors of popularity; but the world would not be content with that: they credited her with all their charms and winning qualities, but also with something grander and beyond comparison; and from the moment her fair cheek was sealed by the gracious approbation of Majesty, all the critics of the Court at once recognized her as the cynosure of the Empyrean.

Monsignore Catesby, who looked after Lothair, and was always breakfasting with him without the necessity of an invitation (a fascinating man, and who talked upon all subjects except High Mass), knew everything that took place at Court without being present there himself. He led the conversation to the majestic theme, and while he seemed to be busied in breaking an egg with delicate precision, and hardly listening to the frank expression of opinions which he carelessly encouraged, obtained a not insufficient share of Lothair's views and impressions of human beings and affairs in general during the last few days, which had witnessed a Levée and a Drawing-room.

"Ah! then you were so fortunate as to know the beauty before her début," said the Monsignore.

"Intimately; her brother is my friend. I was at Brentham last summer. Delicious place! and the most agreeable visit I ever made in my life, at least, one of the most agreeable."

"Ah! ah!" said the Monsignore. "Let me ring for some toast."

On the night of the Drawing-room, a great ball was given at Crecy House to celebrate the

---

[1] "He has written many works of fiction, all, we believe, successful, and many of them among the best of their time; some verse, in which he has rather tried than exercised his powers; and political essays, anonymous, but acknowledged."—*Edinburgh Review*.

entrance of Corisande into the world. It was a sumptuous festival. The palace, resonant with fantastic music, blazed amid illumined gardens rich with summer warmth.

A prince of the blood was dancing with Lady Corisande. Lothair was there, vis-à-vis with Miss Arundel.

"I delight in this hall," she said to Lothair: "but how superior the pictured scene to the reality!"

"What! would you like, then, to be in a battle?"

"I should like to be with heroes, wherever they might be. What a fine character was the Black Prince! And they call those days the days of superstition!"

The silver horns sounded a brave flourish. Lothair had to advance and meet Lady Corisande. Her approaching mien was full of grace and majesty, but Lothair thought there was a kind expression in her glance, which seemed to remember Brentham, and that he was her brother's friend.

A little later in the evening he was her partner. He could not refrain from congratulating her on the beauty and the success of the festival.

"I am glad you are pleased, and I am glad you think it successful; but, you know, I am no judge, for this is my first ball!"

"Ah! to be sure; and yet it seems impossible," he continued, in a tone of murmuring admiration.

"Oh! I have been at little dances at my sisters'; half behind the door," she added, with a slight smile. "But to-night I am present at a scene of which I have only read."

"And how do you like balls?" said Lothair.

"I think I shall like them very much," said Lady Corisande; "but to-night, I will confess, I am a little nervous."

"You do not look so."

"I am glad of that."

"Why?"

"Is it not a sign of weakness?"

"Can feeling be weakness?"

"Feeling without sufficient cause is, I should think." And then, and in a tone of some archness, she said, "And how do you like balls?"

"Well, I like them amazingly," said Lothair. "They seem to me to have every quality which can render an entertainment agreeable: music, light, flowers, beautiful faces, graceful forms, and occasionally charming conversation."

"Yes; and that never lingers," said Lady Corisande, "for see, I am wanted."

When they were again undisturbed, Lothair

regretted the absence of Bertram, who was kept at the House.

"It is a great disappointment," said Lady Corisande; "but he will yet arrive, though late. I should be most unhappy though, if he were absent from his post on such an occasion. I am sure if he were here I could not dance."

"You are a most ardent politician," said Lothair.

"Oh! I do not care in the least about common politics, parties and office and all that; I neither regard nor understand them," replied Lady Corisande. "But when wicked men try to destroy the country, then I like my family to be in the front."

As the destruction of the country meditated this night by wicked men was some change in the status of the Church of England, which Monsignore Catesby in the morning had suggested to Lothair as both just and expedient and highly conciliatory, Lothair did not pursue the theme, for he had a greater degree of tact than usually falls to the lot of the ingenuous.

The bright moments flew on. Suddenly there was a mysterious silence in the hall, followed by a kind of suppressed stir. Every one seemed to be speaking with bated breath, or, if moving, walking on tiptoe. It was the supper hour:

"Soft hour which wakes the wish and melts the heart."

Royalty, followed by the imperial presence of ambassadors, and escorted by a group of dazzling duchesses and paladins of high degree, was ushered with courteous pomp by the host and hostess into a choice saloon, hung with rose-coloured tapestry and illumined by chandeliers of crystal, where they were served from gold plate. But the thousand less favoured were not badly off, when they found themselves in the more capacious chambers, into which they rushed with an eagerness hardly in keeping with the splendid nonchalance of the preceding hours.

"What a perfect family," exclaimed Hugo Bohun, as he extracted a couple of fat little birds from their bed of aspic jelly; "everything they do in such perfect taste. How safe you were here to have ortolans for supper!"

All the little round tables, though their number was infinite, were full. Male groups hung about; some in attendance on fair dames, some foraging for themselves, some thoughtful and more patient and awaiting a satisfactory future. Never was such an elegant clatter.

"I wonder where Carisbrooke is," said Hugo Bohun. "They say he is wonderfully taken with the beauteous daughter of the house."

"I will back the Duke of Brecon against him," said one of his companions. "He raved about her at White's yesterday."

"Hem!"

"The end is not so near as all that," said a third wassailer.

"I do not know that," said Hugo Bohun. "It is a family that marries off quickly. If a fellow is obliged to marry, he always likes to marry one of them."

"What of this new star?" said his friend, and he mentioned Lothair.

"O! he is too young; not launched. Besides he is going to turn Catholic, and I doubt whether that would do in that quarter."

"But he has a greater fortune than any of them."

"Immense! A man I know, who knows another man——" and then he began a long statistical story about Lothair's resources.

"Have you got any room here, Hugo?" drawled out Lord St. Aldegonde.

"Plenty, and here is my chair."

"On no account; half of it and some soup will satisfy me."

"I should have thought you would have been with the swells," said Hugo Bohun.

"That does not exactly suit me," said St. Aldegonde. "I was ticketed to the Duchess of Salop, but I got a first rate substitute with the charm of novelty for her Grace, and sent her in with Lothair."

St. Aldegonde was the heir apparent of the wealthiest, if not the most ancient, dukedom in the United Kingdom. He was spoiled, and he knew it. Had he been an ordinary being, he would have merely subsided into selfishness and caprice, but having good abilities and a good disposition, he was eccentric, adventurous, and sentimental. Notwithstanding the apathy which had been engendered by premature experience, St. Aldegonde held extreme opinions, especially on political affairs, being a republican of the reddest dye. He was opposed to all privilege, and indeed to all orders of men, except dukes, who were a necessity. He was also strongly in favour of the equal division of all property, except land. Liberty depended on land, and the greater the landowners, the greater the liberty of a country. He would hold forth on this topic even with energy, amazed at anyone differing from him; "as if a fellow could have too much land," he would urge with a voice and glance which defied contradiction. St. Aldegonde had married for love and he loved his wife, but he was strongly in favour of woman's rights and their extremest consequences. It was thought that

he had originally adopted these latter views with the amiable intention of piquing Lady St. Aldegonde; but if so, he had not succeeded. Beaming with brightness, with the voice and airiness of a bird, and a cloudless temper, Albertha St. Aldegonde had, from the first hour of her marriage, concentrated her intelligence, which was not mean, on one object; and that was never to cross her husband on any conceivable topic. They had been married several years, and she treated him as a darling spoiled child. When he cried for the moon, it was promised him immediately; however irrational his proposition, she always assented to it, though generally by tact and vigilance she guided him in the right direction. Nevertheless, St. Aldegonde was sometimes in scrapes; but then he always went and told his best friend, whose greatest delight was to extricate him from his perplexities and embarrassments.

.   .   .   .

It was agreed that after breakfast they should go and see Corisande's garden. And a party did go: all the Phœbus family, and Lord and Lady St. Aldegonde, and Lady Corisande, and Bertram and Lothair.

In the pleasure-grounds of Brentham were the remains of an ancient garden of the ancient house that had long ago been pulled down. When the modern pleasure-grounds were planned and created, notwithstanding the protests of the artists in landscape, the father of the present Duke would not allow this ancient garden to be entirely destroyed, and you came upon its quaint appearance in the dissimilar world in which it was placed, as you might in some festival of romantic costume upon a person habited in the courtly dress of the last century. It was formed upon a gentle southern slope, with turfen terraces walled in on three sides, the fourth consisting of arches of golden yew. The Duke had given this garden to Lady Corisande, in order that she might practise her theory, that flower-gardens should be sweet and luxuriant, and not hard and scentless imitations of works of art. Here, in their season, flourished abundantly all those productions of nature which are now banished from our once delighted senses: huge bushes of honeysuckle, and bowers of sweet-pea and sweet-briar, and jessamine clustering over the walls, and gillyflowers scenting with their sweet breath the ancient bricks from which they seemed to spring. There were banks of violets which the southern breeze always stirred, and mignonette filled every vacant nook. As they entered now, it seemed a blaze of roses and carnations, though one recognized in a moment the presence of the lily, the heliotrope, and the stock. Some white peacocks were basking on the southern wall, and one of them, as their visitors entered, moved and displayed its plumage with scornful pride. The bees were busy in the air, but their homes were near, and you might watch them labouring in their glassy hives.

"Now, is not Corisande quite right?" said Lord St. Aldegonde, as he presented Madame Phœbus with a garland of woodbine, with which she said she would dress her head at dinner. All agreed with him, and Bertram and Euphrosyne adorned each other with carnations, and Mr. Phœbus placed a flower on the uncovered head of Lady St. Aldegonde, according to the principles of high art, and they sauntered and rambled in the sweet and sunny air amid a blaze of butterflies and the ceaseless hum of bees.

Bertram and Euphrosyne had disappeared, and the rest were lingering about the hives while Mr. Phœbus gave them a lecture on the apiary and its marvellous life. The bees understood Mr. Phœbus, at least he said so, and thus his friends had considerable advantage in this lesson in entomology. Lady Corisande and Lothair were in a distant corner of the garden, and she was explaining to him her plans; what she had done and what she meant to do.

"I wish I had a garden like this at Muriel," said Lothair.

"You could easily make one."

"If you helped me."

"I have told you all my plans," said Lady Corisande.

"Yes; but I was thinking of something else when you spoke," said Lothair.

"That is not very complimentary."

"I do not wish to be complimentary," said Lothair, "if compliments mean less than they declare. I was not thinking of your garden, but of you."

"Where can they have all gone?" said Lady Corisande, looking round. "We must find them."

"And leave this garden?" said Lothair. "And I without a flower, the only one without a flower? I am afraid that is significant of my lot."

"You shall choose a rose," said Lady Corisande.

"Nay; the charm is that it should be your choice."

But choosing the rose lost more time, and when Corisande and Lothair reached the arches of golden yew, there were no friends in sight.

"I think I hear sounds this way," said Lothair, and he led his companion farther from home.

"I see no one," said Lady Corisande, distressed, and when they had advanced a little way.

"We are sure to find them in good time," said Lothair. "Besides, I wanted to speak to you about the garden at Muriel. I wanted to induce you to go there and help me to make it. Yes," he added, after some hesitation, "on this spot, I believe on this very spot, I asked the permission of your mother two years ago to express to you my love. She thought me a boy, and she treated me as a boy. She said nothing of the world, and both our characters were unformed. I know the world now. I have committed many mistakes, doubtless many follies, have formed many opinions, and have changed many opinions; but to one I have been constant, in one I am unchanged, and that is my adoring love for you."

She turned pale, she stopped, then gently taking his arm, she hid her face in his breast.

He soothed and sustained her agitated frame, and sealed with an embrace her speechless form. Then, with soft thoughts and softer words, clinging to him he induced her to resume their stroll, which both of them now wished might assuredly 'be undisturbed. They had arrived at the limit of the pleasure-grounds, and they wandered into the park and into its most sequestered parts. All this time Lothair spoke much, and gave her the history of his life since he first visited her home. Lady Corisande said little, but when she was more composed, she told him that from the first her heart had been his, but everything seemed to go against her hopes. Perhaps at last, to please her parents, she would have married the Duke of Brecon, had not Lothair returned; and what he had said to her that morning at Crecy House had decided her resolution, whatever might be her lot, to unite it to no one else but him. But then came the adventure of the crucifix, and she thought all was over for her, and she quitted town in despair.

"Let us rest here for a while," said Lothair. "under the shade of this oak;" and Lady Corisande reclined against its mighty trunk, and Lothair threw himself at her feet. He had a great deal still to tell her, and among other things, the story of the pearls, which he had wished to give to Theodora.

"She was, after all, your good genius," said Lady Corisande. "I always liked her."

"Well now," said Lothair, "that case has never been opened. The year has elapsed, but I would not open it, for I had always a wild wish that the person who opened it should be yourself. See, here it is." And he gave her the case.

"We will not break the seal," said Lady Corisande. "Let us respect it for her sake: ROMA!" she said, examining it; and then they opened the case. There was the slip of paper which Theodora at the time had placed upon the pearls, and on which she had written some unseen words. They were read now, and ran thus:

"THE OFFERING OF THEODORA TO LOTHAIR'S BRIDE."

"Let me place them on you now," said Lothair.

"I will wear them as your chains," said Corisande.

The sun began to tell them that some hours had elapsed since they quitted Brentham House. At last a soft hand which Lothair retained, gave him a slight pressure, and a sweet voice whispered, "Dearest, I think we ought to return."

And they returned almost in silence. They rather calculated that, taking advantage of the luncheon-hour, Corisande might escape to her room; but they were a little too late. Luncheon was over, and they met the duchess and a large party on the terrace.

"What has become of you, my good people?" said her grace; "bells have been ringing for you in every direction. Where can you have been?"

"I have been in Corisande's garden," said Lothair, "and she has given me a rose."

THREE YEARS.

BY W. WORDSWORTH.

Three years she grew in sun and shower,
Then Nature said, "A lovelier flower
On earth was never sown;
This child I to myself will take;
She shall be mine, and I will make
A lady of my own.

"Myself will to my darling be
Both law and impulse: and with me,
The girl, in rock and plain,
In earth and heaven, in glade and bower,
Shall feel an overseeing power,
To kindle or restrain.

VOL. V.

"She shall be sportive as the fawn
That, wild with glee, across the lawn
Or up the mountain springs;
And hers shall be the breathing balm,
And hers the silence and the calm,
Of mute insensate things.

"The floating clouds their state shall lend
To her; for her the willow bend;
Nor shall she fail to see,
Even in the motions of the storm,
Grace that shall mould the maiden's form
By silent sympathy.

"The stars of midnight shall be dear
To her; and she shall lean her ear
In many a secret place,
Where rivulets dance their wayward round,
And beauty born of murmuring sound
Shall pass into her face.

"And vital feelings of delight
Shall rear her form to stately height,
Her virgin bosom swell;
Such thoughts to Lucy I will give,
While she and I together live
Here in this happy dell."

Thus Nature spake—The work was done—
How soon my Lucy's race was run!
She died, and left to me
This heath, this calm, and quiet scene.
The memory of what has been,
And never more will be.

THE PASSING CROWD.

BY ROBERT CHAMBERS.

"The passing crowd" is a phrase coined in the spirit of indifference. Yet, to a man of what Plato calls "universal sympathies," and even to the plain ordinary denizens of this world, what can be more interesting than "the passing crowd?" Does not this tide of human beings, which we daily see passing along the ways of this world, consist of persons animated by the same spark of the divine essence, and partaking of the same high destinies with ourselves? Let us stand still but for a moment in the midst of this busy, and seemingly careless scene, and consider what they are or may be whom we see around us. In the hurry of the passing show, and of our own sensations, we see but a series of unknown faces; but this is no reason why we should regard them with indifference. Many of these persons, if we knew their histories, would rivet our admiration, by the ability, worth, benevolence, or piety, which they have displayed in their various paths through life. Many would excite our warmest interest by their sufferings— sufferings, perhaps, borne meekly and well, and more for the sake of others than themselves. How many tales of human weal and woe, of glory and of humiliation, could be told by those beings, whom, in passing, we regard not! Unvalued as they are by us, how many as good as ourselves repose upon them the affections of bounteous hearts, and would not want them for any earthly compensation. Every one of these persons, in all probability, retains in his bosom the cherished recollections of early happy days, spent in some scene which "they ne'er forget, though there they are forgot," with friends and fellows who, though now far removed in distance and in fortune, are never to be given up by the heart. Every one of these individuals, in all probability, nurses still deeper, in the recesses of feeling, the remembrance of that chapter of romance in the life of every man, an early earnest attachment, conceived in the fervour of youth, unstained by the slightest thought of self, and for the time purifying and elevating the character far above its ordinary standard. Beneath all this gloss of the world—this cold conventional aspect, which all more or less present, and which the business of life renders necessary—there resides for certain a fountain of goodness, pure in its inner depths as the lymph rock-distilled, and ready on every proper occasion to well out in the exercise of the noblest duties. Though all may seem but a hunt after worldly objects, the great majority of these individuals can, at the proper time, cast aside all earthly thoughts, and communicate directly with the Being whom their fathers have taught them to worship, and whose will and attributes have been taught to man immediately by himself. Perhaps many of these persons are loftier of aspect than ourselves, and belong to a sphere removed above our own. But, nevertheless, if the barrier of mere worldly form were taken out of the way, it is probable that we could interchange sympathies with these persons as freely and cordially as with any of our own class. Perhaps they are of an inferior order; but they are only inferior in certain circumstances, which should never interpose to prevent the flow of feeling for our kind. The great common features of human nature remain; and let us never forget how much respect is due to the very impress of humanity—the type of the divine nature itself! Even where our fellow-creatures are degraded by vice and poverty, let us still be gentle in our judging. The various fortunes which we every day see befalling the members of a single family, after they part off in their several paths through life, teach us, that it is not to every one that success in the career of existence is destined. Besides, do not the arrangements of society at once necessitate the subjection of an immense multitude to humble toil, and give rise to temptations, before which the weak and uninstructed can scarcely escape falling? But even beneath the soiled face of the poor artisan there may be aspirations after some vague excellence, which hard fate has denied him the means of attaining, though the very wish to obtain it is itself ennobling. The very mendicant was not always so; he, too, has had his undegraded and happier days, upon the recollection of which, some remnant of better feeling may still repose.

These, I humbly think, are reasons why we should not look with coldness upon any masses of men with whom it may be our lot to mingle. It is the nature of a good man to conclude that others are like himself; and if we take the crowd promiscuously, we can never be far wrong in thinking that there are worthy and well-directed feelings in it as well as in our own bosoms.

BEFORE, BEHIND, AND BEYOND.

BY ALFRED AUSTIN.

O the sunny days before us, before us, before us
　　When all was bright
　　From bolt to height,
And the heavens were shining o'er us;
　　When sound and scent, with vision blent,
　　Winged Hope, and perched Content,
　　Joys that came, and ills that went,
Seemed singing all in chorus.

O the dreary days behind us, behind us, behind us
　　When all is dark,
　　And care, and cark,
Or transient gleams remind us
　　Of fruitless sighs, averted eyes,
　　Baffled hopes and loosened ties,
　　Pain that lingers, time that flies,
And the hot tears come and blind us.

Oh! is there nought beyond us, beyond us, beyond us
　　When all the dead,
　　The changed, the fled,
Will rise, and look as fond as
　　Ere Faith put out, and Love in rout,
　　Foes with vigour, friends without,
　　Pique and rancour, make us doubt
Hoc tolerare pondus?

　　　　　　　　　　　—*Interludes.*

THE PLEASURES OF MEMORY.

[Samuel Rogers, born in London, 30th July, 1763; died there, 18th December, 1855. He was the son of a wealthy banker, and his house in St. James's Place was the resort of all the famous authors and artists of his time. He wrote many poems, but the *Pleasures of Memory*, first published in 1792, remained his best and finest achievement in verse. Byron, in his *English Bards*, says that this and Pope's *Essay on Man*, are "the most beautiful didactic poems in our language." Of his other poems the chief are: *Jacqueline*, a tale; *Human Life*; *Italy*, &c. Lord Jeffrey said of Rogers' poems that "they come over us with a bewitching softness, and soothe the troubled spirits with a refreshing sense of truth, purity, and elegance."[1]]

Sweet MEMORY, wafted by thy gentle gale,
Oft up the stream of Time I turn my sail,
To view the fairy haunts of long-lost hours,
Blest with far greener shades, far fresher flowers.
Ages and climes remote to thee impart
What charms in Genius and refines in Art;
Thee, in whose hands the keys of Science dwell,
The pensive portress of her holy cell;
Whose constant vigils chase the chilling damp
Oblivion steals upon her vestal-lamp.
They in their glorious course the guides of Youth,
Whose language breathed the eloquence of Truth;
Whose life, beyond preceptive wisdom, taught
The great in conduct, and the pure in thought;
These still exist, by thee to Fame consigned,
Still speak and act, the models of mankind.
From thee gay Hope her airy colouring draws;
And Fancy's flights are subject to thy laws.
From thee that bosom-spring of rapture flows,
Which only Virtue, tranquil Virtue, knows.
When Joy's bright sun has shed his evening ray,
And Hope's delusive meteors cease to play;
When clouds on clouds the smiling prospect close,
Still thro' the gloom thy star serenely glows;
Like you fair orb, she gilds the brow of night
With the mild magic of reflected light.
The beauteous maid, who bids the world adieu,
Oft of that world will snatch a fond review;
Oft at the shrine neglect her beads, to trace
Some social scene, some dear, familiar face:
And ere, with iron-tongue, the vesper bell
Bursts thro' the cypress-walk, the convent-cell,

---

[1] Rogers never married; and an interesting anecdote of the cause of his celibacy is told by the *Edinburgh Review*. "When a young man, he admired and sedulously sought the society of the most beautiful girl he then, and still thought he had ever seen. At the end of a London season, at a ball, she said, 'I go to-morrow to Worthing. Are you coming there?' He did not go. Some months afterwards, being at Ranelagh, he saw the attention of every one drawn towards a large party that had just entered, in the centre of which was a lady on the arm of her husband; stepping forward to see this wonderful beauty, he found it was his love. She merely said—'You never came to Worthing.'"

Oft will her warm and wayward heart revive,
To love and joy still tremblingly alive;
The whispered vow, the chaste caress prolong,
Weave the light dance and swell the choral song;
With rapt ear drink the enchanting serenade,
And, as it melts along the moon-light glade,
To each soft note return as soft a sigh,
And bless the youth that bids her slumbers fly.

But not till Time has calmed the ruffled breast,
Are these fond dreams of happiness confest.
Not till the rushing winds forget to rave,
Is Heaven's sweet smile reflected on the wave.
From Guinea's coast pursue the lessening sail,
And catch the sounds that sadden every gale
Tell, if thou canst, the sum of sorrows there;
Mark the fixed gaze, the wild and frenzied glare,
The racks of thought, and freezings of despair!
But pause not then—beyond the western wave,
Go, see the captive bartered as a slave!
Crushed till his high, heroic spirit bleeds,
And from his nerveless frame indignantly recedes
Yet here, even here, with pleasures long resigned,
Lo! MEMORY bursts the twilight of the mind.
Her dear delusions soothe his sinking soul,
When the rude scourge assumes its base control;
And o'er Futurity's blank page diffuse
The full reflection of her vivid hues.
'Tis but to die, and then, to weep no more,
Then will he wake on Congo's distant shore;
Beneath his plantain's ancient shade renew
The simple transports that with freedom flew :
Catch the cool breeze that musky Evening blows
And quaff the palm's rich nectar as it glows,
The oral tale of elder time rehearse,
And chant the rude, traditionary verse
With those, the loved companions of his youth,
When life was luxury, and friendship truth.

Ah, why should Virtue fear the frowns of Fate?
Hers what no wealth can buy, no power create!
A little world of clear and cloudless day,
Nor wrecked by storms, nor mouldered by decay;
A world, with MEMORY's ceaseless sunshine blest,
The home of Happiness, an honest breast.

But most we mark the wonders of her reign,
When Sleep has locked the senses in her chain.
When sober Judgment has his throne resigned,
She smiles away the chaos of the mind;
And, as warm Fancy's bright Elysium glows,
From her each image springs, each colour flows
She is the sacred guest! the immortal friend!
Oft seen o'er sleeping Innocence to bend,
In that dead hour of night to Silence given,
Whispering seraphic visions of her heaven
When the blithe son of Savoy, journeying round
With humble wares and pipe of merry sound,
From his green vale and sheltered cabin hies,
And scales the Alps to visit foreign skies :
Tho' far below the forked lightnings play,
And at his feet the thunder dies away,
Oft, in the saddle rudely rocked to sleep,
While his mule browses on the dizzy steep,

With MEMORY's aid, he sits at home, and sees
His children sport beneath their native trees,
And bends to hear their cherub voices call,
O'er the loud fury of the torrent's fall.
But can her smile with gloomy Madness dwell?
Say, can she chase the horrors of his cell?
Each fiery flight on Frenzy's wing restrain,
And mould the coinage of the fevered brain?
Pass but that grate, which scarce a gleam supplies,
There, in the dust the wreck of Genius lies!
He, whose arresting hand divinely wrought
Each bold conception in the sphere of thought;
And round, in colours of the rainbow, threw
Forms ever fair, creations ever new!
But, as he fondly snatched the wreath of Fame,
The spectre Poverty unnerved his frame.
Cold was her grasp, a withering scowl she wore;
And Hope's soft energies were felt no more.
Yet still how sweet the soothings of his art!
From the rude wall what bright ideas start!
Even now he claims the amaranthine wreath,
With scenes that glow, with images that breathe!
And whence these scenes, these images, declare,
Whence but from her who triumphs o'er despair?
Awake, arise! with grateful fervour fraught,
Go, spring the mine of elevating thought.
He who, through Nature's various walks, surveys
The good and fair her faultless line portrays;
Whose mind, profaned by no unhallowed guest,
Culls from the crowd the purest and the best;
May range, at will, bright Fancy's golden clime,
Or, musing, mount where Science sits sublime, ⎫
Or wake the Spirit of departed Time.   ⎭
Who acts thus wisely, mark the moral Muse,
A blooming Eden in his life reviews!
So rich the culture, tho' so small the space,
Its scanty limits he forgets to trace.
But the fond fool, when evening shades the sky,
Turns but to start, and gazes but to sigh!
The weary waste, that lengthened as he ran,
Fades to a blank, and dwindles to a span!
Ah! who can tell the triumphs of the mind,
By truth illumed and by taste refined?
When age has quenched the eye and closed the ear,
Still nerved for action in her native sphere.
Oft will she rise—with searching glance pursue
Some long-loved image vanished from her view;
Dart thro' the deep recesses of the Past,
O'er dusky forms in chains of slumber cast:
With giant-grasp fling back the folds of night,
And snatch the faithless fugitive to light.

. . . .

Hail, MEMORY, hail! in thy exhaustless mine
From age to age unnumbered treasures shine!
Thought and her shadowy brood thy call obey,
And Place and Time are subject to thy sway!
Thy pleasures most we feel, when most alone;
The only pleasures we can call our own.
Lighter than air, Hope's summer-visions die,
If but a fleeting cloud obscure the sky;

If but a beam of sober Reason play,
Lo, Fancy's fairy frost-work melts away!
But can the wiles of Art, the grasp of Power,
Snatch the rich relics of a well-spent hour?
These, when the trembling spirit wings her flight,
Pour round her path a stream of living light;
And gild those pure and perfect realms of rest,
Where Virtue triumphs, and her sons are blest!

FRENCH MEMOIRS.

BY WILLIAM H. PRESCOTT.

The French surpass every other nation, indeed all the other nations of Europe put together, in the amount and excellence of their memoirs. Whence comes this manifest superiority? The important collection relating to the history of France, commencing as early as the thirteenth century, forms a basis of civil history, more authentic, circumstantial, and satisfactory to an intelligent inquirer, than is to be found among any other people. And the multitude of biographies, personal anecdotes, and similar scattered notices, which have appeared in France during the two last centuries, throw a flood of light on the social habits and general civilization of the period in which they were written. The Italian histories (and every considerable city in Italy, says Tiraboschi, had its historian as early as the thirteenth century) are fruitful only in wars, massacres, treasonable conspiracies, or diplomatic intrigues, matters that affect the tranquillity of the state. The rich body of Spanish chronicles, which maintain an unbroken succession from the reign of Alphonso the Wise to that of Philip the Second, are scarcely more personal or interesting in their details, unless it be in reference to the sovereign and his immediate court. Even the English, in their memoirs and autobiographies of the last century, are too exclusively confined to topics of public notoriety, as the only subject worthy of record, or which can excite a general interest in their readers. Not so with the French. The most frivolous details assume in their eyes an importance when they can be made illustrative of an eminent character. And even when they concern one of less note they become sufficiently interesting, as just pictures of life and manners. Hence, instead of exhibiting their hero only as he appears on the great theatre, they carry us along with him into retirement, or into those social circles where, stripped of his masquerade dress, he can indulge in all the natural gaiety of his heart,—in those frivolities and follies which display the real character much better than all his premeditated wisdom; those little nothings which make up so much of the sum of French memoirs, but which, however amusing, are apt to be discarded by their more serious English neighbours, as something derogatory to their hero. Where shall we find a more lively portraiture of that interesting period when feudal barbarism began to fade away before the civilized institutions of modern times, than in Philip de Comines' sketches of the courts of France and Burgundy, in the latter half of the fifteenth century? Where a more nice development of the fashionable intrigues, the corrupt Machiavelian politics which animated the little coteries, male and female, of Paris, under the regency of Anne of Austria, than in the Memoirs of De Retz! To say nothing of the vast amount of similar contributions in France during the last century, which, in the shape of letters and anecdotes, as well as memoirs, have made us as intimately acquainted with the internal movements of society in Paris, under all its aspects, literary, fashionable, and political, as if they had passed in review before our own eyes.

The French have been remarked for their excellence in narrative, ever since the times of the *fabliaux* and the old Norman romances. Somewhat of their success in this way may be imputed to the structure of their language, whose general currency, and whose peculiar fitness for prose composition, have been noticed from a very early period. Brunetto Latini, the master of Dante, wrote his *Tesoro* in French, in preference to his own tongue, as far back as the middle of the thirteenth century, on the ground "that its speech was the most universal and most delectable of all the dialects of Europe." And Dante asserts, in his treatise on *Vulgar Eloquence*, that "the superiority of the French consists in its adaptation, by means of its facility and agreeableness, to narratives in prose." Much of the wild artless grace, the *naïveté*, which characterized it in its infancy, has been gradually polished away by fastidious critics, and can scarcely be said to have survived Marot and Montaigne. But the language has gained considerably in perspicuity, precision, and simplicity of construction; to which the jealous labours of the French Academy must be admitted to have contributed essentially. This simplicity of construction, refusing those complicated inversions so usual in the other languages of the Continent, and its total want of prosody, though fatal to poetical purposes, have greatly facilitated its acquisition to foreigners, and have made it a most suitable vehicle for conversation. Since the time of Louis XIV., accordingly, it has become the language of the courts, and the popular medium of communication in most of the countries of Europe. Since that period, too, it has acquired a number of elegant phrases and familiar turns of expression, which have admirably fitted it for light popular narrative, like that which enters into memoirs, letter-writing, and similar kinds of composition.

The character and situation of the writers themselves may account still better for the success of the French in this department. Many of them, as Joinville, Sully, Comines, De Thou, Rochefoucault, Torcy, have been men of rank and education, the counsellors or the friends of princes, acquiring from experience a shrewd perception of the character and of the forms of society. Most of them have been familiarized in those polite circles which, in Paris more than any other capital, seem to combine the love of dissipation and fashion with a high relish for intellectual pursuits. The state of society in France—or what is the same thing, in Paris—is admirably suited to the purposes of the memoir-writer. The cheerful gregarious temper of the inhabitants, which mingles all ranks in the common pursuit of pleasure; the external polish which scarcely deserts them in the commission of the grossest violence; the influence of the women during the last two centuries, far superior to that of the sex among any other people, and exercised alike on matters of taste, politics, and letters; the gallantry and licentious intrigues so usual in the higher classes of this gay metropolis, and which fill even the life of a man of letters, so stagnant in every other country, with stirring and romantic adventure; all these, we say, make up a rich and varied panorama, that can hardly fail of interest under the hand of the most common artist.

Lastly, the vanity of the French may be considered as another cause of their success in this kind of writing—a vanity which leads them to disclose a thousand amusing particulars which the reserve of an Englishman, and perhaps his pride, would discard as altogether unsuitable to the public ear. This vanity, it must be confessed, however, has occasionally seduced their writers, under the garb of confessions and secret memoirs, to make such a disgusting exposure of human infirmity as few men would be willing to admit, even to themselves.

WHAT WE ALL THINK.

BY OLIVER WENDELL HOLMES.

That age was older once than now,
In spite of locks untimely shed,
Or silvered on the youthful brow;
That babes make love and children wed.

That sunshine had a heavenly glow,
Which faded with those "good old days,"
When winters came with deeper snow,
And autumns with a softer haze.

That—mother, sister, wife, or child—
The "best of women" each has known.
Were schoolboys ever half so wild?
How young the grandpapas have grown!

That but for this our souls were free,
And but for that our lives were blest;
That in some season yet to be
Our cares will leave us time to rest.

Whene'er we groan with ache or pain.
Some common ailment of the race—
Though doctors think the matter plain—
That ours is "a peculiar case."

That when, like babes with fingers burned,
We count one bitter maxim more,
Our lesson all the world has learned,
And men are wiser than before.

That when we sob o'er fancied woes,
The angels hovering overhead
Count every pitying drop that flows,
And love us for the tears we shed.

That when we stand with tearless eye
And turn the beggar from our door,
They still approve us when we sigh,
"Ah, had I but one thousand more!"

That weakness smoothed the path of sin,
In half the slips our youth has known;
And whatsoe'er its blame has been,
That Mercy flowers on faults outgrown.

Though temples crowd the crumbled brink
O'erhanging truth's eternal flow,
Their tablets bold with what we think,
Their echoes dumb to what we know;

That one unquestioned text we read,
All doubt beyond, all fear above—
Nor crackling pile nor cursing creed
Can burn or blot it: GOD IS LOVE!

RELIGIOUS PLAYS AND MYSTERIES.

[Thomas Warton, born at Basingstoke, 1728; died
21st May, 1790. Educated at Oxford University, at
which seat of learning he afterwards became professor
of poetry and of history. He was also appointed to
the living of Kiddington, and presented to the donative
of Hill Farrance. He obtained the poet-laureateship
in 1785, on the death of William Whitehead. His chief
works are: *The Pleasures of Melancholy; The Triumph
of Isis; Newmarket,* a satire; *The History of English
Poetry,* &c. He also wrote several biographies and
other works.]

About the eighth century trade was principally carried on by means of fairs, which
lasted several days. Charlemagne established
many great marts of this sort in France; as
did William the Conqueror, and his Norman
successors, in England. The merchants who
frequented these fairs in numerous caravans
or companies, employed every art to draw the
people together. They were therefore accompanied by jugglers, minstrels, and buffoons,
who were no less interested in giving their attendance, and exerting all their skill, on these
occasions. As now but few large towns existed,
no public spectacles or popular amusements
were established; and as the sedentary pleasures
of domestic life and private society were yet
unknown, the fair-time was the season for
diversion. In proportion as these shows were
attended and encouraged, they began to be set
off with new decorations and improvements:
and the arts of buffoonery being rendered still
more attractive by extending their circle of
exhibition, acquired an importance in the eyes
of the people. By degrees the clergy, observing
that the entertainments of dancing, music,
and mimicry, exhibited at these protracted
annual celebrities, made the people less religious, by promoting idleness and a love of
festivity, proscribed these sports, and excom-
municated the performers. But finding that
no regard was paid to their censures, they
changed their plan, and determined to take
these recreations into their own hands. They
turned actors; and instead of profane mummeries, presented stories taken from legends
or the Bible. This was the origin of sacred
comedy. The death of St. Catherine, acted
by the monks of St. Dennis, rivalled the popularity of the professed players. Music was
admitted into the churches, which served as
theatres for the representation of holy farces.
The festivals among the French, called LA
FETE DE FOUX, DE L'ANE, and DES INNOCENS,
at length became greater favourites, as they

certainly were more capricious and absurd, than the interludes of the buffoons at the fairs. These are the ideas of a judicious French writer, now living, who has investigated the history of human manners with great comprehension and sagacity. Voltaire's theory on this subject is also very ingenious and quite new. Religious plays, he supposes, came originally from Constantinople, where the old Grecian stage continued to flourish in some degree, and the tragedies of Sophocles and Euripides were represented, till the fourth century. About that period, Gregory Nazianzen, an archbishop, a poet, and one of the fathers of the church, banished pagan plays from the stage at Constantinople, and introduced select stories from the Old and New Testament. As the ancient Greek tragedy was a religious spectacle, a transition was made on the same plan; and the choruses were turned into Christian hymns. Gregory wrote many sacred dramas for this purpose, which have not survived those inimitable compositions over which they triumphed for a time: one, however, his tragedy called CHRIST'S PASSION, is still extant. In the prologue it is said to be an imitation of Euripides, and that this is the first time the Virgin Mary has been produced on the stage. The fashion of acting spiritual dramas, in which at first a due degree of method and decorum was preserved, was at length adopted from Constantinople by the Italians; who framed, in the depth of the dark ages, on this foundation, that barbarous species of theatrical representation called MYSTERIES, or sacred comedies, and which were soon afterwards received in France. This opinion will acquire probability, if we consider the early commercial intercourse between Italy and Constantinople: and although the Italians, at the time when they may be supposed to have imported plays of this nature, did not understand the Greek language, yet they could understand, and consequently could imitate, what they saw. In defence of Voltaire's hypothesis, it may be further observed, that the FEAST OF FOOLS and of the Ass, with other religious farces of that sort, so common in Europe, originated at Constantinople. They were instituted, although perhaps under other names, in the Greek church, about the year 990, by Theophylact, patriarch of Constantinople, probably with a better design than is imagined by the ecclesiastical annalists: that of weaning the minds of the people from the pagan ceremonies, particularly the Bacchanalian and calendary solemnities, by the substitution of Christian spectacles, partaking of the same spirit of licentiousness.

I must, however, observe here, that in the fourth century it was customary to make Christian parodies and imitations in Greek, of the best Greek classics, for the use of the Christian schools. This practice prevailed much under the emperor Julian, who forbade the pagan poets, orators, and philosophers to be taught in the Christian seminaries. Apollinaris, bishop of Laodicea, wrote Greek tragedies, adapted to the stage, on most of the grand events recorded in the Old Testament, after the manner of Euripides. On some of the familiar and domestic stories of Scripture, he composed comedies in imitation of Menander. He wrote Christian odes on the plan of Pindar. In imitation of Homer, he wrote an heroic poem on the history of the Bible, as far as the reign of Saul, in twenty-four books. Sozomen says that these compositions, now lost, rivalled their great originals in genius, expression, and conduct. His son, a bishop also of Laodicea, reduced the four Gospels and all the apostolical books into Greek dialogues, resembling those of Plato. But I must not omit a much earlier and more singular specimen of a theatrical representation of sacred history than this mentioned by Voltaire. Some fragments of an ancient Jewish play on the EXODUS, or the Departure of the Israelites from Egypt under their leader and prophet Moses, are yet preserved in Greek iambics. The principal characters of this drama are Moses, Sapphora, and God from the Bush, or God speaking from the burning bush. Moses delivers the prologue, or introduction, in a speech of sixty lines, and his rod is turned into a serpent on the stage. The author of this piece is Ezekiel, a Jew, who is called the tragic poet of the Jews. The learned Huetius endeavours to prove that Ezekiel wrote at least before the Christian era. Some suppose that he was one of the seventy, or Septuagint interpreters of the Bible under the reign of Ptolemy Philadelphus. I am of opinion that Ezekiel composed this play after the destruction of Jerusalem, and even in the time of Barochas, as a political spectacle, with a view to animate his dejected countrymen with the hopes of a future deliverance from their captivity under the conduct of a new Moses, like that from the Egyptian servitude. Whether a theatre subsisted among the Jews, who by their peculiar situation and circumstances were prevented from keeping pace with their neighbours in the culture of the social and elegant arts, is a curious speculation. It seems most probable, on the whole, that this drama was composed in imitation of the Grecian stage, at the close of the second century, after the Jews had been dispersed, and intermixed with other nations.

On the whole, the MYSTERIES appear to have originated among the ecclesiastics; and were most probably first acted, at least with any degree of form, by the monks. This was certainly the case in the English monasteries. ·I have already mentioned the play of St. Catherine, performed at Dunstable Abbey by the novices in the eleventh century, under the superintendence of Geoffry, a Parisian ecclesiastic; and the exhibition of the PASSION, by the mendicant friars of Coventry and other places. Instances have been given of the like practice among the French. The only persons who could read were in the religious societies: and various other circumstances, peculiarly arising from their situation, profession, and institution, enabled the monks to be the sole performers of these representations. As learning increased, and was more widely disseminated from the monasteries, by a natural and easy transition, the practice migrated to schools and universities, which were formed on the monastic plan, and in many respects resembled the ecclesiastical bodies. Hence a passage in Shakspeare's *Hamlet* is to be explained; where Hamlet says to Polonius, "My lord, you played once in the *university*, you say." Polonius answers, "That I did, my lord, and was accounted a good *actor.—*I did *enact* Julius Cesar; I was killed i' th' Capitol." Boulay observes, that it was a custom, not only still subsisting, but of very high antiquity, *vetustissima consuetudo*, to act tragedies and comedies in the university of Paris.

It is more generally known, that the practice of acting Latin plays in the colleges of Oxford and Cambridge continued to Cromwell's usurpation. The oldest notice I can recover of this sort of spectacle in an English university, is in the fragment of an ancient accompt-roll of the dissolved college of Michael-house in Cambridge: in which, under the year 1386, the following expense is entered—"*Pro ly pallio brusdato et pro sex larvis et barbis in comedia.*" That is, For an embroidered pall, or cloak, and six visors and six beards, for the comedy. In the year 1544 a Latin comedy, called PAMMACHIUS, was acted at Christ's College in Cambridge, which was laid before the privy-council by Bishop Gardiner, chancellor of university, as a dangerous libel, containing many offensive reflections on the papistic ceremonies yet unabolished. The comedy of GAMMAR GURTON'S NEEDLE was acted in the same society about the year 1552. In an original draught of the statutes of Trinity College

at Cambridge, founded in 1546, one of the chapters is entitled, *De Præfecto Ludorum qui* IMPERATOR *dicitur*, under whose direction by authority, Latin comedies and tragedies are to be exhibited in the hall at Christmas; as also *Sex* SPECTACULA, or as many DIALOGUES. Another title to this statute, which seems to be substituted by another and a more modern hand, is *De Comediis ludisque in natali Christi exhibendis.* With regard to the peculiar business and office of IMPERATOR, it is ordered, that one of the masters of arts shall be placed over the juniors, every Christmas, for the regulation of their games and diversions at that season of festivity. At the same time, he is to govern the whole society in the hall and chapel, as a republic committed to his special charge, by a set of laws, which he is to frame in Latin or Greek verse. His sovereignty is to last during the twelve days of Christmas, and he is to exercise the same power on Candlemas-day. During this period, he is to see that six SPECTACLES or DIALOGUES be presented. His fee is forty shillings. Probably the constitution of this officer, in other words, *a Master of the Revels*, gave a latitude to some licentious enormities, incompatible with the decorum of a house of learning and religion; and it was found necessary to restrain these Christmas celebrities to a more rational and sober plan. The SPECTACLES also, and DIALOGUES, originally appointed, were growing obsolete when the substitution was made, and were giving way to more regular representations. I believe these statutes were reformed by Queen Elizabeth's visitors of the university of Cambridge, under the conduct of Archbishop Parker, in the year 1573.

MONEY.

Money, thou bane of bliss, and source of woe,
Whence comest thou, that thou art so fresh and fine?
I know thy parentage is base and low:
Man found thee poor and dirty in a mine.

Sure thou didst so little contribute
To this great kingdom, which thou now hast got,
That he was fain, when thou wast destitute,
To dig thee out of thy dark cave and grot.

Then forcing thee, by fire he made thee bright:
Nay, thou hast got the face of man; for we
Have with our stamp and seal transferr'd our right:
Thou art the man, and man but dross to thee.

Man calleth thee his wealth, who made thee rich;
And while he digs out thee, falls in the ditch.
                              GEORGE HERBERT.

EPIGRAMS.

When Jack was poor, the lad was frank and free,
Of late he's grown brimful of pride and pelf;
No wonder that he has forgotten me;
Since it is plain he has forgot himself.

Anon.

Weary of you, dear wife? Oh no, thank Heaven!
But marriage now has made us one;
And I to ennui am given,
Whenever I am thus alone.

Anon.

To this night's masquerade, quoth Dick,
By pleasure I am beckon'd,
And think 'twould be a pleasant trick
To go as Charles the Second.

Tom felt for repartee a thirst,
And thus to Richard said,
You'd better go as Charles the First,
For that requires no head.

Grimm's Ghost.

How D.D. swaggers, M.D. rolls!
I dub them both a brace of noddies;
Old D.D. has the Cure of souls,
And M.D. has the Care of bodies.

Between them both what treatment rare
Our souls and bodies must endure;
One has the Cure without the Care,
And one the Care without the Cure.

Ibid.

The miniature, Phyllis, you're showing us now,
Proves the artist with you well acquainted,
That 'tis monstrously like you we all must allow,
When we see, as we do, that 'tis painted.

KELLY.

"Come hither, Sir John, my picture is here,
What say you, my love, does it strike you?"
"I can't say it does just at present, my dear,
But I think it soon will, it's so like you."

Anon.

" You men are angels while you woo the maid,
But devils when the marriage-vow is said."
"The change, good wife, is easily forgiven;
We find ourselves in hell, instead of heaven."

HAUG.— *Translated by Russel.*

Swans sing before they die: 'twere no bad thing
Should certain persons die before they sing.

S. T COLERIDGE.

I ask'd my love, one happy day,
What I should call her in my lay;
"Choose," said she, "what suits the line,
Only—only call me thine!"

Ibid.

Sly Beelzebub took all occasions
To try Job's constancy and patience,
He took his honours, took his health,
He took his children, took his wealth,
His camels, horses, asses, cows—
And the sly Devil did *not* take his spouse.

But Heaven, that brings out good from evil,
And loves to disappoint the Devil,
Had predetermined to restore
Twofold all Job had before;
His children, camels, horses, cows—
Short-sighted Devil, *not* to take his spouse!

Ibid.

THE SPECTRE BRIDEGROOM.

BY WASHINGTON IRVING.

On the summit of one of the heights of the
Odenwald, a wild and romantic tract of Upper
Germany that lies not far from the confluence
of the Maine and the Rhine, there stood, many,
many years since, the castle of the Baron Von
Landshort. It is now quite fallen to decay,
and almost buried among beech-trees and dark
firs; above which, however, its old watch-tower
may still be seen struggling, like the former
possessor I have mentioned, to carry a high
head, and look down upon the neighbouring
country.

The baron was a dry branch of the great
family of Katzenellenbogen, and inherited the
reliques of the property, and all the pride of
his ancestors. Though the warlike disposition
of his predecessors had much impaired the
family possessions, yet the baron still endeavoured to keep up some show of former state.
The times were peaceable, and the German
nobles, in general, had abandoned their incon-
venient old castles, perched like eagles' nests
among the mountains, and had built more
convenient residences in the valleys: still the
baron remained proudly drawn up in his little
fortress, cherishing, with hereditary inveteracy,
all the old family feuds; so that he was on ill

terms with some of his nearest neighbours, on account of disputes that had happened between their great-great-grandfathers.

The baron had but one child, a daughter; but Nature, when she grants but one child, always compensates by making it a prodigy; and so it was with the daughter of the baron. All the nurses, gossips, and country cousins assured her father that she had not her equal for beauty in all Germany; and who should know better than they? She had, moreover, been brought up with great care under the superintendence of two maiden aunts, who had spent some years of their early life at one of the little German courts, and were skilled in all the branches of knowledge necessary to the education of a fine lady. Under their instructions she became a miracle of accomplishments. By the time she was eighteen she could embroider to admiration, and had worked whole histories of the saints in tapestry, with such strength of expression in their countenances, that they looked like so many souls in purgatory. She could read without great difficulty, and had spelled her way through several church legends, and almost all the chivalric wonders of the Heldenbuch. She had even made considerable proficiency in writing; could sign her own name without missing a letter, and so legibly that her aunts could read it without spectacles. She excelled in making little elegant good-for-nothing lady-like nick-nacks of all kinds; was versed in the most abstruse dancing of the day; played a number of airs on the harp and guitar; and knew all the tender ballads of the Minnie-lieders by heart.

At the time of which my story treats, there was a great family gathering at the castle, on an affair of the utmost importance. It was to receive the destined bridegroom of the baron's daughter. A negotiation had been carried on between the father and an old nobleman of Bavaria, to unite the dignity of their houses by the marriage of their children. The preliminaries had been conducted with proper punctilio. The young people were betrothed without seeing each other; and the time was appointed for the marriage ceremony. The young Count Von Altenburg had been recalled from the army for the purpose, and was actually on his way to the baron's to receive his bride. Missives had even been received from him, from Wurtzburg, where he was accidentally detained, mentioning the day and hour when he might be expected to arrive.

The castle was in a tumult of preparation to give him a suitable welcome. The fair bride had been decked out with uncommon care.

The two aunts had superintended her toilet, and quarrelled the whole morning about every article of her dress. The young lady had taken advantage of their contest to follow the bent of her own taste; and fortunately it was a good one. She looked as lovely as youthful bridegroom could desire; and the flutter of expectation heightened the lustre of her charms.

In the meantime the fatted calf had been killed; the forests had rung with the clamour of the huntsmen; the kitchen was crowded with good cheer; the cellars had yielded up whole oceans of *Rhein-wein* and *Ferne-wein;* and even the great Heidelberg tun had been laid under contribution. Everything was ready to receive the distinguished guest with *Saus und Braus* in the true spirit of German hospitality—but the guest delayed to make his appearance. Hour rolled after hour. The sun that had poured his downward rays upon the rich forests of the Odenwald, now just gleamed along the summits of the mountains. The baron mounted the highest tower, and strained his eyes in hopes of catching a distant sight of the count and his attendants. Once he thought he beheld them; the sound of horns came floating from the valley, prolonged by the mountain echoes. A number of horsemen were seen far below, slowly advancing along the road; but when they had nearly reached the foot of the mountain, they suddenly struck off in a different direction. The last ray of sunshine departed—the bats began to flit by in the twilight—the road grew dimmer and dimmer to the view; and nothing appeared stirring in it, but now and then a peasant lagging homeward from his labour.

When the old castle of Landshort was in this state of perplexity, a very interesting scene was transacting in a different part of the Odenwald.

The young Count Von Altenburg was tranquilly pursuing his route in that sober jog-trot way, in which a man travels towards matrimony when his friends have taken all the trouble and uncertainty of courtship off his hands, and a bride is waiting for him, as certainly as a dinner at the end of his journey. He had encountered, at Wurtzburg, a youthful companion in arms, with whom he had seen some service on the frontiers—Herman Von Starkenfaust, one of the stoutest hands, and worthiest hearts of German chivalry, who was now returning from the army. His father's castle was not far distant from the old fortress of Landshort, although an hereditary feud rendered the families hostile, and strangers to each other.

In the warm-hearted moment of recognition, the young friends related all their past adventures and fortunes, and the count gave the whole history of his intended nuptials with a young lady whom he had never seen, but of whose charms he had received the most enrapturing descriptions.

As the route of the friends lay in the same direction, they agreed to perform the rest of their journey together; and that they might do it the more leisurely, set off from Wurtzburg at an early hour, the count having given directions for his retinue to follow and overtake him.

They beguiled their wayfaring with recollections of their military scenes and adventures; but the count was apt to be a little tedious, now and then, about the reputed charms of his bride, and the felicity that awaited him.

In this way they had entered among the mountains of the Odenwald, and were traversing one of its most lonely and thickly wooded passes. It is well known that the forests of Germany have always been as much infested by robbers as its castles by spectres; and, at this time, the former were particularly numerous, from the hordes of disbanded soldiers wandering about the country. It will not appear extraordinary, therefore, that the cavaliers were attacked by a gang of these stragglers in the depth of the forest. They defended themselves with bravery, but were nearly overpowered when the count's retinue arrived to their assistance. At sight of them the robbers fled, but not until the count had received a mortal wound. He was slowly and carefully conveyed back to the city of Wurtzburg, and a friar summoned from a neighbouring convent, who was famous for his skill in administering to both soul and body; but half of his skill was superfluous; the moments of the unfortunate count were numbered.

With his dying breath he entreated his friend to repair instantly to the castle of Landshort, and explain the fatal cause of his not keeping his appointment with his bride. Though not the most ardent of lovers, he was one of the most punctilious of men, and appeared earnestly solicitous that this mission should be speedily and courteously executed. "Unless this is done," said he, "I shall not sleep quietly in my grave!" He repeated these last words with peculiar solemnity. A request, at a moment so impressive, admitted no hesitation. Starkenfaust endeavoured to soothe him to calmness, promised faithfully to execute his wish, and gave him his hand in solemn

pledge. The dying man pressed it in acknowledgement, but soon lapsed into delirium—raved about his bride—his engagement—his plighted word; ordered his horse, that he might ride to the castle of Landshort; and expired in the fancied act of vaulting into the saddle.

Starkenfaust bestowed a sigh, and a soldier's tear, on the untimely fate of his comrade; and then pondered on the awkward mission he had undertaken. His heart was heavy and his head perplexed; for he was to present himself an unbidden guest among hostile people, and to damp their festivity with tidings fatal to their hopes. Still there were certain whisperings of curiosity in his bosom to see this far-famed beauty of Katzenellenbogen, so cautiously shut up from the world; for he was a passionate admirer of the sex, and there was a dash of eccentricity and enterprise in his character that made him fond of all singular adventure.

Previous to his departure he made all due arrangements with the holy fraternity of the convent for the funeral solemnities of his friend, who was to be buried in the cathedral of Wurtzburg, near some of his illustrious relatives; and the mourning retinue of the count took charge of his remains.

It is now high time we should return to the ancient family of Katzenellenbogen, who were impatient for their guest, and still more for their dinner; and to the worthy little baron whom we left airing himself on the watchtower.

Night closed in, but still no guest arrived. The baron descended from the tower in despair. The banquet, which had been delayed from hour to hour, could no longer be postponed. The meats were already overdone; the cook in an agony; and the whole household had the look of a garrison that had been reduced by famine. The baron was obliged reluctantly to give orders for the feast without the presence of the guest. All were seated at table, and just on the point of commencing, when the sound of a horn from without the gate gave notice of the approach of a stranger. Another long blast filled the old courts of the castle with its echoes, and was answered by the warder from the walls. The baron hastened to receive his future son-in-law.

The drawbridge had been let down, and the stranger was before the gate. He was a tall gallant cavalier, mounted on a black steed. His countenance was pale, but he had a beaming, romantic eye, and an air of stately melancholy. The baron was a little mortified that he should have come in this simple, solitary style. His dignity for a moment was ruffled, and he felt disposed to consider it a want of proper respect for the important occasion, and the important family with which he was to be connected. He, however, pacified himself with the conclusion, that it must have been youthful impatience which had induced him thus to spur on sooner than his attendants. "I am sorry," said the stranger, "to break in upon you thus unseasonably—"

Here the baron interrupted him with a world of compliments and greetings; for, to tell the truth, he prided himself upon his courtesy and his eloquence. The stranger attempted, once or twice, to stem the torrent of words, but in vain, so he bowed his head and suffered it to flow on. By the time the baron had come to a pause, they had reached the inner court of the castle; and the stranger was again about to speak, when he was once more interrupted by the appearance of the female part of the family, leading forth the shrinking and blushing bride. He gazed on her for a moment as one entranced; it seemed as if his whole soul beamed forth in the gaze, and rested upon that lovely form. One of the maiden aunts whispered something in her ear; she made an effort to speak; her moist blue eye was timidly raised; gave a shy glance of inquiry on the stranger; and was cast again to the ground. The words died away; but there was a sweet smile playing about her lips, and a soft dimpling of the cheek, that showed her glance had not been unsatisfactory. It was impossible for a girl of the fond age of eighteen, highly predisposed for love and matrimony, not to be pleased with so gallant a cavalier.

The late hour at which the guest had arrived left no time for parley. The baron was peremptory, and deferred all particular conversation until the morning, and led the way to the untasted banquet.

It was served up in the great hall of the castle. Around the walls hung the hard-favoured portraits of the heroes of the house of Katzenellenbogen, and the trophies which they had gained in the field and in the chase. Hacked corslets, splintered jousting-spears, and tattered banners were mingled with the spoils of sylvan warfare; the jaws of the wolf, and the tusks of the boar, grinned horribly among cross-bows and battle-axes, and a huge pair of antlers branched accidentally over the head of the youthful bridegroom.

The cavalier took but little notice of the company or the entertainment. He scarcely tasted the banquet, but seemed absorbed in admiration of his bride. He conversed in a low tone that could not be overheard—for the language of love is never loud; but where is the female ear so dull that it cannot catch the softest whisper of the lover? There was a mingled tenderness and gravity in his manner, that appeared to have a powerful effect upon the young lady. Her colour came and went as she listened with deep attention. Now and then she made some blushing reply, and when his eye was turned away, she would steal a side-long glance at his romantic countenance, and heave a gentle sigh of tender happiness. It was evident that the young couple were completely enamoured. The aunts, who were deeply versed in the mysteries of the heart, declared that they had fallen in love with each other at first sight.

The feast went on merrily, or at least noisily, for the guests were all blest with those keen appetites that attend upon light purses and mountain air. The baron told his best and longest stories, and never had he told them so well, or with such great effect. If there was anything marvellous, his auditors were lost in astonishment; and if anything facetious, they were sure to laugh exactly in the right place. The baron, it is true, like most great men, was too dignified to utter any joke but a dull one; it was always enforced, however, by a bumper of excellent Hochheimer; and even a dull joke, at one's own table, served up with jolly old wine, is irresistible. Many good things were said by poorer and keener wits, that would not bear repeating, except on similar occasions; many sly speeches whispered in ladies' ears, that almost convulsed them with suppressed laughter; and a song or two roared out by a poor but merry and broad-faced cousin of the baron, that absolutely made the maiden aunts hold up their fans.

Amidst all this revelry, the stranger guest maintained a most singular and unseasonable gravity. His countenance assumed a deeper cast of dejection as the evening advanced; and, strange as it may appear, even the baron's jokes seemed only to render him the more melancholy. At times he was lost in thought, and at times there was a perturbed and restless wandering of the eye that bespoke a mind but ill at ease. His conversations with the bride became more and more earnest and mysterious. Lowering clouds began to steal over the fair serenity of her brow, and tremors to run through her tender frame.

All this could not escape the notice of the company. Their gaiety was chilled by the unaccountable gloom of the bridegroom; their spirits were infected; whispers and glances were interchanged, accompanied by shrugs and dubious shakes of the head. The song and the laugh grew less and less frequent; there were dreary pauses in the conversation, which were at length succeeded by wild tales and supernatural legends. One dismal story produced another still more dismal, and the baron nearly frightened some of the ladies into hysterics with the history of the goblin horseman that carried away the fair Leonora; a dreadful, but true story, which has since been put into excellent verse, and is read and believed by all the world.

The bridegroom listened to this tale with profound attention. He kept his eyes steadily fixed on the baron, and, as the story drew to a close, began gradually to rise from his seat, growing taller and taller, until, in the baron's entranced eye, he seemed almost to tower into a giant. The moment the tale was finished, he heaved a deep sigh, and took a solemn farewell of the company. They were all amazement. The baron was perfectly thunderstruck.

"What! going to leave the castle at midnight? why, everything was prepared for his reception: a chamber was ready for him if he wished to retire."

The stranger shook his head mournfully and mysteriously; "I must lay my head in a different chamber to-night?"

There was something in this reply, and the tone in which it was uttered, that made the baron's heart misgive him; but he rallied his forces and repeated his hospitable entreaties. The stranger shook his head silently, but positively, at every offer; and, waving his farewell to the company, stalked slowly out of the hall. The maiden aunts were absolutely petrified—the bride hung her head, and a tear stole to her eye.

The baron followed the stranger to the great court of the castle, where the black charger stood pawing the earth, and snorting with impatience. When they had reached the portal, whose deep archway was dimly lighted by a cresset, the stranger paused and addressed the baron in a hollow tone of voice, which the vaulted roof rendered still more sepulchral. "Now that we are alone," said he, "I will impart to you the reason of my going. I have a solemn, an indispensable engagement—"

"Why," said the baron, "cannot you send some one in your place?"

"It admits of no substitute—I must attend it in person—I must away to Wurtzburg Cathedral—"

"Ay," said the baron, plucking up spirit, "but not until to-morrow—to-morrow you shall take your bride there."

"No! no!" replied the stranger, with ten fold solemnity, "my engagement is with no bride—the worms! the worms expect me! I am a dead man—I have been slain by robbers —my body lies at Wurtzburg—at midnight I am to be buried—the grave is waiting for me —I must keep my appointment!"

He sprang on his black charger, dashed over the draw-bridge, and the clattering of his horse's hoofs were lost in the whistling of the night blast.

The baron returned to the hall in the utmost consternation, and related what had passed. Two ladies fainted outright, others sickened at the idea of having banqueted with a spectre. It was the opinion of some that this might be the wild huntsman famous in German legend. Some talked of mountain sprites, of wood-demons, and of other supernatural beings, with which the good people of Germany have been so grievously harassed since time immemorial. One of the poor relations ventured to suggest that it might be some sportive evasion of the young cavalier, and that the very gloominess of the caprice seemed to accord with so melancholy a personage. This, however, drew on him the indignation of the whole company, and especially of the baron, who looked upon him as little better than an infidel; so that he was fain to abjure his heresy as speedily as possible, and come into the faith of the true believers.

But, whatever may have been the doubts entertained, they were completely put to an end by the arrival, next day, of regular missives, confirming the intelligence of the young count's murder, and his interment in Wurtzburg Cathedral.

The dismay at the castle may well be imagined. The baron shut himself up in his chamber. The guests, who had come to rejoice with him, could not think of abandoning him in his distress. They wandered about the courts, or collected in groups in the hall, shaking their heads and shrugging their shoulders at the troubles of so good a man: and sat longer than ever at table, and ate and drank more stoutly than ever, by way of keeping up their spirits. But the situation of the widowed bride was the most pitiable. To have lost a husband before she had even embraced him—and such a husband! If the very spectre could be so gracious and noble, what must have been the living man! She filled the house with lamentations.

On the night of the second day of her widowhood she had retired to her chamber, accompanied by one of her aunts, who insisted on sleeping with her. The aunt, who was one of the best tellers of ghost stories in all Germany, had just been recounting one of her longest, and had fallen asleep in the very midst of it. The chamber was remote, and overlooked a small garden. The niece lay pensively gazing at the beams of the rising moon, as they trembled on the leaves of an aspen-tree before the lattice. The castle clock had just tolled midnight, when a soft strain of music stole up from the garden. She rose hastily from her bed, and stepped lightly to the window. A tall figure stood among the shadows of the trees. As it raised its head, a beam of moonlight fell upon the countenance. Heaven and earth! she beheld the spectre bridegroom! A loud shriek at that moment burst upon her ear, and her aunt, who had been awakened by the music, and had followed her silently to the window, fell into her arms. When she looked again, the spectre had disappeared.

Of the two females, the aunt now required the most soothing, for she was perfectly beside herself with terror. As to the young lady, there was something, even in the spectre of her lover, that seemed endearing. There was still the semblance of manly beauty; and though the shadow of a man is but little calculated to satisfy the affections of a love-sick girl, yet, where the substance is not to be had, even that is consoling. The aunt declared she would never sleep in that chamber again; the niece, for once, was refractory, and declared as strongly that she would sleep in no other in the castle: the consequence was, that she had to sleep in it alone; but she drew a promise from her aunt not to relate the story of the spectre, lest she should be denied the only melancholy pleasure left her on earth—that of inhabiting the chamber over which the guardian shade of her lover kept its nightly vigils.

How long the good old lady would have observed this promise is uncertain, for she dearly loved to talk of the marvellous, and there is a triumph in being the first to tell a frightful story; it is, however, still quoted in the neighbourhood, as a memorable instance of female secrecy, that she kept it to herself for a whole week; when she was suddenly absolved from all further restraint by intelligence brought to the breakfast table one morning, that the young lady was not to be found. Her room was empty—the bed had not been slept in—the window was open, and the bird had flown.

The astonishment and concern with which the intelligence was received, can only be imagined by those who have witnessed the agitation which the mishaps of a great man cause among his friends. Even the poor relations paused for a moment from the indefatigable labours of the trencher; when the aunt, who had at first been struck speechless, wrung her hands, and shrieked out, "The goblin! the goblin! she's carried away by the goblin!"

In a few words she related the fearful scene of the garden, and concluded that the spectre must have carried off his bride. Two of the domestics corroborated the opinion, for they had heard the clattering of a horse's hoofs down the mountain about midnight, and had no doubt that it was the spectre on his black charger, bearing her away to the tomb. All present were struck with the direful probability; for events of the kind are extremely common in Germany, as many well-authenticated histories bear witness.

What a lamentable situation was that of the poor baron! What a heart-rending dilemma for a fond father, and a member of the great family of Katzenellenbogen! His only daughter had either been rapt away to the grave, or he was to have some wood-demon for a son-in-law, and perchance a troop of goblin grandchildren. As usual, he was completely bewildered, and all the castle in an uproar. The men were ordered to take horse, and to scour every road and path and glen of the Odenwald. The baron himself had just drawn on his jack-boots, girded on his sword, and was about to mount his steed to sally forth on the doubtful quest, when he was brought to a pause by a new apparition. A lady was seen approaching the castle, mounted on a palfrey, attended by a cavalier on horseback. She galloped up to the gate, sprang from her horse, and, falling at the baron's feet, embraced his knees. It was his lost daughter, and her companion—the Spectre Bridegroom! The baron was astounded. He looked at his daughter, then at the spectre, and almost doubted the evidence of his senses. The latter, too, was wonderfully improved in his appearance, since his visit to the world of spirits. His dress was splendid, and set off a noble figure of manly symmetry. He was no longer pale and melancholy. His fine countenance was flushed with the glow of youth, and joy rioted in his large dark eye.

The mystery was soon cleared up. The cavalier (for in truth, as you must have known all the while, he was no goblin) announced himself as Sir Herman Von Starkenfaust. He related his adventure with the young count. He told how he had hastened to the castle to deliver the unwelcome tidings, but that the eloquence of the baron had interrupted him in every attempt to tell his tale; how the sight of the bride had completely captivated him, and that to pass a few hours near her, he had tacitly suffered the mistake to continue; how he had been sorely perplexed in what way to make a decent retreat, until the baron's goblin stories had suggested his eccentric exit; how, fearing the feudal hostility of the family, he had repeated his visits by stealth—had haunted the garden beneath the young lady's window—had wooed—had won—had borne away in triumph—and, in a word, had wedded the fair.

Under any other circumstances, the baron would have been inflexible, for he was tenacious of paternal authority, and devoutly obstinate in all family feuds; but he loved his daughter; he had lamented her as lost; he rejoiced to find her still alive; and, though her husband was of a hostile house, yet, thank Heaven, he was not a goblin. There was something, it must be acknowledged, that did not exactly accord with his notions of strict veracity, in the joke the knight had passed upon him of his being a dead man; but several old friends present, who had served in the wars, assured him that every stratagem was excusable in love, and that the cavalier was entitled to especial privilege, having lately served as a trooper.

Matters, therefore, were happily arranged. The baron pardoned the young couple on the spot. The revels at the castle were resumed. The poor relations overwhelmed this new member of the family with loving kindness; he was so gallant, so generous—and so rich. The aunts, it is true, were somewhat scandalized that their system of strict seclusion and passive obedience should be so badly exemplified, but attributed it all to their negligence in not having the windows grated. One of them was particularly mortified at having her marvellous story marred, and that the only spectre she had ever seen should turn out a counterfeit; but the niece seemed perfectly happy at having found him substantial flesh and blood —and so the story ends.

THE OATH.

"Do you," said Fanny, t'other day,
"In earnest love me as you say?
Or are these tender words applied
Alike to fifty girls beside?"
"Dear, cruel girl," said I, "forbear —
For by these cherry lips I swear"—
She stopp'd me as the oath I took,
And said, "You've sworn—so kiss the book."

FESTUS.

[Philip James Bailey, born at Nottingham, 22d April, 1816. He is the son of Thomas Bailey, author of the *Annals of Notts.* He studied at the Glasgow University, and was called to the bar in 1840. *Festus* first appeared in 1839 (the eighth edition in 1868), and was at once acknowledged to be a great poem. "With a truth, force, and simplicity seldom paralleled," says Dr. Westland Marston, "we have here disclosed the very inmost life of a sincere and energetic mind." The Rev. P. Landreth says: "There is no poem in any language which gives such a noble and striking idea of humanity under a divine grace which bears it victorious from and through evil, within and without." The scope of the poem is somewhat similar to that of Goethe's *Faust*, from which it differs, however, in many essential principles. Festus is tempted by Lucifer, but is purified and saved, as is Lucifer himself, by divine grace. Mr. Bailey's other works are: *The Angel World*, now incorporated with *Festus*; *The Mystic*; *The Age*, a satire; and *The Universal Hymn*. We have selected the scene from *Festus* in which the hero reveals something of his own character.]

Scene—Home; Dusk

FESTUS, HELEN, *and the* STUDENT.

Festus. I knew one once—he was a friend of mine·
I knew him well; his mind, habits, and works,
Taste, temper, temperament, and every thing;
Yet with as kind a heart as beats, he was
Earthlike no sooner made than marred. Though young,
He wrote amid the ruins of his heart;
They were his throne and theme—like some lone king,
Who tells the story of the land he lost,
And how he lost it.
Student.   Tell us more of him.
Helen. Nay, but it saddens thee.
Festus.   'Tis like enough.
We slip away like shadows into shade:
We end, and make no mark we had begun;
We come to nothing, like a pure intent.
When we have hoped, sought, striven, and lost our aim,
Then the truth fronts us, beaming out of darkness,
Like a white brow, through its overshadowing hair—
As though the day were overcast, my Helen!
But I was speaking of my friend. He was
Quick, generous, simple, obstinate in end,
High-hearted from his youth; his spirit rose
In many a glittering fold and gleamy crest,
Hydra-like to its hindrance; mastering all,
Save one thing - love, and that out-hearted him
Nor did he think enough, till it was over,
How bright a thing he was breaking, or he would
Surely have shunned it, nor have let his life
Be pulled to pieces like a rose by a child.
And his heart's passions made him oft do that
Which made him writhe to think on what he had done,
And thin his blood by weeping at a night.
If madness wrought the sin, the sin wrought madness,
And made a round of ruin. It is sad

To see the light of beauty wane away;
Know eyes are dimming, bosom shrivelling, feet
Losing their spring, and limbs their lily roundness;
But it is worse to feel our heart-spring gone,
To lose hope, care not for the coming thing,
And feel all things go to decay with us,
As 'twere our life's eleventh month : and yet
All this he went through young.

Helen.   Poor soul! I should
Have loved him for his sorrows.

Festus.   It is not love
Brings sorrow, but love's objects,

Student.   Then he loved.

Festus. I said so. I have seen him, when he hath had
A letter from his lady dear, he blessed
The paper that her hand had travelled over,
And her eye looked on; and would think he saw
Gleams of that light she lavished from her eyes
Wandering amid the words of love there traced,
Like glow-worms among beds of flowers. He seemed
To bear with being but because she loved him.
She was the sheath wherein his soul had rest,
As hath a sword from war : and he at night
Would solemnly and singularly curse
Each minute that he had not thought of her.

Helen. Now that was like a lover! and she loved
Him, and him only.

Festus.   Well, perhaps it was so.
But he could not restrain his heart, but loved
In that voluptuous purity of taste
Which dwells on beauty coldly, and yet kindly,
As night-dew, whensoe'er he met with beauty.

Helen. It was a pity, that inconstancy—
If she he loved were but as good and fair
As he was worthy of.

Student.   It was his way.

Festus. There is a dark and bright to every thing;
To everything but beauty such as thine,
And that is all bright. If a fault in him,
'Twas one which made him do the sweetest wrongs
Man ever did. And yet a whisper went
That he did wrong: and if that whisper had
Echo in him or not, it mattered little;
Or right or wrong, he were alike unhappy.
Ah me! ah me! that there should be so much
To call up love, so little to delight!
The best enjoyment is half disappointment
To that we mean or would have in this world.
And there were many strange and sudden lights
Beckoned him towards them; they were wreckers' lights:
But he shunned these, and righted when she rose,
Moon of his life, that ebbed and flowed with her.
A sea of sorrow struck him, but he held
On; dashed all sorrow from him as a bark
Spray from her bow bounding : he lifted up
His head, and the deep ate his shadow merely.

Helen. A poet not in love is out at sea;
He must have a lay-figure.

Festus.   I mean not
To screen, but to describe this friend of mine.

Helen. Describe the lady, too ; of course she was
Above all praise and all comparison.

Festus. Why, true. Her heart was all humanity,
Her soul all God's; in spirit and in form
Like fair. Her cheek had the pale pearly pink
Of sea-shells, the world's sweetest tint, as though
She lived, one half might deem, on roses sopped
In silver dew; she spake as with the voice
Of spheral harmony which greets the soul
When at the hour of death the saved one knows
His sister angels near; her eye was as
The golden pane the setting sun doth just
Imblaze, till heaven comes down again,
All other lights but grades of gloom ; her dark,
Long rolling locks were as a stream the slave
Might search for gold, and searching find. Her frown—

Helen. Nay, could she frown?

Festus.   Ay, but a radiant frown
In common with the stars, which men malign
Who call malignant. Stars are always kind.

Helen. Enough. I have her picture perfect. Cease.

Student. What were his griefs?

Festus.   He who hath most of heart
Knows most of sorrow; not a thing he saw
Nor did, but was to him, at times, a woe;
At times indifferent, at times a joy.
Folly and sin and memory make a curse
Wherewith the future fires my vie in vain.
The sorrows of the soul are graver still.

Student. Where and when did he study? Did he mix
Much with the world, or was he a recluse?

Festus. He had no times of study, and no place;
All places and all times to him were one.
His soul was like the wind-harp, which he loved,
And sounded only when the spirit blew.
Sometimes in feasts and follies, for he went
Lifelike through all things ; and his thoughts then rose
Like sparkles in the bright wine, brighter still.
Sometimes in dreams, and then the shining words
Would wake him in the dark before his face.
All things talked thoughts to him. The sea went mad,
And the wind whined as 'twere in pain, to show
Each one his meaning; and the awful sun
Thundered his thoughts into him ; and at night
The stars would whisper theirs, the moon sigh hers.
The spirit speaks all tongues and understands
Both God's and angel's, man's and all dumb things,
Down to an insect's inarticulate hum,
And an inaudible organ. And it was
The spirit spake to him of everything ;
And with the moony eyes like those we see,
Thousands on thousands, crowding air in dreams,
Looked into him its mighty meanings, till
He felt the power fulfil him, as a cloud
In every fibre feels the forming wind.
He spake the world's one tongue; in earth and heaven
There is but one, it is the word of truth.
To him the eye let out its hidden meaning ;
And young and old made their hearts over to him ;

And thoughts were told to him as unto none
Save one who heareth said and unsaid, all.
And his heart held these as a grate its gleeds,
Where others warm them.

Student.   I would I had known him.

Festus. All things were inspiration unto him:
Wood, wold, hill, field, sea, city, solitude,
And crowds and streets, and man where'er he was;
And the blue eye of God which is above us;
Brook-bounded pine spinnies where spirits flit;
And haunted pits the rustic hurries by,
Where cold wet ghosts sit ringing jingling bells;
Old orchard's leaf-roofed aisles, and red-cheeked load;
And the blood-coloured tears which yew-trees weep
O'er churchyard graves, like murderers remorseful.
The dark green rings where fairies sit and sup,
Crushing the violet dew in the acorn cup;
Where by his new-made bride the bridegroom sips,
The white moon shimmering on their longing lips;
The large o'erloaded wealthy-looking wains,
Quietly swaggering home through leafy lanes,
Leaving on all low branches, as they come,
Straws for the birds, ears of the harvest home.
Summer's warm soil or winter's cruel sky,
Clear, cold, and icy-blue like a sea-eagle's eye;
All things to Him bare thoughts of minstrelsy.
He drew his light from that he was amidst,
As doth a lamp from air, which hath itself
Matter of light although it show not. His
Was but the power to light what might be lit;
He met a muse in every lovely maid,
And learned a song from every lip he loved.
But his heart ripened most 'neath southern eyes,
Which summed their sweets into him all day long:
For fortune called him southwards, towards the sun.

Helen. Did he love music?

Festus.   The only music he
Or learned or listened to was from the lips
Of her he loved; and then he learned by heart
Her words, delicious as the candied dew,
And durable, which gems the rose, on shores
Pacific, where the western sun hath sown
The soil conceptive with the seed of gold.
Albeit she would try to teach him tunes,
And put his fingers on the keys; but he
Could only see her eyes, and hear her voice,
And feel her touch.

Helen.   Why, he was much like thee.

Festus. We had some points in common. When we
      love,
All air breathes music, like the branchy bower,
By Indian bards feigned, which, with ceaseless song,
Answers the sun's bright raylets; nor till eve,
Folds her melodious leaves, and all night rests;
Drinking deep draughts of silence.

Student.   Was he proud?

Festus. Lowliness is the base of every virtue:
And he who goes the lowest builds the safest.
My God keeps all his pity for the proud.

Stud nt. Was he world-wise?

      VOL. V.

Festus.   The only wonder is
He knew so much, leading the life he did.

Student. Yet it may seem less strange when we think
      back,
That we, in the dark chamber of the heart
Sitting alone, see the world tabled to us;
And the world wonders how recluses know
So much, and most of all how we know them
It is they who paint themselves upon our hearts
In their own lights and darknesses, not we;
One stream of light is to us from above,
And that is that we see by, light of God.

Festus. We do not make our thoughts, they grow
      in us
Like grain in wood : the growth is of the skies,
Which are of nature, nature is of God.
The world is full of glorious likenesses.
The poet's power is to sort these out,
And to make music from the common strings
With which the world is strung; to make the dumb
Earth utter heavenly harmony, and draw
Life clear, and sweet, and harmless as spring water,
Welling its way through flowers. Without faith,
Illimitable faith—strong as a state's
In its own might—in God, no bard can be.
All things are signs of other and of nature.
It is at night we see heaven moveth, and
A darkness thick with suns. The thoughts we think
Subsist the same in God as stars in heaven.
And as these specks of light will prove great worlds,
When we approach them sometime free from flesh,
So too our thoughts will become magnified
To mindlike things immortal. And as space
Is but a property of God wherein
Is laid all matter, other attributes
May be the infinite homes of mind and soul.
And thoughts rise from our souls, as from the sea
The clouds sublimed in heaven. The cloud is cold,
Although ablaze with lightning—though it shine
At all points like a constellation; so
We live not to ourselves, our work is life;
In bright and ceaseless labour as a star
Which shineth unto all worlds but itself.

Helen. And were this friend and bard of whom thou
      speakest,
And she whom he did love, happy together?

Festus. True love is ever tragic, grievous, grave
Bards and their beauties are like double stars
One in their bright effect.

Helen.   Whose light is love

Student. Or is it poesie thou meanest?

Festus.   Both
For love is poesie—it doth create
From fading features, dim soul, doubtful heart,
And this world's wretched happiness, a life
Which is as near to heaven as are the stars
They parted; and she named heaven's judgment-seat
As their next place of meeting; and it was kept
By her, at least, so far that nowhere else
Could it be made until the day of doom.

      120

THE MINISTER'S BEAT.

"I am just about," said the minister, "making a round of friendly visits; and as far as our roads lie together, you will perhaps go with me. You are a bad visitor, I know, Mr. Frank; but most of my calls will be where forms are unknown, and etiquette dispensed with."

I am indeed a bad visitor, which, in the ordinary acceptation of the term, means no visitor at all; but I own the temptation of seeing my worthy friend's reception, and the hope of coming in for a share at least of the cordial welcome he was sure to call forth overcame my scruples, especially as in cottages and farm-steadings there is generally something to be learned even during a morning call,—some trait of unsophisticated nature to be smiled at, or some sturdy lesson of practical wisdom to be treasured for future use.

We had not ridden far when my companion, turning up a pretty rough cart-road leading to a large farm-house on the right, said, with an arch smile, "I love what our superstitious forefathers would esteem a lucky beginning even to a morning's ride, and am glad ours commences with a wedding visit. Peter Bandster has taken a wife in my absence, and I must go and call him to account for defrauding me of the ploy. Have you heard anything, Mr. Francis, about the bride?"

More than I could wish, thinks I to myself, for my old duenna, who indemnifies herself for my lack of hospitality by assiduous frequentation of all marriages, christenings, and gossipings abroad, had deaved me for the last three weeks with philippics about this unlucky wedding. The folly of Peter in marrying above his own line; the ignorance of the bride, who scarce knew lint-yarn from tow, or bear from barley; her unpardonable accomplishments of netting purses and playing on the spinnet; above all, her plated candlesticks, flounced gown, and fashionable bonnet, had furnished Hannah with inexhaustible matter for that exercise of the tongue which the Scots call "rhyming," and the English "ringing the changes;" to which, as to all other noises, custom can alone render one insensible.

I had no mind to damp the minister's benevolent feelings towards the couple, and contented myself with answering that I heard the bride was both bonny and braw. The good man shook his head. "We have an old proverb and a true one," said he,—"'A bonnie

bride is sune buskit;' but I have known gaudy butterflies cast their painted wings, and become excellent housewives in the end."

"But there stands Peter—no very blithe bridegroom, methinks!" said I, as my eye rested on the tall and usually jolly young farmer, musing disconsolately in his cattle-yard over what appeared to be the body of a dead cow. He started on seeing the minister, as if ashamed of his sorrow or its cause, and came forward to meet us, struggling to adapt his countenance a little better to his circumstances. "Well, Peter!" said the minister, frankly extending his hand, "and so I am to wish you joy! I thought when I gave you your name five-and-twenty years ago, if it pleased God to spare me, to have given you your helpmate also; but what signifies it by whom the knot is tied, if true love and the blessing of God go with it? Nay, never hang your head, Peter; but tell me, before we beat up the young gudewife's quarters, what you were leaning over so wae-like when we rode forward?"

"Odd, sir!" cried Peter, reddening up, "it wasna the value o' the beast—though she was the best cow in my mother's byre—but the way I lost her, that pat me a wee out o' tune. My Jessie (for I maunna ca' her gudewife, it seems, nor mistress neither) is an ill guide o' kye—ay, and what's waur, o' lasses. We had a tea-drinking last night, nae doubt, as newmarried folk should; and what for no?—I'se warrant my mither had them too in her daft days. But she didna keep the house asteer the haill night wi' fiddles and dancin', and it neither New-Year nor Handsel-Mononday; nor she didna lie in her bed till aught or nine o'clock, as my Jess does—na, nor yet——"

"But what has all this to do with the loss of your cow, Peter?"

"Ower muckle, sir; ower muckle. The lasses and lads liket reels as weel as their mistress, and whisky a hantle better. They a' sleepit in, and mysell among the lave. Nae mortal ever lookit the airt that puir Blue Bell was in, and her at the very calving; and this morning, when the byre-door was opened, she was lying stiff and stark, wi' a dead calf beside her. It's no the cow, sir—though it was but the last market I had the offer o' fifteen pund for her—it's the thought that she was sae sair forwarded amang me and my Jess, and her tawpies o' lasses."

"Come, come, Peter," said the good minister, "you seem to have been as much to blame as the rest; and as for your young town bride, she maun creep, as the auld wives say, before she can gang. Country thrift can no more be learned in a day than town breeding; and of that your wife, they say, has her share."

"Ower muckle, maybe," was the half-muttered reply, as he marshalled us into the house. The *ben* end of the old-fashioned farm-house, which, during the primitive sway of Peter's mother, had exhibited the usual decorations of an *amrie*, a clock, and a pair of press-beds, with a clean-swept ingle and carefully-sanded floor, had undergone a metamorphosis not less violent than some of Ovid's or Harlequin's. The *amrie* had given place to a satin-wood work-table, the clock to a mirror, and the press-beds (whose removal no one could regret) to that object of Hannah's direst vituperations, the pianoforte; while the fireplace revelled in all the summer luxury of elaborately-twisted shavings, and the once sanded floor was covered with an already soiled and faded carpet, to whose delicate colours Peter, fresh from the clay furrows, and his two sheep-dogs dripping from the pond, had nearly proved equally fatal.

In this sanctum sanctorum sat the really pretty bride, in all the dignity of outraged feeling which ignorance of life and a lavish perusal of romances could inspire, on witnessing the first cloud on her usually good-natured husband's brow. She hastily cleared up her ruffled looks, gave the minister a cordial though somewhat affected welcome, and dropped me a curtsey which twenty years' rustication enabled me very inadequately to return.

The good pastor bent on this new lamb of his fold a benignant yet searching glance, and seemed watching where, amid the fluent small-talk which succeeded, he might edge in a word of playful yet serious import to the happiness of the youthful pair. The bride was stretching forth her hand with all the dignity of her new station, to ring the bell for cake and wine, when Peter (whose spleen was evidently waiting for a vent), hastily starting up, cried out, "Mistress! if ye're ower grand to serve the minister yoursell, there's ane 'll be proud to do't. There shall nae quean fill a glass for him in this house while it ca's me master. My mither wad hae served him on her bended knees gin he wad hae let her; and ye think it ower muckle to bring ben the bridal bread to him! Oh, Jess, Jess! I canna awa' wi' your town ways and town airs!"

The bride coloured and pouted; but there gathered a large drop in her eye, and the pastor hailed it as an earnest of future concession. He took her hand kindly, and put it into Peter's not reluctant one. "'Spring showers make May flowers,' my dear lassie, says the

old proverb, and I trust out o' these little clouds will spring your future happiness. You, Jessie, have chosen an honest, worthy, kind hearted, country husband, whose love will be well worth the sacrifice of a few second-hand graces; and you, Peter, have taken for better and for worse, a lassie in whose eye, in spite of foreign airs, I read a heart to be won by kindness. Bear and forbear, my dear bairns —let each be apter to yield than the other to exact. You are both travelling to a better country—'See that ye fall not out by the way.'"

The bride by this time was sobbing, and Peter's stout heart evidently softened. So leaving the pair to seal their reconciliation in this favourable mood, the good minister and I mounted our horses, and rode off without farther parley.

We were just turning the corner of the loan to regain the high-road, when a woman from a cottage in an adjoining field came running to intercept us. There was in her look a wildness bordering on distraction, but it was evidently of no painful kind. She seemed like one not recovered from the first shock of some delightful surprise, too much for the frail fabric of mortality to bear without tottering to its very foundations. The minister checked his horse, whose bridle she grasped convulsively, panting partly from fatigue, and more from emotion—endeavouring, but vainly, to give utterance to the tidings with which her bosom laboured. Twice she looked up, shook her head, and was silent; then with a strong effort faltered out, " He's come back!—the Lord be praised for it!"

"Who is come back, Jenny?" said the pastor, in the deepest tone of sympathy; "is it little Andrew ye mean?"

"Andrew!" echoed the matron, with an expression of contempt, which at any other time this favourite grandchild would have been very far from calling forth: "Andrew! Andrew's *father;* I mean my ain first-born son, Jamie, that I wore mournings for till they would wear nae langer, and thought lying fifty fathoms down in solid ice, in yon wild place Greenland, or torn to pieces wi' savage bears, like the mocking bairns in Scripture—he's yonder!" said she, wildly pointing to the house; "he's yonder, living and living-like; and oh gin ye wad come, and maybe speak a word in season to us, we might be better able to praise the Lord, as is his due."

We turned our horses' heads, and followed her, as she ran, or rather flew, towards the cottage, with the instinct of some animal long separated from its offspring. The little boy before mentioned ran out to hold our horses, and whispered as the minister stooped to stroke his head, "Daddy's come hame frae the sea." The scene within the cottage baffles description. The old mother, exhausted with her exertion, had sunk down beside her son on the edge of the bed on which he was sitting, where his blind and bed-rid father lay, and clasped his withered hands in speechless prayer. His lips continued to move, unconscious of our presence, and ever and anon he stretched forth a feeble arm to ascertain the actual vicinity of his long-mourned son. On a low stool before the once gay and handsome, but now frost-nipped and hunger-worn mariner, sat his young wife, her hand firmly clasped in his, her fixed eye rivetted on his countenance, giving no other sign of life than a convulsive pressure of the former, or a big drop descending unwiped from the latter; while her unemployed hand was plucking quite mechanically the badge of widowhood from her duffle cloak, which (having just reached home as her husband knocked at his father's door) was yet lying across her knee.

The poor sailor gazed on all around him with somewhat of a bewildered air, but most of all upon a rosy creature between his knees, of about a year and half old, born just after his departure, and who had only learned the sad word "Daddy" from the childish prattle of his older brother Andrew and his sisters. Of these one had been summoned, wild and bare-legged, from the herding; the other, meek and modest, from the village school. The former, idle and intractable, half shrunk in fear of her returned parent's well-remembered strictness; the other, too young not to have forgotten his person, only wondered whether this was the Father in Heaven of whom she had heard so often. She did not think it could be so, for there was no grief or trouble there, and this father looked as if he had seen much of both.

Such was the group to whose emotions, almost too much for human nature, our entrance gave a turn. "Jamie," said the good pastor (gently pressing the still united hands of the mariner and his faithful Annie), "you are welcome back from the gates of death and the perils of the deep. Well is it said that they who go down to the sea in ships see more of the wonders of the Lord than other men; but it was not from storm and tempests alone that you have been delivered—cold and famine, want and nakedness—wild beasts to devour, and darkness to dismay.—these have been

around your dreary path; but He that was with you was mightier than all that were against you, and you are returned a living man to tell the wondrous tale. Let us praise the Lord, my friends, for His goodness and His wonderful works to the children of men." We all knelt down, and joined in the brief but fervent prayer that followed. The stranger's heartfelt sigh of sympathy mingled with the pastor's pious orisons, with the feeble accents of decrepitude, the lisp of wondering child-hood, the soul-felt piety of rescued manhood, and the deep unutterable gratitude of a wife and mother's heart!

For such high-wrought emotions prayer is the only adequate channel. They found vent in it, and were calmed and subdued to the level of ordinary intercourse. The minister kindly addressed Jamie, and drew forth, by his judicious questions, the leading features of that marvellous history of peril and privations endured by the crew of a Greenland ship detained a winter on the ice, with which all are now familiar, but of which a Parry or a Franklin can perhaps alone appreciate the horrors. They were related with a simplicity that did them ample justice.

"I never despaired, sir," said the hardy Scotsman; "we were young and stout. Providence, aye when at the warst, did us some gude turn, and this kept up our hearts. We had mostly a' wives or mithers at hame, and kent that prayers wadna be wanting for our safety; and little as men may think o' them on land, or even at sea on a prosperous voyage, a winter at the Pole makes prayers precious. We had little to do but sleep; and oh, the nights were lang! I was aye a great dreamer; and ye maunna be angry, sir (to the minister), the seeing Annie and the bairns amaist ilka time I lay down, and aye braw and buskit, did mair to keep up my hopes than a' the rest. I never could see wee Jamie, though," said he, smiling, and kissing the child on his knee; "I saw a cradle weel enough, but the face o' the bit creature in't I never could mak' out, and it vexed me; for whiles I thought my babe was dead, and whiles I feared it had never been born; but God be praised he's here, and no that unlike mysell, neither."

"Annie!" said the minister, gently loosing her renewed grasp of Jamie's hand, "you are forgetting your duty as a gudewife—we maun drink to Jamie's health and happiness ere we go. We'll steal a glass or two out of old Andrew's cordial-bottle; a drop of this day's joy will be better to him than it a'."

"Atweel, that's true!" said the old father,

with a distinctness of utterance and acuteness of hearing he had not manifested for many months. The bottle was brought—the health of the day went round. I shook the weather-beaten sailor warmly by the hand, and begging leave to come and hear more of his story at a fitter season, followed the minister to the door.

"Andrew!" said he, giving the little patient equerry a bright new sixpence, "tell your daddy I gave you this for being a dutiful son to your mother when he was at the sea." The child's eye glistened as he ran in to execute the welcome command; and we rode off, our hearts too full for much communication.

The day was advancing. These two scenes had encroached deeply on the privileged hours for visiting; and the minister, partly to turn the account of our thoughts into a less agitating channel, partly to balance the delights of the last hour with their due counterpoise of alloy, suggested the propriety of going next to pay at the house of his patron, the laird of the parish, the visit of duty and ceremony which his late return, and a domestic affliction in the family, rendered indispensable. There were reasons which made my going equally proper and disagreeable; and formal calls being among the many evils which are lightened by participation, I gladly availed myself of the shelter of the minister's name and company.

Mr. Morison of Castle Morison was one of those spoiled children of fortune whom, in her cruel kindess, she renders miserable. He had never known contradiction, and a straw across his path made him chafe like a resisted torrent; he had never known sorrow, and was, consequently, but half acquainted with joy; he was a stranger to compassion, and, consequently, himself an object of pity to all who could allow for the force of early education in searing and hardening the human heart. He had, as a boy, made his mother tremble; it is little to be wondered that in manhood he was the tyrant of his wife and children. Mrs. Morison's spirit, originally gentle, was soon broken; and if her heart was not equally so, it was because she learned reluctantly to despise her tyrant, and found compensation in the double portion of affection bestowed on her by her son and daughters. For the latter Mr. Morison manifested only contempt. There was not a horse in his stable nor a dog in his kennel which did not engross more of his attention; but, like the foxes and hares which it was the business of these favourite animals to hunt down, girls could be made to afford no bad sport in a rainy day. It was no wonder that with them fear usurped the place of rever-

ence for such a parent. If they did not hate him, they were indebted to their mother's piety and their own sweet dispositions; and if they neither hated nor envied their only brother, it was not the fault of him, who, by injudicious distinctions and blind indulgence, laid the foundation for envy and all uncharitableness in their youthful bosoms. In that of his favourite they had the usual effect of generating self-will and rebellion; and while Jane and Agnes, well knowing nothing they did would be thought right, rarely erred from the path of duty, Edmund, aware that he could scarce do wrong, took care his privileges should not rust for want of exercise.

But though suffered in all minor matters to follow the dictates of caprice, to laugh at his tutor, lame the horse, and break rules (to all others those of the Medes and Persians) with impunity, he found himself suddenly reined up in his headlong career by an equally capricious parent, precisely at the period when restraint was nearly forgotten, and peculiarly irksome. It was tacitly agreed by both parties that the heir of Castle Morison could only go into the army; but while the Guards or a dragoon regiment was the natural enough ambition of Edmund, Morison was suddenly seized with a fit of contradiction, which he chose to style economy, and talked of a marching regiment, with perhaps an extra £100 per annum to the undoubted heir of nearly ten thousand a year. Neither would yield: the one had taught, the other learned, stubbornness; and Edmund, backed by the sympathy of the world and the clamours of his companions, told his father he had changed his mind, and was going to India with a near relation about to proceed to Bombay in a high official character.

Morison had a peculiar prejudice against the East, and a personal pique towards the cousin to whose patronage Edmund had betaken himself. His rage was as boundless as his former partiality; and the only consolation his poor wife felt when her darling son left his father's house, alike impenitent and unblessed, was that her boy's disposition was originally good, and would probably recover the ascendant; and that it was out of the power of her husband to make his son a beggar as well as an exile. The estate was strictly entailed, and the knowledge of this, while it embittered Morison's sense of his son's disobedience, no doubt strengthened the feeling of independence so natural to headstrong youth.

While Morison was perverting legal ingenuity in vain hopes of being able to disinherit his refractory heir, his unnatural schemes were anticipated by a mightier agent. An epidemic fever carried off in one short month (about two years after his quitting England) the unreconciled but no longer unconciliatory exile; and his young and beautiful bride, the daughter of his patron, his union with whom had been construed, by the causeless antipathy of his father, into a fresh cause of indignation. Death, whose cold hand loosens this world's grasp, and whose deep voice stills this world's strife, only tightens the bonds of nature, and teaches the stormiest spirits to part *in peace.* Edmund lived to write to his father a few lines of undissembled and unconditional penitence, to own that if the path of duty had been rugged, he had in vain sought happiness beyond it, and to entreat that the place he had forfeited in his father's favour might be transferred to his unoffending child.

All this had been conveyed to Mr. Monteith and myself by the voice of rumour some days before; and we had been more shocked than surprised to learn that Morison's resentment had survived its object, and that he disclaimed all intention of ever seeing or receiving the infant boy who, it was gall to him to reflect, must inherit his estate. Mrs. Morison had exerted, to soften his hard heart, all the little influence she ever possessed. Her tender soul yearned towards her Edmund's child; and sometimes the thought of seeking a separation, and devoting herself to rear it, crossed her despairing mind. But her daughters were a tie still more powerful to her unhappy home. She could neither leave them unprotected to its discomforts, nor conscientiously advise their desertion of a parent, however unworthy; so she wandered, a paler and sadder inmate than before of her cold and stately mansion; and her fair subdued-looking daughters shuddered as they passed the long-locked doors of their brother's nursery and schoolroom.

The accounts of young Morison's death had arrived since the good pastor's departure, and it was with feelings of equal sympathy towards the female part of the family, and sorrow for the unchristian frame of its head, that he prepared for our present visit. As we rode up the old strait avenue, I perceived a post-chaise at the door, and instead of shrinking from this probable accession of strangers, felt that any addition to the usually constrained and gloomy family-circle must be a relief. On reaching the door we were struck with a very unusual appendage to the dusty and travel-stained vehicle, in the shape of an ancient venerable-looking Asiatic in the dress of his country, beneath whose ample muslin folds he

might easily have been mistaken for an old female nurse—a character which, in all its skill and tenderness, was amply sustained by this faithful and attached oriental. His broken English and passionate gestures excited our attention, already awakened by the singularity of his costume and appearance; and as we got close to him, the big tears which rolled over his sallow and furrowed cheeks powerfully called forth our sympathy, and told, better than words, his forcible exclusion from the splendid mansion which had reluctantly admitted within its precincts the child dearer to him than country and kindred!

Our visit, had it borne less of a pastoral character, had all the appearance of being very ill timed. There were servants running to and fro in the hall, and loud voices in the dining-room; and from a little parlour on one side the front-door issued female sobs, mingled with infant wailings in an unknown dialect.

"Thank God!" whispered the minister, "the bairn is fairly in the house. Providence and nature will surely do the rest."

It was not a time to intrude abruptly, so we sent in our names to Mr. Morison; and during our pretty long detention on horseback, could not avoid seeing in at the open window of the parlour before mentioned a scene which it grieved us to think was only witnessed by ourselves.

Mrs. Morison was sitting in a chair (on which she had evidently sunk down powerless) with her son's orphan boy on her knee, his bright dark eyes of the little wild unearthly-looking creature fixed in steadfast gaze on her pale matronly countenance. "No cry, Mama Englise," said the child, as her big tears rolled unheeded on his bosom—"Billy Edmund will be welly welly good." His youngest aunt, whose keen and long-repressed feelings found vent in sobs of mingled joy and agony, was covering his little hands with showers of kisses, while the elder (his father's favourite sister) was comparing behind him the rich dark locks that clustered in his neck with the locket which, since Edmund's departure, had dwelt next her heart.

A message from the laird summoned us from this affecting sight, and amid the pathetic entreaties of the old oriental that we would restore his nursling, we proceeded to the dining-room, made aware of our approach to it by the still storming, though half-suppressed imprecations of its hard-hearted master. He was pacing in stern and moody agitation through the spacious apartment. His welcome was evidently extorted, and his face (to use a strong Scripture expression) set as a flint against the voice of remonstrance and exhortation, for which he was evidently prepared. My skilful coadjutor went quite another way to work. "Mr. Morison," said he, apparently unconscious of the poor man's pitiable state of mind, "I came to condole, but I find it is my lot to congratulate. The Lord hath taken away with the one hand, but it has been to give with the other. His blessing be with you and your son's son, whom he hath sent to be the staff and comfort of your age!" This was said with his usual benign frankness; and the hard heart, which would have silenced admonition and scorned reproof, scarce knew how to repulse the voice of Christian congratulation. He walked about, muttering to himself, "No son of mine—bad breed! Let him go to those who taught his father disobedience, and his mother artifice!—anywhere they please; there is no room for him here."

"Have you seen your grandchild yet, Mr. Morison?" resumed the minister, nothing daunted by the continued obduracy of the proud laird. "Let me have the joy of putting him into your arms. You must expect to be a good deal overcome. Sweet little fellow; there is a strong likeness!" A shudder passed across the father's hard frame, and he recoiled as from an adder when worthy Mr. Monteith, gently grasping his arm, sought to draw him, still sullen, though more faintly resisting, towards the other room. A shrill cry of infant agony rose from the parlour as we crossed the hall; and Nature never perhaps exhibited a stronger contrast than presented itself between the cruel old man, struggling to escape from the presence of his grandchild, and the faithful ancient domestic, shrieking wildly to be admitted into it.

As I threw open the door for the entrance of the former, little Edmund, whose infant promises of good behaviour had soon given way before the continued society of strangers, was stamping in all the impotence of baby rage (and in this unhallowed mood too faithful a miniature of both father and grandfather), and calling loudly for the old oriental. With the first glance at the door his exclamations redoubled. We began to fear the worst effect from this abrupt introduction; but no sooner had the beautiful boy—beautiful even in passion—cast a second bewildered glance on his still erect and handsome grandfather, than, clapping his little hands, and calling out, "My Bombay Papa!" he flew into his arms.

The servants, concluding the interdict re-

moved by their master's entrance into the apartment, had ceased to obstruct the efforts of the old Hindu to flee to his precious charge; and while the astonished and fairly overwhelmed Morison's neck was encircled by the infant grasp of his son's orphan boy, his knees were suddenly embraced by that son's devoted and gray-haired domestic.

One arm of little Edmund was instantly loosened from his grandfather's shoulder, and passed round the neck of the faithful old oriental, who kissed alternately the little cherub hand of his nursling and the hitherto iron one of the proud laird. It softened, and the hard heart with it! It was long since love—pure unsophisticated love—and spontaneous reverence had been Morison's portion, and they were proportionally sweet. He buried his face in his grandson's clustering ringlets. We heard a groan deep as when rocks are rending and the earth heaves with long pent-up fires. It was wildly mingling with childish laughter and hysteric bursts of female tenderness, as stealing cautiously and unheeded from the spot, we mounted our horses and rode away.

"God be praised!" said the minister, with a deep-drawn sigh, when, emerging from the gloomy avenue, we regained the cheerful beaten track. "This has been a day of strange dispensations, Mr. Francis; we have seen much together to make us wonder at the ways of Providence—to soften and, I hope, improve our hearts. But after such solemn scenes, mine, and yours, I doubt not, also requires something to cheer and lighten it; and I am bound where, if the sight of virtuous happiness can do it, I am sure to succeed. Do let me persuade you to be my companion a little longer, and close this day's visitation at the humble board of, I'll venture to say, the happiest couple in Scotland. I am engaged to christen the first-born of honest Willie Meldrum and his bonnie Helen, and to dine, of course, after the ceremony. Mrs. Monteith and the bairns will be there to meet me; and as my friend, you'll be welcome as the flower in May!"

After some slight scruples about intruding on this scene of domestic enjoyment, easily overruled by the hearty assurances of the divine and my own natural relish for humble life, we marched towards the farm-house of Blinkbonnie; and during our short ride the minister gave me, in a few words, the history of its inmates.

"I don't know, Mr. Francis, if you remember a bonnie orphan lassie called Helen Ormiston, whom my wife took, some years back, into the family, to assist her in the care of the bairns. Helen was come of no ungentle kin; but poverty had sat down heavily on her father and mother, and sunk them into an early grave; and it was a Godsend to poor Helen to get service in a house where poverty would be held no reproach to her. If ye ever saw the creature, ye wadna easily forget her. Many bonnier blither lasses are to be seen daily, but such a look of settled serenity and downcast modesty ye might go far to find. It quite won my wife's heart and mine, and more hearts than ours, as I shall tell you presently. As for the bairns, they just doated on Helen, and she on them; and my poor youngest, that is now with God, during all her long long decline was little, if ever, off her knee. No wonder then that Helen grew pale and thin, ate little, and slept less. I first set it down to anxiety, and, when the innocent bairn was released, to grief; and from these no doubt it partly arose. But when all was over, and when weeks had passed away—when even my poor wife dried her mother's tears, and I could say, 'God's will be done'—still Helen grew paler and thinner, and refused to be comforted; so I saw there was more in it than appeared, and I bade her open her heart to me; and open it she did, with a flood of tears that would have melted a stone.

"'Sir,' said she, 'I maun go away; I think it will kill me to leave you and Mrs. Monteith, and the dear bairns in the nursery, and wee Jeanie's grave in the kirkyard; but stay I canna, and I will tell you why. It is months —ay, amaist years—since Willie Meldrum, auld Blinkbonnie's son, fell in fancy wi' me; and a sair sair heart I may say I have had ever sin-syne. His auld hard father, they tell me, swears (wi' sic oaths as wad gar ye grew to hear them) that he will cut him off wi' a shilling if ever he thinks of me; and oh! it wad be a puir return for the lad's kindness to do him sic an ill turn! So I maun awa' out of the country till the auld man dies, or Willie taks a wife to his mind; for I've seen ower muckle o' poverty, Mr. Monteith, to be the cause o't to ony man, though I whiles think it wad be naething to me that's sae weel used till't mysell.'

"'Helen,' said I, 'when did Willie Mel-drum find opportunities to gain your heart? I never saw him in the house in my life.'

"'Oh, sir,' said she, 'gin I could hae bid-den in the house, he wad never hae seen me either; but I was forced to walk out wi' the bairns, and there was nae place sae quiet and out o' the gate but Willie was sure to find me

out. If I gaed down the burn, Willie was aye fishing; if I gaed up the loan, there was aye something to be dune about the kye. At the kirk-door Willie was aye at hand to spier for your honour, and gie the bairns posies; and after our sair distress, when I was little out for mony a day, I couldna slip out ae moon-light night to sit a moment upon Jeanie's grave, but Willie was there like a ghaist aside me, and made my very heart loup to my mouth!—'

"'And do you return his good-will, Helen?' said I, gravely.

"'Oh, sir,' said the poor thing, trembling, 'I dare na tell you a lie. I tried to be as proud and as shy as a lassie should be to ane abune her degree, and that might do sae muckle better, puir fallow! I tried to look anither gate when I saw him, and mak' mysell deaf when he spoke o' his love; but oh! his words were sae true and kindly, that I doubt mine were nae aye sae short and saucy as they suld hae been. It's hard for a tocherless fatherless lassie to be cauldrife to the lad that wad tak' her to his heart and hame; but oh! it wad be harder still if she was to requite him wi' a father's curse! It's ill eneuch to hae nae parents o' my ain, without makin' mischief wi' ither folk's. The auld man gets dourer and dourer ilka day, and the young ane dafter and dafter—sae ye maun just send me aff the country to some decent service, till Willie's a free man or a bridegroom.'

"'My dear Helen,' said I, 'you are a good upright girl, and I will forward your honest intentions. If it be God's will that Willie and you come together, the hearts of men are in His hand. If otherwise, yours will never at least reproach you with bringing ruin on your lover's head.'

"So I sent Helen, Mr. Francis, to my brother's in the south country, where she proved as great a blessing and as chief a fa-vourite as she had been with us. I saw her some months afterwards; and though her bloom had not returned, she was tranquil and contented as one who has cast her lot into the lap of Heaven.

"Well, to make a long story short, Willie, though he was unreasonable enough—good worthy lad as he is—to take in dudgeon Hel-en's going away (though he might have guessed it was all for his good), was too proud, or too constant, to say he would give her up, or bind himself never to marry her, as his father in-sisted. So the old man one day, after a violent altercation, made his will, and left all his hard-won siller to a rich brother in Liverpool, who neither wanted nor deserved it. Willie, upon this quarrel, had left home very unhappy, and stayed away some time; and during his absence old Blinkbonnie was taken extremely ill. When he thought himself dying he sent for me (I had twice called in vain before), and you may be sure I did my best not to let him depart in so unchristian a frame towards his only child. I did not deny his right to advise his son in the choice of a wife; but I told him he might search the world before he found one more desirable than Helen, whose beauty and sense would secure his son's steadiness, and her frugality and sobriety double his substance. I told him how she had turned a deaf ear to all his son's proposals of a clandestine marriage, and made herself the sacrifice to his own unjust and groundless prejudices. Dying men are generally open to conviction; and I got a fresh will made in favour of his son, with a full consent to his marriage honourably inserted among its provisions. This he deposited with me, feeling no great confidence in the lawyer who had made his previous settlement, and desired me to produce it when he was gone.

"It so happened that I was called away to a distance before his decease, and did not return till some days after the funeral. Willie had flown home on hearing of his father's danger, and had the comfort to find him completely softened, and to receive from his nearly speechless parent many a silent demonstration of returned affection. It was therefore a doubly severe shock to him, on opening the *first* will (the only one forthcoming in my absence), to find himself cut off from everything except the joint lease of the farm, and instead of five thousand pounds, not worth a shilling in the world. His first exclamation, I was told, was, 'It's hard to get baith scorn and skaith—to lose poor Helen and the gear baith. If I had lost it for her, they might hae ta'en it that liket!'

"About a week after I came home, and found on my table a letter from Helen. She had heard of Willie's misfortune, and in a way the most modest and engaging expressed herself ready, if I thought it would still be acceptable, to share his poverty and toil with him through life. 'I am weel used to work.' said she, 'and but for you wad hae been weel used to want. If Willie will let me bear a share o' his burden, I trust in God we may wrastle through thegither: and to tell you the truth,' added she, with her usual honesty, 'I wad rather things were ordered as they are, than that Willie's wealth should shame my poverty.'

"I put this letter in one pocket, and his father's will in the other, and walked over to Blinkbonnie. Willie was working with the manly resolution of one who has no other resource. I told him I was glad to see him so little cast down.

"'Sir,' said he, 'I'll no say but I am vexed that my father gaed to his grave wi' a grudge against me—the mair sae, as when he squeezed my hand on his death bed I thought a' was forgotten. But siller is but warld's gear, and I could thole the want o't an it had nae been for Helen Ormiston, that I hoped to hae gotten to share it wi' me. She may sune do better now, wi' that bonnie face and kind heart o' hers!'

"'It is indeed a kind heart, Willie,' answered I; 'if ever I doubted it, this would have put me to shame.' So saying, I reached him the letter; and oh that Helen could have seen the flush of grateful surprise that crossed his manly brow as he read it! It passed away, though, quickly, and he said, with a sigh, 'Very kind, Mr. Monteith, and very like herself; but I canna take advantage o' an auld gudewill, now that I canna reward it as it deserves.'

"'And what if ye could, Willie?' said I, 'as far, at least, as worldly wealth can requite true affection? There is your father's will, made when it pleased God to touch his heart, and you are as rich a man as you were when Helen Ormiston first refused to make you a beggar.'

"Willie was not insensible to this happy change in his prospects; but his kind heart was chiefly soothed by his father's altered feelings; and at the honourable mention of Helen's name he fairly began to greet.

"The sequel is easily told; but I think the jaunt I made to Tweeddale with Willie, to bring back Helen Ormiston in triumph, was the proudest journey of my life.

"A year ago I married them at the manse, amid much joy, but abundance of tears in the nursery. To-day, when, according to an old promise, I am to christen my name-son Charlie, I expect to be fairly deaved with the clamorous rejoicings of my young fry, who, I verily believe, have not slept this week for thinking of it. But" (pulling out his watch) "it is near four o'clock!—sad quality hour for Blinkbonnie! The hotch-potch will be turned into porridge, and the how-towdies burned to sticks, if we don't make haste!"

I wish, my dear reader, you could see the farm of Blinkbonnie. lying, as it does, on a gently sloping bank, sheltered from the north by a wooded crag or knoll, flanked upon the east by a group of venerable ashes, enlivened and perfumed on the west by a gay luxuriant garden, and open on the south to such a sea-view as none but dwellers on the Frith of Forth have any idea of. Last Saturday it was the very beau ideal of rural comfort and sere-nity. The old trees were reposing, after a course of somewhat boisterous weather, in all the dignity and silence of years. The crows, their usual inhabitants, having gone on their Highland excursion, those fantastic interlopers, Helen's peacocks (a present from the children at the manse), were already preparing for their *siesta* on the topmost boughs. Beneath the spreading branches the cows were dream-ing delightfully, in sweet oblivion of the heats of noon. In an adjoining paddock graceful foals and awkward calves indulged in their rival gambols; while shrieks of joy from behind the garden hedge told these were not the only happy young things in creation.

We deposited our horses in a stable to whose comforts they bore testimony by an approving neigh, and made our way by a narrow path, bordered with sweet-brier and woodbine, to the front of the house. Its tall good-looking young master came hastily to meet us; and I would not have given his blushing welcome, and the bashful scrape that accompanied it, for all the most elaborate courtesies of Chesterfield.

No sooner were our footsteps heard approach-ing than out poured the minister's whole fa-mily from the little honeysuckled porch, with glowing faces and tangled hair, and frocks pro-bably white some hours before, but which now claimed affinity with every bush in the garden. Mrs. Monteith gently joined in the chorus of reproaches to papa for being so late; but the look with which she was answered seemed to satisfy her, as it usually did, that he could not be in fault. We were then ushered into the parlour, whose substantial comforts and exquisite consistency spoke volumes in favour of its mistress. Opulence might be traced in the excellent quality of the homely furniture, in the liberal display of antique china (par-ticularly the choice and curious christening-bowl); but there was nothing incongruous, nothing out of keeping, nothing to make you for a moment mistake this first-rate farm-house parlour for a clumsy ill-fancied drawing-room. A few pots of roses, a few shelves of books, bore testimony to Helen's taste and education; but there were neither exotics nor romances in the collection; and the piece of furniture evidently dearest in her eyes was the cradle, in which reposed, amid all the din of this joyous occasion, the yet unchristened hero of the day. It is time to speak of Helen her-

self, and she was just what, from her story, I knew she must be. The actors in some strik-ing drama of human life often disappoint us by their utter dissimilitude to the pictures of our mind's eye, but Helen was precisely the perfection of a gentle, modest, self-possessed Scottish lassie—the mind, in short, of Jeanie Deans, with the personal advantages of poor Effie. Her dress was as suitable as anything else. Her gown, white as snow, and her cap, of the nicest materials, were neither of them on the pattern of my lady's, but they had a matronly grace of their own worth a thousand second-hand fashions; and when Helen, having awakened her first-born, delivered him with sweet maternal solicitude into the outstretched arms of the minister's proud and favoured youngest girl, I thought I never saw a picture worthier the pencil of Coreggio. It was com-pleted when, bending in all the graceful awk-wardness of a novice over the group, Willie received his boy into his arms, and vowed be-fore his pastor and his God to discharge a parent's duty, while a parent's transport sparkled in his eyes!

I have sat, as Shakspeare says, "at good men's feasts ere now"—have ate turtle at the lord-mayor's, and venison at peers' tables, and *soufflés* at diplomatic dinners; I have ate stur-geon at St. Petersburg, and mullet at Naples, mutton in Wales, and grouse in the Highlands, roast-beef with John Bull, and *volauxvents* at Beauvilliers'; but I have no hesitation in say-ing that the hotch-potch and how-towdies of Blinkbonnie out-herod them all. How far the happy human faces of all ages round the table contributed to enhance the *gusto*, I do not pretend to decide; but I can tell Mr. Véry that, among all his *consommés*, there is no-thing like a judicious mixture of youth and beauty with manliness, integrity, and virtue! — *Blackwood's Magazine.*

A COURT AUDIENCE.

Old South, a witty churchman reckon'd,
Was preaching once to Charles the Second,
But much too serious for a court
Who at all preaching made a sport:
He soon perceiv'd his audience nod,
Deaf to the zealous man of God.
The doctor stopped; began to call,
"Pray, wake the Earl of Lauderdale:
My lord! why, 'tis a monstrous thing!
You snore so loud—you'll wake the king."

REV. RICHARD GRAVES (born 1715; died 1804).

ANNE BOLEYN.

BY HENRY HART MILMAN, D.D.[1]

Scene: QUEEN ANNE BOLEYN landing at the Tower a prisoner, attended by SIR WILLIAM KINGSTON and guards.

QUEEN.

Here—here, then, all is o'er!—Oh! awful walls,
Oh! sullen towers, relentless gates, that open,
Like those of hell, but to receive the doom'd,
The desperate—Oh! ye black and massy barriers,
But broken by yon barr'd and narrow loop-holes,
How do ye coop from this God's sunshine world
Of freedom and delight, your world of woe,
Your midnight world, where all that live, live on
In hourly agony of death! Vast dungeon,
Populous as vast, of your devoted tenants!
Long ere our bark had touch'd the fatal strand,
I felt your ominous shadows darken o'er me,
And close me round; your thick and clammy air,
As though 'twere loaded with dire imprecations,
Wailings of dying and of tortured men,
Tainted afar the wholesome atmosphere.

KINGSTON (*to the guard*).

Advance your halberds.

QUEEN.

                    Oh! sir, pause—one look,
One last long look, to satiate all my senses.
Oh! thou blue cloudless canopy, just tinged
With the faint amber of the setting sun,
Where one by one steal forth the modest stars
To diadem the sky:—thou noble river,
Whose quiet ebb, not like my fortune, sinks
With gentle downfall, and around the keels
Of those thy myriad barks makest passing music:—
Oh! thou great silent city, with thy spires
And palaces, where I was once the greatest,
The happiest—I, whose presence made a tumult
In all your wondering streets and jocund marts:—
But most of all, thou cool and twilight air,
Thou art a rapture to the breath! The slave,
The beggar, the most base down-trodden outcast,
The plague-struck livid wretch, there's none so vile,
So abject, in your streets, that swarm with life—
They may inhale the liquid joy heaven breathes—
They may behold the rosy evening sky—
They may go rest their free limbs where they will:
But I—but I, to whom this summer world
Was all bright sunshine; I, whose time was noted
But by succession of delights——Oh! Kingston.
Thou dost remember, thou wert then lieutenant.
'Tis now—how many years?—my memory wanders—

---

[1] See *Casquet*, vol. ii. page 53.

Since I set forth from yon dark low-brow'd porch,
A bride—a monarch's bride—King Henry's bride?
Oh! the glad pomp, that burn'd upon the waters—
Oh! the rich streams of music that kept time
With oars as musical—the people's shouts,
That call'd Heaven's blessings on my head, in sounds
That might have drown'd the thunders——I've more need
Of blessing now, and not a voice would say it.

KINGSTON.

Your grace, no doubt, will long survive this trial

QUEEN.

Sir, sir, it is too late to flatter me:
Time was I trusted each fond possibility,
For hope sate queen of all my golden fortunes;
But now——

KINGSTON.

                    Day wears, and our imperious mandate
Brooks no delay—advance.

QUEEN.

                    Back, back, I say—
I will not enter! Whither will ye plunge me?
Into what chamber, but the sickly air
Smells all of blood—the black and cobwebb'd walls
Are all o'ertraced by dying hands, who've noted
In the damp dews indelible their tale
Of torture—not a bed nor straw-laid pallet
But bears th' impression of a wretch call'd forth
To execution. Will ye place me there,
Where those poor babes, their crook-back'd uncle mur-
    der'd,
Still haunt?—Inhuman hospitality!
Look there! look there! fear mantles o'er my soul
As with a prophet's robe, the ghostly walls
Are sentinel'd with mute and headless spectres,
Whose lank and grief-attenuated fingers
Point to their gory and dissever'd necks,
The least a lordly noble, some like princes:
Through the dim loop-holes gleam the haggard faces
Of those whose dark unutterable fate
Lies buried in your dungeons' depths; some wan
With famine, some with writhing features fix'd
In the agony of torture.—Back! I say:
They beckon me across the fatal threshold,
Which none may pass and live.

KINGSTON.

                    The deaths of traitors.
If such have died within these gloomy towers,
Should not appal your grace with such vain terrors;
The chamber is prepar'd where slept your highness
When last within the Tower.

QUEEN.

                    Oh! 'tis too good
For such a wretch—a death-doom'd wretch, as me.

My lord, my Henry—he that call'd me forth
Even from that chamber, with a voice more gentle
Than flutes o'er calmest waters—will not wrong
Th' eternal justice—the great law of kings!
Let him arraign me—bribe as witnesses
The angels that behold our inmost thoughts,
He'll find no crime but loving him too fondly ;
And let him visit that with his worst vengeance.
Come, sir, your wearied patience well may fail :
On to that chamber, where I slept so sweetly,
When guiltier far than now.   On—on, good Kingston.

                – *Anne Boleyn, a Dramatic Poem.*

———

THE GOOD-NATURED COUPLE.[1]

There was once a man called Frederick: he had a wife whose name was Catherine, and they had not long been married. One day Frederick said, "Kate! I am going to work in the fields; when I come back I shall be hungry, so let me have something nice cooked, and a good draught of ale." "Very well," said she, "it shall all be ready." When dinner-time drew nigh, Catherine took a nice steak, which was all the meat she had, and put it on the fire to fry. The steak soon began to look brown, and to crackle in the pan; and Catherine stood by with a fork and turned it: then she said to herself, "The steak is almost ready, I may as well go to the cellar for the ale." So she left the pan on the fire, and took a large jug and went into the cellar and tapped the ale cask. The beer ran into the jug, and Catherine stood looking on. At last it popped into her head, "The dog is not shut up—he may be running away with the steak; that's well thought of." So up she ran from the cellar; and sure enough the rascally cur had got the steak in his mouth, and was making off with it.

Away ran Catherine, and away ran the dog across the field: but he ran faster than she, and stuck close to the steak. "It's all gone, and 'what can't be cured must be endured.'" said Catherine. So she turned round; and as she had run a good way, and was tired, she walked home leisurely to cool herself.

Now all this time the ale was running too, for Catherine had not turned the cock ; and when the jug was full the liquor ran upon the floor till the cask was empty. When she got to the cellar stairs she saw what had happened.

"My stars!" said she, "what shall I do to keep Frederick from seeing all this slopping about?" So she thought a while ; and at last remembered that there was a sack of fine meal bought at the last fair, and that if she sprinkled this over the floor, it would suck up the ale nicely. "What a lucky thing," said she, "that we kept that meal ; we have now a good use for it." So away she went for it: but she managed to set it down just upon the great jug full of beer, and upset it ; and thus all the ale that had been saved was set swimming on the floor also. "Ah ! well," said she, "when one goes another may as well follow." Then she strewed the meal all about the cellar, and was quite pleased with her cleverness, and said, "How very neat and clean it looks !"

At noon Frederick came home. "Now, wife," cried he, "what have you for dinner?" "O Frederick !" answered she, "I was cooking you a steak ; but while I went down to draw the ale, the dog ran away with it, and while I ran after him, the ale all ran out ; and when I went to dry up the ale with the sack of meal that we got at the fair, I upset the jug: but the cellar is now quite dry, and looks so clean !" "Kate, Kate," said he, "how could you do all this? Why did you leave the steak to fry, and the ale to run, and then spoil all the meal?" "Why, Frederick," said she, "I did not know I was doing wrong; you should have told me before."

The husband thought to himself, if my wife manages matters thus, I must look sharp myself. Now he had a good deal of gold in the house: so he said to Catherine, "What pretty yellow buttons these are! I shall put them into a box and bury them in the garden ; but take care that you never go near or meddle with them." "No, Frederick," said she, "that I never will." As soon as he was gone, there came by some pedlars with earthenware plates and dishes, and they asked her whether she would buy. "Oh dear me, I should like to buy very much, but I have no money: if you had any use for yellow buttons, I might deal with you." "Yellow buttons?" said they, "let us have a look at them." "Go into the garden and dig where I tell you, you will find the yellow buttons: I dare not go myself." So the rogues went; and when they found what these yellow buttons were they took them all away, and left her plenty of plates and dishes. Then she set them all about the house for a show: and when Frederick came back, he cried out, "Kate, what have you been doing?" "See," said she, "I have bought all these with your yellow buttons:

[1] This is a popular German story which, being susceptible of many variations, is used by the peasantry as a satire upon silly housekeepers.

but I did not touch them myself; the pedlars went themselves and dug them up." "Wife, wife," said Frederick, "what a pretty piece of work you have made! those yellow buttons were all my money: how came you to do such a thing!" "Why," answered she, "I did not know there was any harm in it; you should have told me."

Catherine stood musing for a while, and at last said to her husband, "Hark ye, Frederick, we will soon get the gold back: let us run after the thieves." "Well, we will try," answered he; "but take some butter and cheese with you, that we may have something to eat by the way." "Very well," said she, and they set out; and as Frederick walked the fastest, he left his wife some way behind. "It does not matter," thought she; "when we turn back I shall be so much nearer home than he."

Presently she came to the top of a hill, down the side of which there was a road so narrow that the cart wheels always chafed the trees on each side as they passed. "Ah! see now," said she, "how they have bruised and wounded these poor trees; they will never get well." So she took pity on them, and made use of the butter to grease them all, so that the wheels might not hurt them so much. While she was doing this kind office, one of her cheeses fell out of the basket and rolled down the hill. Catherine looked, but could not see where it was gone; so she said, "Well, I suppose the other will go the same way and find you; he has younger legs than I have." Then she rolled the other cheese after it; and away it went, nobody knows where, down the hill. But she said she supposed they knew the road, and would follow her, and she could not stay there all day waiting for them.

At last she overtook Frederick, who desired her to give him something to eat. Then she gave him the dry bread. "Where is the butter and the cheese?" said he. "O!" answered she, "I used the butter to grease those poor trees that the wheels chafed so; and one of the cheeses ran away, so I sent the other after it to find it, and I suppose they are both on the road together somewhere." "What a goose you are to do such silly things!" said the husband. "How can you say so?" said she; "I am sure you never told me that."

They ate the dry bread together; and Frederick said, "Kate, I hope you locked the door safe when you came away." "No," answered she, "you did not tell me." "Then go home and do it now, before we go any further," said

Frederick, "and bring with you something to eat."

Catherine did as he told her, and thought to herself by the way, "Frederick wants something to eat; but I don't think he is very fond of butter and cheese: I'll bring him a bag of fine nuts, and the vinegar, for I have often seen him take some."

When she reached home, she bolted the back door, but the front door she took off the hinges, and said, "Frederick told me to lock the door, but surely it can nowhere be so safe as if I take it with me." So she took her time by the way: and when she overtook her husband, she cried out, "There, Frederick, there is the door itself, now you may watch it as carefully as you please." "Alas! alas!" said he, "what a clever wife I have! I sent you to make the house fast, and you take the door away, so that everybody may go in and out as they please:—however, as you have brought the door, you shall carry it about with you for your pains." "Very well," answered she, "I'll carry the door: but I'll not carry the nuts and vinegar bottle also—that would be too much of a load; so, if you please, I'll fasten them to the door."

Frederick, of course, made no objection to that plan, and they set off into the wood to look for the thieves; but they could not find them; and when it grew dark, they climbed up into a tree to spend the night there. Scarcely were they up, than who should come by but the very rogues they were looking for. They were in truth great rascals, and belonged to that class of people who find things before they are lost: they were tired, so they sat down and made a fire under the very tree where Frederick and Catherine were. Frederick slipped down on the other side, and picked up some stones. Then he climbed up again, and tried to hit the thieves on the head with them; but they only said, "It must be near morning, for the wind shakes the fir-apples down."

Catherine, who had the door on her shoulder, began to be very tired; but she thought it was the nuts upon it that were so heavy, so she said softly, "Frederick, I must let the nuts go." "No," answered he, "not now, they will discover us." "I can't help that, they must go." "Well then, make haste and throw them down if you will." Then away rattled the nuts down among the boughs; and one of the thieves cried, "Bless me, it is hailing."

A little while after Catherine thought the door was still very heavy, so she whispered to Frederick, "I must throw the vinegar down."

"Pray don't," answered he, "it will discover us." "I can't help that," said she, "go it must." So she poured all the vinegar down; and the thieves said, "What a heavy dew there is!"

At last it popped into Catherine's head that it was the door itself that was so heavy all the time; so she whispered to Frederick, "I must throw the door down soon." But he begged and prayed her not to do so, for he was sure it would betray them. "Here goes, however," said she: and down went the door with such a clatter upon the thieves, that they cried out, "Murder!" and not knowing what was coming, ran away as fast as they could, and left all the gold. So when Frederick and Catherine came down, there they found all their money safe and sound.

GOOD NIGHT!

BY W. M. PRAED.

Good night to thee, lady! Though many
  Have join'd in the dance of to-night,
Thy form was the fairest of any,
  Where all was seducing and bright;—
Thy smile was the softest and dearest,
  Thy form the most sylph-like of all,
And thy voice the most gladsome and clearest
  That e'er held a partner in thrall.

Good night to thee, lady! 'Tis over—
  The waltz, the quadrille, and the song,
The whispered "Farewell!" of the lover,
  The heartless "Adieu!" of the throng;
The heart that was throbbing with pleasure,
  The eyelid that long'd for repose,
The beaux that were dreaming of treasure,
  The girls that were dreaming of beaux.

'Tis over! The lights are all dying,
  The coaches all driving away;
And many a fair one is sighing,
  And many a false one is gay;
And Beauty counts over her numbers
  Of conquests, as homewards she drives;
And some are gone home to their slumbers,
  And some are gone home to their wives.

And I, while my cab in the shower
  Is waiting, the last at the door,
Am looking all round for the flower,
  That fell from your wreath, on the floor.
I'll keep it!—if but to remind me,
  Though wither'd and faded its hue,
Wherever next season may find me,
  Of England, of Almack's, and you!

There are tones that will haunt us, though lonely
  Our path be o'er mountain or sea;
There are looks that will part from us only
  When memory ceases to be;
There are hopes which our burden can lighten
  Though toilsome and steep be the way;
And dreams that, like moonlight, can brighten
  With a light that is clearer than day.

There are names that we cherish, though nameless
  For aye on the lip they may be;
There are hearts that, though fetter'd, are tameless,
  And thoughts unexpress'd, but still free!
And some are too grave for a rover,
  And some for a husband too light;
The ball and my dream are all over,—
  Good night to thee, lady! Good night!

POSTHUMOUS FAME.

[Sir Thomas Browne, born in London, 19th October, 1605; died at Norwich, 19th October, 1682. Antiquary and physician, knighted by Charles II. He wrote: *Religio Medici*, the Religion of a Physician; *Inquiries into Vulgar and Common Errors; Urne-Burial*, or a Discourse of the Sepulchral Urns lately found in Norfolk, 1658 (from which our extract is taken); and several other treatises on antiquities. Dr. Johnson, who wrote a biography of Sir Thomas Browne, said: "There is no science in which he does not discover some skill."]

To be content that times to come should only know there was such a man, not caring whether they knew more of him, was a frigid ambition in Cardan; disparaging his horoscopal inclination and judgment of himself, who cares to subsist like Hippocrates' patients, or Achilles' horses in Homer, under naked nominations without deserts and noble acts which are the balsam of our memories, the entelechia and soul of our subsistences. To be nameless in worthy deeds exceeds an infamous history. The Canaanitish woman lives more happily without a name, than Herodias with one. And who had not rather have been the good thief, than Pilate?

But the iniquity of oblivion blindly scattereth her poppy, and deals with the memory of men without distinction to merit of perpetuity. Who can but pity the founder of the pyramids? Herostratus lives that burned the temple of Diana, he is almost lost that built it; time hath spared the epitaph of Adrian's horse, confounded that of himself. In vain we compute our felicities by the advantage of our good names, since bad have equal durations; and Thersites is like to live as long as Agamemnon, without the favour of the everlasting register.

Who knows whether the best of men be known? or whether there be not more remarkable persons forgot, than any that stand remembered in the known account of time? the first man had been as unknown as the last, and Methuselah's long life had been his only chronicle.

Oblivion is not to be hired; the greater part must be content to be as though they had not been, to be found in the register of God, not in the record of man. Twenty-seven names make up the first story, and the recorded names ever since contain not one living century. The number of the dead long exceedeth all that shall live. The night of time far surpasseth the day, and who knows when was the equinox? Every hour adds unto that current arithmetic, which scarce stands one moment. And even death must be the Lucina of life, and even pagans could doubt whether thus to live were to die; since our longest sun sets at right descensions, and makes but winter arches, and therefore it cannot be long before we lie down in darkness, and have our light in ashes: since the brother of death daily haunts us with dying mementoes, and time, that grows old itself, bids us hope no long duration: diuturnity is a dream and folly of expectation.

Darkness and light divide the course of time, and oblivion shares with memory a great part even of our living beings; we slightly remember our felicities, and the smartest strokes of affliction leave but short smart upon us. Sense endureth no extremities, and sorrows destroy us or themselves. To weep into stones are fables. Afflictions induce callosities, miseries are slippery, or fall like snow upon us, which notwithstanding is no unhappy stupidity. To be ignorant of evils to come, and forgetful of evils past, is a merciful provision in nature, whereby we digest the mixture of our few and evil days, and our delivered senses not relapsing into cutting remembrances, our sorrows are not kept raw by the edge of repetitions. A great part of antiquity contented their hopes of subsistency with a transmigration of their souls. A good way to continue their memories, while having the advantage of plural successions, they could not but act something remarkable in such variety of beings, and enjoying the fame of their passed selves, make accumulation of glory unto their latest durations. Others, rather than be lost in the uncomfortable night of nothing, were content to recede into the common being, and make one particle of the public soul of all things, which was no more than to return into their unknown and divine original again. Egyptian ingenuity was more unsatisfied, conserving their bodies in sweet consistences, to attend the return of their souls. But all was vanity, feeding the wind, and folly. The Egyptian mummies, which Cambyses or time hath spared, avarice now consumeth. Mummy is become merchandise, Mizraim cures wounds, and Pharaoh is sold for balsams.

In vain do individuals hope for immortality, or any patent from oblivion, in preservations below the moon: men have been deceived even in their flatteries above the sun, and studied conceits to perpetuate their names in heaven. The various cosmography of that part hath already varied the names of contrived constellations: Nimrod is lost in Orion, and Osyris in the Dog-star. While we look for incorruption in the heavens, we find they are but like the earth; durable in their main bodies, alterable in their parts: whereof beside comets and new stars, perspectives begin to tell tales. And the spots that wander about the sun, with Phaeton's favour, would make clear conviction.

There is nothing immortal, but immortality; whatever hath no beginning may be confident of no end. All others have a dependent being, and within the reach of destruction, which is the peculiar of that necessary essence that cannot destroy itself; and the highest strain of omnipotency to be so powerfully constituted, as not to suffer even from the power of itself. But the sufficiency of Christian immortality frustrates all earthly glory, and the quality of either state after death makes a folly of posthumous memory. God, who can only destroy our souls, and hath assured our resurrection, either of our bodies or names, hath directly promised no duration. Wherein there is so much of chance, that the boldest expectants have found unhappy frustration; and to hold long subsistence seems but a scape in oblivion. But man is a noble animal, splendid in ashes, and pompous in the grave, solemnizing nativities and deaths with equal lustre, nor omitting ceremonies of bravery in the infamy of his nature.

Life is a pure flame, and we live by an invisible sun within us. A small fire sufficeth for life, great flames seemed too little after death, while men vainly affected precious pyres, and to burn like Sardanapalus: but the wisdom of funeral laws found the folly of prodigal blazes, and reduced undoing fires unto the rule of sober obsequies, wherein few could be so mean as not to provide wood, pitch, a mourner, and an urn.

Five languages secured not the epitaph of Gordianus; the man of God lives longer without a tomb than any by one, invisibly interred by angels, and adjudged to obscurity, though not without some marks directing humane discovery. Enoch and Elias without either tomb or burial, in an anomalous state of being, are the great examples of perpetuity, in their long and living memory, in strict account being still on this side death, and having a late part yet to act on this stage of earth. If in the decretory term of the world we shall not all die but be changed, according to received translation; the last day will make but few graves; at least quick resurrections will anticipate lasting sepultures; some graves will be opened before they be quite closed, and Lazarus be no wonder. When many that feared to die shall groan that they can die but once, the dismal state is the second and living death, when life puts despair on the damned ; when men shall wish the covering of mountains, and annihilation shall be courted.

While some have studied monuments, others have studiously declined them; and some have been so vainly boisterous, that they durst not acknowledge their graves; wherein Alaricus seems most subtle, who had a river turned to hide his bones at the bottom. Even Sylla, that thought himself safe in his urn, could not prevent revenging tongues, and stones thrown at his monument. Happy are they whom privacy makes innocent, who deal so with men in this world, that they are not afraid to meet them in the next, who, when they die, make no commotion among the dead, and are not touched with that poetical taunt of Isaiah.

Pyramids, arches, obelisks, were but the irregularities of vainglory, and wild enormities of ancient magnanimity. But the most magnanimous resolution rests in the Christian religion, which trampleth upon pride, and sits on the neck of ambition, humbly pursuing that infallible perpetuity, unto which all others must diminish their diameters, and be poorly seen in angles of contingency.

Pious spirits, who passed their days in raptures of futurity, made little more of this world than the world that was before it, while they lay obscure in the chaos of preordination and night of their fore-beings. And if any have been so happy as truly to understand Christian annihilation, ecstacies, exolution, liquefaction, transformation, the kiss of the spouse, gustation of God, and ingression into the divine shadow, they have already had a handsome anticipation of heaven ; the glory of the world is surely over, and the earth in ashes unto them.

To subsist in lasting monuments, to live in their productions, to exist in their names, and predicament of Chimeras, was large satisfaction unto old expectations, and made one part of their elysiums. But all this is nothing in the metaphysics of true belief. To live indeed is to be again ourselves, which being not only a hope but an evidence in noble believers: 'tis all one to lie in St. Innocent's church-yard as in the sands of Egypt: ready to be anything, in the ecstacy of being ever, and as content with six foot as the moles of Adrianus.

END OF VOLUME FIFTH.

GLASGOW: W. G. BLACKIE AND CO., PRINTERS, VILLAFIELD.